A Tender Melody

A Tender Melody

A Tender Melody
BY BIRDIE L. ETCHISON

Piano Lessons
BY GAIL SATTLER

It Only Takes a Spark
BY PAMELA KAYE TRACY

Familiar Strangers
BY GINA FIELDS

HeavenSent
FROM
Crossings

A Tender Melody
Copyright © 1999 by Barbour Publishing, Inc.

Piano Lessons
Copyright © 1998 by Barbour Publishing, Inc.

It Only Takes a Spark
Copyright © 1999 by Barbour Publishing, Inc.

Familiar Strangers
Copyright © 2000 by Barbour Publishing, Inc.

This edition was especially created in 2005 for Crossings by arrangement with Barbour Publishing, Inc.

Published by Crossings Book Club, 401 Franklin Avenue, Garden City, New York 11530.

ISBN: 1-58288-156-1

Printed in the United States of America

A Tender Melody

A Tender Melody

by Birdie L. Etchison

For my sister, Barbara,
Elsie for editing help,
Evelyn for encouragement,
and Keithanne who lives in beautiful Joseph, Oregon

$\mathcal{T}$ t takes a good four years to get over a loss, whether it's from death or divorce."

Pastor Dave's words rang through Laura Madison's mind as she dug holes for the dahlias. He was wrong. It took a lot longer than four years to get over the loss of a beloved husband.

She dug another hole and pushed a tuber into it. She loved flowers and liked having the front yard a riot of colors all year from tulips in the spring, to gladiolas in summer, to dahlias in the fall. Jerry had always been the gardener; consequently, Laura had never spaded the ground, weeded, or even cut the grass until his death. Even now she relied on the help of Renee, her neighbor, who had shown her the best way to dig up the dirt and work compost in. She finished tapping down the earth over the last dahlia tuber when Renee hollered from her porch.

"How about taking a breather? I just put on a pot of tea and have lemon scones hot out of the oven."

Laura straightened and rubbed at a kink in her back. So far her forties had been the pits. This nagging ache in her lower back was noticeable after anything physical such as vacuuming, spading dirt, or hauling bags of groceries from the car.

"Sounds great," she shouted back to Renee. "Let me wash up and get into some clean pants."

The phone was ringing when she entered the house. She removed her dirt clogs first, then her gloves, as she hurried to catch it. She'd been hoping for, yet not quite expecting, a call from northeastern Oregon. The recorder clicked on just as she reached for the phone. A deep, bass voice filled the room.

"This is Reverend Gregory Hall with a message for Laura Madison. I'm responding to the ad placed in the *Chieftain,* our weekly paper. I'd like to discuss the possibility of a position as the pianist in our small community church."

Laura's heart quickened as she started to pick up the receiver to announce she was really there, but something stopped her. She couldn't talk yet.

It had taken weeks of just thinking about it before she found the courage to send for newspapers. She'd then read the "Help Wanted" ads, looking for a position she could fill, knowing she didn't want to be a nanny, sell real estate, or clean motel rooms. A few days later, she'd placed two ads. Now came the next steps: answering the call and going for an interview. Was she up to it? Did she really want to go to the mountains, leave her home in Sealand just three blocks from the Pacific Ocean? What had gotten into her anyway?

She had doubts about this decision, enough so that she hadn't told anyone about her plans to move on. Not even Renee. Especially not Renee.

Laura loved the beach and her community, but every time she passed the fishing docks the memories flooded back. She couldn't bear it any longer. Even with the prayer and support of friends, each day that she strolled the beach, each time she sniffed the salt air, each time she heard a siren or a Coast Guard helicopter, she froze. *Jerry.*

❧

How he'd loved the sea—loved being a commercial fisherman. Always in the back of her mind had been the fear that someday a storm would blow in . . . someday he might not return home.

Then the day came. The knock on her door. Sheriff Dan Olsen stood there, a serious look on his face. "Laura . . ."

She trembled as she motioned him inside. She knew—as women tend to do when it concerns their mate. Jerry had left early that morning on a routine fishing trip out over the bar.

"The weather wasn't bad when he left . . ." she'd said as she closed the door.

"You're right, but a so'wester came in." He held his hat in his hand, fingering the brim as he rotated it in small movements. She knew this was the worst job a policeman had, especially when he knew the victim. She'd had Dan in her Sunday school class; he'd lived just up the street.

"The boat capsized. Jerry helped rescue his crew—told the guys to hang on until the Coast Guard cutter came. And then . . . he . . . well, he didn't come up."

"The others?"

"All accounted for."

The numbness spread through her. "At least he wasn't trapped."

"No, he wasn't."

Laura swallowed hard. "He always said if he had to die at sea, he didn't want to be trapped in the boat."

His eyes didn't quite meet her gaze. "Jerry was a hero, Laura. You need to know that."

Later, after Dan left and her children were there, the tears came. Renee never left her side as neighbors, friends, and her pastor came. Food and flowers were everywhere.

Laura thought about how thankful she was to know that God had been with Jerry. She knew he had drawn comfort from his faith as he died, just as she was now trying to do. The crew couldn't say enough nice things, but nice words didn't bring her husband of twenty years back, nor did nice words lend comfort at night when she reached out to emptiness in the king-sized bed they'd shared.

Renee kept close tabs on her, forcing her to eat. "You have to eat, Laura. You can't sit here all day and stare into space."

That's when the walks started. Even when it rained, she walked, coming home soaked to the skin. When it was windy she walked, letting the wind push her along, or she fought against it as she turned and came back toward home. She hated the wind as a constant reminder of the accident.

The life and boat insurance policies and investments provided more than adequate money for Laura to live on for the rest of her life, but she knew—had come to realize—that she must do something to feel useful and worthwhile again.

Her mind now went over the ad she'd so carefully composed:

Mature woman seeks position as piano player for small church. Experienced. Salary negotiable.

She'd torn up the first letter and started over. She laughed at the word "mature." What would that mean to most people? And "experienced"—she'd stretched the truth just a bit. She'd played piano for her church in the small farming community where she'd grown up. Since then, she'd always had a piano and had played for her own enjoyment all these years. She'd even given her children lessons.

She jotted down the number and name. *Reverend Gregory Hall, Joseph, Oregon.* She smiled as she tried to put a face with the name.

The door opened and Renee popped in. "Did I hear your phone ring?"

Laura nodded. "Yes, that's why I'm still standing here in sweats with dirt-stained knees. Give me a minute and I'll be there."

"Sure thing." Renee backed out the door. "Your yard's going to be beautiful come fall."

Laura winced as she hurried to the bedroom, choosing navy blue slacks and a pale blue sweatshirt. Mornings were still cool in March. She ran a brush through her short brown hair and decided against makeup. She'd do that before going to the post office for her mail.

She walked across the yard and into Renee's house, wondering if she'd ever enjoy baking again. She hadn't baked after Jerry died, not even for the kids. The two younger ones had still been at home, while Kurt was in his first year of college. Now Kurt had graduated and managed a marine supply house, while Jen was chasing down a career in Seattle. Steve, the youngest, had decided to travel before entering college.

Laura sniffed the air. "I love scones, as you well know."

Pale blue living room walls gave way to splashes of orange and yellow in Renee's large country-style kitchen. The teakettle hummed on the stove, the lemony fragrance filling the kitchen.

Renee indicated a chair. "I think it's time we talk, and it always goes better over a cup of tea."

"Talk? What about?"

"Okay." Renee looked exasperated. "We've been friends for a good many years. If you can't talk to me, who can you talk to?"

Laura liked Renee—she'd do anything for a friend, but she was often pushy and would keep at Laura until she found out what she wanted to know. Besides, Laura never could hide her emotions.

"You've been acting funny this past week."

"Funny?" Laura poured a scant teaspoon of sugar into her tea. "In what way?"

"Hey." Her friend reached over and grabbed Laura's arm. "This is me, Renee. Your buddy. The one you share your life with. I know something is going on and want to know what." Renee's round face looked serious, her gaze meeting Laura's. "We haven't been friends for fifteen years for nothing."

Laura swallowed hard as she bit into her buttered scone. "It's time to move on, to do something with my life."

"What? Did you say move on?" Renee sputtered, sending bits of scone across the kitchen table. "Excuse me, but did I hear right?"

Laura nodded, looking at her friend over the rim of her teacup.

"Didn't I just see you planting dahlias?"

"I know. I do things like that to keep busy. That's the whole point. I need more in my life right now than planting flowers, reading books, volunteering, TV, and waiting for a man who will never come home." The last words came out in a squeak.

"Oh, honey." Renee put her arm around Laura. "I know it's been hard."

"No, you don't know. Nobody does until they've gone through it. Even the pastor, with all his wisdom, can't know."

Renee said nothing.

"I still set two cups for coffee each morning, buy the T-bones Jerry liked so well . . ."

Renee nodded. "You're right. I can't pretend to know. If something happened to Derek—" She stood back. "But I can't believe you've been thinking about this without a word to me."

"I know. I wanted to tell you a hundred times, but I feel foolish about the whole thing. Why would I leave the only home I've known for twenty-four years to move to a small mountain town four hundred miles away? It doesn't make sense, nor is it logical."

"Since when is logic any fun?" Renee poured more tea from her favorite teapot, an heirloom from her father's side. "My concern is losing a dear neighbor and friend."

"I'll always be your friend, no matter what."

"I know." Renee touched Laura's hand. "So, where is this place?"

"The Wallowas in the northeast corner of Oregon. It's beautiful. It's also Nez Perce country. Jerry and I visited years ago. Ever been there?"

Renee shook her head. "You know me and Derek are just ol' homebodies."

"That phone call was from a pastor answering one of my ads." Laura trembled as she said it, still not quite believing that someone would answer her ad.

"An ad for what?"

"A job. What else?"

"A job? What kind of a job are you talking about?"

"Part-time, playing the piano. I've kept my piano skills up. Why not use them?"

Renee nodded. "That you have. So, what did this pastor say?"

"Didn't get to the phone in time."

Renee put another scone on Laura's plate. "Then you'd better call him back."

"You think I should?"

"If you've gone this far, you don't want to stop now."

Laura breathed a sigh of relief. "You're the first to know of my plans."

"I gathered that."

"Kurt will be okay. He's got his job, and that keeps him busy on the road two weeks out of four. Then there's Susan. She loves him dearly."

"And the other two are settled. For now," Renee added. "What about the house?"

"I'll leave it empty for the time being. This may not pan out."

Renee kept stirring her tea. "Can't help but think I don't want it to. When would you leave?"

"I'm not sure." Laura downed her second cup of tea and put the rest of the scone in her napkin. "I need to get back now."

"You mean before we talk this through."

"There's nothing to talk through?"

"Oh, yes, there is." Renee grabbed a notebook and pen. "We need to make a list."

"A list? Isn't it a bit late?" But even as she said it, she knew it was futile. Renee was methodical. She shopped with lists, cleaned her house by a list, and made all major decisions after consulting a list.

"I'll number the advantages." Renee wrote the date across the top of the paper. "Then we'll number the disadvantages." Renee ran a hand through her short sandy hair. "You need to do this with any decision: moving, whether you want a baby, a new husband—"

"Hold it!" Laura pushed her chair back. "I get the point, but I'm just not ready for lists or husbands." Laura always thought through decisions carefully. She'd talk about buying a new living room sofa and start looking two months later. Renee would shop one day, and the next morning it would be delivered.

"Thanks, 'Nee, but I'm going home. Talk to you later."

"Here. Was going to give you these anyway since they're your favorites." She handed over a bag filled with three scones. "Be sure to keep me posted on everything."

"I will. I promise."

Laura thought of the message as she made her way back across the yard. The voice had been deep and confident. What was the person like inside? Was she really opening a can of worms? Was this a good choice? She needed to call back, discuss the possible job opening, and see what the pastor's expectations were.

She entered the house, glanced at Jerry's picture on the fireplace mantel, and blew him a kiss. "Honey, I've got to do this. I hope you understand. I'm going to answer this message. For the first time in a long while, I'm looking forward to what tomorrow will bring." She threw her arms wide open. "Lord, I will do this if this pastor—whoever he is—wants me. I feel You have led me this far."

The answering machine blinked the numeral two as she entered the house, indicating that another call had come in while she was out. She pushed the *play* button and the same husky voice filled the room.

"In regard to your ad, I thought of something else. There's a good bed-and-breakfast for you to stay in for a while. Should you decide to remain long-term, a small rental house is opening up at the end of May. Just thought this might help you reach a decision."

Laura looked at Jerry's picture again and let her breath out. Was this a good choice? She'd never know if she didn't take that first step. Later there'd be time to decide what to do about the house, Jerry's fishing gear, the furniture, and the accumulation of possessions one acquires after living forever in one spot. Maybe she'd sell. Maybe she'd rent out the house. But first things first. She needed to make the call, see what this Reverend Gregory Hall had in mind.

"Yes," she said aloud. "I can do all things through Christ who strengthens me."

$$\textbf{2}$$

*R*everend Gregory Michael Hall closed one eye as he stared into the bathroom mirror. Just as he thought. He'd nicked his face shaving. He grabbed toilet paper and dabbed the tiny cut. That's why he preferred a beard: No shaving every morning. A weekly trim sufficed. None of this morning stuff before you had a cup of coffee. Glenn, the best barber in Joseph, had cut his dark hair yesterday and whacked off most of the beard before shaving his face smooth.

"Looks like it's time to give you a shave, Reverend. When the cherry blossoms are blooming in town, the beard goes." It was a spring ritual. No man in Joseph wore a beard during the spring and summer months.

Cobalt blue eyes stared back from the bathroom mirror. The woman—Laura Madison—would arrive today. He had no idea when. He hadn't been able to pin her down. She'd said it all depended on when she left Sealand.

Gregory had made arrangements for her to stay at Ruth's Mountain View Bed & Breakfast. Ruth had opened almost the first "B & B" in Joseph, a huge house on the ridge. Tourists liked the view of the Wallowa Mountains, yet it was close enough to walk into town. Ruth always had a guest room ready, as she had three bedrooms on the second floor and two on the top. She never tired of having guests and would welcome Laura Madison with open arms.

The early morning sun peeked up over the mountain, nearly blinding him with its brilliance. Soon the snow would melt. It was already gone from the valley's low places, but patches clung to the higher spots. Gregory knew he would never tire of the picturesque scene: the lush, verdant valleys fed by clear mountain streams and the wild daisies dotting the meadows each summer. Mornings were crisp, some downright cold, but by noon the sun penetrated the little town.

Gregory liked Joseph in the spring. It was the best time of year. The boys liked it because school would soon be out. He found himself wishing he had someone to share this glorious time of year with. If only—

Gregory wouldn't think of the if onlys. *God, I have much to be thankful for. My boys. My church. The people here. I love them all. And if my heart is a bit lonely, so be it.*

Standing in a T-shirt, he ran a hand through his unruly, thick hair. Thank heaven for Scandinavian ancestors. His father was buried with a full head of snow-white hair. Gregory's had streaks of gray and someday it would turn white.

The boys clattered down from the loft where they shared one large dorm room the whole length of the house. Soon they would leave for school. Joel, the eldest, a seventh grader who was almost thirteen, acted like he was going on thirty. Serious-minded, he was also getting fussy about his appearance, needing to comb his blond hair several times before he was satisfied. His pickiness and his reluctance to do things with the family bothered Gregory. He remembered being that way, but he had never been as quiet or reserved as Joel. It was only in later years that he grew quiet and reflective.

"Dad! Aren't you through in there?"

Gregory glanced at his watch. The bus didn't come for twenty minutes.

"Be just another minute."

"You say that every morning."

"Don't say anything back," Gregory muttered under his breath. Though he was annoyed, he kept his retorts to himself as they did nothing to improve the boy's disposition.

He buttoned his navy blue corduroy shirt, his heart swelling at the memory of watching his eldest being born. It had truly been one of life's greatest moments to see that tiny bit of humanity, the fingers clutching his so fiercely.

Gregory couldn't believe it had been nine years since the boys' mother had died. It had happened so fast. An aneurysm following childbirth was rare but not unheard of, the doctor at the hospital in Enterprise had said. "I'm so sorry, Reverend Hall."

When Gregory had come to Joseph, fresh out of seminary, young and unattached, he thought he was destined to stay that way. The district superintendent had other ideas. "You need to consider marrying," he said. "A pastor needs a wife, and the congregation needs him to have one."

Gregory nodded in agreement. He knew it to be true, but getting over the woman he had loved—who had jilted him—still consumed him. It had been the worst tragedy of his young life. Beth Marie was constantly in his thoughts. Somehow he couldn't think of dating anyone just yet.

Three months later, Shirley Bishop, who worked at the local café, volunteered to help out at the church one day a week. She printed the weekly bulletins and answered his mail. He soon looked forward to her bright smile and sunny disposition, and she helped him get acquainted with the members of the small church. Feeling indebted to her, he asked her to dinner one night, and, since they seemed congenial, he asked her out again. One thing led to another, and soon they made plans to marry. He loved and respected Shirley, but didn't feel the all-consuming love he'd had for Beth Marie. Still, he felt God had led him to this step. Besides, everyone in Joseph thought this girl, with her scattering of freckles and happy-go-lucky smile, was just right for Preacher Hall. Caleb, the youngest, was a constant reminder of his mother.

Shirley had made him a good home, played piano for the small congregation, and taught a Sunday school class. He hadn't realized until after her death how much he actually loved his wife. Even now, after nine years, he missed her. . . . Yet he had never quite forgotten Beth Marie. It was a different feeling, and he decided it was okay.

Since Shirley's death, their boys were the one thing that kept him going, made him work hard, and made him forget his loneliness.

❧

"Dad!" Joel banged on the door. "The bus comes in ten minutes."

"Eighteen," he muttered under his breath.

"Dad!"

"Okay! It's all yours!"

Joel glared as he pushed his way past his father. "I told you we needed another bathroom."

"I thought that was only necessary with girls."

"Yeah. Right."

Gregory entered the kitchen and put the coffee on. Mornings weren't complete without at least two cups.

"Mornin', Dad," Caleb called. He was lacing his shoes and had his backpack on the floor beside him.

"Good morning, yourself," Gregory answered. "Your school conference is tomorrow, right?"

"Yes, Dad," he sighed. "I wrote it on the calendar."

Caleb opened the front door, paused, then came back and kissed his father's cheek. "See ya after school."

"Yeah, sure."

Gregory smiled inwardly. Sometimes he felt as if he were a child and his boys were the father. They admonished him a lot. Of course, he had many things on his mind even before he'd read Laura Madison's ad in the *Chieftain*.

The bus honked, the door slammed, and Joel ran out of the bathroom.

"Thanks a lot, Dad! I didn't get to eat breakfast."

"Grab an apple or some bread."

"Never mind."

"Have a good day," he called after the retreating back.

Gregory poured his first cup of coffee and pulled out the nearest chair. He shoved a bowl aside and mopped up a few droplets of milk. Caleb was sloppy, especially in the morning. Joel was fastidious, as Gregory remembered being.

He reached for his old leather Bible. It was a morning for Psalms.

About half of the passages were highlighted in fluorescent yellow. His eye caught the first two verses of Psalm 25: "To you, O Lord, I lift up my soul; in you I trust, O my God."

Gregory had often considered moving on from Joseph. He was glad that his church wasn't the sort that changed preachers every three years or so. If the people liked you, you might stay until you retired. But was he doing his job? Was he still an effective minister?

He closed the Bible, said his morning prayer, then rinsed out his cup. Grabbing his denim jacket from beside the door, he hurried out into the morning brightness.

It was a mile into town since he'd moved out on the hill, but he needed to walk. It helped clear his mind and started his day out right. One way that he got close to God was through his daily morning walks. The fresh air made him breathe deeply. His boys were thriving, he had his church family, and those in town who knew him, respected him. Though there were some who never stepped inside his church, he knew most were good people. But that wasn't enough. He had to try harder to win souls.

He reached the end of town and thought again about Shirley. He hadn't given her his all, and he would always regret that.

A car stopped, offering him a ride, but he waved them on. "It's dangerous, Pastor, walking out here with no sidewalks."

Gregory shrugged. "They can see me. Thanks for the offer, brother."

Though he'd had coffee, he hadn't eaten. By the time he reached the middle of town, he was ravenous. He'd stop at the Main Street Café to order another cup of coffee and a slice of cinnamon toast. This wasn't cinnamon toast like his mother made, but a Finnish concoction he'd grown to love. He'd discovered it after first arriving in Joseph. The toast was shipped in from Astoria, Oregon, where a Finnish bakery had been making it since 1910. They sent the special item all over the country.

"This toast is what the sailors took aboard the ships," the owner of the café had told him. "It doesn't mold, rot, or ever taste bad. Just right for dipping into coffee." Since then Gregory's breakfast often consisted of two eggs over easy and three slices of cinnamon toast.

"What's happening today, Reverend?" Sally, the morning waitress, asked. "Anything I need to know about?"

He smiled as he broke the toast in half. "Think we have a piano player coming into town."

"Today?" She didn't need to write the order anymore. In fact, now that he thought about it, Sally never wrote the order. She didn't even carry a pad or pencil in her apron pocket.

"Yes, today. Name is Laura Madison. Says she's mature. Now tell me, Sally, exactly what is 'mature'?"

Sally grinned. "I'd say it's anyone over forty."

"Over forty?" Gregory gulped. "That must mean I'm getting close then."

"You? Never."

"I think it's more like fifty-five or maybe sixty."

"If she's coming today, guess you'll know right soon then."

He dipped his toast into the coffee. "Yep, guess you're right."

After breakfast, Gregory called on old man Kelter, who still lived alone though he was ninety-three. Gregory enjoyed visiting the salty gentleman, who had a new story to tell each day. Because he worried about him, Gregory looked in on him two or three times a week. He checked his refrigerator, making sure he had enough food, and made sure his feet weren't swelling. Gregory wasn't a doctor, but he knew anyone with diabetes needed to be careful. Kelter hadn't been diagnosed until he was seventy.

❧

" 'Old-age diabetes,' the doc said," he had said.

"What's going to happen if you can't cook anymore?" Gregory once asked.

John Kelter had thumped the table. "I ain't ever leavin' this here house and if they take me, I'll run off. Ain't going to no hospital to die like my Clara did. Nosiree!"

❧

Gregory found John out in his yard, checking on some bulbs that he'd planted last fall.

"Hi, Preacher!"

"And a top of the morning to you!"

"I heerd tell that a piano player is arriving today."

"How'd you hear that?"

"Word gets around. I may be old and deaf, but I know what's going on."

"Do you want someone to pick you up on Sunday so you can hear her play?"

John squinted as the sun hit the old, crinkled eyes. "Now, Preacher, you know better than to ask me that."

Gregory knew, but that didn't mean he would give up. John was a mountain man in the true sense of the word and worshipped God in his own way. Gregory decided to change the subject.

"Can I take you over to the hospital today or tomorrow for a checkup?"

John squinted again. "No, sir. I have no need for physicals."

"Just thought I'd check."

"I want to die like that Harry Truman did when Mount St. Helen's blew. Die right here in my little house, in my bed or on the sofa, if the good Lord decides that's the best place."

"Okay. I won't bug you about it anymore. Can I bring you dinner one night this week?"

John laughed, revealing a toothless grin. "Now, Preacher, you know the ladies at yore church take care of me real nicelike."

"That's good. Thought they were."

"I'd ask you in, but my favorite game show is coming on in five minutes."

Gregory genially slapped the older man on the back. "I sure wouldn't want to come between you and that game show. I'll see you tomorrow or the next day. And if you're real good, I might bring that piano player around to meet you."

He left the old man standing on his porch, wondering who had encouraged whom. That was the way with the people in this town.

They all encouraged and loved one another. He knew he wasn't an outstanding orator, but he was good with his people. It was just relationships with women he failed at.

He turned and headed back downtown to the church that had become his second home.

$\mathcal{A}$ fter Laura called Reverend Gregory Hall—"Gregory Michael Hall" he informed her on the phone—they made plans for her to come for an interview the following Tuesday. This gave Laura five days to back out, if she wished.

In those five days she visited old friends. Though it seemed a bit premature, she resigned her positions with the church administrative council, on the library board, as chair of the annual Cancer Walk, and as reading tutor at the local grade school. All were commendable positions: all volunteer jobs to keep her busy, keep her from thinking.

She'd finally worked up her courage to contact her children.

"Mom, this is super!" Jen, her daughter, said. "You need to do something adventuresome for a change. Maybe you'll find a man in Joseph—"

"May I remind you," Laura cut in, "that that is the last thing I hope to do."

"Well, you just never know. But I'm happy for you. I really am. Maybe I'll come over when I have some vacation time."

"I'll send an address as soon as I have one."

She couldn't get in touch with Steve, her vagabond son. He was traveling through Europe, staying at youth hostels. The last she'd heard was that he intended to put off college for at least another six months. Laura was confident that Steve would go with the tide; always did, always had.

She hadn't expected Kurt's reaction, however.

"Mom, is this some stunt you're pulling to get my attention?"

Laura looked at her tall son, so like his father with the same hair coloring, the deep brown eyes that could melt anyone's resolve, the square chin. She wanted to take him into her arms as she had done when he was a child and cuddle him. She'd always had a special feeling for her firstborn. Did other mothers feel this way about the first child?

"I am not trying to prove anything, nor am I trying to get your attention. I'm doing this for me because it's time I did something different."

"Susan and I may get engaged."

"That's wonderful, Kurt. She's a nice, Christian girl."

Kurt and Susan had begun dating way back in junior high when she'd first come to the youth group meetings.

"But you need to be here to—"

"To what? Give you an engagement party?"

"No, not that, but just to be here in case I need advice."

Laura shook her head. "Kurt, I can't always be here for you. You need to make decisions on your own, and I know you're quite capable of doing that."

He sighed as only he could sigh. "You've changed since Dad died."

The words hurt. She'd tried to be a good mother, but it was always as if something important were missing. She'd never been able to explain it, not even to Renee. She stood and faced her son now. "I've done my best by you, Kurt, and you've grown into a responsible young man. You have a good job, a good life, and I trust you to weigh things, to pray about it before making a monumental decision. If Susan is the right mate for you, you'll know."

"Did you pray about this change, Mom?"

She caught the edge in his voice. "I certainly did."

"I just don't like it."

"And maybe I won't, either. Maybe I'll be home in a week or two."

Kurt left with an armful of magazines, a few videos, and food from the refrigerator. "I love you, Mom." He set the stuff down and reached over to hug her. "Whatever you do, be careful."

"I intend to do that very thing."

Laura put off talking to her minister. Pastor Dave Reynolds, at age thirty-two, was graying at the temples. He joked about it often: "It's what happens when you don't let go and let God take care of your life. I was so fearful of going bald, but never thought about going gray."

"This is a big surprise," Dave said when Laura entered his office Monday morning. "I heard about your moving, as one always does in a small town. Guess I didn't want to believe it."

Laura smiled. "Figures. Word travels fast in Sealand."

"Isn't all this resigning a bit premature? What if you don't like it there?"

"Maybe I won't; but if it doesn't work out, I'll move back."

"And the kids. What do they think?"

Laura studied a broken fingernail. "Kurt's the only one with reservations."

Pastor Dave nodded. "Kids want their mothers always to be there and never to change their hairstyle or where they live."

"It's my Sunday dinners he'll miss, not me."

He chuckled. "Yeah. You're probably right on that one. Just be very sure is all I suggest."

Laura nodded. "I am. What's the old saying? 'Nothing ventured, nothing gained'? I guess that's where I'm at right now, Dave."

He walked around his desk. "Good. You sound positive about this step. Some of us get in a rut, and you just happen to be altering your life. We'll miss you. Please keep in touch."

"I'll do that."

"And if you ever need a preacher over that way, give me a holler."

"I'll be sure to tell Pastor Hall."

He put his hand on her shoulder and offered a prayer. Laura thanked him and left.

The final good-bye to Renee wasn't as easy. She'd come over several times already with another list. This last time she'd brought coffee, brownies, and a lunch box filled with goodies for the trip.

"You must remember to turn the heat down, put your phone on vacation status, and—"

"Hold it," Laura interrupted. "I'm not a child."

"Oh, I know. I'm just compulsive. You know that," Renee said, then looked away for a long moment. "I'm going to miss you, kid."

"Then come see me."

"You know we'll never do that, but maybe . . ."

They sat on the deck while they talked and munched on brownies and sipped coffee. The hanging geranium looked bright and made Laura smile. "Here. You might as well take my plant. It isn't going to live without daily watering."

Renee stood, removing the hook from the tree branch. "Thanks. I can use another one at the end of the porch, and this is such a glorious scarlet."

"I'm glad I don't have any animals," Laura said. They'd lost Muffy, an adorable cockapoo, the same year Jerry died, and she hadn't been able to even think of getting a replacement. Just as she hadn't wanted a husband replacement.

Laura always traveled light, so Renee now asked what she was taking.

"Mostly my sweats, some casual pants, sweaters, and a few good outfits."

"They may dress up more there than they do here at the beach."

Laura shrugged. "If so, I'll just have to buy something."

"What about shoes?"

"Two pairs."

"What? Two pairs? You can't get by with two." Renee looked shocked.

"I have my walking shoes and my dress-up ones."

Renee pushed her chair back and shook her head. "You gotta take more. Really. You'll need walking shoes, house shoes, ones you work in, walk in, and at least two for church."

Laura rolled her eyes. "Okay. I'll take more. I'm taking basic black. You have heard of basic black? You suppose that will be suitable?"

"How about a touch of purple or that burgundy you look so good in?"

"I don't think so."

Renee looked at her list and crumpled it up. "I don't know why I try with you. You're going to do your own thing, aren't you?"

Laura bit into a second brownie. "Yes, I guess so. Being mature means you don't have to impress anyone."

"I remember when I saw the one suitcase you took on your trip to Florida."

Laura smiled at the memory. "Yeah, I know, you'd need a suitcase that size just for your lists."

Tears sprang to Renee's eyes. "Who will I have coffee with? Or who will watch a video with me?" Renee often came over while Derek watched some sports program.

"Well, who am I going to have coffee with?"

"You'll find somebody. That's the way you are."

❧

By Monday night she was prepared, thanks to Renee and her endless lists. Her car's glove compartment held a new, small first-aid kit Renee had given her and a flashlight—not a simple one, but one that weighed twenty pounds and flashed in case there was trouble.

"Remember to stay in the vehicle and put this sign in the window." Renee looked fearful. "Don't open your window to anyone except a state patrolman."

"I won't. I promise."

The lunch box contained two sandwiches, cookies, apples and bananas, and a small package of cheese. It was enough for four people. "Are you sure you haven't forgotten something?" Laura asked, trying to conceal her smile. Renee did everything so thoroughly.

"I did!" Renee turned and sprinted across the yard to her house.

"Here!" She ran back, holding up a marked map. "This is the best place to stop to rest and stretch."

"I thought I'd drive straight there."

Renee looked shocked. "Most accidents are caused by the driver being tired or sleepy."

"Relax." Laura leaned over and hugged her friend hard. "I'll stop every other hour. How's that sound?"

"And you'll call when you arrive?"

Laura assured her, "The second I hit town."

They hugged good-bye, as Laura would leave early the next morning. She thought about Renee's statement later. Laura did make friends easily; always had. It was she who had gone over to borrow the proverbial "cup of sugar" from Renee when she moved in.

She finished packing. Just for good measure, and because of what Renee had said, she added a pair of boots. Not exactly dress boots, but they were good for mud should she find any.

Laura could hardly sleep that night as excitement bubbled inside her. She felt young and vibrant at the prospect of exploring new territory. What would tomorrow bring?

During her evening devotion, she stumbled across James 4:13–14: "Now listen, you who say, 'Today or tomorrow we will go to this or that city, spend a year there, carry on business and make money.' Why, you do not even know what will happen tomorrow. What is your life? You are a mist that appears for a little while and then vanishes."

"A mist!" she said aloud. "I am but a mist in the scheme of things." How like God to have a sense of humor, to put a smile on her lips before her new undertaking.

4

The car was packed. One Sunday outfit, a black-and-white houndstooth jacket with solid black skirt—the most slimming outfit Laura owned—hung on the hook. A suitcase with casual clothes and plenty of warm sweaters was in the trunk.

The house looked deserted as she backed out of the driveway. The freshly dug dirt where she'd planted dahlias gave it an incomplete look. "I hope I'm doing the right thing, Jerry," she said, talking to him as if he were right there beside her.

She glanced at Renee's house, but the curtains were still drawn.

Guide me, God, she prayed. *Shield me from all harm. And help me to do what is right.*

Heading over the miles, Laura thought about Renee insisting she call the Wallowa County Visitors' Bureau. "You could get snowbound, you know."

"Yes, it is brisk up in that country the first of April," the lady had said. "There's still snow in the mountains and nights are downright nippy, but if you stay on the main road, you'll be fine. I wouldn't try traveling after dark or too early in the morning." She hesitated. "And stay on the main roads. We lost a car last year and haven't seen it since."

Laura gasped, and the lady chuckled, "I was just kidding, of course."

It might have been better if she'd waited until summer, but the job was open now. There was a need for her, and she knew she had to get away. She felt God leading her in this direction. Laura patted the dashboard. "You'll get me there okay," she said, encouraging the car, "I just know it."

As Laura drove across the Astoria-Megler Bridge, she marveled at the sight. The view was awesome with the Columbia River serene on this clear, windless day. A large ship was anchored east of the bridge, and small fishing boats dotted the water. She doubted she'd ever be able to step foot in a boat again. She'd drive into Portland, then take the I-84 freeway heading east. The freeway ran along the Columbia, past Multnomah Falls, and onto Hood River. At The Dalles, she'd be out of the immense trees and rugged terrain.

Laura listened to gospel music as she drove. "What a mighty God we serve! What a mighty God we serve," she sang lustily. Once, it hit her that she was traveling alone and if something happened, she wasn't sure what she would do; however, she believed in prayer and in guardian angels. Feeling confident, she started another song, "Gentle Shepherd."

An hour later, she stopped for coffee. She'd already eaten one of the sandwiches Renee had packed, but she needed to stretch.

The coffee shop buzzed with activity. It was obviously the place the local people gathered in at The Dalles. A man sat in the large corner booth with cameras flashing as a lady held a microphone in front of him.

"He's our local celebrity," the waitress said as she poured Laura a cup of coffee and handed her a menu. "A state representative, home for Easter."

Laura listened while she had her coffee. The politician glanced her way and smiled. She looked away, deciding against a refill.

Laura topped the tank, then headed east, going through Pendleton, over the Blue Mountains toward La Grande. There she'd turn and go north.

"Can't get lost," the station attendant had said. "You'll hit a couple of small towns on your way to Joseph. Just follow the road signs."

When Laura pulled into Elgin, she looked for a place for coffee, wishing she'd brought a thermos.

"What's Joseph like?" Laura asked the lady in the bakery while she munched on a maple bar.

"Small town like this one," she responded. She was frosting the sides of a sheet cake. "I been over there once, maybe twice." She glanced up. "Why? You goin' to move there?"

Laura nodded. "I might."

"Where you coming from?"

"The Washington coast."

"And you're moving here?"

Laura sipped her coffee. She supposed it did sound strange. "Let's just say I need a change."

The lady nodded. "I felt that way when I left Oklahoma."

Laura smiled. "Thought I detected an accent."

"Moved here ten years ago and love it. Small town atmosphere. If you're in a hurry, this is not the place to live."

"I know what you mean." Laura poured another cup of coffee since the pot was close and she didn't want to take the woman away from her cake. "I come from a small place now. I like small. I want to know my neighbor and my neighbor's neighbor."

"It'll be like that in Joseph, for sure."

"What's the picture on the computer screen?"

"That's what's going on the top of this cake."

"It is?" Laura stepped closer, studying the photo.

"Yep. New way of decorating cakes. She pointed to a small machine next to the computer. "People send photos and I put them on the cake. If you wait a sec, you'll see that photo right on top of this cake."

Laura waited.

"Saw how to do this on the Internet and decided to try it. Bought the scanner, and now that's the only kind of decorating people want. This here cake is heading to Portland via UPS. Got an order from a lady up there."

A voice came on the computer, saying the scanner was ready. Laura watched as the cake inched ever so slowly under the scanner.

"Voila! Here it is."

"I must get a picture." Laura zoomed in on the cake and took two photos to make sure at least one would turn out. "If I ever need a cake for a special occasion, I'll be sure to call."

"Joseph isn't exactly close, you know."

"It's a lot closer than Portland." Laura put her camera back in the case and thanked the baker for the demonstration.

She left and wended her way north. On the drive out of Elgin, the flat valley soon gave way to forested hills, then the snow-topped Wallowa Mountains.

Laura pulled off in a turnaround, got out, and inhaled deeply the crisp mountain air. She took a photo to send Renee and the kids, then got back in. Already she knew she'd need a heavier coat than the one she'd brought.

The Wallowa River meandered along the road and fishermen in hip boots, heavy coats, and caps with earflaps lined the riverbank. She waved at one who held up a good-sized fish, and a lump came to her throat. Though Jerry had only fished once with waders in a stream, it brought back poignant memories of that time, and she wondered if they might not have come here again to fish. She'd have to find out what they were catching. At home it was mostly salmon. Boats went out beyond the bar for tuna and bottom fish; some fished for sturgeon from the bank.

Going through more small towns, heading south, Laura felt she was backtracking, but it couldn't be helped. She had the map Renee had marked so well, and there was clearly only one road into Joseph. If she could have cut across from La Grande, the route would have been more direct.

Enterprise was the closest town to Joseph. Laura drove by the courthouse, admiring the large building and sprawling lawn. She got out of the car and stretched her legs. She decided to walk over to a mall, where she found a chamber of commerce and picked up maps and literature about the area.

Laura arrived in Joseph at four. She hadn't figured it would take all day, but neither had she figured she'd be stopping every ten minutes to snap another photo. It wasn't determined that she'd move here; it might be the only time she'd come this way. She wanted pictures to show everyone back home.

A pair of magnificent bronzed horses graced the lawn of a large factory. She'd heard about the bronzed sculptures that were shipped all over the world. She'd have to take a tour after she settled in.

It was too late to find the Reverend Gregory Michael Hall in the church office. He'd be home by now. Or would he be waiting for her? Maybe his wife had cooked dinner and she'd be asked to join them. But she did need to freshen up a bit first and, of course, call Renee.

A bookstore caught her eye on the right, and it seemed to be attached to several other buildings comprising a mall. The restroom sign was a most welcome sight.

Her hair was flying in every direction. That's what happened when you drove with the window at half-mast. She looked tired, with bags under her eyes. It had been a full day. Perhaps Reverend Hall wouldn't notice. She was coming to fill a position, not be scrutinized for her looks.

After applying fresh makeup, Laura stopped in the bookstore. The lady was just turning the "Open" sign around.

"Please excuse me," Laura called out. "I know it's late, but I'm looking for this place." She handed her the address scribbled in her address book.

The woman nodded. "That would be Pastor Hall's home. He's out on the Joseph highway, about a mile. New place. Sits up on the hill. Looks out over the river and Chief Joseph's Cemetery."

"Oh. It's not in town, then?"

"Not quite, but close. Hey, I'm Nancy."

"Laura Madison."

"Are you the lady who placed an ad in the *Chieftain?* Everyone was talking about it."

"Figures you'd already know about me," Laura said.

"We read every line of the paper, you know."

"I'm coming to play the piano at the Community Church. Do you go there?"

Nancy held out a business card. "I live in Enterprise, and coming down here six days a week is enough."

"Do you know Reverend Hall?"

"Oh, yes. Small town, you know. Everyone knows everyone.

You'll soon discover that. Reverend Hall comes in often. Nice enough man, but—"

"But?"

"It's nothing. No, I like him. He's friendly."

Laura still wondered what the "but" referred to as she picked up a book on the counter.

"I'd let you look around, but I'm closing early. School board meeting tonight."

"That's fine. I don't have time to browse now, anyway. But later. I'm an avid reader."

"Good. Here, do you want this coffee? I was going to dump it out. I also have a pizza roll, one of our specialties. They're very popular with the locals."

"Why, thank you." Laura took the coffee and roll. "I am a bit hungry. Never stopped for lunch."

"You're staying the night, of course."

"Yes, at a bed-and-breakfast."

"That would be Ruth's Mountain View."

"Is it a good place?"

"Ruth's the best. Marvelous cook, too." She turned the lights off except for one. "You just go on out there. Can't miss it. There's a fence around the house. He has a dog, you know."

"Thanks for the directions and the coffee and roll."

Laura drove slowly through town, looking at the small cafés, motels, museum, and gas station. It was pretty small, smaller than she'd thought. Enterprise was definitely the larger town of the two.

Laura looked east to the line of mountains. She knew she would never tire of the scene and could hardly wait to explore the area. A road sign pointed to Wallowa Lake. Everyone had told her not to miss the lake. "Even if you're there just a day, you must go to the lake and stop at the small country store. Has the best fudge ever." This from her pastor whom she'd called the night before leaving.

She then saw the sign to the cemetery. Looking to her left, she couldn't miss the house. It sat on a small knoll with a commanding view of the cemetery, the lake, and the hills on the eastern edge. She turned on her signal and climbed the driveway that wound up and around.

She heard barking from within and waited for someone to answer the doorbell. A young boy soon appeared. "Are you the piano lady coming from Washington?" The boy had a rash of freckles across his face and a happy-go-lucky smile.

She nodded. "That I am."

"My name's Caleb. C'mon in."

"Hello, Caleb." Laura stepped inside and shook his hand. "I'm Laura Madison. Are your parents home?"

His smile froze. "Parents? You mean my dad?"

"Well, yes, your dad. And I thought, well—"

"Don't have a mother, you know. She died when I was born."

"Oh." Laura let the shock sink in. "I didn't know. I am so sorry." What else could you say to a child when you've assumed he has a mother? "I guess you'd better take me to your father then."

5

*C*aleb closed the door just as a small, woolly dog raced around the corner and jumped up on her.

"Down, Patsy!" Caleb grabbed the wriggling bundle. "She loves company."

"Caleb, put the dog in your bedroom."

Laura glanced up from petting the excited dog as the man owning the voice entered the room, extending his hand. "Laura Madison?"

"Yes." She offered her hand, and he shook it heartily. "I was expecting you earlier and also expecting someone more—what was the word in your ad?"

"Mature?"

"Yes, mature."

Laura often felt every bit of her forty-five years but was told she looked and acted younger. She could see she had already failed on two counts. The man looked older than he probably was, but it was the brooding eyes that caught her attention. She trembled before answering.

"You were expecting someone with gray hair. Well, I am mature in nature, if not age, and I arrived late because I kept stopping to take pictures."

"I see. You must be a camera buff, then." He ran a hand through his thick mop of dark hair.

Laura nodded. "I met Nancy at the bookstore, and she directed me here."

"We do have a great bookstore. Big selection." His eyes met her gaze. "We can still talk, of course, but tomorrow morning would be a better time."

"Of course." Laura looked away. Reverend Hall was taller than she'd even imagined, and his eyes were deep blue and penetrating. She wasn't sure what she'd expected, but not someone nearly this handsome. He looked as if he belonged in these rugged mountains. His presence unnerved her and she wasn't quite sure why. It wasn't as if he'd lied to her. He just hadn't told her he was a widower.

"I think there's been a mistake—that is—on my part."

"A mistake?"

She looked at Caleb, who'd returned, then back at Reverend Hall. "I assumed you had a wife."

"Oh." He chuckled just as a blast sounded down the hall. Laura jumped.

"That's Joel practicing his horn," Caleb offered. "He practices two hours a day."

"Yes, well, I'm sure Mrs. Madison doesn't need to know all our habits. Would you go check on the hamburgers, Son?" He turned back to Laura. "Guess I forgot to mention that I'm a widower."

Laura tried to smile. "I suppose that doesn't change your need for a pianist."

"It certainly doesn't. We're in dire need, especially this Sunday, as we have new members joining, and I like to have special music. I thought of having a pianist come over from Enterprise, but she'd arrive late and what is a service without the introit?"

Laura felt uncomfortable, almost inconsequential in this man's presence, and wasn't sure why. It was evident that he ran his household with a firm hand.

"I meant to arrive before mealtime."

"Dinner is early because of Caleb's game. Second of the season. Now we'll be on a schedule of early dinners." He turned, raking his hand through his hair again. She decided it had to be his nervous habit.

"Is that baseball?" Laura hadn't realized it was that time of year already.

"Yes. Do you enjoy the game?"

Laura nodded again. "My sons played. I've spent my share of time at the ball field."

"Perhaps you'd like to join us for a hamburger and potato chips. Nothing fancy, but it'd be a way to meet the boys and we can talk about the position."

Before Laura could respond, "Yankee Doodle" sounded from the bedroom.

"He plays well, doesn't he?" she said.

"His face would turn red if he knew you were here listening to him," Caleb offered, looking at her expectantly.

"Dinner?" Reverend Hall repeated.

"Yes, that would be lovely. I even have a pizza roll to add to the table. Since it's so large, we can divide it four ways."

"Go put on an extra plate and don't forget the napkin," the reverend said to Caleb.

The music stopped and a lanky boy with a scowl appeared in the living room, his head down. "Dad, do I have to go to the game—" He stopped when he saw Laura. "Didn't know we had company."

"This is Mrs. Madison, Joel. Laura, this is Joel, my eldest son. Remember I told you she was coming to play the piano since Gert isn't coming back to Joseph and Amanda just didn't work out?"

"Yeah." He thrust his hands in the pockets of his Levi's. "I remember."

"A gentleman offers his hand," the reverend said.

Joel stepped forward, his eyes not meeting Laura's. His hand was limp, but she added firmness to her shake. "You can really play the trumpet."

His face flushed as he hurried from the room.

"He's an okay kid, but needs some refining. . . ."

"That comes later, perhaps, Reverend," Laura said.

"Gregory. You may call me Gregory. No need for formality."

Caleb hollered from the kitchen. "I think these hamburgers are done, Dad!"

Laura smiled. Reverend Hall might teach Joel formal manners, but Caleb was another story. "Could I possibly help in some way?"

"Everything's done," Caleb said, coming back into the room with a uniform on.

"Wow, that was quick," Laura said. Caleb's eyes lit up his whole face, and Laura realized why she had come here. Yes, she'd play the piano for a small community church, but there were two motherless boys who might need her presence more.

Gregory left the room. Laura followed Caleb, having the first feeling of acceptance.

"Of course you're coming to my baseball game," Caleb announced as they entered a kitchen. With pale green walls and an apple border, everything was immaculate, not what one expected in a house without a woman. She pulled out a chair.

"Now, Son, Mrs. Madison is too tired to go to your game."

Gregory glanced over as Laura blurted out, "But I'd like to go. Really, I would."

"Good, then I don't have to," Joel said, shuffling into the room.

"Now, Son, we've had this discussion before."

"I don't want to go."

"Dad, he doesn't have to—"

"He's going and that's final. I'll hear no more about it." Gregory bowed his head. "Let's thank God for this meal."

"If I fail English, it's your fault!"

"Joel! Enough. There'll be time for studying after the game."

The younger boy pushed his chair back and dumped his plate in the sink.

Laura had only finished half her hamburger. She'd forgotten how quickly men and young boys ate. "These are certainly delicious. I need the recipe," she said, feeling uncomfortable.

Gregory laughed. "Just chopped up onions and a dash of ketchup."

"They're so moist."

"I like them that way, and the boys don't care as long as it's food. When their mother died, I couldn't make anything but macaroni and cheese dinners."

"And noodles?"

"No. They didn't like those much, especially the one combination I tried."

"What was that?"

"Leftover split pea soup and chicken noodle; I combined the two."

Laura made a face. "Oh. I don't think I'd like it, either."

"And you threw in leftover rice, Dad." Caleb was back in the room, lacing up his shoes. "It was the grossest ever!"

Laura tried to keep a straight face. It had been so long since her children had been young. She'd forgotten how picky they were, but one could never fail with hamburgers, hot dogs, and pizza. Her Kurt hadn't even liked turkey.

The kitchen was cleaned in minutes while Caleb grabbed his mitt and cap.

"We'll direct you to Ruth's right after the game," Gregory said, holding the back door open for her. "We'll come back here to get your car, if that's okay."

"Sounds fine."

"You'll love Ruth. Everyone does," Gregory said.

Laura met his steady gaze. "She sounds like the town's grandma. We have a grandmotherly type back in Sealand. Her name's Dorothy. She never married, so the church is her family. If you miss a Sunday, she calls to see if you're ill. She keeps track of everyone from her seat in the back row."

"Does Dorothy make cookies?" Caleb asked, punching his hand into his baseball mitt. "Ruth bakes the best chocolate chip cookies of anyone I know."

Gregory nodded. "Yes, but I prefer her peanut butter. I agree that she's the best cook this side of the Rockies. Her cookies are the first to disappear when we have the annual Christmas cookie walk."

"Does she have other specialties?" Laura asked.

"I'd say 'to die for.' " Gregory smiled. Laura realized it was the first time a smile had crossed his face since she met him. "We go to her place Sundays after church for brunch."

"Waffles," Caleb said. "And blueberry pancakes."

"Canadian bacon, hash browns, and fruit compote," Gregory added.

"She doesn't make anything like noodles and pea soup," Caleb said.

"We should get along just fine then." Laura smiled. There was something about this kid she liked, really liked. He so reminded her of Kurt and his exuberance at that age. She noticed Joel hadn't said a word during the exchange, and her heart went out to him.

❧

The baseball field immediately brought back pleasant memories. Boys in uniform were dashing around while the coach told them to pay attention. Pitchers were practicing their throws. Laura thought about Kurt playing up through the Babe Ruth League. Playing left field, he dove for fly balls and hit the ball hard when up to bat. She sighed. What had happened to that sweet, eager child? Nearly engaged to be married to a wonderful girl, he seemed morose, totally unhappy, as if he were searching for something.

The evening was cool and she was glad she'd worn the heavy sweater and brought along her coat.

"Hi, Reverend Hall," the coach called out. "Maybe this is the night that Caleb hits a home run."

Gregory made the victory sign. "He'll come around."

"Is this the new piano player you been advertising for?" The coach leaned over the fence, and Laura had to laugh as she was introduced. Everyone knew about her coming, even the coach.

Gregory left for the concession stand, returning with peanuts, a bag of popcorn, and two long raspberry ropes. "Have to support the team, you know. I work the concession stand one Saturday a month. Little League is big in Joseph, in case you hadn't guessed." He smiled as their eyes met. Laura trembled unexpectedly as she took the popcorn.

"I'm used to the life of a Little League mother." She popped a kernel in her mouth. "I, too, did the concession stand. We had hot dogs for fifty cents then."

"Did you want a hot dog?" he asked.

"Heavens, no, not after that wonderful meal."

Gregory eased back on the stadium seat. It was funny how Laura felt herself going into this phase. It had nearly taken her back ten years to those days when Jerry rushed home from work and met her at the ball field. Most times she had something in the slow cooker, so they would eat the second they got home.

"Your children played ball, then?"

Laura nodded. "Kurt, the oldest, played every sport he could, but baseball was his favorite. He plays on a local softball team now."

"That's one thing parents usually have in common—an interest in the local sports. Joseph people are wonderful at supporting the community, especially school activities."

"It's important," Laura agreed. "How about the churches? Would you say most people are Christian?"

"Definitely." Greg glanced at Caleb, who was up at bat. "Caleb's been in a batting slump, couldn't hit during practice or the game last week, but he'll pull out of it."

The young boy hunched over the plate, winging his bat as he got into a crouched position.

"I have an idea he's going to hit that ball over the fence," Laura said just as the first ball came down the pike.

Cra-a-ack! Caleb slammed the first pitch far into right field, not over the fence, but far enough to bring the first batter in as he darted around the bases to third on a stand-up.

Laura jumped to her feet, clapping and cheering while the team made high fives.

"How about that?" Gregory said after everyone sat down. "He's over his slump."

Laura then noticed she'd dumped over the full bag of popcorn. She laughed as she looked at the golden puffs down on the ground. "I always have been a klutz," she murmured.

"What's a little popcorn?" Gregory asked. "Do you want more?"

"No, I think not. I have an idea I'm not going to be sitting long enough to eat any. Now, a red rope I can nibble on."

An ecstatic Caleb ran to the bleachers to hug his father, though he wasn't supposed to leave the dugout. "I did it, Dad! I finally hit the ball!" He hugged Laura impulsively. "Wasn't that the greatest hit ever, Laura? I mean, Mrs. Madison?" The freckles on his nose seemed to dance.

She ruffled his hair. "That's okay. You can call me Laura. ⌐
it was a smashing hit." For the first time in a very long while,
good inside.

"Happy is he who trusts in the Lord," Laura said then.

Gregory cast a glance in her direction and finally nodded. "I'd say
that's a good assessment, Mrs. Madison."

6

*T*he inning was over and the Blue Chiefs won: 7–6. The parents cheered, pounding each other on the back. A scowling Joel strode up.

"Wasn't that a great game?" Caleb asked his older brother. His gaze was expectant.

"Not as good as last week's—"

"Now, Joel," Gregory interrupted, "just because you don't play baseball is no reason—"

"I'd never play that stupid game. We have to in P. E., and it gags me then."

Laura tried not to notice the disappointment cross Caleb's face or the disgust on Gregory's. She remembered sibling rivalry, how the younger child looked up to the older, always hoping for a few words of praise. It had been that way with her sons, and she saw the same thing happening here, though she didn't know these boys yet.

"Well, I didn't see last week's game," Laura said then, "so I have no way of comparing. I thought it was a wonderful hit and two stupendous catches." She paused momentarily. "Now I'm looking forward to seeing what you do best, Joel." For a brief moment the older boy smiled, but his face froze, as if it was against the rules to be pleased with himself.

"Joel mainly plays trumpet," Caleb said, looking over his shoulder as he hurried back over to his team to help pick up the equipment.

"Playing trumpet is no easy task," Laura said. "It takes a lot of lung power. My youngest son played in the band—"

"Your kids were busy," Gregory broke in.

"Have you played for church?" Laura asked, ignoring Gregory's comment. Sudden inspiration hit.

"No," Gregory said, answering for his son. "Joel isn't much for playing in public. No solos, that is."

Joel scowled. Before she could say anything, he turned and looked in the other direction. She didn't like it when parents spoke for their children. From the looks of things, Gregory had been answering for his eldest son for quite some time now.

" 'God of Our Fathers' is a beautiful piece with a trumpet solo," Laura interjected. "It shows off the trumpet nicely."

"I don't think he'd do it."

We shall see, Laura thought, knowing she'd need to approach this slowly.

"Let's go for ice cream at the Wallowa Lake General Store," Gregory announced. "And then I'll lead you to Ruth's."

"Caleb?"

"He'll go with his team. They go to the café on Main Street."

The sun was setting, but the night was beautiful and invigorating. "I've been eager to see the lake."

"You should go during the day," Joel grunted from the backseat.

Greg pulled up in front of a brown building. "This is the place."

A deer was licking up the remains of a dropped ice cream cone.

"Oh, how sweet," Laura exclaimed.

"Don't get too close," Gregory warned. "You've got to be careful with the deer. Those hind legs can really kick and make you hurt for weeks."

"But they're so tame," Laura exclaimed. "I've never seen deer come right up to you like that."

"That's because they get fed. Heaven help them if they had to go out and forage for real food."

"Hey, Reverend," Oliver called out from inside the store. "Haven't seen you in a week or so."

"Been busy." He turned toward Laura. "Oliver, this is Laura Madison, our new piano player at church. You'll have to come hear her play."

Laura extended her hand.

"Pleased to meet you. And this is my wife, Keithanne."

A short woman with a round, pleasant face smiled. "Happy to meet you, and welcome to the lake."

"It's a beautiful spot." Laura had noticed the lake all the way out. It was so calm and pristine. She wondered if they had storms here that would beat the water up into a frenzy as it did at home.

"I hope you like it here," Keithanne said.

"It's going to be totally different for her," Gregory said. "From the ocean to the mountains."

"Yeah. From beach bum to mountain gal," Laura said, looking around. The store carried a bit of everything one could ever want. "Nice store."

"Thanks," they both chorused.

Laura stared at the trays of fudge. Mocha almond fudge, amaretto, maple nut, chocolate walnut, and more.

"Here, have a sample." Oliver cut off a tiny slab. Laura tried the fudge walnut, then a piece of peanut butter. "Made with fresh Dutch cream," he said proudly.

"It's all so good."

Keithanne had already scooped a cone for Gregory. She looked at Laura. "Ice cream or fudge?"

"Ice cream, definitely. But I want fudge to send to my best friend in Sealand."

She chose chocolate peanut butter ice cream in a waffle cone and mocha almond fudge for Renee. "My friend will be surprised to get this from me so soon," Laura said with a laugh.

"We'd better head back," Gregory said. Joel was already in the car. There were two deer waiting now. "Don't even look at them," Gregory said.

"But, look, one is crippled."

"Yeah, he's been around for a long time now, crippled at birth," Keithanne said from the doorway.

Joel was in the car, munching away on his thick slab of fudge.

"Do you always get fudge instead of ice cream?" Laura asked.

He grunted an answer, which she couldn't quite determine. She would just let it drop; but more than anything, she wanted to be friends with this young boy. Maybe if she continued to talk to him, he'd come around.

It was dusk and Laura could barely see the lake. "This is such beautiful country. I don't remember much about the lake when Jerry and I came years ago."

"It's stayed pretty much the same," Gregory offered. "Did you know there is not one signal light in Wallowa County?"

"There isn't?" Even in her small area at the beach, there were signal lights, one in each town. "Never have been?"

"No, and never will be if we can keep the developers out."

"I hope it never changes. It's beautiful as it is. I wouldn't want it to change in the least bit."

"Tell that to our congressman, then."

Laura thought of the man she'd seen in The Dalles. He looked like a progressive congressman. She wondered if he was behind the potential growth plan for this secluded spot in northeast Oregon.

"How do people make a living here?"

"Tourism," Joel announced from the backseat. "Farming. Some cattle. Lots of mint. No logging."

"There's not much logging anymore," Laura said.

"Yeah. People have to find other ways to make money," Gregory said. "I've seen change since I first arrived and I wish it could stay the same."

"But if people don't have jobs, Dad, they'll have to move on, and then there won't be enough for a church and you'll have to leave, anyway."

Gregory shook his head. "My son, the realist."

"Somebody has to think about the future," Joel said, slouching further into his seat.

Laura finished the last of her ice cream and wondered about the universe. She recycled and had once joined the "Save Our Seals" campaign.

"We're going home, aren't we, Dad?" Joel asked with a scowl. Laura wondered if he ever smiled.

"Yes. We need to stop at the house for Mrs. Madison's car."

After dropping Joel off and getting her own car, Laura followed Gregory back into town, turning right and going up a hill to a house at the end of the road.

The Victorian house, a creamy white with gray gingerbread trim and a wraparound porch, made Laura feel she was going back in time. She could hardly wait to see inside.

Gregory got out and walked over to her car. "Can I help carry something in?"

Closing her trunk, she pointed to her larger suitcase and grabbed the smaller one, then followed him across the lawn and up the steps. The white picket fence around the yard reminded Laura of her grandmother's farmhouse.

A light shone from an old-fashioned porch light. "It's perfectly lovely."

As if waiting for her arrival, a small woman opened the door and peered out. "Well, are you coming in, Pastor, or staying out there all night?"

After introductions, Ruth put her arms around Laura. "I'm the hugging type, dear. I do hope you don't mind. But come in and have a spot of tea. It's a delightful country blend. And freshly baked peanut butter cookies." She reached up to hug Gregory. "Do set the suitcase down in the hall, first." Wisps of gray hair framed her face. She wore a white apron over a flowered housedress. Laura thought that she looked exactly the part of a bed-and-breakfast matron.

Gregory shook his head. "Sounds wonderful, Ruth, but I've got to get home. Big day tomorrow." He glanced at Laura. "I'll expect you in my office at nine in the morning."

"Gregory, be reasonable. Laura must be exhausted. She may want to sleep in, you know."

He looked almost chagrined. "Oh, yes. Well, whenever you make it, that's fine."

After Gregory left, Laura accepted the offer of tea. "We just had ice cream at a wonderful little store by the lake. I feel as if I've done nothing but eat since arriving."

Ruth's eyes twinkled. "You went to the Boeves' then. Yes, it's a delightful place. Great people."

Laura looked at the forest green walls with touches of lavender and rose. Bay windows looked out onto the front yard. "I love it," Laura said.

"Wait until you see your room and the bathroom. A claw-foot bathtub, no less. And chintz curtains to match the canopy bed."

Laura sat with legs outstretched. "I really am tired."

"Your day started early if you left the beach this morning and did all this running around tonight."

"Pastor Gregory—" She wasn't sure how to put it, but she wanted to ask a few questions about him.

"Reverend Gregory Hall is not what he appears," Ruth said as she poured a scant spoonful of sugar in her tea. "He's gruff, brusque, whatever adjective you want to use, but he's as good and kind as they come. You just have to get used to him."

"I love those boys already."

"Then you'll certainly do. Yes, you certainly will."

Laura wanted to ask more questions, but after two yawns, Ruth took the larger suitcase, saying, "Used to carrying these, so don't you worry a whit." Laura followed her up the stairs to a room on the left.

The bedroom was large and airy, painted in delicate yellow with a splash of orange. Laura loved it immediately. Tulips filled a vase on the vanity.

"I may never leave this room at all," she said, responding to Ruth's good-night hug.

Later, after slipping into nightclothes, she thought of the psalm she had memorized as a child in Sunday school. "Give thanks to the Lord, for he is good; his love endures forever."

The down comforter and pillows seemed to pull Laura in. As she sunk into their warm depths, she wondered what tomorrow would bring.

$$7$$

*L*aura slept long and hard that first night in the bed-and-breakfast. The mountain air was soothing, so different from the dampness, fog, and wind at the beach. She liked it here. She had no idea how long she might stay, but for now she felt a thread of contentment stirring inside her. She'd buy and send postcards today and call Renee with the phone number. Nobody had missed her except Renee. She'd have to find another walking buddy.

Following a quick bath in the huge tub, she chose a lime green sweatshirt, blue denims, and her worn-in sneakers. After breakfast, she'd take a short walk through town, acquainting herself with her surroundings, then head to the church and her meeting with Reverend Hall. She was eager to see the church, the inside as well as out, and wondered about the piano. One day away from the keys and she was more than ready to play.

Laura's stomach growled as the smell of bacon floated up the stairs. Bacon and eggs. How long since she'd eaten an honest-to-goodness breakfast? It brought back pleasant memories of Saturday mornings when she and Jerry lingered over breakfast before planning their day. Sundays were filled with church and having brunch afterwards. She grabbed her coat and headed down.

Ruth bustled back and forth from table to stove. "I heard the water running, so I started putting together a good meal before you go look the job site over." She handed Laura a cup of coffee. "If you're like me, you need this to get going in the morning."

"Are you doing all this just for me?" Laura asked, looking at the eggs in the skillet. "You don't have anyone else staying over. Surely you didn't think you had to cook for me?"

"Sit, child." Ruth pointed. "I love cooking. I like having someone to cook for, so be prepared."

Child. Laura had to laugh. How long since anyone had called her *child?* In fact, she didn't think she'd ever been called it.

Ruth set a platter on the table. "Everybody should have a substantial breakfast. No little Continental meal here. Don't believe in them."

"If I don't watch out, I'll weigh two hundred pounds."

Ruth gave her a sideways glance. "You can skip lunch or dinner, but breakfast is a must."

Laura dug into the plate of food, pausing long enough to exclaim how delicious everything tasted.

"You know God works in mysterious ways," Ruth said. "You must believe that. Why else would you end up in Joseph? God sees someone's need, and clear across the state and north of that, a woman needs to get on with her life. I like the scripture from Daniel: 'There is a God in heaven who reveals mysteries.' "

"I don't deny that," Laura said with a nod. "I just hope I fit in."

"I think you already have." Ruth sat across from Laura. "Here. Eat more. There's a lot of food here."

Laura filled her plate again, surprised she was so hungry. At home a bowl of cereal sufficed. She also knew there was no way she'd win an argument with Ruth, at least not over eating the food she prepared. It was as Gregory had said: Ruth liked people. Their problems were her problems, and she was happiest when she was plying them with food.

"I'll help with the dishes," Laura offered, "then I'd better get over to the church."

"Scoot. Don't even think about it. If I get busy later on in the summer, you can clear the table, but I don't expect guests to help."

"I'm hardly a guest."

"To me you are."

Laura pushed her chair back. "Am I going to freeze out there? This is the heaviest coat I own."

"Mornings are cold this time of year. There's a jacket in the hall. I keep a supply of wraps for people who don't realize how cold it is up here in these mountains."

The coat was long, turquoise poplin with a warm flannel lining. "Wow!" Laura exclaimed. "I can play in the snow with this."

"You can still find snow up at the lake."

"I noticed that last night." She added mittens and a black knit hat that pulled down over her ears. "I feel ready for the North Pole."

"If you stick around, you'll get to see some dandy cold weather." Ruth handed her a package. "Some cookies to take to Pastor."

Laura stuck the wrapped package in one of the deep pockets. "I'm on my way."

"Don't get lost," Ruth called out.

Laura laughed at the thought. The church was but three blocks away. Joseph itself consisted of four, possibly five long blocks. There were no other main roads, just the one going through town and toward Wallowa Lake in a southerly direction and one going north and west to Enterprise.

Laura glanced up at the high school on the opposite hill. Several yellow buses were parked up next to the guardrail. She'd drive up there one day soon.

She walked briskly toward the first store. Her breath could be seen in the cold morning air. She took a deep breath and felt the icy cold fill her chest. Yes, this was different from beach living. People might think she was crazy for coming here when people longed to get away to vacation at the coast, but she was going to like it. Once again she felt confirmation that this was where she was needed, where God wanted her to be.

She thought of one of her favorite Scriptures, Psalm 16:11: "You have made known to me the path of life; you will fill me with joy in your presense, with eternal pleasures at your right hand."

The stone church sat like a welcoming beacon on a corner. Laura stood and looked at the old building. Steps led to the main door, and there was a side door alongside the street. It was old. It looked so different from the clapboard church back home.

She ran up the stairs and tried the front door. It opened. She stepped into a small foyer where people could hang their coats and shake off any mud or snow they might carry into the building. She took off the coat and left the hat and mittens on a hook. The cookies were an offering, a conversation starter, if nothing else.

The sanctuary was straight ahead. It was a "U" shape with the pulpit front and center and rows of seats to the left for a choir. Two aisles came to the center. The leaded glass windows on three sides lent a cheery atmosphere. Most importantly, a black piano sat to the left of the pulpit, right under the choir section. No organ, just a piano. It was beautiful, and she couldn't wait to play, but first things first.

"So, do you find our little church to your liking, so far?"

She whirled to find Gregory standing in an open doorway to the right.

"I like it very much." Her cheeks were flushed from her walk, but also from something else. "I hope I'm not too late. Here. Cookies from Ruth."

He nodded. "Something to go with my midmorning coffee break. Perhaps you'd like to join me in the kitchen? Or do you prefer the office?"

Laura shrugged. "Either is fine with me. But no cookies. I just ate one of Ruth's fantastic country farm breakfasts and doubt that I'll need to eat for the rest of the day."

Gregory held the door open, and she caught the scent of aftershave, a nice woodsy, pine smell.

The fellowship hall was large, with a kitchen against one wall and tables and chairs set up in orderly rows.

"This is a lovely church. You must be happy working here."

His eyes glazed over as he handed her a cup of steaming coffee. "I love the church. The area. The people."

"But something is missing?" The minute Laura said it, she wanted to bite her tongue. It was none of her business what lay behind the sometimes sad, lonely look in the deep blue eyes. He was like a chameleon, because now he was smiling.

"My sermons leave something to be desired, but the people stick with me."

"Do I hear a bit of negativity in your voice, Pastor?"

"Yes, that you do."

He finished the coffee and two of the peanut butter cookies while Laura had just one sip.

"I want to hear you play now, if you don't mind. We can talk after you play these hymns, which are scheduled to go with Sunday's message."

Laura wiped her hands and rose. "I've been itching to get at those keys." She smiled. Three of her favorites were listed. "Amazing Grace," one from her Sunday school playing days, "What a Friend We Have in Jesus" was another, and "Sweet, Sweet Spirit."

She went to the sanctuary, pulled the bench out, and held her fingers over the ivories. She'd first run through the scales. Sort of a warm-up like runners stretched before a marathon. This was a test and she wanted to do well.

After the second exercise of running up and down the keyboard, she was delighted that it was completely in tune. A voice called out, "Do we get to hear that every morning as the people come in, or is this your rendition of 'Amazing Grace'?"

Laura stopped playing. Was he being facetious or making fun of her? She wasn't sure.

"I always warm up, like an athlete," she said without turning around. She didn't have to look to see the brooding eyes.

"Whatever, it's beautiful," he said, turning back toward his office.

"Well!" Laura said aloud. "Looks like I've passed the first step."

She played the Gloria Patri, the Doxology, and her favorite seven-chord Amen response. She still hadn't played the hymns, but now everything came out of her, songs she didn't need music for. Songs that uplifted her soul, made her realize how much a part of her life God was. "The Lord's Prayer," "The Old Rugged Cross," "How Great Thou Art," and Charles Wesley's "O For a Thousand Tongues to Sing."

A clapping interrupted the end of the song. She turned to find Pastor Gregory Michael Hall applauding.

"No book? You know all of these from memory?"

Laura stood and bowed. "Yes. I've been playing for the past forty years. How could I not memorize them?"

"Astounding."

"Now I will play the required hymns."

"In what key?"

"Which key do you prefer?"

Gregory raised his hands in resignation. "Whichever you choose."

Laura played another hour, loving the piano, the sound as it filled the church. What a gift this was, to play again in honor of her Lord Jesus Christ.

She closed the lid reluctantly and headed to the office.

Looking up, Gregory motioned her to the chair across from him. "I couldn't be more happy with your playing," he said. "In fact," he closed the book, "would you possibly consider giving Caleb lessons?"

"Caleb?" Somehow she couldn't imagine his wanting to play the piano. "I would think Caleb would choose a band instrument. If not a horn, perhaps a clarinet or something else in the woodwind family."

Gregory leaned forward. "His mother was a pianist, and he's taken it as a fancy to learn. Insists on it. That's been a year or so ago, but there are no teachers here in Joseph."

"Well, I taught my own children, or the two that wanted to learn."

"So you would be an answer to prayer. Make that two prayers."

"Would there be others who might like lessons?" Laura had often thought of teaching in Sealand, but there were two other teachers. By the time her children were raised, there were no openings.

"I'm sure there would be."

"Did your wife play for the church?"

"Yes, and though she was accomplished, she didn't take to it as you did. Never felt she was quite good enough to play for an audience."

Laura looked at a photo on the file cabinet. "I assume this is her?"

Gregory handed it over. "Yes. Taken just before she had Caleb."

A young woman smiled back at her. Love shone in her eyes, giving her a look of radiance and happiness. Was it the loss of her that made Gregory such a quiet, reflective person?

"Very nice." Laura noticed school photos of both sons. Joel definitely had his father's good looks, the same brooding eyes. "I'd be happy to give Caleb lessons if he can work it in between his baseball practice and school homework."

"He will. Caleb can do anything he sets his mind to."

"And Joel?"

"Quite the opposite. He could do it, but he doesn't have the confidence to try."

"Perhaps he needs to be encouraged."

His eyes narrowed. "And you think I don't encourage him?"

"I didn't say that."

"You didn't need to." Gregory leaned over and picked up Caleb's photo, as if to change the subject. "Caleb's like his mother in many ways. He would very much like for me to find a mother for him, but, to be perfectly honest, I have no desire to marry again. Just thought you'd want to know that."

Laura's cheeks flushed for the second time that morning. "Well, I suppose it would be good to let you know I have no intention of marrying again, either. There is no one that could possibly replace my husband, Jerry."

She stood and moved toward the door. Gregory stood also. "Look, I didn't mean to—"

Laura laughed, but it sounded hollow. Could she work for this man? Did she even want to? "It's all right. I believe in being aboveboard with things like that. I'm glad you set the record straight."

The wind had calmed down and the sun shone out of a clear blue sky, but Laura did not want to walk now. All she wanted was to go back to Ruth's and bury her head in the pillow on the comfortable bed. How she missed Jerry. How she missed having someone to bare her soul to. How she missed that special part of belonging to someone, of being one in God. She knew she'd never find another partner who loved God as she did or knew things about her. That's why she would stay single. But it still hurt. From deep within, a longing challenged her, like a haunting melody.

8

*R*uth was dusting the sitting room with a long-handled feather duster when Laura banged in the front door. She hadn't meant to close the door so hard. Ruth glanced around the corner.

"Hello, honey. How'd it go?"

She shrugged out of the mittens, hat, and coat. "My playing passed inspection."

"But?"

"My personality obviously doesn't."

"Oh, my, my." Ruth set the duster down. "Sounds like it's time to put the teakettle on. I was about ready to have some lunch anyway."

"Nothing for me, please. I just want to go upstairs and try to figure out why I thought I should do this."

Ruth came over and put her arm around Laura. "I take it Gregory put his foot in his mouth again. He's quite good at it, you know."

Laura squared her shoulders. "Contrary to what Reverend Hall thinks, I did not come to Joseph to find a husband! I do not want a husband! I do not need a husband!"

"Calm down, dear." Ruth's blue eyes twinkled ever so slightly. "I happen to know if God wants you to have a man in your life again, He'll point the way and I doubt that you'll refuse."

"It had better be pretty clear." Laura tried to relax. "He wants me to give Caleb lessons. Says I play magnificently. Couldn't believe I didn't need the hymnal."

"You don't?"

"Heavens, no. I've been playing all those hymns since I can remember."

"Well, I am impressed now. I was wishing we had a piano here for you to practice on, but sounds as if you don't need to practice anyway."

"One always needs to practice."

"Just as one needs to read the Bible, even if it's been read through before."

"Exactly. I don't want to talk about this just now. I need some time and some space."

"You sure you don't want a cup of my famous potato corn chowder?"

"Not yet. My stomach's in knots."

"It'll just take a minute to heat up whenever you come down."

Laura climbed the stairs and entered the beautifully decorated room. She fell across the bed and let the tears come. What did she want? What did she need? Was this a good step? Was God directing her? If so, why did she feel this pain and rejection? Or was she overreacting?

Jerry used to tell her, "You go to the extremes, honey. You have a problem, say with one of the kids, and rather than try to figure a simple solution, you imagine the worst possible result. That's being awfully negative." Had she been negative when she feared that he might not come back from fishing one day? *What about that, God? You took him from me and I wasn't ready to let go.*

Laura remembered the verse Jerry used to recite to her, James 1:6: "But when he asks, he must believe and not doubt, because he who doubts is like a wave of the sea, blown and tossed by the wind." How like Jerry to find the perfect verse to taunt her with. But God had taken Jerry; and though she was not supposed to question God or wonder, she couldn't help it at times. Right now she missed Renee and her comfort, her wisdom.

Laura drifted off to sleep and woke when the doorbell sounded.

Ruth's voice floated up the stairs as Laura rose, straightened her clothes, and ran a brush through her hair. Her eyes still had dark smudges below. It was a male voice. Probably Gregory, yet it didn't sound like him. Maybe someone needed a room for the night.

Footsteps sounded on the stairs, then a light tap. "Laura? There's someone here to see you. From the paper."

Laura groaned.

"You okay? Still napping?"

She added a touch of lipstick and glanced in the oval gilt-edged mirror. Her eyes didn't have their usual sparkle. She wondered if they had when she flounced out of the pastor's office. She finally descended the stairs.

"Ms. Madison?" A young man with long hair past his shirt collar stepped forward, holding out a hand. "I'm Eddie from the *Chieftain*. I probably should have called first, but I was in the area. I understand you're going to be the pianist for the Community Church."

"Yes, but—"

"You placed an ad in our paper and got results. That's part of the coverage, but I also want to interview you—do a feature for our paper. Can we sit at the table, Ruth?"

"Of course." She indicated the round table in the sitting room. "I'll bring something to drink."

Laura wasn't ready for this. She saw the camera and flash equipment in the young man's case. "I can't do this now."

Ruth came over. "She's had a busy day so far, Eddie. Maybe you could come back in a day or so?"

"Well, sure. But it won't take long. I'll just take a couple of shots and a bit of info—"

Ruth spoke up for Laura. "That's the problem. She isn't ready for a photo. A lady needs time to prepare herself."

Eddie nodded, closing his notebook. "I understand. Sorry I didn't call first."

"You might come to hear her play on Sunday," Ruth suggested, handing him a cup and offering a plate of cookies. "That way you could really get a good story."

Laura had to smile. Ruth was cagey. It was a good way to get the young man into church. "I'd love to talk to you the first of next week," she offered.

"Of course." He spoke with a cookie in his mouth.

"Actually, dear, he came by for some of my peanut butter cookies." She winked. "He knows I bake them on Wednesdays."

"Oh, Ruth," they said in unison.

"You can stay for dinner, if you'd like."

Eddie downed his coffee and jumped to his feet. "Thanks, but I'll take a rain check on that."

"I appreciate your speaking up for me," Laura said once the reporter was gone, and she sunk back into the cushions of the settee. "I just couldn't face something like that right now."

"I know. That's why I ran—what do they call it in football? —interference."

"Yeah, something like that."

"Do you feel better?" Ruth leaned over, brushing the hair back from Laura's face. "You still look a mite peaked to me."

"I think it might take another day to get back to normal. If there is such a thing."

"At least you have two days before Sunday."

"When I'll be under scrutiny."

"If you were interested in someone, I have just the person," Ruth said then. "Our most confirmed bachelor has let it be known—in fact, put it on the prayer chain—that he'd very much like to find a wife."

"Oh, Ruth. I really am not looking for that sort of thing."

"You could do worse than Kenny Thompson."

"I'll be so busy playing and giving lessons that I won't miss there not being someone in my life."

"Perhaps so, perhaps so," Ruth said, dusting the shelf behind Laura's head. "Still, you can't blame me for being a romantic at heart."

Laura grabbed the crocheting out of a bag she'd brought. She was making scarves out of a nice navy blue wool. "No, I guess not."

❧

Gregory watched Laura retreat from his office. He felt like such a— what was it the boys called it?—a doofus. Why had he said that, intimating Laura had come to Joseph looking for a husband? She was probably just as content to be single as he was and had been for the past eight, almost nine years.

He picked up the photo of Shirley, warming at the smile. She had been a wonderful woman, a God-fearing woman, and the one he thought God had selected for him after his engagement to Beth Marie fell through. That had been so many years ago now.

He had a faded snapshot of himself and Beth at the county fair in his wallet. That had been a happy time. Yet wasn't first love the most poignant, the most deeply felt, the most intense? He had never quite forgotten her, though he had been a good and dutiful husband to Shirley.

He put the picture back, his mind going to another smile, a warm smile, indicating an easygoing nature. He didn't know Laura Madison that well, but she had gotten to him, making her way into a tiny corner of his heart in a way no one had since Shirley died. How ridiculous, since he had barely met her. Something about her piano playing, the way her hands flew over the ivories made him realize here was a woman of God. She played flawlessly, but it was the delivery, the way she put her feeling and her heart into it. He had been moved wholeheartedly. God had sent her to this small church in Joseph, Oregon, when she could have played anywhere. He had not known her long, but in those few hours she had been positive and encouraging about Joel, thinking he could play a solo for a future church service. He knew Joel would never do it, but she had seemed so confident. And Caleb, bless his exuberant self, had taken to her instantly. Gregory believed in divine intervention. He'd always said, "What was meant to be was meant to be."

So what had made him say such a thing to Laura? Why did he blunder like this? Why could he get along with most people, but when it came to relationships with women, he was in left field? Maybe she would change her mind now. He wouldn't blame her if she did.

The door opened and Caleb stuck his head around the corner. "Dad?"

"Come on in, Son."

"Is Laura here?"

"No. Did you think she would be?"

The boy slumped into the nearest chair. "I just thought she might have come by to practice the piano."

Gregory leaned forward. "I'll tell you one thing. No, make that two things. And both should make you happy."

"What's that, Dad? Say, do you have any cookies or anything around? I'm starved!"

Gregory produced the last two peanut butter cookies. "Here. Just for you. Guess who made them?"

"Ruth," Caleb said, crumbs falling out of his mouth. "But what's the big news?"

"Mrs. Madison is an accomplished pianist. I enjoyed hearing her play for an hour or better this morning."

"And?"

"She's willing to give you lessons if you still want them."

"Really? Are you making this up, Dad?"

"No. Would I make something like that up? I asked and she said she'd love to."

"She likes me."

"How can you be so sure?"

He wrinkled his nose. "She just does. A guy can tell."

Gregory felt a jolt to his midsection. Maybe that's what bothered him. There had been a magnetism. Laura, unlike him, showed her emotions by her facial expressions. He knew she felt something for him, and it was this fact that made him feel something. A tiny flutter, but still it was something. *No, it couldn't be.*

"I think Laura was happy to go to your game and enjoyed you, all right. She has two boys, you know."

"I can't wait to start lessons. When can I? Huh, Dad?"

"One question at a time, Caleb. How many times do I have to tell you that?" He leaned over and ruffled Caleb's hair. "About time for a haircut, I think."

"When can I start, Dad?"

"Whenever you want, I imagine. After Sunday, that is."

"I say Monday right after baseball practice then."

"You'd better check with her before you make any big plans. See what a good time is for her."

"Oh, Dad! I can't believe it! In one day we have a piano player and I'm going to take piano lessons. Now I can play piano just like my mother did."

Gregory winced. "That you can, Caleb. Yes, that you can."

The boy raced out of his office and whooped all the way down the block. He was probably heading over to Ruth's. He closed his book and shut his eyes. No sense in trying to concentrate anymore today. He'd tackle his sermon topic first thing in the morning, though he liked to have it ready by Thursday. He still had the bulletin to prepare. Well, tomorrow was another day.

9

*L*aura realized after that first Sunday that she needed to shop
for a new dress or suit. A dressy jacket, a skirt or two, a
scarf, and a strand of pearls. She might order from a catalogue. She'd thought it would be more casual dress, like the beach,
but the women in the little community church dressed up and obviously had their hair done on Saturdays.

Ruth had prayed with her that first morning. "Remember what
Matthew says: 'Surely I am with you always.'"

"I know. I think of that Scripture a lot."

Laura met with Gregory thirty minutes before the service to go
over the special music. He looked expectant as she quietly entered his
office. It was different from the other day when she'd flounced out,
and she really hoped he wouldn't bring that matter up. Caleb had
wheeled over to Ruth's all excited at the prospect of taking lessons.
His first lesson was the next day. He didn't want to waste time.

"Thanks for giving Caleb the time he wanted for his first lesson."

"I have no schedule other than Sunday morning and night and
any other special wedding or funeral service."

"Yes, ah, well."

Laura looked into his eyes and immediately glanced away. There
was something there she could not read, and it bothered her.

"I had hoped you could play a fifteen-minute prelude before the
service instead of the usual ten."

"That's fine."

"You know everyone has been champing at the bit, wanting to see
the new pianist."

She had to smile. "This is my big debut."

"You'll pass with flying colors; I have no doubt about that."

"Pastor?" An elderly gentleman tapped on the door as he entered. "I—oh, hello. You must be Mrs. Madison."

"Laura. Please."

"We're so happy to have you. I'm Tom Cantrell."

"I'll be with you in a second, Tom."

"I think I have a piano to go play," Laura said, moving past the gentleman. She was glad she'd brought the black-and-white houndstooth jacket, her best outfit. Laura felt two pairs of eyes on her as she left the room.

She started playing, adding extra chords as the people came in. The only ones she could see without turning were to her left, and those pews filled up fast. New members, she surmised. A murmur of voices soon filled the church. A few people, she figured, were partially deaf, because they spoke loud enough for Laura to hear above her piano playing.

"She's nice-looking!"

"And younger than we thought!"

"Plays better than Gert or Amanda."

"Especially Amanda. Poor little dear really tried, too."

Caleb bounced up, greeting Laura warmly. "I hope I can learn to play even half that good!" His eyes snapped with enthusiasm.

"You will," she whispered, leaning over for a brief second.

He frowned. "How can you play and talk to me at the same time?"

"Because I've been playing many, many years."

"I better go sit down or Dad will get mad at me."

"See you later."

"We're having chocolate cake and white cake and it's all decorated up special for you and the new members," he said.

Laura grinned. "Were you supposed to tell me?"

"Oops!" He covered his mouth. "Maybe not."

Laura looked at her watch. Two minutes and Gregory would come in. When he started walking down the aisle, she changed the tempo to something slow and soft. He caught her eye minutes later, and she stopped playing.

When she played for the singing, she realized how good it was to hear voices again. She never missed a cue as she went through the hymns, following a tall, serious-faced lady who led the singing. She wondered about a choir. She'd have to ask Ruth if they had one.

Gregory chose to introduce her before the announcements. "God has answered many prayers by bringing Mrs. Laura Madison into our midst, and I know you'll enjoy her playing as much as I have already." He beamed at her.

Laura stood and bowed slightly. This was the part she didn't like. She looked out at the congregation, smiling at Caleb, who clapped harder than anyone else did. Joel sat in the back, a frown on his young face. *Does he ever smile?* she couldn't help wondering.

"Laura often plays without the hymnal," Gregory added. "Believe me when I tell you she is accomplished and will bring much happiness and singing to our little church. It's also a special Sunday for another reason, as we'll be welcoming new members."

❧

The singing went fast, and Laura felt happy as she listened to the voices, some loud, some off-key. She sang as she played, as she always had.

" 'Forgiveness' is my text this morning," Gregory began his sermon. "All of us have done something or said something we're sorry for. It is my hope that the one who was offended would be forgiving."

Laura felt color rise in her cheeks. Had he changed his sermon since the day she'd been in the office? She doubted it.

The service ended, the new members joined, and the last song was sung.

"My dear, we are so happy to have you," one after another said, stopping by the piano as she played the postlude following the benediction.

"Thank you, thank you," she repeated.

"You are coming to our special coffee hour," more than one said.

Then Ruth came. "My dear, I am absolutely enthralled at your playing. I'd come to hear you even if I was a heathen."

Laura laughed and stood to hug the older woman. "Do you think I passed muster?"

"Oh, my goodness, everyone is raving about the music. Caleb is very fortunate to have you as a teacher."

Laura knew she'd never remember the names, but she'd remember Clyde, the man who stood over everyone else, and Miriam, who poured coffee and exclaimed over the piano playing. It was good to be needed. She hoped Gregory was happy with the morning's music as well.

"Don't eat too much cake," Caleb said, coming up to her side. "We'll be going over to Ruth's for brunch, you know."

"You are?"

"We always do."

"Oh." She scraped the icing off the cake, then felt guilty for doing so.

"We'll see you tonight," voices called out as she headed for the room where her coat hung.

"Now, Ruth, you sure you want us to come today?" It was Gregory asking about brunch.

"And why would you not come today?"

"Well, it's too much."

"Dad, we gotta go! Besides, I have to discuss my lesson with Laura."

Laura slipped back into the other room. So Gregory was trying to get out of going to Ruth's. It had to do with her. That was fine. He didn't have to like her or she him. She had a job to do, and do it she would.

Since she was wearing her good clothes, Laura had driven to church. She went out the door while the others continued with their coffee and cake. She'd get back to Ruth's and slip into something more casual and comfortable. Thank heavens for Caleb. If he were like his father or older brother, it would be pretty dismal.

Her stomach growled at the smell of a baking ham. She'd had a slice of toast for breakfast and that had been early. Ruth had also baked a rhubarb custard pie, everyone's favorite. "I do hope you like rhubarb."

"That I do," Laura assured her.

"Good. Rhubarb is something you either like or you don't."

Laura wore a pair of brown corduroy slacks and a turquoise heavy knit sweater. After combing her hair, she hurried down to see if she could help set the table. The Halls had just arrived.

"Laura! I looked everywhere for you." Caleb's eager face looked up as she came down the steps.

"So, you're ready for your lesson?"

"You bet."

"Kenny Thompson, the gentleman I mentioned to you, was looking for you, too," Ruth said. "I rather imagine he'll be calling you sometime this week."

Laura shook her head. "I'm not interested, Ruth. Surely you told him that."

"It wouldn't hurt to go have coffee with him," Ruth said.

"He's a bachelor, has land. Lots of it," Gregory added. "Almost married back in the sixties, but his fiancée died in a car accident and he just never dated again. Not that he doesn't want to marry, because he told me that he did."

"Asked to have his request on the prayer chain," Ruth added.

"I say let's eat," Laura said. Anything to get the subject off of her dating.

"I agree," Caleb said. "I'm starving."

"This is your favorite meal," Ruth said as she brought the potatoes and ham out. "And a pie for dessert."

They held hands while Gregory asked the blessing.

After they ate, Caleb asked, "Is the pie rhubarb?"

"I bet it is," Gregory said.

Joel said nothing.

"You'll see," Ruth said with a wink.

Laura laughed when the boys banged their forks on the table.

"We want pie!" Caleb proclaimed.

"We like pie!" Joel joined in.

"We love rhubarb!" Gregory added.

"And I do, too," Laura said.

"Okay, okay," Ruth said good-naturedly. "Yes, it's rhubarb and there's enough for a big slice for all."

Gregory winked at Ruth. "She spoils us all—"

"And loves doing it," Laura said. She'd gotten up to get the dessert plates and forks. Ruth insisted that no one need lick his or her forks around her table. There were always clean ones for dessert.

"You don't like rhubarb," Ruth said, watching Laura's fork in midair.

"Oh, no, but I do. I'm savoring every bite."

The boys dug into their pie, seemingly oblivious to the adult conversation. Laura took one bite and just held it in her mouth. She hadn't had rhubarb custard pie since her mother baked it when she was a girl. It was just as good as she remembered.

After dinner, Caleb pushed his chair back. "Please, may I be excused and can I go skateboarding?"

Gregory shrugged. "This is the way it goes. Every week. Caleb can't wait to use the skateboard."

Joel excused himself and went to the gold room to read.

Laura fetched the coffeepot. One more cup would go good.

After Ruth cleared the table, she brought out the Scrabble game. "I didn't tell you this part, but we play at least one game before Gregory heads for home."

"Scrabble! But I love to play and haven't for ages."

Gregory smiled. "Uh-oh. Something tells me we've met our match."

"Doesn't Joel want to play?" Laura asked. It was one game all three of her children enjoyed. Jerry hadn't, but always joked about the fierce competition the four of them had on Saturday nights. The games stopped when Kurt left for college.

"Joel always reads," Ruth said.

"Did you ask him to play?" Laura asked.

"Probably, a long time ago."

"I'll ask him now," Laura said.

He scowled when she entered the room after first tapping on the door. "We're playing Scrabble and I thought you might like to play."

"I never play."

"Because you don't want to? Or why not?"

He shrugged. There was a lonely look on his face and an intensity that bothered Laura. He needed to talk to someone, and obviously it couldn't be his father.

"I'd like you to be my partner."

He followed her down the hall.

"We're playing partners."

"We never played that way," Ruth said.

"Well, it's simple. You just combine our scores, just as you do yours and Pastor's."

"Sure, why not?" Ruth changed the page for scoring. "I'm always game to try something new."

"I think it's a good idea," Gregory said with a nod.

Joel said nothing, but his face brightened when he drew an "A," which meant he had first turn. "Hey, that was a lucky draw."

"You still have to make the letters fit," Laura added quickly. When Joel wrote "quilt" and received forty-eight points, he beamed.

Laura and Joel won the game, as she had figured they would. She knew Joel would be good with words, just as he was with numbers, and playing his trumpet, and anything else he set his mind to.

When Caleb ran in, he was surprised to see the game already over and even more surprised to see Joel was playing.

"Hey, man, way cool," he said when he noticed Joel and Laura had won by twenty-five points. "That's great. Maybe I should learn to play, too."

"Yes, I think you should," Ruth said. "I won't always be able to play once the tourist season starts."

Laura helped clear up the game and watched while the three left. If she wasn't mistaken, Joel's head was just a bit higher than usual.

L aura enjoyed the evening service because it was less formal. After everyone left, she could hardly wait to get back to Ruth's to relax. She had lots of things to mull over. She thought about Kenny Thompson, deciding it wouldn't hurt to go out for coffee, should he ask.

He asked the following morning.

The voice was deep, yet gruff. She wondered if he'd found it as difficult to call her as she was finding it difficult to talk now.

"Mrs. Madison, I'll be in town, doing some banking. Maybe we could meet at the café for lunch?"

Glancing over her shoulder, she knew Ruth was halfway listening.

"I—well, I have a piano lesson at four."

"Oh, hey, I gotta be back at the ranch long before that."

"Okay. Noon sounds fine."

"He's a good man," Ruth said, after Laura had hung up. "You'd never have to worry about money again or need to play the piano. I imagine the only thing his wife would need to do is learn to ride a horse and maybe lasso one."

Laura laughed. "I suppose he would want someone to ride with him on that big spread. I'm not sure I like horses. Never been on one, if you can believe that."

"That can change with a few riding lessons."

"I'm just not interested, Ruth. Give it up."

"It's just lunch."

Laura was laying out her music lessons, glad she'd packed a beginner's book. Caleb would take to the lessons quickly. He didn't have a piano to practice on at home, but his father said he was looking for a good used one. She had changed into warm tweed slacks, a pair that had been in her wardrobe forever because she never threw things out, when the phone rang.

Ruth's voice called out at the door. "Laura? May I come in?"

"Of course." She set the hairbrush down and motioned for Ruth to sit in the one vacant chair. The bed was dotted with discarded clothes, the music books, her diary, and her Bible.

Ruth chuckled. "You use the bed like I do. Lay it all out."

"Yes, makes it easier. Was the phone for me?"

"Yes. It was Kenny Thompson. Seems he has a dying calf and must make a run to the vet's instead of coming into Joseph to go to the bank. Said he knew you'd understand."

Laura glanced upward. "Thank You, Lord, because I wasn't ready for this lunch."

Ruth patted her arm. "I am glad you aren't upset—"

"Upset? Ruth, how could I be? I know what cattle mean to people who ranch for a living."

After Ruth went back downstairs, Laura wrote Renee a letter, dropped off a line to Kurt and to Jen, and sent Jeff a note at his last known address. She wrote another letter and enclosed one of the photos of her new church to her old one. They'd post it on the bulletin board to let everyone know how she was faring.

At three she walked over to the church.

Caleb was a fast learner. Laura thought he would be. He operated under the theory that he could do anything he set his mind to. Again, she wished Joel had that same confidence.

"You may want to be out on the ball field or shooting baskets," Laura said that first afternoon, "but playing the piano is something you'll have with you all of your life. I don't ask for long practices. Thirty minutes a day is fine. We'll start with scales."

Caleb looked apprehensive. "Scales?"

"Yes, like this." Laura made him stand so she would have plenty of elbowroom as she placed her fingers over the keys. She remembered dreading the scales when she first started piano lessons, but she wondered why now. She explained the treble clef and bass clef, showing Caleb how to hold his fingers poised over the keys.

"Soon you'll have the keys memorized, and later, if you like, we can play duets. You can play the right hand while I play the left or vice versa."

"Hey, way cool! I'd like that." His eyes were shining. "Maybe we can play for church."

Laura nodded. "We'll start at an evening service. People tend to be more relaxed and forgive mistakes."

"You never make mistakes."

Laura laughed. "Oh, yes, I do. You just don't hear them, as I cover them up quick." She rose, motioning for Caleb to sit back down.

"Do you really think I can learn to play good enough for church?"

"Of course. But first things first. We'll learn about flats and sharps and timing. Timing is very important. I'm going to estimate you need two years of practice first."

"Two years? Really?" Being a kid, he was used to instant gratification, and the thought of taking two years seemed almost insurmountable.

"Practice makes perfect. Just like baseball, painting a picture, or, you name it."

Caleb nodded. "Guess I never thought of it that way."

"So, are you ready to begin?"

"Sure."

"Scales are a good warm-up, and you know about warm-ups." She leaned over the piano. "Like this." Music filled the small church. "Of course, you'll have a book. I've brought one about scales and one for beginners. I'll expect you to do one set of scales a week."

Caleb's fingers flew up and down the keyboard, playing nothing in particular. *He has a natural flair, a good touch for it,* Laura thought. But he would. Of course he would, because that's the way he was.

"The only thing I don't like about the piano is you can't play in the band."

Laura nodded. "This is true. Would you rather play a horn or drum or something you can play in a band?"

"Nah. If I'm playing a sport, I can't be in the band, too. Besides, Dad agrees I should learn piano because my mother knew how to play and he says he likes piano."

"You don't have a piano now," Laura said. "Did you ever have one?"

Caleb shrugged. "I think so, but Dad says we lived in a tiny house when I was born and my mother sold her piano."

"Oh, I do hope she didn't sell her very own piano."

Caleb shrugged again. "You can ask my dad. He can tell you. I don't know anything about my mother."

"From what I hear, she was a fine woman and loved you very, very much."

"I know."

Laura opened the beginning music book and started with basic key knowledge. "We always being with middle C." She placed his thumb on the key.

The lesson flew by. Laura could scarcely believe it was already five.

"You can come to church to practice every day. I think it best if you use the old upright in the fellowship hall, though I want to use this one for the lessons."

"Dad will get me a piano," Caleb said.

"Yes. He said he was checking ads for a good used one. Ruth is looking also. Says she's always wanted one for what she calls the music room. So, that's enough for today. Follow my instructions. I wrote them down on this page taped to the back. That way you won't lose it and can't say, 'Oh, I forgot.' "

"I won't forget, Laura."

"Well, you just might. Practice those scales every day, even though you may tire of them." She leaned over and ruffled his hair. He turned and impulsively hugged her.

"Thanks, Laura." Then he bounced up the aisle, holding his two music books close, as if they were treasures. He paused at the doorway and turned to wave. "I hope I do well this week."

"You will, Caleb. I know you will."

Laura half-expected Gregory to come out of his office to make some comments about the lesson, but he didn't appear. Since she needed to practice a new hymn, she sat playing for a few minutes. She seemed to lose all track of time when she was playing. It had always been that way.

A voice interrupted her playing.

"Mrs. Madison?"

Laura turned to find Joel standing there, his head bent.

"Joel, hello. What brings you here?"

"I came over after I finished my homework."

"Yes?"

He shifted from one foot to the other. "Been thinkin' about what you said. About the trumpet solo."

"And you want to play for church?" There was something about this child that made her want to reach out and pull him close. All he needed was a hug, a continual acceptance of who he was, what he could be if only he would try. He had a father, but he needed a mother's tenderness. Some children get by without a mother, but Joel had not fared well. Now there seemed to be this rift between him and his father.

"I'd love to work with you on that. Anytime you're ready."

"Do you think I could really do it?"

Her hand reached out and clasped his arm. "I don't think. I know you can, Joel. I've never been more sure of anything."

He shifted his feet again, but said nothing.

She opened the hymnal. "I've been thinking of Father's Day. We use special music as we honor our fathers. Here, you can see here where the solo parts are." He leaned over. "Here at the beginning." She played it on the piano. "Then at the end of that first stanza, at the end of the second and third stanzas. It's quite effective. The trumpet is the only instrument that can bring this piece to life. It's glorious. I've heard it more than once and it gives me chills every time."

He mumbled. "Would I have to stand up here?"

"Yes, that's what I'd prefer."

"I'll think about it." He turned to go.

"There's plenty of time for practicing. I'll go with your schedule," Laura called after him.

He left the church, head bent again. Laura gathered her books and coat. She could hardly believe Joel had come in on his own. Had his father coached him? Somehow she doubted it.

The aroma of beef stew was in the air when Laura got home.

"It smells heavenly," she said, shrugging off her jacket.

"How did the lesson go?"

"Caleb's a natural," Laura replied. "I don't think there is anything Caleb couldn't do well. He just flows into anything he tries."

"Unlike Joel?" Ruth said.

"That's the neat thing, though."

"Neat?"

"Yes. Joel came. He says he'll practice the solo I mentioned earlier."

"No kidding." Ruth handed over a cup of coffee. "Dinner's about ready, but looks as if you could use this."

"Amen to that." She pulled up a chair. "One is never supposed to compare children, though we so often do. Joel's the eldest, and that usually offers some advantage, but not here. Not in this family."

"Look at Esau," Ruth said. "He was the eldest, but Jacob was the one that God found favor in."

"I believe God finds favor in all of His children," Laura said. "I have never thoroughly understood that story."

"Food was more important than anything else to Esau," Ruth said.

"But Jacob was cunning."

"And Caleb isn't cunning."

"Not in the slightest way. He loves and looks up to his brother. I wish I could see that Joel felt the same, but envy is written all over his face, and it shows in his actions. Caleb is obviously a thorn in his side."

"It's difficult for a boy to grow up without a mother," Ruth said. "Mothers sense problems long before most fathers do. My theory is that Caleb does so well because he never knew his mother. Joel, on the other hand, has memories and knows what it's like to experience a mother's love and understanding."

Laura nodded. "I was the buffer between Kurt and his father," Laura offered. "Smoothed things over more than one time."

"Do you want to eat now, or when?"

Laura hadn't even thought about food until she had gotten home, and she had to admit the smell was tantalizing. Of course, everything Ruth cooked was delicious. "I think I need to eat now, then get busy on some lesson plans for the Hall boys." She smiled and leaned back. She still couldn't believe that Joel had come in voluntarily. It was a good sign.

11

*I*t was May, and Laura had been in Joseph a month. She and Ruth were in the sitting room while Ruth stitched an edging on new place mats and Laura wrote letters.

"I'm getting things done now, because once summer hits, I'll be so busy I won't have time to sit like this," remarked Ruth.

It was the first night they hadn't had a fire in the fireplace. Laura missed the crackling sound and the glow that had relaxed her while keeping her warm.

"You've sure made a difference in the short time you've been here," Ruth said, glancing up. "Some people are like that, you know."

"And you?" Laura set her pen down. "I suppose you think you don't affect everyone you know around here?"

"Well, I don't have any enemies that I know of." She bent back over her work. "We need to go to Enterprise to shop soon."

"I'd love to take you there."

"Good. Now I'm heading for bed." Ruth folded the material. "For some reason I seem to be more tired than usual."

"Yes," Laura said with a smile, "lots happened today."

She watched the kind lady amble out the door. Ruth slept in the small room, which had once been a nursery, at the end of the hall. Laura had no intentions of going to bed this early. She always had been a night owl. Besides, she had some mulling over to do. Her thoughts went back to her husband and children, and Joel and Caleb.

Though Jerry had been a wonderful father, a kind, supportive husband, he had had little patience with his eldest son. Joel, like Kurt, had things to work out. Could Laura help boost his sagging confidence? If so, could she do it without stepping on the Reverend Gregory Hall's toes? More importantly, would he listen to Laura, who was really an outsider? She knew she wouldn't know unless she tried, and she had to try. She just did.

She set her letter aside and turned off the Tiffany lamp. She liked sitting in the darkness, enjoying the quiet. It was a pleasant room with a window bench on the south wall and a row of windows facing east to the mountains. The peaks were huge, outlined shadows against the dark sky. Tonight there was no wind, so the large sitting room seemed much warmer. Thick, long, wine-colored drapes hung from ceiling to floor. Before she went to bed, Ruth usually drew them, but not when Laura was still up. Laura would close them just before climbing the stairs to bed.

"Jerry," she murmured into the growing darkness. "I wish you were here with me, sharing this moment. I miss you so."

The hurt tore at her like a claw, and she fought back the threat of tears. Nights were bad back in Sealand, too. Nights were when they'd shared their day, sometimes read side by side, not interrupting, yet being together. Sometimes they played cribbage, Jerry's favorite game. On occasion they'd watched a video or a TV program. They had been comfortable together. She'd have to ask Ruth if that had bothered her after she was widowed. It had been twenty years, she'd told Laura. Perhaps she wouldn't even remember what it had been like, but then again, perhaps she would. She had a great memory.

Laura's Bible was on her stack of belongings. Its pungent leather was another memory of Jerry and how they'd often read Scripture together. He'd given her this Bible the Easter before he died. "I'm tired of seeing you read from a Bible that's falling apart," he'd said with a laugh.

"You always know what I need the most."

They'd embraced and she felt the beating of his heart against her body. They didn't make love, though she saw desire in his eyes. Why hadn't they? Was it because they were older and let the moment slip by? She didn't know, but often regretted that she hadn't been more spontaneous. If only she'd reached out to him that night, two nights before the boating accident. Now all she had were the memories of those good times, the times of closeness.

Laura's thoughts drifted to Gregory, and she wondered if he missed his wife, if he missed tender moments of passion. Somehow she didn't think they'd been as close a couple as she and Jerry had been. On occasion his eyes revealed a deep inner hurt, but it wasn't a pain like one felt over a loss. There was a problem, a much larger one, that Gregory carried deep inside him. She doubted he'd ever divulge anything, but in the event he did, she was a good listener. Laura had always prided herself on caring about people and being able to just listen and not offer advice.

She leaned back against the comfortable chair, pulling an ottoman over. She turned the light back on. Her Bible opened automatically to Philippians.

"I can do everything through him who gives me strength."

The verse had been Laura's mainstay. When things weren't going well, she clung to that verse and its wonderful, helpful meaning.

She read a few psalms because they uplifted her, then prayed in the darkness. For some reason her thoughts again returned to Gregory and his sermons. His preaching was calm, almost a monotone. Not that he had to preach fire and brimstone, but he could use a bit of inflection. Sometimes she wished she could stay at the piano while he preached instead of going into the audience at the first pew, right where she was in his line of view.

"Give it some oomph," she said aloud. "Make the Word come to life, Gregory. Make the words zing with fervor!"

She wondered what it might be like to be a preacher. It took a special person to answer the calling. She'd never had the desire to be a missionary, though she knew several who had answered the mission call. There were other ways to serve God, and she was doing one of them.

❧

Gregory wasn't sure when he'd first started thinking about Laura in a way other than a friend, a parishioner. There was just something about her smile, the way she brushed her hair off her forehead. It was a nervous gesture, but an endearing one. He also liked how she related to the boys, encouraging them to do well. It had made a difference with Joel.

And she walked with head held high, with such confidence that one couldn't help noticing. Kenny Thompson had his eye on her. Kenny would be good for Laura, and they'd make a nice couple. He liked the idea, but on the other hand couldn't help feeling a twinge of jealousy at the thought of the two of them together.

Gregory had not looked at a woman in so long, the thought both excited and frightened him. How could he even be thinking about her in this way? Yet, how could he stop?

A cup of tea sounded good to relax him enough so he could sleep. The light was on upstairs. He gritted his teeth and opened the door to shut it off. It bothered him that Joel went to sleep with the light on and radio playing. He usually left the radio on, not wanting to climb the stairs.

He went back to the kitchen. Stirring sugar into his tea, he took a big swallow without thinking, burning his mouth. He nearly dropped the cup.

He prayed, *God, what's wrong with me? I never burn my mouth, and rarely do I have insomnia.*

Yet he sort of liked the dizzy feeling, the way his mind kept going to Laura, the way he looked for ways to see more of her. As it was now, he saw her during church services, but that didn't count. They were never alone; someone was always breaking in with various comments. If she came over for dinner or they went to Ruth's, the boys were front and center.

He reminisced back to when he'd first felt love for a woman. Always in his mind were thoughts of Beth Marie. Beth Marie with the beautiful green eyes, following her mother's advice and marrying a man with "more promise."

Lord, if You want me to follow You, please put it into Beth Marie's heart, too, he had prayed as a young, brash man, sure, yet unsure of himself.

Either God had not put it in her heart or Beth Marie had not listened, because her wedding took place at the end of summer. Though he was invited, Gregory stayed away from both the ceremony and reception. Knowing she had chosen another was devastating enough without seeing her in person, all smiles, looking at and kissing another man. *How could she?* had drummed through his head over the years. They had been everything to each other. How could he put her softness out of his mind? How could he ever hope to love another?

He was accepted at a seminary in California. He wanted to get out of North Dakota. He'd been teased about his Midwest twang, and it took weeks of practicing before he sounded like the others. When he reached Joseph, he was ready and eager to serve his first congregation.

Though he wasn't ready to forget Beth Marie, Shirley was there, so helpful, so positive and patient. And God had blessed them with two sons.

He thought again about Joel, how he still irritated him; but suddenly some of the things that bothered him didn't seem important. Why did he always make a big fuss about Joel's leaving the light and the radio on? There were worse things the kid could be doing. And he made good grades. He'd be in line for a scholarship if he kept on progressing well.

He remembered that afternoon at church. He had listened to Caleb's piano playing. The boy pounded, but that was okay. He had a good touch, he'd overheard Laura say. He was glad Caleb had chosen to take lessons.

But it was Joel's coming each week that had shocked him. He had no idea he would agree to playing a solo. Laura hadn't known Gregory was just outside the door, listening as she spoke to Joel. And Joel, always the quiet, unresponsive son, had talked. Unbelievable. He'd wanted to go out and praise his eldest son, but something kept him there, hidden. Many times he longed to pull Joel close, just hold him for a long moment, but he always stopped. Was it the boy's expression, his don't-touch-me attitude? His pulling away the few times Gregory had reached out? Soon he had stopped trying. Maybe he shouldn't have. But how did one turn back the clock and start over again? You had one chance with a marriage, one chance with a kid. If you failed, you couldn't undo the wrong.

Or could you? God never gave up on His children. How could Gregory?

The cup was empty and he still wasn't sleepy. He opened his Bible to the psalms. Some pages slipped out. "Time to buy a new Bible, I think." He could order one from the local bookstore, but he needed to go to La Grande to buy a piano. Maybe Laura would accompany him for the day.

Humming, he set his cup in the sink and padded back to bed. For some reason he suddenly felt better. Yes, Mrs. Laura Madison had made a difference to the Hall family, the church, and most of all to Gregory's heart.

12

*L*aura walked over to the church to practice Friday morning. A guest soloist was scheduled and had brought the sheet music. Laura wasn't familiar with the song and felt she needed to go over it a few times. Then, too, she wanted to plan a lesson book for Caleb to practice when he came to use the piano at the church. She hoped Gregory found a used piano soon. Caleb needed to be able to practice at home.

"Laura!" Gregory stood in the doorway motioning her. "Phone. Kenny Thompson."

Laura cringed. They hadn't dated yet because Kenny had been gone on a business trip.

"Probably wants to ask you out again," Gregory said as Laura moved past him.

"Why would he call me here?"

"I'm sure Ruth told him where you were."

She wished Gregory would leave the office, but he was intent on shuffling through papers, pretending not to pay attention. If only the church owned a portable phone.

"Mr. Thompson?" Laura knew her cheeks were flushed. She took a deep breath. "The movie in Enterprise? Oh, yes, I understood fully about the sick little calf and the business trip."

She turned her back so she wouldn't see Gregory's expression. He'd make her laugh. Laura wished Kenny had never asked her out, nor should she have consented to have lunch with him. She didn't want to hurt him but should have explained she was happy in her single state. He seemed like the type who could be overbearing. She looked over to see Gregory penciling a big "YES."

Laura left church shortly after. Her mood for playing the piano had disappeared.

"What does one wear on a date?" she asked Ruth later. The last time she'd dated was back in the early seventies.

"I'd go conservative," Ruth said. "How about your dark slacks and that nice pastel pink blouse?"

"What do you suppose he'll wear?"

"Jeans, denim jacket, cowboy boots, and of course his hat. The same thing he wears to church. Most ranchers and farmers around here have one attire. Jeans with dirt and cow dung for day wear, clean jeans for church and dates."

"Ruth! Cow dung. How awful."

"You can't miss it, hon."

She remembered how Kenny stuck out in church, being the only one who wore a cowboy hat.

"Wear just a touch of makeup," Ruth added.

Laura changed to a pink, ruffled blouse and sweater vest, then back to a forest green light top and tan slacks.

One thing about Kenny Thompson, he was punctual. Since Laura had changed clothes three times, she was not ready. She heard Kenny and Ruth chatting in the living room as she hurried down the stairs. She never had liked making a grand entrance, nor did she like being late.

Kenny stood, hat in hand, his other hand reaching out to shake hers. "I see you're ready." His smile was hearty, his dark eyes almost smoldering. She'd forgotten he was so short and stocky.

"Yes."

"We don't want to be late. One thing I can't stand is walking into a movie house once the lights are dimmed."

"I totally agree," Laura said. It was the last complete sentence she uttered.

"I expect you want to hear about the ranch and what I do there and that sort of thing," he said as held the car door open. It wasn't his truck; a Cadillac, yellow with wire wheels, waited in front of the bed-and-breakfast. It shone as if he'd polished on it half a day.

"This is my first nice car, and it's been a dandy." He removed his hat for a second, then stuck it back on. "Course I never drive it. I prefer the truck or the Jeep."

"It's nice—"

"Well, back to the ranch; I was born in the very house I now live in. I'm an only son, have one sister who lives in Alaska. Haven't seen her since Ma was buried about three years ago now. I do all my cooking, housecleaning, washing clothes, riding the herd, checking fences. I'm my own boss from one end to the other."

"I see you like ranch life—"

"Shucks, I wouldn't have it any other way. I sometimes think of having a little filly there, cooking my breakfast and taking care of my needs, but most of 'em don't know how to cook nowadays." He glanced at Laura, who was trying to disappear into the seat cushion. "You know how to cook, Laura?"

"Well, I—"

Before she could answer, he was off and running. "That's okay. You play a mean piano and that counts for a lot."

Laura was relieved to see the outskirts of Enterprise. She did not like the way this was going, and they'd only driven seven miles. Kenny Thompson pretty well put his wants and needs on the line. It was her wildest nightmare. He assumed she knew he was looking for someone. Why else would he have asked her out? One didn't spend money on a "filly" if it wasn't for a reason.

He pulled into the parking lot and hopped out to hold her door open. "I've always believed in opening the door for a woman. My pa taught me that when I was this high." He held his hand out. "C'mon, let's mosey on over there." He took her hand and she followed because she had to.

It was a big, callused hand, a strong hand. She couldn't have extricated her hand from his grip if she'd wanted to.

"Hiya, there, Trudy. This here's Laura, the new piano teacher over in Joseph. Been there a while, going to stay a bit longer—"

Laura forced a smile as she looked at the older woman taking tickets. "Just five minutes until the show starts. Better get your popcorn now," she said, nodding at Laura.

Kenny ordered a barrel of popcorn with two squirts of butter, two

Cokes, and a large candy bar. Laura took her drink and the candy and followed him inside.

She couldn't remember later what the movie was about. She kept moving to the far side of the seat as Kenny kept leaning toward her. She let him eat the popcorn, and he ate the whole tub. She found herself thinking about the first time she and Jerry had gone to the movies, how shy they both had been. How she couldn't even quite look at him or he at her.

As the movie went on, Laura remembered "Bridge Over Troubled Waters" as being their favorite song. They'd met on a Tuesday and Jerry was constantly humming the Moody Blues' tune, "Tuesday, Tuesday." But Kenny liked country and western music. On the way here, she'd listened to Billy Ray Cyrus singing about his "Achy Breaky Heart." And Garth Brooks bellowed out something about "The River." Kenny told her they were old songs he'd put on a cassette.

"You enjoyin' this movie?" Kenny asked, loud enough for everyone to hear. " 'Cause if not, we can always pick up a video and go back to my place."

She cringed farther into the seat. How could this be happening? She, a woman of forty-five, out on a date, feeling worse than when she was a teenager. How was she going to get out of going back to his house?

"Actually, I'm enjoying the scenery in the movie," she said, hoping that would sound truthful. And the Montana landscape was beautiful. Of course there were horses in the movie. Laura doubted that Kenny would enjoy a movie without horses or cows.

Afterwards, Kenny took her to his favorite place for ice cream, waving to everyone he saw. He knew all the local people, since he'd lived in the area all his life.

"You're quiet," he said; but before Laura could answer, he began telling about the woman he'd almost married, the one who'd died in a car accident over on the road going to Troy. "Never did find out why she was going to Troy. There's nothing there but a motel and a place for hunters to camp, and fishing in the summer."

"I'm sorry about your loss."

"Well, it's been a long time now. A lot of water has gone under the bridge. And over it!" He laughed then. "Yeah, lots of women around, but I never paid much attention to any of them. But there was something about you, the way you play the piano and all."

Laura licked the butterscotch sauce off her spoon. She wanted more than anything for this night to be over.

"You're a widow, Pastor tells me."

"Yes. We were married twenty years."

"When did he die?"

"Five years ago."

"Then you're probably ready to git married again."

Laura swallowed, then choked on the sweet, gooey sauce. She tried to catch her breath, but coughed harder than ever. "I—I—"

"Don't try to talk." He jumped up and pounded her so hard on the back she thought he'd broken her spine.

Her face was red, her eyes watered, and worse than anything was the awareness that everyone in the place was watching her. She wanted to climb into a hole and hide. At last she had her voice again. "I shouldn't try to eat and talk at the same time."

"I didn't mean to get you all excited. About getting married again, I mean." His hand stole across the table and took hers.

"Mr. Thompson—"

"Kenny. Call me Kenny. Everyone does."

"Kenny, you're a very nice person, but I have no plans to remarry. That's a big step, and I'm quite happy with my life the way it is."

He leaned back and shifted his hat, a habit she found particularly annoying. "People change their minds."

The ride home was a silent one. She expected him to talk more about the ranch, and when she asked what he grew, he hit the steering wheel. "Mint," was all he said. When Joseph came into view, Laura felt relief. At least she wouldn't have to worry about his asking her out again.

He pulled up in front of the dark house, turned the lights off, and put his arm around the back of the seat. He didn't touch her, but she could feel the warmth of his arm, no more than an inch from her shoulder.

"I'm a decent sort of guy. You could do worse than me."

"Mr.—I mean, Kenny, do you believe in God?"

He reared forward as if he couldn't believe she'd asked that.

"Believe in God? Who don't believe in God?"

"Lots of people."

"Of course I believe in God. You saw me in church, didn't you?"

She nodded. "Many people attend church, but it doesn't mean they believe in salvation or have accepted Jesus into their heart."

"Well, I don't know about the salvation or accepting Jesus, but I do believe in God and I believe that Reverend Gregory is a good man."

"Goodness doesn't get you to heaven."

He opened the door and was around to her side before she realized it.

"I'll think about what you said. And I'll be calling you." He took off his hat, leaned over, and kissed her on the cheek. "Thanks for going to the movie with me. I'll see you again."

Oh, please, Laura wanted to cry out, but she said nothing as he walked back to the car and hopped in. She let herself in and sank into the nearest sofa close to the door. If only Ruth were up so they could talk. More than anything, she needed to discuss this over a cup of tea.

Ruth moved out of the shadows of the sitting room. "I heard the car door slam."

"Oh, Ruth."

"What?" Ruth looked expectant.

"He wants a woman. I don't know if he wants marriage, but he definitely wants a woman, and I know I'm not that woman."

For the second time that night, Laura found herself thinking of Jerry and the love they'd had, the marriage that had been wonderful and sacred. She thought of Gregory and how his quiet nature both delighted and frustrated her. She wanted him to bare his soul. Well, after tonight, perhaps she didn't. Kenny Thompson had bared his soul and there hadn't been time for anything else. He was a rich and, in her opinion, an egotistical, overbearing man.

"At least you saw a movie."

Laura giggled. "I can't even tell you one thing it was about."

"No?" Ruth poured water into cups. "I guess it was a dud, then?"

"A real bomb, Ruth. A real bomb."

"Sometimes first dates are like that. I can remember a few."

"No. It's just that I feel we are from two different planets. I know nothing about ranching, and he knows nothing about my life or what I deem important."

"Maybe you have to tell him."

Laura sighed. "Ruth, the man talks nonstop. Did you realize that?"

"No, honey, I didn't. But, then, it's probably because I've never said more than a few words to Mr. Kenny Thompson."

"He would make some woman a terrific husband, I'm sure of it, but she'd need earplugs."

Ruth looked at her and they both burst into laughter.

"Now I'm getting silly."

"Let's go to bed then. Tomorrow is another day and you know what that means."

"No, what?"

"A day to praise God, to be thankful for our blessings, and a day to go to Enterprise for supplies!"

The women laughed again, linking their arms as they went down the hall.

13

The days went fast for Laura. She couldn't believe so much had taken place in such a short time. She'd come wanting to find a new life for herself, to be of service and a blessing to people.

One day a week she read to Mrs. Yates, an elderly member of the church who was nearly blind and needed someone to write letters to her sister in Seattle. She looked in on others who wanted to remain independent and could do so if someone checked on them on a regular basis. Laura also tutored a physically challenged child whose mother preferred to keep her at home. She drove Ruth to Enterprise once a week for supplies for the bed-and-breakfast. She now had four piano students and could have had more, but since she hadn't come to Joseph to simply be "kept busy," she declined. Laura loved to be needed and knew it was God's plan all along.

The time between 1:30 and 3:30 was free. She often strolled through town, stopping by to say hello to Nancy at the bookstore or stopping for a latte. For some reason, she strolled toward the church that afternoon.

There was a light on under Gregory's office door, so she wondered if her practicing would bother him. He usually left the office when Caleb had his lesson, not that she said he must, but he decided it was better for Caleb.

She tapped on the door.

He boomed, "Come in," and she entered to find him poring over a book sitting on a stack of five or six volumes.

"I didn't mean to disturb you, but—"

"No, not at all. You're saving me from a boring time of looking up some information."

She pulled out the chair he indicated and glanced up, her eyes meeting his steady gaze.

"It's just that I wanted to practice a bit—sort of at loose ends, I guess."

"Your playing will definitely not disturb me." He drummed on the open book with the eraser end of a new pencil.

Laura started to get up, but he pleaded with her to stay. "I want to throw a couple of things at you, if you don't mind."

"Sure, what gives?"

The office was immaculate. A bookcase filled with an assortment of books covered the wall under the window. A flowered, ruffled curtain covered the top half. He'd told her earlier that Ruth had made the curtains and had overseen the decorating of his office when he first arrived in Joseph. It was not only clean, but a comfortable place.

"Hope you don't mind sitting for a minute," he said, pointing toward the door. "Glad you left the door open. People do tend to talk in small towns."

Laura smiled. Imagine anyone linking her with the pastor. Not only was he too young, it was apparent he was quite happy with his celibate relationship.

"How can I be of help?"

He drummed the pencil on the book again. "I'd like you to listen to the opening paragraph of this coming Sunday's sermon."

"Very well. Go ahead."

Laura leaned back, crossing her legs while she waited for him to begin. This was a first. He'd never asked her advice on anything with the exception of what to do about Joel's sullenness.

"I very much admire the writings of Dietrich Bonhoeffer. I quote him often."

"Wasn't he involved in World War II?"

"Yes, very much so. He was German and stood up against Hitler and what he was doing to Germany. His beliefs got him executed. My sermon topic concerns our doing what is important, standing up for your beliefs and making your actions count. But my sermon has no life. I must make it come to life, to show the marvelous teachings of this man."

"Use some quotes," Laura suggested. "You sound pretty impassioned to me."

Gregory looked surprised. "I'm a World War II buff."

Laura nodded, her interest piqued. "Read me what you have so far."

He read the quote and summed it up in his own words. He was right. It didn't come to life, and she wasn't sure why.

"I was wondering if you'd ever thought of coming down from the pulpit and standing on the main floor?"

Gregory almost looked shocked. "You mean walk down as I'm talking or start from that vantage point?"

Laura cleared her throat. "Either way works." She could see that Gregory wasn't keen on the idea. Not that he put himself above the people of his church, but he tended to go strictly by protocol, meaning one stood in the pulpit. Always.

"It's just an idea."

"Is that where the pastor stood in your church back in Sealand?"

"Sometimes."

He seemed to be thinking this over. "I guess it would take some getting used to. Maybe he felt uncomfortable the first time he did it."

"Yes, maybe so."

"I shouldn't be a pastor—"

"Don't be ridiculous," Laura broke in. "You are great with your people and they know they can count on you to come for any crisis and pray with them when needed. I feel that one of the most important parts of a ministry is being there when needed. A lot of pastors fail that part of the calling."

He nodded and leaned back in the chair. She'd noticed this before and each time held her breath, hoping the chair wouldn't go clear back, sending Gregory crashing to the floor.

"I try to do what is required of a minister."

"So, back to the sermon."

"Could you read it?"

"I'd be happy to."

"It won't be taking you from any other duty?"

She laughed. "Not hardly. You know my time is pretty much my own since coming here. That's how I wanted it, yet I like helping others."

"And you certainly do that." Gregory leaned forward. "What do you think of Joseph by now?"

Laura laughed again. "I love the people, and the scenery is awe-inspiring." She looked at the pages in her hand. She'd once suggested he might type up his sermon, as once in a while there'd be a long pause in the sermon while he was trying to decipher his notes. That was another reason, she knew, for his not wanting to walk down among the people. Where would he put his notes? She wondered again how he would do if he didn't depend on the notes. What if he spoke from the heart? Would that mean as much to the people? Wouldn't they get just as much out of his talk?

"I'll read this in the fellowship hall and get it back to you before Caleb comes for his lesson."

"I'm not putting you out now—"

She paused in the doorway, looking back. Something about the look on his face gave her the sudden urge to go over and smooth the hair back, to reassure him that things would work out, that they always would with God in control. She resisted the urge.

Noticing her hesitancy, he stood and walked over. "I need to say one thing, Laura, if I may." He was close enough for her to touch that lock of hair, but she didn't. Their eyes met and held.

"Yes?"

"You've done a lot of good for my boys and this church, and I wanted you to know I appreciate it." Before she could respond, he bent down and swiftly brushed his lips against her forehead.

His action so surprised her that she stood immobilized, unable to speak. Gregory was the first to step back. "I know you have things to do. I–I—" He didn't finish his sentence.

Laura's fingers gripped the pages of the sermon notes as she turned and hurriedly left the room.

She decided to make a cup of instant coffee. As the water sang in the teakettle on the stove, she wondered about the kiss. Gregory was appreciative, that was all. He didn't care for her. She knew he thought she was far too outspoken.

Stirring the coffee over and over, her gaze fell on the page with hastily scribbled notes. If only she could convince him he needed to update things. Why not do research on the Internet instead of checking out all those books? She was sure he could find scads of information on this Bonhoeffer.

Laura read two paragraphs, then knew she would make this a special project. She'd use the computer at the bookstore and E-mail her request to a friend in Portland, asking for the needed information. She'd surprise Gregory with it in the next day or so. Perhaps not in time to incorporate into this Sunday's message, but in time for the following week's. If Bonhoeffer was so important, didn't he rate two Sundays?

She read the notes, liking what she read. If anything, Gregory was thorough in his research. She circled important data, then took it upon herself to begin anew. She boxed off the Scripture to the left, like a sidebar, and numbered the points he made, then summarized the contents into one large paragraph at the bottom. She wrote the major points and wrote, *Add to this info from your own words.*

Numbering the pages, she stacked them together with a paper clip. A note scrawled on a separate sheet of paper should encourage him.

> *Great research, Gregory. I think this topic needs two Sundays*
> *Why not continue on with it for one more week? What a great*
> *man he was! Hope you like my number system. L*

He was gone when she walked back to the office. A note on the door said he'd be there at 8:00 A.M. the following morning. In case of emergency, please call the nursing home in Enterprise. She slipped the notes on top of his desk, covered them with a notepad, and left the room. But not before she paused long enough to gaze at two boys smiling from five-by-seven photos. How he loved those boys, yet he had a problem showing it. Not once had she seen him hug Joel. Caleb received hugs and attention only because he was younger and demanded attention from his father. *The squeaky wheel gets the grease,* Laura thought. She looked at Shirley again. The smile was genuine, but there was a look in the eyes Laura wondered about. What had she really been like? Had she been happy as Gregory's wife?

She noticed a new framed quotation and paused to read it:

Life is mostly froth and bubble,
Two things stand like stone:
Kindness in another's trouble,
Courage in our own.

—*Adam Lindsay Gordon*

"I like that," Laura said aloud. "That's a good thought. I wonder who this Adam Lindsay Gordon is."

She closed the door and went to the piano. Playing eased her feelings, soothed her emotions. She remembered those teen years before they'd moved to Oregon, how she'd played; she remembered a happy time when she had played for that small church in the farming town in Nebraska. How she'd loved playing the dear old hymns. They were hymns that a lot of churches didn't play today. Not that she minded those from time to time, but sometimes she missed the songs of Charles Wesley and Fanny Crosby. She felt many old hymns offered more substance than some of the newer songs.

Her mother had loved "When the Roll Is Called Up Yonder," but "Onward, Christian Soldiers" had been the most requested at the small church in Nebraska. It always made Laura want to march around the church, just as "The Battle Hymn of the Republic" did. At that thought, she pounded into the song.

She didn't hear the door open nor did she realize that someone was there, listening, until she heard the floor creak at the end of the latest hymn.

"My goodness, but I never tire of hearing you play." Ruth stood as if transfixed. "I brought a spot of my sun tea over and some freshly baked cookies. Thought you and Caleb might like a snack before you tackle his lesson." She sat on a nearby pew, shaking her head. "Your heart is in your playing. I've never heard anything so beautiful. And if the board of trustees ever says we need an organ, I'm going to veto it with both hands."

"Ruth, you're a peach." Laura left the bench and closely encircled the plump woman's body. "I don't know how I'd get along without you. And I agree with you about the piano."

The side door burst open and Caleb rushed in. Cheeks flushed, he shoved a paper under Laura's nose. "See? I did what you said. I studied before that test and I got a perfect 100!"

"Caleb, I'm so proud of you!"

He beamed while Ruth hugged him, too. "I knew there was a reason to bake something special this afternoon."

"Where's Dad?"

"Gone to the nursing home, probably to visit Bernice," Ruth said.

"Oh, yeah, that's right. But sometimes he waits until I get here."

"You can show him the minute your lesson is over." Laura faced the young boy. "Did you practice your scales like I suggested?"

"Yes, I did."

"And you're ready to start in?"

"Just as soon as I wash my hands."

"Boy, he's wired. Hope you can get him to settle down for a lesson."

"He'll do just fine."

"I'll see you tonight. For supper?"

Laura nodded. "For supper, yes."

Caleb returned, sat on the bench, posed his hands just right, and began the scales. Laura hummed as he ran up and down the keys. Scales loosened up the fingers and the mind. She noted he held his fingers arched, bent just a bit at the knuckle. His back was straight, his head held high. So far he'd taken to all her instruction. Caleb was a child easy to like. She just wished that Joel was as likable. But maybe someday. Maybe someday both he and his father would realize how wonderful they actually were.

Laura smiled as her fingers felt the place on her forehead. Gregory had kissed her there. The gesture touched her deeply and she wasn't quite sure why. . . .

14

*D*o you still want to play the solo, Joel?" Laura asked after several rehearsals. She tried to smile as she stared at his somber face. It was as if she were looking at a blank wall. "The most difficult part is knowing when to start, then later come in. All you need to do is watch me and I'll nod or point if that helps."

"Yeah, I guess so," he finally said, his eyes not quite meeting Laura's.

Laura leaned forward. "Are you doing this for your father? Because you think he wants you to?"

He said nothing.

"I could probably tell him I'll just play the piece the regular way without trumpet accompaniment." She stifled a sigh of discouragement, remembering how hard it was reaching a child when he didn't want to do something but wouldn't admit it. Like going out for a sport or the class play: If she thought it was a good idea, her children would go ahead and do it, then grump all through the season or practice.

"I know you can do a fine job, if that's what worries you. I say go for it. We'll practice as many times as you wish."

There. She'd made a decision for him.

He shrugged. "One more time, then I'm outta here."

"Fine."

Joel stood straight and tall, shoulders thrust back. His face was thin, his whole body lean and hard. The blond hair hung into his eyes, but the back was sheared off as so many of the boys were wearing their hair now. It probably wasn't the most becoming, but if it made him feel good, why not?

There was one tiny bit of hesitation at the second part, but he came through loud, strong, and clear.

"That's going to send chills up people's spines on Sunday," Laura said, wanting more than anything to reassure the boy. "And we still have lots of time to practice."

"Yeah." He carefully wiped the mouthpiece and rubbed the golden body of his instrument. Not once, but twice, using circular motions as he polished it. He was treating his trumpet as if it was his love, his lifeline.

Laura remembered a boy and his sax, a daughter who played clarinet. All her kids had played in the school band. Only Kurt still occasionally took out his sax and played. She knew he could have found a band to play with, but every time she suggested it, he'd shrugged. "Or church. Why not play a solo some Sunday?" He'd really groaned at that one.

Oh, yes, she knew about kids who needed more than anything to talk but kept the words and thoughts bottled up inside. Kurt had never shared his feelings with his father, but Gregory was all Joel had. She doubted that he talked to him. She sensed he was like a gun cocked and ready to go off.

Joel laid his trumpet in the case and snapped it closed.

"We'll practice on Thursday directly after school," she called after his retreating back.

"Yeah. Okay."

He closed the door and the inside of the church was silent again. Laura loved the shape of the sanctuary. It was a wonderful setup and would seat at least one hundred, though the church membership was less than that.

Laura opened the hymnal and played the selection Gregory felt would go along with his sermon that Sunday.

Be Thou my vision
O, Lord of my heart . . .

It was the third verse that had always spoken to Laura's heart.

Riches I heed not, nor man's empty praise;
Thou mine inheritance, now and always;
Thou and Thou only first in my heart,
High King of heaven, my treasure Thou art.

Laura's fingers rippled over the keys as she changed tempo and played a spiritual. *Come stand by me, Lord, yes, come stand by me . . .* Laura played a medley, adding some of the later tunes her kids had loved.

She didn't know how long she played nor did she realize she had an audience until clapping sounded from the back of the sanctuary. She whirled around to find Harvey, the custodian, standing there smiling.

"My mother used to play like that," he said, walking down toward her. "We had a piano at home and she'd practice each night. I'd fall asleep to the sound of her playing. I wish you could have met her."

"My mother played, too," Laura said, the emptiness filling her as it often did when she thought of her mother. "I wish she were alive today to come to this beautiful church and to play one Sunday."

"At least we have our memories."

Laura smiled. "Yes, that we do."

"I came to measure the pastor's office. The board met and voted to put in new carpeting for his birthday."

"His birthday? When is that?"

"Last day of June."

Laura rose from the bench, scooting it back. "Sounds like a great gift to me. I trust it's a surprise?"

Harvey nodded. "Yes, that's why I came now while he's at the school giving a talk to the graduating class."

"Oh. I forgot about that."

"I'll see you Sunday," Harvey said with a tip of his cap.

Laura thought about Gregory's birthday, wondering what she might give him as a surprise. What did one give one's pastor? Some were easy to buy for, but not him. She no more knew what he'd like than a perfect stranger. In many ways, he was a stranger.

Then she thought of the bakery in Elgin. It was a fair piece there, but she was ready to head off somewhere. If the boys had a photo, she could mail it to the lady, have her bake the cake, and then pick it up the day before his birthday. That would be a unique gift, one nobody else would give. Laura hummed as she walked down the steps and across the road to home. She'd run the idea by Ruth, knowing Ruth wouldn't breathe a word to anyone.

"I think the cake is a perfect idea," Ruth said, "though I could bake one twice as good I bet. But I sure can't put no photo on it."

Laura paused, her coffee cup in midair. She always had a cup the minute she entered the house. "I think we should have a potluck after church, and you know we need more than one cake, anyway. This will be the centerpiece, and you and perhaps someone else could bake a cake. You can never have too much birthday cake."

Ruth clasped her hands like a little kid who'd just found a bike under the Christmas tree. "I love to plan parties. I'll get a few women busy on the decorations. We didn't do anything last year for Pastor's birthday, so it's high time."

Ruth started on a list while Laura changed into more comfortable clothes. She still worried about Joel, wondering if he really would do okay with the solo on Father's Day.

On Thursday, Joel arrived five minutes early. He nodded in Laura's direction, and she thought his scowl seemed less grim.

"Hello," she said with a nod. Laura knew one never probed, as there was nothing that made a kid withdraw quicker than a probe, no matter how friendly.

"Hello," he grunted back. He removed his trumpet and it looked shinier than before.

"I never wanted to play trumpet," he said then.

"You didn't?"

"No. It was Dad's idea."

"What would you have chosen?"

"Nothin'."

"I see. Well, shall we start in?"

Laura played the opening two bars. She stopped, then nodded at Joel.

His notes were loud and clear and his head seemed even higher than before. She relaxed just a bit. He lowered his horn and she played the first refrain:

God of our Fathers, Whose almighty hand
Leads forth in beauty all the starry band
Of shining worlds in splendor through the skies,
Our grateful songs before Thy throne arise.

The piece went well and Joel's clear, high notes definitely added something to the old hymn. Laura's hair stood up on the back of her neck.

"That was very good," she said as she played the fourth and final stanza. "Shall we practice again on Saturday?"

He nodded and slumped off, not bothering to remove the mouthpiece or dry off his instrument. The door banged, and she wondered what she'd said or done to make him react that way.

Laura was busy the next few days helping Ruth with the house, as two rooms were rented for that weekend.

"Have no idea what's going on in town. Nothing I know about, but I'm happy for the business."

Laura smiled. "The word has spread about your wonderful pineapple-mango muffins."

"Think I'll make banana."

"Don't you dare!" Laura cried.

Saturday morning she left the guests sitting around the circular oak dining room table, partaking of more of Ruth's muffins, egg and ham omelets, and the rich brewed coffee she bought at the new coffee shop in town.

"I must dash. Time to practice the opening hymn."

"Perhaps you'd both like to attend the service tomorrow. It promises to be a great one, the music, that is," Ruth said to both sets of guests.

Laura didn't hear their answer as she closed the door and ran down the steps.

Joel was waiting at the church.

"Am I late?" She glanced at her watch, knowing she was not. It was the one thing she prided herself on: being on time.

"Nope!" He ran a hand through his shock of hair.

"Well, let's get this show on the road."

"You're funny," he said then.

She looked up from the hymnal, her eyes leaving the page numbers. "Funny? In what way?"

He shrugged. "Just the things you say. What you do."

Was this a compliment? Laura wondered. She had no way of knowing. "My kids always said I was a bit spacey."

He set his horn on the pew and glanced up with such a pensive look that Laura yearned to reach out to hug him.

"I can't talk to my father."

"Why not, Joel?"

"He doesn't understand. He never has."

"What is it you need to talk about?"

"Just things."

Did she dare ask more, or would it make him stop talking? "Do you want to talk to me about it?"

He grabbed his horn and shook his head. "No. Forget I said anything. Sometimes I say too much."

Laura knew it must be difficult for him not having a mother who cared, a mother who would praise him. She knew Gregory was a good father but doubted that he thought praising his sons was part of the job. Caleb didn't need praises, but Joel was a different matter.

The rest of the practice went fine, though the smile she'd caught a glimpse of earlier disappeared and the serious scowl took its place. If only he'd talk! But at least she had let him know she was available. Look at the progress they'd made this week: from not speaking, to a half-smile, to his opening up just a bit this morning.

The solo went well and she smiled, giving the A-OK sign with thumb and index finger.

"I have to leave. There's a meeting at school at one."

"See you Sunday morning," Laura called to his retreating back. She wanted to talk more but knew he had said all he was going to for this time. She was amazed he'd even mentioned the meeting. Before, he just went, not offering any explanation.

She went over the hymns again, then left the church. Today she would not have lunch at Ruth's but would go to The Book Corner and have a cup of coffee and one of their huge cookies. For some reason that sounded good.

As she walked, she wondered what Gregory's Father's Day sermon would be about. She also wondered if he would appreciate the special music, the time and effort his son had made learning the piece, then standing up in front of the congregation when it scared him more than a little. She would make certain that Gregory commented to his son his appreciation. She wondered, also, if the boys had thought of buying their father a gift for Father's Day. So often it was the mother's role to make sure gifts were bought and presented, thank you notes written.

She opened the door and slipped inside the coffee shop, her favorite stop in all of Joseph.

"Good afternoon, Laura!" came the cheerful voice. "The usual?"

"Yes, but make it a double latte today. I think I need it."

15

A house for rent was becoming available the first of July, and Laura discussed the possibility of moving with Ruth one afternoon while they were both in the kitchen baking for that night's youth party. The Joseph youth were meeting with the youth in Enterprise.

The Father's Day service had gone well, with many accolades for Joel. He'd stood proud and tall, and Laura thought she detected a tear in Gregory's eye. She overheard him telling Joel later what a good job he'd done and then beamed when Joel gave her the credit.

The following Sunday they'd celebrated Gregory's birthday with a potluck, and the cake from the bakery in Elgin had been a big hit. The photo was one of him and his sons with the Wallowa Mountains as a backdrop.

While Laura and Ruth were talking, the doorbell rang. Before Laura could answer, Caleb popped in. "I heard there were cookies to sample."

Ruth motioned for him to come to the table and poured him a glass of milk.

"I'll be glad when I'm old enough to go to the youth meetings." He bit into a chocolate chip cookie, then frowned. "Not bad, Laura. Almost as good as Ruth's."

She reached to swat him, but he ducked out of the way.

"I'm going," he said. "I'll be back tonight 'cause I'm not staying alone."

"Good. Maybe we can play a game," Laura said.

Ruth was also setting bread to rise. Someone had offered her a bread machine, which she refused. "I like making my own bread. Just doesn't seem right if I don't knead it."

"So, you're moving out, deserting me in my hour of need," said Ruth, returning to the topic of the house.

"You could rent out my room in an instant, and you know it." Laura stacked the cool cookies. "Besides, it's time I learned to fly solo again."

⤫

Laura had finally received a letter from Jen and a phone call from Kurt. It was ironic that he asked again when she was coming home. He didn't realize how much this was becoming home to her. She had recently added two more students to her schedule, bringing it to a total of six now. Each was progressing nicely and she enjoyed the lessons.

Since the cookies and cake were done and nothing was pressing, Laura walked toward town. She and Joel walked one afternoon a week. It had happened quite by accident.

She'd been on her way to the bookstore one day after school when he caught up with her.

"I never thanked you—"

"Thanked me? What do you mean?"

"For helping me with the solo."

"Oh, that." She turned and their eyes met. Joel seldom looked her in the eye. She felt she'd crossed an important step. She thought of the first practice with Joel. It had been hard working with a morose boy who grunted barely audible replies to her questions. He at least looked at her during the second practice, and by the third practice, had actually smiled.

"You did a wonderful job as you already know," she said now.

"Lots of people said so," he affirmed.

"I knew it would go well. I had every confidence in you. And not even one mistake!"

"Almost did."

"But you didn't and that's the important thing."

"I couldn't have done it without your help."

"I enjoyed it, as you must know. Are you happy with the trumpet, Joel? Remember you said it was all your father's idea—"

"I was just saying that. I like it fine."

"That's great because I think you have a natural bent."

He beamed but said nothing.

The late June sun beat out of a cloudless sky, causing Laura to shade her face with her hand as she greeted Joel. She could never bring herself to wear a shady hat, though she'd been told to more than once.

"Say, let's drive out to the lake and say hi to the Boeves. Want to?"

"Sure."

"A chocolate peanut butter ice cream sounds good to me right now. You can get your piece of fudge and I'll bring a slice back to enjoy later. Should we leave a note for your father?"

"Nah. He knows I'm around."

The deer were waiting out front for people food.

"Hello, friends," Laura called. "We couldn't stand another minute without ice cream and fudge."

Oliver looked up and smiled. "Made a fresh batch last night. It's going fast this week. Here, try my new recipe. It has apples in it."

"Yum!" both Laura and Joel agreed.

"Hello, Joel, Laura," Keithanne said with a wave, after helping a customer. "How are things going with you two?"

"Summer blahs, I think," Laura responded. "My son called last night wanting to know when I was coming home."

Keithanne handed over a double-decker chocolate peanut butter. "Once a mother, always a mother, right?"

Joel had gone to a far aisle to look at some merchandise.

"I cannot believe Joel came with you and he actually looks happy," Keithanne added in a lower voice.

Laura moved closer. "We've been walking the past couple of

weeks. Talking about things. You know, he's such a neat kid—if he could just open up to his father."

More customers came in, so Laura gave Keithanne a quick hug. "See you next trip."

Laura drove over by the lake. The little park was filled with people.

"Let's just stay here by the car," Joel suggested.

"Sure. Sounds fine to me." Laura leaned against the hood, looking out over the vast lake. She never tired of this spot and the beauty of God's creation. She still hadn't made it to Hell's Canyon, one of the world's great wonders, but it was on her agenda. That and going to Troy. It was quite a trip there, but worth it, according to Kenny. She hadn't dated him again, but they'd become friends and that was fine.

"Did I mention I'm renting the Cooper place?"

Joel stopped digging at the ground with his shoe while a smile crossed his face. "No, but that's good."

"Why do you say that?"

"It means you're staying in Joseph longer."

Laura laughed and reached over and impulsively hugged Joel. He flinched, but only for a moment. She moved away. "I think Ruth's hugging has rubbed off on me."

"It's okay." He didn't look her in the eye. "Maybe we should go back."

Joel was quiet on the way home. Laura respected his need for silence and said nothing. "It's a show of true friendship," Renee had said once, "when people can be together and not feel the need for talk."

Laura dropped Joel off, then went home to help Ruth clean.

"You don't need to do this, Laura."

"I know I don't need to, but I want to. Honest."

"Oh! I almost forgot! Your son called again."

Laura shook her head. "That kid never gives up, does he?"

"It's difficult for some kids when a parent isn't at their beck and call."

"I'm not going back just because he thinks he needs me or has a problem with his job or Susan."

Ruth nodded. "Stick to your guns, is the only advice I can give."

Laura would move the following week. It was going to be a busy week with Independence Day and the annual fireworks show at the lake. She could hardly wait to invite Ruth and the Hall family over for a meal. This was definitely a permanent step, and suddenly she realized how it must look. She also remembered the advice from one of the old-timers: "Better wait until you've gone through a winter here before deciding to stay."

Gregory dropped Caleb off at seven. Dressed in casual pants and a plaid shirt, Gregory looked almost like a kid. Laura trembled when their eyes met.

"I need to go to La Grande Monday. Want to come along?"

"Yes, that sounds wonderful."

"I'm going over to look at a piano; I thought you'd know if it was a good buy."

Of course, Laura thought. He didn't want her company. He needed someone to tell him if it was a good piano, a decent buy. Then she remembered she had a busy day scheduled.

"Maybe you forgot that Caleb's lesson's on Monday."

Gregory ran his hand through his hair. "I already explained you'd have to change the day. With school out, it isn't going to matter."

"I also have another student. Crissie Johnson. Do you know the Johnson family?"

He nodded. "Yes. I've been visiting the Johnsons to invite them to church. She's willing, but Dan has a problem with organized religion."

"I think a lot of people feel that way, Gregory. Don't take it personally."

"Can you put the lesson off to another day?"

"I suppose I could. But I still need to be back by 3:30."

"Why 3:30?"

"That's when I'm helping the Girl Scouts with play practice."

He shook his head. "I think you've gotten to know more people in the nearly three months you've been here than I know after being here fifteen years."

"It's getting that way. I'll call the Johnsons. So when should I be ready?"

"Better make it seven if we have to be back early."

"Need anything in La Grande?" Laura asked Ruth. "We're going over to look at pianos."

Ruth looked up. "Sure. I'll give you a list—a short one. Hey, that's terrific about a piano. Won't Caleb be pleased? Does he know about it yet?"

"No," Gregory said. "I don't want him disappointed in case we don't find one."

Ruth laughed. "I bet you will."

"We will."

Caleb came in, skateboard under arm. "I thought you had to get over there quick."

"I'm going, I'm going."

"Why are you smiling?" Caleb asked, looking at Laura, then Ruth.

"Nothing," both said. "We're just happy folks by nature."

Caleb accepted that along with a glass of milk. "I just figured out," he said, looking up, "if I had two lessons a week, I would be able to play for church in one year instead of two."

Laura looked at him, shaking her head. This kid was thinking every minute. He watched her expectantly, waiting for an answer.

"You're right, Caleb. Practice makes perfect."

"Oh, wow! A year. I can hardly wait. Maybe I'll have a piano by then. If I practiced an hour a day, I could maybe play in six months!"

"All right. That's enough. You make my head spin."

Laura helped clean the kitchen, her heart suddenly light. Monday should be an interesting day.

16

*G*regory arrived early and soon they were on their way for the nearly two-hour trip.

"Were your parents farmers?" Laura asked.

They'd just driven out of Enterprise and Laura wanted to know about Gregory's childhood.

"Nope. My father owned a hardware store."

"Mine ran the local grocery store."

"Did you attend summer camp?"

"No, but we had retreats."

"Same here. That's how I met Beth Marie. At a youth retreat."

The seriousness was back, and she noticed how tightly he gripped the steering wheel.

"Beth Marie?"

"We were sort of semi-engaged."

"Oh." Laura stared out the window. Was he going to talk about it? Surely he, as a minister, knew it was better to discuss things than to let them fester away inside.

"She promised to marry me."

"Kids make lots of promises."

"We weren't exactly kids then. I was nineteen."

"Your first love?"

"Yeah. My first serious love."

"And you've not been able to get her out of your mind all these years?"

Gregory took his coffee cup from the holder between their seats and took a sip. "Something like that."

"Then why don't you do something about it?"

"Do something? Such as? What would you suggest?"

Laura tucked her knees up. "All I know is I'd want to find out if I was still carrying a torch for someone."

"She married."

"Maybe something happened. Maybe she's no longer married."

"I don't even know where she lives. Lost all track when my mother died."

"That shouldn't stop you. Look at how people are finding each other, delving into their backgrounds in search of ancestors. You can do lots on the Internet. Put her name out there and see what happens."

He fingered the slight stubble of beard on his chin. "Yes, maybe I should."

Laura pointed. "Look. That man is catching a fish. Let's stop and stretch our legs, okay?" Laura wanted to change the subject. She couldn't imagine feeling that way about somebody all these years. Yet, she knew she had loved Jerry with all her heart; if he had left her at the altar, she would have pined, too.

Everyone was catching steelhead at the fast-flowing river. Laura got a sinking sensation in her stomach. Why had she wanted to stop? Seeing the exuberant smile on the man's face was a painful reminder of how much Jerry had loved fishing. She'd known many times that she should be thankful he died in his boat, doing what he liked best. For every downside there was a good side. That was the good side of his death.

"Seen enough?" Gregory said, walking up next to her. She was aware of his closeness, even more so here than in the car. More so here with the backdrop of high, rocky cliffs, the sound of the rushing stream. Suddenly she had the impulse to turn and touch him. What would it be like to have his arms enfold her? She shook the thought as she turned and raced to the car.

"We're not in that much of a hurry," he said, catching up with her, unlocking her door.

"I know. I just wanted to get the kinks out." She couldn't quite look at him.

"Anytime you want to stop, say the word. I'm not one that gets into a car and drives like a madman until I reach my destination. I've even been known to stop to read historical markers."

"You?" She stared at his profile. "Somehow that surprises me."

"It does, huh?" He looked at her, meeting her gaze.

"It's your turn," Gregory said once they were back on the winding, twisty road.

"My turn?"

"To talk about the love of your life."

"You mean Jerry?"

"Whomever you were married to." He stopped. "Or do you have a secret love in your background?"

She laughed. "Hardly. I knew Jerry was 'the one' on our second date."

"How did you know that?"

"Just the way he was. Thoughtful. Cute. And very much a man of God."

"That was important to you?"

"Definitely. I'd seen marriages fail without God at the helm and knew I must marry a Christian." She nodded at the memory of the tall, gangly boy who had his Bible on the seat beside him when he'd picked her up on their first date. "Besides, it's biblical."

"So it is."

"We knew we wanted to marry, but Jerry wanted to finish college."

"And did he?"

She giggled. "No. We decided not to wait and married at the end of his sophomore year."

"And he went back and finished while you worked?"

"Are you kidding?" She laughed again at the memory. "I got pregnant right off and it was about that time that his uncle asked if he wanted to go into business with him—"

"Which was?"

"Commercial fishing."

"And he did."

"Yes, and, to make a long story short, he took over the boat when

Uncle Al died about ten years ago, and he was happy with that choice. He never wanted to do anything else but fish."

"It must be nice doing what you like and knowing that's what you're supposed to do."

"You don't?" Laura was puzzled. More than once she felt that Gregory questioned his vocation. But if so, why did he continue to preach? God surely would not hold him to a position he didn't feel called to.

"I felt the calling, all right," Gregory said, as if reading Laura's mind. "But somewhere along the way I've had doubts. Major doubts."

"Then it's time to face the issue."

He slowed down and looked at Laura. "Does everything always come so easy to you? Have you always had it all together?"

She bristled at the sound of his voice. "I'm definitely not 'all together' as you put it. Sure I have doubts. Coming here was a big decision and I'm not sure this is where I'm supposed to be."

"Yes, you are."

"What makes you say that?" she sputtered.

"You just fit in. I have an idea you'd fit in wherever you went. Meeting people comes easy for you."

"And not you? Gregory, you're a minister! Ministers have to like people. It's a prerequisite for the job."

"Why do you suppose I'm still here in Joseph?"

"Because you like it."

"No. Because it's safe. I know the people and they know me. To go somewhere else is terrifying."

She couldn't believe he was saying this. No wonder he had that brooding look most of the time. Down deep he was an insecure person—like his son Joel.

He stopped the car abruptly and pulled off in a turnaround. "I can't talk about this and drive."

"Do you want me to drive?"

"No."

They'd parked up against a rocky incline. Wire fencing jutted along the rock as far as Laura could see. She opened the window, breathing deeply of the fresh mountain air.

"So, do you want to talk about your first love or your future?"

His eyes looked almost wounded. "I've never talked about Beth to anyone, not even Ruth in the early days when I first came to Joseph."

"Why ever not?"

He shrugged. "Why ever should I have? You just don't go around blabbing everything. And especially not when you're a minister and the one who is supposed to listen to others."

"Ruth's a good listener."

"I know, and it's one of your best traits, too."

She was older than Gregory. She found herself wanting to know what other traits he liked, but it was inane to think about it.

"I've let things pretty much happen as they did, knowing God was in control."

"You should be the minister, not me."

"You're a good minister."

"Can't write a decent sermon. You know that's true. Look how many times you've tightened up my work. Added something of interest. Like that one on Bonhoeffer. You suggested I go two weeks and I received more comments on that than any other sermon, and I even got a letter in the mail."

"The idea is the important thing and you come up with a good one each Sunday."

"Says who?"

"Me."

He eyed her curiously for a long moment. "Well, thank you, I think. I just wanted you to know I appreciate your help."

"I just happen to have a few English skills. Don't ask me how to do square roots, though."

Gregory started the car, and they headed back down the winding highway. There were so many things he wanted to say, but he felt as if a big load had lifted from his shoulders. It felt good to talk about his youth, about Beth Marie. Maybe he would look into finding her on the Internet.

"Let's stop at the bakery in Elgin. You can tell the owner how surprised and pleased you were with the cake."

"Yeah, sounds great."

At the bakery, Gregory watched the process. "Maybe we should order special cakes for the boys' birthdays."

"Just give me ample time," the baker said, removing the cake from under the scanner.

They left with cups of coffee to go.

As they drove on, Gregory realized he wanted the trip to go on forever. He hadn't relaxed or laughed so much in a long time. They even laughed over their lunch at a local small café.

"Is everything all right?" the waitress asked, and this only made Laura laugh more.

"I feel like a school kid," she said, stirring the thick milk shake she'd ordered along with a hamburger and fries.

A curl slipped down on her forehead. He watched to see if she'd brush it out of the way, but she left it there.

"Why are you staring at me like that?" she asked when the waitress came to see if they wanted dessert.

"You're so positive."

"I am?"

"Yes. It's refreshing."

"You could be, too, you know."

"When are you moving?" he asked, as if wanting to change the subject.

"Next week. The place needs some paint and curtains. Maybe a new couch."

"What about your things at the coast? Are you going over to get them?"

"I've considered that, but renting a U-Haul trailer and coming all that way isn't appealing. Think I'd rather pick up something here at the secondhand store."

"Or we could come down to La Grande again; see what they have at the thrift store."

"Just might do that."

The waitress came and Gregory grabbed the bill. Laura just smiled as she slipped two fives out of her purse.

"No way are you paying for this," Gregory insisted.

"Why not? Everyone goes Dutch, you know."

"I don't."

"You should. If anything, people should pay for the pastor's meal."

He finally agreed to let her leave the tip, and they went on their way to look at the advertised piano.

"I like it," Laura said when they looked at it, "even before I play. Such a beautiful ebony." She sat to play, and soon the house was filled with music.

"If you stay here and play every day, I won't sell it," the owner said.

Laura smiled. "This is for a young boy who plays wonderfully well and needs his own piano."

"I'll knock off a hundred dollars and even deliver," the man offered. "We really need to get it out of here."

"It's up to her," Gregory said. "She's the expert."

"Yes, then. Definitely. The tone is fantastic."

Soon they were on their way home.

"So much for the big city," Gregory said. "I like La Grande, but it's too busy for me. Joseph is just the right size. It has a good feel to it."

"I couldn't agree more," Laura said.

The ride back was spent in silence, both deep in their own thoughts.

Gregory was arguing with himself that he had to be sensible and listen to his head, not his heart. Laura had made it perfectly clear when she arrived that she was not in the market for marriage. No, he would look Beth Marie up instead. That would help get rid of the ache he felt in his heart.

Laura was acutely aware of the man beside her, wishing he weren't so hooked on an old sweetheart. There were so many things she liked about him, but it was foolish to even think about it. Besides, she was determined not to marry.

They made no stops and soon reached Joseph with five minutes to spare.

17

he computer, a gift from the congregation last Christmas, sat on Gregory's desk, often silent and blank. He still preferred to write out his sermon notes in longhand. Someday he might use the keyboard as he wrote, but he was such a poor typist that it took forever to type one line. He'd thought of dictating, but that seemed awkward as well.

The boys used the computer far more than he did. On Saturdays they took turns playing the games. He never minded that they used it that one day. He wished he had Joel's expertise with electronics, specifically computers. E-mail had been a boon. How he enjoyed corresponding with other ministers and a few old friends. Now he would search for one he had loved so long ago.

The morning after the trip to La Grande, Gregory asked one of the computer specialists in Joseph to help him put out a request to find Beth Marie. Fortunately he remembered her married name was Ollinger.

"This an old friend, Pastor?"

"You could say that. I never thought about looking on the Internet until Laura, our pianist, mentioned it yesterday."

"The electronic age is amazing, isn't it?" He leaned back and pointed to the name on the screen with Beth Marie's E-mail address. "There it is. Hasn't changed her name. You're in luck."

Gregory shook his head in amazement. He was so behind with things. He felt he was back in the Pony Express age.

"Couldn't your sons help you here?"

Gregory suddenly felt uncomfortable knowing Joel might see a letter. When he had received the computer, he had been assured that certain controls were in place that would prevent his sons from accidentally wandering onto web sites that were unfit for young people to view, so he didn't have to worry about their going online if they wanted to. As far as he knew, Joel didn't go online, but he wasn't sure.

"Of course, they could help, but they're busy with sports, music, school, you name it."

"Sure. Well, that's it, Reverend."

After the technician left, Gregory composed his letter. He might say no more than *Hello, how are you?* He just had to hear, find out if she was doing okay, and ask her how things were going in the little town of Shelburne. He hadn't been back there since his mother's funeral.

He'd tried to forget Beth Marie. He had buried the yearbooks, photos, and letters she'd written the first year he was away at college deep in his footlocker. Nobody ever bothered it, least of all him. To throw away the memories was unthinkable; but for all he knew, the paper might have turned to dust by now.

Gregory knew it wasn't right to pine away for someone he could not have. *Thou shalt not covet* came to mind many times over the years. He'd preached on the subject once, but only once. It was too close to home; yet he knew God directed His ministers to preach on that which they, too, could learn from.

He thought of Joel, so like himself. All seriousness in his mind, all legs as his body was going through a growth spurt. Joel never spoke what was in his heart. When Gregory suggested he take up trumpet for the school band, his son had agreed. He had never said he preferred another instrument. Perhaps he didn't, yet perhaps he did.

Caleb was a different child altogether. He kept nothing in, voicing his disapproval on a variety of subjects. He would take piano lessons, but only because his mother had played the piano. Yes, he was his own person. He loved God and it was evident in his exuberant approach to others. He was an ideal child in many ways, but exasperating as well. Gregory knew he need never worry about his younger son. He would make his way in this world.

Well, now no longer married, having been widowed for nine years, he didn't think it inappropriate to make this search for Beth Marie.

The answer came back with astonishing swiftness the morning after Gregory had made the request. Yes, there was a Beth Marie Ollinger living in Shelburne. An address and phone number were sent and he felt his heart pounding as he looked at the number and address. Could he really be in touch with her in a matter of minutes? And when he heard her voice, what then?

He decided to wait a day, maybe two, before dialing the number. He had to rehearse what he might say. He'd start off slow, ask how she'd been, how many children she had, things all women like to talk about. He might see if she wanted to keep in touch through E-mail. That could be fun.

Nobody knew about his search, though Laura was the one who had first suggested it. Should he tell her when he made contact, or should he just keep it to himself?

Gregory wasn't prepared for the face that flashed on the screen above her words when he downloaded her message the following morning. He printed it out on the Desk Jet, then held the page in his hand. It was Beth Marie. He'd have recognized that smile anywhere.

Then he saw the salutation: *Grego!* Gregory winced at the memory of her pet name for him. He continued:

> *How many times have I thought about you over the years, wondering if I'd made the biggest mistake of my life?*
>
> *There you are in a small town, making a difference in people's lives. I'm so proud of you for going ahead with the ministry. You knew what you wanted and went after it in spite of obstacles.*
>
> *An irate client shot my husband two years ago. It was difficult, but I've managed to pick up the pieces and go on with things that interest me.*
>
> *I heard you were married, but your wife died, leaving you with two sons. How tragic for you.*

There was more, but he had to digest this first.

Beth Marie was a widow? Of course he'd hadn't heard because he hadn't kept in touch with anyone.

He sat with head down, letting the years pass before his mind. Holding her hand as they ran through the grass at the park. The hayride they'd taken one Halloween, the parties at church, the skating rink where they'd both learned to skate, falling on each other.

She would expect an answer, and as he sat, he thought about what he might say. How he was happy to hear from her, but sorry to hear about the death of her husband. He started typing.

I love the little town where I now preach. The people are genuine. True friends. And— He paused as Laura's face flashed through his mind. Why would he think of her now? Had she come to mean that much to him? No. Not hardly.

I wish I could send a photo of the boys and me, but I am not knowledgeable with these computers. Still learning. Now my Joel has no such problem. Almost thirteen. A good kid, but quiet.

As he began writing about his sons, he realized how many good things he had to say about his eldest. He paused. No sense in telling her everything in one letter. He'd save some for another day. He signed the letter Love, Greg. That seemed okay. It would let her know that he thought of her with more than a passing fondness.

Gregory shut down the computer, covered it, and slipped out of his office. He'd never thought he would be eager to read a letter, but he soon found himself hightailing it over to his office first thing each morning. The letters went back and forth all week long. Then one day the phone rang.

"Gregory Michael, is it really you? It's me. Beth Marie."

"Where are you?" he asked, his excitement mounting.

"At the Portland International Airport. I'm renting a car and driving to Joseph. I'm looking at a map as we speak."

18

*G*regory was stunned. Never had he dreamed of the possibility of Beth Marie coming here. They'd written back and forth the past week, but not once had she indicated anything about a visit. The idea had crossed his mind once, but he wasn't sure he was ready. It would take some getting used to. But now she was coming, just like that.

He had mixed emotions. One part of him was elated and could hardly wait to see her again. The other part wondered about the reaction of his congregation and the town—his sons—and Laura. He wasn't sure why Laura's face popped into his mind. So far, she was the only one who knew about Beth Marie. If it hadn't been for her suggestion, he would never have found Beth.

His next thought was of the house, but she wouldn't be staying there, so he put that worry out of his mind. He'd never hired a housekeeper, though he'd often thought about it. Then he thought about himself. He had changed a lot. He wasn't the tall, skinny, lean kid he'd been then, nor the shy kid, unsure of himself.

He also wondered about Beth Marie's soul. Had she found God? Did she serve Him? When they were kids, he hadn't thought it mattered, but now he knew it did, very much.

He reached for the phone just as Joel came into the study.

"Dad, who's Beth Marie?"

Gregory leaned forward, his heart giving a sudden lurch. "Beth Marie?"

"Yeah. I shouldn't have looked at your E-mail, but I did. She calls you Grego. Nobody ever calls you Grego, or just Greg."

Gregory stared at his eldest son. "You're right. You invaded my privacy and I don't appreciate it. In answer to the second question, I never thought Greg sounded right for a preacher."

"So, who is Beth Marie?" Joel asked again.

"We grew up in the same town, but I haven't seen her for years." He cleared his throat. "She's coming for a visit."

"Here? In Joseph? From North Dakota?"

"Does that sound preposterous?"

"Yes, Dad, it does."

"Why?"

"Well, I just—oh, I don't know. What does she look like, and when is she coming, anyway?"

Gregory dug the picture out of his desk. "This came the other day. And she should be here by nightfall. She's renting a car in Portland."

"That soon?" Joel held the picture close. "She looks younger than you."

"And so she is, by at least two years. No, I think it's three."

"Does Laura know she's coming?"

Gregory looked away. "I haven't seen her to tell her. And why do you object to a friend of mine coming for a visit?"

Joel looked pained. "I just don't want anything to change."

"And what makes you think things will change, Son?"

"Because they do. Just when you get used to something, it all changes."

"Laura will always care about you, if that's what you're thinking about."

"I know that, Dad. I wasn't exactly thinking about me."

"Oh, I see."

Joel finally left and Gregory sat staring into space. Had he made a bad choice? Would Beth Marie's coming change things? He contemplated that for a long moment. Like Joel, he didn't want things to change. For the first time in a long while, he'd felt a state of contentment.

He shook the thoughts from his mind and went over his sermon again, but he couldn't concentrate. Of course Laura would look at the notes Friday and make suggestions. He looked forward to sitting over the table in the fellowship hall while she penciled in comments, then asked if he agreed. He always did. She never changed his content, but her suggestions helped him present his ideas more forcefully. He had decided to preach from Hebrews, the faith chapter. He closed his Bible and paper-clipped his notes. This sermon might be short.

Ruth heard about Beth Marie from Joel, who wasted no time in coming over to tell her. She knew he had to talk to someone, and it was easier for him to tell her than Laura.

"Do you believe someone can fall in love with someone they loved as a kid?"

Ruth pondered that for a moment. "You know, Joel, that's a hard one. I suppose it happens. You read about it, hear about it happening, but people change so much. You know, you can't go back."

"I don't want her to come."

"Honey, it'll just be for a few days, probably. She must have a job back in North Dakota, a family there."

"Her husband died. I read Dad's E-mail."

"Joel! I can't believe you did that. Would you want someone to read your mail without asking?"

His face flushed. "No. I guess not. But there it was on E-mail, while I was looking for an answer from a kid in California. We're going to trade stamps."

After Joel left, it hit Ruth. She hadn't thought about Joel's feelings before. He loved Laura like a mother. He wanted no one to come along to upset everything. In his own mind, he had undoubtedly hoped that Laura and his father would fall in love and marry. She hoped her assessment was right, that this Beth Marie would stay just a few days. Like Joel, she wanted nothing to happen between her pastor and this unknown woman.

Then it hit her again. It had been right here all along and she hadn't even noticed. Laura had fallen right into the mold, the one God had meant for her to fit into. She was the perfect wife for Gregory Michael Hall, the ideal mother for his two young sons. And Gregory loved her and she cared for him, though neither realized it yet.

Ruth finished ironing the kitchen curtains. She felt smug. Like a child with a secret. Far be it from her to say anything, but she'd do her best to see that this Beth Marie didn't stay long.

The phone rang. It was Gregory.

"Pastor, how are you doing today?"

There was a long silence. "Ruth, you'll never believe this, but I just found an old friend on the Internet and she's decided to come to Joseph for a visit."

"That right?" It was difficult to act surprised sometimes.

"Do you suppose she could have Laura's old room? I am sure it would suit my friend just fine."

"For how long, Gregory?"

Another long pause. "She didn't say, but I'm sure she won't be here long. She just wants to see me."

"And she's widowed?"

"Why, yes, how did you know that?"

"A good guess." Ruth seldom lied, but she didn't want to betray Joel's confidence. "Of course I'll have the room ready and waiting. When is she arriving?"

"Sometime this evening."

"Today?"

"Well, yes, she flew into Portland. She's driving over."

"The beds are always clean, the floors are always vacuumed. No problem."

"Thanks, Ruth."

❧

Laura didn't know about Beth Marie Ollinger's arrival, as she had taken one of her elderly patients to the town of Wallowa for a niece's birthday. They had ended up staying the night as a windstorm blew in and the patient wanted to stay.

When Laura arrived back at her cottage, she saw the light blinking on the phone.

It was Gregory. "Laura! I wanted you to be the first to know. Remember I told you Beth Marie had contacted me? I have you to thank for that, and now she's coming—tonight! I want you to meet her whenever you can break away from your busy schedule."

There was a second message, this time from Joel. "Laura, I need to talk to you."

Laura was sorry she hadn't been here for Joel yesterday. It was now eleven. She usually met Gregory at church to go over his sermon. Would he be there today, or would he and Beth Marie be off sightseeing?

She called the house. Nobody home. She called Ruth to see if she knew anything.

"My dear, where have you been?"

She explained, then asked about the newcomer to town.

"Beth Marie is staying here. In your old room."

"How long?"

"My heavens, everyone wants to know that. Gregory said just a few days, but I'm not sure. From the looks of things, she's here to stay!"

"Really?" Laura wasn't sure why, but she felt a sinking sensation in her midsection.

"Not to worry. She's the take-charge type. I thought she might be a clinging vine, but not this woman. She's a Martha Stewart if I ever saw one."

Laura giggled. Somehow she couldn't imagine a Martha Stewart in Joseph. Then she thought of Joel. She also couldn't imagine a Martha Stewart type as his new mother, either. Caleb could adjust, as he always did, but Joel would resist.

"I'll stop over to meet Beth Marie soon."

❧

Laura went over to church for a lesson at three. There was no sign of Gregory, nor was his sermon on top of the piano where he often put it. Distracted, she didn't even notice when Sarah hit some wrong notes.

"Mrs. Madison, aren't you going to scold me for so many mistakes?"

"What? Oh, Sarah, I think my mind wandered. Let's go over it again."

When Laura left after the second lesson, she stopped off at Ruth's. "No sign of them?"

"No. I think they went over to Pendleton and through the Pass to show there is still snow up there, even in the summer."

Laura was home, curled up with a book, when her phone rang. "They're back. It's kind of late, but why not come in the morning and you can meet her at breakfast."

"It's a deal," Laura said. "How about eight?" She knew that was the time Ruth served breakfast to her guests.

"No. Better make it at seven."

"Seven! That early?"

Ruth sighed. "Yes, seems they have another full day of sight-seeing planned."

"Are the boys going?"

"Of course. Gregory insists that it would be rude to do otherwise."

"How is Joel doing? He called here, but I couldn't get in touch with him."

"I don't know how she is with them, but here she chatters constantly. She's been everywhere, knows everything, and is rather—shall we say—opinionated?"

"Well, I guess Joel will survive."

"I hope so," Ruth said.

After hanging up, Laura wondered why the thought of Beth Marie upset her so. Of course it was because of the boys. Their welfare was important to her.

She opened her Bible and read an underlined passage, something she had marked years ago, 1 Corinthians 4:5: "Therefore judge nothing before the appointed time; wait till the Lord comes. He will bring to light what is hidden in darkness and will expose the motives of men's hearts. At that time each will receive his praise from God."

Laura read the passage twice, closed her Bible, and burst into tears. Later she admonished herself, not knowing why she reacted this way to God's word—or was it to Ruth's news? She wasn't quite sure which.

19

eth Marie was up and bustling around in the kitchen when Laura arrived the following morning.

"My dear, you have no idea how happy I am to meet you!" She threw her arms around Laura and gave her a tight hug. "All I've heard about since arriving is 'Laura this' and 'Laura that'—from the boys, you know."

Laura stepped aside and studied the woman before her. She was tall and graceful, not one pound overweight. Her long hair was pulled back and tied with a ribbon, she looked like she belonged on a farm. A white, frilly apron covered a fancy turquoise blouse and black slacks. Sensible shoes with block heels completed her attire.

"I've heard a lot about you, too," Laura replied.

Beth Marie handed her a cup of coffee. "This is decaf, you know. I brought my own special herbs and teas to cook with. So much of the stuff we eat is just plain no good for you."

"I really need caffeine," Laura started to protest, but Beth Marie rattled on.

"You'll get used to living without that horrible caffeine. Anyway," she continued, while opening the oven door and taking a peek, "I'm making my special wheat germ muffins—I can't thank you enough for suggesting that Greg find me on the Internet. I don't know why I hadn't thought of it before. Of course, I thought he'd be happily settled with wife number two and all."

She set the muffins in a bowl lined with a white linen cloth. "I know you'll adore these muffins. I told Ruth we can't have bacon or ham anymore. Turkey bacon is what I cook at home."

Ruth entered the kitchen and met Laura's gaze over Beth Marie's head. "Morning," she said, not as cheerfully as usual.

"I have never had—"

"Never had turkey bacon? Oh, my dear, it's simply wonderful stuff. I also brought my special nonfat cheese, and—well, you'll see."

Laura had a simple breakfast of decaffeinated coffee, special beans grown someplace she'd never heard of, muffins without butter, and tasteless eggs that were not eggs after all. She'd have to go home to find a real breakfast.

Ruth left half of her eggs on the plate, but that didn't faze Beth Marie.

"My dear, you have the right idea. Always leave food on the plate. We Americans eat far too much as it is."

After thirty minutes, Laura had a headache from the endless chatter. Soon she knew every last, minute detail of yesterday's excursion and how "divine" Gregory was for taking her. How "marvelous" the boys were, and how she looked forward to attending church and maybe even playing the piano for one of the services.

"Laura is our pianist," Ruth interrupted. "Perhaps you can play a special number for the offertory."

Beth Marie looked as if someone had slapped her. "Greg told me I could play perhaps next Sunday, but not this one, since Laura would have practiced the music for this week."

Laura said she had to go home; she had lessons to plan.

"That's quite all right, dear. I'll be leaving by 8:30, anyway. Greg is picking me up then; he's such an absolute dear."

❧

Laura kept busy the next few days. The July heat penetrated her skin. Sometimes she missed the cool ocean breeze. She had not once considered going back to Sealand, though Renee wrote every other week asking when she was returning. Then there was Kurt. Kurt with his complaints. She wondered now if she'd spoiled him by taking his side against Jerry. Maybe Jerry hadn't been too hard on him. He had tried to lead his family with the authority that was rightfully his as head of his household. Laura should have left well enough alone.

She sat on her back porch with its view to the mountain range, feet up, while staring at a blank sheet of paper. Beth Marie's words hit her as she tried to write to Renee. The woman unnerved her. She couldn't imagine Gregory being happy with this chatterbox, but how could she question him?

The phone rang and she jumped. It was Ruth.

"I need your help, hon, if you can spare me a few hours."

"What's wrong? You sound agitated. Are you sick?"

"Not sick. Not really. It's just that things are in an uproar here."

"You mean because of Beth Marie?"

Ruth laughed. "Isn't she something else?"

"Not quite what I expected."

"Me either. Me either, dear."

"So? What are you planning?"

"Going to visit my sister for a week or so."

"Now? During the tourist season?"

"Well, I have Miss Efficiency here, so why not take advantage of it? My sis, Molly, hasn't been well, as I may have mentioned to you. Seems she needs me to come."

"Well, Ruth, by all means go. I can help out there. You know I know what to do."

"Yes, but what about Beth Marie?"

Laura laughed. "Well, the turkey bacon definitely has to go. Do you think people are going to like that?"

"That's what worries me."

"Still no word as to how long she plans on staying?"

"Like I told you before, I think this is no mini-vacation. This woman has plans. We used to call them designs."

Laura put her writing supplies away. The letter to Renee could wait. "I'll be right over. We can plan while she's gone."

"Good girl. That's what I had in mind."

Laura hurried over the two blocks and entered the house without knocking.

Ruth poured them both a cup of tea and handed Laura a piece of sliced lemon, though she knew Laura didn't put lemon in her tea. Tears rolled, unchecked, down Ruth's cheeks.

"Ruth! What is it?"

"I didn't want to say this on the phone, but Molly got the results from some tests. It's cancer. That's why I must go to be with her."

"Ruth, I'm so sorry to hear this." Molly was the only family Ruth had left. Of course she'd want to be with her.

"I'll stay as long as you need me, and somehow I'll get along with Beth Marie."

Ruth squeezed more lemon into her tea. "Guess she'll have her wish for playing the piano on Sunday since the bed-and-breakfast keeps pretty busy and people are just starting to leave by eleven."

Laura touched the older woman's arm. "Ruth, that tea is going to be so sour you'll have to use half a cup of sugar to sweeten it."

"Oh." She laid the spoon in the saucer. "He's making a colossal mistake. Why are men so dumb when it comes to affairs of the heart?"

Laura felt a twinge. "He is a grown man, after all. Have you told him about Molly?"

"He, Beth Marie, and Caleb left before the call came."

"What about Joel?"

"He didn't go. Have no idea why."

"Should I take you over to Enterprise so you can leave today?"

"If you wouldn't mind."

"Of course not. Go pack."

On the way back from Enterprise, Laura wondered if Joel was home. On a hunch, she dropped off for her tennis shoes and decided to hike up the hill to the school. The bed-and-breakfast would be okay unattended for an hour.

Brisk walks never failed to calm her spirit when she felt down-hearted, and she never tired of the view from the school, the mountains to the east, the smell of fresh mountain air.

She saw a form hunched over the guardrail, arms folded across his chest. Joel.

"Joel," she said his name softly. He didn't move. She could go away and not bother him, but she knew he knew she was there and not to say something seemed rude.

"Joel," she repeated.

He looked in her direction, and she noticed his eyes were red-rimmed. "Are you okay?" was all she could think of to ask.

He nodded, turning back to the view.

"I won't bother you. Just out walking myself."

"No, it's okay. I like talking to you."

Her heart warmed at his words. "And I like listening." She had to be careful and not say too much or too little. She'd wait and let him begin the topic for conversation.

"I don't like her being here."

"You mean Beth Marie?"

"Yeah. She talks constantly. Hangs onto Dad as if she'll never let go. He acts stupid. Doesn't he see how she is?"

"They were very good friends once."

"I know all that. I read some letters."

Laura understood Joel's reaction. He didn't understand that adults had feelings just like kids, that their feelings of love and caring and needing each other never quite went away.

"He doesn't even care about me and Caleb. He's just there for her."

"What if she were to become your mother?"

"No way!" Joel clenched his fists. "I'd run away. For sure."

"It takes time to know someone."

"I don't want to get to know her. She's—" he fished for an appropriate word— "idiotic!"

Laura stepped up to the guardrail and bent down, looking out over the valley. "What do you think you should do?"

Joel flexed his hands. "I guess that's why I'm talking to you."

Laura was trapped. What could she say to this hurting boy who never felt he measured up to his younger brother, who never felt good enough or that he did the right things for his father? Inside, he was softhearted. He just didn't know how to show his tender side. She wanted to reach over, to move the lock of hair that fell over one eye. She wanted to tell him that she ached for his pain as if it were her own. And, in essence, it actually was.

"I have no answers, Joel. God has the answer you need. You know He never gives us more burden than we can bear, nor does He close a window without opening another."

"I don't believe that."

"I don't think you mean that."

"You love my dad."

Laura jerked up. "What?"

"I can tell."

"Joel, I'm fond of him, but there's never been any feeling like that between us."

"Yeah, sure."

"You're mistaken." But even as she said the words, she felt the tugging deep inside her. She cared a lot more than she'd allowed herself to think or believe.

"He loves you, too, but doesn't know it."

"Joel, you can't know that."

"I watch him watching you."

Her cheeks flushed at the thought. "He admires my piano playing."

Joel shook his head. "It's more than that."

They both walked down the hill together as Laura tried to explain how things weren't always as they seemed. Somehow, she didn't think she'd convinced Joel. When they reached Ruth's, he headed for home while she hurried in to see if there were any messages.

❧

It was dark when Laura heard a car pulling up and voices in the evening air. She'd been sitting in her favorite chair, mulling over what Joel had said, wondering why her head said one thing and her heart another. She couldn't love Gregory Hall. She'd never planned on loving anyone again.

"You must come in, Greg," Beth Marie's voice called out. "I'll fix you some of my special hot chocolate. It's great! No fat. No sugar."

"And no taste," Laura said under her breath. She set her book down and rose.

Gregory murmured something that Laura couldn't quite hear.

The kitchen light came on, and it was then that Gregory saw her. "Laura! What are you doing here?"

Gregory walked over, and Laura felt short of breath at the sight of him. "Ruth's gone to her sister's in Portland. Emergency."

"Oh, no. What happened?"

Laura handed him the letter. "It's all in here."

"My dear, that means you and I must run this bed-and-breakfast," Beth Marie interjected. A smile erupted. She wore a darling two-piece denim outfit, looking perfectly at home in this country. Her eyes shone as she looked from Laura to Gregory and back to Laura again.

"I'll tend to things here, and you can play piano for the services," Laura said.

Beth Marie's eyes grew even wider. "Oh, Greg, that's what I really wanted to do, so you could see how I play and how things could— well, work out!"

Laura could hardly believe it. Talk about brazen! She was moving in lock, stock, and barrel, no doubt about it.

"I guess that'll work," Gregory said. "If it's okay with you, Laura. Laura?"

She knew he was looking at her, waiting for an answer, but Beth Marie answered before Laura could.

"I'll be here to help with the breakfast. That's plenty of time. Oh, this is so exciting!" She clasped her hands.

"That's okay," Laura managed. "You should maybe go over the hymns."

"Hymns?" Beth Marie turned around so quickly, she nearly dropped the teakettle. "Don't you ever play newer songs, Greg?"

Gregory looked almost chagrined. "The people here like the old hymns best. Of course, we can use a newer piece of music once in a while."

"Well, I hate those stuffy old slow hymns. I just know they'll love the songs I know."

Laura excused herself and went down the hall to Ruth's small bedroom, where she'd sleep. Laura got a lump in her throat as she thought about Ruth. It was strange to be here in this room, among her possessions. She looked at the huge doll collection around the room. She hadn't realized Ruth collected dolls. They were on shelves, little tables, rocking chairs. Everywhere. They were beautiful and unique. She'd have to suggest that Ruth put them somewhere so that guests could enjoy them.

She pulled back the quilt and tears came to her eyes as she felt Ruth's worry and concern over Molly. She wanted to have a prayer time, but Beth Marie's voice carried through the walls, so her room was not quiet. She couldn't help wondering what would happen in church on Sunday when Beth Marie insisted on playing the songs she liked. She had an idea it wouldn't matter what Gregory said. Beth Marie would have her way.

O Lord, help us all, she prayed, finally drifting off to the sound of the younger woman's voice going on and on.

20

The days turned into one week, then two, and Laura found it difficult to work with Beth Marie, who felt she was right and wanted everything her way. Kenny Thompson stopped by one day, and Laura chuckled as it looked as if he'd met his match in the talking department.

"Goodness, but that man can talk," Beth Marie said after he left.

She was dressed in a skirt and blouse with a frilly apron around her waist, and Laura had noticed Kenny watching Beth's every move.

"I understand you've dated him."

Laura shrugged. "Yes, but I'm not interested."

"He has money."

"Money isn't everything."

Laura had baked chocolate chip cookies for Caleb because he seemed down at his last lesson. Even having his own piano hadn't cheered him up. Joel also came by periodically and they talked or played Scrabble when Laura wasn't busy cooking, cleaning rooms, or doing laundry. Beth Marie liked the cooking part, not the cleaning.

Laura started planning on a trip to the beach for after Ruth's return. She needed to get away to think, and Ruth was due back soon. She called almost every day to see how things were.

"Molly's doing so much better and urges me to go home," she'd said recently.

"We all miss you, you must know that," Laura responded.

❧

The day before Ruth was due back, Renee called. It was past midnight, Laura noticed on her lighted digital. Shivering, she groped for her robe and made her way to the phone. Ruth, bless her heart, did not believe in portable phones, nor was there an extension in her bedroom.

Shivering, Laura grabbed her robe. Who would call this time of night? Emergency. It had to be. Her mind flitted to the possibilities. One of her kids. The house had burned. Renee was in an accident . . .

"Laura, can you come? Kurt's in the hospital—"

"Hospital!"

"He was coherent enough to think to tell the doctor to call me since he couldn't remember your phone number."

"But what happened? An accident?"

"No, it's some sort of crazy high fever. I just spoke with the doctor."

Laura shivered again, panic threading through her. "What's the prognosis?" She remembered another time, a trip overnight to the hospital when Kurt raged with fever. He seemed to run one at the first sign of illness. The other two had not.

"They're taking tests."

"I'm sitting the bed-and-breakfast, but there's someone who can take over." Beth Marie could handle it just fine. "I'll leave just as soon as I can pack a couple of things."

"And don't worry and drive like a madwoman," Renee said, knowing Laura's inclination to drive fast anyway. "We want you to arrive in one piece. He'll be okay."

"Nobody can be sure about anything except that God makes the world turn. And we can be certain of His love for us."

❧

"Guess this is the end of your sight-seeing tours," Laura said to a yawning Beth Marie, who was walking down the stairs. Of course, she was wearing an elegant frothy pink robe and matching scuffs. "I have to leave. My son's in the hospital." She handed Beth Marie a number. "Just in case you need help."

Beth Marie drew herself up. "Honey, I'm not worried about running this place. It's too bad about your kid."

"Yes, well, these things happen."

"You don't like me, do you?" Beth Marie followed Laura back to her room.

"What makes you think that?"

"I just know. I feel it."

Laura grabbed her suitcase from under the bed. "I'm sorry if I gave that impression."

"I love Greg, you know," Beth Marie said, stepping aside as Laura started throwing clothes in her suitcase, "and I intend to do everything to win him over."

Laura nodded. "That's fair enough. He's been alone a long time and needs someone." Even as she said it, a sudden feeling of loss hit her, one she couldn't quite explain.

"Needs?" Beth Marie scoffed. "Not hardly. How about all those people in his congregation?"

"That's different. He needs a special someone—a wife. All men of the cloth do."

"They have God."

"Yes, of course, but someone tangible is also nice. You've undoubtedly heard of the saying, 'You can be in a room full of people and feel alone'?"

"No, can't say that I have." Beth Marie studied her fingernails as if that was the most important thing in her life.

"Well, if you'll excuse me, I must dress. But rest assured I wish you a world of happiness."

"And I hope your son will be all right."

"Thanks," Laura said as she closed the door. If she didn't, she had a feeling Beth Marie would stand there all morning discussing her needs.

Ten minutes later, Laura grabbed the coffee Beth Marie offered, even if it was decaf.

"And take one of my muffins. It'll fill you up."

"I think I'd like some of the cinnamon toast, too."

Beth Marie wrinkled her nose. "You mean that dry stuff in the box?"

"Yep. It's good. Try it sometime."

Without waiting for a comment, Laura hurried out the door, hopped in her car, fastened the belt, and nosed her car out of the driveway. Why had she gotten into a discussion with Beth Marie this morning of all times? Beth Marie was right. Laura didn't like her much. And she didn't think Beth Marie was what Gregory needed. A tremor ran up her spine as she thought of that afternoon when he'd kissed her forehead. Silly for her to think of that now.

One thing she knew for certain: She couldn't leave without at least leaving Gregory a note about the situation. She swallowed hard. She couldn't go to the house. She didn't want to talk to him face-to-face. She regretted not being able to tell the boys good-bye, but she'd send an E-mail to Joel and a note to Caleb. They'd understand an emergency. Of course, they'd all manage nicely. Why did she think not? Then she remembered Joel that afternoon at the school and his pinched face.

Laura drove to the church, dashed off a line about the phone call, giving few details because she didn't have them anyway. She put the note under the door. Gregory would find it when he came to work on his sermon later this morning. He always worked early, but since Beth Marie had come, his hours were jumbled up and she never quite knew what he was doing or where he was. He'd changed practically overnight to a person who had no schedules, no rules.

The door sprang open as she hurried down the steps. "And what is this? Since when do you go around putting notes under doors?"

Laura stopped without turning. She knew how Gregory would look, his blue eyes with questions in them, a hand raking through his hair, the tilt of his head. Now that she thought about it, leaving a note did seem like something a schoolgirl would do.

She turned and glanced up, her eyes not quite meeting his gaze. "I didn't really think you would be here. I am leaving for Sealand. Kurt's in the hospital. I know nothing more than the note says."

Gregory opened the slip of paper. "Laura?"

"Yes?" Why was she acting this way? Since when could she not look him in the eye? Suddenly and unexpectedly, tears filled her eyes. "I really didn't want to talk to you." There. She'd finally said it.

He came down the steps and took her hand. "Has it come to that?

That we can't talk? That I can't take time to pray for your son, your trip?"

She turned and looked up into his craggy face. "I suppose it has."

"Will you be gone long?"

"I haven't a clue. It's just that I'm needed there and not here."

"Who says we don't need you here?"

"Gregory, I never promised to stay. It was a dream to fulfill, something I wanted to do. I had to get away from the beach and all the memories. Surely you, above all people, can understand that."

There was that word "need." Funny how she had used it twice already today. She supposed everyone needed someone, but she'd tried to believe she was indispensable. Now her eldest son was ill and needed her.

It was time to face some important decisions. Gregory needed her in a different way, if in fact he needed her at all. It wasn't quite in the way she had hoped once, though even in the beginning she'd known it was impossible. Younger men didn't marry older women. It was always the other way around. Yet she knew that he found her attractive. From the first day there had been a magnetism, though they had argued on several occasions. Before Beth Marie, he seemed to hang on her every word, liked to hear her play, enjoyed her working over his sermons, and appreciated the way she could talk with Joel.

She waved the kind of half-wave one does when unsure. She wanted him to say something else. She had the urge to turn, to throw her arms around him, asking him if he really loved Beth Marie. But it wasn't to be.

Gregory didn't want her to leave—not yet. "Laura, don't go thinking you aren't needed here. Everyone will miss you. Surely you realize that."

He longed to go after her, stop her on the steps, take her in his arms. The thought seemed to shatter inside him, moving through his extremities. What was this? He was thinking about Laura in a way he'd never let himself come to grips with.

But what about Beth Marie? She was here now. His dream had always been that one day they would be together again. Why, then, did

Laura's face keep getting in the way? Was she coming back? He really needed to know that. But of course she probably didn't know. He knew her son had wanted her to return since she'd first come. How dire was the emergency?

She choked back tears that threatened. "I'll miss the boys. Please tell them I'll be in touch."

Without another word, her hand left the railing. "I hope you and Beth Marie will truly be happy."

He watched her walk away. As she rounded the corner of the church, he moved to the last step so he could see her get into her car, back out, and head down the street toward town. He waved, but he didn't think she waved back.

A funny, hollow feeling came over him. Why hadn't he held her for just a moment? She'd looked so vulnerable, so in need of being held. Why hadn't he been able to go after her?

The idea was preposterous. She couldn't possibly have any feelings for him. Yet there had been a look on her face when their gaze had met and held, a fierce intensity, yet sweet concern.

Gregory felt his heart sink. *Lord, I'm not reading this right. My life is in more of a shambles than before. How could this happen?* The sun beat down and warmed him on the outside, but his insides felt suddenly cold.

He had a sermon to prepare and dinner with Beth Marie. Knowing her, she'd come around before that and talk about something. She always found something to talk about.

He sighed. Laura's face came to mind again. Why had he not realized how much she had come to mean to him? *God, go with her. Give her peace in her heart. Heal her boy.*

At that, he thought of his own son Joel. She had touched Joel's life and meant so much to him, and Gregory was suddenly worried about him.

$$\textbf{(21)}$$

*L*aura's tears fell as she drove out of Joseph. Thank heavens for the box of tissues she kept in the front seat. She dabbed her cheeks, chiding herself for getting involved. *Lord, I asked for a mission of sorts. You gave it to me, as I knew You would, but why did You let someone else come in and reap the benefits? Is Beth Marie the right woman for Gregory? The right mother for those precious sons?*

At the thought of her own son, the tears started again. It was a good thing she'd become familiar with the road, also good that it was early enough so the road was empty. Kurt had wanted her to come home, and so she was. Home, where she was also needed. But Joseph seemed like home now.

The sunrise was gorgeous, and she cried again at God's infinite beauty. *O Lord, I'm just being an emotional, middle-aged woman. I don't know what I want, so You're settling it for me, making my decisions.* Yet she knew that, though God was in charge of her life, decisions were hers alone to make. Hadn't He let Adam and Eve make mistakes when He could have stopped them?

She stopped once for gas, but pushed on, arriving in Sealand in the middle of the afternoon. The drive across the bridge had made her cry again. She hoped her eyes wouldn't be puffy by the time she reached the hospital. Kurt didn't need to see her like this.

❧

Laura stayed at Kurt's side all night. His fever raged, and she dabbed his forehead with a cool cloth. Nurses came in and checked his vital signs on the hour. She was so grateful for their concern.

Renee had come and gone. Hugging, they had clung to each other.

"I missed you so much, but I sure didn't want something like this to bring you back."

"Me neither."

Renee studied her face. "You look thinner."

"I guess I haven't been eating any of your delicious scones."

"Yeah, sure. It's that preacher, isn't it?"

"Not hardly."

"Well, say what you will, but I wasn't born yesterday."

Pastor Dave and a few other friends came. Everyone prayed with her as she stood vigil. Now she was alone with Kurt, and all she could do was pray and sponge off his face. She felt so helpless. She wondered about Mary and how helpless she must have felt about Jesus, knowing there was nothing she could do to change the course of His life.

What sort of infection is this? Why doesn't it react to any of the medications? Tubes dripped into Kurt, offering him sustenance.

A nurse appeared in the doorway. "Why don't you go home, Mrs. Madison? We can call you if there is a change. You need some sleep."

Home. Laura felt a sudden jolt. *Home.* Exactly where was home?

"I'll stay, if you don't mind."

"Of course." She swished from the room, and Laura stared at the closed door. She reached up and grabbed Kurt's hand. *Oh, please, God, don't take my eldest child from me. I don't know if I can bear it.*

She slipped into a fitful sleep and was slumped over the bed, her hand still holding Kurt's, when Dr. Gleason entered the room.

"I'm surprised to see you still here."

"I couldn't leave him. I'm all he has. His dad—" she choked—"his father was in a boating accident four years ago."

He touched her shoulder. "I remember, Laura."

"Doctor, what if his fever doesn't go down? Will he be brain-dead?"

"The next twenty-four hours are crucial."

"Have you taken all the tests?"

"We're waiting for the results of a spinal tap now."

"When will you know?"

"Soon, I hope. Now, why not go get something to eat? You're a wreck. Do you want him to see you looking like this?"

Laura tried to smile. "No. You're right."

She left to grab a bite to eat from a local café. The hospital was too small to have a cafeteria. Evelyn, a friend she had been on the library board with, nodded from a far corner.

"Laura Madison, I haven't seen you forever." She motioned for Laura to share her table. "I hear you went off to the mountains."

"Yes, I've been in eastern Oregon for the past four months."

"Why there?"

Laura turned her cup upright and nodded when the waitress stood with the full pot in hand.

"It's a long story, but I needed a change."

"Oh."

"Now I'm back because my Kurt's in the hospital having tests."

After discussing the findings thus far and thanking her friend for her concern, Laura ordered a bowl of oatmeal. "With raisins, please."

"I'm sorry to hear about Kurt," continued Evelyn. "Are you moving back then?"

"I really don't know." The ache that had been in her heart on the trip over suddenly returned. "I'm too shattered to make any decisions just now."

"Well, we can always use you around here."

Evelyn rose. "Speaking of meetings, I have to be at the museum in ten minutes, but it's been good to see you again." She hesitated. "I'll certainly pray for your son."

"Thanks."

Laura stirred sugar into her coffee though she never used sugar. She had to do something with her hands. Strange how life had changed for her. She'd been happy here at the coast for many years, yet now she wanted to return to the Wallowa area. But for what reason? Because she missed Joel and Caleb? The church? Playing the piano? Yes, of course. But it was much more. She missed a certain person who had taken up residence in her heart. How could she have let it happen? Could God have directed her path towards one Gregory Michael Hall? But Gregory didn't need her. He liked her, but he was in love with Beth Marie, a.k.a. superwoman.

The oatmeal came with brown sugar on top. "Would you like more coffee?" the waitress asked.

"Yes, that would be nice." She stared at the oatmeal and, though hungry, she doubted she could eat it.

God, Laura prayed for what seemed like the tenth time that morning, *help my son get well. And please help me to know what to do with my life. Give me purpose. Help me to understand. And, above all, help me to get Gregory out of my heart.*

Thy will be done flashed through Laura's mind. Of course she'd forgotten to add that. She forgot a lot of the time. She knew, as she'd always known, that He was there to help her overcome any and all fears. He would walk her along the path, carry her if need be. And He always answered prayers, though sometimes the answer was "No."

"I have to get back," she said when the waitress came, asking if she wanted anything more.

She walked the three blocks to the hospital, pulling her collar up around her neck. Mornings could be cold at the beach. A dampness penetrated her thin coat. It was August and one did not wear a coat in Joseph during this season.

The nurse met her at Kurt's door. "We have the test results back."

"You do? Oh, praise God!"

"The doctor will be with you in a minute."

"But he'll be all right?"

"The treatment has started."

Laura entered her son's room. His eyes were closed, but his face didn't feel as hot.

"Laura, good news!" Dr. Gleason exclaimed as he entered the room. "It's curable, though he's going to need rest."

"What is it, exactly?"

"He has adhesions on the spine. It caused numbness on his right side. With the medication and proper bed rest, he should be okay in a few weeks. Of course, this is a strange case. Usually a fever doesn't accompany this affliction."

Laura smiled. "My son has never had normal anything."

She called Renee to tell her the good news.

"No working for a few weeks, eh?"

"Knowing Kurt, he'll be back on his feet in less time than that."

Later that night, his eyes suddenly opened, lighting up when he saw her. "Mom! I thought I had a dream and you were here, holding my hand."

"It was no dream." She leaned over and kissed his cheek as tears filled her eyes. "I love you so very much, Son."

He held her hand in a tight grip. "What's wrong with me, anyway? I remember feeling woozy, numb, and then nothing."

"A friend found you at work and couldn't rouse you."

Kurt smiled. His face, now wan, looked hopeful. "I just wish Susan was here."

It was then Laura realized her son's girlfriend was missing. She didn't know why she hadn't thought of her before.

"Where *is* Susan?"

"She left. Went to Seattle to find a job."

"Honey, I had no idea."

"That was one reason I wanted you to come home, so you could talk to her or at least tell me what to do."

Laura took his hand. "Kurt, I can't make decisions for you now. It's up to you. If you want her back, maybe you have to go look for her. When you're on your feet again, of course."

"You're right. I guess I have this idea that you have the answer to everything, Mom."

"I don't, Kurt. I never have. It's God who can help you work through a problem, God who gives you a sense of direction. It's time you turned to Him."

Kurt was released the following morning to recuperate at home. Laura brought clean clothes from his apartment. "Just think. Your own bed again. Won't that be nice?"

22

*G*regory was at loose ends and didn't know why. Joel was not speaking to him. Ruth seemed perturbed about something, his parishioners missed Laura's playing, and some said they missed her, period. Even Caleb was quiet.

Beth Marie had taken over. He wasn't sure how it had happened. One day he was completely enthralled with her, so glad they had met again; the next thing he knew, she had altered his sermon subjects and changed the music. The congregation was now singing all new tunes and the words were printed on the overhead. Many members were disgruntled at the sudden changes. Gregory feared a backlash. He decided to stop by and discuss the problem with Ruth. She was always a good listener.

Ruth looked thoughtful. "Are you asking me what you should do in the situation?"

Gregory shrugged. "I suppose you could say that."

"Why not come right out and tell Beth Marie you care for her as a friend? Women understand what that means."

"I don't know if Beth Marie would even hear me if I said that."

"I've got it!" Ruth claimed. "Kenny Thompson. Why not set up a date between the two of them?"

"He's met her—"

"And she him."

"But nothing has come of it."

"Doesn't mean it wouldn't work if we helped a little."

Gregory went home feeling better about the situation. He missed Laura like crazy, far more than he'd ever thought possible. He'd been calling the hospital each day to check on Kurt's condition but had refrained from asking for Laura. Still, he felt compelled to go see her in person. He wanted to see if she felt the same way. Now if that wasn't silly thinking!

He could close his eyes and see her smile, see the way her hair tossed in the wind, the warmth she passed on to everyone she met. She took the time to listen. She'd made Joel care about living. She'd brought them together as father and son.

Gregory got home to find Caleb watching cartoons.

"Where's Joel?"

"I don't know."

"Did he come home from his walk?"

Caleb shrugged. "Don't know, Dad."

He went up the stairs to the boys' bedrooms. Joel's was neat, the opposite of Caleb's. Joel had everything in place, and his desk was straightened with two books on top. Two pairs of shoes were side by side under the bed, no dirty clothes on the floor. A book was open to Shakespeare's *Macbeth*.

There was no note on the desk or bed or on the pad on the kitchen bulletin board.

When Joel didn't come home by seven, Gregory was concerned. Where could the kid be?

He finally got in the car and drove through town and out by Wallowa Lake. No sign of his son, nor had anyone seen him. He stopped at Ruth's again. She hadn't heard from Joel, either.

Where could he go? What stone had he left unturned? He prayed, which he should have done in the beginning. *God, help me to know where Joel is.*

Driving up the hill to the junior-senior high school gave him a funny feeling. With school out, the buses were parked in the garage, and an empty parking lot gave the whole area a look of abandonment. He saw Joel quite by accident, though he knew God had directed him there. Joel stood at the far end of the school grounds, looking out over the mountains. Hands in his pockets, he stared into space. He didn't even turn when Gregory walked over.

"Joel. Why are you here?"

Finally he looked at his father, his shoulders stiff, his body un-yielding. "I always come here to think. So does Laura. And I don't want to talk about it."

"Don't or won't?"

"What's there to say?" He turned and Gregory saw the trace of tears on the young boy's face. He longed to go to him, to pull him close, and it was then as if a voice was directing him, saying, *Do it. If you feel love, show it.*

"Joel," he said again, reaching out his arms. Then the boy was there, and they clung to each other, tears intermingling.

"I had no idea you were in pain. I wish you could come to me."

"Dad, I miss Laura. I've tried to like Beth Marie. She told me how you two would have married if her mother hadn't interfered, and I know she loves you, but I don't like her."

It was a long speech for Joel.

"I don't love Beth Marie, Son."

"You don't?"

"I did at one time, and I thought I might rekindle what we once felt for each other, but it hasn't happened. Like you, I feel an intense loneliness for Laura. I want to bring her back. I want her to stay here in Joseph, be part of my life. Our life."

Joel's face split into a wide grin. "Dad, she'd do it, I know she would."

"How can you know? One never knows for sure."

"I do know. I just do, Dad. C'mon, we gotta go and bring her back."

That night Gregory called the hospital and was told Kurt had been released. The nurse refused him Kurt's home phone number, so he called information.

This phone call would be one of the most important calls he'd made in his life, and God was behind his decision. He just knew it. He'd take it one step at a time. He and the boys would visit her at the coast and meet Kurt. They would talk.

But, before that could happen, his first step was to talk to Beth Marie.

"But we belong together, Greg," Beth Marie said, a pout on her full, red lips. "You've always loved me. You said so yourself."

He looked at the woman in front of him. Not one hair out of place. Her long navy blue skirt reached the top of fancy leather boots. Her deep purple shirt was frilly. Her cheeks were rosy, but it was blusher, not natural. She was nothing like Laura.

"We've changed, Beth. I don't think we want the same things anymore."

"I can be a good minister's wife—"

He nodded. "Perhaps too good."

She laughed, throwing her arms around him. "How can anyone be too good?"

"Maybe 'good' isn't the right word. I just know it wouldn't work for us."

She left his home, holding her head high. "I'll change your mind. Just you wait and see."

"I doubt it," Gregory said under his breath.

In the morning, Laura was making pudding, as Kurt's diet had to be light, when the phone rang. Kurt answered in his bedroom.

"Sure. I'm doing fine. Yes, my mom is here."

Laura grabbed the kitchen extension, certain it must be one of her friends who had learned she was back in town.

"Laura? How are you? And how is Kurt doing?"

Her heart lurched as she recognized the deep voice. "Gregory. And how are you?"

"I asked the first question."

She closed her eyes, visualizing his face, the thick thatch of hair. "Kurt needs plenty of rest and should be fine in a week or so."

"I called every morning to check on his condition."

"You did? But nobody told me."

"I know. I wanted it that way."

"How are Joel and Caleb?"

"Caleb says if you don't come back, he wants to sell the piano."

"Oh, sure." Her heart began pounding.

"So Kurt is going to be okay? Would you say the crisis has passed?"

"As far as I know." She wondered what his questions were leading to, but she wouldn't ask. "I'm staying with him for a few days until he gets on his feet again."

"I'm coming there. The boys, too."

"Coming here? But what about church?"

"A pastor over in Enterprise is filling in. His church has a special revival going on this week."

"But—"

"Don't you want us to come?"

Her heart lurched again. "I was just wondering about Beth Marie. Will she be along?"

"She's gone home."

"Home?"

"Yes, but she's coming back."

"I see."

"No, you don't, but I don't want to explain it on the phone. I want to see you in person. We'll be there tonight. Oh, and Ruth sends her love. Her sister's prognosis is good. They think they got all the cancer."

"That's terrific news. Give her my love, too."

"Must finish packing. And Caleb is wired. I may let him run behind the car on the way."

Laura laughed, then said good-bye.

❧

When Gregory's car was packed, the boys climbed in, eager for a long ride to the coast. As they rode, Caleb kept saying over and over, "Dad, you mean you love Laura and she might be our mom?"

"I don't know, Caleb. We won't know until we get there."

❧

Kurt's eyes were on Laura when she came into his bedroom, bringing a bowl of pudding.

"So, Mom. What's going on? Your cheeks are pinker than I've ever seen them."

"Oh, Kurt. God answers prayers in the most unusual, wonderful ways, just as He will answer your prayer about Susan. I know He will."

"But what's going on?"

"You'll see. This evening. We just have to wait."

"Wait?"

"Wait for Gregory, Joel, and Caleb to arrive."

As Laura cleaned the kitchen, she knew she'd be counting the hours until Gregory Michael Hall and his two wonderful sons arrived.

(23)

hey arrived that evening, tired, hungry, and "gritty" as Caleb put it.

Laura embraced first Caleb, then Joel, and gave a quick hug to Gregory.

"Hi, I'm Caleb!" said the boy, wasting no time in introducing himself to Kurt, who sat propped up on his couch.

"I've been hearing about you over the past few hours."

"Good things?" Gregory asked, extending his hand.

Laura watched as Kurt sized up the older man.

"All good things," Kurt said.

Laura thought Kurt's color had improved since he'd come home.

"Your mother and I have some unfinished business to discuss," Gregory said. "The boys know and have agreed to stay here and keep you company—if that's all right."

"Of course," Kurt said, looking from his mother back to the preacher.

He helped her on with a light jacket, and they took Laura's car as she headed for her favorite spot on the beach.

"This is, or used to be, my thinking place," she explained. It was dark, but a near-full moon shone down from a dark sky. They stayed in the car because it was warmer.

"I've done a lot of thinking. Praying. Talking to the boys."

"Yes?" She wondered if he could hear her heart beating.

"I love you, Laura. Plain and simple. I don't know how you feel about me, but I know you love the boys and they need you. I need you, but more important I want you to be part of my life, to share in my joys, my concerns, and just everything that comes to the Hall family." He took her hand and held it tight. "I don't expect you to answer now. You must be very sure. My heart would break should you change your mind down the road."

"And Beth Marie? What about her? How do you know you are over her?"

His expression changed. "I was foolish, carrying a torch all those years. I know God will forgive me, and I pray that others will, too."

"I'm sure they will if there's something to forgive."

"I suggested to Kenny Thompson that he might ask her out when she returns with her belongings."

Laura laughed. "Beth Marie is just the one to help run that ranch!"

"Yes, she is. And she can also play the piano on occasions such as . . . well, I was thinking about a honeymoon in Vancouver British Columbia, should a certain person say 'yes' to my proposal."

Tears filled Laura's eyes as she turned and lifted her face for his kiss. A real kiss, not just one from her dreams or a kiss on the forehead like that day in his office.

"I think that certain person would say 'yes' should she get a proposal from the right man."

"I don't have a ring."

"That can come later."

He kissed her again, noticing how the moonlight hit her hair, making it almost shine, but not nearly as much as her face.

"I think we should go back and make an announcement to our sons."

"Our sons," Laura repeated. "Yes, I like the sound of it."

"And I think we should offer a prayer of thanks to God, our Creator. I, for one, thank Him for a certain ad that appeared in the *Chieftain*."

"And I thank Him for your answering that ad." They bowed their heads and prayed.

Afterwards, Gregory asked, "Should we have a small wedding or invite the whole town?"

Laura giggled. "We may as well invite the whole town. We might even get as many people as the Chief Joseph Pow-wow! And I want Ruth to bake the cake and my friend Renee to be my matron of honor."

"Done!"

"Do you hear that?" Laura asked.

Gregory listened. "Hear what?"

"It's singing. I think angels are singing a happy melody in heaven."

Gregory took her hand again. "You should write books with that imagination," he said, and she couldn't help noticing the wide smile on his face, as the moonlight lit up the streaks of gray in his hair.

"Let's go back and see what happens."

As they passed the place where they'd found Jerry washed ashore, Laura felt a gentle regret surface, but she supposed that would always happen. This place and the things that had happened here were part of her. She'd be back. The beach would always be home to her, but now she was ready to return to Joseph and to the new life that beckoned.

Ruth's Rhubarb Custard Pie

Make a double crust and line a 9" pie pan with bottom crust.

Filling:
Beat 3 eggs slightly.
Add 3 tablespoons milk.
Mix and stir in:
2 cups sugar, $1/4$ cup flour, $3/4$ teaspoon nutmeg.
Wash, chop up ($1/4$" chunks), and mix in 4 cups pink rhubarb.

Pour filling into pastry-lined pie pan.
Dot with 1 tablespoon butter.
Cover with top crust.
Bake until nicely browned. Make sure pie is bubbling.
Best when served slightly warm.

Temperature: 400°
Time: 50–60 minutes.

Piano Lessons

by Gail Sattler

Dedicated to the memory of my own piano teacher,
Miss Isabel Kachinowsky, who made the music so much
more than mere notes on the page.

$\mathcal{J}$ ed parked his truck but remained seated behind the wheel as he stared at the house. Back when they were teenagers, he and Liz had done nothing but fight. He'd been the worst kid brother imaginable, and he didn't know how it happened, but through phone calls and constant letters, it was almost unbelievable they had become so close as adults while living apart.

The kids' bikes lay strewn in the middle of the front yard, and squeals of laughter along with the dog's barking echoed from the back.

Suburbia. Happy family life.

Enter Uncle Jed.

Would he be a happy family addition, or an intrusion? Liz had invited him to stay, and after all, he would be earning his keep, but he wasn't sure he would like the big city of Vancouver. Even though Liz's house was in the suburbs, like his new job, it was too close to the city to suit him.

Leaving his belongings in the truck, he approached the house slowly. He would start his new job in a few days, but for now he felt like a poor, displaced relative.

He knocked and waited.

Liz answered the door with a huge smile, greeting him with a big bear hug before he had a chance to say a word.

"Jed! We've been so excited waiting for you. Come on in!" Liz turned to yell at the top of her lungs. "Mark, Betsy! Uncle Jed is here!"

Their screeches gained in volume until they rounded the corner and pounced, almost knocking him down the stairs.

"Hey, ragamuffins! How's it going? And how's school? Got your diplomas yet?"

"Uncle Jed!" Betsy faced him with a scornful expression, her hands on her hips emphasizing her disdain. "They don't give dippalomanas out for kinnergarnernen."

Liz shook her head, scowled at Jed, then smiled at Betsy. "That's pronounced 'dip-lom-a,' and Uncle Jed will teach you to say it properly. And he can work on the word 'kindergarten,' too."

Jed laughed. He loved to goad Betsy into using big words. "So, Mark, how's calculus?"

Mark scrunched his eyebrows, scowled in an expression that mirrored his mother's, and said nothing.

He ruffled Mark's already messy hair. "You mean they haven't got you doing calculus in grade three? What good is that school, anyway?"

"Uncle Jed!" Mark crossed his arms and tried to look angry, but his quivering grin gave him away. Jed mussed his hair even more.

Liz craned her neck over Jed's shoulder to see his truck. "Bring all your stuff?"

"Yup."

"In one load?"

Jed tried to give his shoulders a casual shrug and forced himself to smile. His 4X4 was big, but not that big—not that he had a lot of stuff left. "I sold everything big and put the rest away in storage. All I need is my clothes, bedroom furniture, and my stereo. I didn't think you wanted my couch and stuff in your family room."

"The sale go all right?"

"Yeah, I was lucky."

It had almost been too easy, but he could see God's hand at work. After the plant closed, causing massive unemployment and a downturn in the local economy, he somehow had managed to find a buyer for his condo immediately, selling it for just enough to cover his outstanding mortgage. He'd also managed to find another job before his last penny ran out, albeit in the city. He moved as soon as the money came through. The only problem would have been finding a decent place he could afford to stay in only a short week before starting his new job, but Liz had taken care of that.

When her sitter quit only three weeks into the school year, Liz was desperate. Now that Betsy had started kindergarten, only the more costly day cares would provide transportation back and forth to the school—if she could even find an opening without being relegated to a waiting list.

Problem solved. Jed's new job on the evening shift would allow him to be home all day to baby-sit. Liz and Frank arrived home in plenty of time for Jed to drive the fifteenminute trip and arrive on time for the second shift. All he had to do was start supper for the family, and of course keep up his share of the housework, and he had free rent and all his meals paid for until Betsy started full-day school next September.

The entire drive into town he had been lost in thought, both grateful and amazed everything had fit into place so smoothly and quickly. He dared not question why all his prayers had been answered, especially after he'd been so stupid.

Liz and Jed both started to speak at the same time. "I really appreciate . . ." They laughed in unison. Liz's eyes sparkled, lightening his spirit by one more notch.

"You first," he said.

Liz smiled up at him. "I was going to say, little brother, that I really appreciate you moving in to do this for me. I'm going to enjoy living with you again, because it's far cheaper to pay for your meals than to pay for day care." She cocked her head to one side. "Your turn."

Jed heaved a sigh of relief. He still worried about being an unwelcome guest or a financial burden, but Liz had again eased his fears. He wondered how she knew what he was thinking. Perhaps the reason they fought constantly when they were growing up was because they thought too much alike.

"I was going to tell you how much I appreciate you sharing your home and committing your family to putting up with me for a year. And don't count your chickens about the cost of keeping me. You haven't calculated the cost of my laundry." Jed pretended to have to pry his shirt off his chest, as if it were wet.

Liz hit his shoulder with a stuffed toy she had been carrying. "Frank will be home at 4:30, but if you want, we can start moving in the boxes and smaller things now."

As they walked out to the truck, Jed thought about Frank still at work. "So, why are you home? I thought you would be at work, and I was going to let myself in. I was really surprised to hear the kids at home." He jingled the contents of his pocket, fingering the shiny new key Liz had mailed him.

Liz sighed. "I couldn't find a sitter, so I had to take a few days off work until you got here, and they weren't very happy about it. If it's okay with you, I'd like to get back tomorrow. Are you ready to jump right in?"

He handed down a suitcase. "No problem. Just run down the routine for me. After all, what else do I have to do, except find a place for what little stuff I brought?"

As they walked back and forth together unloading the truck, Liz gave him the rundown on the daily routine. "Frank and I leave at 7:00. That means you have to get Mark up and get him ready. He has to be out the door for school at 8:20. Betsy usually wakes up when he leaves. Mark eats lunch at school, and Betsy has to be at school by 12:30. You'll have the afternoon to yourself, until you pick her up at 3:00. Mark gets off at 3:00 also, but he walks home with his friends. So if you can start supper, Frank and I get home at 4:15. Monday is soccer, Tuesday is Mark's piano lesson, Wednesday he may go over to a friend's house, Thursday is . . ."

"Whoa! I think I'm going to have to write all this down. How do you keep up? No wonder your sitter quit!"

Liz turned and stuck her tongue out at him. "You took the job, little brother."

Jed grinned at her. "I know." It was great to be home.

❧

Jillian checked her watch as she listened to little David pounding out each note of the song he was supposed to have practiced all week. She put on her best teacher's smile.

"David, I thought you said you practiced your piano lessons every day."

"I did. But I only played it once every day."

Jillian wanted to hit her head against the wall. If he had practiced this song seven times over the past week, it surely would have sounded better than that. Instead she smiled at him again. "I'm going to have to ask you to repeat it for next week. I know you can do it with no mistakes. And don't forget to tap your foot. All the notes have to be on time with your foot. Okay, David?"

"Yes, Miss Jefferson."

"Your time is up now, and I see your mom's car in the front. Now, you practice it every day, and more than once." She closed the book and stood, prompting David to stand as well. "Good night, David."

"Good night, Miss Jefferson."

Jillian waved good-bye to the last student of the day. As she closed the door, her smile faded, and she immediately headed to the medicine cabinet to get something for her pounding headache.

Why did little David have to play so loud? It wouldn't be so bad if at least he got some of the notes right the first time. She wondered where his parents had the piano, and how they could stand it. It was almost as if he pounded every key as loud as possible on purpose, just to be annoying.

Her students ranged from kindergartners to high school students, beginners to advanced. By sheer coincidence, all her worst pupils were on Monday, and all her best ones were on Tuesday. She loved Tuesdays. But children grew up so quickly; soon they would all improve their skills or quit, and these days of headaches and frustration would be long forgotten. Once her schedule filled to capacity, she wouldn't be taking on so many beginners.

The best part of teaching piano lessons from her home was not having to fight traffic or worry about pleasing the boss. She only needed a few more students, and her appointment book would be as full as she wanted.

Sitting at the piano, she packed up the beginner lesson books, tidied up the pile of pass stickers and various other rewards for hard work, then selected a small pile of her own favorites. A Bach classic, her favorite Chopin collection, and a few praise books. After a day like today, she especially needed those. As she played, the music soothed her shattered nerves, and her mind drifted ahead to the next day's schedule.

On Tuesday, the best day of the week, she most appreciated her lesson with Mark Edwards. Even at eight years old, Mark demonstrated real talent, along with a desire to excel. Eager, intelligent, he had a real love for music. If only all her students could be more like Mark.

❧

Jed held Betsy in his arms, and they waved to Liz and Frank as the car backed out of the driveway. It had been 3:30 in the morning before he had his stuff organized enough to go to bed. Now, only three and a half hours later, Betsy was up for the day.

"Uncle Jed?"

Jed answered and yawned at the same time. "Yeah, Pumpkin?"

"Are you really going to live with us until I get to stay in school all day?"

"You bet."

"Are you going to like living with us?"

"Sure." He yawned again.

"Can you help me ride my bike?"

"Yup."

"And play baseball like Mark?"

"Yeah, sure."

"I can print my name. My teacher says I'm doing real good. Can you help me print my phone number?"

"Yeah, sure."

"With a pen?"

"Yeah, with a pen."

"And when will you teach me to tie my shoes?"

Why was the kid asking these hard questions? Didn't she know what time it was? "Tomorrow." Jed lowered her feet to the floor. Was she always such a yacky little thing so early in the morning? Liz had told him Betsy didn't get up until much later.

The alarm on his wristwatch beeped as Jed stifled another yawn, signaling time to get Mark up for school. "Tell you what. I'll give you a nickel if you go wake your brother up for me." He remembered Liz waking him up for school one morning by pouring water on his head. Betsy was too young for that, for now. Maybe one day . . .

"Mark! Mark!"

Jed flinched at the volume of Betsy's voice as she screamed loud enough to wake the dead, never mind an eight-year-old boy.

"Shut up!"

"Wake up! Uncle Jed said so!"

"Shut up!"

"Uncle Jed! Mark told me to shut up!"

"Did not!"

"Did too!"

"Shut up!"

"Uncle Jed! He did it again!"

What had he done? What had he gotten himself into? How long would it take to pack up all his stuff again? Jed slumped, sitting heavily on the couch. He waited for Betsy to run into the kitchen and Mark to shuffle along before he started to push himself up to follow.

A bang sounded from the kitchen, followed by a huge thud, then a crinkling sound.

"Uncle Jed! Mark spilled the cereal!"

"Shut up, you fink!"

"Uncle Jed! Mark told me to shut up!"

"Knock it off!"

"And he's calling me names!"

Jed groaned. "I'll be right there."

As Jed entered the kitchen, he observed Mark furiously scooping the cereal off the floor and shoveling it back into the box with his hands, while behind him the dog licked it off the floor, eating as fast as she could.

Surrounded by a ring of cereal on the floor, Betsy jumped up and down, shrieking, and grinding it into small crumbs, sending bits and pieces all the way across the room. "Uncle Jed! Uncle Jed!" she cried out, waving her arms in the air.

Jed closed his eyes. What now? If he could find something else to feed them, he would clean up later. He wondered if Liz had another box of cereal hidden somewhere. With a little imagination and determination, Jed found some bowls and a box of instant oatmeal. Carefully reading the directions, he plugged the kettle in to boil, and waited.

According to the clock on the wall, they were fast running out of time. Jed measured and poured the water, turned his face back to the table, and opened his mouth to speak, but Mark was gone.

Mark's voice drifted from the living room. "Uncle Jed, I think the dog was sick."

Jed checked the clock. Now they were really running out of time. "What? Where?"

"In front of the TV, on the rug."

Not now. Why was this all happening? Was cereal bad for dogs? If so, how come the kids could eat it with no ill effects? He grabbed the roll of paper towels and strode into the living room, where an ugly blob lay on the rug in front of the television. Jed's stomach flipped over. Good thing he hadn't eaten yet, or he would have been next, right along with the dog.

Mark stood to the side, his hands covering his mouth and his shoulders shaking. Jed tried to keep from puking himself as he looked down at the mess. As Mark started to laugh out loud, Jed became more suspicious.

"Mark!" he shouted. "This is plastic! I'll get you!" He started to chase after Mark, feeling bits of dry cereal crunching under his bare feet as he ran, but Mark managed to keep one step ahead of him. Mark dashed into the bathroom and locked the door, howling with laughter the whole time.

Betsy stood on the coffee table, pointing at the closed bathroom door. "I'm telling Mom! You're gonna get it!"

Jed sucked in a deep breath. He was never having kids. Never. "Come on, Mark, it's time to eat and get ready for school."

Mark opened the door a crack and peeked out.

Jed ran one hand down his face as he squeezed his eyes shut. "Come on, Mark. Just get ready for school."

Without a word, Mark shuffled into the kitchen. By now the oatmeal was cold, and both of them ate only a couple of small spoonfuls, complaining bitterly the entire time. Jed sagged in his chair while they argued over who got to look at the brightly colored box.

As Jed watched, he had a nagging impression that there was something he should have been doing, but for the life of him he couldn't remember what it was. Mark pushed the bowl of cold oatmeal to the center of the table with a loud scraping sound, then returned to his bedroom to get dressed. Jed checked the time again, worried that Mark was going to be late if he didn't move a little faster.

"Come on, Mark, move it!" he called out, trying to keep the irritation out of his voice.

Running out of his room, Mark turned to the front door.

"Did you brush your teeth and comb your hair?"

"Oops." Mark ran into the bathroom, and came out in record time. Jed wondered if the toothbrush was even wet, but didn't push it.

Mark grabbed his backpack from the kitchen floor and stopped dead. "Uncle Jed? Where's my lunch?"

Jed leaned his head back and slapped his palm to his forehead. He knew there was something he was supposed to have done.

As quickly as he could, he dug through the fridge and found the sandwich Liz had made, then threw in an apple and a couple of cookies. He found a thermos in the cupboard with a picture of some superhero on it, filled it with milk, and rammed it into Mark's backpack.

"I'm going to be late now. You have to drive me."

"What? I'm still in my pajamas!"

"I'm going to be late."

"What about Betsy?"

"You have to bring her."

"She's still in her pajamas!"

"But Uncle Jed! I'm going to be late! You're going to make me get lines!"

Jed stared at Mark with his mouth hanging open, on the verge of telling Mark it was his own fault, but he stopped. Lines. He would never live it down, especially on his first day taking care of them. Jed ran into his room and quickly tossed on the first thing he touched. He bundled Betsy's coat over the top of her pajamas and slipped her sneakers over her bare feet.

"Let's go. We can still make it."

He hustled the kids into his truck and arrived at the school as the bell rang. Mark leaped out of the truck and ran into the school yard, and Jed turned around and drove back to the house.

"Well, Pumpkin, we made it." He pulled into the driveway. "What do we do now?"

"You forgot to let Missy out."

Was this a problem? "So?"

Betsy's big brown eyes opened wide at him, reminding him of a chubby-cheeked chipmunk. "I hope she didn't go peepee on the rug."

That was all he needed. This time it wouldn't be fake. He hurried with the key, listening to the dog barking furiously from the other side of the door. As he opened it wide, Missy ran into the front yard to relieve herself. At least one thing had gone right this morning.

Maybe he had bitten off more than he could chew.

Coffee. He needed coffee. Bad. Maybe ten coffees.

"Uncle Jed?"

He clenched his teeth, then forced himself to relax as he looked down at Betsy. If he heard one more "Uncle Jed" he was going to scream. "Yeah, Pumpkin?"

"Can I watch TV?"

"You bet."

In silence, Jed hung up Betsy's coat, slid her sneakers by the door, and settled Betsy in front of the television. He started a pot of coffee and sat down, elbows resting on the table, his chin cupped in his palms, and watched it drip. The heady aroma of coffee soon filled the room. Had it really only been an hour since he had been dragged out of bed?

❧

Jillian smiled, inhaling the fresh morning air as she opened the window wide. Tuesday, her favorite day. Her smile widened at the thought of her first lesson later that afternoon. Mark Edwards, her favorite student.

The hardest part of teaching piano lessons for a living was finding things to keep her busy all day, and then as soon as school was over, working nonstop, often not taking the time for supper until lessons ended at 8:00. She paid the price for working such short hours on the weekends, however, which were filled with lessons from early morning till midevening. Many Sundays she spent time after church with students who needed extra help, especially at exam time, but it was worth it. She managed to earn a living from her home, even if it did mean seldom keeping company with other adults. In many respects, she welcomed the chance to keep to herself. No one asked her out anymore, and she liked it that way.

Jillian sighed. After running a few errands today, she had tentative plans to visit her sister. Except for Sue's screaming children, she enjoyed those visits. It also made her appreciate the calm, well-behaved kids she taught.

As the day wore on, despite the best of intentions, Jillian ran out of time, arriving back at home with barely enough time to get a pot of coffee started before her first student knocked at the door.

"Hello, Mark," she greeted him cheerfully as she sat in her chair beside the piano. "How is that new piece coming?"

"I really like it, Miss Jefferson, and I think I'm doing okay, except I don't have my book again. Can I borrow yours?"

Jillian picked through her pile of extra books. "Did the sitter forget to pack it again? I think maybe you're going to have to try harder and remember to pack your books yourself from now on."

Mark grinned. "No, the sitter quit. My uncle is staying at our house to look after us. I guess he forgot. He had a bad morning. I thought he was gonna, you know, like, hurl, when he saw what Thomas lent me."

Jillian didn't even pretend to understand as she opened her spare Level Three book to the correct page. "Well, let's get started. Can you do it hands together?"

She watched him work the selection with amazing ease, especially for the first week on a new and difficult number.

They discussed what needed improvement, and Jillian carefully complimented him on what he did well. After reviewing a couple of songs from past weeks, the lesson progressed quickly, and they soon ran out of time.

Her next student waited patiently, sitting in the chair next to the door. Jillian dismissed Mark and called Ashley up to the piano.

❧

"Uncle Jed!" Mark called as he walked in the door.

Jed cringed. "Yes, Mark."

"You forgot my piano books. Miss Jefferson is mad at you. She said I have to pack my music books myself now."

"Is that so?"

"Yeah, she's real strict."

Jed looked at Mark's smiling face. He looked like a pretty happy kid to have just come from a grueling piano lesson. "You know, I haven't heard you play for a long time. Want to play something for me? How about what you just played for your teacher?"

Mark glanced over at the piano, where his books were still sitting open to the correct page. "Sure."

Jed listened to him play. For an eight-year-old, the kid sounded good. As he recalled, Liz started him at the beginning of grade one, so he had been playing for nearly two years now. For a strict teacher, this Miss Jefferson must have what it took to put up with active kids like Mark. Mark obviously enjoying playing the piano, and he did well.

"So what's your teacher like?"

Mark opened his eyes wide. "Miss Jefferson? Her feelings get hurt if I don't practice, and she expects me to remember all the hard stuff. She makes me sit still, and both feet have to touch the floor." Mark paused to think. "And she's old."

2

*A*fter a few weeks of baby-sitting, Jed was ready to climb the walls. Mark and Betsy got away with all that nonsense the first day, but since then, their behavior had greatly improved. He had been tested, he put his foot down, and that was the end of it.

With the family all settled into their new routines after the flurry of the beginning of the school year, Jed managed to get Mark off to school with no more shenanigans, entertain Betsy all morning, feed her lunch, and take her to school with no difficulty. During his solitary afternoons, after his daily devotions and Bible reading, he discovered there were only so many times he could wipe the same counter. All he did was walk from room to room, when he wasn't pacing. And it gave him too much time to think.

The new job was going to work out, but his assigned menial duties didn't help his frustration level one bit. The other men were companionable enough, but they lacked any spark or vision for the future. Stuck in a dead-end job, not a single one of them seemed to mind. At least for him, the job was only temporary until next September, when he would enter college, provided he could get back on his feet. He would do anything to see that it happened, and this time nothing would stop him.

Jed mentally kicked himself for being such a pushover as he straightened the towels in the bathroom, then stood back to admire Liz's decorating scheme. One day he'd have a house like this. Never again would he let anyone take advantage of him as he had in the past.

He stood in silence in the empty house, wondering what he should do next. The guys had invited him for a beer before work, the same as they did most days, but Jed turned them down. Not only did he consider it a bad idea to drink before work, he just plain-old didn't drink. He didn't want to be labeled a religious fanatic, but as a Christian, his decision had been made. At twenty-six, he definitely was no angel, but he did his best to live his life according to God's direction.

Working the afternoon shift effectively put an end to any potential social life. Aside from the fact that he didn't know anyone in this city except for his sister and her husband, the only church activity during the daytime was the ladies' Tuesday morning Bible study and coffee time. He simply wasn't that desperate. Yet.

Jed picked up a few Lego pieces and tossed them into the box in Mark's bedroom, then paused for a split second, actually considering dumping the box and building something. Jed shook his head, almost screaming in frustration. Surely he was going around the bend. All alone with nothing to do. All day. Every day. He'd never considered himself a social butterfly, but he always found it easy to meet people. He liked the activity and atmosphere of a large busy church, where there was always something going on, but working the evening shift put an end to his participation. Give it a couple more days, and he was going to welcome the opportunity to dust the top of the door frames. With Liz's meticulous housekeeping, he couldn't finish up anything except for what they had previously agreed upon, and that wasn't much.

In the solitude of the empty house, as he passed the lonely piano, Jed tried to plunk out a melody with one finger. Before he left for work, Jed often listened to Mark practice his piano lessons. Mark had shown him a few notes, but Jed felt too awkward to ask the kid to teach him a tune.

As he passed the piano again, Jed tried to plunk out a melody with one finger. As a boy, he had wanted to learn to play the piano, but his parents didn't have the money or a piano. Now that he was alone, no one could listen or watch him make a fool of himself.

He dug through the drawer in the kitchen and found Liz's address book. Flipping the pages one at a time, he finally found what he was looking for under "P." Piano teacher, Miss J. Jefferson. Jed dialed the number.

Jillian heard the phone ringing as she fumbled with her grocery bags and the bulky key ring. She deposited her groceries on the floor and picked up the cordless phone beside the piano, but it was dead. Not wanting to miss the call, she ran up the stairs to answer before it stopped.

"Hello?" she answered breathily, trying not to sound like she was panting.

"Is this Miss Jefferson, the piano teacher?" a male voice asked.

"Yes, speaking. Can I help you?"

"Do you have any openings?"

Her heart beat faster. Another student! She prayed he was going to ask for a day that still had a space available. Jillian held her breath for a second to try to steady her voice. "Yes, I do. What day would be best?"

The caller paused, as if thinking. "Doesn't matter. Every day's the same to me. How about tomorrow?"

She knew the answer without checking her schedule. "Yes, I have an opening tomorrow. How does 4:45 sound?"

"Too late. Let's see. I've got to work around kindergarten hours, so somewhere around 2:15?"

Jillian shuddered at the thought of taking on another five-year-old. The kindergarten kids had such a short attention span, and at the beginning of November, most of them hadn't learned enough of their alphabet to know what notes they were playing. Their legs were too short for their feet to touch the floor, and they wiggled the entire lesson. Often, after being in kindergarten all morning, by midafternoon they were too tired to concentrate.

Did she have the energy for this? Jillian fumbled to dig a pen and a scrap of paper out of her purse, which was still slung over her shoulder. "Yes, that would be fine. And the name?"

"Jed Davies," the deep voice of the caller announced.

She hesitated before writing it down. A few kids that age had already had lessons, and were getting pretty good. She tried to convince herself that it was entirely possible that this would be one of them.

Hopefully he knew enough of his alphabet so she wouldn't have to waste the first lesson on simple ABC's.

Jillian shrugged her shoulders as she scribbled with the pen, trying to convince it to write. It was unusual for the father to be calling to enroll a child for lessons. She smiled to herself as the pen finally began to write, thinking how nice it would be if more fathers showed a little enthusiasm for their children's musical education.

Jed listened to the scratching noises, wondering if old Miss Jefferson was writing an entire novel, rather than just his short name.

"Fine, Mr. Davies. And do you have a book?"

Silence hung over the line, until Jed realized that by saying "Mr. Davies," Miss Jefferson was speaking to him. He hadn't thought about a book. Liz probably wouldn't mind if he borrowed Mark's old book. In fact, she would probably laugh. "Yes, I've got one."

"Good. I'll see you tomorrow at 2:15. Thank you for calling."

Jed hung up the phone. Old Miss Jefferson had been a little out of breath when she answered the phone. He tried to picture the little old lady who would be teaching him piano lessons. Jed laughed out loud as he tucked the phone book back into the drawer. Wait until he told Mark and Liz this one.

As he glanced at the clock, he welcomed the time to go pick up Betsy from kindergarten since, except for work, this was his only opportunity to talk to other adults.

Jillian retrieved her spilled groceries, then prepared to psyche herself up for her Monday lessons. Someday some of these kids might be good. Someday they might remember their piano teacher with fond memories. Someday their feet would touch the floor.

❧

Jed approached Miss Jefferson's house carrying Mark's old book under his arm. Mark made him drive by yesterday on the way to soccer practice just so he could show off his teacher's house. Jed sucked in a deep breath and knocked.

A young woman about the same age as himself or maybe a bit younger answered the door. Her wavy, shoulder length auburn hair framed a perfect oval face. Wide, gorgeous green eyes stared up at him. He thought the woman could have been on a makeup commercial, only she wasn't wearing any. Her figure was model perfect, but she was too short to be a model, probably only about five-foot-five or so.

His mind wandered back to his conversation with Mark. This woman had to be old Miss Jefferson's daughter. But Mark had said "Miss" Jefferson. Was she a niece or something? He didn't know what to say, or who to ask for, Miss or Mrs. Jefferson, or her mother. Or her aunt?

His brain froze as she stared at him, expecting him to say something. He tried to shut out the impulse to get to know her better. He wasn't interested in available women. He was here for piano lessons.

"Can I help you?" she asked.

Jed swallowed and shuffled the book from one hand to the other. "I'm here to see Miss Jefferson."

Jillian blinked to stop herself from staring. When she opened the door for her newest student, the sight of the boy's father had rendered her speechless.

Mr. Davies was breathtakingly handsome. And tall. And not what she had anticipated. A fabulous mane of wavy light brown hair framed his strong dark features, and snug-fitting jeans showed off strong muscular legs.

And he was rather young-looking for the father of a five-year-old, but it was possible. She estimated his age at about the same as her own or maybe a bit older, probably about twenty-five. And where was the child? "I'm Miss Jefferson."

Jed opened his mouth, but no words came out. He swallowed again, hating himself for being so suddenly tongue-tied. "You're Miss Jefferson?" he blurted out. His gaze traveled up and down her one more time, before he fixed his eyes to her face. "I was expecting someone, um, older. Um, I mean, uh, your hair is brown, uh . . ." Actually, he didn't know what he meant! Jed's cheeks grew warm, and he was sure his ears were beet red as well. On top of it, he was stammering like an idiot. Mark had told him the piano teacher was old. Was the kid blind? But then again, Mark thought kissing girls was disgusting.

Miss Jefferson's eyes widened, showing off a deep sea green that nearly took what was left of his breath away. She inhaled sharply, then turned her head, searching for something behind him. "Where is little Jed?" she asked.

The corners of Jed's mouth quivered. He was six-foot-one. "I've been called many things in my life, but 'little' was never one of them. I'm Jed." He smiled down at her, extended one hand, and waited.

Jillian tilted her head back to let her gaze travel up to his face at the same time as she lightly touched his hand, giving him the limpest handshake of her life. Although she wondered why he had blushed when she introduced herself, now the heat crept up her face as well. She retracted her hand abruptly.

"Oh," she mumbled. As she made eye contact, his quirky little smile nearly made her knees give out. "You're an adult." She cringed inwardly at her brilliant observation. "I was expecting someone, um . . . someone younger. You were asking about kindergarten hours." Jillian mentally kicked herself. At first she thought his stammering was cute. Now she was doing no better.

"My niece is in kindergarten, so I need to do lessons when she's in school."

Jillian blinked twice in rapid succession. Niece? "The lessons are for you?" She kept staring, lost in the deep blue of his eyes until a wisp of her hair blew into her face, drawing her attention to the fact that they were still standing in the open doorway. "Oh, I'm so sorry, please come in."

She led him to the piano and motioned for him to sit beside her on the bench. "I don't have any adult students. Please excuse me, I'm afraid you caught me off guard. Shall we start?" She smoothed her sleeves in an effort to compose herself.

The bench creaked with his weight as he sat. They both looked at each other, stood, then Jillian pulled the bench further back to accommodate the length of his legs, and they sat down again.

Jillian concentrated on the obviously used lesson book that her new student placed on the piano. "Can you read music?" she asked, wondering if he had taken lessons as a child and given up.

He shook his head. "No. I'm a beginner. Mark showed me where middle C is. That's all I know." He plunked out middle C with his index finger.

"Mark?"

Jed nodded, turned his head, and smiled at her. "Yeah, Mark Edwards. He's my nephew. Plays well, doesn't he? He's the one that gave me your name. He thinks this is real funny, that I'm going to take piano lessons from his teacher."

Jillian tried to collect her befuddled brain as her newest student flashed a dazzling white smile at her. Mark Edwards? This was the uncle who didn't pack his music book last week? The one who was staying with them because the sitter quit? Her voice came out in a croak. "Yes, he is one of my better students."

He continued to smile at her, and Jillian fought to keep from becoming undone. She turned her body to the piano and focused on the keyboard. "Well," she mumbled, "let's get started." She played some notes on the piano, asking him to name them, then asked a few questions to see what he knew so far.

Next, she placed his hands on the keyboard and showed him the proper hand position, curving his fingers and placing them individually on the keys. He had wonderful hands for a man. His skin was soft, and she admired the little bit of hair showing from under the cuffs of his shirt. She tried to stop herself from blushing at noticing such a thing.

"Now, Mr. Davies, you must maintain proper posture. Keep your back straight, no slouching. Elbows in, feet flat on the floor at all times."

He laughed at her seriousness. "Please, call me Jed. I'm not old enough for anyone to call me Mr. Davies. And I can see what Mark meant about you being strict. He isn't very happy about you making him sit still and keep his feet on the ground."

Jillian tried to smile back. "I guess you should call me Jillian. I'd feel silly if you called me Miss Jefferson like the kids do. And Mark does very well sitting still and maintaining his posture when he is playing. He is very well-behaved."

Well-behaved? Jed remembered the plastic dog vomit and the

subsequent chase around the living room on his first morning at the house. It would be years before he forgot that one.

He sat still as Jillian opened the book and showed him the first few songs, all of which required only one hand, four songs in all. Before he knew it, the lesson was over.

"This is it?" he asked.

"That's half an hour. Actually, we covered much more than I usually do in one lesson. Now you have to practice for a week, and come back and play these songs perfect for me."

Jed couldn't believe it. Was that all there was to playing piano? "If this is all I get to do, can I have another lesson when I'm done, even if it's not a week? I've got nothing else to do all day."

Jillian faced him. It was true, the first lessons were very simplified, but this series was a good progressive course. She wished he had brought a book more suited for adults. "Well, I don't generally . . . but I suppose I could make an exception. When you're ready, call in the morning and we'll see if we can set something up."

Jed checked his watch, noticing that it was time to go to the school to pick up Betsy. "Great." He stood. "I'll do that."

Jillian's heart beat far too fast as she escorted him to the door and watched him leave, taking long lazy strides as he walked. To say this was not what she expected would be a massive understatement. As hard as she had tried to concentrate, she'd found herself being distracted by his closeness as she tried to teach him the basics. Her face flushed as she remembered calling him Little Jed. Little Jed, indeed!

Jed walked quickly once he rounded the corner on his way to the school. He didn't know why he'd tried so hard to look casual as he left Jillian standing on her doorstep, but he could feel her watching him as he walked down the street. He just knew.

How in the world was he going to learn anything with a teacher like that? Throughout the entire lesson, he'd found it difficult to concentrate on the lesson, hypnotized by her sweet melodic voice and gentle manners. He'd forced himself to listen to what she was saying, rather than how she was saying it.

His lips tightened and his pace became more determined. He could not allow this distraction. If he ever got the urge to get back into the dating scene, Liz said she knew a number of nice single women at her church whom she wanted to introduce to him. When he was ready, that would be the route he would take. Later. Much later. Like when he graduated from college. And got a good job teaching in a big high school. And then, only after many years. Maybe when he became the department head. Or principal.

If he could get past Jillian's annoying sweetness, piano lessons were going to be fun. And he was going to have to speak to Mark about his definition of "old."

He arrived at the school with perfect timing to take Betsy home.

❧

Mark raced out the school door and straight to Miss Jefferson's house. He had remembered to put his music books in his backpack all by himself this morning.

His teacher was waiting for him.

"Hi, Miss Jefferson!" he called as he walked up to the piano, throwing his backpack on the floor beside the bench. "Was Uncle Jed here today? He said he was going to take piano lessons. He's going to use all my old books." He gazed up expectantly at her, but Miss Jefferson only smiled politely at him and nodded. "Yes, Mark. He was here." She patted the bench and smiled again, so it didn't look like she was going to thank him for showing Uncle Jed all the notes. "And did you practice those hard ones this week?"

Mark didn't want to pout like his little sister. "Yes," he mumbled. "I had to practice lots to show Uncle Jed how much fun it was to play piano. He kept asking me to play stuff for him."

"Oh, really? Was he impressed? Did you do your best?"

Mark nodded so fast his hair fell into his eyes. "Yes, I practiced real hard." He sat straight and tall, both feet on the floor, and played his best for Miss Jefferson, showing her how well he had played for uncle Jed.

Jillian was impressed as she watched Mark play. It seemed having his uncle take lessons was going to be good for Mark. However, the unsettled feeling his Uncle Jed had left might not be so good for her.

"Very good, Mark, you passed them all! I can tell you worked very hard." She placed a large colorful sticker on each of the pages as he grinned excitedly. "Now, let's start the next page. I think it's going to be a fun one."

Jillian continued on with Mark's lesson, and tried to put thoughts of his uncle Jed aside. Would he really call before next Tuesday? Against her better judgment, she hoped he would.

She sent Mark on his way on time and welcomed her next student.

❧

Jed heard the door slam over the sound of running water as he washed the potatoes he was preparing for supper.

Mark's loud voice almost caused him to drop the knife. "Uncle Jed! Uncle Jed!"

"I'm in the kitchen!" Jed shouted back. "What do you want? I have to get ready for work."

"Uncle Jed! I passed them both!"

Jed wiped his hands so he could admire the new stickers in Mark's book. Would he get stickers for passing? He hoped not. What would she do when he passed?

The sound of a car pulling into the driveway made him rein in his thoughts. If that was Liz and Frank getting home, that left him ten minutes to make it out the door to be on time for work.

Jed turned the heat down on the potatoes and gave the roast a poke with a fork to check its progress. Roast beef sandwiches for lunch tomorrow.

Packing his lunch pail, Jed wondered if this was a good time to get some information out of Mark, who was sitting at the table admiring his new stickers.

"So, Mark," Jed said as he casually searched the fridge for the bag of apples, "Miss Jefferson seems like she's a good teacher. She's pretty too. But she really isn't that old."

"But, Uncle Jed! Look at her! She has to be almost as old as Mom. I'll bet she's as old as you."

Jed straightened his back and cleared his throat. He swiped his hair back, then patted the top of his head, just to make sure there weren't any thin spots he didn't know about. As far as he knew, there were no gray ones either.

When Mark stared up at him with a stunned expression, Jed couldn't take it anymore. "Get out of here!" He stepped forward, pretending to chase Mark, lunch pail in hand. Mark squealed, prompting Jed to give chase for real, until he almost collided with Liz and Frank in the hall.

"Hi, Jed." Liz flattened herself against the wall as Jed skidded to a halt. "So, how was your piano lesson? You did go today, didn't you? And what did you think of Miss Jefferson?" He watched Liz bite back a grin. "She certainly has a way with children."

Jed narrowed his eyes to stare at his sister. "I'm leaving," he mumbled, just loud enough for her to hear.

She pointedly ignored him as she peeked into the oven. "Have a nice night at work then. See you."

"Yeah. Save some for me, will ya?"

"Bye, Jed," Frank said absently as he walked past Jed and opened the lid of one of the pots on the stove. "What's for supper?"

Jed didn't answer.

As he drove to work, Jed anticipated the next afternoon. After he dropped Betsy off at the school, he could start practicing his piano lessons.

❧

Friday finally came. Not that the beginning of the weekend made much difference, since Jillian scheduled a full day of lessons Saturday, making it her busiest day.

She had just switched on the coffeemaker when the phone rang.

"Hi, Jillian? It's little Jed."

Jillian's face flushed, and she was relieved he couldn't see her. She had a feeling she would never be able to forget calling him that. "Yes, Jed?"

"Got time for a lesson today? I'm getting bored with these four one-handed tunes."

Obviously he had no clue that every afternoon was open. "Yes, today would be fine. Same time?"

"Yeah, sure. See you later. Bye."

Jillian dressed in her oldest jeans and rattiest T-shirt, deciding to keep to her original plan of scrubbing out her window frames, a job she had been putting aside for months. While she was in the process of dumping the dirty water down the drain, the doorbell rang. She cringed as she looked at the clock. If it was Jed, then he was early, and she was wearing her grubbiest clothes. But no matter. She couldn't leave him standing outside just because she wasn't ready.

Jillian answered the door with her heart in her throat. So much for her dignified professional image. "Hi, Jed. Come in. I'm afraid I lost track of the time, and I'm not ready."

He stood at the door, also dressed in jeans, but he wore a neatly pressed cotton shirt instead of a stained old T-shirt, and he, at least, was clean. He shrugged his shoulders. "Sorry. I think I'm a bit early."

"Well, come in." She couldn't very well leave him in the living room while she ran off to change. They would have to do the lesson as she was.

Instead of sitting beside her on the piano bench, Jed stood to the side, gripping his book with both hands. She followed his gaze, first to her accumulation of music books on her bookshelf, then to the praise book she had left open on the piano. She usually felt awkward about people seeing her church music, but thankfully Jed didn't say anything.

"Can you play something for me?" he asked, catching her off guard.

Jillian bit her bottom lip. "I guess so," she replied. "Anything in particular you'd like to hear?"

"Well," he drawled as he continued to study the pile of books, "how about something I could expect to be able to play a few years down the road?"

Jillian didn't want to hurt his feelings, but she hadn't a clue what level he could expect to be at. She had no idea if he had any real talent; after all, this was only his second lesson, and they hadn't even started yet. How committed would he be? How much time did he intend to practice every day? There were too many unknowns. And what was a "few" years? Two? Three? Five?

"That's a tough one. Can I just pick a favorite number of my own that isn't too difficult, and play it for you? If you work hard, you should be able to do this one in a few years."

Jillian selected a book and played a simple sonata by Mozart. "That's about the grade five Royal Conservatory level. Or would you rather hear something more contemporary?"

Jed's face lit up like a Christmas tree. "Wow," he mumbled as he scanned the open page. Jillian couldn't tell if he thought the written music looked too complicated or not. "Will I really be able to play like that?"

Jillian smiled, enjoying the opportunity to play for an appreciative student, rather than a parent who was merely listening to be polite. Although she had been asked to play piano for the worship service at church, she had declined, wanting to remain in the background. Never again would she be displayed in front of people, not even the moral and upright people at church. At least she knew the motives of her students, which was only to share her love of music and nothing more.

She started playing another selection at the same difficulty level. Jed lowered himself to her chair beside the piano. Out of the corner of her eye, she could see him leaning back, his long legs stretched out in front of him, smiling as she played, his eyes closed. She turned her concentration back to her music, before she completely lost her place.

At the closing diminuendo, his eyes opened and he continued to lie back, a lazy smile lingering on his face. Jillian tried to ignore her unwarranted impulse to smooth his hair.

"Do you really think I'll be able to play like that someday?"

She swallowed, mentally kicking herself for her thoughts. He was her student and nothing more. She swallowed hard and closed the book. "If you practice hard and keep at it, I don't see why not."

"Can you play me one more before my lesson? A favorite of yours? Do we have time?"

"Sure. This is called Moonlight Sonata."

The Beethoven classic was her current favorite, helping her to relax after a trying day. Jillian poured her heart into the music, and let the piano sing the melancholy melody. When she released the final chord, silence permeated the room.

"Wow, that was beautiful. You play as well as you teach." His starry-eyed smile made Jillian blush.

She cleared her throat. "Maybe we should get on with your lesson."

"Yeah, sure."

Jed sat beside her on the bench, and he proceeded to play the first two-line song without making a single mistake. Jillian tried not to be too impressed.

"Now play it again, and I'll play my part down here."

The duet sounded as good as could be expected for the first lesson in the book. All four songs progressed in the same manner, without error, and Jillian found herself hard-pressed not to grin at his enthusiasm, as well as his sense of humor about having to learn the easy beginner selections.

"I'm afraid that's it."

"Yup. Time for me to go get Betsy. See you next lesson."

They stood simultaneously, and she immediately missed his warmth.

"Yes, see you Tuesday, Jed." She didn't want to count the days until Tuesday. She accompanied him to the door.

Jed closed the door behind him and walked toward the school, trying to appear calm and carefree. He wondered if she was as curious about him as he was about her. And what was that book that was open on the piano, before she picked that classical number? He had been too far away to read the words, but the title of the song seemed like something he'd sung in church. He wondered how he could find out more about her.

But it didn't matter. Jed's smile turned to a hard frown. He'd learned his lessons the hard way, and he wasn't about to have a repeat performance. From now on, he would concentrate only on his lessons, not on his teacher.

3

"I can't play this!"

"But it's in the book. The book is progressive, and you should play everything in it, in the right order, for the maximum benefit from each lesson. Try it, you may even like it."

"I'm *not* playing 'Pop Goes the Weasel.' "

"You played 'Willy the Whale.' That one was fine."

Jed sat upright and folded his arms across his chest. "This is different. I'm a grown man. Grown men do not play 'Pop Goes the Weasel.' "

Jillian mumbled to herself, "And real men don't eat quiche." Up until now, Jed had progressed quickly with his lessons. An eager student, he had been more than prepared each lesson, even doing two lessons a week to hurry through the easy stuff at the beginning stages. In only a month and a half, they were nearly done with the first level.

"What did you say?" he asked.

"Nothing." She stopped to think for a minute. "If you play 'Pop Goes the Weasel' without making any mistakes after only one lesson, I'll promise not to tell anyone."

He balked. "Not good enough."

"Well, then I'll give you some homework on it. After you play the first part of the song, I want you to figure out the rest of it that isn't written in the book, and play the entire song for me next week. It's called 'playing by ear' and it's good for you."

"My mother is the only one that can tell me what's good for me," he groused.

"Jed." Jillian tapped her foot, but it had nothing to do with the beat of the music.

He grumbled under his breath again. "Mark was right. You are a slave driver."

Jillian narrowed her eyes to glare at him, but he returned her scowl with his dazzling white smile. She didn't smile back. He could turn on all the charm he wanted to, he wasn't going to *weasel* out of this one. And Jed really did know how to turn on the charm. Trouble was, she didn't think he was aware of it. Aside from a few jokes and some very short conversations, he kept personal details of his life as private as she did. She didn't know why, but it made her all the more curious about him, even though she kept telling herself she didn't want to know.

She tried to keep her mind on the lesson, where it belonged. "Tell you what. I'll play it first. I'm an adult, and I have no qualms about it. Listen."

Instead of merely leaning over to plunk out the beginner version from the book, Jillian rose from her chair, sat beside him on the piano bench, and played an embellished version of "Pop Goes the Weasel," exaggerating her demonstration with a rousing flourish of chord aggrandizement and brilliant accompaniment. Quite satisfied with her performance, Jillian folded her hands in her lap and turned to smile sweetly at him, hoping this would inspire him to greater things. His stupefied expression caused her to bite her lip to keep from laughing.

"You amaze me. Will I be able to do that someday?"

"I'm going to say the same thing I've said before. If you practice and work hard, then there is no reason why not. You just have to go through the book, learning each lesson step by step."

"Okay, you win. I'll play 'Pop Goes the Weasel.' But you still won't make me like it."

Jillian smiled back at him again. His beautiful smile always made her weaken. And the way his gorgeous blue eyes crinkled at the corners would send any woman's heart aflutter. Her eyes widened then narrowed at the direction of her thoughts, thoughts she refused to have ever again. "That's it," she said sternly.

He said the same thing at the end of every lesson. She followed every syllable in her thoughts as he spoke, almost mouthing his words. "Yup, time for me to go get Betsy."

As usual, she watched him walk down the street toward the school until he rounded the corner. Soon the selections in the book would become more difficult, and Jed would reach the point where each lesson would require enough work to keep him busy for a week. Trouble was, Jillian couldn't decide if that was good or bad.

⤫

Busy making supper, Jed didn't notice Liz and Frank come in the door until he heard Liz's voice behind him, causing him to drop the spoon into the pot he was stirring.

"Hi, Jed." Liz peeked into one of the other pots as he tried to fish the spoon out with another one.

"Oh. Hi, Liz. Frank. How's work?"

Frank, as usual, said nothing. He disappeared into the living room to read the paper. Liz looked like she was sagging.

"I'm exhausted," she moaned. "I'm just glad it's Friday. You look quite perky, though. And what was that tune you were humming? Sounded like 'Pop Goes the Weasel.' "

⤫

Jillian was gobbling down her lunch in the fifteen minutes she allotted on Saturday between morning and afternoon sessions, when the phone rang.

"Hello?" She answered the phone between bites, trying not to sound impatient. If she didn't finish her lunch before the next student arrived, she would go hungry. This job did not allow for coffee breaks. A trip to the bathroom proved equally difficult. But she couldn't let the answering machine get the phone, in case it was a student canceling his lesson.

Jed's cheerful voice rang out on the other end of the phone. "Hi, Jillian."

Jillian almost choked on the last bite of her sandwich. What was he doing calling on Saturday? After the scene he made yesterday, she hoped he wasn't phoning to complain about "Pop Goes the Weasel." "Yes, Jed, what can I do for you?"

"I know you're trying to rush down your lunch, so I won't keep you. I was wondering if you'd like to join me for dinner tonight after your lessons for the day are over."

Dinner? Like a date? The thought of Jed asking her out hadn't crossed her mind as a possibility. "I'm really in a hurry before my next student gets here, so I don't have time to talk about it, but my answer is no. I don't date my students."

Jed paused only briefly. "I'm not asking for a date. I'm just asking if you would like to join me for dinner. I'm bored and lonely, and I was hoping you'd feel sorry for me."

Jillian checked her watch, counting the seconds. Her next student was due to arrive any moment. "No, Jed, I don't think so." She estimated she had one minute to gulp down her milk and run to the bathroom.

"Aw, come on. I'm all alone and I don't even know where to go in this town."

Jillian heard the sound of a car stopping and cutting the engine. "I don't think it's a good idea." The car door slammed. Then another.

"Aw, come on. Please? I promise to behave."

The doorbell rang. Jillian glanced toward the door and shuffled her feet. "Oh, all right. I'll be finished at six o'clock. And I'll need a few minutes to get ready."

"Sounds great. I won't keep you. Bye." A click sounded as he hung up.

"Bye," Jillian answered to dead-air space, mentally kicking herself as she replaced the receiver. She wondered if he questioned her excuse about not dating her students. Would he know the oldest of her students, except for himself, was only fifteen and female?

She literally ran to answer the door for her first student of the afternoon, but found it difficult to concentrate on the lesson. If it wasn't a date, then what was it when a man invited a woman out to dinner on Saturday night? And the next time she considered a date, she

would be sure she knew the man and he came with full recommenda-
tions from at least ten reliable sources. She knew nothing about Jed
and practically nothing about his family, other than one of her other
students was his nephew, and they paid on time. At the sound of a
horrible discord, she focused her full attention on her student, where
it should have been in the first place.

Jed arrived on time at 6:00. However, her lessons were running a
bit late, so Jed sat waiting in the hallway in the chair reserved for incoming students. Even though he remained quiet, she could see him
out of the corner of her eye, and she found him distracting. Like a
typical man, Jed sat with his long legs stretched out in front of him
and slightly apart as he leaned back in the seat with his hands casually
clasped behind his head, the picture of lazy contentment. How could
a man with such masculine appeal be so . . . nice?

Jillian tried her best to concentrate on the broken and uneven performance of her student. "I think that needs a bit more practice, Deborah, but you've come a long way in one week. What do you think?"

"Yes," Deborah replied. "I've been working on the hard parts, but
I should have it better for next week."

"Next week, then. Our time is up. Keep up the good work."

"Thank you, Miss Jefferson, I will."

With that, Jillian closed the book and the girl picked it up, prepared to leave. Jed straightened in the chair but did not stand as Jillian
saw her student to the door. When the door closed, they stared at
each other, neither of them speaking. Jillian's mouth refused to move
as a million thoughts raced through her mind. If the only reason she
had agreed to accompany him to dinner was because he had badgered
her into it, why did she look forward to the evening so much? The
thought scared her.

Jed stood. "Are you hungry? I have no idea where to go in this
city, so it's up to you to pick someplace good."

Jillian composed her thoughts. "Sure. I just have to freshen up
and I'll be right back."

She walked stiffly to the bathroom, trying to hold herself properly,
in case he was watching her. After a few composing breaths, she
checked her reflection in the mirror. She wore no makeup and her

hair was a mess. Although her hair was naturally wavy, she would have liked to run a curling iron through it, but she didn't have time with Jed waiting. Then she wondered why it mattered. Jed was a student, nothing more. She brushed her hair to fluff it up and hastily applied a little lipstick.

Trying to quell her jitters, she rummaged through her box of earrings, but ended up simply wearing the ones she already had on. This wasn't a date. She was Jed's teacher, and it was only dinner, and she had no intention of trying to impress him. She stood back to give herself one final check in the mirror.

Jed wiped his sweaty palms on his pants, although he didn't know why he was nervous. As it was, he still didn't know why he'd asked her in the first place. He wasn't sure he could trust his own judgment anymore, but after nearly two months of piano lessons and pumping Mark with questions, he'd decided to take a chance that Jillian was safe.

He made his decision based on the fact that even though they enjoyed each other's company during lesson time, she'd made herself perfectly clear on many occasions that she had no interest in him other than as a student, which was fine with him. Jed tried to convince himself that was exactly what he wanted, although the thought stung, just a little.

And to top it off, now Liz was mad at him because they'd hardly spent any time alone together since he got here. If she found out he was taking the piano teacher out tonight instead of her, she'd hit the roof. The guys from work had invited him out for a couple of beers, too. And here he was, standing in Jillian's front hall, shuffling his feet like a kid on his first date.

Jillian stepped out into the hall and sucked in a deep breath. "I guess I'm as ready as I'll ever be." She still wondered about the wisdom of seeing Jed outside of lessons, but his teasing sense of humor made her laugh like no one else, and against her better judgment, she looked forward to an evening with him.

Unlike Graham, Jed never tried to impress her, or made promises he had no intention of keeping. And why was she comparing Jed to Graham? Jillian clenched her teeth. She had no intention of dating Jed. Ever.

Jed removed his jacket from the coatrack and slung it over his shoulder. "Let's go."

Jillian slipped her feet into the nearest pair of shoes, speaking without raising her head. "I'm not so sure this is a good idea, Jed," she mumbled. The last time she let her guard down she had met with disastrous results, and she refused to let that happen again. She enjoyed Jed's company too much to risk crossing that line.

She sensed a lack of movement from Jed as he stood with his hand on the doorknob. "It's just dinner. Relax, Jillian. We can discuss the intricacies of 'Pop Goes the Weasel' if you want, but I'd prefer we didn't."

Discussing "Pop Goes the Weasel" was the furthest thing from her mind, but she would if she had to. A knot formed in her gut, and she wondered exactly what they would discuss; her suspicion that this really wasn't a good idea solidified into certainty. What did she know about him, except that he could carry on with amiable chitchat, and that he really was serious about learning to play the piano, at least so far? However, it was too late to back out now, so she would make the best of the evening. She would have dinner with Jed, and from that point on, she would only see him during lessons.

Jillian sighed in relief at her sensible conclusion. "Shall we go?"

After she locked the door, she followed Jed to a huge, snappy four-wheel-drive truck parked in front of her house. She realized that since he walked to every lesson, she hadn't known what kind of car he drove, or if he even owned one. Now she knew.

She grasped the door frame and hoisted herself way up into it, swishing her long flowing skirt underneath her as she scrambled onto the seat. "Nice truck," she commented, fishing for something to open a safe topic of conversation. Personally, she preferred her economy compact car, which was much closer to the ground. Why did men pick vehicles you needed a ladder to get into?

Jed watched Jillian struggle to climb into the passenger seat. He could tell she wasn't impressed with his truck, but after all that had happened recently, it was the only material goods he had to his name besides a few pieces of furniture. He wasn't even sure she was very impressed with him, either.

He walked around to the driver's side. She couldn't have made her intentions any more clear, and it hurt. But wasn't that what he wanted? To stay clear of any close personal involvement? He was going to need a whole year of careful managing to recover from what Brenda had done to him, and he didn't want to go through that again, emotionally or financially. Nothing was going to stop him from fulfilling his dream this time. Nothing. Including and especially Jillian Jefferson.

4

$\mathcal{T}$he roar of the engine startled Jillian as Jed turned the key to start the large truck. He stepped on the clutch, threw the stick shift into gear, and turned to her. "So, where should we go?"

She directed him through the city as Jed good-naturedly complained about the traffic, as if he had to worry driving his huge monstrosity of a truck. One of the few things she knew about him was that he had previously lived in a small town in northern British Columbia, and she wondered if it even had rush hour traffic.

As she expected, a line awaited them when they arrived at the restaurant. Jed added their names to the waiting list, and Jillian wondered what to do to kill time until it came their turn for a table.

She had enjoyed his lighthearted banter in the truck, even his teasing about her height and her difficulty climbing into the high cab. Jillian struggled to think of a way to get back at him.

As a popular piano tune came on the background music, an idea came to her. "So, seen any weasels lately?" she asked, humming his favorite song, just to get his goat.

He quirked one eyebrow in response. "Yeah, but I chased it around a bush in the backyard for fun, then I popped him. He's gone now."

The hostess chose that moment to call their names, preventing Jillian from making a reply.

As they were seated, another waiter delivered a colorful castle-shaped kids-meal box to the family at the next table. The child delved into it, going for the ice cream first before the mother removed the container from his tiny fingers and placed it in the center of the table.

The child complained at the same time as he started to shovel the fries into his mouth.

Jed sighed as he watched. "Mark and Betsy would love it here," he said.

"I've been wondering why you're doing that."

"Doing what?"

"Baby-sitting." Jillian studied Jed as he sat across from her. Tall, good-looking, intelligent, and single. And he had a job, so he wasn't desperate for money. While she was curious, lesson time was not the time for such a personal question. Even though it was probably none of her business, she'd wondered from the first time she met him why he was baby-sitting.

"Well, they're not exactly babies. Mark is in grade three, and Betsy is in kindergarten. They're just not old enough to be left alone. It's not bad, although I must admit sometimes they do drive me a little nuts. That's why I decided to take piano lessons." He grinned and winked. Jillian nearly choked on her water.

"So you decided to take piano lessons to help keep you sane." Now she had an answer to that question, which only led her to wonder about other things. "You still haven't explained why you're doing baby-sitting."

"It's not really a very exciting story." He shrugged his shoulders. "When the mill where I worked shut down, I sold my condo and managed to find a job here in town. At the same time, my sister's sitter quit. Seems she thinks it's cheaper to have me live there than pay for day care. She asked me if I would baby-sit in exchange for room and board until next September. They feed me, except I have to start supper on weekdays. So here I am. End of story."

"Why September? That's nearly a year away. What's happening in September?"

Jed's back stiffened. "I've registered for college, and I'm going to finish up my degree in education."

"Education? I thought you had a job." Jillian had no teaching degrees. Of course she had her bachelor's degree in music, but she'd never taken any teaching courses.

"I plan to be a high school teacher. I'm going to teach English."

Jillian imagined a string of giddy teenage girls hanging around Jed after class. The boys would probably suffer from slight cases of hero-delusions as well. As it was, Mark worshipped the ground Jed walked on. She heard a little more about Jed every Tuesday during Mark's lesson. She would have liked Jed even if she had never met him. According to Mark, not only could he cook, but he wasn't afraid of housework. She imagined women waiting in line for him.

Her lips tightened as she stopped her mind from wandering. She would not be waiting in line, picking a number.

"So, what do you do besides piano lessons, your night job, and baby-sitting?"

"Not much. I don't get out much." Jed paused and started to play with his silverware. "I hope there isn't something or someone I'm keeping you from tonight."

Jillian would have laughed, except it wasn't funny. Aside from piano lessons, her calendar was bare. If he was referring to the possibility of a boyfriend, he couldn't be more wrong. The men who asked her for a date only wanted one thing, and when she didn't give in, they were no longer interested in her. She had simply stopped opening herself up to more disappointments, and she was happy that way.

She sighed, then caught her breath, hoping Jed hadn't noticed. At first, she had thought Graham was different, but in the end, the wounds he inflicted were worse than all of them combined. "No, the opposite, I'm afraid to admit. Since I decided to teach piano lessons for a living, most of my evenings are taken up, and by the time Saturday night rolls around, I'm usually too tired to go out."

The waiter arrived with their orders, halting their conversation for the moment. At first she was hesitant, but she made a quick decision to bow her head for a few seconds of silent prayer before she ate. The same split second her eyes closed, Jed's hand touched her wrist. Her eyes shot open.

"Jillian? Are you doing what I think you're doing?"

Her head lowered again. "I just paused for a moment of thanks," she mumbled.

"Can we pray together?"

Her heart caught in her throat. She knew Mark's family attended church, but she didn't know if Jed also participated in church life, nor did she know the depth of his commitment, or if it included praying in a public restaurant. Not only that, she wasn't sure she was ready to pray with him, because praying with someone encouraged a closeness she didn't want to share with Jed. But she couldn't refuse without looking churlish. She gulped and nodded.

Jed bowed his head. "Thank You, Heavenly Father, for this time of fellowship, this good meal, and the abundance You provide for us. Amen."

All she could do was raise her head, blink, and stare.

His ears reddened as he reached for his fork. "Hey, with two hungry little kids waiting to eat, we don't do long prayers. Don't you hate when you go out after church, and by the time the prayer is finished, your lunch is cold?"

"I guess."

Jed caught her off guard with his wide smile, starting to eat and continuing on as if there had been no interruption. "So, if you don't get out much, how would you like to have lunch together sometime during the week? I drop Betsy off at 12:30 every day, and don't have to pick her up until 3:00. Or maybe we could do something else, although to tell the truth, I still haven't figured out what there is to do in the afternoon. I usually do my share of the housework, and practice my piano lessons like a good boy." He finished off his statement with an exaggerated wink.

Jillian turned her head down and mumbled into her plate. "There's not too much to do during the day." All she did during the day was housework, shopping when necessary, and occasional visits with her sister.

Jed grinned back at her, his bright blue eyes flashing. "Well, maybe we could play tennis, or go for a walk or something. I don't know. I'm open to suggestions."

She almost said no, but the more she thought about it, the less appeal lonely afternoons held compared to spending the time with Jed. Since teaching piano lessons involved sitting for hours, the possibility of a little exercise sounded better and better. Tennis seemed a little extreme, especially since it was nearly Christmas, but she was open to suggestions. "A walk sounds nice. Sometimes I go out to walk around the mall, just to get out and moving around."

"If you like to walk, we're about finished here. Want to go for a walk now?"

Jillian checked her watch. "Now? It's dark out."

Jed smiled that dazzling white smile she was growing so fond of. "It seems like a nice neighborhood, and it's not raining. Unlike you people who were born and raised in the Vancouver area, I'm used to icy cold and being up to my armpits in snow this time of year. And don't worry about it being dark; I don't think anyone will bother us. Don't forget, you'll have Little Jed to keep you safe. And if you don't think I can protect you, we can borrow my sister's dog."

The comment about "Little Jed" made her smile. The casualness of his attitude completely disarmed her, so she pretended to consider it. "Hmm . . ." She tapped her index finger to her chin. "Maybe. What kind of dog?"

Jed covered his heart with his palm and pretended to look hurt, making Jillian wonder if he'd ever taken acting lessons. "You'd pick the dog for protection over me?"

"Depends. Is it a Doberman?"

"It's a mutt. A Heinz 57, mixed-heritage mongrel. An ordinary, hairy brown dog."

His ridiculous hangdog expression made her snicker. "You win. Let's go for a walk. Without the dog."

Jed paid the bill, and they left. Jillian gazed out the window the entire drive back to her house. Stars shone overhead in the clear sky. The air was nippy, but it was still above freezing. She supposed she was spoiled, never having lived anywhere else. There had been some snow last winter, but it barely covered the ground and was gone within a day. And unlike most people, she had the luxury of not having to worry about driving to work in it, and Jillian liked it that way.

Jed locked his door, pocketed the keys, and ran around to Jillian's side. "Ready?"

Still seated in the truck, she looked both ways down the block. "Where do you want to go?" she asked. Not that it really mattered.

He raised his hands in the air, then flopped them down to his sides. "Anywhere but to the school."

Jillian couldn't help but giggle as Jed held out his hand to help her out. Against her better judgment, his playful expression made her take his hand. "Then I guess we go that way." She pointed.

He didn't let go of her as they started to walk, and rather than protest over something so silly, she allowed him to hold her hand as they walked slowly and wordlessly down the street. They walked in silence, the only sounds being the clicking of her heels on the cement and the drone of the odd car in the distance.

When they approached a playground, Jed stopped. "Want to go for a swing?" He held out one arm in the direction of a large metal swing set.

Jillian checked from side to side, then up at him. "Us? Now?"

"Yeah, sure. Why not?"

Jillian studied the swings. She hadn't been on a swing in years, and at this hour, no one would see them. She could almost feel the brush of air on her face and the rush of weightlessness.

She nearly gave in to temptation, but good sense overruled. "I don't think so. I can't go on a swing in a skirt." However, Jillian's gaze remained glued to the vacant swings.

"Just wrap your skirt underneath you, and you'll be fine. I'll bet you haven't been on a swing in years." Jed smiled down at her, and she looked up, her gaze fixed on his eyes. He squeezed her hand, then released the pressure. "Come on, it'll be fun. I'll push you. . . ." His voice trailed off as his smile widened.

Jillian's heart fluttered in her chest. He was right: it had been years since she'd been on a swing. As a girl, she'd enjoyed many solitary hours swinging. She hesitated. If she gave in, no one would see. Forgetting the dignified image she tried so hard to uphold, she dropped his hand and ran to the swing.

Tucking her skirt underneath her as much as she could, she wiggled her bottom into the rubber seat. "All set!" Jillian held the chain tightly and tilted her head backward, unable to wipe the smile off her face as Jed grasped the chain and pulled her back.

"Ready?"

"Ready!" Jillian held her breath as he pulled her further back and held her suspended for a few moments.

"Go!" With Jed's firm but gentle push, Jillian dipped down, then swung up, exhilarated by the feeling of weightlessness before she drifted down and back again with the swing.

Jillian wiggled her feet as Jed continued to push her while she swung gaily back and forth. Stopping at the swings had turned out to be a great idea, something she never would have considered doing. She closed her eyes as she neared the top, then opened them and tilted her head back as she started to descend, floating backward to have Jed push her higher.

Feeling as free as a child, suspended for that brief moment in time before she drifted backward and down again, Jillian sucked in a deep breath of the cool air and kicked her feet. One shoe went flying off. "Oh no! Stop! Jed! My shoe!"

As she floated back, Jed's hands grasped her by the hips, lowering her to a halt. Thankfully, he couldn't see her blush in the darkness. With any luck, he would stay behind her while she looked for her errant shoe.

She leaned forward to hop off, but Jed didn't let her go. "Don't step in the sand in your stockings. I'll find it. What color is it?"

Jillian held out the foot with the shoe still on it. "Well, this one is blue, so the one that fell must be the same. I realize that there must be lots of shoes out there, so knowing the color is dreadfully important."

Jed stood in front of her and gave her a comical dirty look but said nothing.

"Really, Jed," she chided him. "Ask a stupid question, you get a stupid answer."

"It wasn't a stupid question. If I was looking for a tan shoe the same color as the sand it would be impossible to find in the dark. If I was looking for a black shoe, it would be easy to find, and if I was looking for a white shoe, it would only be marginally difficult."

"Jed, it's December."

"What? So?"

"You can't wear white shoes past Labor Day."

"Oh? Excuse me. Who wrote that rule?"

"It's been in effect since the beginning of time."

Jed mumbled something under his breath as he continued to look for the missing shoe in the dark. "Found it," he called, shaking the sand out of it as he walked toward her. Instead of handing it to her, he bent down on one knee, picked up her foot, rubbed his thumb in a massaging motion along her instep, then slid the shoe onto her foot. He grinned up at her and then bowed. "Cinderella," he said with a grin and a slight nod.

Jillian gulped. She wanted to say *Prince Charming* but couldn't speak the words. He'd turned what would have been a dull evening into a fairy-tale night, bringing back a childhood simplicity she had long forgotten.

Jed stood and backed up a step. "Don't kick your feet this time, okay? Don't think I didn't notice you kicking your feet."

He walked behind her again to pull her back with another gentle push, starting her off again. After a few more pushes, Jillian drifted back and forth at a comfortable height, restraining herself from kicking her feet.

A movement caught her attention. Jed whooshed past, riding the swing beside her, gaining more height with every repetition, until he was slightly higher than she was.

"Watch this!" he called out. As the swing reached the highest point, Jed jumped. "Bonzai!" he yelled, flying through the air with his hands and legs spread-eagle. He landed on his feet, continuing the momentum with a single somersault, and then stopped, standing with his hands raised high in the air. He turned around and bowed dramatically, grinning from ear to ear. "I knew I could still do it!"

Jillian feared her heart would pound through her chest. She clutched the chain with a death grip, forcing herself to gulp for air. When Jed went flying into the air like a reckless kid, all she could see was the image of him breaking his neck while she was helpless to do anything about it. And he had the nerve to be proud of himself.

She cleared her throat to find her voice. "Are you crazy?" she squeaked out. "You could have killed yourself doing a stupid stunt like that!"

"Hey, I knew what I was doing!" The silly grin remained while he shrugged his shoulders. "I've done this a million times!"

Jillian continued to drift back and forth on the swing, not sure she could find the strength in her legs to drag herself to a stop. "And how old were you?"

He stood before her and laughed. "I don't know. Fourteen?"

Jillian didn't feel the least little bit like laughing. She felt like wringing his fool neck, the same neck he could just as easily have broken. "And you obviously haven't grown up since then."

"Hey! I wouldn't have even thought of doing that in front of the kids." He shrugged his shoulders, then rammed his hands into his pockets. "Bad example and all that stuff. Besides, you're just jealous. I'll bet it's something you've been dying to do and are too afraid to try."

"I am not!"

"Chicken." He had the nerve to cluck.

"I'm not chicken."

"Prove it."

"Don't dare me, mister."

"Me? I would never dare you to do anything."

Jillian said nothing. His attitude alone was a dare. It was dark. No one would ever know.

"I'll catch you." Jed planted his legs firmly apart and held out his arms, waiting in an open invitation.

"If you drop me, I'll never forgive you."

"I found your shoe, didn't I?"

Jillian wondered what that had to do with anything as she pumped herself up higher.

"Here I come!" And with that, Jillian slid to the edge of the seat, stuffed her skirt between her knees, and pushed herself off. "Bonzai!" she called out. Time stretched in the exhilarating rush of being suspended in midair, and down she went.

True to his word, Jed caught her with no difficulty. Solid as a rock, he stood firmly rooted to one spot, catching her with ease. Slowly and gently, he lowered her to the ground, gripping her firmly around the waist. Jillian's breath caught in her throat at the contact. He smiled down at her as her feet touched ground, and Jillian tried to convince herself that the increase in her breathing was from the excitement of the leap, not the landing.

Grateful that the darkness would hide the color she knew rose in her cheeks, she bent to smooth any crinkles from her skirt. "Well," she mumbled, "both shoes are still on my feet."

Jed apparently didn't notice her discomfort. "Want to try bungee jumping next? I hear it's fun."

Jillian patted her hair down. "I don't think so, Jed. This little dare-devil adventure should keep me satisfied for the next ten or so years. And we should go. If we make any more noise, someone is going to call the cops. We both live in this neighborhood." She lowered her voice. "Besides, I have to get up early for church in the morning."

Jed sighed. "Yeah," he mumbled. "Me too."

Careful to avoid his hand, Jillian walked beside Jed in silence the whole way back to her house. She would have to reconsider future dealings with Jed. As a student, she could ignore him, but as a Christian, she didn't know which way to turn. Her head told her that she would be safe to trust him, but her heart told her that her higher expectations would only lead to bigger disappointments.

She unlocked her front door and pocketed her keys. As she pushed the door open, Jed's soft voice murmured into her ear. "Can I see you again tomorrow?"

"I don't think so, Jed." Part of her wanted to tell him to wait until his next lesson, but part of her didn't want to wait that long.

"Lunch Monday?"

Jillian opened her mouth to protest, but the wrong words came out. "Sure. Lunch Monday sounds fine."

She waited for Jed to politely say good night, but instead, he lifted her hand to his lips and kissed it.

"Good night, Jillian, see you Monday. And think about bungee jumping; you're a natural."

Before she could properly unscramble her thoughts, he turned, strode to his truck, and drove off.

Jillian stood on her doorstep, staring at the huge truck until it rounded the corner. What had happened? The prim and proper piano teacher had just jumped screaming from a swing into a man's arms at midnight—and enjoyed it. Her heart still pounded from his small kiss to her hand! Was he doing this on purpose?

She shook her head, reminding herself of what was bound to happen if she let things continue. Next lesson she would make it clear that they would not see each other except for lesson time.

Next lesson, she would talk to him. Unfortunately that would be after the lunch date she had already promised him.

5

*O*nly the living room lamp was on, and that was on the lowest setting. Jed sucked in a deep breath as he gently inserted the key in the lock and turned it, praying the rumble of his truck hadn't woken the dog. And if that hadn't, surely the key would. He gritted his teeth as Missy scratched the door, but fortunately the dog didn't bark. She had taken a month before she stopped barking at him when he arrived home from work at 2:00 in the morning, and now instead, she jumped on him and showered him with wet dog kisses. Jed didn't know which was worse.

He shucked off his cowboy boots and pushed them into the row of shoes beside the door with his foot. As strange as it had been at the beginning, he kind of liked the feeling of not living alone. He'd had his own condominium for almost four years, but living alone, it had never felt like home.

He patted the dog to quiet her whining and tiptoed downstairs to the den, which was now his bedroom. Between the double bed, dresser, stereo, and his large television, he could barely move, but it was home.

Once he tucked himself in bed, he couldn't sleep, even though he was tired. The evening had not progressed like he'd expected. He might have had a few ideas of his own before he arrived at Jillian's house, but if God had other plans, it wouldn't be the first time. The way things had turned out threw him for a loop.

Jed lay on his back in the dark, staring at the ceiling. What had come over him to act like that? Normally, he was a pretty responsible, respectable kind of guy. Whatever had possessed him to jump off the swing? He was a little too old to be showing off, but young enough to get carried away.

He covered his eyes with his forearm. Why had he kissed her hand like that? He could tell by her reaction that he'd surprised her, but he'd surprised himself even more: He'd been on the swings in the park at midnight with Jillian Jefferson, the piano teacher.

Jillian. He sighed and rolled over onto his stomach. What should he do? During lesson time, Jillian always remained quiet and reserved, but this evening proved what he had suspected all along. Underneath that prim and proper teacher lay a woman full of wit and whimsy. Warm and responsive, she'd held his hand. And she was a believer.

Jillian was hard to resist, but resist he must. He'd fallen for Brenda, but in the end, she'd squandered everything he had to give her, and more. If it hadn't been for Brenda, he would already be in college, but instead, if he worked hard enough all year, he might be able to start next September. He wasn't going to let himself be in the position ever again where a woman made a fool of him. Not that Jillian would ever be so devious. She had too much dignity to do what Brenda had done.

Dignity? Was he referring to the woman who jumped off a swing at midnight? With those high heels, if he hadn't caught her properly, she could have been hurt.

He smiled at the memory of holding her before he lowered her to the ground. Fortunately, the cover of darkness had prevented her from seeing his expression. At the time, he was sure he had been wearing his heart on his sleeve, something he couldn't afford. His last experience had cost him a year off his life and a piece of his heart, and he wasn't willing to chance a repeat performance.

He would get together with Jillian to have lunch only because he had already promised, and then he wouldn't see her except for lesson time.

Jed finally fell asleep, dreaming about sharing a swing in the dark, accompanied by soft strains of gentle piano music in the background.

❦

Luckily, Jillian arrived at the coffee shop at the same time as Sue. Church had been late getting out, and she hated the thought of leaving Sue waiting. They picked a table against the window and settled in, ready to enjoy a quiet couple of hours without Sue's four children.

"Enjoying the peace and quiet?" Jillian asked her frazzled sister, already knowing the answer.

Sue rolled her eyes, then turned her attention to her donut. "I can't stay as long as usual. I have to do some shopping without the kids. I hate Christmas shopping, but I'm almost done, record early, too, if I can find what I want. Are you going to walk around the mall with me after we finish our coffee?"

Jillian groaned. "I went for a walk yesterday, and like a fool, I was in my high heels. My feet are killing me!"

Sue licked the whipped cream off the top of her donut, closing her eyes for a second to savor it. When she opened her eyes again, she stared unwavering, straight into Jillian's face. "What's his name?"

Jillian nearly choked on her coffee. "Whose name?"

"The tall man you went out with yesterday." Sue sucked a dribble of chocolate icing off the tip of one finger.

Jillian's cheeks reddened. "Did you have spies out after me or something?"

"You're so transparent, Jillian; you always have been. I could tell from your face that it was a man, and when you admitted you wore high heels, I knew he was tall or else you would have worn something more practical. Then when you said your feet were sore, I knew it was a long walk, so I know it has to be serious. I didn't get my Big Sister Certificate for nothing."

They both smiled, remembering the gag gift Jillian gave to Sue on Mother's Day—a certificate for excellency in the role of big sister. When their parents divorced, their mother remarried, but her new husband didn't want children from a previous marriage around, so they lived with their father, who really hadn't wanted to be bothered with children either. Seven years older, Sue had been as much a mother to Jillian as a sister, and now they were inseparable.

Jillian swirled the last bit of coffee around in the bottom of her cup, studying it as it swished. "He's actually one of my students, Mark

Edwards' uncle. And yes, he's tall. We went for a walk last night, that's all." She purposely missed telling Sue about holding Jed's hand, or about how she jumped off the swing into his arms. And she didn't want to make too much out of Jed's kissing her hand. Just thinking about it, though, gave her goose bumps.

Sue licked her fingers again after finishing the last bite of her donut. "You're avoiding telling me about him. Now I know it's serious. And you really should have had one of those donuts. They're fabulous. Now are you going to come with me or not?"

"I don't know how you stay so skinny, eating all that junk. You make me jealous, you know. And yes, of course I'm going with you around the mall. You shouldn't even have to ask, if I'm so transparent. Besides," Jillian winked, "I need more stickers for my students."

Sue sighed. "Always the dedicated teacher. On your only day off, yet."

"I can't help it. How many people could say they love their job as much as I do? And working from my home, too."

Sue snorted as she reached under the table for her purse. "Let's go. If we find what I need quickly, we can come back for another donut."

Even though it usually meant shopping, Jillian always enjoyed her sister's company. However, on Sunday, Jillian would have preferred seeing her sister and her family in church. Although Sue respected Jillian's beliefs, she didn't see a need for God in her own life, and she refused to discuss it. Graham had claimed to be a Christian, which hadn't helped Jillian's efforts to share her faith with Sue. In fact, it was something else in her life that Graham had destroyed.

Jillian's only consolation was to occasionally take Sue's kids to Sunday school with her, hoping some of it would rub off on her sister, except deep down she knew Sue only agreed in order to get some time alone with her husband.

Of course, Jillian continued to pray for Sue and her family daily, praying from the depths of her soul that Sue could find the same peace that God had given her.

They walked and walked until Sue found all the items she needed, and Jillian collected enough reward stickers to replenish her stockpile.

True to her word, Sue made sure they finished their excursion back at the coffee shop where she purchased another donut. Jillian meant only to have another coffee, but caved in and ordered a donut as well.

"So, when are you going out on another date?"

"It wasn't a date, Sue. It was just a walk."

Sue rolled her eyes again. "Yeah, sure."

Jillian's face paled at Sue's use of Jed's favorite expression. She tried to act calm and pass it off. "I'm not dating him. He's just a student. Nothing more."

"I'm not dating him," Sue playfully mocked, then stuffed another piece of donut into her mouth. "I used that same line when I was dating Geoff, and I married him in the end. But suit yourself. I don't know who you think you're fooling."

Sue knew her too well, but this time Sue was wrong.

"He feels the same way. We're only going to see each other at lesson time." She dropped her voice to a whisper. "And lunch tomorrow," she mumbled.

Sue laughed as she gulped down the last of her coffee and checked her watch. "I gotta run. See you next week. Have a nice lunch date."

❧

The flashing message light greeted Jillian upon her return home from the mall. Jed's cheery voice inquired whether she would be interested in joining him for a burger if she got home in time for supper.

This would be a good opportunity to tell Jed that she didn't want to see him except for lessons. She looked up the number and called him. Mark answered the phone.

"Can I speak to your uncle Jed, please?"

She heard muffled scraping as Mark put one hand over the phone, but his scream still pierced her eardrums. "Uncle Jed, it's for you! It's Miss Jefferson! Uncle Jed! Miss Jefferson wants to talk to you!"

Jillian winced. Now the entire household knew who was calling for Jed. She heard a muffled click as Jed picked up the extension phone.

Jillian's eardrums nearly burst again when Jed yelled. "I've got it! You can hang up now, Mark!" Through the ringing in her ears, another click sounded. Jed's smooth and cheery voice came on in a lower volume. "Hi! I see you got my message."

After the big production with the entire household, Jillian didn't want to tell him her decision over the phone. She would tell him away from prying eyes and curious ears. Her stomach rumbled, one donut and two cups of strong coffee being a poor substitution for a decent lunch. Jed's original offer began to gather appeal. "Yes, is it too late to take you up on that burger?"

"Not at all. We haven't eaten yet. Have you?"

"No."

"And how do you feel about catching a movie after? We'll still have time."

"Catch a movie?" She paused to think. She had already committed herself to the burger. She tried to stall to give herself time to think. "Depends on how fast it's going, I suppose."

Jed's soft chuckle made her heart flutter. "I'll be over as quick as I can then, so it won't get away. See you in a few minutes. Bye."

Even though he chided himself for being slightly rude by hanging up so fast, Jed patted himself on the back for ending the conversation before Jillian had the chance to change her mind. The second he hung up the phone, Jed dashed into the bathroom. He rubbed his chin and shaved for the second time that day, not that she would get close enough to notice. He applied a little gel to his unruly hair, and decided he needed a haircut. Tomorrow.

He stepped back to look at himself, running his hand over the faded picture on his T-shirt. Not classy. He ran back to his bedroom and selected a crisp cotton shirt, which might have been a little on the dressy side for a burger and a show, but it felt nice and looked good with his new jeans. Making one last check to make sure the kids hadn't smeared anything on them, he tucked in his shirt and vaulted down the stairs, straight for the family room.

Liz and Frank's heads turned in unison away from the television as he rummaged through the pile of newspapers, searching for the movie section of Saturday's paper.

"I won't be home for dinner," he mumbled as he pulled the paper out of the pile.

"Well, you sure look nice, Jed. Where are you going?" Liz asked.

"Oh," he mumbled, trying to avoid the issue. "Nowhere special, just out for a burger with Jillian. When was the last time you took some papers out to the recycling bin?"

"Jillian? Jillian who?" Liz's voice trailed off. She blinked, then sat straight up on the couch. "Do you mean Miss Jefferson, the piano teacher? Is that why she called you? To ask you out for a burger?"

"Uh, yeah, something like that."

Jed pulled the movie page out of the middle of the paper. "Got it. Don't wait up for me. Bye." He ran out, leaving his sister with her mouth hanging open and one finger in the air.

❧

Jillian rummaged through her closet, frantically searching for the right thing to wear. She wanted something attractive but not too fancy, yet comfortable enough to sit in at the theater. Since Jed said he'd be right over, she didn't have a second to waste.

On an impulse, she picked a baggy pink sweater and a snug short denim skirt, yanked them on, then ran into the bathroom to touch up her makeup and comb out her hair. She stepped back to study herself in the mirror. A little spritz of perfume, and she'd be ready.

The second she sprayed the perfume, she regretted it. Why was she in such a tizzy to get ready? After dinner, she planned to tell Jed that she didn't want to see him except for lesson time.

Jillian stared at her reflection in the mirror. The last time she got all in a fluff about getting ready for a man was for Graham, and in the end he was more concerned with the outward package than the person within. In going through all this effort to look her best, she was perpetuating the trend. With that thought in mind, Jillian had filled the sink to wash off the makeup when the doorbell rang.

Jed stood at the door, waiting, his heart pounding. What was he doing? Yesterday he'd given himself a good speech about not getting involved in a relationship, but he'd lain awake half the night thinking of Jillian. He tried to convince himself he only had one reason for asking her to dinner, and that was to avoid getting out of the house alone.

Jillian opened the door, and Jed thought he'd been hit in the chest with a sledgehammer.

"Hi, Jed. That was quick. I barely had enough time to get ready."

His mouth opened, then closed before he said something to make himself look like a drooling idiot. Between the dark but subtle makeup accents on her eyes and the muted-colored lipstick, she had transformed from moderately beautiful to drop-dead gorgeous.

He shoved his hands in his pockets. "Yeah, I see you're ready."

"Did you get a haircut?"

Jed ran his hand over his hair with a nervous laugh. "It's amazing what a little gel will do, isn't it?"

She clasped her hands in front of her in a gesture so feminine and sweet, Jed had to struggle not to reach out and touch her.

"Where are we going?" she asked. "Or do you want me to decide?"

Jed couldn't have decided if his life depended on it. The way his thoughts were running, he should have headed straight for the evening service at church. "It's your neighborhood. You pick. Or maybe we should go inside and choose a movie now, so we know how much time we have first."

"I'm afraid I didn't pick up the weekend paper. I have no idea what's playing."

Jed pulled the folded-up movie page out of his jacket pocket. "I brought it from home. I wasn't sure if you would have it or not."

"Good idea. Come on in."

He thought he could finally relax when she turned and walked into the house—but she looked just as good in back as she did in front. As he followed her past the piano and into the kitchen, he gritted his teeth and reminded himself she was his piano teacher.

They spread the movie page on the table. They didn't take long to agree on a comedy they'd both seen a preview of on television. Jed tore their selection out and stuffed it in his jacket pocket. Standing, he held out his hand to her. "Let's go. I'm starving."

"Jed, why did you call me?"

Jed couldn't stop his cheeks from heating up. He shrugged his shoulders, trying to act casual. He really didn't know why he'd called, because he had told himself he was going to avoid her. "Liver," he said lamely.

She grimaced. "Liver?"

"Yeah, Liz is making liver for supper, and I'd have to eat it and act like I liked it in front of the kids. I do a lot of things for those kids, but I refuse to do that." He placed one palm in the center of his chest and held the other in the air. "As a Christian, I'm not supposed to lie."

Jillian tried not to smile at his imitation of a boy scout. For one thing, he was twice the height of any scouts she'd ever seen, and for another thing, boy scouts didn't wink. Unable to stop the quiver at the side of her mouth, she broke out into a laugh. "Pizza?" she asked between giggles.

"Yeah, sure."

Jed held the door open for her once they reached the truck. Jillian grabbed the side of the door frame, but when she started to lift one leg to step up into the huge four-wheel-drive truck, she discovered the hard way that she had chosen the wrong skirt. She couldn't extend her legs wide enough apart to lift her foot onto the frame.

Trying to control her blush, and failing miserably, she backed up a step, glancing at Jed over her shoulder. "I can't get up. I think I should go change my skirt."

"No!" Jed exclaimed, then lowered his voice. "No," he said again, more calmly. "I'll boost you up. If you don't mind."

Not sure which would be more embarrassing, running into the house to change or having Jed help her up, Jillian nodded.

Without a word, Jed stood behind her and placed his hands on her hips, and with a little push, boosted her up enough to step into the truck. Before she knew it, Jed was already behind the wheel, the driver's door closed. "Ready?" he asked.

Jillian gulped, trying to ease the fluttering in her stomach. Stiffly, she nodded and fastened her seat belt with shaking hands. "Yes, let's go."

6

"So, how was your visit with your sister?"

Jillian dabbed the corner of her mouth with her napkin. "Very nice, thank you. I meet her at the mall every Sunday after church, and she always gets the gooiest and most fattening donut she can find because she doesn't have to share it with her kids."

"I think I can appreciate how she feels." Jed grinned.

"She's got four kids, and she needs the break."

Jed laughed. "Mark and Betsy are great kids, but some days I think if I hear one more round of 'Uncle Jed, Uncle Jed!' I'll scream."

Jillian nodded. "I know what you mean. After seeing other people's kids every day, sometimes I think I'd like to scream, too. But I wouldn't ever do anything else."

"So, does your sister go to the same church as you?"

Jillian wondered at his sudden change of subject, grateful for it at the same time. "No. She doesn't go to church at all."

Jed paused, a piece of pizza halfway to his mouth. He put it back on his plate and folded his hands on the table. "How long have you been a Christian, Jillian?"

"I guess about four years. How about you?"

"All my life."

She envied him. The routine, the stability, the bond of a family that loved God and loved each other was something she saw all the time but had never experienced. The faith his parents modeled and instilled in him as a child extended to the next generation, because she knew from Mark that his whole family attended church regularly as well.

Likewise, Jed would probably marry a nice Christian woman and have nice Christian kids. She suddenly felt jealous of the unknown woman. "Must have been nice."

He smiled, his gaze becoming unfocused for a few seconds before he made eye contact with her again. She could only imagine the fond memories he held. In order for Jed to be baby-sitting and living with his sister's family, they no doubt had grown up very close.

"Yeah," he said, still smiling, "it was."

Soon only a few stray crumbs and one lone mushroom stem remained on the round tray. Jed paid the bill and led her outside. As Jed opened the passenger door, Jillian froze, having forgotten until this exact second her problem with her entrance into his truck. She eyed the step, knowing that again she would need Jed's help. She regretted her decision not to change her skirt when she had the chance.

Jed bowed. "Milady," he said a little too courteously as his head came up. He was obviously trying to stifle a smile. Without asking if she needed assistance, his hands grasped her firmly by the hips and he boosted her up once more. The touch was innocent enough, but it sent shivers through Jillian anyway.

They arrived at the theater in plenty of time. Jillian slithered down from the seat to the ground, the trip out much easier than the trip in.

Once inside, Jed followed Jillian instead of leading the way to the back, where he preferred to sit. Being so tall and broadshouldered, he liked to be courteous to any unlucky short people who had the misfortune to get stuck sitting behind him. He said nothing, though, leaving the decision up to her.

Instead of scanning the theater, Jed watched Jillian nervously checking out the location of the empty seats, taking note of a few couples already starting to get cuddly in the back row. Her posture stiffened, she grabbed his hand, and then she led him to the back row. "I chose the back because you're so tall."

Jed pressed his lips together, but he couldn't help himself. "Was that an invitation or a warning?"

The way her eyebrows knotted and her lips tightened indicated that it was indeed a warning. He raised one hand in the air in his good-old-boy-scout routine. Not that he'd ever been a scout. "Your virtue is safe, milady."

"Don't push your luck, Jed."

He watched Jillian as she sank into her seat. She intrigued him. She fascinated him. She was intelligent and fun. To his surprise, she had encouraged him when he told her about his preparations for college next fall. Of course she had a higher education with her bachelor of music, so she knew the commitment involved, in addition to the expense of obtaining a degree.

True to his word, Jed behaved himself, enjoyed the movie, and kept his hands to himself. As the houselights came on, Jed wondered what he could do to further stretch out the evening. He slowly led her outside into the parking lot.

Jillian's voice broke his train of thought. "What are you grinning about?"

"I'm hungry."

"Hungry? After all that pizza?"

"I feel like a big sticky donut."

"You don't look like a big sticky donut."

"Aw, come on. Ever since you mentioned it when you were talking about your sister, I've been thinking of donuts."

Jillian opened her mouth to protest but changed her mind. Despite her intentions to tell him that they wouldn't be wise to see each other outside of their lessons, she didn't want the evening to end. Besides, one could never eat too many fattening donuts. Jillian rested her hands on the door frame of the truck, waiting for Jed to boost her up again, telling herself that next time they went out together, they would take her little car, and he could be the passenger.

She glanced over her shoulder, trying not to appear nervous as she watched him stuff his keys in his pocket. What was she doing making plans, even if they were only in her mind? Twice a week for piano lessons was enough.

Once inside, she fastened her seat belt, watching Jed easily swing himself into the truck and start the engine. She couldn't believe how effortlessly he had hoisted her up; she hadn't had time to make even a cursory hop. Jed had picked her up and placed her on the seat of the truck as if he were lifting a child.

His voice broke through her thoughts. "What are you staring at, Jillian? Do I have popcorn in my hair or something?"

She couldn't help her blush. "You lifted me so easily; it made me wonder if you worked out or something."

Jed chuckled. "Only on the job. Most of the tool caddies weigh more than you do."

Despite her best efforts to keep herself trim, Jillian knew she weighed a few pounds more than the books said she should, but she had no intention of telling that to Jed.

Unconsciously, Jillian pointed her finger to the right and inhaled to speak, but Jed shook his head. "This time I don't need directions. I know where the all-night donut shop is."

Immediately upon entering, they discovered a group of young men causing a ruckus in the corner, which was not the relaxing atmosphere they had hoped for.

With one hand on his arm, Jillian whispered as close as she could get to Jed's ear, "Let's bring a couple of donuts back to my place, and then I can make some decent coffee, too."

He leaned down and whispered his reply in her ear. "Only if you let me pay."

A deal she couldn't refuse.

She followed Jed to the counter to purchase their selections. When she reached for the napkins, the dispenser was empty. "I'll be right back; just get something chocolate for me," she said to Jed and walked to one of the tables to help herself. As she tugged a couple napkins out of the holder, conversation among the rowdy crowd in the corner stopped.

"Hey, babe, these ones are better."

Jillian raised her head to see everyone staring at her. Rather, they were staring down the neckline of her sweater as she leaned over, leering and making rude comments among themselves, loud enough so she could hear them, too. Standing abruptly, she pressed her hand to the neckline and turned toward Jed, who was busy talking to the clerk, laughing as he fished through his wallet. He wasn't looking in her direction.

As she turned her head forward again, two members of the obnoxious crowd left their table and approached her. She could smell the liquor on their breath from five feet away.

Jillian stepped backward, but found herself pressed against the wall. Since they were in a public establishment, she knew she probably wasn't in any real danger, but still, she didn't want to be humiliated if they tried to touch her.

Her attempt at confidence dissolved as the largest of the group continued to approach until he was within a foot of her. Jillian started to open her mouth to call out to Jed, but no sound came out. The stench of liquor nearly made her gag.

"Hey, babe, want some help?" he sneered. Her stomach churned.

From the counter, she heard Jed mumble something, and in a flash he stood beside her. "Let's get out of here." With his arm around her waist, he ushered her out as the onlookers watched in silence. As the door closed, the whistles, catcalls, and lewd remarks began.

Jed inserted the key into the lock on the passenger door. "I'm sorry, Jillian. I wasn't paying attention, and I should have been watching."

She rested one hand on his arm as he turned the key. "It's okay, Jed. It all happened so fast, and I really wasn't in any danger, even if they were a disgusting bunch."

Already standing beside her, Jed turned, then tipped her chin up with two fingers, positioning her so she was staring up into his face. In the glow of the distant streetlights, his blue eyes glistened, and his expression caused her heart to miss a beat.

"Jillian . . ." Jed's voice trailed off as his eyes closed and his head lowered. The butterfly touch of his lips on hers almost made Jillian sink to the ground as all the strength left her legs. When he pulled away, Jillian missed the brief contact; without thinking, she lifted her chin and leaned into him.

In response, Jed's hand moved from her chin to her nape, and his other hand, still holding the bag from the donut shop, brushed the small of her back. He tilted his head and kissed her fully on the mouth.

All coherent thought drifted out of Jillian's mind; the fact that they were standing outside in the parking lot registered, but barely, as she raised her arms to drape them around the back of his neck—and then she kissed him back. Jed's arms tightened around her as she rose on her toes and let herself drown in his kiss, until the sound of a car horn startled them apart.

Jillian backed up a step and stood frozen, unable to comprehend what she had just done. Jed backed up slowly, his eyes wide. Jillian wished she knew what he was thinking.

He stiffened, then opened the truck door. Jed reached inside, then turned back to her. "Donuts are in. You're next." As before, he lifted her with ease and gently guided her onto the seat.

Jillian cleared her throat, trying to appear calm, although inside, she was a bundle of nerves. "Am I being foolhardy inviting you over at this late hour?"

Jed started the engine, then turned to smile at her. "I don't think so."

His smile did funny things to her equilibrium. Feeling suddenly warm, Jillian started to roll the window down, thinking the fresh air would help her come to her senses. She looped her fingers over the window when it was three-quarters of the way down and inhaled deeply just as she heard the sound of footsteps.

"Hey, honey, where ya goin'?" the slurred voice of the guy from the donut shop drifted in. In the blink of an eye, his hand shot through the window and he grabbed her wrist before she realized what was happening. Jillian let out a startled squeak and tried to pull away, but he didn't let go.

In a flash, Jed's arm shot across her and grasped the drunk's wrist in an iron grip. He twisted until the man let go, but Jed didn't release him. Instead, he gave the man's wrist a few firm squeezes.

"That wasn't very nice," Jed growled. "Do you have something to say to the lady?"

The man cursed a blue streak and called Jillian a number of rude names. Jed increased the pressure and twisted again. "Well?" he snarled.

"Sorry! Ow! Sorry!"

Jed thrust the man's arm out the window. "You're lucky I'm in here and you're out there."

The drunk stumbled back into the donut shop. Jillian's heart pounded and her hands shook as she rubbed her wrist with her other hand. Shock started to take effect as the back of her eyes burned. She didn't want to cry, not here, not in front of Jed.

"You okay?" he asked. He reached one hand toward her, but Jillian automatically flinched, then regretted it. Jed leaned back in his seat and gripped the steering wheel with both hands.

Jillian nodded, not wanting to talk about it for fear of bursting into tears. "Let's just go home," she finally gulped.

Jed filled the entire trip home with light and cheerful conversation, helping Jillian put the unpleasant incident behind her.

She slid out of the truck one last time, her hand carefully clutching the hem of her skirt to protect her modesty. As she started to push the door shut, Jed caught it and pulled it open. "Wait," he mumbled.

Jillian's breath caught and her heartbeat quickened as Jed's hand moved toward her. He stepped beside her and started to bend down. Was he going to kiss her again? Jillian nearly melted at the thought. She started to move closer to him, but to her surprise, he didn't touch her. He reached past her, then leaned into the truck.

Grinning, he pulled out the bag of donuts from behind the seat and held them in the air. "Now, we can go in."

Jillian forced herself to smile. Was she doing the right thing?

7

*W*ithout letting go of the bag of donuts, Jed toed off his cowboy boots, pushed them neatly in place on the shoe tray with his foot, then followed Jillian as she headed to the kitchen at the rear of the house, passing through the living room first.

By now, the living room was very familiar to him. Or at least, what should have been the living room. Converted to a serviceable music studio, it contained a shelf full of music books, a small couch for parents to sit and watch the lessons, Jillian's small chair, and taking up most of the room, the large shiny black grand piano. Since she only used the room for lessons, he wondered if they were going to stay in the kitchen with their coffee and donuts, rather than sit on the couch beside the piano. "I guess you never entertain in there," he commented on their way past.

Jillian turned her head slightly but did not stop walking. "No, the living room is for business only. The things people usually put in a living room are in the next biggest room, which really is the den. I have to make do with the rooms I have—it's not a large house."

Jed sat at the table and watched as she poured the water into the pot and then into the coffeemaker. The first time he met Jillian, he'd thought her beautiful. As the days and weeks went by, and the more he got to know her, the less he thought about it, although on days like today, her beauty nearly took his breath away.

Unlike Brenda, Jillian did not flaunt the beauty that God blessed her with. Quite the opposite, in fact. Until today, Jed had never seen her wearing makeup or flattering clothes.

He blinked twice, then wondered why in the world he thought of Brenda. Brenda no longer mattered to him. By moving in with his sister after losing his job, he'd managed to make a clean break and get on with his life. He had plans, and could see his future mapped out before him without looking back.

Jillian turned to face him. "There, the coffee's on. In a few minutes it will be ready, although I don't know why I'm making coffee at this hour."

Jed lifted his wrist to check the time. "If this was a weeknight, then it would be about time for my last coffee break. One cup of coffee won't keep me up. How about you?"

"One cup shouldn't bother me."

He started to reach for the bag of donuts, but something in Jillian's expression made him withdraw his hand and wait for her to speak. "You look like you're going to ask me something." He hoped it wasn't something he didn't want to hear.

"Jed, this has been on my mind all evening."

He forced a smile, his suspicions getting stronger. "Uh, yes?"

"About yesterday."

Now he knew he didn't want to hear it. Yesterday had been fun, but judging from Jillian's stiff posture and the firm set to her mouth, she wasn't about to discuss fun. "Why do I have the feeling that you're not going to tell me you're ready to try bungee jumping?"

"Jed, I'm really not the type to go jumping off swings in the middle of the night. I wanted to say I don't know what came over me, and that I'm not normally like that."

As far as he could recall, they'd had a lot of fun, even when she lost her shoe. "So I guess that means skydiving's out too." Not that he would ever try such a thing himself, but why was he disappointed?

"Jed, I'm trying to be serious."

"Well, skydiving may be a little extreme. Tennis?"

Her mouth opened, then shut, as if she changed her mind about what she was going to say. He hoped she wouldn't accuse him of trying to be dense on purpose, because that was exactly what he was trying to be.

Jed took advantage of her hesitation. "If I can't find my racket, I'm sure Liz has one I could borrow. I had to pick through my stuff carefully, so a lot of things are packed away in storage." He didn't care if he had to go buy another racket, maybe even two, one for Jillian as well, even though he knew he had to count every penny.

"Don't you think tennis is a summer sport? I can't see playing tennis wearing a coat. After all, it is winter."

"Oh. Right, I keep forgetting because there's no snow on the ground here. Well, I'll think of something else." He reached for the bag of donuts before she had a chance to respond. "Isn't that coffee ready yet?"

"I . . ." Her mouth snapped shut again. She turned to open a cupboard and reached for a pair of mugs.

Fortunately, she appeared to be in no rush as she poured the cream into a pretty little bowl with pink flowers on it, and set it beside a matching sugar bowl in the center of the table. He had the impression she had more to say, and that he'd like it even less than her denial she had enjoyed yesterday evening as much as he had. He tried to fight the premonition that a serious brush-off was coming. As much as he had neither the time nor the money to get involved in a relationship, he wanted to spend more time with Jillian.

She set everything on the table, then opened her mouth to speak again. Jed hastily opened the bag and stared inside. "Donut?" he asked, not giving her a chance to speak first.

Jillian sighed loudly, then turned to fetch some plates while Jed continued to stare at the donuts. He didn't want to hear what she had to say. Was she going to tell him to back off? Had he blown it by kissing her? He didn't move or raise his head, but he followed her with his eyes as she bent over and reached into the back of a cupboard for the napkins.

He still didn't know what had come over him, but when that drunk approached her inside the donut shop, he'd surprised himself with a surge of protectiveness. He'd had to kiss her afterward.

Why was he still looking at these stupid donuts? He didn't even want them. The only reason he suggested they buy some donuts was to extend the evening.

Jillian delicately placed two plates on the table, forcing him to look up. He handed her the bag of donuts he had been staring at for so long. "Here. You pick first."

In silence, she held the bag open, peeked in, then hesitated. "There's six in here. I thought you were only going to buy two."

He shrugged his shoulders, not sure of how to respond but not wanting to take his eyes off her. "I couldn't help myself. They all looked so good. I couldn't decide."

She picked out the smallest one and handed the bag back to him. "That's all I want. Take the rest home for your family. If you leave them here I'll eat them, and then I'll be sick."

Jed thought of offering to nurse her back to health but thought better of it. "Then I think I'll take the stickiest one now so the kids don't get it. Liz would kill me if she found chocolate fingerprints all over the place. She'd make me wipe down the walls."

"A woman after my own heart."

"Hmph. No comment."

She bit into the donut, sparing Jed from having to play any more verbal tag. "So, what church do you go to?" he asked. He wanted to learn everything he could about her.

For a second, she stopped chewing, then sipped her coffee and swallowed. "Huntington. It's across the street from the arena."

Jed closed one eye, trying to picture the area. Liz had told him a little about most of the churches in the area, so he knew about Huntington, but not much. "That's small, isn't it?"

She bit into the donut again and nodded. "How about you? I'll bet you go to that big one near the mall with Mark and the family."

"Yeah. I tag along with Liz's family on Sunday. So, you like it there? Do they have a ladies' Bible study once a week? I know you can't do anything in the evenings."

"No, they don't have anything like that there."

"I'll bet you play piano for them Sunday mornings, though."

"Actually, no, I don't."

"You don't? They have a whole band at my sister's church. I would think you could really get into that. They're all dedicated God-loving people, and they really know how to bring the congregation into a meaningful time of worship. And Doreen, the piano player, is going to be needing a replacement soon because she's really big and pregnant." Jed linked his fingers and held his arms in a circle in front of his stomach.

"Pardon me?"

"I should introduce you; you'd like her. Doreen and her husband, Edwin, are really into dogs, and he keeps telling everyone she's going to have a whole litter."

Jillian's mouth hung open, and Jed broke into a wide smile.

"Whenever he says that, she threatens to have him fixed, which always gives everyone a good laugh. The worship team is quite a lively bunch."

Jillian's face turned red. "Huntington's is small and quiet. The guitarist is good, but not outstanding."

"Why do you go to a small place like that?"

"The pastor preaches a good message, and there aren't any single men."

Their eyes met, and they finished their snack without further comment. Jed wasn't sure he wanted to know the reason behind that statement. The quiet, middle-of-the-night atmosphere of her kitchen was too intimate for such a discussion, especially after putting his foot in his mouth making that comment about Edwin and Doreen. He usually didn't babble, and his idiocy only proved how nervous he was.

Jillian delicately licked the tips of her fingers, doing funny things to Jed's insides. "This was a nice idea," she said quietly, then licked one finger again. "Thanks for the treat."

"You're welcome. And on that note, I should go. I have to get up early to get Mark off to school, and it's already well past midnight."

"How do you do it?"

"Do what?"

"Work so late every night and then get up early. When do you sleep?"

Jed felt his ears heat up. "I'll admit to the occasional afternoon nap after I get back from dropping Betsy off at school. But I still practice my piano lessons."

She smiled but didn't say anything, which was just as well.

"See you for lunch tomorrow, then?" Jed mumbled as he stepped into his cowboy boots. For a second, his heart clenched when he thought she was going to say no. He released his breath when she nodded and opened the door.

"Good night, Jillian." He leaned toward her, but she backed up a step. Jed didn't want to push his luck, so he nodded back and stepped outside.

"Good night, Jed. See you tomorrow."

Jed walked to his truck and started the ignition. He knew he wouldn't fall asleep quickly, and he knew it wouldn't be from too much caffeine.

꧁

Not being one to tempt fate, Jillian was ready and wearing a sweatshirt, jeans, and sneakers when Jed arrived to pick her up.

She never did figure out what went wrong, but the chance to tell him that she wouldn't be seeing him outside of lessons had never come up during their late-night conversation. Today would be different.

As she vaulted herself up into his truck, without his assistance this time, Jed started the conversation by teasing her about her jeans and the pink lace around the pockets. To top it off, when she complained and defended herself, he threatened to make her walk, then laughed at her when she became flustered. By the time they arrived at the local hamburger joint, she was laughing so hard she couldn't bring herself to spoil the mood.

Despite the questionable quality of the hamburger and fries and the bad coffee, Jillian couldn't remember the last time she had so much fun. They laughed and joked and teased each other throughout the entire meal, and stayed far longer than necessary in a fast-food establishment.

For some reason, she was hesitant to leave. To her dismay, especially since she didn't want to like him too much, Jillian discovered they shared much in common. Jillian had been fascinated, listening to Jed as he shared his funny stories. He ended with his dreams to study literature and his goals when he became a teacher.

Curiosity having got the better of her, she asked enough questions to find out what happened to make him move in with his sister. Apparently, he had been working at a goodpaying job out of town, trying to put enough money aside for college, but he hadn't quite made enough when the mill closed. However, when he told her about the last few months at the mill, Jillian was left with the impression he purposely left something out, because at one point he became distant and evasive. Then he had changed the subject so fast she didn't know what hit her.

Before she knew it, Jed had jumped to his feet and pointed out the time, obviously worried that he would be late picking up his niece from kindergarten. Before she had time to think, he grabbed her hand and they dashed out the door, running hand in hand through the parking lot. He mimicked Betsy's reaction to seeing her Uncle Jed pick her up in the truck instead of walking, because he always walked, even in the rain. He described Betsy's own special umbrella with little yellow ducks wearing raincoats on it. Even though Jillian had never met Mark's little sister, she could picture her, cute as a button.

She stared at his taillights as he rounded the corner on his way to the school, wondering not only where the afternoon had gone but also how the opportunity never came up to have that serious little talk with him.

She inserted the key into the lock. Jed's next lesson wouldn't be until after Christmas; he'd had to cancel his Tuesday lesson because of something going on at the school. She found herself humming "Pop Goes the Weasel," then forced herself to switch to a Christmas carol.

❧

"Hi, Jed. You're right on time, as usual."

Jillian watched as Jed toed off his large cowboy boots and pushed them onto the mat with his foot. Trying to be discreet, she checked his boots as he hung his jacket on the coatrack, and bit back a smile when she noticed that the right boot had a prominent and permanent scuff mark on the back. As she did every lesson, Jillian sat in the chair beside the piano bench and smiled at him with her practiced teacher smile.

Jed turned to her with an animated grin. "I practiced, Miss Jefferson!"

Jillian wondered when he could possibly have found the time during the hectic holiday season, but she said nothing. Everything had been such a rush for her as well. She had delivered a small Christmas gift to all of her students, and as usual, some of them had given her small token gifts in return.

She had been surprised to receive two gifts from the Edwards household. Mark had given her a chocolate Santa, and Jed had given her a small Christmas tree ornament that played an electronic Christmas carol when a small button was pressed. She would never again hear "Silent Night" without thinking of him. But the tree was down now and the Christmas decorations all put away, and now lessons could start with renewed enthusiasm for the new year.

Just to see what kind of response he'd get, Jed raised his hands to the keyboard, smiled playfully at Jillian, and winked. He'd missed her. Even though he'd phoned a number of times, with all the rush and bustle of the Christmas season they never did have a chance to get together. And until today, when the kids had gone back to school, he'd had to stay home to baby-sit. But he'd had plenty of time to think about her.

"Jed, you're slouching. Holidays are over, and it's time to concentrate."

Jed grinned, straightened his back, and returned his thoughts to the music in front of him. Mark had been right. Mark warned him that "Miss Jefferson gets superstrict about sitting still after the holidays are over." Unlike Mark, though, he had no trouble settling down and keeping his feet on the floor.

"Come on now, Jed. Don't forget your proper hand position."

He tried not to laugh. He had no trouble with his hand position either. Most of the time he placed his hands wrong on purpose, just so she'd touch him. He noticed at some point she saw through him, and started to verbally remind him instead of actually repositioning his hands. She called it a "friendly reminder" when he playfully complained about her nagging.

He sucked in a deep breath to help focus his concentration. If he did these three songs to her satisfaction, including the dreaded "Pop Goes the Weasel," he would pass Book One. He had tried his best to practice with everyone home, but he'd had to battle Mark for the piano. The noise and activity nearly drove him to distraction. At least Betsy had been interested enough in a new video he had bought for her to let him practice uninterrupted for a while this morning.

He made a few mistakes on the first song, but she took him at his word that he had played it perfectly at home, and she passed him anyway. Of course, playing it by himself at home would never compare to the duet during lesson time. He always enjoyed the fancy stuff she played an octave lower to fill out the sound, once he got it right. She promised that one day he would be able to do the same.

Jed managed to play the second song without error, but Jillian still pointed out his uneven timing and a number of other inconsistencies, which he knew without her "friendly reminder."

He tried not to be disappointed. "Does this mean you're not going to pass me? It wasn't that bad, was it?" He wanted to pass Book One so bad he could barely sit still. He was so sick of the kiddy stuff; he wanted to play something good.

"Of course, it wasn't that bad, but I know you can do better. As an adult, my expectations are higher for you than the kids, even Mark. You have to remember that no matter how good you do at a song, you will never, ever, achieve perfection. There will always be something you feel you could have done better. Music is personal. No matter how near perfect you get it, every time you play it, it's different. Sometimes it changes with the mood you're in at the time. Am I making sense?"

Jed thought about it. Maybe he could see her point with the complicated stuff that Jillian played, but he didn't see how that affected "Pop Goes the Weasel." "I think so," he replied uncertainly. "I know I'm playing these kiddy songs different here than at home with Mark and Betsy running around screaming. At home I was annoyed and getting mad at them, and here I'm nervous."

Jillian crossed her arms and stared at him. "They're not 'kiddy' songs. They're 'beginner' songs. And what do you mean, I make you nervous?"

He grinned back. "I guess it's this thing I have from back in high school. Teachers are so intimidating."

"But you want to teach high school literature."

"And I should be good at it. I can be very intimidating too if I want to be."

Jillian stared blankly at him, and he couldn't even begin to guess her thoughts. "That's enough," she said. "Let's get back to the lesson. It's almost time for you to go, and I'm still waiting in anticipation to hear your favorite song."

He knew which one she was referring to without asking. Jed grimaced. "It's not my favorite song. And I don't have to worry about the time today. Betsy is going to a birthday party after school, and I don't have to pick her up. If you don't mind, I thought I'd stay for Mark's lesson."

First, she grinned, then her smile quickly dropped to a frown. "Good. Then you can see how well Mark behaves at his lesson. Often he runs here from school; I can tell because he's panting, but he won't admit it." She sat back in her chair, tapping her chin with her pencil, waiting for him to play.

He couldn't stall any longer. "Here we go," Jed said flatly, taking a deep breath as he positioned himself properly. " 'Pop Goes the Weasel,' the whole thing, adding the missing verse, playing by ear." He hesitated, then destroyed his proper posture by turning and sitting almost sideways on the bench to look at her. "You know, I've been humming this stupid thing all weekend, trying to figure out the whole song, so I hope you're satisfied with yourself." Without waiting for a reply, he turned back to the piano and repositioned himself in a huff.

Jillian tried unsuccessfully to repress a smile. "Temper, temper. Remember, the mood you're in affects the way you play the song."

"Then this weasel is going to really go 'pop,' " he grumbled under his breath, "and it will serve him right."

Jed prepared himself to start playing one more time, resigning himself to the fact that she really was going to make him play the silly song. He had the unwritten part all figured out and memorized at home, and now he would see how well he did under pressure, with Jillian sitting behind him, her arms crossed, listening and analyzing him.

Jillian listened to a meticulously played "Pop Goes the Weasel," the missing lines perfectly filled in. She really couldn't justify his constant complaining about it. She'd been humming it to herself all week, too.

"That was great, Jed! Now I'll play the accompaniment." As happened every time she played her part of the duet, her leg pressed up against his as they sat side by side on the bench. Even though this happened twice a week, she still found the sensation unnerving, not to mention distracting.

Together, they played the song again, Jillian following his lead, making a rousing musical "pop!" at the end of the song.

"Do I pass now?"

"You sure do."

Jed lifted both hands in the air in triumph. "Yippee! I've finished the kiddy songs!" He turned and gave Jillian such a heart-stopping smile, her breath caught. Slight crinkles at the corners of his gorgeous blue eyes emphasized how genuine his smile was. "So, what do I get for passing the book? You never gave me a single sticker. Mark shows me his stickers every week, you know."

"I don't know," Jillian gulped. "Suggest something."

Jed wiggled his eyebrows, only adding to the allure of his wide smile. "Dinner?"

"Dinner?" she echoed weakly.

His eyes twinkled. "Name the place. Your treat."

"*My* treat?" She wondered what she was getting suckered into. "I'll think about it."

The smile dropped to an exaggerated pout. "What do you mean, think about it? What do I get for passing?"

Jillian reached over and patted him on the head like a dog. "Congratulations, you pass. Good boy."

They both burst into peals of laughter, her hand still resting on the top of his head. His hair felt wonderfully thick and soft, and she twirled a few strands in her fingers, amazed at the feel of it. Wavy and untamed, the gentle shade of light brown blended perfectly with his clear blue eyes. Her fingers played with one of the flowing waves, which always seemed to have a mind of its own. No matter how she twisted it, it always sprang back to where it wanted to go. Strong and unfettered, it suited him.

Jed's eyes drifted shut, and he automatically leaned his head into her hand. As much as she liked to look into his dreamy blue eyes, with his eyes closed, Jed's expression became totally unguarded. The sweet half-smile on his face along with his unconscious sigh was Jillian's undoing.

She felt herself shudder as his hands slipped around her waist. She closed her eyes and leaned into his solid chest as she continued to play with his hair.

At the same moment, they both opened their eyes and murmured each other's names. Her eyes drifted shut again as she welcomed his kiss. The part of her that warned her against becoming involved with Jed lost the battle as his kiss deepened and he stroked her back, sending hot shivers all the way through her.

Jed pulled away first, and Jillian immediately missed the contact. Rather than separate from him completely, she remained still, only inches from him.

When he kissed her again, Jillian melted completely into him. Her heart pounded as he showered her with countless short, gentle kisses.

"Eeewww! Gross! Uncle Jed! Miss Jefferson!"

Jillian and Jed bolted apart. Mark stood in the hall entrance, staring at them with his mouth hanging open.

Out of the corner of her eye, she saw Jed running his fingers through his hair to brush it back off his face. "Guess what, Mark?" Jillian noticed a quaver in Jed's voice as he spoke. "I passed Book One."

Jillian's brain refused to function, and words would not form. Her best student had just caught her sitting at the piano kissing his uncle Jed, and not just a peck on the cheek, either.

Mark didn't move. He clutched his book to his chest and stood stock-still, his eyes wide. "Well, forget it. If you ran out of stickers, you're not kissing me!"

Jillian was mortified. She couldn't think of a single thing to say.

Jed jumped to his feet. "It's okay, Mark. She only kissed me because I asked her to. Right, Miss Jefferson?"

Trying to regain her composure, she looked up at Jed. "Um, yes, Uncle Jed. That's right." She sucked in a deep breath and wished she could settle the frantic thumping of her heart. "Don't worry, Mark, I still have lots of stickers. Come on, have a seat and let's get started."

She couldn't face Jed as Mark sat on the bench, watching her out of the corner of his eye as he squirmed into position, apparently still not certain if he could trust her. Jillian tried to control the shaking of her hands as she smoothed her hair back, then settled into her own chair beside the piano bench. Jed sank down onto the couch reserved for parents who stayed to watch the lessons.

Coming down from the adrenaline rush, Jillian's knees trembled as she tried to concentrate on Mark and his piano lesson and not on his uncle Jed, who patiently listened as Mark diligently played the songs he had practiced so hard.

When she wasn't watching him, Jed watched Jillian as she struggled to maintain her dignity with Mark. However, he could tell by her shaking hands and slight tremble in her voice that she wasn't entirely successful.

If he could have, Jed would have kicked himself. What had happened? And why couldn't he laugh about it? Any other time, Mark's performance would have had him rolling in the aisles, but instead, his insides churned. Jillian was upset, and he was responsible. He knew how much her solid upright image meant to her, and knew he was on shaky ground as it was in his efforts to get closer to her.

If he were alone, he would have retired to a quiet place to pray for guidance. Since he couldn't, he did his best to calm his mind and ask God for help, and then, most of all, for wisdom.

Jillian pointed out a few more things for Mark to work on, then dismissed him. Her next student was waiting.

Jed wished he could say something before he left, but Mark already had left the piano. The next student was settling in, so Jed followed Mark to the shoe tray and stepped into his boots. He tried to make eye contact, but Jillian avoided him.

Very politely, Mark opened the door in silence. "Come on, Uncle Jed," he said in a stage whisper, beckoning to him. "It's time to go!"

As Jed closed the door behind him, he finally met Jillian's eyes. She wasn't smiling.

8

*J*ed walked home, his steps heavy, as Mark hopped along beside him, bouncing with his excitement over the new stickers in his book. Jed did not share his enthusiasm.

"See, Uncle Jed, I passed, and she didn't have to kiss me," Mark chattered. "And now you're all done with Book One! That's so totally radical, Uncle Jed! When we get home, I'll get Book Two out for you. There's way better songs in it. I'll show you the best ones, and show you my cheater notes. Just don't tell Miss Jefferson about them. And then we can . . ."

Jed did not feel very radical. He let Mark prattle on, barely paying attention to what the kid was saying. All Jed could think of was Jillian. He was falling hard and fast, despite his resolution to avoid getting involved in a relationship. Time and time again, Jillian proved she was nothing like Brenda. Jillian was in a class by herself. Professional, dignified, intelligent, and beautiful. And honest and unselfish. And from what he had seen so far, a dedicated Christian. No one could compare.

For himself, Jed didn't care that Mark saw them, or what Mark thought, but if Jillian cared, then it mattered. He wondered why it made such a difference; after all, Mark was his nephew, so it wasn't like Mark was just any student. But the fact that she was upset about it made the difference. What could he do? He'd have to have a talk with Mark, and then if he explained things to Jillian, maybe she'd feel better.

". . . and then you start to play some of that Bach and Beethoven stuff, and some of it is really neat, but some of it is really boring, but Miss Jefferson will tell you how good it is for you to play all that stuff and then she'll set that ticking thing and make you do it real fast, but then it really does start to sound good. And then in Book Four it gets even harder and she starts making you do scales with tons of black notes and . . ."

How could he convince Mark to keep this a secret? Like any typical eight-year-old boy, once you said the word *secret,* it became a general bulletin through the whole school population and entire neighborhood. Bribery? No, he would tell everyone the reason he got whatever he picked out. Threats? Another bad idea.

"Uncle Jed? Don't you want to hear about Book Four?"

Maybe the kid would forget all about it. Maybe it was already forgotten. He was constantly forgetting about his homework and making his bed. Kids forgot things all the time.

"Uncle Jed? Uncle Jed? Aren't you listening?"

"Huh? What, Mark? I'm sorry, I guess I didn't hear. What was that again?"

"I said, why didn't you just wait for her to get you a different sticker? Why did you let her kiss you? Gross!"

Maybe he wouldn't forget that quickly. "Mark, I asked her to kiss me."

"Eeww! Why? She's got great stickers. Girls got germs, you know. And cooties."

"I like to kiss Miss Jefferson." At Mark's horrified expression, Jed tried to scramble for another idea. "Doesn't your dad ever kiss your mom?"

"Oh. That. Yeah, he does."

"Well, it's kind of the same thing."

"Oh."

Jed could almost see it like a light going on inside Mark's head. Finally, he was getting somewhere. "It's no big deal, Mark. Really. It's nothing."

"Oh. Okay."

Mark walked in silence the rest of the way home. Jed thought Mark looked very serious for a little kid. He was too young now, but in a couple of years he would start having girlfriends of his own. Jed prided himself on handling it so fast. Now he could get on with his bigger problem of convincing Jillian, which would be the hard part.

As soon as they entered the house, Jed hurried into the kitchen to start supper. Instead of going outside to play, Mark sat at the table and watched him. Jed thought his behavior unusual, but since he was starting a bit late, he didn't have time to concern himself. He had barely got everything going, his lunch packed, and was hurriedly trying to gulp down his coffee when Liz and Frank walked into the kitchen.

"Hi, Jed. How was your day?"

"Fine. Don't forget to pick Betsy up at 6:00; remember, today is Angela's birthday party. And I'm almost on my way." Jed grabbed his lunch pail and rushed to swallow the last gulp of his coffee before he dashed out the door.

Mark piped up. "Guess what, Mom, Dad?"

Frank and Liz started to peek inside the oven and pots on the stove. "What, Mark?" Frank asked absently.

"Uncle Jed and Miss Jefferson are getting married."

Jed choked on his coffee, spitting most of it into the sink, and dribbling some of it down the front of his shirt.

Liz dropped the pot lid and gasped. "Jed? Why didn't you tell me?" She stood straight and placed her hands on her hips, feet slightly apart. "Have I been missing something? Is there anything you want to tell me? Or do you have some explaining to do, little brother?"

Jed tried to speak through his cough, barely getting the words out. "Mark! I'm not going to marry Miss Jefferson! What gave you an idea like that?" Jed wheezed for air as another fit of coughing seized him.

"You said it was just like Mom and Dad. And they have to because they're married."

Liz took advantage of Jed's inability to speak. "What do Mom and Dad have to do, Mark?"

Mark made a face. "You know! Kiss!" Mark opened his mouth and let his tongue hang out, grabbed his own neck with both hands as if choking himself, then crossed his eyes.

Jed's face burned as Liz and Frank stared at him. The tightening sensation in his throat wouldn't allow him to speak.

"I can hardly wait to hear this one," Liz said, crossing her arms and narrowing her eyes.

Mark continued on, unaware of Jed's predicament. "When I got to my piano lesson, Uncle Jed was kissing Miss Jefferson because he passed Book One. I told her she better not kiss me; I want stickers for passing. I know she's got a *huge* one of Mario and Luigi, but Uncle Jed said it was okay for her to kiss him because he asked her to. And it was just like you and Dad, you know, cause, like, you and Dad are married, and that's how babies are made, you know."

"Oh?" Liz looked down at Mark, then back at Jed, then pressed her lips tightly together. "Well, Uncle Jed? Want to tell me all about passing Book One?"

Thankfully, Frank had the sense to be quiet. Jed cleared his throat. "I'm going to be late for work!" he grumbled as he ran the dishcloth over the wet dribbles on the front of his shirt, then threw it in the sink. He made a grab for his lunch pail for the second time, and stormed out.

All the way to work, Jed's guts churned. If Liz and Frank hadn't guessed there was something happening between himself and Jillian before, they knew for sure now. But, worse than that, now Mark knew, and knew too much. Now the whole school, and probably every one of Jillian's students would hear about it. Jillian would be devastated.

Would Mark tell the whole school his uncle Jed was marrying his piano teacher? Or worse? Liz and Frank had better straighten the kid out about the reasons for kissing a girl. Although come to think of it, what were his reasons?

Jed ran in and punched his time card with only a minute to spare. He threw his stuff in his locker, changed into his work boots, and hurried to his station. Another night of the same old thing. Today he'd have to make an extra effort to keep his mind on his job.

❧

With relief, Jillian bade good-bye to the last student of the day. All evening, she hadn't been able to concentrate on anything except the heart-wrenching embarrassment of being interrupted by a child, a student no less, caught in the most exhilarating kiss of her entire lifetime, not that she'd been kissed that often. Now that she was finally alone, she could deal with it rationally. Her stomach flip-flopped thinking about it as she leaned with her back against the door.

Jillian covered her face with her hands and sagged into the door. She never did get around to telling Jed that she didn't think it wise to see him outside of piano lessons. And now this! No matter how much she liked him and enjoyed spending time with him, she wasn't going to risk her reputation or her heart for him. She had to come to a decision on which way she would proceed with Jed.

Her decision was redundant; either way, she lost. She could keep with her original plan to refuse to see him again except for piano lessons, but she didn't think she could handle the strain of seeing him twice a week and knowing there would be no more, now that she knew how much fun he was to be with. Her only other option would be to tell him to find another teacher, so she would never see him again. Jillian sank lower as she continued to lean against the door. She couldn't handle that, either.

She shuffled into the kitchen to make herself some tea to help her relax, but only stared into the bottom of the empty cup. She opened her Bible to read, but none of the words made sense. Instead of sitting up all night and moping, she decided to go to bed. She would be able to think more rationally in the morning.

Yawning as she hopped into bed, she switched off the light, but she found she couldn't close her eyes. Every time she did, all she could see was Jed with his eyes closed, his untamed hair falling onto his forehead and a lazy smile on his face. Either that or the horrified look on Mark Edwards' face as he stood in the entrance hall. She tried praying about it, begging God for answers, but she only came up with blanks.

At 2:07 A.M., Jillian turned to the clock radio for the hundredth time. Rather than stare at the ceiling all night unable to decide what to do, she shrugged on her housecoat and shuffled into the kitchen to make herself some chamomile tea in the hope that it would help her sleep.

Sitting at the table, she watched the kettle, waiting for it to boil. Outside, a rumbling sound echoed, then stopped in front of the house.

Jillian ran to the front window to peek through the blinds: Jed's truck. The interior light came on as the door opened. Jillian yanked her fingers out of the blinds and ran to the door, clutching the neckline of her housecoat to her throat when he knocked on the door. For a second, she considered leaving him standing outside, but she opened the door anyway.

A rush of cold air whooshed in as Jed stood in the doorway, staring at his feet. Splotches of dirt streaked his shirt, and his jeans were so ratty they had holes in them. His typically unruly hair lay flattened in places, and he smelled like a grease pit. The only clean part about him was his cowboy boots.

"What are you doing here? It's two in the morning!"

He shoved his hands in his pocket. "I know. I was on my way home from work and saw your kitchen light on. Can we talk?"

9

*J*ed held his breath, hoping she wouldn't slam the door in his face.

"Now?" she asked. She stared up at him, eyes wide, her hands clutching desperately around the collar of her housecoat.

He studied the toes of his boots. "I had a feeling you wouldn't be able to sleep."

"Come in, Jed," she sighed, then stepped back to allow him entry. Jed closed the door behind himself, toed off his boots and kicked them onto the tray, then followed her into the kitchen, where the kettle whistled on the stove.

"Do you want some herbal tea? It's caffeine free."

All he could do was nod and watch as she busied herself making the tea. She looked cuddly and sweet in her baggy housecoat and bare feet. For the first time since he met her, her hair was a mess, but even still, she was the most beautiful woman he had ever known. Not only that, she wasn't making excuses for her appearance.

She turned her back to reach a couple of mugs in the cupboard. As she lifted her arms, the hem of her housecoat raised up, showing her cute little bare toes beneath it. His heart caught in his throat.

When she placed the steaming cup of tea in front of him, he took a slow sip, then swallowed it too quickly, scorching his throat, rather than spit it back into the cup. "This stuff tastes like boiled straw! How can you drink this?"

"It helps me sleep. And I like it."

Jed cradled the cup in his hands, painfully aware of Jillian staring at him as he took another cautious sip. He hoped the second sip wouldn't be as bad, but the strange taste of the tea made him grimace in distaste. He set the cup on the table, wondering how to refuse to drink any more without hurting Jillian's feelings.

As much as he needed to talk to her, now that she sat in front of him, staring at him, he couldn't think of a single thing to say. After a full shift, he was filthy, and since it had been a particularly busy night, he didn't smell too great, either. Jillian, on the other hand, looked great. Pleasantly mussed and bundled in a granny-style housecoat that was probably thicker than his overcoat, she still somehow managed to carry about her an air of dignity.

"Bunny slippers," he said as he leaned back in the chair. He folded his arms across his chest, trying to cover the coffee stain and other assorted splotches, although the condition of his clothing was the least of his worries.

"What?" Jillian started to raise her cup to her lips, then froze. "Bunny slippers? What are you talking about?"

"You need bunny slippers. They would suit you. You know, the kind with the floppy ears and big eyes that look up at you when you cross your ankles on the coffee table."

"I do not put my feet up on the coffee table."

"Well, then, you should start."

"Jed, it's two in the morning. I don't think you came here to discuss ridiculous footwear."

"No, I didn't." Jed stared into the half-empty cup, then sloshed the liquid around as he tried to think. "I know you were upset about Mark, uh, walking in on us like that."

Jillian didn't answer. Instead, she appeared to be paying too close attention to the pattern on her cup. She blinked a couple of times, and Jed's stomach tightened.

"He's just a kid," Jed blurted out. "And I had a little talk with him on the way home." And he had. He merely omitted telling her that things didn't exactly turn out the way he had planned. He hoped Liz and Frank had had a chance to have a better talk to Mark about kissing girls.

When she didn't respond, Jed reached across the table to touch her hand, but she pulled it away. His throat became so tight he wondered if he would be able to manage the words. "Do you want to pray about it? It always helps."

She clutched her cup again. "I don't think I'm ready to pray with you, Jed."

He knew exactly what she meant. He often participated in group prayer, praying for people he barely knew, if at all. This was different. This was personal. Intensely personal. Praying together with someone close lent itself to a certain intimacy, one he couldn't even begin to reason out. And in a group situation, the results of such prayers usually didn't directly affect him. This time, Jed not only wanted to pray for peace for Jillian, he needed to. The more he thought about it, the more important it became.

He also needed answers. He wanted to know why she resisted his efforts to draw her closer. He didn't think it was him in particular, but he couldn't be sure. While she didn't exactly push him away, she didn't encourage him either. But more than anything, while he was curious about why it bothered her so much, he wanted her to have some peace about the incident with Mark. From her reaction, and the fact that she was still bothered so much about it, he had a feeling things went far deeper than just a little embarrassment.

So, while Jillian stared into her cup, her eyes fixed on its contents, Jed lowered his head slightly, closed his eyes, and prayed alone.

When he opened his eyes, Jillian was still staring into her cup. The sight of her made him want to get up, pull her out of the chair, hold her tight, and kiss her again, if he didn't smell like lubricant and other assorted unmentionables.

She looked up at him, her eyes big and round. "What if word of this spreads to my other students?"

"So what if it does? You're entitled to a social life."

"But not at the piano, and not with a student's uncle."

Her words didn't bode well at all. "It'll be okay, Jillian, I promise."

She didn't answer. Instead she stood, hugged herself, then looked toward the door, then back at him. Jed decided he could take a hint, before he was asked to leave and never come back. He couldn't take that. "I guess I had better go; it's late."

He walked slowly to the door, listening to the shuffling sounds of Jillian behind him. She didn't say a word to him as he let himself out. He thought about turning around to say something, but the door closed as soon as he cleared the doorway, and the lock clicked as it engaged. He walked slowly to the truck, then tightly gripped the steering wheel for a few minutes before he started the engine.

It would be quite some time before he fell asleep tonight.

❧

Jed and Betsy stood in the window and waved at Liz and Frank as they drove off to work. Again, Betsy woke far too early, especially after last night. Not only had he been extra late getting to bed, but he had also lain staring at the ceiling for hours. He was getting to know every bump and lump of stucco on a personal basis.

Jed yawned, making no effort to hide it from Betsy. "Hey, Pumpkin, I'll give you a nickel if you go wake Mark up. I'll give you two nickels if you do it without any yelling."

Betsy giggled. "You watch me, Uncle Jed!" She tiptoed down the hall, still giggling.

He smiled through another yawn. Betsy could be such a good little girl when she wanted.

For a minute there was silence.

"You little monkey brain! Get outta here!"

Betsy shrieked and ran down the hall and jumped into Jed's arms, laughing wildly. "I didn't yell! I didn't yell!"

Jed closed his eyes, afraid to ask, but he had to know. "What did you do?" He remembered one morning from his youth when Liz had kept snapping the elastic on his underwear until he couldn't stand it. Did kids still do that to each other?

"I pulled his blankets off and tickled his feet. You owe me two nickels!"

He could live with that. "Tell you what. After Mark leaves for school, how about if we go to the mall and I'll let you spend those two nickels?"

"Oh, boy! Can I buy a new doll?"

It was a struggle, but he tried to look serious. "Not with two nickels. You're going to need more than that for a doll."

"Then I had better go get my bank!" Betsy jumped out of his arms and ran to her bedroom. Jed could hear the shaking and rattling of coins as she emptied the contents of her bank onto the floor.

Mark shuffled into the living room, rubbing his eyes. "I hate her. She's a brat."

"She's a little girl, and she's your sister." Now he knew how his parents felt, only in their case, Liz was the eldest, and she never let him forget it. But even though she was older, by the time he reached thirteen, he was taller. Much taller. And then he didn't let her forget it. At times, he pitied his parents.

"At least I don't have to kiss her."

Jed cringed. Obviously, Liz had not spoken to him like he'd hoped. He wanted to have another little talk with Mark about this kissing business, but this was not the opening he had planned.

"Then who would you want to kiss?"

Mark tilted his head, as if it would help him think better. "Well, Dad thinks that in a couple of years I might want to kiss Kimmy Albertson, but then Mom poked him and said for him not to give me any ideas."

"Do you like Kimmy?"

"Yeah, she's cool. She burps even better than Rodney."

Jed smiled. Nothing like true love. "Pretty cool for a girl, huh?"

"Yeah, for a girl."

"Come on, let's get you out the door on time."

Once Mark left for school, Jed stretched and decided to make a pot of coffee. He was going to need at least that to get him through the morning.

After sufficient coffee consumption, he helped Betsy tie her shoes as they prepared to go to the mall. Betsy could barely sit still, anticipating buying some new doll she had seen on television, which he hoped was not too expensive. He had a feeling this was going to be a costly trip.

"Got your seat belt on, Pumpkin? Let's go."

Betsy chattered all the way to the mall, going on and on about that doll. By the time they arrived, Jed was sick of hearing about it. He allowed her to pull him all the way to the toy department, skipping. Jed refused to skip, no matter how great this doll promised to be. Fortunately, the doll was not overpriced, so Jed bought it for her as a treat. He picked out a small model for Mark to be fair to both kids.

"Come on, Pumpkin, now it's time to buy what Uncle Jed came for. Want to help me pick the right color?"

"Yes! That'll be fun!"

"Hurry up, it's almost time to go back and get you to school. Want a hamburger for lunch?"

"Do I get the kids meal with the toy?"

❧

Jillian looked at the clock. She could almost hear Jed saying "Yup, time for me to go get Betsy"—except it was the wrong day.

How he got enough sleep to keep going was beyond her. Jillian couldn't survive on so little sleep from day to day, week after week. And yet, Jed had committed himself to this routine until next September, until he went to college, an entire year.

When Jed said he would do something, it was considered done. She envied his family. His commitment to them was not only commendable but done with such a spirit of love that Jillian was almost jealous of his sister.

Jed appeared happy and settled in his arrangement. She had met Liz once briefly when Mark started lessons a few years ago, and although Jed mentioned they were very much alike, she couldn't remember Liz. Jillian tried to imagine a feminine image of Jed but couldn't. As she stared off into space, she pictured Jed, his dazzling smile, his brilliant blue eyes, and his unruly brown hair, a lock of it constantly hanging in his face. Even without him there, she had to suppress an urge to push it back into place.

"Hi, Miss Jefferson. I practiced everything extra hard this week. Which one do you want to hear first?"

Jillian blinked, then tried to discreetly check the clock before focusing on her incoming student. She had to get her images of Jed out of her mind and get down to business.

"Good afternoon, Sheila. Pick whichever one you want first. Come and sit down and we'll get started."

❧

As the last student of the day left, Jillian locked the door, leaned her forehead into the back of the door, and yawned. She couldn't remember the last time she had been so tired.

With the events of yesterday, and then her very, very late night after Jed left, she felt ready to drop. She barely found the energy to make herself a peanut butter sandwich for dinner, spending the balance of the evening on autopilot before she crawled into bed.

Sometime in the middle of the night, she half woke to listen for a few seconds to what sounded like the low rumble of Jed's truck. Through the fog of interrupted sleep, she tried to work up the energy to peek out the window, but the sound faded and disappeared. She rolled over and went back to sleep and dreamed of Jed and sitting on the swing.

Sunlight was pouring in the window by the time Jillian awoke. After she dressed, Jillian put on a pot of coffee and stepped outside to retrieve the mail and newspaper. As she wrenched the paper out of the slot, a volume of flyers tumbled down around her feet. Grumbling about the volume of after-Christmas sale flyers, she bent to gather them. Sorting them with one hand, she reached up to the mailbox without looking.

Her hand jerked back when she came in contact with something fuzzy in the mailbox. A pair of bunny faces stared back at her. She pulled them out, but they weren't stuffed toys; they were slippers. She found a note attached.

> *Instructions—place one on each foot and position carefully on a solid coffee table. Improper usage voids warranty.*
>
> *Love, Jed*

Jillian stood on the doorstep, staring at the large blue faces, complete with big wide eyes, pink noses, and floppy ears. Bunny slippers? They looked ridiculous in her hand. Jillian couldn't begin to imagine how ludicrous they would look on her feet.

Jillian read the note again. Was this Jed's way of trying to cheer her up? She held the slippers at arm's length, and the utter silliness of the faces got the best of her, forcing her to grin. At the sound of a car going by, Jillian realized that she was still outside. Quick as a bunny, she backed up into the house and shut the door.

She stared at the note again, and her grin faded. *Love,* Jed? Did he sign all his little notes this way, or was the situation with him spiraling even more out of control? She hugged the slippers and walked into the kitchen. They were too cute to scuff along the floor.

Jillian placed them on the counter beside the coffeemaker, continuing to stare at them as she poured her coffee. The bunnies stared back.

She'd never seen anything so preposterous in her life. Bunny slippers. While she was sure, knowing Jed, he had meant to cheer her up, she couldn't imagine anyone giving her such an odd gift. In the past, when anyone, especially a man, gave her a gift it had always been something expensive, fancy, ultrafeminine, and with strings attached.

She dropped the bunny slippers on the floor, then slipped her feet into them. She shook her head, and shuffled over to the couch and as instructed, lifted her feet and rested them on the coffee table. The bunnies looked back at her, just like Jed said they would. They were absurd. Definitely undignified. And warm and fuzzy. And comfortable. Jillian wiggled her toes inside them and leaned back on the couch. She loved them.

Without getting up, she leaned over to the phone on the end table and dialed Jed's number.

A little girl answered. "Hello?"

"Hello, Betsy. Can I speak to Uncle Jed?"

"How did you know my name? Who is this?"

Jillian smiled at Betsy's plight, amused to be getting the third degree from a little girl. "This is Miss Jefferson, the piano teacher. Your Uncle Jed told me your name. May I speak with him, please?"

"No, you can't."

Jillian's smile dropped at the thought of being screened without knowing why. "Why can't I speak to him, Betsy?"

" 'Cause he's having a shower. Wait. The water stopped." The phone crashed with a loud bang in Jillian's ear and Betsy screamed for

Jed in the background. She listened to a series of loud thumps, as Betsy screamed to Jed that she had to tell him something.

Jillian's own face heated up and she considered hanging up rather than listen, when she heard Jed's voice in the distance. He gently admonished Betsy for calling him out of the shower unless it was an emergency. Jillian strained her ears to hear Betsy telling Jed it was the piano lady, who was still on the phone, waiting. Silence hung in the air.

"Hi, Jillian." Jed's embarrassment radiated over the phone. Jillian struggled to remember why she called in the first place.

Jillian looked down her legs at the bunnies, still resting on the coffee table, and wiggled them. "Thanks for the bunnies, Jed. They're adorable. This was so sweet. I don't know what to say."

He laughed in response. "You're welcome. Enjoy them. You'll have to model them for me."

"Anytime you want. But I should let you go. You're probably leaving a puddle on the rug."

Jed remained silent for a few seconds. "Oh, yeah. Kids, no tact. You busy this afternoon?"

"Uh, no, why do you ask?"

"How about modeling those slippers for me and then we could decide from there?"

"Well, I don't know."

"Come on, Jillian, I've got to see those slippers on you."

Jillian wiggled her feet, which were still on the coffee table, causing the bunny ears to flop. She grinned. "I guess so. Bye, Jed."

"Bye, Jillian."

Jillian smiled as she hung up the phone and wiggled her bunnies once again.

10

*J*illian answered the door, proudly wearing her new slippers. In response, Jed laughed when she pointedly looked down and wiggled her feet.

She looked up at him. "Here's Flopsy and Mopsy, but where's Cottontail and Peter?"

His wide smile nearly caused her to melt into a little puddle. "You have to model them on the coffee table, or remember, you void the warranty."

She couldn't imagine doing anything so horrible as to void the warranty. Jed stood before her with his arms crossed over his chest, waiting, but his playful smirk gave him away. After all his efforts to sneak them into her mailbox, she couldn't disappoint him.

Jillian led Jed through the house to the den, where she plopped herself down on the couch, leaned her head back, and carefully placed her feet, complete with bunnies, on the coffee table.

"There. Satisfied?"

"Satisfied. Let's go." Jed stood.

"Go?"

"I'm starving. Let's go grab some lunch. My treat."

Jillian stood, watching Jed as he started to walk to the front door. "But you didn't even give me a chance to properly thank you for the slippers."

"It's no big deal. You said thanks over the phone." Jed turned around completely to face her, resting both hands on his stomach. "Come on, I'm famished. Or do you want to wear those silly things out in public?"

Jillian's bunnied feet refused to move. That was it? He didn't expect anything in return for his gift? Not even a kiss? A choking feeling gripped her throat. No one had ever given her anything and not expected something in return. No one. She tried to fight the tears welling up in her eyes and failed.

"Jillian, what's wrong? Are you crying?" Jed stood before her in the blink of an eye. With one hand resting gently on her shoulder, he tenderly wiped a lone tear with the back of his finger as it slid down her cheek.

His gentle touch was her undoing. Her lower lip started to quiver and her eyes burned. Jillian buried her face in his chest, threw her arms around him, and let herself lose control. His arms tightened around her, making her sob harder.

Jed tightened his grip and stared down at the top of Jillian's head, completely at a loss to figure out what he'd said or done. They were only slippers, and they'd cost him less than an hour's wage. In fact, he thought he was being funny by slipping them into her mailbox in the middle of the night, only Jillian wasn't laughing. But she had been earlier. The last thing he wanted to do was upset her. The stupid slippers were meant to cheer her up, but apparently they'd had the opposite effect.

A warm spot seeped through his shirt, wet from her tears. Jillian's whole body shook as she continued to cry uncontrollably. Her muffled voice vibrated against his chest. "I'm so sorry, Jed. I feel like such a fool." Her hands released their grip around him, then she grabbed a handful of the front of his shirt and pressed her face into him again.

Unable to figure out what to say or do, Jed kept one arm around her back, and stroked her hair with the other. "Want to talk about it?"

She shook her head, still pressing her face against his shirt. "No, it's not important." Her whole body trembled as a new wet spot formed from yet another burst of tears.

"Jillian, if it upsets you this badly, I think it is important. Come on, you can tell me." Actually, he wasn't sure he wanted to know, because if it was this bad, he didn't know if he could deal with it, and he seriously doubted he could possibly be of any help. He took advantage of her inability to speak to pray for guidance and especially for wisdom. He seemed to be doing a lot of that lately.

Jillian sniffled and drew in a shuddering breath. Jed cringed as she readied herself to speak.

"This is the first time someone has ever given me a gift and not expected anything in return."

Her voice had been so soft and muffled that Jed barely heard what she said, but he had a nagging suspicion there was more to it than that. Gently, he continued to stroke her hair, waiting for her to continue.

"My parents split up when I was a kid. My mother's new husband and family always came first, and she didn't want us living with them, so Sue and I lived with our dad. Mother didn't visit often, but whenever Roger forced her to come, she always brought an outrageously expensive gift or a wonderful toy. She taunted me, usually in front of Roger's kids, to make me want whatever she brought real bad, and then she wouldn't give it to me until I gave her a big kiss and said 'I love you.' Then she'd gloat, her duty done, and we wouldn't see her for months."

Jed stroked her hair. "What about your dad? Didn't he do anything about that?"

"My father didn't want kids underfoot either. He was always so busy or out with different women, we hardly ever saw him, either. Sue and I were passed from sitter to sitter, and nanny to nanny. He gave us every toy imaginable just so we'd go away and leave him alone. I didn't want a room full of useless toys. I wanted my dad."

Jillian stopped to sniffle, then continued in a voice so soft he barely heard what she said. "The other kids were so jealous they wouldn't play with me, except when I got another new toy. I had to be satisfied with my music, and my sister."

Jed felt her trembling as another wet spot developed on his shirt with her muffled cries. As a child, his family had often done without, especially compared to some of the other kids in the neighborhood. But they'd been happy because God was in their midst.

Still stroking her hair, he tried to think of something that would help. "As a kid, that's gotta hurt. But surely there's been someone else that was special. A man?" Even though he knew she didn't have anyone to call her special at the moment, Jed thought a woman like Jillian would always have a lineup of suitors. Somehow, the thought irked him.

She sniffled again. "Every man I went out with made it very clear he wanted something for everything he did or gave to me. I seem to bring it out in them."

"You can't base all this on the experience of just a few jerks, Jillian."

She sniffled again, and her voice wavered as she spoke. "I was in love once, Jed, at least I thought I was. His name was Graham. He came from a nice stable home in a nice stable neighborhood, and went to a nice established church. I even thought we would get married. One day he told me he had something for me, and I thought it was an engagement ring. But it wasn't; it was a very flimsy negligee. He made his intentions very clear when he started undoing his shirt and insisting that he expected me to model it. I knew what he thought would happen next. And it didn't involve marriage or any commitment, at least on his part."

Jed couldn't think of a thing to say as he looked down at her tearstained face. The thought of a man trying to take advantage of Jillian made his blood boil. "What did you do?"

Jillian smiled weakly through her tears. "I didn't think I'd done anything to warrant that kind of suggestion. When I recovered from the shock, I ripped the negligee in half, then threw it back to him, box and all. Then I tried to leave. He was furious." She sniffled as her lip quivered. "He blocked the door and threatened me, so I ran into one of the bedrooms and locked the door. He started trying to break the door down, screaming vile things, what he was going to do with me when he got hold of me." She hugged herself, and her eyes temporarily became unfocused, staring at some unknown spot on the wall. She refocused and stared into space beyond Jed's shoulder, and her lower lip trembled again. "I was terrified, so I escaped out the window. I never saw him again."

"You jumped out a window?"

"It was ground level. Fortunately for me."

Jed drew her close once more, hugged her tight, rested his chin lightly on top of her head, and squeezed his eyes shut. Little snippets of conversation starting falling into place, things he hadn't understood at the time, but now he could. No wonder the incident with the drunk at the donut shop terrified her so much. His heart ached for her. He had no idea she carried such deep hurts on her shoulders, things he couldn't relate to after growing up in a very loving home. Sure, he'd done battle with Liz countless times, but that was only sibling rivalry, and never amounted to anything serious. They hadn't had much, as a family, but they had each other, and what was given was given freely.

"Jesus loves you, Jillian, and there are no strings attached."

"I know that, Jed, and you have no idea how much that gives me comfort; it's only been Him that's held me together. But, still, I'm not very good at dealing with people. And I know I'm not handling this very well. I don't know what to do, especially when you're being so . . ." she sniffled ". . . nice."

He had no idea what to say; all he could do was to trust that God would give him the right words. First John 4:15 came to mind, one of his favorite verses. "If anyone acknowledges that Jesus is the Son of God, God lives in him and he in God." It was so simple, yet so powerful. "God loves you, Jillian. He's given you salvation through Jesus Christ, and all the love that goes with His Son. It's a gift. All you have to do is take it."

Jillian sniffled and nodded her head against his chest. "I know. It took me a while to accept that, but I have. I guess there's just still . . . scars on my heart. Thank you, Jed," she whimpered.

They stood in silence, allowing Jed to give Jillian the time she needed to calm herself. He was positive that so many things in his own life were gifts from God, including the developing friendship with Jillian. In addition to being better able to understand her, he could see this was a good release for her. While not exactly fun, this conversation was necessary for both of them.

Jillian sniffled and pushed herself away from him. "I'm so sorry, Jed. You said you were starving. Would you like to go out for something to eat?"

Jed touched the wet splotches on his shirt. He wasn't about to go out in public like this. Jillian didn't look too great herself, with her puffy red eyes, tearstained face, and shiny nose. "I have a better idea. Want to stay here and just have a sandwich or something fast?"

Jillian swiped at her eyes with the back of her hand. "Maybe we should. I probably look terrible, don't I? I'm so sorry for falling apart on you like this." She sniffled again.

Jed touched her cheek with his fingertips. "Don't be. It probably feels good to get it off your chest, doesn't it?"

"Yes, in a way, it does. Thank you, Jed." Jillian kept her eyes averted, and her eyes settled on the blotches her tears had left on his shirt. "I think I made a mess on your shirt. I'm so sorry. That might stain. I should wash it."

Jed was not about to start undressing in front of Jillian, especially after hearing her story about the negligee. He covered one of the wet spots with his hand. "Don't worry about it. I'll just keep my jacket done up when I go get Betsy. I have to change into a different shirt for work, anyway. Either that, or if you splash some old coffee down the front of me, no one will know the difference." He forced himself to give her his Boy-Scout smile, even though he really wasn't in a teasing mood.

She swiped at her eyes with her forearm and cleared her throat. "Excuse me, I'll see what we can come up with for lunch."

Jed's stomach grumbled at the mere mention of food. He followed Jillian into the kitchen, then watched helplessly as she rummaged through the fridge, despite his offer to help. As she fussed about the kitchen, he tried to imagine what it would be like to grow up so lonely and neglected. He could also understand her apparent unwillingness to trust him. The biggest problem was, he wondered what he could do about it.

His parents were still happily married, and he phoned or visited them whenever he could. Throughout his childhood years, there never seemed to be money for extras, but they certainly never did without anything they needed. As a family, they enjoyed their time together, participating in a variety of activities, both in and out of church. Above all, his parents, through love and by example, imparted to him the love of God in his life. For that, Jed would be eternally grateful.

From what Jillian had said, it seemed she had enjoyed none of the same privileges, and his heart ached for her. He knew she was close to her sister, but they seemed to be drawn together by bad circumstances as much as anything else. He wondered at what point she had learned to trust in God, although it really didn't matter. The fact that she knew God's love and depended on Him now was what counted.

Lunch conversation stayed at a minimum, centering around small talk, and Jed didn't try to steer the conversation deeper; he wanted to give Jillian the time she needed to recover from her crying jag. As well, he also needed time to digest everything he had learned.

By the time they finished, only fifteen minutes remained before Jed had to leave to pick Betsy up from the school. Despite Jillian's protests, he insisted on helping clean up and wash dishes. The whole time they worked together, Jillian deliberately avoided eye contact.

The sensible part of him said this would be a good time to back off. He had plans for his future, and they didn't include a woman with extra baggage to carry. She couldn't have made more clear that she wanted to keep him at arm's distance, but when push came to shove, she wasn't exactly telling him to go away. Jillian had enough problems of her own, and as far as Jed could see, she didn't know what she wanted herself, beyond her career. But Jed knew what he wanted, didn't he? And that was paving his road to college with no distractions. Wasn't it?

He washed the last dish and drained the sink, then watched Jillian. She still fought the odd sniffle as she put everything away in silence. His grand plans for the future might be modified, but he realized that for the moment, he had only one goal in mind.

Jed stopped Jillian as she stacked the last plate in the cupboard. "You know what I want to do right now?" he asked.

Like a frightened doe, she turned her face to look over her shoulder, her big round eyes still red and puffy from crying. His heart clenched, and he reached to her waist, turned her so that she faced him, and pulled her into him, pressing them together from head to toe. He tilted his head and leaned his cheek onto the top of her head. "To hold you," he murmured into her hair.

Jillian leaned into him, enjoying the comfort of Jed's touch. Another rush of confusion washed through her as his arms wrapped around her. "Watch it. If you're not careful, you might get another wet spot on your shirt."

He nestled his face into her hair. "I'll take my chances."

The press of tears no longer threatened Jillian, now that she was nestled safely in the comfort of Jed's arms. She cherished the support he offered for the moment, and refused to think about tomorrow, after he had time to think things through.

His voice rumbled in his chest as he spoke. "It's time for me to go get Betsy." She inhaled deeply, taking in the faint scent of fabric softener along with the stronger fragrance of his aftershave before they separated.

As he walked away, Jillian wondered if he would ever come back.

❧

Immediately upon awakening, Jillian dangled her legs off the bed and tucked her feet into her new bunny slippers.

Instead of concentrating on her itinerary, after she got dressed she shuffled into the den and sat on the couch, her ankles crossed on the coffee table, and stared at the bunnies on her feet. If the silly things weren't so large, she would have been tempted to sleep with them on. Jillian wondered if she was losing it, because she had never been sentimental in her life. Not only that, but the ludicrous slippers destroyed the dignified image she had worked so hard for. Strangely enough, she didn't care if any of her neighbors saw her. The bunnies were a gift from Jed.

Today was Friday, and all she could think about was Jed's piano lesson. After her overly sensitive reaction to his simple gift, she doubted he would come. The more the day wore on, the more agitated she became. At the sound of a knock on the door, the pile of music books in her hand hit the floor, scattering around her. She ran to the door, nearly tripping on the bunnies.

Drawing a deep breath, Jillian opened the door. "Hi, Jed. You're a bit early." Jillian was grateful he was. A few minutes more, and she would have driven herself completely insane.

"Hi." His gaze dropped to her feet. "Blue is your color, I think."

All she could do was smile weakly up at him, her heart in her throat. Jed's brilliant white smile quickened her heartbeat, leaving her light-headed. She stepped back to let him in, because she could no longer stand still.

"Want to know why I'm so early?"

Her feet froze and her hands started to tremble. Half the night and all day, she had agonized over his reaction to her uncontrolled outburst, and she dreaded his decision after he had time to think about it. But if he chose to keep his distance after witnessing her unstable reaction to an innocent gift, wasn't that what she wanted all along? If so, then why did she feel so heavyhearted? It terrified her to think he would quit lessons.

"You promised me something."

Jillian tried to think as she stared blankly at him. Her mind zinged in a million directions that had nothing to do with promises.

"I'll give you a hint. I passed Book One."

Book One. Jillian struggled to remember that far back. The day he passed Book One he had played "Pop Goes the Weasel." He had been a bit testy at first, but as he played it, he loosened up, and after that he had kissed her. She didn't dare guess what he was thinking.

"You said you'd take me out to dinner."

"Dinner," she echoed.

He grinned as if he didn't have a care in the world. Jillian thought she could have hugged him, but she didn't dare touch him.

"When?" she asked weakly.

"Saturday. Do I get to pick where?" He raised his eyebrows.

All she could do was nod.

He shook his head. "No. You choose. Not only do you know the better places; you're paying."

She already felt like her head was spinning without the added verbal runaround. "Then why did you ask if you got to pick?"

"Just testing." He shrugged his shoulders.

Her mind went blank. She couldn't have thought of a response if her life depended on it. "I think we should start your lesson. I'll decide where we're going later."

Jillian tried very hard to concentrate on the lesson, but she couldn't. After everything that had happened with Jed, she had too many things to consider. Already, they were running behind, but Jed was one student she couldn't let go overtime, because he had to leave on time to pick up Betsy no matter what. She focused on a section Jed found difficult, and made an attempt to encourage him to try harder.

Jed tried very hard to concentrate on the lesson, but he couldn't. He could only concentrate on Jillian. She was obviously still rattled, even though he had tried his best to keep conversation light. However, she wasn't as focused as usual. He'd even managed to tease her, but it didn't work. She spoke too quickly, her movements were too jerky, and her piano playing too mechanical. He listened as she attempted to explain what he was doing wrong, but her instructions went in one ear and out the other.

What was happening? All he had wanted to do was take piano lessons. When had that changed? Once he finally got up the nerve to ask her out, separate from lesson time, he was glad he did, because they had a lot of fun together. After the incident at the donut shop, not only did he feel he had to protect her, he wanted to, even needed to. Beyond becoming protective, he'd become territorial, and that wasn't good. Then he'd kissed her. As if things weren't complicated enough, she willingly kissed him back. Both times. And he wanted to do it again, and again.

Jed blinked hard, then shook his head in an attempt to return his concentration to his lesson.

As she tried to think of another way to explain something he wasn't understanding, she licked her lips, and Jed's brain froze. He stared at her mouth, and his thoughts wandered again to the way he kissed her on their last lesson, which had been great, until Mark interrupted. Her vulnerability and openness about what troubled her drew him all the more.

"Jed, are you listening to me?"

He blinked and forced himself to smile. "Yeah, sure. I was just thinking. What did you say again?"

"I give up. I think we're done, anyway."

Jed focused on her face, first on her wide green eyes, then on her full lips. She must have known what he was thinking about, because she inhaled suddenly, then touched her fingertips to her bottom lip.

Unable to resist, Jed lightly grasped her hand, pulled it down, then ran the fingers of his other hand lightly over her bottom lip. Her eyes widened, but she didn't shy away. It was all the encouragement he needed. He whispered her name, pressed his thumb gently into her soft lower lip, brushed his fingers down to her chin, and kissed her.

A beeping sound forced them to separate.

Jillian stared at him, her face red, her unsteady breathing doing strange things to Jed's thinking processes. "What is that?" Jillian asked. "Do you have a pager or something?"

Jed blushed. "I set the alarm on my watch. Just in case I lost track of the time."

"Betsy," she said weakly.

"I don't want to phone and disturb your lessons tomorrow, so can you tell me now how I should dress for dinner?"

"I haven't decided yet, but no jeans, and wear a tie."

"Suit jacket?"

"Do you own one?"

"Believe it or not, I do." He grinned.

"Well . . ." Jillian tilted her head and held one finger to her chin. It only increased Jed's desire to kiss her. "If you want, but it's not necessary. I don't want to go anywhere so exclusive that you would feel embarrassed if I paid the bill."

He'd never considered if he would feel awkward about a woman paying the bill in a restaurant, because it had never happened before. "Don't worry about it. I think I can handle it."

"You'd better go. I'll see you tomorrow, Jed."

He could hardly wait.

11

The doorbell chimed as Jillian completed the final touches on her hair. Instead of merely curling it, she had swept it up for a more sophisticated image. After one final glimpse of herself in the mirror, she hurried down the stairs.

When she opened the door, her breath caught. Beneath his open coat, Jed wore a dark dinner jacket, accompanied by a crisp white shirt and silk tie. His flawlessly pressed slacks fit him perfectly, and for a final touch, polished black shoes replaced his usual scuffed cowboy boots.

Her eyes traveled back up his tall frame, taking in every detail until she gazed into his face. Clean shaven and sporting a recent haircut, he looked immaculate, even respectable, except for the Mickey Mouse on his tie. His grin made her foolish heart flutter.

"Wow," she exclaimed softly. "Little Jed?"

Jed studied Jillian with an appreciative stare, not so sure this was such a good idea, after all. He recalled the first time they met, his first impression of her, and how different she looked now. His heart slammed in his chest as he tried to take in everything at once.

While not revealing, the soft fabric of her dress flowed over every curve, accenting her hourglass figure. With her hair swept up in some kind of wavy style that begged a man's touch, it was all he could do to keep his hands at his sides.

How did she expect him to take her out for dinner with her looking like that? He could barely breathe, never mind function like a human being.

"Wow," he echoed playfully, struggling to keep the rasp out of his voice. "Miss Jefferson. You look good enough to eat." Her gorgeous green eyes widened as Jed realized what he just said. He looked pointedly away from her and pulled at his collar to ease the choking sensation in his throat. "Shall we go?"

She nodded, then tilted her head with a slight motion to the side. "I have to check and make sure the back door is locked. I'll be right back."

Jed watched her from behind as she turned and walked down the hall, appreciating every feminine movement. Upon her return, he held her coat for her as she slipped it on, then he let her rest her tiny hand on his arm as she stepped into a pair of high-heeled shoes the same color as her dress. He knew she didn't try, but she would turn the head of every man in the vicinity. His breath caught when she smiled up at him. He hoped he would live through the evening without a heart failure.

"Jed? Are you feeling okay? Your face is flushed. If you're not feeling well, we can do this another day."

Not on his life. Jed let his breath out in a whoosh of air, not realizing he had been holding it. "I'm okay, just got a tickle in my throat." He pressed his fist into the center of his chest and made a small cough to clear his constricted airways before he choked. "So, where are we going? Do I need directions?"

Jillian gave him a backward glance as she locked the front door on the way out. "Downtown. We're going to the new revolving restaurant. You keep mentioning bungee jumping, so I'm assuming you're not afraid of heights. It will also give you a good view of the skyline. I timed our reservation so we can enjoy the sunset."

Trying to be the perfect gentleman, Jed helped her up into his truck as delicately as possible. "Sounds good." From what he heard, being at The Loft would make it hard on his male pride if she paid the bill there, but he had been adequately forewarned. But truthfully, he'd only been teasing Jillian about treating him. He would be the one paying—not that she couldn't afford it. Come to think of it, knowing what she charged for lessons, if she ever chose to expand into full-time hours, she would be making much more than he would as a high school teacher, even after he earned his degree. In the back of his mind, he asked himself why he would care.

The breathtaking ride up the glass elevator on the outside of the building provided them with a magnificent view of the city as they quickly rose above the height of the surrounding buildings. Once inside, the hostess seated them at a window table.

The city stretched out below them. With the sun almost set, the horizon glowed in hues of bright pink and vivid purples. Tall downtown skyscrapers dotted with lights were majestically silhouetted against the skyline. The head waiter informed them the restaurant would make approximately one full revolution in the time it would take to finish dinner.

Jed gazed out the window. "I've never been on one of these things before. I know it's moving, but you really can't tell unless you look real closely at the table and the window frame. I wonder how fast we're turning."

Jillian had no idea. Dressed in well-fitting jeans and the usual cotton shirt, Jed normally would turn any female head, but dressed to the nines as he was today, he made her head spin, without the additional movement of the restaurant. She felt like a lovesick puppy, gazing starry-eyed at him across the table. Just because he didn't discard her after her emotional outburst was no reason to idolize the man, but she couldn't help but continue to stare, starstruck, at him.

He seemed not to notice. All his attention was focused outside the large windows. "This is quite the bird's-eye view from here. I wonder if we'll be able to see Liz's house." He turned and grinned at her. Jillian's heart skipped a beat. "Or your house."

Before she could reply, the waiter returned to inquire about bar selections and present them with their menus, allowing Jillian time to compose herself. They both ordered coffee to start, and the waiter left.

She reached across the table, brushing her fingers against his arm as she spoke. "Order whatever you want, Jed. This is my treat, and the sky's the limit. You deserve it. I've never heard 'Pop Goes the Weasel' done so well in my life."

Jed grunted. "Come on now, Jillian, I feel silly playing all that kiddy stuff. And you're going to be sorry you said that. What if I ordered the most expensive thing on the menu? You're going to wish you had simply given me a sticker."

She laid her menu flat on the table. "Don't feel silly; everyone has to start somewhere. It's not so simple when you're first learning. I played all that kiddy stuff too, you know."

"I know you did," he grumbled, "but when you did it you were probably eight years old. I'm a little older than that."

"I was six. As you can probably guess, I poured my heart and soul into the piano as a child. And that's beside the point. If it's any consolation, I admire you for starting now, as an adult. You've got guts. I hope you stick with it."

Jed turned his head to look out the window. "What every man wants to hear from a woman," he mumbled. "He's got guts."

Just like a little boy who didn't like being told he couldn't have a cookie before dinner, Jed's head lowered, and his lower lip stuck out. In all his masculine attire, Mickey Mouse tie aside, Jed's image presented quite a contrasting picture to his little-boy pout. Jillian bit her lower lip, but failed to control her laughter. First, she giggled, sputtering to hold back, then she covered her mouth with both hands. In the end, she burst into laughter, anyway. At that moment the waiter arrived to take their orders, giving her time to collect herself.

Resting her finger on the menu, she gave the waiter her order between giggles, then watched him write down both orders. When he left, Jed was staring at her.

"I love to watch you laugh. You know, you're as pretty as your name."

She couldn't help it. She blushed.

"Your name is so delightful. Jillian Jefferson. It suits you. What's your middle name?"

Jillian's cheeks heated up even more. "It's silly. Forget it."

"No, come on, tell me."

"June. My full name is Jillian June Jefferson."

"Alliteration. Effective. And beautiful."

Jillian's mouth gaped. She ignored the "beautiful" comment—but alliteration? She hadn't heard the term since high school. Up until now, she couldn't imagine Jed teaching high school literature. Maybe it wasn't so far off after all. "Well, what's your middle name? And I'll bet Jed is short for Jedediah."

He sighed and closed his eyes. "Jedediah. Beloved of the Lord."

"Come on, Jed, your middle name. I told you mine, so you can tell me yours."

"Ezekiel," he mumbled. "It means strength of God. My mother really did her homework."

Jillian snickered. Jed shrunk in his chair. "Jedediah Ezekiel Davies. Your initials are J.E.D., the name Jed. I like it."

"My mother thought it was cute." He sneered on the word "cute."

"Yes, it is cute." Jillian tried not to giggle again, but failed. "It suits you."

Jed straightened, sitting tall in the chair, emphasizing his size and the masculine width of his shoulders. "Get serious. Do I look 'cute' to you?"

All she could do was stare. He was a long way past cute.

Jed lowered his head. "Let's change the subject," he mumbled.

Her eyes softened, then became misty. "You're a nice man, Jedediah Ezekiel Davies."

Fortunately, their dinners arrived, sparing him the need for a response. The only time anyone ever used his horrible name was when his mother was furious at something really stupid he'd done, but when Jillian said it in that honey sweet voice, it was different. Her words and tone rushed over him, piercing him all the way to his soul. And his heart.

Jed said a short prayer of thanks over their meal. By the time they finished dinner and dessert, they had indeed made one complete revolution, just as the waiter promised.

When the bill came, Jillian scooped it up before he had the chance to touch it. Before he could protest, Jillian silenced him with a look that would have stopped a herd of wild elephants, then smiled sweetly at the waiter and handed him her credit card.

She turned to him when the waiter left. "I told you this was my treat, Jed. You deserve it. Now, don't insult me by trying to be gallant."

Jed tried to smile and hoped it didn't look as phony as it felt. He really hadn't been serious, nor had he thought she would take him seriously. "Next weekend, will you let me take you out and it'll be my treat?"

She shook her head. "No. I didn't do this to take turns. I wanted to treat you because you deserve it for all your hard work. Now be quiet and quit complaining."

Jed tried to appear casual on the outside, but inside, he was all choked up. Of course, it was only dinner, but this was the first time a woman had ever treated him to anything other than small birthday gifts. Brenda certainly never had.

At the time, he thought he'd fallen in love, and he thought Brenda loved him back. At first, they'd had fun together, and he gladly shared everything he had with her. Before long, she started asking for things, small things, then more expensive items she claimed to need, and then later, she claimed to be desperate and asked him for what she called a small loan, just for a few months. Since he was saving for college, however, the loan had not been small for him.

The next day he stopped by Brenda's house after work to discover Brenda and everything she owned—and everything of his she'd borrowed—were gone. Even though she'd asked for it, he hadn't given her the key to his condo, and he was glad now he hadn't, or else she would have cleaned that out, too. He hadn't been able to find her. No one, not even her parents, knew where she went, but her neighbor, a supposed friend of hers, a man, mysteriously packed up and moved out the same day.

She'd said she loved him, and he'd believed her. From that day on, he swore he'd never allow himself to be used like that again. She had bled him dry from both his heart and his bankbook, at the same time, forcing him to postpone his dream of a college education. The next day, he'd been told the plant was closing, and as corporate secretary, Brenda would have known that beforehand. Half the town, himself included, was suddenly unemployed. Through God's grace, he found another job quickly, except he had to sell his condo and move quickly. If it wasn't for Liz's needing a sitter, he could never have saved enough money for college while paying for a place to stay in Vancouver, where accommodation was far more expensive.

The waiter returned with Jillian's credit card and the receipt for her signature. Jed couldn't help but stare as she tucked it into her wallet, then back into her purse.

Jed was flabbergasted. What he felt for Brenda could in no way compare to how he felt about Jillian; he really hadn't been in love at all, he realized now. Friends, yes, and she'd played on his sympathies and tugged on his heartstrings to get what she wanted. But that was all. His feelings for Brenda were nothing like what he felt now for Jillian.

All his defenses came crashing down as Jillian smoothed her skirt, then folded her hands on the table, and smiled sweetly. His throat constricted. His last excuse was gone. He had no choice left but to admit to himself he was helplessly and hopelessly in love with Jillian Jefferson, the piano teacher.

"Ready to go?" she asked, completely unaware of the confused state of his heart. Jed stood and escorted her to the elevator door.

"How would you like to go up a floor and walk around the observation deck?" Jed asked as they waited for the elevator. He needed time to think. He couldn't let the evening end yet.

Jillian smiled and pressed the "up" button.

When the elevator door swooshed shut behind them as they entered the observation level, Jed gently grasped Jillian's hand. She didn't pull away, so he slowly led her around the perimeter, gazing out the window at the bright lights of the city shining below.

Alone in the semidarkness of the observation deck, talk was unnecessary, allowing Jed to enjoy Jillian's company in silence. They walked slowly, hand in hand, looking out the window of the observation room. No noise disturbed them, no appointments loomed, no schedules needed to be met. Except for the slight drone of the restaurant under them, they could have been alone in the universe, the city lights stretched out beneath them, miniature cars inching their silent way on the streets far below.

Jillian stopped to point out a few of the older landmark buildings in the area. When she leaned on the rail, then touched her finger to the glass, Jed slipped his hands around her waist. She didn't protest. He wanted to never let her go. She slid within the circle of his hands until she faced him, then rested her palms on his chest, keeping them a respectable distance apart. Jed didn't feel like being respectable.

His voice came out much lower pitched than it should have. "Is this where I'm supposed to thank you for a lovely evening, or do I wait until we get home? I've never had a woman take me out before, and I'm not sure what to do." He forced himself to smile. "And I'd like to know what you're going to do to top this when I pass Book Two."

Jillian's voice also came out soft and husky, doing more strange things to his insides. "I don't know. We've barely started."

His fingers found their way into her hair. "That's true, we haven't really." Jed couldn't believe the direction of their conversation. The lesson book was the furthest thing from his mind. The thing foremost in his thoughts was Jillian's sweetness, the silky feel of her hair, and the slight herbal fragrance of her shampoo. As he ran his fingers over the silken strands, Jillian's eyes drifted shut, and before he could talk himself out of it, Jed closed his eyes, lowered his head, and kissed her. When her arms floated up around his neck, Jed wondered if he'd died and gone to heaven. In the background, soft music played, adding to the atmosphere of romance.

He'd never been the romantic type, but Jed couldn't stop his emotions from spiraling out of control. Before someone walked in on them, Jed reluctantly ended the kiss, but rather than let the moment end, he held her tight. She fit just right in his arms, her head neatly tucked beneath his chin. Deep in his heart, he knew tonight was special.

Ever since she'd lost control and poured out her sad story to him, he'd found himself praying for her at the oddest times. At some point, his prayers had changed. Rather than only wanting to provide comfort and stability to her, he had started to pray that she would respond to him on more than a mentor level, that she would see him as a friend, then as more than just a friend, as the soul mate to share his hopes and dreams and his future. He wanted so much to pour his heart out to her, to shower her with words of love and devotion, but he doubted she was ready to hear them.

He ran his hands up her back, then released her. "I think it's time for me to take you home."

More than ever before, Jed impressed Jillian with his manners, both when he escorted her back to his truck, and when they arrived at her house. He appeared at the door of the truck, extending his hand to help her out before she even realized he was there. He'd been strangely silent on the drive home, but more than silent, what little he did say was ominously serious.

Although unsure of whether or not to invite him in, she didn't want the evening to end, so Jillian invited Jed in for a cup of tea. He graciously accepted, without commenting on how much he hated her favorite blend. The omission worried her.

As she poured the water, she peeked over her shoulder at him. His size dwarfed her small kitchen. She compared his appearance today to the last time he had been in her kitchen. On his way home from work that night, he hadn't looked like this. In contrast to his almost elegant attire tonight, his clothes then were worn, torn, and dirty. But it wasn't his garments that made the difference; it was something else, something she couldn't put her finger on.

"Relax, Jed, you're making me nervous," she quipped, trying to sound light. She wished she could figure out what it was.

Jed leaned back in the chair, raising his arms, linking his fingers behind his head. He rested his feet on one of the chairs, crossed his ankles, and grinned. "Better?"

Jillian stared. Even the silly pose could not undermine his size and attractiveness. His dimples and white smile nearly made her heart stop. The usual lock of hair dangled rakishly onto his forehead, magnifying his good looks. "You have big feet," she stammered.

"What?" His grin dropped, he wiggled his toes, then smiled again. "At least you didn't say I have a hole in my socks."

Jillian waited for the kettle to boil, then poured water into the teapot to steep, and after a few minutes, poured the tea into two cups. The entire time, Jed said nothing, a sure indication that something was up. Slowly, she raised her teacup, hoping she could control the shaking of her hands as she gently sipped her tea. Jed straightened in the chair, following her lead.

On his first cautious sip, he grimaced, squeezed his eyes shut, and shook his head. "Yuck! This is that boiled straw again!" He opened his eyes and set the teacup on the table. "First, you make fun of me; now, you're trying to poison me."

"I beg your pardon?" Jillian gently lowered her cup to the saucer.

His sour expression did indeed indicate he seriously thought he was being poisoned.

Jed closed his eyes and shook his head again. The one stray lock of unruly hair bounced with his movement. "This is the same putrid concoction you gave me before."

She couldn't help but smile. The old Jed was back.

As if trying to save face, he took another cautious sip, then again grimaced in distaste. "This brew rates up there with 'Pop Goes the Weasel.' Just so you appreciate me, I'll let you know, I'm only drinking this to be polite."

Appreciate him? Jillian appreciated him in ways she dared not admit. To distract herself, she took another sip of her tea. "For your information, it's good for you. It's a special blend, a selection meant to be enjoyed, an herbal mixture meant to aid relaxation. And don't tell me that only your mother can tell you what's good for you. I'm your teacher, and don't you ever forget it."

"Oh, so you're not trying to poison me, you're trying to put me to sleep." His eyes twinkled as he spoke.

"If you do go to sleep, at least I'll know it's the tea, and not that I'm boring you," she retorted, unable to suppress a grin.

Jed lowered his cup to the table, then reached across to cover both her hands with one of his. His large hand dwarfed hers completely. "You'll never bore me, Jillian."

Unable to respond, she yanked her hands out from under his, but in doing so, her elbow caught the edge of her teacup. The cup rattled against the saucer, then tipped, spilling the tea, sending a large puddle flowing over the tabletop. Jed jumped to his feet a split second before a waterfall of hot tea cascaded onto his chair, then dribbled onto the floor.

Jillian raised both hands to her lips. "Ooh, Jed, I'm so sorry!" She tried to stand, but Jed stopped her by resting one hand on her shoulder, preventing her from moving.

"Missed me by a mile. You stay there, I'm already up. I'll get it, before this wonderful substance strips the finish off the table."

Using her dishcloth, Jed carefully wiped up every drop, rinsed the cloth, and hung it over the faucet. He pulled down a section of paper towel, and dutifully wiped the chair and floor. "Done," he stated simply, wiping his hands on the towel.

Jillian's face flamed. Not only had she been so clumsy and spilled her tea, but she sat and watched while her guest cleaned up after her.

"Want me to pour you some more?" He picked up the teapot and sloshed it around. "There's still some in here. You didn't have a tea cozy on it, but it's probably still warm enough." He rested his hand on the outside of the teapot, feeling its warmth, then nodded. "I think I can sacrifice not having a second cup if you want it." He grinned and started pouring it without waiting for her to reply.

Sitting in the chair, Jillian's throat constricted as she watched him carefully pour the tea. She didn't know how to handle her time with Jed. He spent time with her because he enjoyed her company, and he sincerely didn't want anything she wasn't willing to give. Totally undemanding, he was fun to be with, but yet he had a serious side, both dependable and respectable. His faith in God was solid and secure, and he lived his life to honor God to the best of his ability. Although in an unconventional way, he was an invaluable support to his family, committing himself to the long term. He could be trusted. Unconditionally.

Slowly and innocently, he had worked his way into her heart. "Thank you," she choked out in a whisper. Hopefully, he couldn't hear the strain in her voice.

He rinsed out the teapot and set it upside down in the drain board. Jillian didn't want the tea, but she forced herself to drink it. Jed resumed his position in the now-dry chair, pushed his cup to the center of the table, and watched her as she sipped in silence.

"You know, I never realized how late it was. I guess I'm used to being up in the middle of the night, working the hours I do." He stood, pushing the chair in. "I should be going."

"Yes, it is late." Despite the lateness of the hour, and the supposed soothing effect of the tea, the last thing Jillian felt like was sleeping.

She walked him to the door. He stepped into his shoes, then turned. "Good night, Jillian."

She stood beside the door, hypnotized, unable to look away. Jed turned to stand close to her, the sparkle in his eyes fading along with his smile.

Very slowly, his arms surrounded her. "I want to kiss you good night, Jillian." She noticed it wasn't a question, and if it had been, she couldn't have denied him. One hand gently drifted up her arm, brushed her throat, then cupped her chin as his eyes closed. Her eyes fluttered shut just as his lips descended on hers. Delicately, he kissed her, gently and tenderly. She was lost. He pulled away long enough to whisper gently against her lips, "I love you, Jillian."

Somewhere in the background, she heard her own voice answer back, "I love you too, Jed." She started to kiss him back when she realized what had just happened. She couldn't love him, and he couldn't love her. Panic gripped her. Not Jed. She valued his friendship and his steady companionship too much to venture past what had already been established, past the point of no return. Jed had the capacity to do more damage than anyone she'd ever known.

Jillian slid her hands to his chest and pushed. "We both have to get up for church in the morning."

Jed stiffened, then separated, but instead of fully backing away, he held both her hands between them with both of his. "Jillian?"

"I think you'd better leave." She needed time to think, and to ask for help, and in order to do that, she had to be alone with God.

His confused expression was almost her undoing. "Maybe we should talk."

Jillian shook her head. "I don't think so. Not today. Not now." She clamped her lips together before she started to babble.

Still holding both her hands with one of his larger ones, Jed gently brushed the hair off her temple, then ran two fingers down her cheek, resting them under her chin. "Will I see you tomorrow?"

Her heart pounded so hard, she thought he could surely see it. All the heat drained out of her until she shivered. "I don't think so," she squeaked.

"I see." He nodded, dropped his hands, then left.

Jillian stood in the open doorway, watching the taillights of his truck disappear into the night. The cool air against her face helped quell the sudden rush of despair as he disappeared around the corner. She'd sent him away.

She rushed inside and slammed the door shut, leaned against it, and gulped for air. What had she done? Burying her face in her hands, Jillian did the only thing she could. She talked to her Best Friend.

Dear Jesus, help me. Things are going too fast. I don't know what I should do. I can't handle this alone. As You do every time I ask, please guide me, show me what is in Jed's heart, and if it is in Your plans, if it is in Your will, tell me what to do.

Then Jillian picked up her Bible, sat on the couch, and read 1 Corinthians 13:4–7 a dozen times. Could she ever achieve those high standards for love?

12

*J*illian walked into the sanctuary in silence, ignoring the sociable chatter around her. Sitting quietly in the pew, she tucked her purse beneath her, staring forward. As she waited for the service to begin, her head swam with conflicting images. Graham, declaring his love, demanding and expecting physical proof of hers, followed by the threat of violence if she denied what he claimed as his right. Jed and his soft words, his unspoken friendship and tenderness, demanding nothing, then holding her close when she fell to pieces and cried in his arms. She had needed him, and he'd been there for her.

No one had ever been there for her before. No one but Jesus. On the other hand, people freely called her when they needed something. At the university, she'd tutored many other aspiring music students. She'd volunteered whenever she was asked for church-related activities. Even as a child, her father loved to show off his cute little budding talent on the piano, then once the crowds were gone, off to the nanny she went. No one wanted her for what she was—simply Jillian Jefferson.

Graham, whom she had thought was a fine upstanding Christian man, let her down when he should have been different. But Jed was different from Graham. In her mind, she knew it, but in her heart, she struggled to let go of her fear. If she trusted Jed, would he be the next to disappoint her? If so, she wouldn't survive. Not again, and not from him.

Jillian closed her eyes to pray, but before she gathered her thoughts, a familiar deep voice beside her nearly caused her heart to stop. "Hi, Jillian. Mind if I sit here?"

"Jed!" A few heads turned at the volume of her squeaky voice. She lowered her pitch a few octaves. "Jed," she whispered. "What are you doing here?"

Standing tall beside her, he looked down, then lowered himself to sit in the pew beside her. "It's Sunday. I'm attending church." He slid in close beside her.

Last night, she'd opened her heart and soul to God, talking to Him at length about Jed. She'd done a lot of Bible reading and a lot of praying, and she could feel God telling her to listen to Jed, to open her heart, put all her past hurts aside, and allow herself to love him as he surely loved her. Surely that couldn't be so hard.

She started to fold her hands in her lap, but Jed grasped her left hand to hold it with his right. "I missed you."

Her throat tightened, and her heart pounded. "You just saw me last night," she whispered.

He chuckled gently, then rubbed her hand with his other one, being careful not to let go. "That was nine hours ago."

She gulped, her throat tight, almost totally constricted. "Oh, that long?"

"That's too long. We should be going to church together."

"You should be in church with your family."

"We could be family."

She turned to face him, but he was staring down at their joined hands, absently toying with her fingers. She wanted to yank her hand away, but she couldn't. Family? What did he mean by that? The only way they could be family was if they got—

The service started, drawing Jillian's attention forward. Throughout the worship songs, every time they stood, then sat, he didn't release her hand. Throughout the sermon, his grip remained gentle, but firm. During the prayer time, he squeezed her hand a number of times, as if she needed a reminder of his presence. When they stood for the closing hymn, Jed released her hand, but Jillian missed her pitch on the high note when he slipped his arm around her waist.

As soon as the pastor closed the service, with the last strums from the guitar softly accompanying his words, Jed turned to her. Again he held both her hands, then ran his fingers over her wrists. "Jillian, I need to talk to you. Alone. I wonder if—"

"Jillian! Good to see you! And who's your friend?"

Jillian forced a smile as she turned to face the pastor, who had just arrived beside them. "Pastor Lucas, this is Jed Davies."

She listened politely as the pastor welcomed Jed and then asked a few questions as they chatted. Jed responded politely to the questions about his church affiliation, and thanked him for the warm welcome to their small fellowship. Pastor Lucas laid his hand on Jed's shoulder, giving it a friendly squeeze as he kept talking.

A female voice interrupted their conversation. "Aren't you Dorothea and Peter's boy? I heard you've moved in with your sister, Elizabeth, isn't it?" All three heads turned to see the woman who was approaching, speaking as she walked.

Jed glanced back and forth between Pastor Lucas to Jillian, then back to the woman. "Yes, that's right. But I'm sorry, I don't remember you."

"I'm Christine Engels. I live next door to your Aunt Madge. How are your mom and dad?"

Jillian watched the light go on in Jed's eyes as he apparently remembered the woman. Jillian saw her chance for escape. She wouldn't be leaving him with strangers, so she didn't have to feel guilty about deserting him. She stepped back. "Excuse me, I'm meeting my sister for lunch, and I'm already late."

Jed gave Christine a polite smile. "If you'll excuse me, too, Christine, I'm sure I'll see you another time, okay?"

Christine nodded, and Jed accompanied Jillian to the parking lot.

On the one hand, Jillian wanted to know what Jed had to say, but on the other hand, she was almost afraid to ask. She unlocked her car door, quickly glanced at the time, then turned to face Jed. "We're alone now, Jed. What did you want to tell me?"

"Uh, I don't think this is quite the place . . ."

"I'm sorry to rush off, Jed, but Sue is already waiting for me. But I really want to hear what you wanted to tell me, especially if you made the special effort to come here, instead of going with your family this morning."

Jed grasped her hands, checked from side to side to make sure no one was watching, then fixed his eyes on her. Jillian blinked, then met his gaze.

He cleared his throat. "I didn't feel right about the way we parted last night, and I wanted to make sure you were okay."

That was all he wanted? To make sure she was okay? His concern broke down the last barrier. She couldn't speak as she stared up at him. Despite the fact that they were still standing in the church parking lot, she wished she could kiss him, just to show him how much she loved him.

She felt him give her hands a gentle squeeze, and his voice lowered so much she could barely hear him. "I love you, Jillian. Did you mean it when you said you loved me?"

Her throat tightened, but she had no doubt of her answer. "Yes, Jed, I did," she mumbled. "I just don't know what to do about it."

"Well, when a man and a woman fall in love, they start thinking of a future together. You know my plans for a teaching career. College will take a few years, so before we get into a long discussion, I'd like you to think about that, and what the future will hold for us."

Jillian felt all the color drain from her face. Us?

"You sound like you want to discuss something long term. Marriage . . ." She allowed her voice to trail off.

Jed smiled, then touched one finger to her cheek. "That's what usually happens, Jillian. Two people stand before God and declare their love, their commitment, and their trust in each other. You do trust me, don't you?"

She looked him straight in the eye, and nodded her assent. He wore his heart on his sleeve, the love for her was plain to see. His sincerity took her breath away. And it scared her.

"I've got to go, I'm already late. I'll phone you when I get back." She ducked into her car and headed for the mall.

When she got there, Jillian hurried into the restaurant as fast as her high heels would allow.

"Hi, Jillie. You're late."

"Something came up. Sorry about that. Hope you weren't waiting long."

Sue shook her head. "Not too long. So. How's the tall man in your life? Anything interesting to report?"

Jillian fumbled with her purse as she placed it on the seat beside her. "No."

Sue snorted. "No?"

Normally, she would discuss anything with Sue. This time, she simply couldn't.

Sue sipped her coffee, peeking over the rim of the cup as she spoke. "Too bad. So, he's still just a student, huh?"

"Something like that," Jillian mumbled.

Sue laid her menu down. "I can't stay too long; I have a million things to do. Geoff's mother took the kids for the afternoon, so I have to take advantage of that while I've got it."

The entire time she spent with her sister, Jillian's thoughts kept drifting back to Jed. She couldn't help but think of his closing question before she had to rush off. Did she trust him?

Since she met him, she'd progressed from simply enjoying his company to missing him when they weren't together. They'd gone from the usual amiable chitchat during lesson time to her pouring her troubles out to him, and yet he liked her anyway, and then declared his love. When they'd shared their goals, she had to admire him for his decision to make the sacrifices necessary to obtain his education for his teaching career, something she knew he'd be good at.

She knew he found her attractive, just as she found him attractive, yet he didn't push her beyond the limitations she'd set, or put aside the godly principles he held. She couldn't help but love him.

And he'd been the one to bring up long-term commitment. It was she who was holding back. Why?

Did she trust him?

The answer was yes, beyond any doubt. And she did want to marry him. And she wanted to give him the chance to ask her properly, which wasn't in the church parking lot.

Jillian smiled at the realization. Sue looked at her strangely, but didn't ask what was going on in her head, which was fine with Jillian. She could hardly wait to get home and phone Jed.

After the quickest lunch she'd ever had with her sister, Jillian rushed back to where she'd left her car. As she reached in her purse for her car keys, she touched a plastic wrapper. Jillian squeezed her eyes shut. In her rush, she'd forgotten to replenish her stock of reward stickers for her students, which was why she'd left the empty packet in her purse, to remind herself. She glanced at her watch, then to the mall across the street. If she ran in, a ten-minute delay could save her two hours tomorrow. Jillian crossed the parking lot, wishing she had worn more sensible shoes.

After she purchased her stickers, she walked quickly through the mall back to the exit. As she passed the food court in the center, a familiar head of unruly brown hair caught her attention. Her breath caught in her throat, and her mood lightened. It was Jed.

This could be her opportunity to apologize for her unenthusiastic response when he wanted to discuss their future together. Spending the time with her sister had been exactly what she needed. Although Sue was reasonably happy in her marriage, Jillian knew with the strength of God's love to support their marriage, she and Jed would form a bond that would be impossible to break, and when troubles came, together they would lean on God to help them along.

She no longer feared leaving herself vulnerable to Jed. She trusted him in every way. She felt both honored and humbled that such a man would choose her.

As she approached where Jed sat, he stood, as if ready to leave. Her feet skidded to a stop and her heart skipped a beat. He was not alone. He was with a woman.

Jillian blinked and stepped backward, partially hidden behind a large plant. Frantically, she searched for another way to make a discreet retreat, but she couldn't move without him seeing her. She was trapped.

Jed threw his head back and laughed. Jillian's face burned, not wanting to eavesdrop. She was so close that she could hear every word he said, yet he obviously didn't see her. All his concentration was focused on the woman he was with.

The woman stood, also laughing. The woman was everything Jillian was not. Tall, dark-complexioned, and model-slim, the woman exuded natural grace and confidence as she touched Jed's arm.

Jillian could hear Jed still laughing.

The woman spoke. "It's been too long since we got together, just the two of us."

Jed's laughter subsided as he wiped his eyes. "Much too long. I couldn't believe it was you; I was so surprised to see you here."

The woman replied, giggling. "I could say the same about you! All our failed plans to get together, and we bump into each other like this."

Jillian gasped. They planned to meet? How long had this been going on?

Jed stopped laughing, and patted his jacket pocket. "You wouldn't believe what I bought."

"You're full of surprises today, Jed. I have my ways; I'll get it out of you."

He shook his head and laughed. "No, you can't. I'm wise to all your tricks. You'll never pull one over on me again."

Something in Jillian's stomach went to war. So this was an old relationship. She knew Jed had a relationship that had an unhappy ending about the same time he lost his previous job. Was this her? Had they renewed their relationship, and were they now making up for lost time?

Jed picked up a few parcels, and handed them to the woman. When their hands touched, their fingers joined together between them. Jillian felt sick.

Jed's eyes sparkled, his face radiant. Jillian had never seen him so happy. The backs of her eyes burned, but she didn't dare move to wipe them.

"I'll tell you later, after I've had time to think about it some more. And in the meantime, we'd better get going and get you home before you're missed. We'll make real plans for next time." He let go of her hands, and they turned toward the exit.

The woman laughed again, then reached toward Jed's pocket, the same one he had just patted. He covered it with one hand, then raised his other hand and wagged one finger at her. "Don't touch. Mine."

"I think I have an idea what that is. Ain't love grand!" she exclaimed, then giggled. They left, laughing about things Jillian could no longer hear, so intent on each other they fortunately didn't see her, hiding behind the large bushy plant.

As Jillian watched them exit the mall her stomach tightened. And he had asked if she trusted him. Was this why? Because she shouldn't have? If she hadn't chanced upon Jed and the other woman, would she ever have known? Or had he changed his mind?

The other woman. Jillian nearly choked. Holding her head high, she hurried back to her car, managing to hold back the flood of tears and anguish until she inserted the key in the ignition. What she had felt for Graham paled in comparison to the love she felt for Jed. She realized she hadn't loved Graham at all; she'd only thought she did because he was the first one to pay her attention.

Jed. She did love him, but for some reason, he'd changed his mind about loving her. Did he finally get fed up with her inability to get a grip on herself? Or had he been seeing both of them at the same time all along?

She drove home as fast as she could; as soon as she stepped into the front hall she burst into tears once again. The other woman's words echoed through her head. *Ain't love grand?*

No, love was not very grand at all.

❧

"Are you sure she didn't call while I was gone?"

Mark shook his head violently, sending his hair askew in a halo around his head. "No, Uncle Jed, she didn't call. Honest."

Jed checked his watch for the millionth time. How long did this lunch with her sister take? He'd made it home in plenty of time to catch her call, yet the phone remained silent. No messages registered on the machine, and he'd checked it at least a dozen times to be sure it worked. Jed sucked in a deep breath, picked up the phone, and dialed Jillian's number.

Jillian wiped her face on her sleeve and answered the phone with a shaking hand, hoping whoever it was wouldn't notice the tremor in her voice.

"Jillian? Hi, I've been waiting for you to call."

Her heart stopped, then started up in double-time. "Jed," she choked out. "I've been too busy."

"Are you free now? Can I come over? I'd like to talk to you."

She knew what he wanted to talk about. Either he was going to tell her he was seeing someone else and tell her good-bye, or he would pretend nothing was going on, spouting lies of love and devotion. Her emotions were still too raw to listen to either option. "No, not tonight." The less she spoke, the more chance she had of holding her composure. She bit her lip to keep it from quivering.

She heard Jed hesitate. "Tomorrow then?"

"No, not tomorrow, either."

A few seconds of silence hung on the line. "Tuesday?"

"Yes, I'll see you at your regular lesson time on Tuesday." She had managed to keep herself under control so far, but she knew she would soon lose it. Hearing his voice, all she could picture was him laughing and smiling at the other woman. Tears burned her eyes, and squeezing them shut wouldn't stop the flow.

Jed's voice lowered into a smooth husky tone, filled with concern. "Jillian, is something wrong? Talk to me."

Jillian couldn't. "I have to go." She hung up the phone as quickly as she could without slamming it into his ear, then unplugged it. Childish, perhaps, but she needed the time to sort everything through and get control of herself once more. Tuesday would come soon enough.

❧

Jillian checked the clock again. In only a few minutes, Jed would arrive for his regular lesson. After two sleepless nights, she felt like a zombie, yet her nerves were so keyed up, she couldn't keep still.

Every time she tried to plan what to say to him, she came up with a different answer. No commitment had ever been directly stated, but still she felt deceived.

Jillian closed her eyes, shook her head, then absently began picking through her pile of music books and stickers, sorting them into meaningless piles to keep herself busy. At the sound of Jed's knock, a handful of paper fluttered to the floor.

Jed walked in.

She stared past him, then sat in her chair beside the piano bench. "Please sit down, Jed," she stated formally.

"Hi, Jillian. I missed you. Did you have a good visit with your sister?"

"Yes, thank you. We should start right in, because we're working on your new book today." She leaned forward and opened the book, smoothing it open at the right page.

His hand touched her shoulder. "Jillian . . ." Jed mumbled in a choked voice, "talk to me."

She couldn't talk to him. Every version of every conversation she rehearsed flew out the window. Clearing her throat, Jillian put on her best teacher smile, ignored his plea, and recited the same lesson she'd done so many times before with so many children. When the clock on the wall indicated 2:45, she turned and smiled at him as best she could. "That's it," she said, trying to sound light.

Jed turned to her, his expression so sullen it nearly broke her heart. "Time for me to go get Betsy," he mumbled.

"Now that you're on the next level, I think we should cut the lessons back to once a week." As much as she wanted to see him, it hurt too much. "I'll see you next Tuesday."

"No, Jillian, I can't wait until next Tuesday. Can't we talk about this?"

Jillian choked. Her eyes burned, but she would rather die before she let him see her cry again. No matter what her head told her, in her heart, she still loved him, even though his heart belonged to someone else. As a Christian, supposedly someone who valued fidelity and trust, how could he be so casual about it?

Jed reached forward and grasped both her hands in his. "Can we have lunch together tomorrow?"

She yanked them back. "I don't know. You really should go get Betsy."

Jed straightened his back. "Yes, I should."

He walked to the tray, slipped his cowboy boots on, and left. Jillian sat and stared at the piano, then at Jed's scarf, taunting her from the coatrack beside the door.

$$\textbf{13}$$

*J*ed exchanged greetings with the other men, at the same time throwing his lunch pail carelessly into his locker. The men laughed and joked as they sat on the bench and changed into their safety boots, ready to start another night. Today he did not join in their lighthearted banter. His mind was on other things.

After lacing his safety boots, he placed his cowboy boots in his locker and stood still. With his hands braced on the opening, he lowering his head, squeezed his eyes shut, and drew a deep breath. What had happened?

Tuning out the clatter around him while he still leaned half into his locker, Jed prayed. He prayed for guidance and for answers. Sure, he knew Jillian's hesitations to accept his love, but he could understand and accept that. Then, just when he finally started to hope she had managed to overcome her past experiences, she froze him out. The closeness he thought they'd developed was gone. Why? And, most importantly, what could he do about it?

"Wake up, Jed. Time to get moving!"

Jed opened his eyes and turned his head to see that everyone except for Dave had left the room to start their shift.

"Yeah, sure. Be right there." Jed closed his locker and walked to his workstation.

The night passed even more slowly than usual. He couldn't stop thinking of Jillian, but he came to no conclusions to explain the abrupt change in her attitude. Finally, he decided to come right out and ask her face-to-face what was wrong, or what he'd done to cause this sudden withdrawal.

When only a few minutes remained till the end of the shift, Jed heard a voice drifting down from the ceiling, calling his name. He looked up to see three members of his crew standing on the narrow catwalk, trying to adjust the fitting that held the cable to the center of the structure.

"Hey, Jed! Ya wanna come up here and help out?"

"Be right there." Jed called from the ground level. "What's up?"

"The walk feels a bit shaky—can you grab a toolbox and give us a hand?"

Jed couldn't believe his eyes. One of them had loosened the center supports in an effort to adjust it. If it was out of alignment, it was the duty of the senior man to report it to the maintenance department. Jed quickened his pace to fetch the toolbox, taking the stairs up two at a time.

One of the men started walking to him as they saw him approaching, and met him at the edge. He extended his arm to take the toolbox from Jed.

Jed handed it to him. "Are you sure you should be up here? You should leave it for maintenance. It's the end of the shift, anyway." The weight lifted from his arm as the other man took the toolbox, turned around, and started walking back to the center of the span.

Jed stood at the edge with his hands on his hips. It didn't feel right or safe. This was a job for someone who knew what he was doing.

Suddenly, with a creak of groaning metal, the catwalk swayed. All three men stumbled to the side at the same time, their weight jarring against the railing together. The toolbox flew over the side and crashed to the floor far below.

The sudden weight slamming against one side made the structure tilt further, and Jed heard a pop as the support they had been repairing came apart. A groan of fatigued metal sounded near Jed's feet. As he looked down, he saw that where the catwalk was connected to the concrete platform the metal joint had sheared. Only one bracket remained to support the catwalk, and it was bending. The structure was going to go down, and there were three men on it.

"Run!!!" he shouted at the top of his lungs. Then Jed did the only thing he could think of. He grabbed what he could of the railing, held on tight, pulled backward to brace himself against the weight, and prayed for strength. If he could hang on long enough, they could run off. The three of them would be killed from this height if the walkway came down with them on it, four stories up.

He felt the jarring of their footsteps all the way to the roots of his clenched teeth. He couldn't yell at them to run faster.

The joint gave way, leaving the entire weight in Jed's hands. He refused to let go with one man not all the way off. The weight pulled him forward off his feet and slammed his body down on the concrete floor. With the crashing impact, Jed saw stars. Between the pain in his chest and his face, his vision blurred, and he had difficulty breathing. He could taste blood and dirt from the concrete floor against his face. Jed never saw if the last man made it off or not. Everything started to go black. He tried to fight it.

The force and weight of the railing dragged him forward before it wrenched out of his hands, and the structure plummeted down and shattered, crashing to the ground below.

Jed gasped for breath, lying on his stomach, his head and arms hanging over the edge of the platform. He tried to move, but nothing would respond. He hurt so bad he couldn't focus, call for help, or even move.

Someone grabbed his ankles and dragged him away from the edge. As his arms went up above his head, the pain in his shoulder was so intense it made him nauseous. Everything started spinning. He thought his head would split in two. He threw up, and everything faded to black.

❧

Jillian woke up exhausted after a fitful sleep. Through all her tossing and turning, she had come to a decision. She simply could not teach Jed piano lessons anymore. After losing her heart to him, confiding in him, and now knowing that he loved someone else, she could no longer bear to carry on as if nothing had happened.

Worst of all, he had deceived her.

Jillian swiped tears from her eyes, unable to stop her lower lip from quivering. What was wrong with her? She was a hardworking, God-fearing woman. She tried her best to be honest and treat people fairly and to respect people's feelings.

As a stabbing reminder, Jed's scarf still hung on the coatrack by the front door, taunting her.

As she got dressed, she decided to spare herself the drawn-out agony. Rather than have Jed come to her house, she would go to him, tell him she didn't ever want to see him again, and leave.

Jillian checked the time. She knew Jed got Mark off to school, so she chose to do it now and get it over with.

For a minute, she remained in her car after she parked it in front of the house, allowing herself to take a few deep breaths to compose herself before she saw him one last time. She still loved him. He had said he loved her. She sucked in a deep breath and closed her eyes, asking God for strength. One day she would work on forgiving him, but for now, she would tell him how he'd hurt her, and she would leave. She'd rehearsed her speech in her head a million times during the night. Now she would steel her nerve and do it.

Jillian stepped out of her car and carried the scarf over her arm to the front door. Holding it close, she could smell his spicy aftershave, another reminder of the closeness she had lost. Refusing to let herself cry, she held her head up high, determined to be strong. She would face him and tell him she was sorry she somehow disappointed him and say good-bye. She sucked in one last breath, for composure, and pressed the doorbell.

A dog barked, and a man who was not Jed came to the door, making her wonder if she had the right house.

"Miss Jefferson?" he asked hesitantly, recognizing her, even though she did not recognize him.

"Yes?" she mumbled, her mind blank.

"Looking for Jed?" It seemed she did have the right house after all.

"Yes, I am." She still couldn't think of a single thing to say.

"I'm Frank, his brother-in-law, Mark's dad. We've never met, but we've spoken to each other on the phone a few times. Please come in." He led Jillian inside, but did not smile a greeting. Barely polite, he seemed lost in thought and was barely aware of her existence.

Jillian stiffened her back and stood as tall as she was able. "Can I see Jed?" she managed to squeak out.

"He's not here—he didn't come home from work last night. I just got off the phone. There was an accident."

Jillian heart missed a beat, then pounded in her chest. An accident. Jed was hurt. Or worse, had he been killed? No! Her knees wobbled, and she felt sick.

Frank looked at her, his face rigid. "He apparently got hurt when a walkway collapsed. His actions saved the life of a man who was on it when it started to fall. They say Jed's injuries aren't life-threatening or anything, that he's not that badly hurt, but he is under sedation. I want to go see him, but I don't know what to do with Betsy. I don't know what to expect. If he's all connected to tubes and full of bandages I don't want her to see him yet, and I can't find a sitter."

Jillian gulped. Praise God, Jed was okay. Suddenly, nothing else mattered, not his deceit, not the other woman. She had to go see him. "If you don't mind, I'd like to go see him, and if you have a message, I'll be more than happy to relay it."

Frank looked at her and she looked at him. She waited while he thought of something to say. "Just tell him we're proud of him."

Tears welled up in her eyes. "Is he at General?"

"Yes, but they didn't say which room, and I was too dumbfounded to ask."

"I'll go now."

"Yes, and I've got to phone Liz. They didn't phone until early this morning to say they'd taken him to the hospital, and we were really worried. We got up to get ready for work, and it was only then we realized Jed hadn't come home. When the phone rang we knew something was wrong, because he would never stay out all night and leave us in the lurch for baby-sitting. Earlier, no one could tell us how badly he was hurt. Liz will be relieved to know it's not serious."

Jillian thought she had the tears under control, but they started up again. When it came to his family, Jed would always keep his promises and do what he said he would. Why couldn't he have been so faithful and loyal to her?

The drive to the hospital seemed to take forever. She found out which room he was in, and when she arrived at the ward, she located a nurse.

"I still don't know what happened, the extent of his injuries," Jillian croaked out in a whisper.

The nurse walked behind the desk and flipped through a file. "Hmm," she mumbled, in a businesslike tone. "You'll have to speak to the doctor on duty." She replaced the file to its slot, crossed her arms, and looked Jillian straight in the eye, as if waiting.

Jillian shuffled her feet, then turned her head back and forth to check both ways down the hall. "I don't see a doctor. Do you think you could page him or something?"

The nurse grumbled. "I know where he is. Wait here." She walked off, leaving Jillian alone by the nurses' station.

Jillian followed the nurse with her eyes, and when she was out of sight, Jillian quickly checked for anyone else around, then hastily pulled Jed's file from its slot.

The sheet containing a list of his injuries was right on top. The writing wasn't too sloppy, so she hurriedly scanned the list. Four broken ribs, a dislocated shoulder, multiple stitches to his hands, and his nose was broken.

Not taking the chance of getting caught reading any more in the file, she hastily replaced it in the nick of time as the nurse reappeared around the corner.

"I can't find the doctor, but Mr. Davies is resting. You may go in now."

That was all Jillian needed to hear. She hurriedly slipped into his room and stood beside him. His eyes were closed, and he seemed unaware of her presence.

He looked terrible. Most of his face was obscured with bandages that covered up his nose completely, and both his eyes were blackened, although she had heard that sometimes happened when noses were injured. His torso was completely wrapped because of his broken ribs, and his left arm was bound rigidly to his body. Both hands were completely bound by castlike bandages that covered his fingers like mittens.

If he were sleeping, she wouldn't wake him. Rather than speak, she reached out and smoothed that unruly lock of hair off his face.

His eyes opened a slit. "Jillian? What are you doing here?" he mumbled.

She tried to keep her voice from cracking. "I'm here to see you."

His eyes closed. "You don't want to see me. I feel like I've been run over by a truck."

Jillian bit her bottom lip. "Shhh." She stroked his hair again. "I love you, you know."

His eyes remained closed. "I love you, too," he mumbled, then dozed off, with what Jillian thought was a smile on his face.

She continued to watch him, forcing herself to push aside the vision of him with another woman. She couldn't help herself, she loved him no matter what. Perhaps there was a logical explanation, perhaps there wasn't. The most important thing, for now, was that he was going to be all right.

Jillian checked the time, then sat in the chair beside his bed. She didn't know how long he would sleep, but she couldn't stay all day because she had students coming. In order to cancel lessons, she needed more notice, since most of them came directly from school. She considered leaving a note for Jed, although she had no idea what to say.

As she was digging in her purse for a pen, his eyes opened. "Are you still here?"

Startled, she looked up. "How are you feeling?" It was a stupid question, because he really did look like he had been run over by a truck, just like he had said earlier. How did she expect him to respond?

"I'm going to have a bump on my nose," he groaned.

"What?"

"My nose. I'm going to have a bump on it."

Jillian watched Jed lying in the hospital bed, completely immobile and covered in various types of bandages and wrappings. "A bump on your nose? You're worried about a bump on your nose?"

"I liked my nose the way it was. Now it's going to have a bump on it." His eyes closed again, and he drifted back to sleep.

The sound of footsteps caused her to turn her head. A middle-aged man entered the room and came to a stop beside Jillian.

He shoved his hands in his pockets. "I'm Roy, Jed's supervisor."

"Hi. I'm Jillian." She wondered how to introduce herself. His friend? His teacher? Or something more, but what? Jillian swallowed hard and said nothing.

Roy turned his attention to Jed's still form. "How is he? The nurse said he was awake."

"He just drifted back to sleep."

Jed heard both Jillian and Roy's voices, but the sedatives and painkillers they had given him did their job. His head spun, and his eyes refused to open. He wondered if he did open his eyes, if the room would continue to spin, and he'd be sick. Instead of trying to do something he wasn't capable of doing at the moment, he listened to the conversation, dazed.

"How did this happen?" asked Jillian, her voice shaky.

Roy cleared his throat. "He tried to hold up the catwalk by himself when the structure started to collapse. It worked for the few seconds needed for the last man to run, jump off, and get dragged to safety, but Jed sure got banged up in the process. I came to tell him he made the difference."

Jed vividly recalled that split second when the last bracket gave way, the sensation of trying to stop it before it broke, and the agony as the weight sent him flying into the cement floor. He didn't know if the last man had made it off. When he woke up briefly in the ambulance, the attendants didn't know. Now he knew, and through the fog in his head, he thanked God for having made a difference.

He felt Jillian's fingers in his hair, and he tried to respond, but couldn't.

Her fingers stilled. "I don't know if you can hear me, Jed, but I have a message for you from Frank. He says they're very proud of you. And I have to get going now, because I have students coming soon, but I would think that your family will be coming tonight. I'll be back tomorrow."

He felt the cool air where her fingers had been, and the room fell silent. Jed allowed himself to fall asleep, anticipating her return, knowing everything would be all right after all.

❧

Jillian woke earlier than she had in years. She didn't think she'd ever been up before sunrise. It probably took longer to warm up the car than to walk the short distance, but this early in the morning, she couldn't bring herself to walk.

Tapping lightly on the door, she listened for a sign of movement inside the house. She was startled when sounds of barking echoed through the door, and then the door shook when the dog landed against it.

"Down, Missy!" It was Frank's voice, accompanied by scratching sounds and whining noises as the door opened. Frank pulled the dog back by the collar as he spoke.

"Hi, Jillian. We really appreciate you doing this for us. We're going to have to do something really special for Jed when he gets home. His being here has lifted such a burden off us about the baby-sitting. Since he's been living here, I think we've forgotten what a hassle it was in the morning. We haven't even given baby-sitting a second thought."

With the dog pulled away, Jillian walked in and placed her shoes neatly on the tray. "Yes, he takes his commitment very seriously, and he really loves the kids."

"And they really love him." As they walked up the stairs together, Jillian looked around. The house was quiet, so fortunately the ruckus with the dog at the door had not woken Mark and Betsy.

"I'll give you a quick tour of the house, and then we've got to be on our way. Liz will give you the routine."

Jillian followed Frank into the kitchen, where a woman who was obviously Liz was bending over into the fridge.

Liz turned at the same time as she stood. Tall, slender, dark hair. Jillian almost fainted. This was the woman Jed had been with at the mall.

14

"Hi, Jillian, or should I say Miss Jefferson?" Liz held out her hand as a greeting. "I'm embarrassed to say that I've only met you once briefly, when Mark first signed up for lessons. The first thing I want you to know is how much we appreciate you doing this for us."

Jillian's mind reeled in shock as she shook Liz's hand. The other woman was his sister! How could she have been so stupid? How could she have been so untrusting? Just because Jed said he and his sister were a lot alike was no reason to assume they also looked alike.

Looking at Liz up close, now that she knew, of course, Jillian could see the family resemblance. She tried to regain her composure. "Hi, Liz, it's nice to meet you again."

"Yes—but it was supposed to be under better circumstances."

Jillian wondered what Liz meant by that comment. "You had better give me a rundown on the routine for the day so you can make it on time for work."

As Liz gave Jillian the schedule for the day, Jillian tried not to smile. Most of it she already knew from Jed, especially the afternoon schedule.

Before they left, Liz woke Betsy up and introduced her to Jillian so she would not awaken to find a stranger in the house. When Mark got up, he was delighted to have his piano teacher there to get him ready for school, although he took special care not to let Jillian see him in his pajamas.

After Mark was out the door and on his way to school, she made a pot of coffee and Betsy joined her at the kitchen table.

"Uncle Jed talks about you all the time, you know."

Jillian studied Betsy's face. She wasn't sure she wanted to hear this. "He talks about you, too."

"He does?"

Jillian gave a sigh of relief. She had managed to distract Betsy. "Yes. He says you are doing very well in kindergarten, and your teacher is very proud of you."

"You're Uncle Jed's teacher. Are you proud of him?"

Maybe this had backfired a little. Jillian tried not to let her nervousness with the little girl show. "Yes, I am."

"He thinks you're a good teacher."

"Well, I think he's a good student."

"He likes you, you know."

Great. Woman talk with a five-year-old. "Well, I like him too. Say, how would you like to help me make some cookies? I'll bet you know where your mom keeps everything, don't you?"

"Yes! I love to bake cookies. Uncle Jed tried to make cookies once. They were kind of awful. But Missy liked them. Except she barfed up the walnuts."

Jillian managed to keep a straight face. She knew Jed started supper every day, but maybe it was too much to expect that his culinary skills extended beyond that.

They took all morning to get one batch of cookies mixed and baked and the dishes done, but it was worth the mess and effort to keep Betsy busy. After a quick lunch, Jillian drove Betsy to school and then continued on her way to the hospital to visit Jed.

The entire trip, she tried to sort out what she was going to say to him. She had behaved like a jealous fool, and now she was going to have to swallow her pride and face him.

Lunch was being served as she arrived at his ward. She could hear him complaining before she walked into his room.

"How do you expect me to eat this? This isn't funny!" he griped, but she could tell he had a smile on his face without even looking. The nurses were giggling.

"The department decided to hold a raffle to see who was going to come in to help you. Proceeds go to Children's Hospital Fund." There was more giggling.

Jillian heard Jed mumble something about not being very amused, and she walked in to see for herself what was going on.

Jed looked up, causing the two nurses to turn around.

"Oh, she's here," one of them sighed. "Looks like the lunch raffle's off. Maybe suppertime." Then they both left, pushing the lunch cart out the door.

Jillian frowned and glared at Jed. "What's going on in here?" She folded her arms against her chest.

Jed had been propped up to a sitting position in the bed. He let his head drop backward. "I hate this place!" he grumbled. "Let me out of here!"

"Why?"

"With one arm strapped up like this, I can't move without someone helping me, and I can't touch or hold anything with my hands wrapped up solid. I feel like I've been mummified! I can't move, I can't eat, I can't do anything!"

Jillian tried to stifle a laugh. If this was the way he was talking to her, she could only imagine what he said to the nurses. However, she was going to have to check out this raffle.

"I can feed you. What's for lunch?" Jillian peeked under the lid of the lunch tray and laughed. Soup and a sandwich. No wonder he was complaining. And coffee, too. How would he drink that without using his hands? She couldn't imagine drinking coffee through a straw.

Jillian lifted up the sandwich so he could take a bite. He made a wry face, but took a bite anyway.

"They barely have enough food on here to feed a pigeon. And you are not going to spoon-feed me that soup. This is so humiliating," he grumbled.

Their conversation for the balance of the afternoon mostly consisted of Jed's semi-good-natured complaining.

Jillian looked at the time. "Say 'that's it,' " she ordered.

"That's it?" he questioned.

"Yup," Jillian stated. "Time for me to go get Betsy."

"What? You?"

"Liz and Frank couldn't get a replacement for you on short notice, so I volunteered until you're up to it."

"Jillian, I don't know what to say."

"Say nothing then. Actually, they're very nice people."

"Of course they are. Frank couldn't have found a better wife than Liz. She's great. You know, we used to fight constantly when we were kids, but now, we've become the best of friends, as well as brother and sister."

Jillian's smile faded. She couldn't put it off any longer, and since he had started the topic of his sister, it forced her to say what she had been agonizing over.

"Jed, speaking of your sister, I'm afraid I have a confession to make."

"What about Liz? You two didn't have a fight, did you?"

Jillian looked down, unable to face him as she spoke. "You're probably wondering why I acted so cold to you the other day. Well, I feel so stupid about this, but I saw you and Liz together on Sunday as you were leaving the mall. From what I saw I thought you were seeing someone else, and it looked like you were exchanging words of love, and," Jillian paused and swallowed, her voice dropping to a whisper, "and I was hurt. And very jealous." She shrugged her shoulders but couldn't look up at him. "I didn't know it was your sister. I'm so sorry." Tears welled up in her eyes, and she couldn't blink them away.

"Look at me." Jed's words were soft and gentle.

Jillian couldn't face him. She swiped the tears away with her sleeve.

"We probably made quite a scene, Liz and I, carrying on at the mall, and I think I can remember what we said as we were leaving. If that's what you saw, I think I can understand why you felt that way. But you missed the best part of the conversation. We were talking about you."

Jillian blinked, but a tear escaped and ran down her cheek.

"Come here. I wish I could hold you properly, but I'll do my best."

As Jillian sat on the bed beside him, he rested his unbound arm around her as best he could.

"I love you, Jed. I'm so sorry."

"I love you, too. And don't worry about it anymore. Now, the air is clear. It's okay. Now, come here and kiss me."

Jillian stood, bent at the waist, then kissed him lightly and briefly on the mouth. "I have to go get Betsy. I'll be back tomorrow. Oh, and give me your keys so someone can pick up your truck at the plant."

"You have to get them yourself. Right there, in the drawer."

"See you tomorrow."

"Yeah, bye."

Jillian walked around the nurse who was standing near the doorway and left.

❧

Jillian arrived at the hospital the same time as the day before. However, this time she was not allowed to go into Jed's room, as the doctor was in with him, checking him over before releasing him.

She sat in a chair by the nurses' station and listened. Jed was complaining again. First something tickled, then something pinched. Next, he refused to do something, followed by a question about why he was not allowed to do something else. Then she heard a nurse asking him to be quiet and quit moving. Jillian was glad she wasn't the one looking after him.

Finally, the nurse at the desk allowed her to enter. Jed was sitting upright in the bed with a grumpy look on his face and considerably fewer wrappings than the day before. A doctor washed his hands in the sink, and a nurse picked up the scraps of the bandages that had been removed.

"Hi, Jed," Jillian said, trying not to laugh at his dour expression. "Liz sent you some clothes. I've come to take you home."

"Yes! Freedom!" Jed shouted in triumph.

She waited in the hall for him to get dressed, but since his hands were still heavily bandaged, she helped him slip on his boots and tied the laces. "That's it," she said as she stood. "Not only that, it's time to go get Betsy."

Jed shrugged his shoulders. "What a classic line."

She led him to the parking lot, where he stopped dead in his tracks. "This is my truck! You drove my truck."

Jillian blushed. "My car is so small I didn't know how you would fit in it. I hope you don't mind."

She wasn't sure how he'd feel about her driving his truck, because some men were kind of funny about that kind of thing. Instead of being angry, though, Jed looked down at her and laughed. "You probably looked ridiculous, a little thing like you, driving a big truck like this. I'll bet you got some strange looks on the way here, didn't you?"

"Yes, as a matter of a fact, I did. I was tempted to show off, too, but I drove your precious truck with lots of TLC; I didn't do any racing with it. But I could have driven right over top of the competition." When he laughed again, Jillian knew she'd done the right thing.

"Let's go."

When Jillian drove up to the school, Jed waited inside the truck while Jillian went into the building to get Betsy. When they returned, Mark was sitting inside beside Jed. Apparently he'd noticed the huge lumbering vehicle as he was coming out of the door, and all his friends had to check it out.

On the way home, Mark and Betsy were asking Jed a million questions. When they arrived at the house, Jillian made coffee while Mark and Betsy went into their rooms to play. Once it was finished brewing, Jillian handed Jed a cup, after arguing with him over whether or not he would be able to hold it. They lounged back on the couch and Jillian turned on the television.

Suddenly, Jed's eyes widened as he stared at the time on the VCR. "Look at the time; you're late for your lessons! You'd better get going."

"No, I canceled my afternoon lessons. I wanted to stay with you until after Frank and Liz get home." She raised her hands and slowly brushed both of Jed's cheeks with her fingertips.

"Wow. Personal attention from the teacher. I could get used to this." Jed smiled and Jillian's heart melted. She leaned toward him at the same time he leaned to her, joining together for a wonderful kiss, a kiss that was sweet and made up for the waste of lost time. Briefly, they separated, their eyes drifted open, shut again, then they joined again in a warm embrace, anticipating the next kiss. A thump on the floor interrupted them.

"Gross! Uncle Jed! Miss Jefferson! That's sick!"

Jed and Jillian bolted apart. Jillian's stomach clenched. Out of the corner of her eye she saw Jed wince, suck in a deep breath, and press his arm against his ribs with the abrupt movement.

Mark stood in front of them, a large ball in his hand and Betsy at his side, both of them wide-eyed, staring at their every movement. To her dismay, Jillian had forgotten about them.

"Eeww!" Mark exclaimed, with the same disgusted look on his face as the other time he had interrupted them. "Uncle Jed, why are you letting Miss Jefferson kiss you again? You said you didn't want to marry Miss Jefferson."

Startled, Jillian backed further away. Jed's face turned red, but he didn't say a thing. She remembered when Jed brought up marriage, and at the time it had frightened her and they agreed to discuss it later. It hadn't come up again between them, but to have Mark not only mention it but say Jed had no intention of marrying her made her wonder what had been said. Why would he have said something to Mark, and most of all, what?

Betsy grabbed Mark's T-shirt and started yanking on it. "I heard Mom and Dad talking about it. Wanna know what Mom said?"

Jillian glared at Jed. All the color drained out of his face.

She jumped to her feet. She had made a mistake about his sister, but to hear from the children's mouths that Jed had said he had no intention of marrying her, with no immediate denial on his part, was more than she could take. She took a step back. "I think I had better leave."

"Jillian, wait!" Jed jumped to his feet, then tottered slightly. "Please, Jillian, wait. I have to get something, and I'll be right back. Promise me you'll wait right here." He looked at her with such a tortured expression that Jillian conceded. She hugged herself with both arms and leaned against the wall to wait for his return.

His movements were labored as he tried to hurry down the hall, then slowed as he made his way down the stairs. He returned with a small bag, and sat on the couch. He patted the seat beside him, and held out a small bag.

"Take it, Jillian, with all my love."

Jillian sat beside him, and as she took the bag from his hands, her own hands started to shake. She recognized the logo as belonging to the large jewelry store in the mall. Peeking inside, she could see a small velvet box.

"Open it." Jed's deep voice trembled.

As she picked up the box, Betsy and Mark stepped closer to see what it was. With all eyes on her, Jillian opened it. It was a small heart-shaped ring, with a small sparkling diamond set in the middle. It was delicate, and it was beautiful.

Jed's bandaged hand rested on her knee. "Jillian, I'd like to plan for the future, and I want you to be in my future. I had intended to talk about it later, and, well, now that we're together, I can't wait. Jillian, will you think about marrying me?" he said in a low husky voice. "This wasn't the way I intended to ask you something so important, but it couldn't be helped. I can't let you walk away from me again."

Jillian's vision blurred as she raised her head to look into his eyes.

"You bought this at the mall," she choked on the words, "the day I saw you there with your sister."

"That's right. It's just a little promise ring, because it's going to be a long time before I finish my education. If you'll wait for me, I wanted to give you this ring as a promise. But if you say yes now, we can go together so you can pick your own engagement ring."

Jillian swallowed, hard. "Yes, of course I'll marry you. But your education comes first, before an engagement ring."

One side of his mouth tipped up in a lopsided smile. "It's taken care of. I was going to take out a student loan, but as it turns out, yesterday I had another visitor in the hospital. An old friend stopped by and it seems she saw the error of her ways, turned her life over to Jesus, and paid back a lot of money she owed me. So, don't you worry about that."

Jillian's heart pounded. God had carried her through her trials and hurts, and helped her to rise above them. Now she could love Jed as he deserved to be loved. God had given her the best gift of all, and she didn't have to do anything to receive it. She'd received the gift of love, both through the salvation of Jesus Christ, and the commitment of a wonderful, God-fearing man. Her voice dropped to a choked whisper. "I love you so much, Jed."

"I love you, too, Jillian."

At the same moment, they both turned their heads to see Mark and Betsy, who were staring at them with their mouths hanging open, still watching, and listening to every word.

"Okay you two, beat it, or you're going to have to watch Uncle Jed kiss Miss Jefferson."

Mark ran away first. "Yuck! No! Anything but that!" he screamed as he ran. Betsy shrieked, following his example, and ran after him.

Then Uncle Jed kissed Miss Jefferson like she had never been kissed before.

It Only Takes a Spark

A Spark

BY PAMELA KAYE TRACY

To my parents:
Albert H. Tracy and Rosemary A. Tracy (1927-1992)
When I said I wanted to sing, they listened.
When I said I wanted to draw, they provided pencils.
When I said I wanted to write, they gave me paper,
and through it all they gave me love.

And to my aunt and uncle:
Arnold Wilfong and Catherine Wilfong (1915-1993).
Every child needs cheerleaders. You were mine.

1

$\mathcal{I}$'ll be there in four more months." Isobelle de la Rosa expertly propped the phone between her ear and shoulder while propping her feet on her boss's desk and twirling a strand of black hair around her finger. "Mom's doing much better, and Carole's baby is due any day now."

Carole Martin waddled into the office, smiled as if she knew a secret, and set a stack of books on the large table that took up most of the office's space. Pressing a hand to the small of her back, she waited for Izzy to finish talking.

"I gotta go," Izzy sang into the phone, winking at Carole. "You know how my boss is."

"Was that Connie?" Carole put one hand on the table for balance and knocked a bulging folder to the floor.

"Yes." Izzy jumped up, came around the desk, and bent to retrieve the papers littered across the carpet. She carefully returned them to the stacks of things to do already towering on the head librarian's desk and scolded, "You're in your eighth month. You should be sitting down."

"There's too much to do." Carole frowned at the phone as if it had committed a crime. "If you're really going back to Phoenix come January, I've got to train the new girl, learn the computer system, and at least finish converting some of the card catalogue entries onto disc. All that and have a baby, too." Carole glanced at a photograph on her desk. Her husband, robust and graying, posed with a politician's smile. Their two college-age children flanked him. Carole grinned and shook her head. "Pregnant at forty-five, what was I thinking? Oh, well, Jake says it will keep us young at heart. Izzy, I can't locate any of Erma

307

Bombeck's books on the computer. Will you come out and initiate a search for me?"

Carole left the room. Izzy said a quick prayer. She'd tried to see to it that her boss didn't spend much time on her feet. Carole had gotten slower with each pound gained, until her blossoming body mainly took up residence behind the checkout counter and dealt with patrons. That left Izzy to do everything else. Carole's desk had lately become Izzy's. The stress of dealing with learning the new computer system, bar coding the hundreds of books, convincing seasoned patrons about the wonders of the electronic age, and responding to the newspaper's editorials about censorship inspired Carole to turn more of the duties over to Izzy. The amount of work piling up on the desk testified a real need for organization.

Glancing at the calendar, Izzy tabulated how long she'd worked at Mayhill Library. One year, six months.

Izzy brushed a quick hand through her long hair and again reminded herself that she certainly didn't fit the stereotype for a small-town librarian. Yet, Carole seemed to approve of Izzy's charge-ahead attitude and tendency to clutter.

Carole paused at the door. "Izzy?"

Izzy looked longingly at the desk. "No problem. I'll be right out." She grabbed the stack of telephone messages from on top of the computer, intending to return the calls between checking out books.

Straddling the stool behind the counter, Izzy keyed in the author, Bombeck, and allowed her eyes to roam over the mahogany bookshelves and vaulted ceiling. Mayhill Library had opened its doors in 1911, and until last year, little had changed. Izzy was fascinated by the still-talked-about exploits of the first librarian, Rosemary Mayhill, who had started the library with just two hundred books. For forty-one years Rosemary—now honored via a huge painting that hung behind the check-in desk—had added books to the shelves from her own funds and invited migrant workers to come in on Monday evenings to learn to read. Catherine Wilfong had taken over in 1952. Carole Martin had been in charge for the last six years. When Izzy had been hired, temporarily, her task was to bring the library into the twenty-first century. A happy glow tinted Izzy's cheeks. She hadn't changed the library's personality, she'd just made it more user-friendly. It had taken months of heated debate to convince Carole's husband to appropriate funds for updating the library. Only after Izzy convinced Carole of the need to modernize had part-time Mayor Jake Martin agreed to consider allotting tax dollars to technology.

Jake didn't like change. He wanted the library and his wife to stay exactly the same. After all, he was demonstrating his liberalism by letting Carole work. Before Catherine retired, he'd allowed Carole to make the long drive to Lincoln to take the necessary classes to qualify for a degree in library science.

Izzy always winced when Carole told the story and used the word *allowed*. If Jake had been Izzy's husband, he'd have walked around with a frying-pan necklace for most of his days.

A blue-haired woman pushed two romances and a home decorating book across the counter. "Hello, Izzy."

Izzy took the books. "Hello, Mrs. Hepfield. How are you today?"

"Call me Agatha and not so good, but I don't want to talk about it." The woman rolled her eyes then forced a smile before saying, "I'm so pleased that you've painted the children's area. Those crayons with the names of books instead of the names of colors are just a marvelous idea."

"Thank you, Agatha." Izzy felt a tinge of regret. She'd miss this place when she went home.

"Yes, I like the changes." Agatha reached over and laid her hand over Izzy's. "Rosemary would be proud of you."

"You knew Rosemary?" Izzy exclaimed, but Agatha was already walking away—her aged ears beyond hearing.

Mondays were typically slow. Izzy completed her phone calls and began pricing some of the books she intended to add to the back room where used paperbacks were sold. Carole sorted books. The sounds of Whip Thompson snoring over a newspaper added to the atmosphere.

The swish of the front door opening didn't inspire Izzy to look up. That door would open a hundred more times this day without her noticing.

"Excuse me." A deep voice said.

Izzy looked up. The man, carrying a stack of at least fifteen books, towered over Carole. His rugged features spoke of hard work and hours in the sun. The arms that held the books balanced the load easily. Izzy bit her lip. She'd been in Mayhill almost two years. No way could she have missed this man. He handed Carole two books, stretching out a tanned, bare arm—taut with muscles—that captured Izzy eyes.

Carole grinned up at him. "Parker Strickland," she scolded. "I'll bet you haven't been in a library since high school."

"Only once or twice," he acknowledged, balancing the stack of books.

Carole took a few off the top and loaded them into the cart, managing to fumble a few onto the carpet.

He dumped the rest of them in a cluttered pile and bent down to retrieve the dropped books. He glanced around the library as if trying to decide if he wanted to stay. His brown eyes stopped their surveillance when they came in contact with Izzy's. Interest flashed, but quickly disappeared, momentarily replaced by a guarded look that tugged at Izzy's heart.

"This is Isobelle de la Rosa," Carole introduced, drawing Izzy close. "She's Clara Bryant's daughter."

Parker Strickland nodded, a handful of reddish-brown hair finding its way to his brow before he brushed it back. "Pleased to meet you."

Carole began checking the books. "Parker, these are way overdue!"

A frown marred his handsome features. "How much?"

"Let's see. Some were due . . . Parker! These are more than two years overdue!"

His frown deepened. "How much?"

"The ones that are years overdue we charge the price of the book," Izzy said, stepping closer. "The others are just a nickel a day."

"How much?" Parker repeated, pulling out his checkbook.

Carole ignored the computer and figured the total on the library's ancient calculator. "It's one hundred and fifty-two dollars."

He wrote the check without flinching, although Izzy thought she saw a moment of anger highlight his expression. This man hid his emotions well. He handed the payment to Carole and nodded good-bye.

The women watched him walk away. "His wife died a few years ago," Carole confided in a practiced whisper. "He just moved back to town."

Izzy stared after the man. The sadness that leapt from his eyes haunted her. This man didn't know the happiness the Lord could bring. He leaned against the wall, skimming one of the upcoming events announcements promoting the Mayhill Centennial. Folding it, he put it in his pocket before walking out the door.

"He's a looker." Carole hadn't missed Izzy's interest. "I've known his family for years." She moved closer to Izzy, her expression full of eagerness. There was nothing Carole enjoyed more than sharing the joys and sorrows of the Mayhill townsfolk. "Oops." Carole bent. "Missed one." She held up another book that had tumbled out of her grasp as Parker handed them to her. "Wait, this isn't one of ours." Carole frowned as she turned a blue book from front to back in her hands. "Here." She thrust the book toward Izzy.

From one glance, Izzy knew the book didn't belong in the library. It was a journal. She kept one herself. Only instead of a plain, blue cover, hers depicted a Victorian woman, sitting in a garden, head bent while writing.

"Is this Mr. Strickland's?" Izzy asked.

"I think so, but I didn't look."

Izzy opened the journal, intending to see if the front page identified the owner. Instead of a name, the first paragraph jumped out at her, a brittle scrawl that took up too much space, the tips of the letters sharp with anger.

I made it through another day. Another day. I think I'll make it through tomorrow. The next day—I'm not too sure about. I have the gun. I can use the gun. If I can't make it through the week.

The journal dropped from her hands as if it had suddenly turned hot. Izzy closed her eyes, feeling the color drain from her face. For a moment, she thought she heard the sound of her father's laughter.

Carole stared at the journal, concerned. "Well, is it Parker's?"

"I don't know. There's no name." Izzy picked up the book, deliberating about whether to share what she'd read.

"Never thought he looked like the type to keep a journal." Carole moved closer, eyeing the book with interest.

"Why not?" Izzy held the journal firmly.

"I've known him all my life. He's older than my Tom. Still, they played baseball, basketball, football. Never seen either of them crack a book. Of course, Parker went off to college. Maybe he developed the habit there."

The book felt brittle in Izzy's hands. Suddenly, she didn't want to claim possession of such private thoughts. "I'll see if I can catch up with Mr. Strickland."

Carole nodded, moving out of the way.

Izzy sprinted across the new mauve carpeting, pushed the library door open, and dashed across the grassy landscape of Mayhill Park. Parker Strickland was climbing into a pickup. Trucks seemed to be the vehicle of choice for Mayhill, Nebraska, men. Her small car always appeared dwarfed in the parking spaces. The men who asked her out always seemed surprised when she turned them down, as if the size of their vehicles should impress her. Instead, as she drove through the streets, she felt very much like the mechanical rabbit the greyhounds chased. A small morsel to be won.

"Mr. Strickland! Mr. Strickland!" she called.

Parker had one foot on the floorboard as he began to ease into his truck. He glanced back when he heard her.

"Mr. Strickland!" she called again.

"Yes."

"Is this yours?" She held up the journal.

Parker slowly took it, cracking it open. His eyes skimmed the page, and he frowned. "Oh, yeah, thanks." He tossed the journal on the passenger side. It skidded off the seat and landed on the floor. He climbed the rest of the way in.

Only after he started the engine and began to back out of his space did Izzy react. "Mr. Stickland," she said loudly, "are you okay?"

"Just dandy, ma'am." He shot her a puzzled glance as he drove away.

Izzy shook her head, thinking of what she had read in the journal. Someone should tell his family. She did bowl with his mother and father, but that wasn't enough to make her feel as if she knew them well. How could she confront mere acquaintances and confess that she'd gotten the information about their son from reading a page from his journal? Journals were supposed to be private. Parker Strickland had made it this long without her interference. Surely, he'd make it through the rest of the day while she considered what she might do. She headed back to the library, stopping under the big pin oak tree.

"Hi, Miss Izzy." Billy McKenna grinned toothlessly at her. Delta, his mother, read a book at a nearby park bench while Billy played in the falling leaves of September. School had started last week, making the park a daytime shrine to peace and quiet—except for the occasional toddler who rambled along the play area followed by a mother.

Izzy smiled at Delta and tousled Billy's hair, enjoying the childish texture of his deep brown curls. The sun shone down and highlighted hints of red in Billy's silken strands.

"You okay?" Delta put her book down and pushed a strand of blond hair from her eyes.

"Just thinking."

Delta took a deep breath and looked around with appreciation. "This is my favorite time of the year."

Izzy nodded and watched as a yellow and red leaf swirled gracefully to the ground. How different this land was from Arizona. It was just six years ago, during a 122-degree summer heat spell, that she had sat across from her mother at the kitchen table trying to convince Mom to do something . . . to live again. Izzy had been twenty and going to Arizona State University. Mom had been spending too much time alone. Izzy had forced her mother to leave Phoenix to go on that cruise.

"Mom, you need to explore," a much younger Izzy had argued. "Get away from the doing the same old thing day in and day out."

"I'm fine," Clara de la Rosa had protested, staring with dismay at the airplane ticket that would transport her to California. "You want me to go alone?"

"This is a cruise for people your age." Izzy had encouraged, adding, "You'll have a blast!"

"I don't want to be with strangers," Clara had protested. Three weeks later, Izzy had kissed her protesting mother good-bye at Arizona's Sky Harbor Airport. Clara had grumbled, handing the stewardess her boarding pass and declining to check in her old, avocado suitcase. She clutched her luggage in an unwilling fist and refused to wave to Izzy.

The cruise had worked too well. First, her mother had phoned from Mexico, bubbling incoherent praises about a man named Harve. Next, two days after Clara should have been home, the sounds of celebration came over the phone, and suddenly Izzy had a stepfather. Clara moved out of the hot, desert mobile home in Apache Junction, a retirement community east of Phoenix, and traveled to the grasslands of the Midwest with her new husband.

Despite her reservations, Izzy liked Nebraska. Every summer since her mother's marriage, she'd left the heat of Phoenix and flown to Mayhill. But she'd never dreamed that one day she'd leave the malls and sunshine of Phoenix to reside in a town of a mere twenty thousand hardy souls who barely noticed the deep chill of winter that blanketed their town almost six months of the year. Two years ago, when Clara had suffered a heart attack, Izzy had packed up and moved without regret. Nothing could replace family, and Mom was all she had left.

That was all in the past. Mom had been walking every day, and now she and Harve were in Florida attending his oldest daughter's wedding. Then, they were off to Kentucky to spend time with his other daughter and her family.

Izzy was free to go back home. But she couldn't, not until Carole had her baby. When Izzy had first arrived in Mayhill, all she had done was take care of her mother. After six months, things had calmed down, and Izzy had applied at the city hall. She'd been thinking of taking a clerical job for a while. But Mayor Martin had happened upon her resume, and instead of a job she could easily walk away from, she'd started at the library.

"It's just temporary," Mayor Martin had insisted. Reluctantly, Izzy tried to pretend that she hadn't locked herself into a situation that she'd have a hard time escaping. But escape it she would, as soon as Carole ended her maternity leave.

A gust of wind shook Izzy from her wonderings. The leaves rolled against her shoes. A vibrant variation of red, gold, green, and yellow marked the changing of the season.

"Billy, stop that!" Delta's voice came loudly. Billy plopped to the ground at the base of the big tree in the middle of the park, its lowest limb out of his reach.

"Aw, Mom," he whined. "All the kids climb this tree. I want to."

"You're not old enough." Delta looked her son up and down. "Or tall enough."

"How's Billy liking kindergarten?" Izzy asked.

"He loves it. I took him out early today for a doctor's appointment. I didn't see any reason to take him back. Besides, there'll only be a few more days like this before snow."

"God truly made a beautiful day." Izzy nodded and looked at her watch. "I've got to get back to work. See you." Briskly, she headed toward the library.

Carole looked up, worried, when Izzy breezed through the double doors.

"Was it his?"

"Yes." Izzy leaned against a shelf. "Is he always that sad?"

"I thought he was doing better. Today must have been a bad shift. He's a fireman."

Izzy thought about those broad shoulders. A fireman? That made sense. She'd feel perfectly safe if he scooped her up and carried her down a ladder. Unbidden, the image of the corded muscles of his arms flashed though her mind, and Izzy sat down on the stool with a thud. *Where did that thought come from?*

Carole looked around the silent library, then said suddenly. "Parker met his wife in college. Julia died coming back from Lincoln during a snowstorm. Parker blames himself. He seems to think that if he had been with her the accident wouldn't have happened."

Captivated, Izzy stopped rearranging. "Would it have?"

"Julia was from southern California. She didn't know how to drive in the snow. From what Parker's mother told me, he'd asked Julia to stay home that day, but she'd wanted to go shopping. Imagine that! Risking a blizzard to buy a new dress." Carole opened her mouth, as if she had something more to say, but thought better of it. "Let's just say she wasn't used to taking the weather into consideration."

Izzy nodded. Parker Strickland obviously wasn't over his wife's death, not if he wrote such dismal entries in his journal.

❧

Parker hated days off. He would just as soon work and keep his mind occupied. Mayhill didn't have many fires, but he doubled as a paramedic, and that kept him busy. Two months ago he'd participated in the community effort to save the livestock of the area's farmers. He, Jeff Henly, and Ty Horner had driven to farm after farm and turned the hose on panting animals, hoping to keep them from dying of heat. When winter rolled around, there'd be other emergencies such as downed power lines and distant residents unable to drive to the hospital.

He flicked the turn signal on, heading for Summers Cafe. He'd grab a late lunch and then go to his parents' house. As he turned the corner, the blue book that librarian had returned to him slid toward his boot.

Parker shook his head, bending to retrieve the journal. He wished the librarian had thrown it away.

He thought he caught a whiff of that librarian . . . what was her name? Isobelle de la Rosa? Her perfume lingered around the book. She didn't look anything like her mother. Parker remembered when Harve had brought Clara home. The community had been in an uproar for months. They hadn't quite recovered from the knowledge that a retired, widowed farmer would even want to take a cruise before Harve returned with a big-city bride. Parker recalled seeing Izzy a few times when she'd been in Mayhill visiting her mother. He'd been happily married to Julia then. He wondered how he'd missed seeing her around town since he'd moved back, then reconsidered. He didn't frequent any of the places singles hung out.

Was she single?

It bothered him that the urge to find out her marital status crossed his mind.

Isobelle had been cute. She'd tripped across the park's grass in high heels with beige pants hugging an athletic build. She looked healthy enough, but health wasn't enough to battle cold Nebraskan winters. He recalled how the wind had caught the fringed vest she'd worn, blowing it back so that her white shirt was exposed to contrast with her tan neck. She lived up to her name, de la Rosa. She smelled like a rose. Her long, black hair, high cheekbones, and olive complexion spoke of distant ancestors, rich in Hispanic blood and mystique.

Parker looked out the side window and slammed on his brakes. He'd been thinking about the librarian and driven right past the cafe. He didn't care if she were single or not!

He turned the truck around and finally pulled into one of the cafe's parking places. The journal fell back to the floor. Parker pushed it under the seat. He would deal with it later. Izzy was nothing like Julia, that was for sure. Parker sat in the truck, staring at the cafe. He'd lost his appetite. What was it that woman had called after him? "Mr. Strickland, are you okay?" Hah, she had called him mister. She must think he was fifty years old.

"Just dandy," he'd answered.

He had lied.

❧

"Has Parker Strickland gone to counseling?" Izzy fed Mr. Whiskers, the library's rabbit. It had been hours since the fireman had left, yet she couldn't get him off her mind.

Carole raised an eyebrow. "What for?"

"The grief from dealing with the loss of his wife."

"I don't know. He's been away for so long. He moved to Lincoln, went to school, and now he's back. Say," Carole filed the audio cassettes in the bin. "You're sure asking a lot of questions. Has he gone and sparked your interest?"

Izzy tried to smile. She'd overdone the questions. She should have known better. What else was Carole to think with Izzy prying into the fireman's history?

"No, no, please don't get any matchmaking ideas. I was just curious, that's all. I thought I'd met just about everyone in this town."

"He's Kenny Latkam's cousin."

Izzy took a step back.

"I know," Carole laughed. "Those two boys are as opposite as can be. Kenny's an only child, and then there's just Parker and his sister. Their parents doted on them. Parker and Rhea turned out okay. Oh, sure, Parker sowed his wild oats. But Kenny, whew, I wouldn't let my daughter within ten feet of him! He finally stopped bothering you, didn't he?"

"After I filed a complaint with the sheriff."

"Kenny wouldn't hurt a fly. He's just spoiled rotten. It's probably a good thing he's leaving town. He and his cousin Chris used to get in more trouble. . . ."

Izzy nodded, not really listening, but glad that Carole's thoughts had shifted from Parker Strickland to his cousin and away from Izzy's interest in the fireman.

When school let out, the patronage doubled. Gum-smacking students prowled the aisles, looking for term-paper material. Already the *Phantom of the Opera* video was in demand. A quick-fingered senior boy with hair longer than Izzy's had snagged it at five minutes after three, and now twelve names graced the reserved list. It looked as if Mayhill seniors intended to avoid reading the book. A tall football player frowned brutally at the card catalogue, roughly shoving in a drawer and turning to glare at Izzy as if she'd purposely hidden the card for whatever book it was he wanted. Izzy hoped he'd be kinder to the computers after they were installed.

At seven o'clock Izzy played the recording bidding the final patrons farewell and put the monies collected for fines into the safe. When everyone was gone, she checked on the rabbit, set the alarm, and followed Carole out the back door.

Izzy didn't go straight home on Mondays. In order to get to know the town and its people, she had followed her mother's example and made an effort to get involved with the community. Bowling seemed an easy way to make friends, so she'd let her landlord, Whip Thompson, talk her into joining his league. Now she had more friends over sixty-five than she knew what to do with. Her collection of crocheted washcloths was extensive, and if her car ever decided to break down, a flock of undershirted men appeared like vultures to surround the dead machine and debate. The more she got to know her parents' friends the more she liked them, although she did long for friends her own age. She missed Connie Decker, her best friend back in Phoenix. Connie didn't bowl, she was into twelve-step programs, usually having to do with diets. Connie didn't crochet washcloths, she collected dolls. Connie had never read a book from the comfort of a park bench or stopped to watch red and yellow leaves fall to the ground. She was too busy supervising the day-care center at church. Izzy hated being torn between two places.

Tonight, watching her team members laugh and talk about their day, Izzy felt out of sorts. She kept an eye on Francine and Blake Strickland, looking for some indication that they were worried about their son. Nothing. The two wore matching green sweaters and looked as if they could pose for a seniors' fitness magazine. They didn't notice her stares.

Izzy missed picking up the ten pin by inches. Whip sent his ball down the alley for a strike. Her game was off, but that made sense. For the first time in over a year, her mind was on a member of the male sex. With a half-smile, she thought back to the guys she'd dated since moving to Mayhill. Most of them very nice, but nobody with enough charisma to keep her from concentrating on striving for that 300 bowling score. Until Parker Strickland. And it wasn't his charisma she was worried about.

"Where's your mind tonight, girl?" grumped Whip after Izzy missed an easy spare.

"You feeling all right?" asked Agatha, wiping her bowling ball off with a crocheted towel. It was embarrassing. Tonight both Agatha and Whip had bowled better than she, and Agatha's ball weighed barely six pounds.

"Just a long day," Izzy replied.

When the final game ended, Izzy removed her bowling shoes,

struggling with the nagging feeling that she needed to do something. She, alone, knew that Parker Strickland was suicidal, and instead of seeking the man out and talking to him, she'd gone bowling. She stopped at the public telephone just inside the bowling alley's entryway and looked up Parker's address and phone number. She wrote it down on the receipt part of her checkbook. His house was miles out of town.

Izzy pulled out of the parking lot and drove to the corner. Checking her watch, she bit her lip. It was just after ten. She just needed to make sure he was okay. Otherwise, she wouldn't get any sleep. She turned away from her own home and headed toward Parker Strickland's address.

The road was void of streetlights. Izzy relied on the moon and her headlights glancing off fields and trees. In a way, driving through the rural roads at night seemed an adventure. She squinted, trying to see, but the darkness settled around Parker's place, making everything a silhouette. All she could tell was that it was a large farm. As she came closer, she noted that lights burned in almost every window. Izzy checked her watch, not surprised that the man was awake. She had once dated a military fireman and knew they kept erratic hours. She drove past the house and turned into a side driveway, backed up, and turned the car toward home. To her dismay, Parker Strickland came out of his house and stood on the porch with his hands on his hips. He'd seen her, and since she had driven past the McKennas' place, he knew whoever was on his road must be visiting him.

Wishing she was anywhere else, Izzy considered driving by. She could put her foot to the gas and zoom by. He might not notice who she was. With sinking heart, Izzy realized he'd know her car. Everybody knew her car. Maybe it was time to get rid of the Peugeot and get a truck. No, that would mean she was adapting to small-town America.

She inched closer to his house, and he stepped off his porch, sauntering to the road and her car. Izzy braked and leaned over to roll down the passenger side window.

Parker bent, crossing his arms over the door. "You lost, Ms. de la Rose?"

"It's Miss de la Rosa and, no, I'm not lost." The minute the words left her mouth, Izzy wanted them back. He'd just given her the perfect reason for being on a seldom-used back road. She'd blown it. "I'm not lost," she repeated. "I–I–I just came out here to tell you that you owe another two dollars' worth of fines on those library books."

2

*D*ark branches waved with the wind behind Parker. His face didn't change expression as he reached in his back pocket and withdrew his wallet to extract two dollars. "You drove all the way out here to collect a library fine?"

"Carole said you hardly ever use our facilities. I wanted to make sure you were aware of our policy."

Parker laid the money on the passenger seat. "A simple overdue notice would have sufficed." He stepped back, shoved his hands in his back pockets, and studied her car.

"What's wrong?" she said.

"This car's going to be useless in the winter."

"Don't worry about me. I don't go far." The pane of glass slid into position. Izzy pushed on the gas and drove away, watching Parker in the rearview mirror. He stood in his front yard, an unyielding, diminishing figure.

"I can't believe what I just did," Izzy mourned aloud, embarrassment making her hands shake. Why had she driven out to his house? What had possessed her? Even worse, the bad feeling in her gut did not go away. Her foot hovered over the brake, then settled on it. "Okay, Lord, I'm pretty sure what You'd do. It's not as if he can embarrass me any further tonight." She turned the car around. "And just maybe I can help him."

All his lights were still on. Izzy pulled into the driveway. She sat a moment, contemplating, then grabbed the two dollars from the passenger seat and stepped out of the car.

As if he'd been waiting for her, Parker came out the screen door and stood at the edge of the porch. His hands were jabbed tightly in his pockets. He didn't look as if the word *welcome* was in his vocabulary.

She made it all the way to the bottom step before he spoke. "Do I owe more money or are you lost?"

Izzy took a breath. "Neither." She held out the two dollars. "I don't make it a habit to lie. You made me nervous, and I said the first thing that came to my mind. You didn't owe the library two dollars. Please, take it back."

He took his hands out of his pocket and crossed them over his chest. He reminded her of her father. The stance he'd taken whenever she was trying to tell him why she'd missed curfew; why she'd gotten a C on her report card; why she thought it was okay to wear makeup.

"Look," Izzy went on quickly, waving the money as if it were a white flag. "I'm really embarrassed. I came out here to see if you were okay."

"Okay? Why wouldn't I be okay?"

"Well, you know, you acted a little funny today at the library. Kind of sad."

"Oh, and you follow sad people home from the library?"

"I didn't follow you home!" Izzy stepped back.

"No?"

"I went bowling, and then I looked your address up in the phone book."

"All because you were worried about me?"

Izzy smiled hopefully and nodded. Surely, he would remember that he had turned in the journal and what was written on the first page. "Yes, all because I was worried about you. Do you need any help?"

"What kind of help are you offering?" He stepped to the edge of the porch.

Too close in Izzy's opinion. She took a breath. Every fiber of her being told her she was safe, but still she felt vulnerable standing in Mr. Strickland's front yard. "Maybe I could arrange for one of the deacons at my church to come have a Bible study with you. You'd be surprised at how—"

"No, that won't be necessary," Parker said slowly. "I'm fine. Nothing to worry about. I don't need your help."

She had no choice. The man obviously was annoyed with her. Sticking around would only annoy him more. Izzy forced the two dollars in his hand, ignoring the shiver that ignited when his warm fingers closed over hers. She yanked her hand away and hurried back to her car. As she pulled back out onto the dirt road, she didn't allow herself to look back. She was too afraid she'd see the man laughing.

Lord, I could have handled that better. One more chapter in the story of Isobelle de la Rosa's life. Forever acting on impulse and repenting at leisure. Paul wrote to the Ephesians, "Therefore do not be foolish, but understand what the Lord's will is." Izzy took a deep breath. A carefully constructed plan would have worked better with Parker, instead of a late-night spontaneous encounter. Well, she'd put him on the church's prayer list and see what happened.

She calmed down as she drove through the silent night and entered the city limit. In Phoenix, even this late, the roads would be busy. She waited at the stoplight in the center of town, noticing a few cars still in the Summers Cafe parking lot. The place doubled as a club at night, but she'd never been there. The light turned green, and she drove the last block to her apartment. Whip owned a white clapboard two-story Victorian. Izzy had almost refused to rent from him once she found that they had to share a kitchen, but she'd fallen in love with the home when he showed her around.

She pulled into the driveway and sat in the car a moment. The porch light burned, bidding her enter. None of the downstairs lamps were on, except for the kitchen's. It looked as if she'd manage to catch Whip asleep. He was a great landlord. An angel in disguise. Within a month of her moving in, he'd convinced her to participate in a weekly Bible study, taught her how to make banana bread, and coached her in the intricacies of playing checkers.

Izzy often came home to find a casserole warming in the oven or a plate of meat loaf with her name written on a paper napkin in the refrigerator. Sharing a kitchen wasn't half bad. Whip assured her that if she wanted privacy all she had to do was notify him in advance, and he'd spend the evening at his son's house. Izzy couldn't imagine telling the man to leave his own home, since he'd been nothing but polite to the few visitors she'd had. When her best friend Connie had come for a visit, he'd taken her all around while Izzy worked. Connie had gone back to Arizona spouting wheat prices and wearing a John Deere hat.

Izzy let herself in through the back door that opened into the kitchen. A piece of peach pie waited on the table. She poured a glass of milk and sat down with fork in hand. If Whip kept up the culinary treats, she'd soon be forced to buy a new wardrobe. A size bigger! The sugary goodness had a calming effect, helping her to pretend that tonight hadn't been a complete fiasco. She knew Parker Strickland was still alive. Alive and *alone* in a distant farmhouse.

She finished the peach pie and climbed the stairs to her apartment. Her living room light glowed. Izzy knew she'd left it off and felt fairly certain that Whip had stolen up here to make sure she didn't enter a dark room. She shrugged out of her sweater, not sure if she liked her landlord acting like a parent. After a year of living with her mother and Harve, she had moved to Whip's upstairs apartment to regain independence and sanity. Radar meowed from the flowered couch, blinking away the effects of sleep and jumping down to wind his way around her feet.

"Did Whip feed you?" Izzy asked as she turned on the television.

The big black and white cat got up on his hind legs, patting Izzy's knees, informing her that he wanted to be carried. She picked him up and walked into the bathroom, checking his food bowl, not surprised to find fresh water and an open can of cat food. Lately, Whip had started cooking liver for Radar. It was only a matter of time before the feline began to share residency with the man downstairs.

She changed into her pajamas. Picking up her Bible, she settled down on the couch. She had been reading the Old Testament, but for some reason, tonight Izzy felt more inclined to turn to the writings of Paul.

Paul was her favorite apostle, along with Peter. They made mistakes, yet knew truth when it stared them in the face. Idly, Izzy stroked Radar's soft fur as she read about the cost of being a disciple. She wondered what Paul would say to Parker? What advice would the apostle give? One thing for sure, Izzy couldn't forget the lost look in Parker's eyes. Nor could she forget the warmth of his touch on her fingers. Somehow, Izzy knew, she had to help him.

He must have adored his wife.

Izzy knew what it felt like to love and lose. She knew what it was like to have the floor ripped from under her. Without her family and the Lord, she'd have been lost. Her weekly Bible study with Whip had brought her even closer to knowing peace. Parker had family, but he didn't seem to have the Lord.

Izzy fell asleep in the living room with her Bible open, the light on, and the television blaring.

❧

Parker stayed outdoors for a long time, sitting on the front porch. After Julia died, friends had taken to visiting at odd hours. He'd never invited anyone but family into the house. After realizing a visit to Parker's meant standing in the front yard, the visits had tapered off.

He'd been watching television when he'd seen the car lights coming up his road. He'd recognized her Peugeot. With mixed emotions he'd gotten off the couch and walked outside to wait. For a moment he'd thought she wouldn't stop. As he'd walked to her car, he'd told himself to be polite, neighborly, invite her to sit on the porch. But the minute his mouth opened, the habit of misery had made itself known, and he'd been indifferent to her, making sure no one got close to him again.

He'd known from the start that she had not driven all that way to tell him he owed the library a two-dollar fine, but this business about his being sad didn't reason out either. He wasn't sure what she was after.

What a crazy day. What really bothered him was that she'd been on his mind since he'd left the library. Her scent had lingered in his memory all day. It had stayed with him during lunch and when he went over to his parents' house. It was great to be back in Mayhill and with family. All he needed was to keep busy and be with family, even if his family included his worthless cousin Kenny.

Kenny! Now there was a mess. Parker had spent a good part of the morning cleaning the one-room garage apartment Kenny rented from Agatha Hepfield. He'd packed the old clothes, thrown out all the newspapers, and gotten rid of the furniture. Kenny had done nothing but take what little he'd thought he'd need at boot camp. From what Parker understood, Kenny had spent the night in town with some woman instead of with his family. Kenny deserved boot camp in Parker's opinion. At least the town would get some peace. And maybe Kenny would grow up. The apartment had been a mess with half-eaten food cemented to plates under the bed. Dried milk had added permanent stains to glasses littering the dresser. Plates amassed with stubby cigarette butts tumbled old ashes onto Parker's fingers. Agatha had appeared at the door numerous times, shaking her head in sorrow and looking as if she might cry. Parker shooed her away and spent the entire morning clearing out that one small room, and the only reason he'd done it was because he didn't want his aunt Edna to see further proof of what a slob her son was. If Kenny hadn't already left, Parker would have hunted him down.

After finishing Kenny's apartment, Parker had dropped off the books at the library, grabbed lunch, and then stopped off at his parents. His parents' house had not been a place of joy. He'd hoped to drop off some of Kenny's belongings without having to face Edna, but Aunt Edna had been sitting in the living room, weeping over the indignities her son might suffer in the military.

"Kenny should have gone to college," she had sniffed into her tissue.

"Now," Parker's mother patted her sister on the shoulder, "lots of boys choose the service as a way to see the world." Francine Strickland had looked up, her gaze falling on Parker, and said, "Parker thought about it for a while. His dad and I told him it was up to him. He happened to choose college."

Aunt Edna glared at Parker, her frown suggesting that if he'd chosen the service, Kenny would not have followed in his footsteps. "He applied for a position with the city. I don't know why he wasn't hired."

"I have some of his stuff in the back of my truck. You want me to load it in your car?" Parker wasn't about to inform Aunt Edna that Kenny's police record kept him from being considered for the fire department's opening. Too many of the powers that be knew Kenny's disposition and, although they felt bad for Edna, they believed the good of the community would be threatened if Kenny were to don a fireman's uniform. Not that Kenny could have passed the oral interview, anyway. It was just dumb luck that had Parker taking the position Edna wanted for her son.

"It's unlocked." Edna waved her sodden handkerchief.

Parker carried three boxes over to Edna's car.

"Parker, you staying for supper?" Mom asked.

Parker rubbed his stomach, mumbled about eating at Summers, and casting a wary eye at Aunt Edna, left.

A farmhouse full of memories awaited him at home. Memories stamped with the exquisite taste of his wife. He remembered her excitement. She'd so loved the rolling countryside that she'd sat right down at the kitchen table after they'd gotten married and wrote down a list of everything she wanted for the farm. Half the things they didn't need, like a tractor. Other things, like a horse, would surprise her when it came time to actually caring for the animal. Parker had put her off with the excuse of time.

"We'll get these things one at a time," he'd assured her, and she'd wrapped her arms around his neck in happiness. Now as he lived in the farmhouse alone, he wished he'd given her everything.

No wonder Isobelle de la Rosa's visit had him pondering. The library definitely rated as the high point of the day. Parker stood up. Leaving his musings on the front porch, he entered the silent house. Blinking his eyes against the glare of the television, he realized he wasn't a bit sleepy.

Two hours later, Parker carried the last box of Julia's knickknacks out to the shed. He'd gone through every room, packed her personal belongings and taken down all her pictures, save the three on the living room wall. Undoubtedly, he'd done enough packing today. Maybe it was time to let go a little. He undressed in the living room. He hadn't slept in the bedroom since Julia had . . . left. Even when he'd moved to Lincoln to finish his schooling and attempt to leave Julia's memories behind, he'd found himself not liking to sleep in the bedroom. Couches were much more comfortable. There, he never turned in the middle of the night to reach out only to discover an empty half of the bed.

He slept lightly, partly from habit, partly from training. The rooster over at McKennas' place woke him. Parker's mouth felt dry. Wearily, he rolled off the couch and went to the kitchen for something to drink. Sitting at the table meant for two, he downed a glass of milk. His dreams had awakened him too often during the night. Oddly, Isobelle had been in them, not his wife. Her late-night visit had stayed on his mind longer than he wanted. There was no reason for an absolute stranger to affect him. Why had she *really* driven out to the farm? He quickly washed his glass before heading to the bedroom to dress. Looking in the mirror he saw a man who didn't need anybody. A man who could only bear to lose a love—once.

Parker pulled a dark blue T-shirt over his head. He'd avoid that woman like the plague, even if her perfume made him want to sing.

❧

Izzy loved being first to the library in the morning. She liked turning the lights on and finding the books standing up straight in military rows, acting as if they'd protected the building during the midnight hours. She liked the waiting smell of a room that was built for the sole purpose of having people stroll over its carpeting as they contemplated their next written-word adventure.

"Good morning, Rosemary." She greeted the painting of the first librarian. "What did you read overnight?" Izzy leaned forward, pretending to listen. "What? You read the Bible?" Looking around, Izzy confided, "Me, too."

Izzy went around the building, checking to make sure everything was in its place. She started the coffeemaker and went into the office to attempt clearing off Carole's desk. She'd be alone with only a student worker once Carole went on leave; neither volunteers nor insurance were part of the Mayhill Library budget. She had to get everything in order.

The rattling of a key announced Carole's entrance. Izzy smiled, listening as Carole silently put away her purse and sneaked to the back room to pour a much-needed cup of coffee.

"One, two, three," Izzy counted, imagining Carole taking a drink at every number, gradually waking up.

Finally, Carole passed by the office door on her way to the overnight drop box to collect the books that had been returned after hours. "Morning, boss." Carole kidded. Seeing Izzy seated at the desk never bothered the head librarian.

Izzy waved as the phone rang. The morning started with a conversation with Jake Martin, transitioned into updating files and ended with a phone call from one of the librarians from the University at Lincoln. They were putting together a list of Nebraska authors. Izzy was double-checking the spelling of the G authors when Carole stuck her head in and smiled. "You ready for lunch?"

Four hours had passed!

"Or do you want me to go first?" Carole rubbed her stomach.

"Are you hungry?"

"Well, Jake said that if I managed to get away at noon, he'd meet me."

Izzy glanced at her watch. "You go ahead. I'll go when you return."

There were two patrons in the library, and a sleeping Whip was one. Delta McKenna was the other. As soon as Delta selected and checked out her choice, Izzy was on her toes, ushering her friend out the door. Checking to make sure Whip still slept, she headed for the microfiche files and looked up the last five years of the *Mayhill Daily*. She sat before the terminal and chewed her bottom lip. Should she look up Parker's past in the local newspaper? Would finding out more about him help her figure out why he had written such dismal words in his journal?

Izzy sneaked another glance at Whip. The library was part of his morning ritual. He slumped in the chair, chin resting on his shirt as his chest rose and fell with reassuring snores. Izzy inserted the fiche and began. Julia Strickland glowed from the page of marriage announcements. She and Parker had married during their junior year, before he'd even graduated from the University of Nebraska in Lincoln. The small-town paper burst with news about the couple's early days. Izzy followed the newlyweds through the purchase of the farm, and Julia's first automobile wreck—which had taken place during the winter and on to . . .

"What are you doing?" Carole interrupted, breathing over Izzy's shoulder. "Hmmm, checking up on Parker?"

"I was just curious," Izzy defended herself, jumping up and knocking her pencil to the floor.

"If I were single, I'd be more than curious."

Izzy tried to act nonchalant as she switched off the scanner. "He was cute. I just thought I'd check him out."

Carole dropped onto the chair at the next computer and lifted her blond hair high. "What do you want to know?"

"How depressed has he been since his wife passed away?"

"Oh, Izzy. What a question! He took it hard, of course. Who wouldn't? He's done okay. I think it was smart of him to get away for a couple of years. His ma wasn't too happy that he didn't come home more often, Lincoln only being a few hours away, but now she's proud of him. He trained to receive his emergency care license while there. Rhea McCoy's his sister, and he's related to the Walker brood over in Waco, Nebraska. It's about seventy miles east of here. You've heard of Chris? The one who ran around with Kenny and caused all that trouble."

"I don't think I've met Chris Walker." Izzy bent and picked up her pencil. "Rhea's never mentioned that she had a brother."

"She has. You just don't remember. I guess you were too busy thinking about escaping back to Phoenix."

Whip snorted, stood up stiff-leggedly, and walked out the front door with a look of bemusement on his face.

Carole watched his progress with a giggle and went to get the spare newspaper. "You'd better go grab some lunch."

Izzy grabbed her purse, irritated that Whip might have been awake during their conversation about Parker's past. She walked out of the library as Carole reached for the phone. What Izzy needed was chocolate. What she didn't need was for the whole town to know that she was checking up on Parker.

After sliding into a booth at Summers, Izzy studied the menu she already knew by heart. The noise of camaraderie echoed around her. Most of the time she packed a lunch and ate in the park, liking the company of birds and squirrels, but last night she'd been restless.

She'd slept right through the alarm this morning, waking only after Whip had banged on the downstairs ceiling with a broom. Scrambling into her clothes, she hadn't even had the time to thank him for waking her, let alone prepare a lunch.

She watched the people, nodding at the ones who nodded to her. Did any of them know to worry about Parker? She ate quickly, paid the bill, and went out blinking into the sunlight. Glancing at her watch, she realized that she had over twenty minutes before she needed to return to work. She started to step across the street to the park, thinking that she had plenty of work to do, but instead, as if guided by some unseen force, she headed for her car.

The fire station was three blocks away from the library. Izzy had driven by it numerous times without ever giving it a once over. She hunkered down, hoping to cruise by without attracting attention to herself. Ty Horner polished the already gleaming machine, while Jeff Henly seemed to be rolling the hose into some sort of doughnut shape. Both were testimonies to bodybuilding. They preened as water dripped down their muscles and soaked dark blue T-shirts. Izzy knew them. They made weekly trips to the library. It seemed that education and being a fireman went hand in hand. If they were the last ones in the library, they saw her safely to her car. They were both married, and at the moment their wives looked very much like Carole from the side view.

Parker sat alone on a bench in front of the brick building with the etched words *Mayhill Fire Station Number One*. It looked as if he was sewing the button onto some huge sort of jacket. His legs were stretched out before him, crossed at the ankles. He looked so alone. The comparison between the two laughing, wet firemen and Parker hit Izzy in the gut with all the finesse of a line drive. The man needed her help. No one else seemed to be paying any attention to him.

❧

Parker watched the Peugeot drive by with only the top of a jet black head visible. He'd glanced over at Ty and Jeff to see them switch from easy male bantering to flexing in the blink of an eye. Parker almost laughed at Ty using the firehose as a freeweight, but kept his face perfectly solemn as the woman whom he needed to ignore drove by. Just what was she doing? Why wasn't she sitting up? She could cause a wreck driving like that.

"I don't think she drove by for us." Ty turned the hose in Parker's direction, purposely sending a spray of water at his friend's feet. "Just say the word, Parker. Jane and I will be glad to invite Izzy over. Help fix you two up."

"Doris says you had a whopping library fine," Jeff added from on top of the engine. "That's an expensive way to score a date. I think you might have a fighting chance."

"Izzy? She calls herself Izzy?" Parker grumbled at his mates, intent on convincing them that he had no interest in the woman. He didn't want her to be called Izzy. Izzy made him think of a warm woman in his arms, head thrown back as she smiled. Her wild, raven hair tempting him into commitment. Isobelle sounded more refined. More like someone he could keep at a distance.

"Yeah, Izzy." Jeff winked an eye. "She moved here a few months after you left. Her ma's Clara Bryant. You know, Harve's new wife. Izzy's kinda hard to get a handle on. I haven't seen her even once after hours at Summers Place. Of course that might be because your cousin Kenny was hassling her. Smart girl. She ran. Dad says she's a pretty good bowler."

Parker hadn't visited the Summers nighttime bar scene since he'd returned. He didn't want to answer questions or nod at people trying to express their concern with kind words.

So Izzy didn't bother going out either. She probably found the nightlife in Mayhill a little less invigorating than in Phoenix. *Isobelle,* he told himself, *I must think of her as Isobelle.*

"You don't need to worry about me. I'm not after her." Parker stood.

"You done?" Jeff looked at the turnout jacket.

"I'm done." Parker went inside, staying close enough to the open door to listen.

Jeff and Ty watched him, grinning. Parker went into the office and tried to read their lips through the glass.

"It's about time," Jeff was saying.

Ty cleared his throat. "He'll never do anything about—"

"Unless we help," Jeff finished.

Parker looked out the window and wondered why the two men were shaking hands.

❧

"I need part of tomorrow afternoon off." Carole peeked in the office door, looking almost afraid to enter.

"Are you okay?" Izzy taped clip art to her authors' flier. She'd finally finished it two days ago.

"I have a doctor's appointment at one. I'll return when it's over. Just think of it as my lunch hour."

Izzy looked up from the memo she'd received proclaiming that funds were unavailable for the computers she'd requested for library patron use. Mayor Martin wrote that the library's spending this past year already exceeded the former ten years and that it was time to limit funding. Izzy took off her glasses and rubbed her eyes. "Do we have anything planned?"

Carole shifted uneasily. "The kindergarten class from Mayhill Elementary is coming on a field trip."

"When did we schedule that? I'll be the only one here!"

"It's not that hard," Carole protested.

"I know it's not that hard, but what if somebody wanders in and needs assistance? I can't very well leave a class of five-year-olds in the middle of a fairy tale, now can I?"

"You won't be alone, the teacher will be here. And besides, our patrons are very patient. They'll realize that you're busy. Everyone knows I'm going to the doctor. You worry too much." Carole carefully turned and headed back to the front desk where Mrs. Hepfield waited.

Izzy brought up a new screen on her computer and began typing a reply to Jake Martin, citing statistics about the necessary skills needed by high schoolers and how computers were a must for employment and educational opportunities. Currently, Izzy knew the high school was scurrying to keep up with the latest technology. Izzy wanted to offer after-school tutoring about computer use, but without computers there could be no class. Mayor Martin needed to make some decisions fast. Izzy only intended to stay in Mayhill four more months. After the New Year, she was heading back to sunshine and no shoveling.

~❦~

Chief Robert Parrish strolled into the fire station, checked the big calendar on the wall, and turned to Parker. "Are you on call tomorrow?"

"Yes." Parker looked up from his crossword puzzle. He had Monday off, but during the rotation of the four city employees, the man off duty remained on call.

"Your sister spoke to me at church this morning. She wants someone to come talk to the kindergarten class about fire safety. They plan to bring the kids here in a few months, so they don't need the engine. Since it's your sister's class, I thought you might like the assignment."

"No problem. I'll teach them to Stop, Drop, and Roll." Parker liked going to the schools. He'd always wanted children of his own, but he made do with Rhea bringing her two over to the farmhouse to explore the outdoors. He'd even fixed up the spare room with some of their toys for when they stayed over.

"Rhea wants you at her classroom about twelve-thirty." Robert penciled Parker's name on the duty roster and went to change clothes.

Jeff came in the back room and gathered up his lunchbox and belongings. "Going to the school tomorrow?"

"Yeah."

"Better you than me." Jeff took off the black boots he'd been wearing to wash the engine and put on his high-tops. He watched as Parker took his notebook out of the top pocket of his shirt to record tomorrow's appointment. "I just wish I could come along and watch you squirm."

"Squirm?" Parker said, raising an eyebrow.

Jeff chuckled as he left the room.

3

*W*hat do you mean Delta McKenna canceled? I'm supposed to give a talk about fire safety, not chauffeur kids to and from the library." Parker felt himself growing agitated at the thought of facing Isobelle de la Rosa.

"Listen." Rhea McCoy shook a ruler at him, not looking the least bit sorry that she was putting him in a fix. "Delta said the vet was supposed to be there before noon, but he didn't show. She can't just leave. I need another driver, so big bro, since you're already here, it's gonna be you."

Parker looked around the classroom. Children sat on the floor, building with blocks or coloring in books. Others stared up at him with wide-eyed admiration. He felt trapped. Last week, he'd vowed not to go near Izzy, now his sister was forcing him to walk right into the crazy librarian's domain.

"All right! Everyone find their partners." Rhea clapped her hands. Immediately children started putting away the toys and grabbing for fingers. "Hold hands!"

Parker felt a tug on his thumb and looked down at one of the little boys Rhea had assigned to him. Billy McKenna stared up at him through inch-thick glasses. The boy was sucking his thumb and bending his knees in a weird aerobic bounce. "I gotta go to the bathroom," he chirped around his thumb.

"Take him, quickly," Rhea urged.

Parker walked with Billy down the hall and let him go unattended into the boy's room. Billy lived, with his mother and grandparents, at the farm next to Parker and spent a lot of time shooting plastic arrows at the trees behind Parker's field. Delta McKenna often moseyed into Parker's yard on the pretense of fetching Billy.

"You want me to fix you some supper, Parker?" Delta would ask, her eyes hopeful. Parker might have been tempted. He had known Delta all his life. But her name was too closely linked to his cousin Chris's. There were those in town who spoke of the amazing resemblance of Billy's hair to that of Parker's cousin.

Rhea popped her head around the corner and shooed three more little boys in his direction. "They're riding with you."

Billy came out of the bathroom, holding his pants together until Parker could force the rusty snap to connect. He swung Billy up in his arms and walked out of the school building trailed by the rest of his passengers. If Billy was Chris's son, Chris didn't know what he was missing. In Parker's opinion, Billy was a great kid who needed more of a male influence.

"Are you really a fireman?" two boys asked in unison as Parker loaded them into his extended cab.

Billy answered. "Yes, he's really a fireman, and he gets to wash the big, red truck all the time. And he never has to wash dishes."

The other boys looked impressed. Parker blinked, amused that Billy was spending time peeking in the kitchen door when he wasn't shooting the plastic arrows. Turning the key in the ignition, Parker heard Billy add, "And he gets to slide down the pole."

Parker glanced around, saw the kindergartners staring at him with awe, and decided not to tell them that Fire Station Number One didn't even have a pole. For two more blocks the little boys talked about washing the fire truck.

Parker pulled into a parking place. Four pairs of eyes spotted the playground. "Can we go play first?" Billy asked.

"We'll have to talk to Mrs. McCoy about that." Parker helped Billy while the rest of the boys scrambled past him. One towheaded imp actually took three steps in the wrong direction before Parker was able to grasp a back belt loop and tug the child in the right direction.

"Welcome to Mayhill Library." Izzy grinned easily, her eyes wandering over the expressions on the children's faces. She gave Rhea a quick hug and turned to nod at the parent drivers. Her brows went up when she saw Parker.

"These are all kindergartners," Rhea explained, distracting Izzy. "They will be learning their sounds this year, and a few of them will take the big step into reading. They're excited about coming here today."

"You know Tonya. Have you met my brother?"

"Yes, just one week ago." Izzy forced a tight smile at the man.

Parker enjoyed watching her squirm. "And I'm still just dandy."

"Yes. Well . . ." Izzy shrugged before addressing the schoolchildren. "Follow me. This is the children's section. Whiskers, our rabbit, has been looking forward to your visit. He counted the books last night and wants you to know our library has over 15,000 books. Some have only pictures, and others have only words."

The children looked aghast at the thought of a book not having pictures. Parker followed as Izzy led them down the aisle with books suitable for small hands and curious browsing. He watched her gather the children into a circle and show them the three books she planned to share. All the adults, including his sister, vanished. He felt uncomfortable as if he should leave too, but he didn't. Just wait until he got hold of his sister. She'd probably arranged for Delta to cancel.

Parker sat on an undersized chair, knees nearly to his chin, and watched. It was harder than he'd anticipated. Her white dress, with the bold red flowers, moved invitingly every time she turned the page of the book. When she kicked off her sandals halfway through the second book, Parker found that he couldn't take his eyes off her ankles. He was too old for this. He'd married at twenty-two, became a widower at twenty-six, moved to the big city at twenty-seven, returned home at twenty-eight, and now the thought of tempting fate and falling in love again felt like too much of a chance. Being a fireman gave him enough excitement. He didn't need the worry of a woman, and he could tell by the upswept hairstyle of Isobelle de la Rosa that she wasn't one to stay home in the evening. She'd want to go to plays in Lincoln, eat dinner in town at least once a week, and probably try to attend all the town meetings. She'd . . . probably drive too fast in the snow.

At the end of the third story, he glanced around searching for his sister. He located her leaning against the checkout desk holding a few paperbacks to her chest and laughing quietly with Tonya Summer. Behind him, Izzy urged each child to find two books to take home. Rhea walked up, calling her class to attention. Library cards were passed around, books were checked out, and the visit ended.

Four little boys surrounded him, handing Parker their books, and shifting from foot to foot. Parker recognized the movement. He steered them toward the rest room, wishing for assistance but finding none. He held the books while the children tarried. Finally, Parker exited the library with a sigh of relief, pushing the little boys ahead of him. Billy turned around. "I hafta go to the bathroom."

"You just went." Parker looked back at the library with dismay. He did not want to go back in.

"I only went a little."

"I'll watch the others. You take him in." Rhea smiled encouragingly. "We've decided to let the children play for a while."

With a whoop, the kindergartners raced for the monkey bars. Billy looked uncertainly after his friends and then back at the library where the bathroom waited. "I gotta hurry!"

Izzy sat behind the desk, head bent as she sorted through the applications for library cards that Rhea's class had just turned in. She looked up when Parker and Billy entered. "Lose something?"

"Just need to use the facilities." He hurried Billy to the back, leaning outside the door and waiting impatiently.

"How are you doing today?" She was right beside him, her voice falling gently on his ear, sounding too comforting. He hadn't even heard her coming.

"I'm just dandy."

"You keep saying that."

"I was doing dandy the last time we talked, too."

She fidgeted with the sleeve to her dress, rolling it up and then pushing it back down. "This is a nice town. I like it here."

"Billy." Parker knocked on the door, needing to distract himself from her perfume. "Hurry up."

"I just remembered that Mama told me I had to say the ABCs before finishing," Billy hollered.

"What letter are you on?" Parker said, hoping the boy was on the letter U.

"You made me forget, so now I gotta start over."

Parker turned to look at Izzy, frowning down at the woman who stood a full foot shorter than he. "Don't you have something you need to be doing?" The words came out gruffer than he'd intended.

Izzy didn't blink at his tone, instead her eyes seemed to say she understood. "I'm supposed to make sure everyone who comes to the library has the assistance they need. Can I help you find anything?"

"No." He stared, hard, trying to convince her—and himself—that she wasn't needed.

"What do you do in this town for fun?"

Billy chose that moment to come through the bathroom door. Parker bent, grateful for the timely interruption and snapped the boy's pants shut. "I work."

~&

"He works." Izzy mumbled to herself, adding the names of the children to the computer. A few of them had library cards. Izzy made note of those names, determined to drop a postcard to the parents telling them how much the library enjoyed their patronage. The students who were new to the system received a "Welcome to the Library" package.

Parker hadn't smiled when he picked up that child. Imagine holding a sticky-fingered imp and not enjoying the wiggling motion. The poor man. Izzy didn't think Parker realized how much he was missing by hiding behind the facade of pain. She had driven by the fire station twice since last Tuesday, but she'd hoped not to run into him—in person—again so soon. After watching him in the library, she knew the attraction she felt wasn't just because of the alarming paragraph she'd inadvertently read, but the man himself.

"He works." Two proofs of address slipped through her fingers and swirled to the floor. Izzy bent down to retrieve them.

"Who works?" Carole came up behind her.

Izzy smiled, but didn't answer.

Carole smirked knowingly. "Did you have fun with the kiddos?"

"Of course. Did you have fun at the doctor?"

"Er, can you believe it? I waited a half hour and never got to see him. Some sort of emergency came up. I'll bet Tonya Summers came along with her little girl."

"Uh-huh," Izzy nodded.

"Did Delta McKenna help out?"

"No. Didn't see her."

"Well, tell me about your afternoon!"

"I helped fifteen children pick out thirty books. The poor rabbit got poked by numerous fingers. Your husband called to tell you he got the tickets to the play you wanted to see in Lincoln. He seemed really surprised to find out you had a doctor's appointment."

"Guess I forgot to mention it to him." Carole stuck her purse under the counter and headed back for the coffeepot.

Izzy could hear Carole's laughter escaping as she tried to pour herself a cup. *Great*, thought Izzy, realizing she'd been the victim of a setup. *Just great! Carole's pushing me at Parker because she thinks we're a match made in heaven, and I'm practically throwing myself at him because I'm afraid if somebody doesn't start paying attention to him he'll have a nervous breakdown or something.* It was the "or something" that had her worried.

She pushed aside lingering thoughts of Parker Strickland and concentrated on catching up on some of the more pressing matters.

It was after seven when she got home. Radar had left tufts of hair by the front door. Izzy picked them up and threw them away, washing her hands at the sink. Scooping the cat up, she nuzzled him under her chin. "Are you hungry?"

A disgusting slab of liver lay shriveled in his dish. Izzy deposited the cat back onto the floor and dumped the liver in the toilet and flushed. Radar meowed piteously, chagrined that the treat had slipped by him. Izzy poured hot water in the sink to soak the dried-up liver resin from the dish. "Liver. Ugh, I hate liver."

❧

The McKennas' rooster woke Parker, and he wished the bird would develop fowl laryngitis. He'd left the school yesterday a jumbling mass of nerves and driven for miles into the countryside trying to organize his feelings. Some of the farmhouses he'd passed had been the caches for Julia's furnishing quest. She'd been so intent on filling the house with antiques. Izzy didn't look as if she'd care for old sewing machines and hall trees. More likely her domain featured contemporary white and track lights. No matter how many stubbled wheat fields he sped by, he'd been unable to drive thoughts of the librarian from his mind. He'd returned home after midnight, falling on the sofa, glad that he'd awake to a double shift.

It only took twenty minutes to get to work. Parker's great-great-grandfather, Darby Mayhill, had helped build the fire station. Pictures of old volunteers and employees smiled from gray frames. When his father was young, the fire station had been manned strictly by volunteers. Mayhill had experienced a growth spurt during the seventies, thanks to fast food chains desiring prime locations near the interstate. Now working alongside the sheriff and his posse of volunteers were four full-time employees. Robert Parrish served as chief, and Tyler had signed on as an engineer. Jeff worked as captain. Parker was the paramedic. His usual shift was twenty-four hours on, twenty-four hours off with every other weekend free. Ty was attending a workshop in Lincoln, and Parker had volunteered to cover his shift. It was just as easy to sleep in the fire station's cubicle as it was to sleep on a sofa in a lonely living room.

Parker made a notation in the logbook, stating that the school's request had been unfulfilled due to unexpected parental interference. He would explain to Robert and see if the chief wanted a more detailed report.

He'd eaten lunch at Summers, wishing Izzy would walk in, sit across from him, and ask if he were okay. Why did it seem so important to her how he felt? The fire station remained calm all afternoon. Reruns played on the television while Jeff drank coffee and worked on updating the files. Parker went in the back and lifted weights until it was time for supper. Just as the firemen picked up their forks to eat, the phone rang.

❧

"What do you mean you've been trying to get him down all afternoon? How did he get up there?" Izzy tried not to sound upset. The old man was excited enough for both of them.

"I didn't let him out. It was a plain, ordinary day. I went to the library, read the paper, my usual thing. When I came home, I happened to hear him meowing up there. I called him, but he wouldn't come down, then I went in and cooked some liver, thinking to entice him."

"Radar," Izzy called, stepping closer to the tree and peering up through the branches. Radar was a dark silhouette. Izzy put one hand to the tree, thinking to climb up.

"This is an old tree, Izzy. Some of those branches probably wouldn't hold you."

The dark branches waved at her, daring her to climb up. That, combined with her fear of heights, stopped her. "I'll go call Carole. She'll get Jake to bring over his ladder and get Radar down."

"Ah, Izzy." Whip looked at the ground. "I already called the fire department."

Whip's words were still hanging in the air as the fire truck came around the corner and halted in front of the house. Almost in one accord, the neighbors peeked out doorways and windows before moseying over to stand on the sidewalk in case advice was needed.

"Is there a fire?"

"What's all the commotion?"

"Hey, Parker, you really need the truck just to rescue a cat?"

"It's no fun without the engine," Robert joked, shooing the spectators back.

Parker eyed the tree, and Izzy could tell he was considering the dimensions and wondering how he'd get that cat down while maintaining his dignity.

"What do you feed that thing?" Parker frowned.

Whip saved her from answering. "I've been cooking him liver at least twice a week."

"Look, Mr. Strickland," Izzy spoke up. "I didn't call you, and I'm sorry that we've disturbed your evening. I'm sure Radar will get down. Why don't you—"

Whip interrupted, "Izzy! What are you saying? Radar is an indoor cat. What if he decided to come down in the middle of the night? He could get lost." Whip turned to Parker. "You can't leave him up there."

Izzy opened her mouth to protest. Parker glanced over at Robert. Izzy waited for the captain to intercede and make a decision, maybe even take over. But Robert looked to be enjoying the spectacle.

A drop of rain hit Parker on the nose. The fireman squinted, looking up the tree as a few more drops splattered across his forehead. Exasperated, he grumbled, "Radar, you named your cat Radar? Can't you call him and get him to come down?"

Izzy smiled haughtily and looked up, calling sweetly, "Radar."

Meow, came the answer.

"Come down here," Izzy ordered.

Meow, meow.

"He says he won't come down." Izzy crossed her arms and glared at Parker. "My cat has a mind of his own."

"I ought to just leave him up there," Parker muttered.

"That's fine with me. He'll come down when he's ready. I doubt if he'd let you get hold of him, anyway."

"I've rescued plenty of cats from trees."

"My cat doesn't need rescuing. He'll be fine."

"Izzy," Whip interrupted. "It's going to pour any minute."

"Whip, if it rains, the cat will come down. No problem."

"Why don't we just set a dish of food down. He'll come, if he smells something to eat." Parker looked at Whip. "You have any of that liver left?"

Izzy said, "Radar is a cat, not a dog, Mr. Strickland. You can't trick him with food."

"I take it you think cats are superior?" Parker challenged.

The look she shot him let him know she did.

It also inspired him to retort, "As an experienced firefighter I can attest that I've never been called to rescue a dog from a tree."

"Yes, well, those who are afraid to risk adventure seldom find any excitement in life."

"Are you saying dogs are passive?"

"No, actually I was thinking of you."

Silence surrounded them. All the neighbors waited for the next sentence. Robert pushed away from the truck and stepped closer to listen.

Parker reached up to grasp the lowest branch of the tree, ignoring the rain. As he hoisted himself up, he looked one last time at Izzy.

Izzy stood on the ground seething. She hoped Radar bit him. She hoped. . . .

"Got him!" came a cocky yell.

Radar didn't look happy coming down the tree in Parker's arms. The fireman held his victim firmly, since the cat seemed bound and determined to stay at the top. Parker's attempts to hold the animal reminded Izzy of something from a B movie. By the time Parker jumped to the ground, he had a long scratch on his cheek and a furious feline tucked under his arm while his other hand held a fistful of fur. He handed cat and fur to Izzy.

Whip clucked sympathetically, patting Parker on the back. "Come on in, my boy. I'll doctor those scratches, and then you and Robert can sit down for a slice of my peach pie."

"You didn't do much to earn your piece of pie," Parker complained to Robert as they followed the old man inside.

Izzy stroked her cat. "You've upset Radar," she accused.

"I wouldn't have missed this evening for anything," Robert chuckled.

Whip pulled out a chair at the table and urged Robert into it, while directing Parker toward the back bathroom where the bandages awaited. Izzy sat her cat down on the floor and stomped upstairs.

Behind her, Whip chuckled. "That cat's claws are very sharp. Let me put something on those scratches."

She heard Parker mutter, "I'm all right."

❧

Parker sighed and followed the old man down the hall.

Whip fumbled with Mercurochrome. "She sure sets store by that cat. I'll bet you're a hero in her eyes. She's a nice girl."

Great, thought Parker, *first my sister and now Whip Thompson.* The whole town seemed to be in on some diabolical plan to coerce him and Isobelle de la Rosa into couplehood.

Whip finished and beckoned Parker to follow him back into the kitchen. Robert sat in front of his empty plate, bliss written across his face, crumbs decorating his mustache. "You have to taste this pie."

Parker knew how good Whip's pies were. He'd spent many a Saturday afternoon in this kitchen as a boy, with Thelma Thompson stuffing him with pies after he had mown their yard. That's what he'd charged back then. Two dollars and a piece of pie.

"Izzy!" Whip went to the stairs and hollered.

"What?" Her voice tumbled down into the kitchen.

Parker noticed Robert's face contorting with a smirk. Good grief, could it be that his boss was in on it too? And yesterday at the station Jeff had wanted to come along to the school and watch Parker with the children. It was suddenly all too clear. Rhea had never intended to have him teach the children to "Stop, Drop, and Roll." She'd planned on tricking him into going to the library right from the beginning. He had to admire how fast his friends had put that plan together.

"Come on down for some pie!" Whip called up the stairs.

"I don't want any, thanks."

Parker smiled, knowing he was the reason she didn't want any. It felt good, being one up on her for the first time. He dug in, savoring the peachy goodness.

Robert cleared his throat. "We need to be going."

Taking one last bite, Parker wiped his mouth with a napkin. He stood, holding out his hand for Whip to shake. After that was done, he walked over to the stairs. "Miss de la Rosa," he called.

"What?" Impatience oozed from the word.

"If my dog ever gets stuck in a tree, I'll be sure to call you."

Robert pushed him out the door, whispering, "You don't have a dog."

"She doesn't know that."

❧

The puppy woke Parker up. Its lumpy paws were more effective than McKennas' rooster. "Down, Brute."

He'd gotten the puppy yesterday, taking his day off and answering an ad he'd found in the paper. The more he'd thought, the more he'd wondered why he didn't want Izzy to find out that he'd lied to her.

The dog had spent the drive home howling or burying its wet nose on the side of Parker's neck while flopping puppy paws raked at the leather seat. A few times the puppy had climbed into the extended cab, as if looking for something. Parker had winced, but let the puppy whimper. Maybe the dog was lamenting the fading scent of his mother or possibly the motion of the car upset his stomach.

Parker rubbed Brute's head, thinking of the way the puppy's mother had followed her offspring all the way to his truck and how the ancient farmer had told him not to worry, that the dog was a good-natured mutt.

The farmer had spit on the ground and advised, "He'll be a big dog. Just look at his paws. Lots of Golden Retriever in his bloodline."

Lying on the couch, Parker watched the puppy snuggle closer. He reached over and laid his hand on the puppy's head and tickled Brute behind the ears, then he kicked back the covers and threw his feet over the edge of the couch. Brute jumped down and scampered to the door, whimpering to go out.

"I don't think so," Parker said. Yesterday, when they'd pulled up in front of the farmhouse, Parker had made the mistake of letting the puppy jump from the car on its own, and as a consequence had spent the next two hours trying to get Brute to come out from under the porch.

Parker had finally crawled under the wooden lattice, amid the dirt and scurrying bugs, and dragged Brute out by one paw. He didn't intend to tell Izzy about the experience, because it had taken far longer to retrieve Brute than it had to rescue Radar. And there was no pie after.

Brute had been a mess, too. His blond mongrel hair stood in clumps. Twigs and grass stuck in his whiskers. Parker plopped Brute into the kitchen sink and turned the faucet on. Afterwards, he took the squirming puppy out into the yard, attached the collar to a long rope, and went back inside. For all of twenty minutes.

He hoped the noise also disturbed the rooster. He decided a trip to the library was necessary, to look up the information. Maybe he'd even have to ask a certain librarian for help, and of course he'd mention the joy of having a puppy. The puppy who didn't like being tied up outside.

The puppy that had shared Parker's couch.

4

"Yes, Izzy, this is Jake Martin." The mayor's voice boomed over the phone line, excitement accentuated in each word. "I've got a two o'clock appointment scheduled with Mark Dalton of the *Mayhill Daily*. Fred Rasmussen will also be there. Can you come? We're going to discuss next year's celebration of Founding Day. Do you realize that Mayhill's first settlers stopped their wagons on this spot roughly one hundred years ago?"

"How could I *not* know?" Izzy laughed. Jake had started promoting the centennial last January. Already storefronts displayed pioneers holding shovels with banners that proclaimed, "Mayhill or Bust."

She flipped open her planner and stared at her schedule. Thursday. It had been a week since Parker Strickland had rescued her cat. She had seen him around town a few times, or at least she'd seen his truck. Last Sunday she had gone to church and had written Parker's name on a prayer card. Funny how every time she added a commitment to her planner, she thought of Parker.

"Okay, Jake, I can make it this afternoon." The only unusual venture planned for today was a three-thirty appointment with a high school girl about part-time employment. Carole could do the interview if Izzy didn't get back in time.

Izzy pushed aside a pile of flyers announcing extended library hours every Tuesday and located last Friday's paper. Mark Dalton dominated the front page with stories of Mayhill's past glories. She scanned the writing, smiling at the mention of a reported sighting of Jesse James by one Margaret Summer. From the arrest of a Nazi criminal to the smiling photo of Greta McKenna representing Big Red in a

Miss America pageant, Mayhill proved it had done its part promoting the pride of Nebraska.

Izzy felt a spark of loyalty. She hadn't been born in this state, but in many ways she felt at home here. Her mother had never been happier.

❧

"They're waiting for you." Agnes Hepfield said.

Izzy smiled. Agnes looked so prim and proper behind the huge cherrywood desk. She'd volunteered to be a secretary on the two days Jake worked at the courthouse. The elderly woman had been his full-time secretary at Martin's Insurance Firm until she'd retired.

Mayhill Courthouse resided right across the street from the library and displayed its history gallantly, from the etched date of 1911 that existed above the door frame to the chipped white pavilion where James McKenna and his band played jazz every Saturday night during the summer.

Jake Martin's office was awash with blue marble. The shiny floor looked like a museum's. A painting of George Washington gazed with dignity over the furnishings. Izzy found herself scrutinizing the signature, almost expecting to see an autograph by the first president himself.

Jake leaned back in a leather chair, hands folded sternly in front of him. Mark Dalton scribbled in his notebook and didn't bother looking up at her entrance. Fred Rasmussen wheezed from the corner where he was getting a drink from a distilled water cooler.

"Glad you could make it." Jake rose from the chair, arm stretched out in greeting, pure politician stance.

Mark nodded, quit writing, and looked up. "I'll be glad to turn over copies of the old *Daily*s when you begin research and—"

"Do you think I could have a cigarette?" Fred interrupted.

"Don't worry," Jake said, seeing Izzy's distressed look. "His daughter made him quit. Now all he does is chew on them."

"Women," Fred complained.

"Izzy." Jake cleared his throat. "Mark jumped the gun a bit. We called you here because I, er, Mark had the bright idea of doing a biography of Rosemary Mayhill's life. We thought that since you've done such a good job of refurbishing the library, you might like to be in charge of writing up her history. What do you think?"

"A better woman never lived." Fred Rasmussen feebly sat down in the seat next to Izzy's.

"What kind of history?" Izzy tried to pretend she wasn't interested. She knew the talk of politics. She didn't like it, but she knew it. Truthfully, the thought of being commissioned to research the finer points surrounding the first librarian of Mayhill intrigued Izzy. Rosemary Mayhill had been years ahead of her time. The cornerstone of both the town and the church.

"We were thinking that we'd focus in on at least five past citizens and expound on their good works for the community. Sort of a 'they made a difference' topic. Rosemary Mayhill and Alias Summer were voted as unanimous choices. Mark thinks you'd be perfect as the writer of Mrs. Mayhill's mini-biography. He's going to do Alias's."

Mark nodded. "During the Saturday-evening celebration, we'll role play the parts of the forefounders."

"What do you think?" Jake leaned forward eagerly. The light in his eyes told Izzy he was sure that this event would help keep him mayor for years after the spectacle.

"Sounds like a lot of work," Izzy said.

"You could work on it during business hours." Jake smiled.

Izzy opened her purse and took out her planner, slowly opening the book and studying her schedule with a pretend scowl. "I'm only going to be here four more months, and with Carole gone, I'll be very busy at the library. Now that school's started again, I've got lots of students needing help, plus with the onset of winter, patrons check out a large number of books, anticipating being inside during blizzards."

"I'm waiting for you to order that new book by that fancy New York lawyer," Fred spoke up. "Be sure you get it in large print."

Mark settled back in his chair, watching Izzy with an interested expression.

"Mayor Martin, my time is very valuable." Izzy leaned forward, looking at Jake Martin with raised eyebrows. "The task is extremely appealing, but I may have to pass. Oh, by the way, when do the city commissioners plan on finalizing next year's budget?"

Jake picked up a pen and tapped it against his desk calendar.

"That's all been decided," Mark began and then choked.

"Some decisions have already been made." Jake started examining his hand with intent interest.

"Just how thoroughly did you discuss my motion for three computers to be installed for patron use at the library?"

"We haven't made any firm decisions about monies allotted to the library yet."

Izzy stood, sticking her planner back in her purse and smiling at Jake. "I originally requested five, you know."

"Three seems like a reasonable number," Jake responded.

"How long do you want the report on Rosemary Mayhill to be?"

"You can go over the details with Mark." Jake came around the desk and shook Izzy's hand. "He'll be in charge of the final program."

"Let's get Fred over to his apartment, Izzy. I'll fill you in on my ideas, and maybe you can make some suggestions." Mark stuck his notecards in his pocket and helped Fred stand.

The retirement home squatted two buildings down from the city hall. With a young person on each side, Fred slowly made his way outside. "When I was born, only five thousand people lived in Mayhill. It was pure farm country then, had just one restaurant and that was run by the Summers family as an offshoot of the store."

Mark and Izzy smiled at each other over the bent gray head, and then Mark cleared his throat before loudly saying, "Fred, how'd you like to meet Izzy and me for dinner tomorrow night?"

"Excuse me," Izzy frowned, "tomorrow night I—"

"Will certainly want to meet with Fred to ask him questions about Rosemary Mayhill," Mark finished her sentence.

Fred took two steps up the retirement center's walk. "You young people let me know if your argument ends with a yes to dinner."

"We'll pick you up at seven," Mark said.

"We'll let you know," Izzy butted in.

Fred waved good-bye, chuckling advice. "Take charge, my boy."

"I could be busy tomorrow night," Izzy said, turning toward the library.

"It's not your bowling night. You never go to Summers'. Your parents are in Florida. I think you're available."

Izzy sputtered indignantly, "Why you snoop! How do you know all that? What gives you the right—?"

Mark laughed and easily threw his arm around her shoulders companionably. "Welcome to small-town America. There's not much to be known. I bowl on Tuesday nights and always check the boards to compare high scores. You're a good bowler, by the way. Carole's been a friend of my family's for years. She likes to talk, so I know all about the things you do for fun. I hear you're getting pretty good at crocheting dishcloths. As for your parents still being in Florida, I'm a reporter, Izzy. I'm supposed to snoop. Now, what about dinner? Fred Rasmussen will be the perfect chaperone."

❧

Parker sat in his truck watching Izzy with dismay. What was she doing with that weasel, Mark Dalton? It was almost too much to bear when Dalton threw his arm around Izzy's shoulders. In Parker's opinion, Mark rated just a little bit above Kenny.

Parker sighed. It was probably for the best. He didn't want to be interested in Izzy, anyway. Now that he knew she was seeing Mark Dalton, Parker would just stay away from the library. He had a new puppy for companionship. He didn't need or want a woman, especially not one who wanted him to give his time to a Bible study. He knew the Bible. His parents occasionally attended services. He refused to be a hypocrite: living one way; feeling another.

The puppy yawned in agreement. Parker petted the top of the dog's head and started the engine. He'd go visit his folks and then head home.

❧

The minute Mark got into the car, leaving Izzy free to return to the library, she let out a silent whoop. She'd been planning on researching the woman's life on her own. There were many magazines interested in publishing the stories concerning pioneer women and to think that she could use working hours to get the job done.

"Well, did Jake talk you into it?" Carole handed books back to a patron and smiled at Izzy.

"He certainly did."

"And how many computers did he agree to?"

"What! How? Oh, Carole, you're a charmer. How did you know I'd use those computers as leverage?"

"Because you're a smart girl. I hear Parker rescued your cat last week."

"Hurrumph."

Carole wagged a finger. "I know Mark Dalton is not the right man for you."

"Guess what? I know that too."

"Good," Carole teased. "I'd hate to think of your settling for Mark Dalton when Parker Strickland's a possibility."

A loud sneeze echoed off the library's walls. Carole and Izzy glanced over to where Whip was exiting his chair. "Parker's a good man," Thompson said. "He has great taste in pies." He headed for the door, throwing back over his shoulder. "And women."

Izzy felt embarrassment steal up her cheeks. She forced herself to remain calm. "Carole, if you don't leave my love life alone, I will go out with Mark Dalton."

Carole wasn't fooled. "I doubt that."

"Mark's a fine man. An excellent journalist. A fine judge of bowling scores. We share many like interests."

"Mark has a girlfriend in Lincoln. Seems to think he's fair game until the wedding day, which is in June. Parker is more reliable."

"He's impossible," Izzy muttered.

"He's what?"

"Nothing. And, it doesn't matter anyway. I'm moving back to Phoenix soon. Don't you have work to do?"

Carole grinned and began emptying the drop box. "Sure, and so do you. Oh, Delta McKenna wants you to call her."

Izzy stepped behind the front desk and helped a patron who suddenly appeared from behind the biography section.

Carole returned to the desk, and Izzy went into the office. It seemed as if she was getting less and less of her own work completed. Unless she took matters in hand, and quickly, she'd have little time to work on Rosemary's life.

A stack of messages waited atop her computer. Two were personal, and she dispensed of them quickly. One was a thank-you from Jake Martin, and the last was from Delta McKenna. Izzy took a breath and dialed Delta's number. Delta probably wanted to do a movie or something. She had lived in Mayhill all her life. She'd turned up pregnant during her senior year of high school and refused to tell who the father was. Most of the bowling league women seemed to think it was a boy from Waco named Chris Walker. Izzy remembered that Agatha had said Chris was Kenny's cousin. That would make Chris a relative of Parker's too. Parker's roots sank deep in Mayhill history.

Others claimed the father was Carole's boy, Tom. Carole denied that and said it was probably Chris, but that Delta had dated anyone who walked. Whip said it was nobody's business. Izzy agreed, and was proud of the way Delta held her head high and dared anyone to look down on her or her boy. She'd begun attending church again merely a month ago. Her Christianity was fragile. Izzy sometimes sat next to her during services. Delta struggled, that Izzy could see. The old life called, and commitment was still divided.

"Thanks for returning my call so quickly," Delta said. "Dad wants to attend the gun show in Lincoln Friday night. Mom and I thought we'd get some shopping done. Would you be willing to stay with Billy for the weekend?"

"I really—" Izzy tried.

"I know how last minute this is and how busy you are, and normally I wouldn't think to bother you, but Bushy is about to have her first batch of kittens. The vet says it will most likely be this weekend, and Billy so wants to be here. I just know if we leave, Bushy will give birth, and Billy will be devastated."

"Well, I—"

"We'll be glad to pay you."

"Delta, that's not it. I have plans for tomorrow night and—"

"Of course. I'm sure Bushy will be fine, and Billy can be there the next time. Dad was planning on getting the cat fixed, but perhaps I can convince him—"

"I'll be glad to do it." Izzy knew when to give in.

"I'll drop the keys by the library this afternoon. Tomorrow, Billy will walk to the library instead of taking the bus home. I can't tell you how much we appreciate this."

Izzy hung up the phone, feeling drained. Jake Martin better beware. If Delta McKenna ever took a mind to run for Congress, he wouldn't have a chance against her if it came to bargaining.

❧

Billy obediently sat in the children's section and looked at a picture book.

Izzy kept a sharp eye on him, checking to make sure he was behaving. He stayed close to the rabbit. Maybe the kid would be a veterinarian when he grew up. Suddenly, Izzy began looking forward to the evening. Mark had agreed to pick up Fred and bring him out to the McKennas' farm. Izzy would purchase plenty of food at the grocery store and intended to make a four-course meal. She rarely got the opportunity to cook, and she wanted to go all out. She'd worked her way through college via the restaurant route. She'd waitressed, cooked, bussed, and even managed. Sharing a kitchen with Whip had curtailed her culinary daring. Besides, with the old man cooking, she'd already put on eight pounds since she'd moved in.

"Are you ready?" she asked Billy after making sure Carole knew she was leaving.

"Yep," Billy lisped toothlessly, digging in his back pocket and extracting a wrinkled piece of paper. "Mom said you hadn't been ta the house before so she drew ya a map."

Izzy took the damp piece of paper, wondering where the wetness came from, yet glad she didn't know. Delta had drawn a detailed route to the McKenna farm.

"You live," Izzy cleared her throat, suddenly remembering, "behind Parker Strickland's place?"

"Yes, maybe tomorra we kin go over and play with his puppy."

"I don't think so," Izzy managed, turning into the local grocery store's parking lot.

Izzy didn't use the map to find the McKennas' house. Her twilight romp to Parker's house, to collect a made-up library fine, was a vivid memory. The McKennas lived right next door, albeit a quarter-mile down the way. Izzy had turned around in their driveway.

Of course, the place looked different in the fading daylight. It was nestled amid a landscape of green grass and winding driveway. The dirt road shot pebbles from under Izzy's tires as she skidded toward the white garage. An old well stood to the left of the two-story house. The smell of animals and nature hit Izzy full force when she parked her car alongside the barn. Clouds were gathering in the distant skies.

"Park behind the barn," Billy ordered. "You can see my rabbit hutches."

"Have you lived here all your life?" Izzy helped Billy out of the car.

"Yes, Mama made the big mistake when she was seventeen, and we've lived here ever since." Billy took Izzy's hand and led her to a homemade wooden structure.

Izzy knew the big mistake was Delta getting pregnant out of wedlock. From Billy's tone, she didn't think he thought of himself as the big mistake, just of his mama as making one that he was as of yet uncertain about.

After Billy introduced Izzy to seven bunnies, all named after dwarves, he took off running for the front door. Izzy fumbled in her purse for the key, but Billy careened into the house without halting.

They don't lock the door, Izzy said to herself in amazement.

Lights came on in every room as Billy ran through the house. Izzy followed more slowly taking in the layout. She touched a finger to the floral wallpaper of the kitchen and imagined the sense of generation after generation blending together to make what existed now. The very smell of the air tingled with history.

She went back outside and emptied the car of its groceries. Leaving everything on the kitchen counters, she came to the living room and sat down on a large couch. The television looked comfortable next to the obviously homemade brick fireplace. Dark pictures, depicting stern-looking ancestors in black and white, graced the walls.

A glance at the clock put Izzy on her feet again. She had just a few hours to prepare supper for her visitors. Billy entered the kitchen and proudly displayed five favorite stuffed animals while Izzy measure, poured, chopped, and stirred.

Only the sounds of crickets and locusts blanketed the night air around the McKenna farm. Thunder sounded once, then faded to nothingness. Izzy stood on the back porch, wiping a cold hand over her damp brow. The kitchen had warmed up soon after she'd turned on the stove. The smell of lasagna permeated the musty air. The dark sky taunted her with blue and gray clouds that moved threateningly toward the fading moon. The moon hazed in the distance.

Billy tripped out to the porch, carrying a protesting, extremely pregnant cat. "Bushy wants to be near you."

"Let's sit and wait for Mark and Mr. Rasmussen."

"My grandma says Mark Dalton better go home when Mr. Rasmussen does."

From the mouth of babes, Izzy thought. "Don't worry, he will. Put that poor cat down and come inside."

The cat went under the porch. Billy led Izzy inside. She checked the lasagna. Billy pulled a building block game from under the coffee table and set about creating some sort of oddly shaped car. Izzy divided her time between the kitchen and living room.

It was just after seven when headlights glowed from miles away. Izzy knew they belonged to Mark. No one else would be out on a night like this, with a storm threatening to appear, especially on a country road that led nowhere, and Parker's truck sat silhouetted in his driveway, a testament that he was home. The glow danced as the driver hit ruts in the curving road that had once served only wagons.

"I forgot about that road," Mark laughed, stepping out of the car.

Izzy opened Fred's side. The old man's hand sailed through the air as he tried to find a firm foundation to brace himself against. Izzy offered her arm.

"No," he grumbled. "Mark."

Mark came around the car and helped Fred out. "He's not real comfortable with equality, yet." Mark led Fred to the door.

"Delta's grandmama used to have the best barn dances." Fred looked around in admiration. Billy heard the reference to the great-grandmother he'd never met and positioned himself behind Fred's feet, dangerously close to the wavering cane.

"Put Fred at the table," Izzy ordered.

"Don't forget to turn off the stove," Fred advised.

Izzy looked at Mark with alarm. Was there something wrong with the oven? Mark shook his head helplessly.

Once the food hit the table, Fred forgot about the stove and plunged in with a joyous abandonment that awed Izzy. Izzy opened her mouth, then shut it. She didn't want to embarrass the elderly man. Reaching over, she took Billy's hand and whispered a quick prayer of thanks for the meal. Mark stopped eating but didn't join in.

Fred didn't notice at all. No one had ever shown so much appreciation for her food before. He didn't even complain because she'd gone a little liberal with the amount of ketchup she used in the sauce.

Billy turned up his nose at the Italian fare and settled for a peanut butter and jelly sandwich. The continuing thunder kept Izzy on the edge of her seat, smiling brightly, and trying to act as if nothing bothered her.

After the meal, she led everyone into the living room, and they gathered around the coffee table, Mark and Izzy with notebooks in hand, Billy stroking a bloated feline and keeping his building blocks from straying too close to Fred's feet.

Mark began the questions, "Did you know Alias Summer?"

"Not really. . . ."

Two hours later, Fred dropped off in the middle of a sentence. His "not really" reference had expanded into a blow-by-blow account of the many dealings he'd had with the man. His history narration started with his childhood, as a young boy shoveling snow. Later, he detailed the life of a doctor trying to contend with a self-diagnosing patient. They never got around to discussing Rosemary Mayhill.

Izzy fumed silently, trying hard to keep her temper in check. The book of Psalms described the Lord as being slow to anger. Izzy believed the teaching, lived it, but sometimes had a hard time enjoying it. The nerve of Mark, allowing her to cook the meal and then to be forced to listen to an old man discuss only aspects pertaining to Mark's portion of the historical assignment. Every time she'd tried to direct the questions to Rosemary, Mark had smoothly turned the topic back to Alias.

"He's falling asleep, and Billy's been asleep for over an hour," Izzy whispered. "Time for you guys to leave."

Mark grinned, raising an eyebrow in a suggestive pose that Izzy hadn't witnessed since college. The man who attempted to impress her back then hadn't been successful either.

Izzy opened the front door—surely, Mark would take the hint—and stepped out onto the porch. Mark followed, without Fred. She counted to ten, but that didn't help. Sunday school had told her that patience was a virtue, but it continued to be a virtue Izzy lacked.

"Mark," Izzy said, "very few men have irritated me as thoroughly as you have this evening. I can with complete assurance predict that you and I have no future. I think you're a complete jerk." A clap of thunder added emphasis to her words. "And it's time for you to leave."

"I don't understand," Mark pretended.

"You poor thing. I believe you've dated girls who lie to you about your appeal. You know exactly why I'm irritated at you. Next time you want to interview somebody, have your mother do the cooking. I hear crow is especially easy to prepare. Now leave."

Mark came a little closer, amusement and something else dancing in his expression. Izzy frowned as she realized that he hadn't believed a word she'd said. She was too tired to mess with this. Back in Phoenix, the public library had hosted numerous safety seminars. Izzy had attended more than one. A woman had many options to take if she felt threatened. In the middle of nowhere, on an almost stormy Friday night, Izzy wished she had a whistle or can of mace. Not that Mark deserved that, but . . .

She'd first utilized her screaming skills in the backyard of her Arizona home at age eight. Playing in the desert had been fun. With her friends, she'd chased lizards and dug holes. She and her two best friends happened upon a little snake while following the exploits of a roadrunner. Anna had screamed first, but no one noticed, so Izzy had taken a deep breath and let loose a sound that summoned three sets of parents.

The last time Izzy screamed had been at the Phoenix Library when one of her mother's friends had came for her . . . to tell her that her father had . . . to tell her . . . that her father was dead. That scream had been so heart-rending that no one had even given the automatic "shhh." Izzy had done a lot of screaming the week her father had died. Then she'd stopped, until tonight.

Mark's hand on her shoulder released her from her thoughts. She tilted her head back and screamed. Mark jumped. Billy started crying, clearly frightened by what he'd heard. Fred didn't move.

"Izzy," Mark grumbled as he backed away, "you'd think I was going to hurt you."

"You did hurt me," Izzy ground out. "You hurt my feelings and my dignity. I'll definitely add you to my prayers, but I don't think we need to work together anymore."

"Fine by me. I'll send you written guidelines about what to do. You need to stop being so uptight. I thought you'd be grateful for a little excitement. Mayhill must be pretty dreary after Phoenix."

"Grateful? When I meet your girlfriend from Lincoln I'll ask her how grateful she is."

Mark went rigid and stiffly reentered the living room. "Come on, Fred." He shook the old man's shoulder and then hurried the dazed older man out the door.

The rain started as they drove away. Even in the uneven mist, Izzy could see the lights going on one by one at Parker Strickland's farm.

5

arker heard the truck drive away from McKennas' place. Unless he was mistaken, Mark Dalton had just spent the evening at his neighbors. That didn't explain the scream. If there had been more than one holler, Parker would have rushed over. As it was, the screaming stopped right before Mark left.

Still, something didn't feel quite right. The scream hadn't sounded like Delta or her mom, and her dad certainly wasn't one to shout. Parker paced for a few moments before deciding he'd take a walk in the McKennas' direction, make sure everything looked all right.

Brute tumbled at his feet. In the back of his mind, Parker considered leaving the puppy shut inside, but the dog loved being outdoors. Brute had quickly figured out how to work Parker. A short whine and every wish was appeased. Brute no longer missed his mother. Parker fulfilled his every need.

The night seemed to grow darker as Parker crossed through overgrown fields. It had been seven years since any crops had been planted, and according to his dad, now would be a good time to put his land to use. Parker had no intention of becoming a farmer. He just liked the farmhouse and the privacy of many acres between him and the city.

Rain pelted his face, and Parker almost turned around, went back home. Nothing looked amiss.

He saw the woman on the porch and stopped short. It sure wasn't Delta or her mom sitting there. Besides, Delta usually had a date on Friday night. His gut let him know who it was before he even recognized the long, dark hair and athletic body. What was she doing here?

Thunder crashed and lightning appeared to make the moment look as day. He watched Izzy sitting on the porch, arms tightly wrapped around her own body, and realized she was frightened. All of Parker's instincts told him to go comfort her. He wouldn't. She'd obviously survived thunderstorms without him. She was already in his thoughts more than he wanted her to be. Parker turned, took two steps, paused, pivoted around. Brute made up Parker's mind for him. The small bundle of fur ran ahead, then jumped up and pounced on Izzy's knees.

A sense of foreboding came over him. Brute had wiggled, muddy-pawed, into Izzy's lap and planted a sloppy kiss right on Izzy's chin.

"Are you coming up, Parker?" Izzy's voice clashed with a streak of thunder. She held Brute in her lap and crossed her feet at her ankles.

"Storms scare you?" He stepped out of the shadows.

"A little," she said. "This your dog?"

The wooden slats of the porch creaked under his feet. He looked around, but the only place to sit was alongside Izzy on the porch swing. He settled for the top step, stretching his legs out and wishing she didn't make him long for things he couldn't have. "I heard a scream."

"That was me."

"What did Mark do?"

"He made me mad."

"And so you screamed?" He shifted, sitting Indian style and trying to figure out the truth behind her flippant answers.

"A trick I learned in a defense class. It worked, didn't it? He's gone."

"Who was with him?"

"You're full of questions tonight."

Parker felt his face growing red. The careless splattering of rain turned into a downpour at that moment, saving him from obvious embarrassment. "I'm the only neighbor who came to investigate," he pointed out. "I think that gives me the right to ask a few questions."

"You are the only neighbor," she pointed out. A healthy burst of thunder inspired Brute to bury his nose in Izzy's hand. Izzy stared off in the distance, watching the lightning and chewing her bottom lip.

Parker kept watching her, wondering why she was interested in Mark Dalton and how she'd wound up here at the McKennas' place.

❧

Any other man would have settled down beside her in the porch swing, not Parker. He preferred to sit on the porch with his feet in the mud. Still, she was grateful that he was here. Dark places with thunder-and-lightning sound effects had never been her favorite locations. She wanted him to stay because his presence made her feel safe, and she wanted him to stay because his haunted eyes seemed to cry out for her.

"Let's go in," she heard herself say.

Parker cleared his throat, "Maybe I should—"

"It's dark, it's raining, and your dog's asleep."

Brute had burrowed his way under the porch swing and between two potted plants. Puppy snores added music to the night sounds.

"What's his name?"

"What? Oh, his name is Brute."

"You named a golden retriever Brute?"

"So?"

Izzy tried not to chuckle. "It just doesn't fit."

"Well, I'm not quite sure how your cat came about the name Radar, but I didn't mention that as I extracted him from the tree."

Izzy smiled, glad that Parker was touchy. It was a good sign. "I'll bet the McKennas have Monopoly," Izzy suggested.

Parker stood, slipping out of his muddy boots and nodding. Izzy led the way inside, formulating all the questions she could ask him about his late wife, and about why he always seemed so sad.

While they'd been outside, Billy had come into the living room and laid on the couch. Izzy straightened the blanket over his sleeping form and went to find the game.

"I'll get some candles," Parker called.

Izzy shivered. Candles. What could he . . . ?

The lights went out.

In the flashing darkness, Izzy froze. She could hear Parker fumbling and then the striking of a match.

"Izzy?" came a whisper.

"Over here," she whispered back.

The light from the flickering candle found its force, and Izzy turned to see Parker, so silent in his stocking feet, loom up behind her.

"Why are you so frightened of the storm?" he asked.

The shadows from the candle played across his face, highlighting such a serious look that Izzy wanted to touch his chin. She wanted to witness the beginning of a smile change his stoic expression to one of joy.

"Why are you always so sad?" she countered.

He frowned, "I'm not sad. I just don't . . . Listen, we can play Monopoly. It will keep your mind off the storm." He walked into the living room.

Funny, with Parker sitting on the floor across from her, the night didn't seem so scary. The lightning highlighted his hair. The strands were still damp from the heavy rain.

"What piece do you want?" Parker changed the mood from moonlight to reality.

"I'll be the thimble." Izzy handed out the miniatures and located the dice.

His body seemed to take up so much of the living room. Izzy almost felt suffocated, as if his very being demanded her complete attention. She leaned against the sofa while he lounged with his back to the silent television. His eyes were shaded. The stubble on his chin told of his need to shave.

Izzy cleared her throat and started with a safe topic. "So how long have you been a fireman?"

"Almost three years."

Izzy acquired Baltic and St. James Place. "Do you like living in Mayhill?"

He didn't answer until she handed him Park Place. "It's home."

Brute whined from outside. Parker eased his body off the floor and ambled to the door. Izzy watched. The man moved with the ease of a panther. She was getting much too interested. Brute slid in, jumped on the couch, and curled puppy style at Billy's feet.

The clock said midnight. The game had effectively taken her mind off of the storm and now the rain was letting up. Izzy tried to stifle a yawn, and she handed him the last of her money as rent. "Parker, that was a lot of fun."

It looked as if he started to nod, but thought better of it and changed the gesture to a shrug, although he said more in the next sentence than he'd spoken all evening. "I think I'll head home. The storm's mostly over. Let me take Billy upstairs."

Without waiting for an answer, he scooped the little boy up. Izzy felt her heart beat as she watched the man gently rest Billy's head against his shoulder. This was a scene right out of her daydreams. Billy's chin quivered in sleep, and Izzy carefully pushed an errant strand of hair out of Billy's eyes. Parker stared down at her, questions in his eyes.

"You know where his room is?"

"No," Parker whispered.

"Up the stairs, to the left."

The flames from the fireplace shot out an amber of light into the room. Izzy watched the two heads as they bobbed up the stairs. Two reddish-brown heartthrobs. She stood on one foot then another. She'd been with Parker for hours and knew practically nothing about him, except that her quest to save him had doubled. Under his gruff exterior nestled the heart of a teddy bear. If she were to liken him to an apostle, she'd choose Luke, the healer. He didn't like to see people hurting, which was why he hurt so much and probably why he'd put a lock on his heart so he wouldn't chance getting hurt again.

Billy nodded awake before Parker reached the top of the stairs. Izzy heard the muffled words, "You're not Mark."

"Not even close," Parker agreed. After a few minutes, during which time giggles and things dropping echoed down the stairs, Parker came back into the living room, nonchalantly looking around.

"Your boots are on the porch," Izzy said.

She followed him out the door, watching as he sat in the swing to put his boots on.

He stomped away some of the mud that had caked on his boots. Izzy stepped closer. He looked up at the sky and glanced at Izzy warningly. "It's still raining a bit."

She backed away, silently, wanting to appear a shadow.

He hadn't worn a jacket. "I had a nice evening," he murmured, as if it had been a planned meeting.

She nodded mutely. He stood uncertainly and then started across the porch. He hesitated when he got to the steps. Then with a suddenness that left her breathless, he turned, took two big steps in her direction, hooked his hand securely around the base of her neck and brought her mouth to his.

The few drops of rain that shivered on her arms all stood to attention. Izzy felt herself leaning into the kiss, drinking in the taste of him. Her knees brushed against him, and she let her body become enraptured with his as her skin fought to touch him.

Abruptly, he pushed her away. He glared down at her sternly before he turned and marched into the field. Brute followed, dancing excitedly amidst the dripping trees, unaware that his master could accept and return the love of a dog more than he could the possible love of a woman.

❧

Every time his boot sank in the mud, Parker made a fist. What had happened back there? She'd asked more questions than his mother, and he'd fielded all of them. Julia hadn't surfaced even once. So why had he kissed her? She was as innocent as the sky was blue. He should have moved off that porch without looking in her eyes. His boots had already been on, his dog had lain at his feet. There was absolutely no reason for him to turn around, clasp her to his lips, and kiss her. No reason, except that for the first time in years his chest didn't hurt every time he breathed. Except that now the scent of roses put a smile where a smile previously hadn't been welcomed or wanted.

Parker looked up at the skies and wondered what God was up to.

❧

Izzy stayed in the office the next day. Every time the door opened, she jumped. Parker's kiss had kept her awake all night. This morning when she had prodded Billy out of bed, he had confided, "My mama likes Parker, too, but she says he's boring."

Then he'd checked his cat, disappointed at nature's delay. On the way to the library, he'd asked all kinds of mindless questions. She'd answered each one patiently, hoping he wouldn't mention Parker anymore. She didn't know if she had the courage to go back to the McKennas'. What if Parker came over again? Worse, what if he didn't?

She took Billy to Summers for lunch. Two of his school friends were there. When it was time to return to work, she gave halting permission for him to play with them at the park in front of the library. She spent the rest of the afternoon working the front desk and watching out the door as Billy and his friends tried to climb the huge, gnarled tree.

"I use to climb that tree when I was in britches." Fred Rasmussen's voice jerked Izzy from her scrutinizing.

Izzy strained to watch as Billy jumped at the limb for the umpteenth time. "He can't quite reach the lowest branch."

"Did you get that book I wanted in large print?"

"Not yet, Mr. Rasmussen." Izzy scooted around on her chair and took the books from Fred's arms. He was one of their better patrons, at least for returning books on time. Something slithered to the floor. Izzy bent, picking up the single page and stared aghast at the paperback book it came from, especially when she noticed that all the pages were loose.

"Mr. Rasmussen, what happened?"

"Arthritis. I can't hold the books comfortably anymore."

Carole walked over, and took the paperback from Izzy's trembling hand. "What did you do?"

"If I tear the pages out. I can hold them more easily."

His cane tapped a Morse code of aged independence as he hobbled to the door.

"What . . . ?" Carole began.

Izzy found it far easier to forgive Fred than she had Mark last night. After a quick round of "What would Jesus do?" she said, "We'll see to it he only checks out the books that are beyond repair. He can read them before we dispose of them."

Carole swallowed her laughter and nodded.

When the library closed at six, Izzy grabbed her coat, fed the rabbit, and rushed out the door, barely responding to Carole's good-bye.

"My mama drives this fast," was Billy's only comment as they sped towards the McKenna house.

Izzy checked the speedometer and slowed down.

Parker's house stood empty. Billy supplied the answer. "It's his shift."

Twenty-four on, twenty-four off. There went her plans to invite him to church tomorrow morning.

Saturday evening dragged on, with only the television to offer entertainment, but Sunday came too quickly. She'd learned all sorts of things following Billy around the farm. She'd learned how to gather an egg. It had taken her fifteen minutes to grab the innocent oval from the unthreatening chicken, but she'd done it. She'd climbed an elm tree to investigate Billy's treehouse, made from wood and old John Deere parts.

It almost felt like noon when she pulled into the church's parking lot. Billy trustingly tucked his hand in hers and entered the foyer. She made sure he was safely cocooned in Sunday school and then headed for her own class.

One thing Izzy knew about every church she'd ever attended, and that was: It was hard to be single. Izzy had sat through many a lecture about how to stay a couple. Today was the first time she'd felt vulnerable. As if she'd forgotten to bring something, someone, to church. During all the other "Making the Marriage Work" sermons, she'd dreamed about meeting her future husband. Today, she felt almost ill. The smiling couples, sitting on gray folding chairs, and nodding at the minister's words, had they always known they were meant to be together? Had God directed them toward each other, and when their eyes met had they known? What if she'd met the man God had chosen for her and somehow not recognized him? What if there were no significant other for her?

Izzy wished her mother weren't in Florida. She could sure use some advice, and she wasn't sure she could find the Scripture that pertained to Parker Strickland.

Delta McKenna and her parents pulled into the driveway late Sunday afternoon. Izzy and Billy were watching cartoons on the television. Billy eagerly jumped up and ran outside to leap into his grandpa's arms. Delta's father nodded curtly at Izzy. "Did the cat have the kittens?" the man demanded in a gravelly voice.

"No, Grandpa." Billy wiggled down. "But Parker came over Friday night and said my action figures collection was neat."

Delta smiled as she walked Izzy to the Peugot. "We really do appreciate it that you stayed with Billy. Parker's a nice guy. He seems to be smiling a bit more lately."

"I don't know him very well. There was a storm. He came over when the lights went off." Izzy slid into the driver's seat. She backed up and around before heading down the driveway to the road. The McKenna women stood together on the lawn, waving. Izzy waved merrily back and caught just a few words of their muted conversation. As she left the Mayhill countryside, she wondered what Delta had meant by the overheard words, "Carole sure did have a good idea."

Izzy still pondered the words on Monday morning when she entered the library. She avoided the office, not wanting to miss Parker, should he decide to come to the library. He didn't. Later, making a few wrong turns on the way home, she noticed that he wasn't sitting in front of the fire station.

She didn't see him for almost two weeks.

&

The library didn't have much on Rosemary Mayhill, but the newspapers did. Izzy purchased a spiral notebook and wrote a year on every page, starting with 1885, the year of Rosemary's birth, and ending with 1983, her death. Each time she found mention of Rosemary, she made note of the date and recorded the event on the page corresponding with the correct year. The outdated newspapers were filled with tidbits. Izzy discovered Rosemary's favorite recipe for apple pie, and how often the woman had hosted the church's bake sales. The births of Rosemary's seven children were front-page items as was the loss of two of them to childhood diseases. When Rosemary lost a toe to frostbite, the *Mayhill Daily* was there.

After Izzy finished reading Rosemary's obituary, she sorted out the information and kept what was interesting, deciding to go to the elderly residents of Mayhill and find out more details about the events. She still needed a clearer picture of the habits and personality of Rosemary.

Over the phone Fred acted a little disappointed after finding out that Mark Dalton would not be there. Izzy did the cooking, preparing a tuna casserole to die for. Whip pitched in and whipped up a key lime pie. By the time Izzy went to fetch Fred, the kitchen aromas had her stomach growling.

A thump from Whip's fingers inspired Fred to join in the prayer. Izzy peeked during Whip's words. Fred wasn't bowing, he was staring at the food appreciatively. His fork found action before the final strain of "Amen" left Whip's mouth.

The men didn't talk while they ate. Finally, Fred sat back. "That was delicious." He took a handkerchief out of his back pocket and patted at his lips, missing a sliver of bread hanging on the edge of his lip.

Izzy sat down across from Fred and opened the notebook. "Tell me what you remember about Rosemary."

Fred grinned, slurping down a gulp of iced tea. "Old Rosemary knew how to get around the townspeople. If you didn't return a book on time, she'd come knocking at your door with her little library card list. Only two people managed to be forgiven for losing a library book. One was a migrant worker who fell in love with the words of a poet. For years Rosemary would get this dreamy expression on her face and start speculating where the book might be. She imagined it in hay wagons of Kansas, on dirt farms in Tennessee, orange groves in California. She enjoyed the musings so much that she forgave Miguel for stealing the book."

"And the other book?"

"I think I'll have another piece of that pie if you don't mind." Fred took out his handkerchief again, this time he got the piece of bread.

After three bites, Fred sat back with a contented smile and continued. "It was well after Rosemary's retirement. Oh, but she bothered Catherine Wilfong, who was the librarian who took over after Rosemary stepped down, with her suggestions and rearrangings. Nary a day went by that Rosemary didn't mosey down to the library to help out, not that Catherine wanted her to. Catherine felt quite capable of running the library herself. I suppose the second lost book really falls under Catherine's jurisdiction, but it was Rosemary who claimed credit." Fred was the only one to chuckle at the joke. "Rosemary was already well into her eighties, maybe already ninety. Her great-great-granddaughter Francine was expecting her first child. Francine was only seventeen, and everyone was worried. I was in Chicago at a conference. Those were the days." Fred nudged Whip as if they shared a secret.

"Francine wasn't due for another month, but babies being what they be, the little one decided to come early. The whole family, including Rosemary, headed for Lincoln in the dead of winter. They went to the big hospital there and in the wee hours of the morning Francine Strickland had a son, while someone stole her purse."

Izzy's head jerked up. *Strickland?* Could this possibly be Parker's mother?

"Yep, those big cities are full of crime. While Francine was cooing over Parker, an ingrate was running off with her purse. A library book was in it. Rosemary 'bout tore into Catherine when the woman started to send out an overdue notice."

"So," Izzy tried to make her voice sound steady, "Parker Strickland is Rosemary Mayhill's great-great-grandson?"

"Yep. Francine's maiden name is *Mayhill*."

Izzy's pencil broke. Fred didn't notice and continued giving insights into Rosemary's history. Izzy set the pencil aside, and Whip handed her a pen. An hour later, Fred still rambled on. He switched from detailing his own life to discussing Rosemary's to straying to other elderly residents. In the back of the spiral notebook, Izzy recorded some of the more colorful stories, thinking she'd give some suggestions to Jake about who to feature during the centennial.

It was late when Izzy returned to her apartment. Radar chomped on hard cat food. Izzy changed into her nightgown and got down on her knees beside the bed. Usually, her prayers came easily, but maybe she'd been praying the same words for so long, they were rote. The people of this small town were getting a piece of her, Izzy realized. Her prayer started with a thanks for her landlord, and a concern for Fred's health, but when she turned her prayer to concerns for Parker, she didn't know where to start.

⁃❧

The accident happened just outside of Mayhill. Parker elevated Delta's head while wiping aside bangs and blood. Her color was good. He busily checked her vital signs. If the situation back at the car weren't so somber, Parker would have whooped when Delta opened her eyes and blinked at him once before returning to unconsciousness. Convinced that Delta wasn't in immediate danger, he glanced at the car.

"Come on!" Ty yelled, trying once again to pry the driver's-side door open. The driver slumped over the wheel.

Robert yelled, "Wait a minute! I wish backup would get here. Jeff, radio York, see what's taking them so long."

The electrical pole moved as Ty again placed one leg on the car's fender and tried to pry the door open.

"Watch it," Robert warned. The pole leaned dangerously. The momentum of a speeding car cracking into its foundation had left the man-made fixture as unstable as a rotting elm tree half sawn through at the bottom.

Precious moments ticked by while Robert readied the gas motor for the jaws of life a distance away. Officer Rowe returned from cordoning off the area. Ty helped steady the machine when Robert placed the jaws in the seams of the car's door and like a jackhammer began forcing the car door to give. Everyone breathed a sigh of relief when the jaws slid open the door, like an elevator opening, so that the young man was free.

Robert eased off just as the door creaked open. The young man flopped out. Robert caught him gently by the head, leveling him, and muttering. "I thought he was pinned." Going down to one knee, Robert felt for a pulse in the boy's neck.

"Move over." Ty joined Robert by the victim's side, immediately checking, starting CPR.

"Kyle," Ty whispered.

"The air evac will be too late," Robert said.

Parker looked from Ty to Robert. Both men were pale and shaken. They knew this boy. He'd marched in holiday parades with his lips connected to a tuba. He'd played football at Mayhill High, before going off to Lincoln on a scholarship. If only his grades had been passing, he'd have been there now, instead of lying on a dirt road with the breath knocked out of him forever and the evidence of empty beer cans, covered with blood and hair, on the floorboard. Parker and Ty went back to Delta. Right now, she was their priority.

"I don't want his name over the airwaves," Robert hissed. "I'll be the one to tell his mama, not some idiot with a squawk box who happened to catch an emergency transmission and couldn't wait to spread the news."

Ty nodded gloomily.

"And Delta's folks?" Officer Rowe joined the conversation.

"You know them better than most, Parker," Robert retrieved the paperwork from the engine. "Get on the phone. Call your mother. Have her get Delta's parents and fill them in on what's happening. What's your take on Delta?"

"She'll live. Her pulse is strong, but she's bitten through her top lip, and I'll bet her front teeth are in the car somewhere amidst the beer cans. Other than that only an X-ray will tell."

"It's four in the afternoon. On a Tuesday!" Ty said. "Why were they out drinking?"

No one answered. Robert went back to the truck. Officer Rowe stayed by Kyle, halfheartedly rechecking the boy's pulse, and then slowly covering the body with a sheet.

The sound of a tractor filled the air. Parker looked up annoyed, ready to chase the trespasser away until he realized it was the farmer who'd placed the call.

Chester Wilfong brought a gallon of cold water and a Bible. "Wife says if you be needing anything, just let her know."

Robert nodded, taking the gallon of water and turning it upright to get a swig.

The helicopter radioed its location.

Mayhill's ambulance arrived just in time to wave good-bye to the helicopter. Doctor Phil Taylor knelt beside the body. "First traffic death this year," he remarked. "Why'd it have to be someone so young?" He didn't expect an answer.

"I'll never get used to this," Parker murmured.

"And if you ever did," Robert said, "it would be time to change vocations."

Parker's shift ended at eight. He felt exhausted enough to pull his truck over to the side of the road and sleep there, but knew he needed to get home, at least to feed Brute.

At ten, the Lincoln television station covered the death of one of Mayhill's own. Pictures of Kyle flashed across the screens. Mention of his failure to succeed at the university didn't occur. The coverage of weeping parents jarred Parker.

Julia had had to be pried from a smashed vehicle. He hadn't been there to hold her head. No beer cans had rattled on the floorboard, their worthless noise claiming responsibility for one more senseless death. He'd become a fireman because of her. Because when Robert Parrish had knocked at his door, with all the compassion of a lifetime featured in his brown eyes—that had been the life thread that enabled Parker to walk out the front door and get in the back of the police car that took him to the scene of the accident, where Julia had lain stiff and cold in the back of an ambulance.

After the raw taste of pain left his throat, Parker pushed himself up and went into the kitchen to down two cold sodas in a row, ignoring the effect of acid on the raw edges of his throat. He opened a third and went into the living room, staring vaguely at the movie that followed the Tuesday night news.

❦

Izzy hadn't known the young man, although she almost felt she had after listening to Carole's tears and tales. Jake Martin had come to retrieve Carole, sure that a time of mourning was necessary for his wife. After all, she'd taught Kyle in Bible school. An American flag went to half-mast outside the city hall, and the Boy Scouts immediately took out tin cans and started canvassing the neighborhoods. The parents were farmers. Money came by season and now was an uncertain time. Izzy played the closing tape to an empty library. Parents had called children home, mostly to stare at, and to appreciate the look of their offspring. Carole held her stomach as she walked out the front door. "I don't think I'll be in tomorrow," she advised. "And . . . this child will never drink anything but Kool-Aid and orange juice."

Izzy nodded. Carole was already past due and shouldn't have been working anyway. The doctor had pushed back the due date. After locking the library door and facing the sunlight, Izzy went home.

Whip had fixed meat loaf. They both sat at the kitchen table, with unmoving forks, pondering the meaning of life and feeling strangely guilty of some wrongdoing. Whip because his old age seemed ripe for death, and yet he lived on. Izzy because she had dear friends in Phoenix who sat behind the wheels of cars with the taste of liquor on their tongues and the fear of death far away. Friends who didn't understand why she preferred going to a movie rather than going to a bar. Friends who didn't understand the lure of Sunday school on a sleep-in morning. And to think, she'd thought the town of Mayhill to be so far removed from Phoenix.

The devil didn't check the map for size and population.

Izzy took a breath and stood up. The phone rang. Whip answered it. Izzy heard him grumble about good ideas and being there.

"Are they going to have a special service at church tonight?" Izzy looked at the barely touched meat loaf.

"Yes, at eight." Whip scooped the meat loaf into a covered dish and pushed it in her hands as she headed out the back door. "Parker will say he doesn't need it. Just leave it on the kitchen counter. He'll eat it."

Carefully, Izzy laid the meat loaf on her passenger side seat. Kyle wouldn't be eating meat loaf anymore. The streets were strangely silent as she drove toward Parker's. Every light in his house was on.

Izzy slowed down and eased her foot off the gas, unsure if she should turn around or if she should go ahead and attempt knocking on his door. The smell of the food enabled her to push her foot to the pedal and turn in his driveway.

His curtains were open. Izzy saw his body lapped over on the couch, head hung low, hands reaching listlessly to the floor.

She knocked.

He didn't move.

She knocked again, and then she opened the door and went into the living room. "Parker," she whispered.

He raised his head. Bloodshot eyes called out to her.

"Parker, have you eaten today?"

"Who invited you in?" he muttered.

6

"Nobody invited me in. I just came." Izzy tightened her grip on the casserole dish.

"You're not wanted."

If anyone else had made that statement, Izzy would have turned and marched out the door, with a heroic slam. Instead, she clutched the meat loaf, trying to decide what to do. The look of the living room inspired her to stay more than anything. It had the look of loneliness.

"I heard about the accident." She took one step closer.

He jerked to a sitting position. His eyes penetrated hers, flashing irritation. "You don't take hints very well, do you?"

Izzy felt hot tears beginning to form. She squeezed her eyelids shut, willing the sadness to disappear, telling herself that he acted this way because he'd forgotten any other way.

He left the couch with one fluid motion. Using the shirt material bunched at her shoulders, he walked her backwards. "I want you to leave," he said slowly. "I don't need you."

His voice said one thing; his eyes another.

"Let go of me," she whispered. "You're just trying to scare me. You shouldn't be alone."

"You don't even know me." His fingers pressed into the skin of her arms. "And I don't want to know you."

He didn't mean it. Izzy wasn't sure how she knew that, but she did. Never before had she so wanted to reach out and make a difference, to fill a need, to touch a soul. This man had the ability to make her vulnerable. And she was helpless to stop him and clueless as to how to help him.

It was possible that in many ways, he was more vulnerable than she.

She whispered, "I know you need a friend."

"I need to be left alone." His hands left her shoulders.

"Hungry?" she gasped, thrusting the plate of food at him.

He backed away, shaking his head. A look of disgust, anger, loathing, and hatred filled his eyes. Not aimed at her, no, but at himself.

Izzy again offered the meat loaf. "Parker, it wasn't your fault."

"I don't want your meat loaf, and I don't want your pity." He jerked away from her, jostling her.

The meat loaf fell to the floor. Its crash resounded through the silent house and made Izzy flinch. The plastic wrap came undone. Meat lumped on his hardwood floors.

Izzy went to her knees. "Oh."

Parker hauled her back to her feet. "Leave it."

She had made things worse, again. She should have called one of the deacons. Phil Taylor would have been glad to come. For that matter, why weren't Parker's parents here? This man was too alone. Why didn't they realize what he was thinking about?

Brute howled from outside. Doggy noises distracted Izzy, but not Parker. He kept a grip on her upper arm while he ran his other hand through his hair. It stood straight up, sweat plastering it together. His jaw twitched. Right now, Izzy knew Parker was running on adrenaline and raw need. This is what happened when you didn't know the Lord. There was no one to reach out to, until you grasped at the first sign of humanity. And usually you grabbed rough.

She remembered the anger she'd felt at her father's death. How she'd wanted to hurt someone, in order to divert the pain.

"Parker, stop." Izzy pushed against him. What she really wanted to do was cradle his head between the palms of her hands and whisper that everything would be okay. That he could cry and tell her what was in his heart. "I came to tell you that they're holding a candlelight service in Kyle's memory tonight. Come with me."

He shook his head.

Tears streamed down her cheeks. Her throat constricted, and she let out a ragged breath, the sobs hitting the silence of the room. "Come on, Parker. Please."

"What are you doing, lady? You don't know me! You think it's that simple. You think I can just go to this vigil, and suddenly it will be all right."

He pushed away. Her head banged against the screen door sharply. The latch, already creaking under the pressure of holding her up, shuddered and came undone. Izzy tumbled out of the door, falling flat on her back and biting her tongue.

Parker hadn't lost his balance. He jerked the door open, staring down at her without expression. "Are you okay?"

"I think so." Izzy swallowed.

"Good. Now go home." The screen slammed shut, followed by the thud of the wooden door.

Izzy picked herself up and limped away. She should be angry. He had pushed her away, had pushed her out the door. But she wasn't angry, she was enlightened. A man who felt this much pain at the death of a child must have a sensitive heart. Once he answered God's call, this man would be a mighty Christian.

But Izzy didn't have a clue how to reach him. How to touch the vulnerable part of the man and soothe his pain. And it bothered her how much she wanted to.

Izzy didn't pray on the way to her church. She felt the presence of the Lord beside her and knew He was crying, too.

❧

Parker stared out the screen door as Brute did his business. Breaths came and went in jagged bursts. Something had to change. Every time he saw that woman, he acted irrationally. Isobelle de la Rosa: the bearer of meat loaf and talk of redemption.

"I'm sorry, Julia." He walked over to stand in front of one of the few pictures he'd left hanging. Julia's laughing eyes were caught forever in a picture-perfect moment as she flung her arms with abandonment around Parker's neck. His father had taken the photo at Mayhill Park, just two months before Julia and the car slid off the interstate and became another statistic for winter accidents.

His fist pounded against the wall, unmindful of the plaster giving way under his strength. Now, beside the picture of a couple locked in loving embrace, a portion of the wall caved in as easily as the front end of Julia's car had. Parker walked to the back door, ignoring his hand's dull pain. It was better to have an aching fist than an aching heart. Brute answered Parker's whistle, bounding up the steps and decorating Parker's pants with mud and stickers before heading to his dish, stopping in shocked dismay and trotting expectantly to sniff at the large bag of dog food.

"Okay, okay." Parker started walking into the kitchen.

Brute followed, puppy paws skidding on the floor and sending him close to the meat loaf. While Brute ate with unabashed pleasure, Parker picked up the plate. He turned the television up, hoping the noise would drown out his conscience. She had smelled so good. Her scent lingered in the living room. He hated being alone, but no way was he heading into town to sit on a hard bench pew and listen to the weeping of survivors. They'd had a candlelight vigil for Julia. Parker hadn't gone, but his parents had. They had brought an envelope full of money to the farm. The church's idea of help: prayer and money.

He'd only wanted one thing: Julia back.

He'd enjoyed being married. From the first time he'd looked at Julia and realized that he preferred to spend Saturday nights in stocking feet, watching old movies on the telly instead of prowling with the guys, to the evenings when he'd eaten her mealtime experiments—he'd been a happy guy. Content. Growing comfortable with a member of the opposite sex had become the most natural state of being to him, until his cocoon had been cruelly ripped open by a patch of ice on the interstate.

The noise from the television reached him, drawing his attention to the screen where pictures of the afternoon's accident victim flashed. Parker picked up the remote and clicked the set off. The silence surrounded him, an accusing nonsound that created the picture of Izzy lying on his front porch where he'd allowed her to fall. For a moment he resented the fact that, lately, Isobelle de la Rosa had haunted his dreams more than Julia. Much more than Julia.

Brute came racing out of the kitchen, crumbs of meat loaf dribbling down his whiskers. He skidded sideways on the wooden floor and landed with a thump against Parker's socks.

Parker ignored him until the whining hit operatic tones. Brute jumped on the sofa and circled the cushions three times before sticking his nose against Parker's leg and falling asleep. Parker soon joined him.

～❧

Carole opened the office door and peeked in. "Why are you hiding back here?"

"I'm not hiding," Izzy protested, rubbing her eyes.

"It was a late night," Carole murmured, massaging her stomach.

The candlelight service had ended at midnight. Half the town had shown up. Izzy figured the other half were still in shock. Parker hadn't shown up, although Izzy, ever hopeful, kept checking the foyer.

"That it was." Izzy rubbed her forehead.

Carole shrugged and backed out before Izzy could ask any questions. Carole was supposed to be home on bed rest until the baby came. She was going stir crazy, Izzy knew that. Okay, she'd let the "real" head librarian putter around for a while, like maybe twenty minutes. Then, Izzy would send her home. But for now, Izzy needed the down time. She wished she had been able to sleep last night. After she'd driven home, she'd eaten a grilled cheese sandwich and paced until dawn. This restlessness was alien to her. The feelings just didn't fit into her easy division of what was right and wrong. Oh, she knew the difference and how to act, but for the first time, doing right didn't come without repercussion. For the first time, she was attracted to a man who didn't have Jesus first in his life.

She had tried to think of the married couples of the Bible and found herself reaching. The heroes of the New Testament, so many were single. Finally, she settled for reading the account of Priscilla and Aquila. And when she set the Bible down, she felt somewhat renewed. A goal, her goal, was to have a mate as dedicated to the Lord as she was.

Izzy had held the Bible tight. She knew the words within. And she knew that what she was longing for wasn't for the best. Parker Strickland wasn't meant to be her mate. He might be a great rescuer of cats, a super Monopoly player, and a man who agonized over the pain of others; but he wasn't open to the teachings of the Bible. He ignored the topic every time she brought it up, which had been twice.

And, according to his journal, he was suicidal. Izzy had carefully placed her Bible on the end table. The Bible was clear about that topic. Man's body was a temple. You shouldn't mess with the temple.

Reminiscing was not getting the library open. Izzy yawned and stood up. The library opened in ten minutes; best get Carole home before regulars came in and lured the woman into conversation. Conversation that would center around Kyle.

"Does Jake know you're here?" Izzy pushed a library cart full of books behind the checkout counter.

Carole thumbed through the lost and found drawer. "He said I could come visit you for a half hour, if I promised to sit and not drink coffee."

"Okay, you've got about five minutes left." Izzy restocked the pencil holders. "I'm working on the piece about Rosemary Mayhill. Do you remember her?"

"I hear about her every night while Jake decides just how he's going to convince me to role play whatever it is you're writing about her. Apparently, he also wants there to be a conversation between a young Rosemary and an old Rosemary. I'm not sure I'm flattered about the part I get to play. The only thing I remember about her is that she gave me a chunk of peppermint candy once when I was waiting for my mama to check out some books."

"Hmmm." Izzy chewed on the pencil's eraser. "You're the fourth person to mention peppermint candy. Maybe I'll arrange for complimentary ones to be passed out while I give my presentation."

"Good idea."

"Anything else?" Izzy asked eagerly.

"Not from me."

"Think Jake would remember anything?"

"Ahem," Carole cleared her throat. "Ah, Izzy. Jake wouldn't remember much because . . . Jake is, er, seven years younger than I am."

Izzy raised her eyebrows. "Really? I never would have guessed that. I think that's wonderful. You know women outlive men by seven years, so you're a perfect match."

The advice didn't cool Carole's blush. "I tried dating other guys, but from the first time I saw him I guess I knew. He was playing baseball with my little brother, Jerry, and one of the guys hit a ball through my bedroom window. It landed right on my bed. Knocked off two of my dolls. One had a china face, and it cracked into tiny slivers of what looked like veins. Suddenly, my favorite doll looked more like a wicked witch than my treasure. Jerry came running in, asked me if I was hurt, grabbed the baseball, and left. Two of his little friends were behind him. I remember Jake asked me if I still played with dolls, and I told him no, but that one had been special.

"I guess Jerry sneaked in and got it later. Jake had asked him to. About a week later my doll sat on the bedspread with a new coat of pink paint smeared across its cheek with eight-year-old skill. I still have that doll. Whenever Jake and I have an argument, I go to grandmother's whatnot cabinet and stare at that disfigured face and realize that I have the best husband in the world. You'll have that someday." Carole walked to the exit.

Izzy didn't move. Imagine knowing, having, a love like that. Carole opened the door to leave. "By the way, I think Parker's crazy about you." Carole giggled as she left.

Izzy's pencil dropped to the floor and rolled under the desk. Opening the drawer, Izzy felt for another. There were no more. Izzy went back to the office to get a new box. Her elbow knocked against two of the many books that cluttered the desk. After a moment she gave up looking for a box of pencils, or any loose pencils on her desk for that matter. Any pencil risking refuge on her desk was buried under a mass of "things to do." Izzy scooted her chair back and dropped to her knees, stretching for the two fallen books.

She heard the door open, figured it was Carole, and called impatiently, "You're supposed to be home."

"I thought maybe I should apologize."

Parker's voice penetrated her ears. She sat up, hitting her head with a resounding thump that sent stars to her head and tears to her eyes.

"Hello, Parker." She grabbed the desk and used her hands to drag herself to a standing position. She looked at Parker. He held a baseball cap nervously in his hands and stood ramrod straight. He was the last person she wanted to see. Right?

He stopped reshaping his hat. "I wasn't myself last night. I just wanted to say I'm sorry, and it won't happen again."

"Uh, thanks, I think." Izzy bent, picked up the books from the floor, and set them back on the desk. They teetered precariously. Parker took one step and balanced them with his finger.

"Look, Parker," Izzy took a deep breath, "I didn't mean to bother you, I—"

"You didn't bother me—"

"Yes, I did. You've asked me to leave you alone and I haven't, but listen, I want to ask you something."

"What?"

"The other day, you turned in a—"

"Oh, Parker, I'm so glad you're here." Carole came unannounced through the door. "Izzy's doing some research on your great-great-grandmother. You've got some family records and photos out at the farm, don't you? Sure you do. Why don't you invite Izzy out there to look them over?"

❧

Parker drove away shaking his head. All he'd wanted to do was to put things right. He'd overstepped some boundaries, and it had been really rude to let Izzy lie on his porch after his door had burst open and she'd taken a tumble.

He was a paramedic! Even if his blood was boiling out of control and all the carefully constructed walls were crumbling, he should have reached out a hand and checked for injuries. Face it, the woman got under his skin. And now he'd agreed to let her stop by and go through the old family photographs.

He frowned. The apology hadn't gone quite as he'd expected. He'd wanted to humbly say his words, then slink out, but after Carole had walked in, all thoughts of setting things to right had fled. Why had he agreed to let Izzy come over? He didn't need a woman as intense, as flowery—what had Whip called Izzy?—as *good* as she was. He didn't need anyone at all, but especially not her.

Maybe he should stop fighting it, go ahead and take the girl out. See how compatible they were. No, he shook his head. Izzy was not a country girl. She might be having fun now, joining bowling leagues, sharing meals with old men, but soon she'd want a selection of malls and fancier restaurants. Besides, according to every person he knew, Izzy planned on leaving town after Carole came back from maternity leave.

The light turned red. Parker stopped the truck, glancing over downtown's Main Street. He didn't want to go home. Didn't think he could stand the silence, or the broken wall plaster by Julia's photograph, or the still-slick floor where Izzy's meat loaf had been enjoyed by Brute until only a few crumbs remained. Summers Cafe looked too busy. Parker checked out the street again. When the light changed to green, Parker pulled up next to the curb.

He'd been getting his hair cut at Matt's Barber Shop since childhood. He remembered the first time he'd followed his father into the room swirling with the heady smell of shaving cream and hair oil. He'd sat on a black folding chair and read a comic while Matt snipped at what was left of Grant Strickland's hair. Dad had admired the cut, made a quick rearrangement to the top, and then turned to plop Parker into the brown vinyl barber's chair where three Lincoln phone books waited. Matt had draped a dark cape under Parker's chin and begun cutting the brown curls that his mother adored and Rhea envied. To Parker, sitting in the barber shop had been the first step into manhood. He'd listened to the snip of the barber's shears while staring at his wrinkled boots and noticing they were smaller versions of his father's. He'd left the barber shop that first time feeling taller.

"Hi, Parker, thought you'd started cutting your hair yourself." Matt trimmed the white sides on Whip's head. Parker sat down without answering and idly thumbed an ancient comic, wondering if it was left over from his childhood.

Whip stared with bright chuckles in his eyes. Parker looked away, wondering if Izzy had told Whip that he'd thrown the meat loaf on the floor during a fit of passion.

Matt looked out the window. "Winter's coming."

"Yep," Parker agreed.

"I hear Izzy's writing a story about Rosemary. You're having her over tomorrow night? Are you taking her to your folks' house, or to your place?" Whip grinned foolishly, as if the idea had been his.

"That Izzy, she's a looker." Matt held the scissors in the air and studied Whip's gray locks with a short black comb suspended in the air.

"My place, but it's nothing to get excited about. I'll show her some old pictures, she'll write a cute story, and that's it." Parker felt the pressure building. He'd just left the library, and already people knew Izzy was coming over to his house tomorrow night.

❧

The house was dark when Izzy pulled into the driveway. Grabbing a soda, she headed upstairs. She turned the television on and sat cross-legged on the floor in front of the coffee table and opened her spiral notebook.

She'd accomplished quite a lot the last few days. Over half the notebook pages had at least something scribbled on them. She began rewording her research. In red, she highlighted some potential questions for Parker, knowing he wouldn't be able to answer them, but maybe he'd take her with him over to his family's house to ask them.

What she wanted the most was to make sure that she had enough questions to keep him occupied and his mind off . . . well, off her.

Izzy sat back. Why did she want Parker to take her to his parents' house? She knew Mr. and Mrs. Strickland. She bowled with them. Radar crawled into her lap. She didn't bother to push the cat away as she usually did when she was working. She wanted Parker to take her to his parents' house because she wanted them to get used to her. Because no matter how much she denied it, she was falling in love with Parker.

In love with Parker?

In love?

Izzy laid her head on the coffee table. Love with a man who often told her to leave him alone? No, he didn't just *tell* her to leave him alone, he *ordered* her to leave him alone. And allowed her to fall to the ground without offering a hand to help her up! And treated her without respect! And didn't go to church!

"Oh, Radar," she moaned, scooping the cat into a hug. "What am I going to do?"

The cat wiggled free, not in the mood to be pampered. Izzy watched the tail go straight up in the air as Radar went to look disdainfully at the store-bought cat food that had replaced the liver Whip had been feeding him. Izzy rolled her eyes. Lately no one seemed to appreciate the food she gave them. Thinking about food reminded her that she hadn't really gotten much nourishment from the frozen dinner. She pushed herself up off the floor and headed downstairs.

$\mathcal{P}$ arker drove down the street, glancing in the mirror occasionally to admire his haircut. It looked good, better than when his mother trimmed it. He shook his head; things were changing, whether he wanted them to or not.

Turning off Main Street, Parker pulled his car in front of the familiar structure that had been his home for the first eighteen years of his life. It was a yellow clapboard monstrosity, added on to by expanding branches of the Strickland family. He parked the truck in the street, dismayed at the sight of Aunt Edna's car in the driveway. He sat a moment, contemplating, then he got out of the car and headed up the sidewalk.

His foot rested on the first porch step and he paused, once again considering turning around. Aunt Edna's voice carried from the living room, blasting through the open screen door. Parker winced.

"This is ridiculous! How dare they claim Kenny to be undesirable for service! They only gave him three weeks!"

"Now, Edna," Grant Strickland soothed, "you said yourself you didn't want Kenny going overseas. At least now you know there's no chance of that."

Parker left his hand on the doorknob, listening to his father, and steeling himself for the family argument he was about to join. He stepped inside. No one in the living room turned to acknowledge him.

Edna stood in the middle of the room. Her fists were clenched. "Do you think that comforts me?" Her cheeks went red with rage as she noticed Parker with a glare. "The paper will print lies, and everyone will think my boy's unfit!"

Slouched in the green easy chair, Kenny balanced a beer bottle on his knee and dangled a cigarette from his lips. His eyes already red and wild. The reddish-brown hair that so resembled Parker's stood at attention, the only part of his body still looking military.

Edna moved to stand in front of the television, an unyielding granite of indignation. Her hand shook as she waved a piece of paper in Parker's direction with short, threatening jerks. "We're going to fight this!"

The phone rang, startling Parker's mother and saving Parker from having to answer. Francine grabbed at the receiver, knocking it to the ground with a clang. She nervously settled it to her ear. "Hello."

Parker watched her eyebrows rise as she listened intently to the person on the other end, occasionally opening her mouth to offer a response, but never getting the chance. After a few minutes, without saying good-bye, Francine numbly put the receiver back to the phone and whispered, "That was Blanche McKenna."

Edna eased up, shaking the paper at Parker, and glanced uneasily between Francine and Kenny. "What did she want?"

"They're coming over." Francine pushed herself up off the couch and began picking up the newspaper that Grant had dropped on the floor.

"Did she say why?" Grant asked.

"Delta's not doing too well. They need to go to Lincoln for a few weeks to be with her."

"What's that got to do with us?" Grant quizzed.

"Not us," Francine said softly. She shot a worried glance at Kenny, looking disapprovingly at the cigarette.

Kenny set his beer on the end table, carefully twirling the bottle so that it rested on the round ring of condensation already there, and stubbed out the butt on a plate. "What's wrong with Delta?" he slurred.

"She was in an automobile accident." Parker spoke for the first time.

"That has nothing to do with us!" Edna snapped. "Kenny wasn't even back in town!" She walked over and snatched the beer bottle from his grasp.

"Shut up, Mother." Kenny stood, ambled to the kitchen and returned with a cold one.

Edna's mouth closed. The paper in her hand dropped to the floor. Francine took her sister by the shoulders and led her into the kitchen. Grant followed.

Parker picked up the official-looking piece of paper and glanced over it quickly.

"I didn't do nothing," Kenny defended himself after Parker placed the dishonorable discharge notice on the television.

"Of course not." Parker rolled his eyes.

"She flirted with me and when I acted on it, she complained. Said I wouldn't leave her alone. Why else would a woman join the service, if not to find a man?"

Parker didn't answer. He'd rather have a woman defending the nation than Kenny, but this was not the time to tell Kenny that.

"Why do you think the McKennas are coming over?" Parker changed the subject.

"How should I know?"

"It must have something to do with you."

"I hardly ever see Delta. She hasn't talked to me since she had the kid. Over five years. I didn't even know she was in the hospital."

"Don't you want to know how she is?"

Kenny raised red-rimmed eyes. "Sure, tell me."

"Her concussion is mild. That's not worrying the doctors, but she wrenched her back upon collision. They're diagnosing acute lumbar strain. She'll go through months of therapy trying to restore easy movement. Her front teeth are missing. I guess Mr. McKenna went to the yard and dug through the car hoping to locate them, but no luck—"

"When was the last time you had anything to do with Delta?" Grant came back into the room and sat on the arm of the couch, interrupting their conversation and glaring at Kenny.

"High school," Kenny mumbled, lowering his eyes.

"She hasn't written, contacted you, anything, since?"

"No, she and her parents avoid me like the plague."

"Well, it looks like—"

The squeal of tires and slamming doors silenced Grant.

Thomas McKenna didn't knock. He jerked open the screen door and strode into the room. His usually serious eyes focused on Kenny in a heated stare. He ignored Parker and Grant. Blanche was only a step behind, holding Billy's hand.

"We're leaving for Lincoln tonight," Thomas ground out.

"Thomas, Billy can come with us—" Blanche said.

"Delta needs us. She's alone in that hospital up there, and driving back and forth is wiping you out." Thomas glared at Kenny, before touching his wife's shoulder.

Kenny didn't look up.

"We warned Delta about you," Thomas continued. "She wouldn't listen. Said that underneath it all you were a real nice guy—"

Edna and Francine came to the kitchen door, staring into the living room with worry. Blanche picked up Billy. She stepped toward Edna and Francine, but looked at her husband. "I'm not sure about this, Thomas."

Without a word, Edna and Francine moved aside to let Blanche pass. Billy stared back at the living room as if knowing that it was his future they were going to play ping-pong with. Giving Kenny one last openmouthed stare, Edna hurried into the kitchen. For the first time, Parker thought about Billy's age and how Kenny had hung around Delta in high school. No, that couldn't be it. If Billy belonged to any of Parker's relatives, he belonged to Chris. Delta had only hung around Kenny for a short time. *Of course,* Parker realized, watching Kenny's ears turn red, *a short time is all that is needed.*

Thomas stood in the middle of the room, looking ridiculously like Edna a few minutes ago. The man seemed ready to explode. "Mr. McKenna," Parker said gently. "Maybe if you'll just tell us what's going on, we can help."

"Can't you guess, Parker?" Grant went to the middle of the room and touched Thomas' arm, motioning him to the couch. "Billy is Kenny's son, isn't he?"

Thomas nodded, all the anger vanishing, as if no energy remained.

"Why are you coming to us now?" Grant sat down next to Thomas. Parker watched as Kenny closed his eyes.

"Oh, I know the Strickland family would have wanted to do right by my girl, but I don't consider Kenny part of your family," Thomas continued.

Kenny didn't move, but his bloodshot eyes opened and glared at Thomas.

"I would rather claim Delta didn't know the father than have the town know Kenny was the one," Thomas said.

Kenny reached, without looking, for the bottle of beer and took a drink.

"We stood by her." Thomas looked as if he was trying to convince himself. "She wanted to keep the baby. We went along with it. Mother thought things would be all right. Delta took over the books, got her GED, and actually was doing a pretty good job of raising Billy. We thought things were going just fine."

He no longer spoke to the family. Thomas spoke to the ceiling, his eyes taking in every detail, as if he were embarrassed. "We didn't raise her to be wild. Her older sisters were never that way. Billy did a lot to calm her down. We thought someday—prayed that someday—she'd meet the right man, settle down, and all her drinking and partying would stop.

"We never intended to let anyone know that Billy belonged to Kenny." Thomas gave Kenny another scorching look. "She didn't drink until she started up with you. Now she's in the hospital."

"She's going to be—" Parker started to say.

"I know that." Thomas tried to pull himself together. "But don't you see? Her behavior tells us that we expected too much of her. It's time for Kenny to pitch in and help. If people talk, so be it. Delta needs our attention now."

Grant stood, went into the kitchen, and came back with a cup of coffee. He handed it to Mr. McKenna. "And what do you want from us?"

"It's time for Kenny to take responsibility for his actions, at least monetarily. Delta's not going to be able to work for quite a while. Kenny must start paying her some sort of child support."

"He'll pay the child support," Edna said from the kitchen doorway. Kenny finally moved, "Mom, we're not sure . . ."

"Oh, yes we are. You think I wouldn't recognize my own blood? I've noticed the resemblance, but I thought Chris . . . To think I've been a grandmother for five years. I put too much stock in the gossip of others. All this time I've been harboring a grudge against Chris for not living up to his raising, and it was my own boy. Blanche and I have made some decisions. When Delta's out of the hospital, we'll sit down and firm up what needs to be done. In the meantime, just tell us what you need."

❧

Izzy pulled the car into Parker's driveway. The farm looked deserted. Surely he hadn't forgotten that he'd agreed to meet with her and let her go through his family photographs. Brute's high-pitched barks sounded from around back. Izzy got out of the car and followed the noise to survey the vacant backyard and empty garage. She'd just driven all this way for nothing. Parker wasn't home.

The distant chirping of birds convinced her that the trip hadn't been completely worthless. Parker's farm had enough scenery to keep her occupied until his return. Izzy laid her purse on the back step and sat down to wait. Surely Parker would be home soon. Stretching her legs out in front of her, she surveyed his land and bounced her keys against her knees liking the way the clang contrasted with the music of nature. Parker's place went on for miles. Trees formed one continual backdrop for the sky. The scent of dirt and foliage erased the tension at the base of her neck. The country had a lot to offer. She slipped off her sweater and leaned back. Taking a deep breath, she tried to picture what it would be like living here. This was God's country. If she lived on Parker's farm, she would never turn on the television. She would put a quilting frame on the front porch and glory in the sunsets.

After almost an hour, Izzy was tired of waiting. She grabbed her purse and headed back to the car. It was only six o'clock. Daylight was fading fast. She had never driven farther than Parker's house; maybe now would be a good time for exploring. Instead of heading home, she turned the opposite way and bumped along the uneven dirt road. A few times she passed the remains of a long-deserted building. If it had been the middle of the day, she'd have climbed out of the car and investigated. Maybe Rosemary's migrant worker had stayed here. According to Izzy's father, search far enough back in the de la Rosa history, and there were plenty of laborers.

The first hint of twilight made her decide to turn around. A driveway beckoned her, she whipped in, intending to turn around, but the porch light went on. Izzy didn't even know who lived here. A stooped, gray-haired woman in a flowered housedress stepped out on the porch. Izzy let out her breath. It was Catherine Wilfong, the woman who'd been the librarian after Rosemary. Before Carole.

"Hi, Catherine," Izzy called getting out of the car. Maybe she could ask Catherine some of the questions she had about Rosemary.

"Izzy. I've been wishing we could talk. How's the library? I keep telling my husband that I want to get to town. Come in. We were about to have supper. Glad to have the company."

If her stomach hadn't growled at that moment, Izzy might have begged off. Catherine's cooking was famous throughout Mayhill. A self-published cookbook occupied a special shelf at the library: Catherine's recipes, written down for the next generation. It was checked out often.

"Is Parker home already?" Catherine moved away from the door and welcomed Izzy in.

"No." Izzy didn't even pretend that she hadn't just been at his house. "I waited for nearly an hour. When he didn't come home, I decided to explore the area."

"Gladys Hepfield called when she saw you driving out of the city limit. She was surprised you didn't know Parker wouldn't be home."

"Where is Parker?"

"He's at his parents' house, and Delta's parents are there, too."

Izzy felt remorseful for a moment. She needed to call Delta's parents to let them know she was praying for Delta. She followed Catherine into the kitchen. "Why are Delta's parents over at the Stricklands'?"

"I don't know the whole story." Catherine said the words, but her eyes lit up. "Gladys says that the truth about Delta's son is about to be found out. Apparently, it's time for the father to pitch in. Funny, I always assumed it was Chris."

Izzy blinked, but tried not to let her emotions show. "Why are they at Parker's house?"

"Why, I suppose Parker is the father." Catherine began setting hot dishes on the table. "What's wrong?"

Izzy pictured Parker: sitting in his house agonized because he hadn't been able to save Kyle; missing his wife so much that he contemplated ending his own life; playing Monopoly all night to keep a neighbor from being scared. That type of man wouldn't, couldn't, turn his back on his own child. "Catherine, I don't think Parker is the father." No, not Parker Strickland. Izzy remembered the way he had sat on a tiny chair in the children's section of the library, surrounded by small children, pretending to be interested in the exploits of an orange dinosaur. She remembered how he had climbed the tree to get her cat. No, Parker Strickland was not Billy's father, because if he was—Billy's paternal heritage would never have been a secret.

"Evening, Izzy." Catherine's husband walked through the back door and smiled. "You waiting for Parker? He'll likely be a while."

Catherine nodded. "We enjoy company. Don't get much out here."

Izzy smiled and picked up a dish of mashed potatoes. She wasn't quite sure how she came to have such a strong conviction concerning Parker's innocence, but the sincere belief set well in her heart.

❧

Parker groaned when he saw Izzy's sweater on his porch. He'd completely forgotten that he'd invited her over. He picked the sweater up and let himself in through the door.

"Izzy," he called. Though why he bothered was a mystery. Her car wasn't outside. Silence greeted him. Obviously she hadn't entered the house. Probably she hadn't gotten over the big-city belief in locked doors. He put her sweater on the counter and opened the refrigerator.

Two peanut butter and jelly sandwiches later he felt better. He picked up the phone and dialed her number. She'd be relieved to know she hadn't lost her sweater. Except, no one answered.

He thought back on the evening's events as he listened to the continual ringing. The McKennas had stayed quite a while, talking over how to ease Billy into knowing his true father. Thomas admitted that he'd never intended on just dropping Billy in Kenny's lap. All along he'd wanted Edna and the Stricklands to be the ones to pitch in and help. The rest of the family, except for Kenny, had still been making plans when Parker had left.

A scratching on the back door reminded Parker that Brute needed in. He hung up the phone, stretched, and ambled to the kitchen, opening the screen.

"Down." He laughed as the puppy jumped against his knee. After a few moments of play, Brute settled down allowing Parker to reach for the phone again.

"Hi, it's me," he said when Izzy answered. "You left your sweater."

❧

Izzy hung up the phone. Parker had called her. For the first time, he had reached out to her. She was surprised at how good that made her feel, how special. Never mind that the main topic had been her sweater.

The house was silent. Izzy turned out all the lights and sat down with Radar in her lap. The cat burrowed his nose into the crook of her arm and snoozed happily. Izzy leaned back, not wanting the television or the radio to disturb her meditating. After a few moments of staring at the ceiling, she put the cat on the couch and went in the bedroom to pull out the box of old photograph albums from under her bed. She loved looking at the pictures of her mother and father on their wedding day. Clara's red hair had been almost to her knees. Izzy's father, Rueben de la Rosa, looked like a movie star in his rented tux. They had been so happy. Rueben had wanted lots of children, but they had only been blessed—their words not hers—with one. She had been her father's little girl. Oh, and he had been strict. She had to wear dresses to church when the other girls wore jeans. She had been the last allowed to wear eye shadow. The boys she dated had to come to the door. Touching a finger to the likeness of her father, she remembered the sound of his voice, the lingering scent of his aftershave, the way he had always touched her on her shoulder as if to remind her that he was there.

He would have liked Parker Strickland.

❧

"You got your ears lowered." Ty Horner teased as Parker entered the fire station.

Absently, Parker ran his hand through the shorn locks. With everything that had happened, he had forgotten. His parents hadn't even noticed.

"It was getting a little long." Parker shrugged.

As Robert slammed his locker shut, he surveyed Parker. "Out to impress anyone? Wife said she saw Izzy de la Rosa heading down the road your way."

"She was coming to see me, but I was at my mother's."

Ty and Robert nodded, the smiles leaving their faces, and said in unison, "We heard."

Robert put a hand on Parker's shoulder. "What's Kenny going to do?"

"Mom called this morning. Edna came over and got them out of bed about six. He just took off."

"That's better than having him live with you," Ty said.

"Yeah, but Thomas is bringing Billy over to Edna's today. She's going to start baby-sitting."

Robert frowned. "Edna's well past sixty."

"I know, and she had a hard time when Kenny was a baby."

"I remember," Robert said. "What a surprise. The doctor told Edna she couldn't have children, and then when she was forty-two, along came Kenny."

"She spoiled him," Parker said to Ty, as if the other man didn't know.

"She's more excitable now than she was then. Having a child in the house will just about send her over the edge," Robert went on.

"Will your folks help Billy, then?"

"I don't know," Parker said. "I just don't know."

Robert nodded in sympathy. "If you need time off, we can arrange it."

"I need to work."

❧

"The baby's dropped." Carole rubbed her stomach. Her face glowed with happiness. "They said I should get packed and ready. Can you believe they want me to go to Lincoln just because I'm over forty? I feel great!"

Shaking her finger at Carole, Izzy said, "I just found *Moby-Dick* in the pet-care section. I had forgotten the joys of having a student assistant."

Carole laughed. "I'll bet Shannon was concerned because there were no books on how to care for your pet whale."

"Funny," Izzy tried to look stern.

"So," Carole said nonchalantly, "what's going on with you and Parker?"

This time, Izzy's stern look was real.

The edge of Carole's mouth raised. "Okay, I give in. I won't pester you any more for information you don't want to share. But if I find out you told someone else first, I'm going to bean you with this *Moby-Dick* book."

Giggling, Carole started to leave. She gave a little jump when she got to the door and patted her stomach. "Oh, he kicked, hard. He's ready; now if he'd only do something about it."

Carole stopped with that. Izzy had the funniest feeling that Carole had been imputing the same characteristics to Parker as she had to the baby. Carole's knowing grin changed the funny feeling to a convinced feeling.

"Bye," sang Carole.

"That woman's too happy," Izzy mumbled as she started entering the overdue notices. That finished, she began replacing the due date peals in the back of popular paperbacks. Country music played in the background. Izzy had fought for the music. Jake Martin claimed he'd never heard of a library with music. He said libraries were places where the word *Shhh* should be revered.

Izzy made sure the music was so low that it wouldn't disturb patrons. It really could only be heard when everyone was quiet. During peak library hours, no one noticed it. Jake Martin himself had strolled in one busy Saturday afternoon and remarked that he appreciated Izzy not using the radio. Izzy wisely kept her mouth shut and didn't tell him that the only reason he couldn't hear it was that he was not honoring the *Shhh* tradition.

8

*I*t was past time to get back to work. Izzy had spent too much time staring out the window, looking for Parker to bring her sweater. Actually, she cared little about the sweater; she cared more that Parker was coming. Circling the desk, Izzy settled back in her chair and picked up her book order forms. Saturdays were supposed to be busier. At least busy enough to keep her mind off an appealing fireman.

She'd finish updating the new releases. The phone rang as she chewed on her pen. Izzy waited a moment before answering it, wanting to compose herself just in case it was Parker. "Hello."

"Izzy," Mayor Martin's voice boomed, "how's our story going? Mark says he's making progress. I thought maybe we'd meet for breakfast on Monday and go over the presentations. Carole told me your idea about handing out peppermints. I think that's perfect. Can you meet at eight?"

"Jake, with Carole on maternity leave, my time is precious."

"By the way," Jake gushed on, "are you ready for three new computers?"

"I'll be there," Izzy promised, "but can we make it ten o'clock? I have other things to do on Monday morning. The story's coming along just fine." Opening a desk drawer, Izzy took out a spiral notebook. She braced it against a stack of books to the side of her computer and started typing in all the information she'd gathered. She eliminated the outline form and wrote it as if she were telling a story to a friend. She frowned after she'd written five pages. The facts were all there, but the substance was missing. She couldn't catch the essence of Rosemary Mayhill if she didn't talk to the family, look at the photographs, and dig deeper for the emotional side of Rosemary, not just rehash the time line of good deeds documented in the news-paper.

Maybe it was time to arrange a visit with Francine Strickland. Parker's mother probably had more memorabilia than Parker. Plus, getting to know Francine would give Izzy more insight into Parker's personality. The man she was dreaming about—was falling in love with—certainly didn't appear the type to be suicidal. So, what should Izzy do about the journal's desperate message? Could Parker have written it when he was in high school? Izzy sighed. The more she got to know Parker, the more confused she became. Nothing made sense.

She had set out to save Parker Strickland's life, now she worried more about his soul. She grabbed the telephone and jabbed at the numbers. No one answered the Strickland phone. Izzy glanced over at the clock. Two hours until the library closed.

The time dragged. Izzy managed to clear a corner of the desk and finish writing the grant proposal for the funding of a new multi-cultural section for the library. She hadn't left the office once. Shan-non poked her head through the door a few times, asking senseless questions. Izzy almost suspected that the student aide was worried about her.

"Ahem."

This time when Shannon interrupted, Izzy looked up disgruntled.

"Six o'clock." Shannon pointed to her watch. Getting off on time on a Saturday was important to the girl.

"Has everyone left?"

"Twenty minutes ago."

"You go ahead and take off. It will only take me a minute to close up." Izzy stuffed the spiral notebook into her bag and stood up. If she hurried, it would still be daylight when she knocked on the Strick-lands' door.

❧

Parker recognized the car. He had meant to take her sweater over, but time had gotten out of hand.

"Why's Miss Izzy here?" Billy came and yanked the curtain aside to stare out.

"We'll soon find out." Parker watched Izzy pat her hair into place. She glanced up when Billy opened the drapes.

Parker opened the door before she could knock. "You do get around, Ms. de la Rose."

"It's *de la Rosa*. I was hoping to talk with your mother. I wanted to see if she had any pictures or memories of Rosemary she'd like to share."

"Mom left for Lincoln. Dad's out shopping for Billy. Seems to think it's pretty exciting, finding he has a grandnephew."

"I want to go see Mom," Billy said, a frown creasing his brow.

Parker looked down as if he'd forgotten the boy standing there. "I know you do, Buster. Delta says she'd rather you not miss any school."

"Not fair," Billy muttered. "She's my mother and nobody tells me anything."

"Your mother feels well enough to say that you can't miss school," Izzy said. "Sounds like she's doing fine."

Billy went to the couch and sat down, arms crossed and lips pouting. Brute jumped up next to the boy.

"Come in," Parker said pretending to be gruff. He wanted to feel nonchalant—uninterested—instead he was pleased that she'd come to the house. "I'll run up to the attic and get the hope chest that has Rosemary's things in it."

He took the stairs two at a time. He knew right where the small chest was. Picking it up, he carefully made his way to the hallway. He watched Izzy as she tried to soothe Billy.

"It's not easy when Mom's sick, is it?" Izzy played with the strap of her purse.

Billy rolled his eyes.

"Oh, you think I don't know," Izzy tried to sound hurt. "I'm in Mayhill because my mother got sick. She's all better now. As a matter of fact, she feels so good that she went to Florida on a long vacation. As soon as she's well, I can go back to Phoenix."

"Why would you want to go there?"

"That's where my job is. My friends. It's where I made my home."

"You work at the library. You're friends with Parker. If your mom is here, how can your home be somewhere else?"

"That's only temporary."

Billy frowned, clearly not understanding. "What's temprary? What do you mean?"

"Carole can run the library when I leave. Parker and I have a different outlook on life, but you're right, he is my friend. Mom has Harve, but I always come to see her for the holidays."

"Where's Phoenix? Is it next to Lincoln? That's not too far away. Parker can still see you."

"Phoenix is a lot farther than that, Billy." Parker set the hope chest carefully on the floor. He eyed Izzy with disapproval. "Izzy thinks big cities are better than small towns. Don't you, Izzy?

"Ah, spiderwebs." Billy looked at the chest with interest, saving Izzy from having to answer.

"They'll take just a moment to clean away." Parker went to the kitchen and came back with a handful of paper towels. "No one's been through this thing in years. Rhea used to get the clothes out and prance around in them. I'll bet she's forgotten."

"It's beautiful." Izzy admired the intricate designs. An engraved array of flowers decorated the front; the scars and knicks of time added jagged flaws to the wood.

Parker gave the chest a second look, clearly unaware of the magic. "It should be tossed."

"Oh, no, Parker. It's a treasure. Just think of what it would look like after being refinished."

Billy got down on his knees beside Izzy. Together they unlatched the lock and raised the lid. A fine spray of dust rose in the air. Watching Izzy dig through his family treasures brought back memories. Her words about refinishing sounded too much like Julia. Only Izzy was smarter than Julia. Izzy would be going back to Phoenix soon. Back to the malls and traffic jams. Away from snow. Away from him.

"That's Grandma—when she was young! She has some pictures like this on the living room walls!" Billy shouted delightedly, coming across a picture of Rosemary with Blanche.

Parker went into the kitchen and poured a cup of coffee. Sitting at the kitchen table, Parker stared past his mother's crinoline curtains and watched the stars. The scene in the living room hurt too much.

"Parker?" Izzy said from the door.

"Yeah?" Parker looked up.

"It's getting late. I'd like to come over again to talk with you when you're not so busy. Can I take these two journals home?"

"Sure, go ahead."

"Thanks. Oh, and Parker."

"What." Impatience tinged his voice.

"Why don't you come to church with me Sunday morning?"

He stared at his coffee cup. Crazy woman, still thought that all the answers could be found in prayer. "I'm sorry, Izzy. I'm not interested."

Izzy waited, seeming to want him to say something, do something. When he made no move, she backed away. She looked down at the ground. "We keep saying 'sorry.' "

"It's best that way. You'll be leaving soon, remember?"

Her face fell, and all the sparkle left her eyes in a blink. She seemed to want to say something. Parker waited, giving her time, but she turned and went back into the living room.

He heard her softly saying good-bye to Billy as she gathered her belongings and left. Billy came into the kitchen, carrying the old photo of Rosemary and Blanche.

"Can I haf this picture?"

Parker almost retorted that Billy couldn't haf the picture, but must take it all. "Sure, Billy. Keep it."

"Grandma looks like Mama."

Parker took the picture. "She sure does. You look like her, too."

"Good," Billy said a little strongly. "I don't want to look like Kenny."

"Kenny's got some problems, Billy. Someday he'll straighten up, and you'll be proud he's your papa." Parker didn't believe the words even as they exited his mouth. He wanted to, though. He remembered when young Kenny used to tag along. They had fished, played tag, climbed the old tree at the library.

"Grandpa says it's Kenny's fault that Mama was in the accident. Grandpa said it was Kenny started Mama to drinking."

Parker didn't know how to respond. Just what was keeping Dad, anyway?

"It's getting late." Parker stood, taking Billy by the hand, hoping that being tucked into bed would calm Billy's trembling lower lip.

"I don't want to go to bed. I want my mother."

"Your mother's in Lincoln." Parker guided Billy toward the stairs. "She's in the hospital being taken care of by doctors. Doctors who will make sure she's all right."

"She needs me."

Parker opened the guest room door. "You're right. She needs you to be a good boy and go to school."

"There's no school tomorrow. It's Sunday."

Parker felt lost. Billy was right. There was no school tomorrow, and Parker was off. He'd have the care of the boy all day. The boy who was asking questions.

Billy reluctantly got into his pajamas and crawled in the strange bed. He frowned at Parker, as if it were Parker's fault that everything was going wrong.

"Night, Buster." Parker tried to sound reassuring.

"I want my mother," Billy whimpered one more time.

Parker silently made his way downstairs, relieved to hear the front door open. "Where have you been, Dad?"

"You wouldn't believe it. I knew a growing boy needed lot of milk and vegetables, so I went to the store. I couldn't make it through an aisle without someone stopping me to ask me what was going on with Kenny."

Parker watched his father. Grant never was a good liar.

"Dad."

"Okay," Grant sighed. "I ran into Carole Martin at the grocery store. She told me Izzy was visiting you and suggested I give you a little privacy."

"Privacy? Dad, Billy was here."

"Wasn't that child in bed at eight?"

"Ah." Parker hadn't even considered what a six-year-old's bedtime should be.

Grant shook his head, handed Parker the bag of groceries, and headed up the stairs.

Parker carried the food into the kitchen and set the bag on the counter. He'd just put the milk away when he heard his father holler down, "Parker! Where'd you put Billy?"

"He's in Rhea's old room!"

"No. He's not."

Parker flew up the stairs, Billy's last words playing through his head. Parker had no doubt. Billy had crawled out the bedroom window and taken off to find his mother.

~&~

Izzy stuck the cup of hot chocolate in the microwave. Parker had turned down her invitation to church. That didn't mean she would give up. Statistics claimed that most new Christians came to the faith because a friend reached out to them. She would keep reaching. Parker was a smart man. He could only resist the truth for so long. Right? Izzy wished she knew the answer.

The microwave beeped. Izzy took the hot chocolate out and blew at the steam. Whip had prepared some food, too. She covered the spaghetti and put it in the refrigerator. Carefully, she carried the cocoa up to her apartment. Radar waited impatiently at the top of the stairs, meowing scoldings at a mistress too long gone. Izzy set the cocoa on the coffee table and took Radar in her lap.

"It's okay, boy. I'm home now. Where do you want to be scratched? Behind the ears?"

After a few minutes of fur rearranging, Izzy settled back and chose the older-looking diary. Opening it to the first page, she began reading. It didn't take long to become absorbed. Rosemary had strayed from the usual day-to-day listing of events, instead she had penned a first-person narrative. Izzy grinned, Rosemary had no doubt been a fan of Louisa May Alcott.

It was midnight when the blinking lights went down the street, sending a red and white glare into Izzy's living room and making her put down the diary. She got up and went to the window. One of May-hill's police cruisers slowly drove down the street. Izzy shivered. That was another thing she didn't miss about Phoenix, the sound of a helicopter circling overhead whenever a major crime had been committed. Izzy wondered what the policeman was looking for, or whom?

She put her shoes back on and silently went down the stairs. She'd just reached the last step when the phone rang, its shrill sound making her jump. Whip's phone never rang after midnight. Concern prickled up her spine.

Whip stumbled into the living room. Izzy couldn't see him, but she could hear him. He'd probably slipped into his robe and slippers, just in case Izzy walked in on him.

"What?" he rasped into the phone.

Izzy leaned forward. She could barely hear.

"No kidding," Whip's voice rose. "They've called out the volunteers? How long has he been missing? No, no, I'm glad you called. I'll put my pants on and start checking all the backyards in my neighborhood. Sure, I'll wake her up, but I don't think she knows anything. The fact that she's interested in Parker has nothing to do with Billy running away."

Izzy stood. Interested in Parker? Billy had run away! She rushed into the living room.

"Ask them how long Billy's been missing?"

"They discovered the boy missing at about 9:30 P.M."

"I left there at nine o'clock," Izzy said. "Billy was upset about his mother, but we thought he'd gotten over it. He wanted to go see her." Her eyes widened. "You don't think the child's heading for Lincoln, do you?"

Whip said a few more words into the phone and then hung up. "That's what Parker thinks. The state troopers have been informed. Still, there's a good chance the little boy will stop to rest before he even makes it out of town. That's what we're hoping for. I'm going to check the neighborhood."

Izzy watched Whip hurry into his bedroom to change. Calmly she picked up the phone, paused to say a prayer, and dialed Parker's number.

Francine answered.

Izzy cleared her throat. "Hello, Francine. This is Izzy de la Rosa. I just found out about Billy. Is there anything I can do?"

"Officer Rowe's on his way over to your apartment now." Francine sounded out of breath. "He wants you to try to think of anything Billy said tonight while you were over. Maybe he—" Francine choked off, weeping loudly into the phone. "Oh, what am I going to tell Delta? When I left her tonight . . ."

"Izzy," Carole's voice came over the wire. "Francine isn't able to talk. You answer all the police officer's questions and then call us back."

Personally, Izzy agreed with Parker. Billy was attempting to find his way to Lincoln so he could see his mother. She liked the police officer's idea too, that Billy would get tired and stop to rest.

The police cruiser stopped in front of the house. Whip opened the door and invited Officer Rowe and Grant Strickland in. The interview took only ten minutes.

"Yep," said Officer Rowe, "everything you said matches what Parker remembered. Don't worry. We'll find the boy."

Whip handed the men mugs of cocoa and walked the officer to his car. Izzy stayed on Whip's couch a moment. She knew she should call Francine, fill the woman in on what the officer had said, but she wanted to do more.

She wanted to find Billy.

And she had an idea.

9

*W*hip wasn't the only one out searching for Billy. Flashlights galore bobbed up and down the Mayhill streets. A chorus of "Billy!" rang out in disjointed ranges of octaves. Izzy pulled her sweater closer.

Izzy paused, watching Whip. She looked up to the starry sky and closed her eyes. *O Lord, please watch over our Billy. He's so young and afraid. Keep him safe, Lord. Help us to find him soon. And, please Lord, be with his family. They have so much to worry about right now. Let them feel Your protection and love. Help me to feel it, too.* She almost uttered "Amen," but a nagging thought stopped her. She was forgetting something, someone. *And Lord, please be with Parker. Help him to recognize Your ways and to lean towards Your guidance and love. Amen.*

Whip rambled over to the hedge that separated his yard from the one next door. His raspy voice crooned "Billy" as if he were looking to wake a child from slumber.

Izzy didn't for a moment think that Billy was asleep. She'd run away from home once, when she was young. At Christmastime, no less. She hadn't thought to wear a coat that long ago day either as she ran through the darkened streets to her friend Melanie's house. Once she'd gotten there, she'd been too afraid to rap on Melanie's window. So she'd turned around, hurried toward home, and crawled back through her bedroom window. No one ever found out about her late-night escapade. Being outdoors past your bedtime wasn't conducive to sleep. Izzy couldn't remember what traumatic happening had inspired her to climb out of her window, but she did remember that once she got scared, all she wanted was home.

Billy wouldn't think about sleeping either, unless he found a place he considered safe. And no one was home at his house. Where else would he go?

The school!

Connie claimed that school represented a safe haven to many children. Funny time to be thinking about her best friend back in Phoenix. Connie was always laughing over the exploits of the kids in her class. Izzy stuffed her hands in her pockets and walked briskly toward Mayhill Elementary. She didn't turn into its parking lot though, for others had had the same idea, and a kaleidoscope of beams bounced over the playground. The principal stood at the front door talking to Officer Rowe.

For a brief moment, Izzy contemplated yanking on Officer Rowe's sleeve and suggesting they contact Billy's friends, but no doubt, they'd done that. Izzy thought back to the days she'd watched over Billy. What had they done? Where had they gone? The McKenna farm was probably being scrutinized. Where else could he be? Without conscious thought, Izzy headed for the library. A bitter Nebraska wind followed her progress, sending chills down her neck and keeping her pace hurried. She stuffed her hands in her pockets, wishing she'd worn gloves.

The silence of Mayhill Park greeted her. Maybe she should go inside the library and call Francine to see if Billy had returned home yet. It would feel good to spend a moment in the library and out of the chill. Izzy stood, shivering, staring at the dark trees and blowing leaves. She could hear someone on a microphone in the distance, calling Billy's name. The wind increased. She closed her eyes, picturing Billy playing while Delta watched over him. When she opened her eyes, she stepped off the sidewalk and traversed the grass. The old, gnarled tree stood ominously in the middle of the park. She looked up into the towering tangle of limbs and leaves.

"Billy," she whispered. A few leaves swirled down to brush against her face and made her jump. "Billy." She cleared her throat and said it again. "Billy!"

"I want down, Izzy."

Weak-kneed with relief, Izzy leaned against the tree, sucking in breaths of cool air, calming herself. "Billy! I'm so glad I found you! Can you make it to the bottom branch?"

"No. My pants are ripped, and I'm scared."

Izzy reached up and took hold of the bottom limb and struggled to pull herself up. Her frozen fingers felt stiff against the tree. She managed to wrap both her arms around the branch, but when she attempted to swing her feet up they only went halfway. She tried again, making it a little farther this time. Her feet kicked erratically in the air while her hands tore against the rough surface of the old elm. "I'm coming, Billy."

Looking around, Izzy spied one of the big trash cans. Maybe she could turn it over and use it as a step up. She started walking towards it, but Billy's frantic voice stopped her.

"Don't leave me!"

"I'm not, Billy. I'm going to get the trash can." She hurried across the park. The steel container seared her fingers, as if she'd touched an old metal ice-cube tray. She tugged, trying to twist it around, but a chain held it firmly to the park bench, which was cemented to the ground.

A fingernail broke as she gave one last exasperated pull. "Billy, I'm going to have to go for help."

"No," he called frantically. "Don't leave me."

Izzy looked around. Surely with all the searchers out, someone would be near enough to hear her call. "Help! Over here! I've found him!"

The wind picked up force, blowing hair in her mouth as she screamed. She put her hands on the tree branch again and tried to remember how she'd climbed trees when she was little. This time she grabbed the branch and used the tree trunk to walk her way slowly up and then twisted around so that she straddled the branch. For a moment she held on to the branch as if it were the neck of a horse, trying to regain her balance.

"Izzy, what are you doing?" Parker got there just one minute too late to save her from having to climb.

"Billy's in this tree. He's ripped his pants, and he's scared." Izzy pushed herself up so she was sitting.

"Billy, you okay?" Parker called.

"I want down. I hafta go to the bathroom. And I'm cold."

Parker stepped closer to the tree and held his hands up for Izzy to lower herself into. She scooted her body, hugging the branch as if it were a lifeline. She wrapped her legs tightly around it and then carefully let herself twist and slide until she was hanging from the branch upside down so that when she landed in Parker's arms, he'd cradle her fall.

She didn't want to drop. Not that she didn't trust him—she did. And she knew that he wouldn't let her fall. It made her feel vulnerable in a different way. She closed her eyes and let go. She landed in his arms easily, and for a moment, the chill of the night disappeared. He hugged her to him, as if she weighed no more than a child. Izzy wanted to wrap her arms around his neck, kiss him, and bury herself in the warmth he represented.

He gently stood her on the ground and pulled off his gloves. "Here, hold these." Grabbing the lowest branch, he pulled himself up without a grunt.

Izzy pulled his gloves on and watched him make his way to the shadow that was Billy.

"Hurry, Parker. I hafta go to the bathroom bad."

Once Parker had Billy in his arm, he scooted down the tree. He carried the boy as easily as he had carried Izzy's cat. When he got to the bottom branch, he handed Billy down. Billy let Izzy help, then jumped to the grass and pressed his knees together firmly. "Izzy, please."

"Can you get in the library?" Parker asked.

Izzy took Billy's hand and hurried him to the back door where she punched in the code and flipped on the light. Billy rushed toward the children's section. Not the closest bathroom, but the one he knew best. Izzy entered the dark main room and leaned against the counter. Parker came right behind her.

"Do I need to dial nine for an outside line?"

"No." Izzy reached behind the counter and got the phone.

While Parker calmed his mother, Billy sang the ABC song in the background.

"I was so scared," Izzy admitted, once Parker hung up.

"Why didn't you call somebody when you found him?"

"Every time I started to walk away he got upset. I yelled for help and then tried to get up to him."

"I heard you." Parker took off his jacket and put it over her shoulders. "What made you think of that tree?"

"I was praying, then I thought about a friend I have in Phoenix who runs a day-care center. Everything clicked. When Billy's at the park, he tries to climb that tree. Delta said it's kinda like a passage into growing up. I knew Billy couldn't make it to Lincoln, or even to the outskirts of town, so I tried to think of a place that would make him feel safe."

Parker calmly touched a finger to her chin. "Billy was easier to rescue than your cat." He urged her face toward him and held her chin. The touch reminded Izzy of safety, and love, and commitment. She thought back to her father. Would Parker—? No, surely not. His eyes were tender for the first time. There was hope! This man wasn't lost. His lips settled on hers.

Izzy leaned into the kiss, savoring the bond between them. Then, she felt a tug at her jacket.

"I'm done." Billy was still shivering.

Izzy figured he was too chilled to comment on catching them kissing. He would probably wait and bring it up when there was a crowd of people around.

"Let's get you home, Buster." Parker picked Billy up and hugged the child to him. "Coming, Izzy?"

The Strickland home glowed with the activity of frenzy. A police cruiser was parked in front. All the neighbors gathered on their front porches, two-stepping to the beat of a cold, October night, while they watched Parker carry Billy in.

"He asleep, Parker?" The strain of rushing back from Lincoln to face the terror of looking for a missing child showed in Francine's eyes.

"Yes, Mom."

The phone chose that moment to shrill. Francine grabbed it quickly, but too late. Billy jerked awake. "Is it Mama?"

Francine had no more informed the caller that Billy was fine and hung up, when another call came. "Billy's going to have a tough time falling asleep." Francine frowned at the phone.

"Leave the phone off the hook," Grant advised.

"That's not fair to the people who are out looking. They've been checking frequently to see if Billy's returned. If they can't get through, they might keep looking. No, honey, I've got to answer the phone. Our friends are worried, too."

Officer Rowe sat in the corner filling out paperwork. "Parker, take the boy to your place. Let him get a good night's sleep."

Parker nodded, "Good idea. He'll be happier out in the country."

"Izzy," Carole added, standing up to tuck a crocheted blanket around Billy's shivering form. "I wonder if you'd mind going along. Billy seems quite taken with you. Maybe you can help keep his mind off his mama for a while."

"Why, Carole, I can go along to Parker's and you—" Francine laid the phone on her shoulder, muting her words.

"Now Francine . . . ," Carole walked over and sat down next to Francine.

Parker let Carole's words fade away. He'd seen her well-placed kick to his mother's shins. Thing was, he was perfectly willing to let Izzy accompany him home. Maybe just for tonight and maybe forever. Tonight when he'd looked up into the tree and seen Izzy clutching the branch for dear life—and a moment later when he'd cradled her in his arms—he'd realized that he'd fight to keep her here in Mayhill. Here with him.

"I'll follow in my car," Izzy insisted.

"I appreciate this." Francine started gathering Billy's belongings. "Poor tyke. His whole world's turned upside down."

❧

Izzy kept Parker's taillights in her sight, muttering scoldings at him for driving much too fast. She pressed down nervously on the gas pedal. *Well,* she thought, *this is probably the only time I'll travel seventy miles an hour without worrying about being stopped for speeding.*

Parker gently lifted Billy from the front seat as Izzy pulled her car in behind his. He waited for her to come alongside him. "Kenny doesn't know what he's missing." Parker's eyes rested on Billy and then speculatingly on Izzy.

"You're right." Izzy started up the steps. She paused in front of the door.

"It's open."

"Oh. Yeah." Izzy felt uncomfortable opening the screen. The living room light glowed a welcome. Brute waited, panting by the coffee table. He started toward them, but a word from Parker changed his mind.

Parker edged her aside as he headed toward a door that opened to a bedroom.

Glancing around the masculine living room, Izzy realized she hadn't really gotten a good look the other day. There were a few feminine touches, but most all the furniture was covered with neat stacks of clothes. He kept a neat house, except for the clothes. Brute sniffed at her feet. Idly, she bent down to scratch behind his ears. She could hear Parker talking to Billy as he undressed the child and helped him to bed.

She moved a stack of shirts off one of his chairs and sat down.

"I pretty much live in the living room." Parker stepped back into the room. "My bedroom's clean. You want to see it?"

"Er, no."

"I put Billy in the spare room. Rhea's kids stay there once in a while." Parker shifted from one foot to the other. "Are you hungry?"

"A little." She really wasn't, but it would be more comfortable sitting at the table, trying to make idle conversation, than it would be sitting on the couch staring at a television that only received three channels. No doubt, reruns from the seventies would be playing. Nothing romantic about them. Izzy bit her lip. She hadn't been this nervous since high school.

"How about ham and eggs?"

"Sounds good."

Parker's kitchen had a gray linoleum floor with a big trapdoor in the middle. The cabinets—except for two at the end, newly refinished—were painted a dingy, peeling white. One didn't close all the way, and Izzy could see the plates and glasses perfectly aligned inside. Brute pranced by his doggy dish, knowing that whatever the master ate, Brute ate.

"They used to keep food down there." Parker stepped hard on the trapdoor.

"I've heard of that."

"I don't go down there very often. The steps are very narrow. I'm thinking I'll enlarge them and turn the room into a cellar."

"That would be nice. There's never enough storage space."

"That's what Julia has—" Parker's voice tapered off. He stared at Izzy as if seeing her for the first time.

"Parker, I can go, if you don't need me here."

"No, please. You're the first date I've had since—"

"This isn't a date."

"No," Parker sighed. "It isn't, but I'd like to take you out. A movie, maybe. Dinner?"

"I don't know." Izzy sat at the scratched, wooden table. "Parker, can I ask you something?"

"Anything."

"What do you think about God?"

Parker turned and cracked eggs into a skillet. The sound of popping and sizzling barely dented a silence so tangible it could almost be touched. "I *don't* think about Him."

The emphasis on the word *don't* gave it away. Izzy rubbed her finger over a deep scratch bearing the initials KL. She tried not to sound too eager, but surely this was an opening. "Did you ever?"

"You are the strangest female. I believe in God. Okay? I just don't think He has much time for me."

"That's not true!"

"Now's not the time, Izzy."

It was too soon for this conversation. She should have waited. This was why she hesitated at inviting more friends to church. She didn't know the right words. This man carried baggage that she didn't understand. If she had understood, maybe she would have been able to help her dad.

Unfortunately, what haunted Parker was the memory of a deceased wife.

Izzy wished she could remember the words spoken to her by her church family after her father's death. The minister had stayed by her.

She remembered that. What had the minister here done? She'd have to find out. Of course, in all honesty, Whip had done more to restore her sense of peace than the minister back in Phoenix had. Since starting her Bible study with her landlord just six months ago, she had learned more about forgiveness and strength than she had the previous twenty-five years of her life.

Izzy stood up and made her way to the guest bedroom. Billy lay curled on his side, thumb in his mouth. Izzy could imagine tucking in her own son or daughter and saying good night in this room. She would paint it blue with a Noah and the Ark scene on the wall.

Leaning back, she let her head rest against the closet door. Why did Parker have to be suicidal? She could deal with anything but that. He didn't act depressed. Not like her. No, she wouldn't think about the past. She'd almost managed to forget about his journal tonight. Until he'd brought up Julia's name.

Billy moaned in his sleep, and Izzy moved closer to put a hand to his forehead. He didn't feel warm.

"He's okay. I took his temperature when I put him to bed."

Izzy jumped. "I didn't hear you walk in. I know, poor little guy."

"He's had a rough week, that's for sure."

The phone rang. Parker picked one of the stuffed animals off the floor and laid it next to Billy before leaving the room.

Izzy followed, listening to his one-sided conversation.

"Yeah, everything's okay...He's here...Delta's gonna be fine... Izzy's here, too . . . You're kidding! Carole did...I'll tell Izzy."

"What is it?" Izzy asked when Parker hung up the phone.

"It was Robert. They've taken Carole to the hospital in Lincoln. Seems she's been in labor for hours and didn't bother to tell anyone."

"She's so excited." Izzy studied a picture of a much younger Parker, standing between his parents, wearing a sailor's outfit. "I think it's neat she's getting a chance for a second round of motherhood."

"Yeah." Parker didn't look convinced.

Izzy took a deep breath, inhaling the smell of ham. "You think the food's ready?"

"I'm sure it is." Parker led the way to the kitchen.

Izzy followed more slowly. She would eat even if the eggs were runny, and then she'd go. The room was so charged with emotion that she couldn't think of a word to say. She hated feeling ill at ease. He made her so aware. It wasn't fair. She'd never been at a loss for words just because of a man's presence. She almost couldn't breathe.

"You want ketchup?"

"Of course." Izzy sat gingerly at the rickety table and tried not to notice the creaking sounds the chair made as it adjusted to her weight.

"Be careful. That chair belonged to my great-grandma. I never sit in it. Afraid to."

"It belonged to Rosemary?"

Parker raised his eyebrow. "That's right. Tomorrow morning, take a look at the brass bed Billy's sleeping in. It belonged to Rosemary, too."

Izzy rubbed her fingers along the edge of the table.

"Don't get too mushy," Parker warned. "The table used to belong to Edna." Parker set down two plates of food and sat across from her. Izzy picked up her fork and started rearranging her food.

"You cut the ham up in little pieces and mixed it into the eggs." Izzy stared at her plate.

"It's easier that way. I already had the sharp knife."

"This is the way I eat my ham and eggs." Izzy reached for the ketchup bottle.

Parker got it first and squirted a healthy amount on his eggs. He held the bottle just out of reach. "It will cost you."

"What?"

"Yep, you want the ketchup, I get a date to the movies."

"You like ketchup on your eggs?" Izzy croaked.

"Sure, change the subject. As for the ketchup, I know, it's weird."

"No, it's not. I like it, too. And I'll think about the movie."

Parker grinned, as if they shared some secret and handed the bottle to her without making her promise a movie. "You know," he said. "I think I knew you were going to be a problem when you drove out here to tell me I still owed the library two dollars."

"A problem?" Izzy whispered.

Parker nodded, then said, "I don't want you to be in my thoughts. I don't want to worry about you. But that kiss at the library . . . the one Billy interrupted. Izzy, I want to kiss you again."

"Parker, you don't know me." Izzy felt the world spin out of control. She had daydreamed about this moment. Now it was happening. This couldn't be happening.

He looked into her eyes.

Izzy's skin tingled. He looked so sincere.

"I want to know you," he continued. "Tell me you're not seriously considering returning to Phoenix. You're happy here, aren't you?"

"I'm happy, but—"

"I didn't think I'd ever feel this way again." Parker put his fork down. "After Julia died, I thought I'd spend the rest of my days alone."

Izzy picked up the glass of milk Parker had put in front of her. Idly holding it in front of her, she stared at it, watching the bubbles foam against the rim.

"Are you all right?"

"Parker, when did all this come about?"

"I don't know. I saw you in the library, and then when you kept driving by the fire station. I thought you were crazy. The night you screamed and scared Mark Dalton away, I thought you needed protection. Then, you brought that stupid meat loaf over."

"Parker, I don't know what you want."

"Why? Do you have a boyfriend back in Phoenix?"

"No."

"Then, why?"

Izzy pushed her plate away. "Parker, how well do you know my mother?"

"I like Clara. I even visited her in the hospital in Lincoln when she had her first heart attack. That was before you moved down here."

"You've never talked to her about my . . . dad?"

"No. Why?"

Izzy's cheeks felt as if the air of the room had suddenly been sucked out, leaving nothing left in the atmosphere for her to breathe.

"Izzy, what is it?" Parker put his hand over hers.

"I—" She pulled her hand out from under his. "Ah, Parker, my father killed himself six years ago."

Sympathy shone from his eyes. He put his hand back on hers and leaned forward. "Izzy, I'm so sorry. That must have been hard. Do you know why?"

Izzy blinked. Parker acted as if suicide was a surprising thing, a thing that happened to others. She felt saliva pool in the back of her throat. Suddenly, it was hard to breathe. "I've got to go!" Izzy jumped up, her legs catching the edge of the chair and knocking it over. She backed up, her foot tangling in the chair leg, and she went to the floor on one knee.

Parker's strong hand caught her at the elbow and guided her back up. "Izzy, you need to talk. Have you been holding all this in? Does your mother know you're still upset?"

"Leave me alone, Parker." The tears dripped into her mouth, the salty flavor closing her throat even more. She rushed through the living room, grabbing her purse and tripping down the front steps to her car.

He watched as her taillights bounced out of sight. Whew. Of all things, he hadn't expected her to fall apart on him.

"Parker!" Billy's voice, terrorized, came from the bedroom.

"I'm here," Parker yelled.

Billy was sitting up, sweat dripping down his forehead, the stuffed animal clutched tightly in his arms. "I heard something. I want Izzy."

I want her, too, thought Parker, but didn't say it. "She had to go home."

"What day is tomorrow?"

"Well, I think the tomorrow you're asking about is already today. But, it's Sunday."

"Oh." Billy frowned. "We've been going to Sunday school. Afterwards, can we drive to Lincoln to see Mama?"

"I don't know, Billy. We'll have to see how everyone's schedule looks. What we can do is call your mama's room and see how everything's going. See if she's strong enough to see you. It wouldn't make much sense to drive all the way there, if she was sleeping."

"I wouldn't mind. I can watch my mama sleep."

"I know you would, Buster. You're a good boy."

Parker sat on the edge of the bed and took Billy's hand. Young fingers curled around Parker's thumb, and he felt Billy relax. Parker stayed until the boy's steady breathing signaled sleep.

Pulling his shirt over his head, Parker walked to the living room. He tossed the shirt in the corner. It landed on top of the clothes Izzy had stacked there. She'd only been in his house an hour and already it felt better. He could help her. He knew what it felt like to lose somebody. It just took time to get over the loss, but friendship and love were the best medicines.

Man, Parker thought, listen to me. *I'm telling myself the same things that everybody told me after Julia died.*

Izzy hid it well. He'd never have guessed she was carrying that much grief around and for so long. Parker stripped down to his boxers and sat on the couch, pulling the blanket off the back and starting to cover himself.

For a moment he lay there with the room closing in on him. He stood. If he was going to help Izzy get over her loss, he'd better start working on his own. The first thing he could do was start sleeping in his bedroom again. On the bed he'd shared with Julia.

❧

Whip sat on the front porch. Agatha Hepfield waited next to him.

"Some excitement today, eh, Izzy?" Agatha rocked her chair forward so that she looked past Thompson and at Izzy.

"Enough excitement for me." Izzy nodded, knowing that her red eyes would be blamed on the weather.

"You like little Billy?" Agatha grinned wickedly.

"He's a good kid," Izzy agreed.

"Takes after Parker," Whip said. "Although, technically, I guess Parker's more like a second cousin twice removed, or something. Maybe he's a first cousin, once removed."

Izzy didn't want to hear about Parker. She said good night and went inside. Whip had laid out a piece of pie for her. She grabbed it and a soda before climbing the stairs to her apartment. Radar curled around Rosemary's journal, deep in slumber. Izzy changed into her pajamas and collapsed on the couch, but she was soon scooting up and switching the light back on. She couldn't sleep, so she might as well read. Purposely, she pushed Parker's image away. This time she took the newer-looking journal and got comfortable.

Radar settled on her stomach. His footsteps dug into her chest, making her gasp.

One thing for sure, Izzy decided after rearranging Radar and reading two pages, this journal didn't belong to Rosemary. The first date recorded was in the 1980s. No name decorated the front. Izzy decided to read a little farther before putting it away. The handwriting looking vaguely familiar.

At first, all the entries spoke of school, baseball, catching snakes. Izzy squinted. She wasn't reading the best handwriting. The little boy who'd written this, and it had to be a young boy, because no girl she knew got such joy out of scaring her mother with a snake, certainly wasn't gifted in the art of forming letters.

The boy didn't write every day. According to the dates, he'd write for a couple of days and then put the journal away for a month or more. Izzy skimmed to the middle of the books. It took her into the boy's future, to about 1981. The boy wrote about not liking school, about liking girls, and about having to work part-time at the McKennas' farm. Izzy felt prickles go up and down her arms. Was she reading Parker's journal? She really should stop, she told herself. *One more,* she decided, *I'll just read one more page.*

She turned to the next entry, surprised to discover the boy changing to a slanting cursive. Of course, the date recorded was 1989. The boy wrote about his cousin Parker leaving for college and about his buying a gun.

She wasn't reading Parker's journal—she was reading Kenny's journal. And the handwriting matched the handwriting of the journal Parker had turned into the library. The journal with the entry about suicide.

Izzy felt the pie stick in her throat.

Parker wasn't suicidal.

Kenny was.

10

*I*zzy could see the hazy, white sun from her bedroom window, but wasn't sure it radiated any life. Or maybe *she* didn't radiate any life. A sleepless night, a nagging suspicion that she had been irrevocably wrong about Parker, and a yearning for morning to put things right had tormented her thoughts. She dressed quickly, grabbing a soda and trying to blink away fatigue. She put on her coat, tucked her hands into mittens, and wrapped a scarf around her neck. Time to face the music. Shivering, she jumped in the car. The heater hummed, almost drowning out the Christian radio station. Izzy drove, blowing white air into the atmosphere, wondering if she could make a smoke ring with the visible chill. Nebraska was one cold state.

She'd been so wrong about Parker. She had believed that he was suicidal! If he slammed the door in her face, she'd understand. She'd sit on his front porch and cry, but she'd understand. This whole relationship, or nonrelationship, was crazy.

Izzy hit the steering wheel with the palm of her hand. Love wasn't supposed to be this hard. She had prayed for a Christian man who would be her spiritual mate. Instead, she was in love with a torn, rugged fireman who believed in God but didn't follow the faith. The car hit a huge hole in the dirt road. Her purse bounced to the floor. Yeah, here she was driving through the crooked country roads of a community she'd sworn she wouldn't settle in, heading toward the house of the man she wanted to marry.

She'd thought she'd turned everything over to God. But the last few days only proved that she'd kept a piece for herself. It wasn't her fault that her father hadn't been strong enough to face devaluation in the work place. Money had been the cause for ruin of so many men. Look what it had done to Judas.

Often, Izzy thought as her car cruised by the waving branches of tall trees, she'd felt remiss about her religion. So many of her friends accepted God without qualms. Izzy had a problem accepting perfect peace. She tended to let things worry her. Parker was probably a lot like that.

His house looked deserted, with a grayish bitter wind sending the last of October's leaves tumbling across the porch. In the distance, a rooster heralded the morning. Izzy stepped out of the car and slowly made her way to the front door. Clutching her coat closed with one hand, she rang the doorbell.

Parker answered almost immediately, hopping up and down on one foot while holding his boot in his hand. "Izzy?"

"I've got something to tell you. Do you have a minute?"

"I wish I did. The station just called. With everything that's going on, they're shorthanded. I was just getting ready to wake Billy."

He hopped away from the door.

"Parker, I've treated you unfairly." Izzy trailed after him.

"I won't argue." He grinned.

Izzy felt the blush start at her neck and travel to her cheeks. She followed him. "No, I don't mean that. Do you remember the day you turned in all the books at the library?"

"Sure. That's the day I met you." His eyes turned a frosted brown as he took in her padded appearance. "Hand me your coat?"

With nervous fingers, Izzy jerked off her mittens and unbuttoned her coat. Unwrapping the scarf, she tossed it and the rest of her wraps onto a chair. She felt herself melting as he slowly started scrutinizing her from head to toe. She cleared her throat and tried to go on. "Parker do you remember that book I returned to—"

The phone rang. Parker picked it up. Izzy sat down on the couch to wait.

"Mother . . . really? I've got to go to work. Hold on a minute." He turned to her. "Would you be willing to stay with Billy for a little while this morning? Mom's not feeling well."

"Sure," Izzy said, thinking she'd do anything to smooth over what she was about to confess. "I'll watch him. I'll take him to church with me."

"No problem, Mom, Izzy's going to stay with him. Why don't you just call here later this afternoon when you start to feel better, and Izzy will bring him over. Okay, bye."

As soon as he hung up, Izzy said, "Parker, what I was trying to say—"

Static filled the room, then the clear sounds of Robert Parrish barking out orders from the squawk box on top of the television. Parker quickly responded. "Strickland here. I'm on my way."

"Parker, about that journal."

"Izzy, I wish I could stay and talk, but there's a three-car pileup over by the Waco Turnpike. I've got to get to the station. I promise, the moment I can, I'll call you and we'll meet for lunch or something." Then, as if it were a habit, he leaned down and kissed her good-bye—on the lips.

He was out the front door before Izzy could say another word. She fought the urge to touch her mouth.

"Wait," she called after him.

He turned, zipping his coat and pulling on his gloves. "What?"

"I need a key."

He looked quizzical as he opened the car door and started to step up into his truck.

"To your house," she finished.

"No, you don't," he laughed, his chuckles sending white puff rings into the air. "Just close the door. No one will bother anything."

The wind caught at his hair, Izzy held the wooden door and kept it from blowing all the way open. "Parker! I'm going to pray for those people who had the accident and you. Be careful."

He touched his brow in a two-fingered salute, slammed his door shut, and sped down the winding road.

Izzy closed the door behind her and went to check on Billy. He felt a little warm, but slumbered peacefully. Brute lay cushioned between Billy's legs. Idly, Izzy scratched the dog between the ears. Suddenly, all the events from the night overcame Izzy. Her shoulders sagged and her eyes felt dry. She went back into the living room and looked at the couch. Feeling a little daring, she turned to the open door that led to Parker's bedroom.

It was a big room with only a bed in it. Clothes were folded and stacked on the floor.

He needed a woman.

No, he needed a maid.

Izzy went to the pile of shirts lying on the windowsill. Plucking one off the top, she held it up, considering. She had more than three hours to kill before church. Billy was asleep. She unsnapped her pants and kicked them off before shrugging out of her shirt. She slipped his button-down shirt over the top of her head and crawled into bed. Into Parker's bed. The scent of him wove a spell around her, and she fell asleep with a contented smile on her face.

❧

Parker whistled as he drove back to Mayhill. Robert and he had arrived at the accident just as the car fire was dying down. The state police had restricted the area. Parker had sent the ambulance on its way. It carried the injured, fortunately none seriously hurt. Parker thought briefly about Izzy's comment concerning prayer for this couple. Nah, that couldn't have made a difference. After thoroughly dousing the smoldering vehicle, the firemen turned their engine toward home. Mayhill waited just five miles ahead. Already Parker could see the grain towers like a lighthouse beacon welcoming him home.

"You're looking good this morning, Parker," Robert teased. "Wife said Carole Martin sent Izzy out to your house last night to help with the kid. Could it be she stayed all night?"

"No," Parker said, "she didn't stay all night. Izzy's not like that." Then, laughing at the disappointed look on Robert's face, he added, "But she did come back this morning."

"Finally!" Robert exclaimed. "Ty and Jeff have been after me the last few weeks with all sorts of ideas to help fix you two up, but I told them you didn't need any help."

"I'm going to marry her, Robert. Just as soon as I can." Parker started coughing, his own words surprising him.

Robert threw back his head and howled with laughter. "You Stricklands always did make up your minds quickly. Izzy's a fine girl."

"I told her I'd meet her for lunch today. That okay?" Parker felt a sweat breaking out on his forehead as he realized the implications of what he was saying.

"She'll have to come to the station. Jeff and Ty have been at the job forty-eight hours straight. I sent them home. It's just you and me, and I have a pile of paperwork. With this weather, I'd rather have you stick near the radio."

"That's fine. Izzy won't mind."

Robert rolled down the window and stuck his head out into the cold. The wind sent his hair flying back, and the chill from the outside seeped around Parker.

"It's a good thing they took Carole into Lincoln last night," Robert yelled. "They've been predicting our first storm, say it's going to arrive within the next twenty-four hours."

"I love the first snow of the season." Parker smiled as the image of Izzy standing at his front door bundled into winter wraps crossed his mind. He tugged on Robert's sleeve, bringing his boss back into the truck. Then he paused. He used to love the first snow. He'd hated the snow since Julia died. Could it be he was finally looking forward to winter?

Robert left his hand outside for a few moments, fingers spread. "This one feels different. Like it's going to be a whiteout."

Parker didn't like the worried expression on Robert's face. His boss seldom tried to predict occurrences, but it seemed as if Robert was filled with concerns today. Come to think of it, pulling a forty-eight straight really wasn't that tough. Why was Robert so concerned about Jeff and Ty?

Mayhill was waking up as Parker and Robert drove back into town. The line at the fast food restaurant was forming as people stopped to get their one-minute breakfast. Parker saw the minister of Izzy's church drive by as Robert pulled into the station. Parker checked over the engine while Robert went inside to file a report.

The police call came in at eleven. Parker relayed it over the station radio . . . a barn fire on route five . . . man injured . . . hay. Robert drove this time. Parker called his house from the truck's phone as they sped back in the direction of the earlier car fire. He expected to leave a message, sure that Izzy was at church. Instead, she answered.

Parker liked the thought of her answering his phone. "Lunch is off. Did I wake you?"

"No," she sound distracted.

"Izzy, is something wrong?"

"Billy's feverish. What should I do?"

"Give him plenty of fluids. Keep him in bed. Don't let him walk on the bare floor. We're responding to a call. It could be a while. I'll phone you when it's over. If he gets worse, take him into to town to my mother."

"Okay."

"Izzy," Parker lowered his voice, knowing Robert was listening. "I love you." His throat constricted on the words.

"I think I love you, too."

He let out his breath. "We'll work on that *think* part," Parker promised. "Bye."

Parker set the phone down.

"Your mother's not sick, you know?" Robert said.

"What do you mean Mom's not sick?"

"Whip spread the word that Izzy came back home disheartened last night. Carole was sure upset that her plan to get you two talking didn't work. But then this morning Agatha saw Izzy leave, heading in your direction, and called your mother. Your mother called Jeff." Robert took a deep breath, exaggerating his commentary. "Jeff knew you were being called in and decided that there's was no better way to get you two acting like a couple than to put you in charge of Billy."

"That's ridiculous."

"You still sleeping on the couch?"

"I didn't last night."

"Okay, then I'll tell Ty, Jeff, Carole, Agatha, Whip, Rhea, and your mother that you don't need any more help." Robert made a big production out of counting off his fingers at the recital of each name.

If Parker had been driving, he'd have put his head down on the wheel and moaned. "You're really enjoying—"

"Look," Robert pointed, suddenly animated, "no wonder York radioed for help."

Black swirls of smoke billowed toward the clouds and blended into the sky. Robert steered the fire engine a safe distance from the burning barn and jumped out. Parker ran around to the back and hooked his arm into the coils of hose. Running toward the action, Parker felt the first wave of heat hit his cheeks with stinging tentacles of airborne fire.

"Didn't expect to see you all so soon," one of the York firefighters yelled. Jeff and Ty pulled up in Jeff's car. Jeff joined Parker.

"Gonna be one of those days! Luckily, this is the old barn. The farmer built a new one and was just feeding out of this one. There's not much hay inside," reported a York fireman.

"Thank God," Parker murmured. He hated burning hay. "Anybody hurt?"

"Farmer took quite a knock to the head. He was out here caring for the stock. Says he heard something and when he went to check it out, interrupted a man going through an old desk he keeps in the tackroom."

"Wife home?" Robert yelled.

"No, she's shopping in town. We have an officer looking for her."

The York fireman relieved Parker of the hose. Parker joined Ty and a group of men busy breaking open bales of hay to scatter them so they could be doused thoroughly.

"Good time for it to snow," Robert yelled from behind them.

Parker nodded as he watched his chief hurry over to the pond where York's engineer was readying a hose for suction.

"Parker?"

"What, Mike?"

"Just thought you'd better know. The farmer gave a good description of the man who probably started the fire."

Parker felt the water pressure easing as the engine emptied. "So?"

"It sounds like your cousin Kenny. Sheriff's put out an APB."

"Kenny! You sure?"

"If I wasn't sure, I wouldn't tell you, Parker. You might want to get to your aunt Edna as soon as you can."

"And the troopers have already been called?" Parker asked.

"Arson's a serious offense."

~&~

Izzy came awake with the graceful yawn of a woman content. She hugged Parker's pillow to her face and drank in his scent. His bed. She'd spent the night, well really the day, in his bed. Rolling out of bed she tugged on her jeans before going to check on Billy. He slumbered on. Izzy felt his forehead again. He was still a little warm.

"Billy." She shook his shoulder.

"Wha–at," he grumbled.

"You hungry?"

He fell back asleep before he could answer.

Padding silently through Parker's house in her stocking feet, Izzy felt so thankful she could almost purr. Izzy let the dog out, filled his bowl with dry dog food, and shook her head at the dimming skies. How had she slept past suppertime? Amazing. The search for Billy, combined with worry about Parker, must have been more taxing than she realized. She had her work cut out for her, now, that was for sure. Opening the bottom cupboards, she found Parker's supply of soup and grabbed a can of chicken broth.

"I'm not hungry," Billy mumbled when she woke him up.

"You need to eat."

"How's my mom?"

"Tell you what," Izzy promised, "you eat half this soup, and we'll call her."

Billy winced, but obediently pushed himself to a sitting position and weakly took the bowl of soup from Izzy's hands. "Half?"

"Half," Izzy said.

Parker's clothes were still in the corner where she'd tossed them last night. Izzy gathered them up and went looking for the washer and dryer. She tried the bathroom in Parker's bedroom first. Next, she went out to the garage. Last, she investigated the back porch. Surely the man owned a washer and dryer. Shrugging, she headed back to check on Billy. He managed to maintain his upright position, but his head was nodding dangerously close to the soup. Izzy relieved him of the bowl and started to tuck him in. The wet spot of soup on his T-shirt stopped her.

"Billy, wake up."

"Izzy, I don't feel good." He shivered.

"I know. Your shirt's wet. Let's just take it off and then you can go back to sleep. By the way, where's Parker's washer and dryer?"

"At the fire station. He showed me," Billy mumbled.

"He doesn't have a washer and dryer here?"

"In the basement."

"Basement?" She didn't remember any basement.

"Yeah, you know, where they used to keep canned goods. That's where we keep ours."

Ah, the cellar. "Oh." She tucked the covers up over Billy's shoulders and went back to the kitchen. Looking at the floor, she located the handle that lay flat in a slight indentation on the floor. Izzy bent, grabbed it with a firm hand, and tugged upward as hard as she could. It resisted, and she pulled harder. The metal handle dug into her hand. Izzy almost gave up, but now she was curious. It took two broken nails and more than five minutes, but she finally managed to open the trapdoor.

The steps went straight down, a ladder effect instead of gradual descent. As her foot touched the ground, the idea of a flashlight came to her and she climbed back up. She found Parker's flashlight in a kitchen drawer, next to a pair of rolled-up socks and an empty aluminum foil box.

A chill followed her down the steps. As her foot touched the ground for the second time, she began to doubt the need to do Parker's laundry. He probably did it at the station house. They had a washer and dryer there. And she seemed to recall Parker saying he didn't come down here much. Well, he didn't do laundry much, so that didn't mean anything. She swung the flashlight around and squinted in the darkness trying to detect some type of light switch.

Instead, the flashlight beam found the leering face of Kenny Latkam.

❧

It was growing dark, but the fire was out. Parker grimly held the heavy hose, fatigued beyond belief. This time his cousin had gone too far. Not Parker, nor Edna, nor Mayor Martin would be able to ease Kenny through with only another misdemeanor on his record. Arson was a serious crime, and not one society could afford to ignore, even if the guilty party happened to be a hometown boy.

Parker wiped the sweat from his brow and noticed Robert's worried gaze. His boss's predictions had come true once too often today. The snow that fell from the sky gathered on the ground quickly, and already the firemen's footsteps could be seen.

"We're finished up here, Parker," Robert called.

This time York had the bulk of the paperwork. Numbly, Parker hopped into the front seat, closing his eyes and letting his head fall against the seat cushion.

"Robert, do you think it was Kenny?"

"You know it was."

"I don't think Kenny would set a fire."

"I doubt Kenny meant to. Still, if the boy wasn't trying to rob the farmer in the first place, he wouldn't have been near the barn. Chances are, Kenny dropped his cigarette as he tried to run."

"Do you think—?"

"I think it's time Kenny faced up to his troubles. There's not a thing you can do this time, Parker. Probably would have been better if Kenny had faced the music a long time ago."

"But Aunt Edna—" Parker began.

"Spared the rod and spoiled the child," Robert finished.

"Did you know Kenny was Billy's father?"

"I was one of the few."

"How long have you known?"

"Since Billy was born. You remember Delta's senior year, don't you?"

"Not really."

"That's right," Robert gripped the steering wheel. "You were newly married, living up in Lincoln. Delta kicked up quite a stir. She didn't keep a steady boyfriend, but went out with them all. She went out with Jeff, Mark Dalton, your cousin Chris from over in Waco. Her dad was fit to be tied. He'd ground her, she'd sneak out the window. Twice she disappeared for a week, only to turn up at her parents' doorstep, refusing to tell where she'd been or who'd she'd been with."

"How do you know all this?"

The knuckles on the steering wheel turned white. "She dated Russ."

Parker stared ahead, knowing how hard it must have been for Robert to admit that his son had been involved with Delta during that time.

"We were worried that Billy might belong to Russ," Robert went on, eyes fixed on the road. "I was there when Billy was born. It was in January. Delta went into labor, and they were headed toward Doc's when the car skidded in the snow and went into a ditch. We got her to the emergency room in time. I happened to be nearby when Delta mumbled his name. I didn't say anything. If Delta wanted the father to know, she'd announce it. Fact is, she was smart not to. Having Kenny for a father will be a millstone around that boy's neck.

"The town spent a few months speculating on whose baby Billy was: Chris, Russ, Mark, Kenny. Finally folks settled on Chris. Kenny didn't pay any attention to Billy. Chris was the logical choice. He went off to college in Texas and never came back. Delta didn't deny it. The few of us who knew let sleeping dogs lie."

Parker shook his head. "What a mess."

"Parker, you don't think Edna would help Kenny get away?"

"Not once she knows arson's involved. She's pretty shook about him being Billy's father and her not knowing she had a grandson all these years."

The snow swished off the windshield and the two men finished the rest of the journey into town in silence.

❧

The flashlight hit the ground and rolled. Kenny quickly picked it up and idly tossed it from one hand to the other. "Nice shirt."

Izzy backed up, feeling the wooden beams of the steps dig into her shoulder blades. In the shadowed basement Kenny looked bigger. She had never met the esteemed cousin Chris, but Kenny looked like a smaller, somewhat-erased version of Parker. Tonight he looked as if he had been stepped on, beaten, and thrown away. His white T-shirt was streaked with dirt, and the bottom of his pants were torn and still wet. "What are you doing down here, Kenny?"

"I just wanted a little peace and quiet. What are you doing down here?"

Izzy glanced around. No washer or dryer. She should have known that. Parker had said he planned on redoing the cellar. "Oh, Billy said the washer and dryer were down here." Quickly, Izzy turned and put her foot on the first narrow step.

Kenny came up behind her. The scent from his body seemed tangible: cigarettes and fear, with a chaser of alcohol. Together they climbed to the kitchen.

"What are you going to do, Kenny?"

"They won't be looking for you. You're going to drive me out of here."

"What are you talking about?" Izzy looked out the kitchen window, hoping more than anything that she'd see Parker's truck pull in.

"We'll go to Denver." Kenny didn't answer her question.

Izzy clamped her lips shut and glared. Inside, her brain went into overdrive. *Lord,* she prayed, *what's happening? What should I do? Please, please, keep us safe. Don't let him hurt Billy.*

Kenny only chuckled. He went into the living room, heading with a sense of self-assurance that let Izzy know that while she'd been sleeping he'd been going through the house—and maybe even her purse.

With one halting step, Izzy moved toward the back door. The prayer had made her feel better, but not completely safe. She could do this. Billy was the most important factor. She had a spare car key in a magnetic box hidden up under the front grill. All she had to do—

"You wouldn't leave me alone with Billy," Kenny called.

Izzy froze. "Why not?"

"I've had a lot to drink. Oh, and if I hear you even go near the phone, I won't let you pack."

"What! Kenny, what's going on? What's wrong with you? This isn't funny—"

"Shut up!"

Billy came, sleepy-eyed, to the doorway of the bedroom. "What's he doing here, Izzy?"

"Come on, Billy. We're going to—"

"You're going to do nothing but what I tell you to do," Kenny yelled.

Sitting down on the couch, Izzy beckoned for Billy to join her. Kenny ran into Parker's bedroom, but immediately stuck his head out the door, "Don't even think about moving." A few minutes later he came back in the room carrying a pillowcase bulging with clothes. He began opening cupboards and stuffing food into the corners. "Grab whatever you want for the kid. You've got two minutes and then we're out of here."

Izzy slowly stood, wanting to run but afraid to move. "Billy, just stay where you are." She wanted to show him she wasn't afraid. Taking one step in Kenny's direction, she said, "Why are you doing this?"

"It's time I got away. A small town suffocates you, especially when your whole family oohs and aahs over Parker and Chris. I wasn't fast enough for the football team, I wasn't tall enough for basketball, but I could hold my liquor. I'm not the kid's father, no way, no how. Delta was with Chris before she was with me. Nothing's ever been fair around this place. We'll get to Denver, you'll see. No one's going to stop us. Not while we got the kid."

Izzy backed up. The overpowering odor of whiskey suddenly

pushed her into the realization that Kenny was out of control. She'd seen drunk before, and Kenny was about a quart beyond that.

"I'll go to Denver with you, but I don't think we should take Billy. The kid will just get in the way."

For a moment Kenny looked thoughtful, then he frowned at her. "The McKennas are rich. They'll pay a ransom for Billy."

"Billy's your son, Kenny!"

"Well, then my mom will probably fork out some money, too. You're wasting time. You've got one minute to get your stuff together."

Izzy ran for the living room, plopping down in the chair and cramming her feet inside her boots. Shoving her arms through her coat sleeves, she tried to think rationally. They'd have to stop for gas somewhere. She'd get Billy out of the car—

"Come on!" Kenny came out of Billy's room, holding the terrified boy tightly and scowling. "I have nothing to lose, Izzy. Don't even think about leaving me alone with Billy."

"I'm not thinking about leaving you. I'm wondering if we should grab some blankets. It's supposed to snow tonight."

"Get the blankets. Now!"

With a handful of covers, Izzy stumbled after Kenny. She was sure there had to be a way out of all this, but for the life of her she couldn't think of what it was. Billy was using both hands to try to push himself away from Kenny. Tightening his grip, Kenny ignored the terror in Billy's eyes and opened the car door.

"Let me drive, Kenny." Izzy wanted to hit him.

"I don't think so. You learn some pretty neat things in boot camp. I especially enjoyed the survival games. Got really good at tying knots." With a wicked grin, he pulled some rope out of his jacket pocket. Roughly, he wrapped it around Izzy's wrists before winding it about Billy's. He shoved them in the front seat, wound the rope between the door handle, and slammed and locked the car door before climbing behind the wheel.

"Don't even think about gas stations or fast food joints. In the time it would take you to get that knot undone, if you could manage that, I'd be back. You're with me now, and nothing's changing that."

"Kenny, it's starting to snow." Izzy's fear made her voice crack.

With a rebel yell, Kenny turned the key and pressed the Peugeot's gas pedal to the floor. "I like driving in the snow."

As the car skidded down the gravel driveway, Izzy shot a quick glance back at Parker's disappearing house. With a sinking heart, she realized that in Kenny's drunken state, it was very doubtful they'd make it to anywhere near Denver.

11

*E*dna had married well. Each time Parker pulled into the circular driveway he felt as if he were visiting somebody else's aunt. Today, the house had a neglected look to it. Like lost party favors, newspapers littered the sidewalk in front of the door. Leaves covered the basin of the decorative fountain. The chiseled, white, ceramic angel no longer spewed liquid in the air and seemed to shiver from the cold. Usually Edna's house qualified as a showplace. Not today.

Parker left his truck in front of the triple garage, and shoving his hands into his pockets, slowly walked to the front door. Too often he'd been the one to bring Aunt Edna bad news. When he was younger, she'd called him a tattletale and closed the door in his face. Later, during his teenage years, it had been his fault that Kenny often had to be left on the front step, too drunk to find his house key. It didn't matter whether Parker had been with his cousin or not. He was older and always received the blame.

Raising the antique knocker, Parker dropped it, three times. No one answered.

Edna had to be home. It was Sunday night, late. Leaving the step, Parker walked around to the backyard and peeked in a window at a dark kitchen. "I don't believe this," Parker mumbled. The first gnawing tendrils of worry surfaced as he hastened back to his truck to retrieve Edna's spare house key from the glovebox.

The house had at one time belonged to a wealthy rancher. He'd built the clapboard home to impress the wife he'd ordered from the East. There were more rooms than necessary and enough open space to confuse a family of mice. It never felt quite like a home to Parker, more like a museum.

He found his aunt in her late husband's den, huddled at the desk and shaking.

Edna had always been high-strung. Parker wondered how long this anxiety attack had been going on.

"Parker." Edna took a long breath, it looked painful. She stood up and started to pace. "Things will be fine in the morning."

For a shocked moment, Parker stood in the middle of the room. Fine? Who was she kidding? Pictures of Kenny and of Dale, her late husband, smiled at Parker from the desk.

Edna might be bossy and overbearing, but she didn't deserve this.

"I'm going to make you some hot tea, Edna. Now, I want you to stop worrying. We'll find Kenny."

Her gray hair, usually efficiently coiled about her round, red face, now hung in limp imitations of shocked steel wool. "I don't know where Kenny is. They kept asking. I just don't know."

Parker stepped back, feeling helplessness mix with anger. With a stiff-legged turn, he headed toward the kitchen and dialed his mother's number. Francine promised she would be there in fifteen minutes. Parker figured more like five.

He dialed his own number next. Izzy was probably frantic with worry. He wanted to hear her voice, have her tell him that everything was fine, and that she had a pot of chili—or something—on the stove, just waiting for his return. He knew what she'd say if he told her about Kenny. She would offer to pray. He would listen. He could do that.

Her earlier prayer—the one about the accident—had been answered.

Maybe he would ask her to pray for Edna, and for Kenny.

A busy signal came from the other end. Well, he'd get back to her later. He glanced at the clock. It was well after eleven. There had been more excitement in Mayhill, the last week, than there had been in the entire last year—make that decade. He added water to the teakettle and turned on the gas stove.

Edna was still shaking when Francine arrived. Parker watched as his mother bent over Edna, talking soothingly as if to a baby, and having her sister sip tea. "Come on, Edna. You just need a nap. Nothing to be ashamed of. Sleep will make you feel better." Francine walked Edna to her bedroom.

Parker remained in the den, tapping his foot on the floor, anxious to leave Edna's house and look for Kenny, to do something physical.

The police would be back in the morning. He was almost surprised that they weren't still here. There was nothing of Kenny's in this room, except the photographs. Edna, although she had a blind eye where Kenny was concerned, had kept charge of the family's holdings. A quick perusal of Kenny's old room added no insights.

He met his mother coming out of Edna's room.

"She awake?" Parked tried to peek into the bedroom.

"No," Francine replied. "But it's not a peaceful sleep, either. Why'd you come here?"

"To see if she would tell me more than she told the state troopers."

Francine's eyebrows shot up. "You don't think she'd lie?"

"No, I don't think she would lie, but I do think she would purposely forget to mention any details they didn't specifically ask."

"I cannot believe Kenny started that fire."

"There's not positive proof, but it doesn't look good."

The phone rang. Francine's mouth hung open, primed to ask more questions. Parker picked up the receiver. "Latkams'."

"Parker!" Robert Parrish's voice boomed over the receiver. "The police have traced Kenny's car to the McKennas' and—"

"Good, I'll be right there."

"Not so good," Robert went on. "Kenny's not there."

"Where do they think . . . ?" Parker's voice faltered. He knew where the police would go from McKennas'. They'd go to his house, right next door. The house he'd left just this morning. The house where Izzy and Billy had waited for Francine to call when she felt better. The house with the busy signal.

Parker picked up the phone and called Whip. It took a while, but finally the old man's yawning voice growled an answer. Parker didn't waste time on a salutation. "Have you seen Izzy and Billy?"

"Why, no, I thought they were with you."

Parker muffled the phone against his heart for a moment, then shot off another question. "But you called?"

"Yes, earlier, but the line was always busy."

Francine's eyes brimmed with tears. "Parker, is everything all right? Do you need me to head over—"

"Stay with Edna," Parker shouted, slamming down the phone. "If she wakes up, call Robert!"

The streets were slicking up as Parker frantically attempted to make record time to his house. For a moment he regretted his choice to live so far away from the community. If he'd purchased the house down the street from his mother's, he'd already be home and figuring out what was going on. He hated losing control. It made him vulnerable. Caring for Izzy was making him vulnerable, but also alive. Her with her talk of God, her love for children. Her smile.

Parker sped up as the beginning of his property came into sight. Every light was on, and two cruisers blocked his drive. Not caring if he slid off the road, he floored it and almost hit the back of Officer Rowe's patrol car, parked just inside the drive. Jumping out of the truck he slipped in the snow and started going down. In a flash, Brute was out the front door and jumping against Parker's knees. Catching hold of the car door handle, Parker hauled himself up and hurried toward his front door, with Brute prancing excitedly at his heels.

"Parker," Officer Rowe opened the door, frowning. "We've been looking for you."

"I was at Edna's. Kenny's not there."

"We've traced him here. Why don't you—?"

"Izzy! Billy!" Parker pushed past Rowe and looked inside the guest bedroom. The messed-up bed looked empty and accusing.

Officer Rowe grasped Parker's elbow firmly. "You mean Billy should be here, in the care of Isobelle de la Rosa?"

"They're not here," Parker said brokenly.

Puppy barks came from the kitchen. Parker rubbed his lip, trying to think about what Kenny might have done. The barks continued. Officer Rowe took a notebook out of his shirt pocket and said, "When did you last speak with Izzy?"

"Before noon. I called her while we were heading toward the York fire."

"Did she sound all right?"

Parker held up his hand letting Rowe know he needed a moment to think. Brute wouldn't be announcing his hunger from the kitchen. The puppy would be sinking his teeth into the hem of Parker's pants and dragging his master toward the bowl. "Something's wrong."

Rowe nodded, following Parker to the kitchen. Brute whined and scraped his paw against the floor right above the cellar trapdoor.

"What is it, Brute?" Parker bent down and tugged at the latch. It gave easily, letting Parker know it had been opened recently.

"Let me—" Rowe began, but Parker had already descended.

The glaring light cast shadows around the cobweb-laden cellar. Rowe stepped off the last stair and joined Parker in scrutinizing the small room. Brute barked from the kitchen, clearly wanting to join them but hindered by the steep steps.

"Over there." Rowe nudged Parker in the direction of a stack of old boxes.

A blanket lay on the ground. An empty pack of cigarettes was pushed to one side.

"Kenny's brand." Parker nodded.

Rowe climbed back upstairs. "I'm going to radio this in. Kenny stole a car in Lincoln. Wrecked it a few miles down from the barn he tried to burn. Catherine Wilfong picked him up and dropped him off at Summers this afternoon, probably about the same time you were putting the fire out. Now we know he's been here. It looks as if he was planning to stay for a while, but something interrupted him. I'm willing to bet Izzy stumbled onto to him. What do you think?"

"She drives one of those little Peugeots." Parker pictured the little car, and in his mind's eye, it shrank to child size.

"What did you remember?" Officer Rowe took a small notebook out of his shirt pocket.

"Those cars are lousy in bad weather. Too small." Parker winced as the picture of Izzy's Peugeot came to mind. The little red car could have skidded off the interstate and her body might be slumped across the front seat. Parker didn't waste any more time contemplating. With three steps he was out the front door and running into the darkness.

Rowe raced behind him. "Just what do you think you're doing?"

"He not only has Izzy, he has Billy!" Parker had one foot in the truck, ready to hop in, when a thought came to him. He grabbed his flashlight, stepped down, and hurried over to where Izzy had parked her car that morning. The tracks had been snowed over, but enough of a faint outline remained, evidence that someone had put that car in reverse and backed out at top speed. The fact that he could still see the impression gave him hope. They might have left an hour ago, or if luck was with him, as little as a half hour. Kenny wouldn't go back to Lincoln. He'd already been there and caused enough trouble to be noticed. Besides, Mayhill people loved to visit Lincoln. With all Kenny had done, he needed to go somewhere and get lost. Parker knew Kenny was heading for Denver, heading for Denver in a totally unsuited vehicle. Parker looked back down at the tire tracks.

She was an Arizona girl in a midget car without snow tires, and his idiot cousin was at the wheel.

Parker hurried to his truck. Brute scampered at his heels. Opening the door, Parker leaned against it for a moment, gathering his thoughts. Brute jumped in. Parker finally swung in behind the wheel. He put his hand on the ignition key, paused, then bowed his head to pray.

❧

Kenny took the exit to Grand Island. The town, only an hour from Mayhill, was one Izzy never visited. And in this darkness, she couldn't identify a single distinguishing feature.

Izzy tightened her grip on the door handle and tried to scoot farther away from Kenny. In troubled slumber, Billy nestled closer. Kenny didn't seem to notice.

"Why are we stopping?" Izzy tried not to sound worried.

"Snow's getting worse. Best fill the tank now and try to outrun the blizzard. We're not staying, and you're not getting out of the car. Thanks to the new pay-at-the-pumps systems, I won't even need to go inside the station." Kenny reached in his pocket and extracted her bank card. "I just slide this in, punch a few numbers, and we're done."

"Billy has to go to the bathroom."

"He can hold it."

"I have to go, too."

"Tough."

At that moment, Izzy thought she'd never disliked anyone as much as she did Kenny. She stared out the window and started to pray, but the prayer choked in her throat and became more a plea for help.

The city of Grand Island provided numerous filling stations and restaurants just off the interstate exit. Kenny drove slowly, looking left and right, frowning at the lines of cars pulling into motel parking lots and convenience stores.

"What are you looking for?" Izzy wanted to feel Billy's forehead, but her hands were firmly connected to the door.

"A gas station without any customers."

It took him a few miles, but finally he pulled into a forlorn station toward the downtown section. He parked as far away from the office as possible and reached over to unroll her window.

"Kenny, it's freezing!"

Jumping out of the car, he ran around and pushed her card into the slot. "What's your pin number?"

"I don't remember."

He grinned mercilessly, and pushed his jacket open just enough to show the butt of a gun. "Number?" he repeated.

Izzy blinked. How could she have figured he didn't have a gun? She remembered reading about it in his journal, and if he was crazy enough to write about suicide, he was probably crazy enough to threaten his own child.

"This isn't funny, Kenny." Izzy straightened up and gave him a stern look. "Untie the rope, now! I'll explain everything to Parker. He can help you."

Kenny glared at her. "I don't want Parker's help. I never did. I can take care of myself and you."

"This is kidnapping. Kenny, do you know what kind of a jail term kidnapping brings?"

Kenny's unruly hair danced wildly in his eyes as he shook his head negatively. "No. Prisons are overcrowded. I'm under the influence and known to be suicidal. A good lawyer will get me off."

"Who will pay for the lawyer—?" She stopped. Edna had the money.

"Give me the pin number."

"Loosen the ropes, and I'll give you the number."

For a moment, she thought he wouldn't do it. Then, he shrugged. She held her breath as he opened the passenger-side door. Cold air swished in. Izzy stiffened. After a few moments of fumbling, Kenny left her right hand tied to the arm rest, but separated her and Billy.

"You bug me," he threatened, "and I tie you even tighter than before."

"Please, leave Billy untied."

Kenny shook his head, but Izzy noticed that he tied Billy's hand in front of him, with a much looser loop. He also moved the boy to the backseat.

She thought about asking if she could move to the backseat, too, but one look at her kidnapper stymied that notion. She gave him the ID number. His bloodshot eyes looked crazed. In his state of mind, he didn't know or care what he was doing. A lawyer would have a strong case.

"Izzy, will we be all right?" Billy mumbled.

"Don't you worry," Izzy comforted. "God has a special angel in the car with us, and he'll make sure nothing bad happens. I've been talking to God since we got in this car. He will take care of us. You talk to Him, too. He'll listen, Billy. This is just a . . . a funny adventure."

"I wish Grandpa would hurry up and come get us," Billy said, staring out the window. "I'm telling God to send him right now."

"Good idea." Izzy didn't really want Thomas McKenna. She wanted Parker, and strangely enough, she expected him. Maybe that was why she wasn't more scared. She heard the nozzle clink against the pump as Kenny finished. The car shook, Izzy turned and looked toward Kenny. He pointed a threatening finger, then looked up and down the street before dashing into the tiny store that ran from the gas station's office.

Izzy looked in the same direction as Kenny had gone. The street was deserted. She stuck her head out the window. A bitter wind scorched her cheeks with ice particles. She opened her mouth, wanting to scream. The wind took the words and flung them right back at her. Tugging at the rope, she fought to untie it, succeeding only in shredding her right hand as the tough rope tore into her skin.

"I told you I tied good knots." Kenny easily slid behind the wheel. He pulled a six-pack out of a brown paper sack, separated a bottle, and twisted the top off. Taking a swig, he added, "Sorry, didn't think about asking you if you wanted anything." He took another long drink and then offered her the open bottle. "You want some of this?"

Izzy managed to gingerly roll up the window. Her hands felt swollen from just the short time she'd wrestled with the rope. Kenny told the truth. He did tie good knots.

"No, I want to go home." Izzy clutched the door handle as Kenny spiraled the car crazily onto the main street and back toward the interstate.

"Don't you ever shut up?" Kenny's lip went thin with anger. He took another gulp from the bottle and shot Izzy a dirty look.

The snow came down in close-knit clusters of flakes, making it impossible to see more than a few feet ahead. The streets were now completely empty. Izzy envied the wise folks secure in the comforts of their homes, snug in bed. By far, this was the most terrifying event that had ever happened to her. She'd been raised in a home where church and family came first. Money had figured in, maybe a bit too much, especially at the end, but growing up, she had always felt secure. Were there families where alcohol made every day as desperate as this one? Was there really so much of nothing in Kenny's soul, that he would willingly endanger his own child?

"Can we turn the heater on?" Izzy tried to keep her voice steady.

Kenny finished the beer and belched. "I'm not cold." He stuck his hand in the bag and pulled out another bottle.

"Why don't you let me drive? I promise—"

"I know all about women and their promises." Kenny turned back onto I-80, and into the whiteness, beginning to sing off-key.

Izzy looked behind her. They'd just left Grand Island. Thanks to the darkness and snow, all proof that it existed was blocked. The lack of visibility hindered road signs from being seen. Izzy glanced at her watch. Well after two. Maybe Billy would fall asleep. He didn't need to be awake during all this.

"There's a rest stop ahead. Can we please stop?" Izzy said.

Kenny paused between words and seemed to consider. "If there's no one around, I'll stop."

He didn't. Truckers, more sensible than Kenny, had taken over the parking lot and were sleeping away the bad weather.

Kenny started singing in a uneven voice that quickly reverted to off-color songs.

He finished his second bottle and went for a third.

Izzy tried to keep her voice steady. She didn't want Billy picking up on her worry. "Billy, can you put your seat belt on?"

"No."

"Have you tried?"

"No."

"Well, try."

The rope around Izzy's arm tightened, digging in and irritating her already chafed wrist.

"I can't put it on with my hands tied, and I'm cold." Billy sobbed.

"Please try, Billy." Izzy watched as Billy twisted his body up and tried frantically to bring together the two straps. He'd just get one strap where he wanted it, and then he'd lose it when he reached for the connecting belt. "Don't give up. You're doing fine."

"Got it!"

Kenny turned more sullen by the moment. He turned to glare at Billy and opened his mouth to say something, but with his attention off the road, for only that one second, he allowed the vehicle to meander toward the emergency lane. No other cars had traveled over the accumulating snow on the interstate's edge. The Peugeot's tires slid off the road. Izzy screamed. Kenny jerked forward, grabbing the wheel and doing exactly the opposite of what he'd been taught. Instead of going with the spin, he spun the wheel clockwise. The out-of-control car picked up speed and bounced off the pavement and onto the flat land surrounding I-80. The grassy snow didn't slow down progress. Before Izzy could form her second scream, the car went nose down in a ditch, finally stopping. Kenny slumped against the steering wheel, and silence entered the car along with the smell of alcohol and urine.

"Billy, are you all right?"

"I wet my pants."

"That's okay. I almost did, too." Izzy gingerly turned around to look at Billy.

He looked fine, a little white around the edges, but physically unharmed. He had even slipped his hand out of the loosely tied rope. Izzy tugged at her hand, but it was still bound tightly to the door. She felt the blood dribble down her wrist. The impact had caused the rope to tighten, and because the rope wasn't about to give, her skin had.

"Are you bleeding anywhere?" Izzy tried to sit up. She felt weak, but managed to turn around and give Billy a thorough going over.

"Nope. Is he dead?"

Izzy put out two fingers and felt Kenny's neck for a pulse. Touching him made her jumpy, but the steady beat of his heart made her breath easier.

"He's not hurt, he's passed out from the beer. We've got to get out of here." Izzy tried to work at the knot.

"If I was wearing my jeans, I could give you my jackknife."

"That would be good," Izzy agreed. With a weak smile, she looked Kenny over. He was out cold. She could reach him. She just had to stretch. With a shaking hand, Izzy started searching his pockets. Just as her hand closed over the pocket knife, secured in the pocket of his jacket, Kenny started to snore. Izzy felt the knife slip from her fingers as the sound startled her. "I can do this," she whispered.

"You're really brave, Miss Izzy. You're the bravest librarian I've ever seen," Billy hung over the seat, watching her every movement.

"Thanks." Izzy didn't feel brave. She slowly went for the knife again. "Got it!" She held it for Billy's inspection. Izzy opened the door. They both frowned. The car's dome light shone on a blade that looked dull.

The snow blew into the car like an infestation of tiny white specks. Izzy tried to ignore the cold, but her hands shook. It took over fifteen minutes to cut the rope. Hot chocolate, her mother's quilt, and a roaring fire, that's what she wanted. Staying here would not get it. "Come on, Billy."

"My pants are wet."

"Grab another pair out of the pillowcase." Izzy rubbed her hands together, surprised that she could think rationally enough to remember that they'd brought extra clothes.

Billy changed his pants faster than she'd ever seen a child dress. While he dressed, she opened the glove compartment and grabbed her flashlight. He climbed over the seat and together they crawled out of the car.

"Your hand looks really bad," Billy observed.

"It will be okay. Come on, Buster." She adopted Parker's pet word, hoping it would help keep Billy's spirits up.

Her tennis shoes sank into what felt like slushy ice. The snow brushed under her pant leg. Izzy took a deep breath as the cold melted around her sock, pricking against her ankle like tiny knives. Tears of frustration started in her eyes. God had gotten them out of the frying pan, but there was still the fire to contend with. The flashlight seemed inadequate against the weather. It's beam didn't seem able to penetrate the darkness.

"Are you crying?" Billy wanted to know.

"It's been a bad day." Izzy tried to sound casual.

" 'A very bad, rotten, no-good day.' " Billy recited from a book Izzy had read aloud to him the weekend she'd baby-sat.

They were both miserable before they reached the side of the interstate. Izzy held tightly to Billy's hand, wondering if they should attempt to make it back to the rest stop, or if they should try to flag down a motorist. In this weather they were more likely to be run over than noticed.

"Do you like to sing, Billy?"

"Ah-ha."

Izzy had just started "Jesus Loves Me" when a bright pair of headlights penetrated the swirling snow. Izzy tugged on Billy's hand and ran toward the road. Miraculously, the truck pulled off to the side. Izzy blinked away the snowflakes that were threatening to blind her and stumbled toward the vehicle. The driver's-side door opened, and Izzy could just make out the dome light inside. One driver and a dog. No! Izzy squinted. One Parker and a Brute! Izzy started to run, but Parker was already there grabbing her into his warm arms and picking up Billy.

"I found you." He blanketed her in his arms. For a frozen moment, his unshaven chin gently scratched against her face. "I prayed. For the first time in years, I prayed."

"Parker," she whispered. "I can't believe you could see us in this weather."

Even with Billy clutched to him, Parker's lips closed over hers and suddenly, for a brief second, she wasn't cold.

The weather couldn't be ignored for long, and as she began to shake, she managed to say, "How did you find us?"

He took the flashlight from her hand. "I'd say that this is powered by more than batteries. I saw the light plainly. It was like a beacon."

She shivered, not just from the cold. "Kenny's back there. He might be hurt. And, Parker, he has a gun."

Parker helped them into the truck and tucked a blanket securely around their shivering forms. He climbed in and quickly radioed his location and stated that he would check out the situation and then attempt to get any injured party to Grand Island. Brute excitedly washed the wet snow from Billy's face, only making the boy shiver.

"I'm leaving the heater on. I'm going to go get Kenny. I doubt if he's hurt. His body was probably too relaxed from the alcohol to feel any pain. You didn't hit anything did you?"

"No, we just went a little ways into the ditch."

"I was scared," Billy said. "But Izzy said it didn't matter because she was scared, too, and that there was an angel in the car with us. I didn't see him. I tried not be scared. I told God to send Grandpa after us, but it's okay that He sent you."

"Well," Parker said slowly, "I'm glad it's okay. After the kind of day you've had," Parker tousled Billy's hair, "you'll be known as the bravest boy around. I'm sure proud of you for taking care of Izzy."

The moment Parker slammed the door and walked away, the truck lost its security. Billy's eyes had been gleaming proudly while

Parker praised him, but now he snuggled closer to Izzy and buried his head in her side. Brute put a paw on Billy's leg and rested his head against the boy.

Billy stared out the window for a moment, then asked, "Why did Kenny take us? What was he going to do?"

Izzy stroked Billy's hair, allowing her hand to pass briefly over his forehead. He still felt warm. Poor little tyke. Three weeks ago his biggest obstacle had been conquering the old elm in the library's park; now he'd been separated from his mother, found out he had the world's worst father, run away, been kidnapped, and all this before he'd even lost his first tooth.

"Kenny took us because he wanted attention," Izzy said.

"What?" Billy sat up.

"Remember how you yelled at Parker that you wanted to go see your mother?"

Billy nodded.

"You wanted his attention, so you yelled. Kenny likes to yell, too, only he does it while drinking. When he took us, he was yelling for attention."

Billy didn't look convinced, but he was listening.

"And remember how you ran away to go looking for your mother?"

Billy smiled proudly.

"Kenny was running away, taking us with him, because he needed help and didn't think anyone was listening."

"I guess he doesn't know that God will listen," Billy said thoughtfully.

*P*arker came back carrying Kenny over his shoulder, as if his cousin weighed no more than a sack of flour. With sudden insight, Izzy realized that rescuing Kenny came naturally to Parker. He'd probably been doing it since childhood. Another reason Parker made such a good fireman.

"Will Billy be okay if I put Kenny inside?" Parker tried to duck down enough to look at Billy's face. Kenny's head banged against the top of the truck. Kenny moaned but didn't wake up.

Izzy tilted Billy's head up and caressed his forehead. With the innocence of a child, Billy slumbered peacefully, looking as if the day had been typical. Brute lay in the boy's lap, a sleeping watchpuppy. No sign of stress creased Billy's brow.

"If we're careful, Billy won't even know." Gently, Izzy scooted Billy over so that he was near the steering wheel.

Parked loaded Kenny into the extended cab. Brute whined and rearranged his position.

"I'll hurry," Parker promised, getting in the truck and seeing the worry in Izzy's face as she brushed Billy's bangs out of his eyes. Then he glanced at the thickness of night that waited on the deserted interstate. "But it will be a slow hurry."

They continued on toward Kearney before finding an emergency cutoff that allowed them to turn around and head the opposite way. Parker didn't talk. He hunched forward, looking as if he was cradling the steering wheel as he tried to make out the road before him.

"Do you think my car's all right?" Izzy couldn't take the silence anymore.

"No, we're going to get you a new one. A truck." Parker gripped the steering wheel tighter.

"I don't want a truck. I like my car. We just slid into a ditch. I know it will have a little front-end damage, but surely it can be fixed."

"If we fix it, you can only drive it in summer. You'll need a truck for winters."

"Parker, what are you talking about? Why will I need a truck for winters? Plus, if I get a new vehicle I'm quite capable of choosing my own. I chose the Peugeot."

Briefly, Parker took his eyes away from the road. "Yes, that's obvious."

"Are you mad at me?" Izzy whispered with a huff. "The accident wasn't my fault. What is this, 'We'll get a new car? You can only drive in summer.' This morning—"

Parker hit the brakes, maintaining perfect control of the truck as he swerved over to the emergency lane and braked. "I was trying to make it to Grand Island before I did this. I don't want Billy to wake up and see Kenny, but. . . ."

Without another word, Parker pulled Izzy to him, planting a firm kiss on her lips, which warmed her all the way to her toes. His cold fingers came up to caress her cheeks as he took possession of her mouth.

"Parker," she murmured.

He tore his lips away. "I love you, Isobelle de la Rosa. When I found out that Kenny had taken you, I imagined that little car of yours against a tree and your pretty face sheet white, and—" Parker stopped. "I prayed, Izzy. And He answered. You were right all along. I couldn't have found you without His help. Still, I never want to worry about such a thing again. When we're married, if you want to go to Lincoln to shop, I'll take you. But if you need to get around town, it's going to be in a four-wheel drive, painted cherry red, so that if you ever go off the road I can find you."

"Married? Married!" Numbly, Izzy repeated the word as she tried to savor the warmth that marked the place his lips had been a moment earlier. Here it was, her first proposal that she might accept—

and she sat in the front seat of a truck, holding a little boy while a madman slumbered behind her. "Parker, are you proposing?"

He kissed her again, quickly, tenderly, holding one hand behind her head. Brute whimpered. Parker pulled away, looking at her, and then took his foot off the brake, giving his attention to the white road ahead. Slowly, the truck began the tedious crawl back on the interstate. As they pulled off the Grand Island exit, the grayness lifted a bit, and Izzy saw a piece of morning white sky. Another night spent in chaotic adventure. Things were looking better, even for a Monday.

"Yes, I'm proposing. Are you going to answer?" Parker asked.

"I'm cold."

"Besides that."

"I'm hungry." This should be a moment of gladness, but fatigue nestled deep. Marriage to Parker? She could imagine that. But, was he ready? Had he comes to terms with man and God? He was pretty excited about finding her and quite willing to give credit to God. But what about later, when he had time to think?

A flashing red and white beam highlighted the truck's cab. Izzy glanced at the side mirror and said a little prayer of thanks that a cruiser had them in sight. Parker pulled over into the parking lot of a fast food restaurant. Another cruiser joined the first and pulled in behind them.

Izzy stayed in the truck, holding Billy. She watched as Parker animatedly spoke with the police officers. After a few minutes they came and pulled Kenny out of the cab. Two cops shook their heads and lifted him between them to walk back to their cruiser.

Parker got behind the wheel. "We have to follow them to the station. You need to fill out a complaint; not that they intend to hold him just for kidnapping."

"I almost feel sorry for him," Izzy said.

"I used to, but after the scare he gave me today, I'm through picking up after him."

Parker parked the truck on the street in front of the Grand Island Police Station. Billy scrambled out of the truck, a bit woozy. He let Parker carry him inside. The station lobby had hard, green plastic chairs pressed against olive-colored walls reminiscent of the sixties, with dark forest tile underfoot. Izzy took Billy on her lap while Parker went to the pay phone to call his mother.

Billy looked around. "What's going on?"

"We're at the police station in Grand Island. They arrested Kenny, and we have to tell them what happened."

"Will we get to go home then?"

"I don't know." Izzy looked outside. Snow pelted against the door panes, making Izzy feel as if she were trapped inside one of those snow-scene paperweight decorations. Water globes, that's what they were called. But she could not recall one that had a jailhouse for setting.

Parker left the pay phone and walked to the counter. Two women were busy typing at desks. He cleared his throat and leaned over to ask them something. Izzy couldn't make out his words, but the answer seemed to annoy him. She watched as he flipped out his identification and tapped his finger impatiently on the counter. One of the women picked up a phone and dialed. After a moment she relayed some information to Parker, who shook his head in irritation before walking back to Izzy.

"They're really backed up." Parker shook his head. "She's calling the captain now, but it looks as if we'll need to take a room at one of the local motels and wait until a more reasonable hour to give them your statement."

"Do you think there are any rooms available? We saw lots of cars pulling into motels when Kenny got gas earlier."

"The local police keep a motel room on retainer, just in case." Parker didn't explain the "just in case" and Izzy immediately fantasized about Texas Rangers transporting criminals back to the state line or hostile witnesses held against their will until trial date.

An elevator door opened. So enthralled with her meanderings, Izzy hadn't even noticed that there was an elevator. A tall, brown-haired man with dark circles under his eyes stepped out. He walked over and shook Parker's hand, nodding at Izzy.

"I just got off the phone with—" he checked a small notebook, "an Officer Rowe. He gave me everything I need to book Kenny

Latkam. We still want a statement from you Miss de la Rosa, but that can wait until later. We've arranged for a room at the Holiday Inn. Do you know where that is?"

Parker nodded, leaning over and pulling Izzy up.

"Unfortunately, due to the weather, they've only got the one room. It has two double beds. Will that be a problem?" The captain looked at Izzy, and then Parker, as if imagining a binding between them.

"No," Parker said. "As long as they don't mind my dog. He's in the truck. We're tired. We just want to sleep. Thanks for postponing the report until tomorrow."

"Yes, that is a problem," interrupted Izzy. "Parker, I'm sorry. I trust you and all that, but . . ."

The captain nodded. "Let me make a call. There's a fire station just down the road. What with you being a fireman, I'm sure they'll let you bunk there for the rest of the night. Here's my card. Get something to eat and give me a ring."

Parker took Billy from Izzy and they went back to his truck to head for the Holiday Inn. He had stayed here twice before. Both times he'd testified concerning criminals wanted by both Mayhill and Grand Island police. He pulled in a reserved spot by the front door and lifted Billy out of the truck. The "No Vacancy" sign blinked orange and off.

❧

Snow crunched underfoot as Izzy followed Parker inside. Objecting to sharing the room had come automatically. The words had, that is. She knew her beliefs. Unfortunately, her imagination longed for something else. Still, telling him she wouldn't share a room with him, even platonically, and with Billy as a chaperone, sent him a message. He knew where he stood. Where she stood. Even her overactive imagination knew what Jesus would do.

Billy perked up the moment Parker opened the door to their room.

"I want down. This is great. Just wait until show-and-tell at school. I've never stayed in a motel before. Can I sleep in the bed by the window? Can we turn the television on?" Billy jumped from one location to another with Brute at his heels. Before Izzy or Parker could answer his questions, he peeled his coat off and tried to take a hanger down from the closet. "Hey! These hangers are broken. This one won't come down."

Parker hung up Billy's coat.

Billy ducked under his arm and went to jump on the bed. Brute followed, letting out a loud woof, and trying to keep up with Billy. The coarse orange and brown bedspread slid to the side.

"Billy, stop. People are trying to sleep."

As if a puppeteer had cut the strings, Billy settled on the bed. Brute ran back to Parker, then returned to Billy.

"It's been quite a day—er, night." Izzy straightened the bedspread. "He's wide awake now." She watched as Billy investigated under the bed. Checking her watch, she said, "Parker, it's almost five in the morning. I don't know whether to put Billy to sleep, or feed him breakfast. It's going to take a while for him to wind down."

"Do you want to go down to the restaurant and get something to eat, or shall I go over to McDonald's and pick something up?" Parker hesitated in taking off his coat.

"I'd rather eat in the restaurant. That okay with you, Billy?" She felt his forehead. He felt fine. Amazing.

"Restaurant! Sure. Do they have spaghetti?"

Poor kid, who knew when he'd get his internal clock adjusted? Spaghetti for breakfast? Truthfully, Izzy thought as she went into the rest room, Billy had been so brave, he deserved whatever he wanted. She looked in the mirror. Splashing cold water on her face, she tried to wipe some of the grime off. "Parker! Maybe we should eat in. I look terrible."

Parker's face suddenly joined hers in the mirror. He stood inches taller than she, and the effect looked like a studio portrait. "I think you look beautiful. You didn't answer my question about getting married." Parker stepped closer, propping one hand against the bathroom wall.

Izzy ducked under Parker's arm. "I think going out to eat is just the thing for Billy. You need to talk to him about Kenny, explain that your cousin is sick."

"I'll do that." Parker looked thoughtful. "You don't think Billy's going to need counseling or anything, do you?"

"Not with all the attention your family is going to give him when we get back."

"And his new cousin?"

"I'm hungry." Izzy poked him in the ribs. "Put Brute in the rest room and let's go."

The Holiday Inn restaurant was just opening for breakfast. A hostess informed them it would be a few minutes. Billy went down to his knees by a basket of giveaway toys. Parker sat down next to Izzy on the vinyl bench and put his arm comfortably about her shoulders.

"Do you know how scared I was when I figured out that Kenny had your car, with you and Billy in it?" Parker took her hand.

"Not nearly as scared as I was." Izzy leaned back, closing her eyes, enjoying the feeling of Parker toying with the sensitive skin of her palm.

"That's true. Why did you go down into the cellar?"

"I wanted to do your laundry."

"My laundry?" Parker gave her a funny look. "Whatever for?"

"Billy had spilled his soup. I wanted clean clothes for him, and I wanted to get the house in order so that nothing would distract me when you finally came home. I needed to talk to you."

"You didn't need to do my laundry."

"I know I didn't need to. I wanted to."

"What did you so desperately intend to tell me this morning?"

"I wanted to explain my actions. Parker, do you remember when you returned all those library books?"

"How could I forget? Kenny's library fine cost a month's worth of groceries."

"When you turned the books in, I didn't realize they were Kenny's."

Parker shrugged. "So you were upset at me for having massive library fines?"

"No!" Izzy disentangled her arm and turned to face him. "Remember how I chased you down and handed you back one of the books?"

"I remember."

"Did you look to see what that book was?"

"No. It belonged to Kenny. It was private."

"You're right. It was Kenny's journal. I opened it to see if there was a name, but there wasn't. I read the first paragraph by accident. It was all about suicide. I thought it was yours."

"You thought it was mine? Why?"

"I'd never seen Kenny's handwriting. I'd never even seen him in the library. You were returning the books. You paid the fine, and you were so sad. I just assumed it was yours."

"So you started pestering me because you thought I might kill myself?"

"Yes."

Parker pulled her closer to him and put his arm around her again. "I think that's sweet."

"You're not mad?"

"Of course not. I was worried that you were afraid of relationships, because of what your father had done. Now that I know you thought I had some of the same emotional problems that your father did, I can see why you were so skittish. Since we have all this out of the way, are you going to marry me?"

"Strickland," the hostess said over a microphone. It sounded unusually loud against the silence of the restaurant.

Billy ran up with a fistful of plastic toys.

"He can only take one," the hostess said.

Izzy whispered to the hostess. "He's had a really bad day."

"Yes, but—"

" 'A really bad, rotten, no-good day,' " Izzy repeated.

"I read that book." The hostess smiled as she led them to a corner booth.

❧

Izzy had crawled into the bed by the door. Billy took the one by the window. After a few minutes of horseplay, he settled down. Izzy's eyes were closing when Billy started complaining that he couldn't sleep with the outside light throwing its glare at him. They changed beds. Now, the feeble glow from the flickering motel sign shone on Izzy. She was no longer tired, and thoughts of Kenny and Parker played over and over in her mind. Breakfast had ended too quickly. The need to get a drooping Billy into bed had stalled Parker from attempting any more marriage proposals. Izzy wondered what Parker was thinking about.

She'd wanted him to propose! Only not in twenty-degree weather with his cousin passed out in the extended cab. He hadn't mentioned Julia, either. Just when had he decided to chance marriage again? He'd been so distant that day in the library. An unsmiling man with a chip on his shoulder. The suddenness of his change in disposition unsettled Izzy. Could he have found peace that quickly? And what kind of peace had he found? It was too much, too new. Maybe she could have the preacher . . .

A fierce knocking woke her up. Stumbling, she wrapped the blanket around her and went to the door. "Wake up!" Parker stood there, offering chocolate doughnuts and a carton of milk.

Izzy cleared her throat. "What time is it?"

"Half past three. You've been asleep for over seven hours."

"Have you checked the weather?"

"Yes. It's stopped snowing. The Grand Island police are waiting for us, and Billy needs to get home so we can find out about his mother. I tried calling the hospital, but no one answered the phone in Delta's room. My folks aren't home and neither are the McKennas."

"Give us a minute."

"I'll take Brute for a walk and meet you in the lobby."

Not even as a child had Izzy liked putting on the same clothes twice. "First thing I'm going to do when I get home is take a shower," she yelled at Billy from the bathroom.

"You look fine," Billy said, sounding much like an adult.

Once they were downstairs, Parker backed up Billy's words. Standing up to greet them, he touched her hair and said, "You're the best-looking woman here."

"You know," Izzy said, giving Parker a long look, "you just might have possibilities."

"Does that mean you'll marry me?"

"That means I'll allow you to buy me a diet soda from that machine over there."

Parker saluted before walking to the machine.

"If you marry Parker," Billy said, "can I still come over and eat peanut butter jelly sandwiches for breakfast . . . ?" Billy took a deep breath, and Izzy had a feeling the best part was coming. "And not clean up afterwards?" Billy finished.

Parker handed her a cold soda and answered for her. "If Izzy marries me you can come over in the morning and have pop-tarts. That's what Izzy eats. Right Izzy?" He opened the door of the motel and ushered them out.

"How do you know?"

"Whip. He's real concerned that you didn't cook much." Parker opened the truck door for her.

"He's always cooking." Izzy didn't like the disbelief on his face. "Parker, I can cook. Ask my mother. Ask Fred Rasmussen. Ask Mark Dalton." She listed everyone she could think of as they got in the truck.

Parker frowned when she mentioned Mark Dalton's name. "I don't care if you can't cook. I'm a good cook. Most firemen are." He started the engine, waiting a moment for the truck to warm up.

"He makes great peanut butter and jelly sandwiches," Billy agreed.

The brick police station seemed a more friendly place without the swirling, night snow as a background. They rolled the window down just a bit, wrapped Brute in a blanket—which he promptly shook off—and went inside. The same brown-haired captain greeted them from the elevator, and rode with them down to a tiny office. He sat behind an ancient wooden desk and handed Izzy three blue information sheets to fill out. Parker watched over her shoulder as she filled in the personal data.

The captain cleared his throat. "Your cousin's in the holding cell. If you want to see him, I've told the duty officer to let you in. It might be a while before he's transported back to Mayhill."

Parker nodded. "I'd appreciate that."

With Parker gone, it was easier to tell the captain about Kenny's behavior. Billy sat, all grown-up like, in the wooden chair next to Izzy and nodded at her words. The interview didn't take long. To Izzy's surprise, the captain was more interested in the information she'd written down than in what she told him. The last thing he did was hand her a white card that had his phone number on it and a report number.

"If you remember anything else, Miss de la Rosa, contact me." His beeper sounded and he nodded that she could leave.

Parker paced the waiting room. "Let's go."

Silently, Parker helped Izzy and Billy into the truck, his actions making it clear that he didn't feel like conversation. They left Grand Island with the distant October sun laughing down at the feeble attempt of the snow to remain a blanket. Slush flew from both sides of the truck as Parker headed for Mayhill.

"Parker, what happened?" Izzy shed her coat.

"He thought I was there to bail him out."

"Doesn't he know how much trouble he's in?"

"I don't think he does." Parker shook his head and repeated sadly, "He really thought I was there to bail him out." They drove the rest of the way home with the radio tuned to a country station focusing on heartbreak songs.

Officer Rowe waited, sitting inside his patrol car, in front of Izzy's apartment. Parker had barely stopped the car and hopped out to shake the man's hand before Francine screeched to a halt and ran toward Billy.

"Edna's at our house. I think she's having a nervous breakdown. Delta's doing fine." Francine's hand shook as she pulled Billy into her arms. "Mr. and Mrs. McKenna got home last night. I filled them in on all that's been happening."

"Grandpa?" Billy grinned. "Can I go home now?"

"Why don't you take him, Parker? I need to ask Izzy a few questions, and your mother's beat." Officer Rowe reached for the pen in his shirt pocket.

Parker looked ready to argue, but then he looked at his mother. "Izzy, is it—?"

"Go ahead, Parker. I'll be fine."

Whip came out of the house and wandered down to the conversation. "Catherine's doing fine. She's called twice and told me to tell you to take the day off. I think she's enjoying coming out of retirement."

Officer Rowe nodded. "I did stop by the library this morning on the off chance that you'd returned last night, and I'd missed you. She was mumbling something about only the coffeemaker being worth keeping and that libraries need books, not computers."

"Will you be okay, Izzy?" Parker held Billy's hand.

"I'll be fine." Izzy started to follow Officer Rowe into the house. She paused at the front door.

Parker stopped to talk to his mother. Izzy went back to the porch, sat in the rocker, and watched them. The cold seeped through her coat.

"Hurry up, Parker!" Billy climbed in the truck and hugged Brute.

"Just a minute." Parker left his mother and walked back to the porch.

"I've got some cream to go with that coffee, just inside." Whip motioned at Officer Rowe.

"I don't use cream."

"Today's a good day to start," Whip recommended, giving Officer Rowe a look of elderly authority that the policeman decided to obey.

Parker's mother drove off.

"Izzy," Parker said stepping onto the porch, "will you marry me?"

"Hmmm," Izzy said, folding her hands in front of her.

Parker got down on one knee. "Will you marry me?"

"This is happening so fast." Izzy tried to smile. He looked so handsome. She wanted to freeze the moment and sit down and admire him. It wasn't just his looks. It was a strength he had, both physically and mentally. She touched his hair and thought that although she'd just been through a terrifying couple of days she had never been happier. She squatted down and looked into his eyes. "You know how little girls dream about the man they're going to marry, write their names in the margin of notebooks, and wonder how many children they might have?"

"Somewhat," Parker acknowledged, helping her up.

"I always did that, but there was one other thing. Parker, there's not supposed to be just two in a marriage."

"What do you mean?"

"I mean, I only believe a marriage can work if God is the third member of the union."

"Now you're going a little fast. I can promise I'll think about it." Parker reached out, gently took her hand, and brushed his lips against her knuckles.

"Okay," Izzy said, "then I can promise I'll think about it too."

Parker raised one eyebrow. "For how long?"

"As long as it takes you."

$\mathcal{T}$he white dress trailed two inches onto the floor.

"Rosemary was taller than you," Francine said, the pins in her mouth moving up and down with each word. The Strickland living room looked as if a fabric-store tornado had descended.

"I'm not sure I should wear this for the centennial." Izzy studied her reflection in a handheld mirror, fingered the ancient lace around her neck, and fidgeted.

"If you're changing your mind again, you get to tell Jake." Carole bounced seven-month-old Jessica Kayla Martin up and down on her knee and cooed.

"This dress belongs in a museum," Izzy argued. "What if I spill something on it?"

"Rosemary already did," Francine said, fingering a yellowing spot near Izzy's knee. "I hope I can get that out without the material tearing. I can't believe you found this dress. I'd forgotten about that old hope chest."

Clara Bryant handed Francine the measuring tape. "That dress looks like it was made for you."

"Mom." Izzy rolled her eyes.

"She's right," Francine agreed. "I couldn't have squeezed into this bridal gown on my wedding day if I tried. You're the perfect choice to reenact the highlights of Rosemary Mayhill. What a coincidence you noticed that Rosemary's wedding day happened to fall on the same day as the centennial. We're thrilled to have you join our family." Francine smiled warmly at Clara. "I can hardly wait for Thanksgiving. Just imagine all of us around the dinner table."

"I don't know if I can do this." Izzy fingered the white lace that clung against her arm.

Walking backwards, Edna butted the screen door open and let everyone know she had been eavesdropping. "Sure you can. Isobelle, you're going to make a sensational bride. I can't believe it was just seven months ago you were going to leave." Edna laughed, watching Izzy turn red. "I heartily approve of Parker's choice for a wife. Where is he?"

"He took one look at his mother, armed with her sewing basket, and mumbled something about the garden and fertilizer." Izzy rolled her eyes. Parker hadn't wanted a big production for his wedding, but after Mayor Martin visited the library and mentioned to Izzy how nice a separate information desk would look next to the biography section, Parker knew he'd be getting married the old-fashioned way, complete with homespun trousers and suspenders.

"I went through mother's jewelry and found this." Edna held out a silver locket. "And look." Edna waved a curled, old black and white photograph in front of them. It showed Rosemary and Darby Mayhill. "See." Edna puffed, exasperated that she had to point out the minute details. "The necklace. She's wearing it."

"That's fantastic," Carole admired the picture. "Izzy, do you have everything you need for Saturday night?"

"I can't believe I let Jake talk us into getting married the evening of the centennial. There's so much going on." Butterflies hit Izzy's stomach with the force of an air force squadron.

"It's perfect," Francine said, "especially since the Wilfongs are letting Parker borrow their old buggy."

Izzy closed her eyes and tried to remember how she'd reverted from being a single woman whose greatest concern was that her cat liked liver and became, not a blushing contemporary bride, but an imitation turn-of-the-century bride.

"This dress can count as the something old." Francine finished pinning.

Carole added, "The veil is new."

"You've got something borrowed," Edna said, holding up the necklace.

"And I'll lend you something blue." Delta came in dragging a reluctant Billy along.

"I don't want to come in," Billy protested. "I want to go in the backyard and play with Parker and Brute."

"It will only take me a moment to pin his pants." Francine stepped back, releasing Izzy from scrutiny.

"Billy," Izzy said. "I really do appreciate you being our ring bearer."

"Aw, that's all right."

Edna took Billy under the shoulders and stood him on the stool Izzy had just vacated.

"You'll be the best ring bearer ever," Edna bragged.

"Mama, I gotta . . ." Billy squirmed.

"Go ahead," Delta urged.

Billy scampered down the hall.

"He's still having trouble sleeping. Doctor Taylor says he'll get over it. Other than that, he seems to have forgotten all about that day."

The women all nodded solemnly.

"Kenny's doing better," Edna defended her son. "Whip's been visiting him at the prison and seems to think Kenny figured out that it's time to grow up."

"That's wonderful." Francine hugged her sister. "We've been attending a Bible study with Whip, too. You ought to come, Edna." Francine giggled. "Do you remember when Rosemary would take us to church on Sundays? We'd be dressed in our Sunday best and afraid to move. I didn't realize how much I missed it. Worse, I don't even remember when we stopped going. We missed a Sunday, then another Sunday, and suddenly we didn't even think of attending church. Between Whip, Izzy, and Parker, it looks as if the Lord is showing us where we belong."

Izzy smiled and looked at her reflection in the mirror. In just two days, she would would be Isobelle Strickland. In the last seven months, she had watched Parker go from a questioning man sitting in a Bible study to a devout man convincing others of his newfound love. Jesus first, yourself last, and others in between. He took joy in his new freedom. He had written a letter to Julia's parents and sent them some of her belongings. His thirst for scriptural knowledge had overflowed and caught Izzy in the current. His life gave evidence of Ephesians 5:14: "Wake up, O sleeper, rise from the dead, and Christ will shine on you." Parker had been baptized just one month after proposing to Izzy for the first time. Since then, nothing had stopped his spiritual growth.

"A, B, C . . ." Billy's singsong voice echoed down the hall.

"I got his report card," Delta bragged. "Guess what subject his first grade teacher commended him in."

"Music," Carole shouted, only a breath ahead of Francine and Edna.

"As a librarian," Izzy scolded Carole, "you should have said 'reading.' "

❧

Mayor Martin sat, not in the front row, but in the second row. His neck, wrinkling like a turkey's, turned every thirty seconds while he scanned the aisle, anxiously waiting for Izzy to appear in the back door.

Parker waited by the preacher. Every time Jake Martin turned his head, Parker plucked at the bow tie collar that was choking him. Next to Parker stood Robert Parrish, Ty Horner, and Jeff Henly, all looking equally uncomfortable in their turn-of-the-century-groomsmen outfits.

A hum carried over the church. Parker scanned the audience, amazed to see that every pew was packed, and that with nowhere else available to sit, people were standing against the wall.

"What do you think is keeping her?" Jake whispered to Carole.

Parker strained to hear Carole's answer. If she had one, he wanted to know too.

"It takes a woman a while to get ready for her wedding. Especially if she's wearing an heirloom bridal gown."

"She did a great job acting like Rosemary today." For a moment, Jake relaxed.

Carole fixed Jake with a stern look. "With Parker at her side, she felt very much like a part of Rosemary's family. I can't believe you made her wear a 'Vote for Martin' pin."

Jake squirmed. "It didn't look so bad. Did you notice her saying some things during her speech that weren't in her research?"

The baby hiccuped. Carole cradled Jessica against her shoulder and nodded. "I noticed that, too. I wonder where she located more information. I had no idea that Rosemary was three years older than Darby."

The church's hum grew louder. Jake looked back and nudged Carole. "There she is."

Every head turned. Parker stood straighter. Izzy's skirt occupied almost the entire doorway. Billy and the little Summer girl waited for the nod from Francine that meant they should walk. Parker swallowed. Izzy had never looked more beautiful than tonight. And the lion's share of her beauty was inside. She'd given him so much: love, commitment, and the Lord.

Izzy gave Billy a gentle push. Billy took a few steps and then hurried back to Izzy. The little boy tugged on the lace sleeve of Izzy's bridal gown. Parker watched as Izzy listened for a moment and then nodded. Billy disappeared out the door.

"What's going on?" Jake Martin's hiss brought disapproving stares.

Over the heads of the witnesses, Izzy's eyes met Parker's. I love you, she mouthed.

I love you, too, he mouthed back.

His collar stopped choking. The organist hit one note, stopped, and leaned forward to listen. The entire church followed the woman's example.

"A, B, C, D . . ." Billy McKenna's singsong voice, at a distance, entertained the guests at Parker and Izzy's wedding.

Familiar Strangers

BY GINA FIELDS

To "Ma" and "Pa"—Thanks for accepting me as one of your own and for giving me such a wonderful husband.

$\mathcal{M}$ ama, are you going to marry Jeff?"

Sara Jennings tucked the pillow-soft comforter around her daughter's small body. "I don't know. Maybe someday."

Chloe promptly wormed her arms from beneath the binding cover. Like her mother, she didn't like feeling confined.

"That's what you always say," the four year old said.

Sara eased down to sit on the edge of the bed. "I know it is, but I haven't made my mind up yet." She scooped up a one-eyed giraffe from the foot of the bed and nestled the tired-looking toy into her daughter's waiting arms. *Poor George,* Sara thought. She really should find a button and replace his missing eye.

"But if you marry Jeff," Chloe persisted, "then I would have a daddy, like Missy and April."

Sara sighed. How did one explain to a child so young why she didn't have a daddy when her two best friends from her Sunday school class did? The same way she always did, Sara decided, wondering how much longer she could get away with the same answer.

"Sweetie, do you remember what I told you the other day about some boys and girls having two parents and some having only one?"

Chloe gave a doleful nod.

"It doesn't mean you're any less special than the children who have both a mommy and a daddy. It just means I get to love you twice as much."

Chloe dropped her gaze to the spiked hair atop the giraffe's head. "I know," she responded in an I've-heard-it-all-before tone. "But I still want a daddy."

Sara's shoulders rose and fell in dejection. Ever since Jeff Chandler, the widowed director of a Chicago homeless shelter, had asked Sara to marry him six weeks ago, she and Chloe had had this same conversation several times over. And Chloe's answer was always the same. *"I want a daddy."* Not *"I want Jeff to be my daddy."*

Chloe's vague answer left Sara wondering if Chloe wanted Jeff, in particular, for a father or if she simply wanted *"a daddy."*

Since the marriage proposal, Sara had watched closely for signs of a developing parent-child relationship between Jeff and Chloe, but so far she'd seen little evidence of any. Sure, Jeff and Chloe were close, in an uncle-niece sort of way. But that special bond, like Jeff shared with his own two adolescent children, simply wasn't there.

And that alone gave Sara pause in making her decision.

If and when she ever decided to marry, the prospective husband would have to acknowledge and accept he was getting a package deal—a wife and daughter. Sara would rather die an old maid than have Chloe feel inferior to stepsiblings. Or anyone else, for that matter.

Sara leaned over, and Chloe rubbed noses with her mother. "Good night. Sleep tight," Sara chimed. "And don't let the bed bugs bite!" they finished together.

Giggling, Chloe reached up and rewarded her mother with a hug and a butterfly kiss on the cheek. Then, turning to her side, she snuggled George the Giraffe to her chest and closed her eyes.

Sara reached over to turn off the yard-sale lamp that sat on the nightstand she had borrowed from her landlady, but then she paused to study her daughter. Chloe's long, tawny lashes curled against rosy cheeks, and her hair had grown so that it flowed like silk around her shoulders. Hard to believe they'd already celebrated her fourth birthday. Where was the baby that had nuzzled at her breast, cuddled on her shoulder, offered her toothless grins? Where had the last four years gone?

Into one mindless day after another, Sara silently answered her own question. A cycle of perpetual routine she had come to accept as her destiny.

And today had been no different.

She had gotten up at six A.M., showered and dressed for work, and had breakfast with Chloe and Evelyn Porter, the regal, elderly lady from whom Sara rented two rooms. Then Sara had bundled up Chloe in a thick sweater and warm toboggan—because, even in late May, Illinois mornings could be brisk—and together they had walked to one of the four houses Sara cleaned weekly in the upscale Chicago suburb where they lived.

While Sara scrubbed toilets, dusted furniture, and battled cobwebs, Chloe, as usual, had been content watching one of her favorite cartoon videos or playing with one of the games Sara brought along. But as always, guilt had pricked Sara's conscience at least twice that day because her daughter spent so much time entertaining herself.

As a single mom, Sara found meager comfort knowing she was doing the best she could do. After all, any plans she had made, any goals she had set for herself, had been ripped from her grasp five years ago. Now her plans and goals all centered on Chloe.

When Sara had finished her household tasks, she and Chloe walked back to Mrs. Porter's, where Sara helped her landlady prepare supper. Then, after the three shared the evening meal and the kitchen was put back in order, had come Sara's favorite time of day, when she tucked Chloe into bed with a hug and a prayer.

Another ordinary day. A day like any other. Nothing grand or spectacular about it.

In fact, Sara knew of only one truly grand and spectacular day since she'd come to live with Mrs. Porter almost five years ago. That was the day Chloe had been born. That day, that hour, that single moment had marked a new beginning for Sara. The instant she looked into her daughter's eyes, she knew God was giving her a second chance at life. She could either take it or throw it back in His face and continue mourning the life she had lost.

Sara had decided to take it.

And now, looking down at her daughter's face, she didn't have one single shred of regret. Reaching over, she brushed a strand of hair from Chloe's cheek and she was reminded, not for the first time, how different she and her daughter were. Chloe had straight blond hair and huge sapphire-blue eyes, while Sara had corkscrew curly brown hair and light brown eyes. Except for their slight frames, Sara couldn't find a single physical similarity between her and her child.

Did Chloe favor her father? Only God knew.

Pulling the comforter up a few more inches on Chloe's shoulders, Sara shook off the melancholy spirit stealing over her. She would not waste time feeling sorry for herself; she had too much to be thankful for: a man who loved her enough to want to spend the rest of his life with her; a friend in Evelyn Porter, who had offered Sara a home when she was homeless; and a perfectly healthy daughter who gave her a reason to face one tedious day after another. A surge of love rose in Sara's chest and almost overflowed in the form of tears. All things considered, she was pretty well blessed.

She leaned down and planted a soft kiss on her daughter's cheek. Chloe's eyes fluttered open, then slowly drifted down again as the child slipped from twilight sleep into dreamland. Sara switched off the lamp and crept from the room.

Stifling a yawn, she went down the red-carpeted steps leading to the first floor. There was still plenty she needed to do: fold the laundry, unload the dishwasher. But those things could wait until morning. This had been a long day, and Mrs. Porter's chamomile tea smelled too delicious. All Sara wanted to do was pour herself a cup of the pungent brew and curl up with the suspense novel her landlady had brought home from the library that day.

Massaging her nape, Sara padded in socked feet across the marble foyer floor into a kitchen dimly lit by a single twenty-five-watt bulb that glowed from the range hood. Sara smiled as she ambled to the stove. Mrs. Porter might be "financially secure," as the refined lady so modestly put it, but when it came to cutting monetary corners, she was downright miserly.

Sara, on the other hand, was frugal because she had to be. She reached into the cabinet for a cup and saucer. Someday, when she saved enough money to buy herself and Chloe a home of their own, light would be an item on which she would not scrimp. Not only on the inside of the house, but on the outside as well. Abundant sunlight and wide-open spaces. One day, she and Chloe would have both—if Sara had to scrub a dozen toilets a day to get them.

"Sara?"

She was stirring a teaspoon of honey into her tea when Mrs.

Porter's genteel, high-pitched voice filtered into the kitchen from the adjoining room.

"I'll be right there." Sara put her spoon in the sink.

"You may want to hurry!"

Frowning, Sara glanced over her shoulder at the open doorway leading to the adjoining family room. Were her ears deceiving her or was that a note of urgency she'd heard in Mrs. Porter's voice?

"Please," Mrs. Porter added in what sounded like an afterthought, as though she'd suddenly realized she had stepped out of character by using a tone other than her usually calm and proper one.

Gingerly balancing her cup on her saucer, Sara headed for the door.

Her landlady sat in a plush recliner, her eyes riveted on the television screen. The glow from a nearby floor lamp's low-wattage bulb reflected off her short white hair like a silver halo.

"Is something wrong, Mrs. Porter?" Sara asked.

Her gaze fixed on the screen, Mrs. Porter said, "I think you'll want to see this."

When Sara glanced toward the TV, she thought she knew why Mrs. Porter had called to her. On the screen was one of the most peaceful coastal scenes Sara had ever seen. Foamy waves lapped lazily over cream-colored sand, then slipped quietly, almost reluctantly, it seemed, back out to sea. Vigilant seagulls sailed over the water, and restless palm leaves danced in the wind.

Mrs. Porter knew Sara loved the ocean, knew she dreamed of seeing it one day for herself. Every time she saw a picture of the rocky cliffs bordering the Pacific or read about the mysteries of the blue Atlantic, longing filled her heart. But only in her imagination could she walk the endless stretches of beach, revel in cool water tugging at her ankles, lift her face to the wind's salty kiss.

Her shoulders rose and fell as a wistful sigh escaped her chest. *Someday,* she told herself. *Someday . . .*

A suave-looking gentleman appeared on the screen. The wind kicked up the front of his well-groomed gray hair as he strolled up the beach. "We come to you tonight from the tranquil beaches of Quinn Island, South Carolina," he said. "A place where southern hospitality is in abundant supply, and residents of this small, close-knit community pride themselves on maintaining one of the lowest crime rates in the Southeast."

He stopped and squared off to face the camera. "But almost five years ago, on the night of August eighth, tragedy struck Quinn Island with as much force as the battering winds of a class five hurricane, when one of their own, Lydia Anne Quinn, disappeared *without a trace*." The face of an attractive young woman, smiling like she held the world by its reins, flashed on the screen.

Sara stared at the screen for a moment in stunned silence. Then she blinked, and her world tilted, teetered on its side for a few precarious seconds, then tumbled from its axis, sending her stomach into a wild tailspin. She felt the blood drain from her face, and the cup and saucer slipped from her limp fingers. She was vaguely aware of searing liquid scalding her denim-clad right knee and seeping through the wool of her socks.

This can't be happening, she told herself, thinking any second now she'd wake up. When a sharp edge of broken china penetrated her sock and bit into her heel, she realized she was not dreaming. The day she had both longed for and feared had finally arrived. And life as she knew it was about to change. *Forever.*

Because the face on the TV screen . . . was hers.

⮞

Still strong and agile at seventy-two, Mrs. Porter had helped Sara to the sofa before the younger woman completely collapsed, then fetched a Band-Aid for Sara's bleeding heel. The two women now sat side by side, holding hands, as they watched bits and pieces of Sara's life—the one she'd lived before waking up in a Chicago hospital five years ago.

Once Sara had watched every missing-person show televised in the Chicago area, thinking maybe, just maybe, a story would evolve that would lead to her identity. Even if she didn't have a family looking for her, she figured, surely *someone* would have noticed her absence—a boss, a coworker, a friend.

But, after a while, when episode after episode passed without revealing anything that might be of consequence to her past life, she grew weary of the waiting, the anticipation, and then the letdown. So she'd stopped watching, stopped waiting for someone to find her, and she accepted that whoever might have known her in her past life had either given up searching—or hadn't cared enough to ever begin to search. Now, here she was, on national TV. Someone *had* cared enough. Enough that they had never given up looking for her.

Aside from the throbbing of her now-bandaged heel, she was too shocked to feel anything but numb.

"Lydia Anne Quinn led a charmed and privileged life," came the skilled voice of the screen host. "She was born twenty-nine years ago on April second, the oldest daughter of William Quinn, the partner in a successful charter fishing business, and his wife, Margaret Quinn, a former teacher who left the classroom to become a full-time mom after Lydia was born."

"I'm twenty-nine years old," Sara whispered in awe. Her doctor had estimated her age, and every year Mrs. Porter insisted Sara celebrate her birthday with Chloe. Just last month, Sara had celebrated her twenty-seventh.

But she wasn't twenty-seven—she was twenty-nine. And her birthday wasn't April twenty-sixth, like Chloe's—it was April second.

After five years in ageless limbo, she finally had a beginning.

A portrait of herself and three other people, obviously her family, flashed on the screen. Her father appeared to be only a couple inches taller than her mother. He had the same curly brown hair and light brown eyes as Sara. Her sister, a tall, willowy blond, favored her mother.

Sara studied the portrait intently to see if something in one of the faces would kindle a spark of recognition, a sense of connection. But she felt nothing. They were all total strangers to her.

"Lydia was a high achiever," the host continued. "A straight-A student, head cheerleader, and homecoming queen her senior year in high school. She graduated summa cum laude from South Carolina State University. At the time of her disappearance, she owned and operated Lydia's Boutique, a prosperous dress shop located on Quinn Island's mainland. And she was planning to marry this man"—the scene changed to a handsome young man—"Attorney Daniel Matthews, who was the last person known to have talked to Lydia the night of her disappearance."

Sara's breath caught in her throat. She had been engaged . . . to an attorney . . . and he was *beautiful.* He wore his dark brown hair cut short on the sides, a little longer on top, and combed back in a side part—with the exception of one rakish lock that dipped toward his right brow. His wedge-shaped jaw, olive complexion, and prominent cheekbones hinted at an ancestry other than pure Anglo. Native American, maybe? His brown eyes held a touch of sadness that made Sara's pounding heart roll over.

"Lydia was on her way home from New York," the young attorney explained to the off-camera interviewer. "She'd driven up three days before to attend some fashion shows and order new designs for her dress shop. Normally, she would have flown, but she'd just purchased a new car the week before and wanted to drive it."

His educated southern drawl had a smooth, velvet-edged quality that captivated Sara. Without thought, she pulled her hands free from Mrs. Porter's and leaned forward a couple of inches, her own hands clasped tightly in her lap. Daniel Matthews was seated, she noticed, on a sofa in someone's living room. Whose home was he in? His? Hers? Her parents'?

"Her mother usually took these trips with her," he went on, "but Mrs. Quinn had undergone hip surgery a few days before, and she wasn't able to go along. Her sister Jennifer stayed behind to run the shop. So this was a solo trip for Lydia. Her first."

An indefinable emotion clouded his features. He paused, dropping his gaze to some point below the camera lens. Seconds hung in suspension while he appeared to struggle with his private thoughts. Then he raised his head and lifted his shoulders a few inches, as though summoning the fortitude to plow ahead. "Before she left, I bought her a cellular phone so she could check in with her parents or me while she was on the road, or call someone if her car broke down.

"The night she was expected home, she phoned me around eleven o'clock. She had crossed the South Carolina state line, but she had run into a traffic jam. She said she was going to get off the expressway somewhere above Darlington and try to work her way around it.

"I knew some of those rural roads could be deserted, especially so late at night, so I tried to talk her into staying on the interstate. But she told me not to worry, that she had a map."

He closed his eyes, and a raw grief flickered across his face. He swallowed hard, then wet his lips. Somehow, Sara sensed he was steeling himself against his next words.

Finally, he opened haunted eyes. "The last words she said to me were, 'I'll call you when I get home. I love you. Good-bye.'" His voice, as he delivered his final statement, was raspy with emotion.

Sara took a deep shuddery breath and pressed a trembling hand to her chest. Unexpected tears warmed her eyes. This man had loved her. Deeply. She could see it in his grieving expression, hear it in his tortured voice. And she had loved him, had told him so just before something dark and horrible had taken away what might have been a precious memory.

The scene switched to a foreign-made sports car sitting alongside a dark, deserted stretch of highway. The driver's door stood open. The host stepped into view on the right side of the screen.

"But Lydia didn't make it home that night," he said. "Instead, Daniel answered a knock on his door three hours later to find the Quinn Island sheriff and a deputy standing on his doorstep. The news they had to deliver was not good. They had received a call from the Darlington Police Department. Lydia's car had been found, abandoned, alongside a sparsely populated stretch of highway outside the Darlington city limits."

As the host spoke, a patrol car pulled up and stopped behind the sports coupe. Two actors portraying police officers got out and approached the abandoned vehicle cautiously. They continued playing their role while the host resumed the story.

"The driver's door was standing open, and Lydia's purse and cellular phone were found on the front passenger seat. Next to the flat rear tire on the passenger's side, a crowbar with traces of hair and blood was found."

Sara's hand rose and touched the jagged scar on her left temple, the one doctors had said probably robbed her of her memory. Had the crowbar delivered the blow? What about the four-inch laceration on the back of her head and the one over her right ear, the bruises and broken bones . . . ?

Like hot water breaking into a boil, anger exploded in Sara's chest. The crowbar had not delivered the damaging blows to her defenseless body, the hands that held it had.

The doctors had told her she'd been brought into the hospital in the wee hours of August twelfth. According to the story unfolding on the TV screen, that had been a little more than two days after her disappearance. For forty-eight hours she must have been in the hands of her assailants. During that time, she had been stripped of all she was, all she had been, all she had loved.

A raw ache rose in her throat. Closing her eyes, she wrapped her arms around her waist and bit down hard on her lower lip. Faceless demons still haunted her. Demons that had robbed her of her memory, her past. The results of their actions, however, had left an irrevocable mark upon her life.

She squeezed her eyes shut tighter and started rocking, trying to shut out the harsh reality that wrapped around her like a fog. She had a family who loved her . . . and a fiancé who was still searching for her.

After almost five years of struggling to put some sort of life together for herself and her daughter, she had been found. She knew with certainty she was going home, but she also knew that things would never be as they once were. Not for her. Not for her family. Not for a man named Daniel Matthews. Because she was not the same woman who had left them half a decade ago. A sob tore from her throat. Could her parents, her sister, her fiancé accept the woman she had become—and the horrible things that had happened to her?

She felt Mrs. Porter's arms slip around her shoulders, and she turned her face into the crook of the older woman's neck. She was going home to a place she knew nothing about, a family of strangers, and a man she had promised to marry. What kind of homecoming would it be?

And what would they think about Chloe?

❨ 2 ❩

*A*t a television station in Manhattan, Daniel Matthews stood in the *Without a Trace* studio room, his gaze on a big-screen television boxed inside a pewter-gray wall. Arms crossed and feet braced shoulders' width apart, he watched as the story of his fiancée's disappearance unfolded. Behind him, eight telephone operators, stationed in two rows of four each, sat at individual computer terminals, headsets in place, waiting for the first call to come in.

Odd, Daniel thought as Lydia's picture gave way to a portrait of her and her family, *how losing someone you love can make time stand still.* He still looked for her face in every crowd and around every corner. Still surfed the net for countless hours in hopes of finding a clue to what had happened to her. Still waited each night for the phone to ring, for her to tell him she had made it home safely after all. At least once each day, he relived that fateful night when she'd been abducted from her car on a deserted stretch of highway north of Darlington.

He scrubbed a weary hand down his face, his mind buzzing through the brutal days that had followed. After six months of relentless searching proved futile, the sheriff had tried to convince Daniel the worst had happened. That Lydia had been killed and whatever was left of her would probably never be found. But Daniel refused to believe that. Only when a body was discovered and positively identified would he accept that she was gone from him forever.

"How're you holding up?"

Daniel looked to his right, wondering how long Bob Siler, the head producer of *Without a Trace,* had been standing next to him. "I'm okay," Daniel answered, massaging the back of his neck.

"Really? You don't look okay."

A grin pulled at one corner of Daniel's mouth. He knew Bob's words were spoken out of concern and not criticism. Their frequent communications over the last few months had led to an amicable friendship.

"It's just the anticipation," Daniel said. "You'd think after five years I'd be used to it."

But he wasn't, and he doubted he ever would be. Every time a clue trickled in, hinting at what might have happened to Lydia, his reaction was always the same. Sweaty palms, a stiff neck, and a heart that pounded so hard his ears burned.

Then would come the letdown, a gut-wrenching twist to his insides that left his chest feeling hollow when the clue led to another dead-end.

"Daniel, you know what the chances are," Bob said as though reading Daniel's mind.

"Yeah, I know," Daniel replied. *Slim to none.* That's what everyone, including Bob, had told Daniel. In fact, from the start, Bob had been so negative about a program segment on Lydia's abduction, Daniel had been shocked when the producer had called two months ago to tell him the network had decided to air the story.

Of course, six months' worth of weekly calls from Daniel to the station might have had something to do with the decision. The show's producers had eventually figured out the persistent attorney wasn't going to give up until the story of his fiancée's disappearance was told. Since all else had failed, Daniel figured getting her picture on national TV was his best chance of finding her—maybe his last chance.

"I just want you to be prepared," Bob said.

Daniel chose not to respond. How did one prepare himself for the unknown? He jammed his fists into his pockets to keep from drying his damp palms on his dark dress slacks. "How long does it usually take before the calls start coming in?"

"It varies. Sometimes immediately. Sometimes a couple of hours. We've even had a few come in several days after a program aired."

A picture of Lydia's dress shop flashed on the screen, and a painful knot rose in Daniel's throat. The wedding gown she'd planned to wear less than a month after the date of her disappearance still hung in the back of that shop. Would he ever see her march down the aisle in it?

A buzzer indicated an incoming call. Pinpricks of anticipation raced up the back of Daniel's neck. Both men turned, but only Bob hurried to the operator who had answered the call. Daniel stood waiting, praying, his head throbbing from a sudden rush of blood.

Then Bob looked Daniel's way and motioned him over. Daniel sprinted across the room to join Bob, who was huddled over the operator as she transferred information onto the computer.

"What did you say your name was, ma'am?" the operator asked, then typed in *Elizabeth Bradford.*

"And you're calling from where?"

Riverbend, Illinois.

"I know that area," Bob mused. "It's a ritzy suburb north of Chicago."

Ritzy, Daniel repeated to himself. Lydia would like ritzy. He held his breath.

"You said Ms. Quinn looks like someone you know?" the operator continued.

Yes.

Daniel clenched a fist, ready to punch the air with glee.

She looks like Sara Jennings, my cleaning lady.

Daniel's mounting hopes dissipated like a warm vapor in a cold wind. The last thing Lydia would be was a cleaning lady. She hated housework. In fact, before her disappearance, she had paid someone else to clean her one-bedroom apartment once a week to keep from having to do it herself.

The sudden drop from elation to disappointment left Daniel shaky. He ran trembling fingers through his hair.

Bob glanced back over his shoulder. "You don't think it's worth following up?"

Daniel released his pent-up breath with force. "No. The last thing you'd find Lydia doing for a living is cleaning houses."

"Anything's possible," Bob said. "I think we should at least look into it."

"Sure." Daniel hunched his shoulders. "Why not? Like you said, 'Anything's possible.'"

But Lydia? A cleaning lady? He didn't think so.

Spirits weighed down, he lumbered back across the room and resumed his vigil in front of the large-screen television and waited for the next call to come in.

❧

Daniel closed the lid on his suitcase. Last night, he'd waited at the studio for two hours after the show ended. Aside from the strange call from the lady in Riverbend, Illinois, there had been no other calls. Bob had told him not to lose hope so soon, but the sympathy in the producer's eyes had belied his true thoughts. *Lydia's gone,* his expression had said. *Time to move on.*

Daniel ran a weary hand over his face. Maybe Bob was right. Maybe it was time to move on. Daniel just didn't know how without Lydia.

A knock sounded on his motel room door. He opened it to find the bellhop, standing at attention, his uniform as fresh and crisp as a navy captain's.

"Your cab is ready, sir."

"Thank you." Daniel turned to retrieve his suitcase.

"I'll get that, sir." In the blink of an eye, the bellhop slipped past Daniel and claimed the luggage.

Unaccustomed to being waited on, Daniel checked various pockets for his keys, wallet, and plane ticket to keep from cracking his knuckles, a nervous habit he'd picked up shortly after Lydia's disappearance. Before stepping outside into the hallway, he slung his navy blazer over his shoulder and turned one last time to scan the opulent suite the *Without a Trace* network had provided for him. Lydia would have loved the room. The blue velvet window dressings, the mottled marble fireplace, the plush white carpet. She was a woman at home in elegance.

In his mind's eye he saw her pirouetting in delight around the room like a gypsy, a long red dress swirling around her slim ankles and her shiny highlighted hair flowing about her pale shoulders. When she was in a good mood, her laughter and energy were contagious.

"Did I forget something, sir?"

Reluctantly, Daniel turned his attention back to the bellhop standing a few feet down the hall. "No. I was just double-checking, but I think we got everything."

When he looked back into the room, his dancing gypsy was gone.

He pulled a deep breath into his tightening chest, then slowly released a long sigh. "Good-bye, my love," he whispered.

As he closed the door, an eerie sense of finality swept through him. And as he walked away, the words *Move on, Daniel. Time to move on,* seemed to follow him down the hall.

He pressed a generous tip into the bellhop's hand and slid into the car. "Kennedy Airport," he told the cabby. The driver eased his car out into the noisy New York traffic.

They had barely traveled a mile when Daniel's cell phone rang. He dug it out of his blazer pocket and flipped it open. "Hello?"

Silence filled his ear.

"Hello?" he repeated after five seconds.

Silence still, but he thought he heard someone breathing on the other end of the line.

"This is Daniel Matthews. May I help you?"

The line went dead.

Frowning, he pulled the phone away from his ear and pressed the caller ID button. He didn't recognize the number, but the area code triggered something in his memory. After a moment of thought, he realized it was the same area code as the woman who had called the studio the night before. But Daniel wasn't sure about the rest of the number. Could it be the same woman? If so, why was she calling him and not the TV station? And how did she get his number?

Only one way to find out. He hit the button that dialed the number on the display screen.

"Hello." The voice sounded like that of an elderly woman.

"Hello," he returned. "This is Daniel Matthews."

"Yes, Mr. Matthews," came a cheerful reply. "My name is Evelyn Porter. It's so good to finally speak to you."

"Thank you," he said, totally confused. "How did you get this number?"

"Directory assistance."

"Of course," he said, remembering he was having his home calls forwarded to his cellular phone. "What can I do for you?"

"Nothing, really."

Daniel clenched his teeth. Was this someone's idea of a joke? If so, he was in no mood. Tempering the rising anger in his voice, he said, "Then why did you call?"

"I didn't."

"Then who did?"

"The young lady who lives with me."

"And that would be . . . ?"

A slight pause, then, "Why don't I just let you talk to her."

Daniel waited while a muffled, inaudible conversation took place on the other end, then a faint click sparked a distant but distinct memory.

An earring. Lydia's earring always clicked on the receiver when she answered the phone. He sat up straighter in the seat.

"Hello?"

His lungs shut down and his heart slammed against his chest. The voice was hers.

"Hello," she repeated a little louder. "Is . . . anyone there?"

"Lydia? Is that you?"

"I . . . think so."

I think so? What kind of answer was that?

The pressure against his ribs reminded him he wasn't breathing. Slowly, he exhaled. "I don't understand."

"It's a bit complicated, Mr. Matthews. I'd rather not get into it over the phone."

Conflicting emotions tumbled through him. She'd called him *Mr. Matthews*. So formal. So impersonal. Was this another false alarm?

Someone looking for a generous handout or public attention? He'd had enough of those in the past five years to last a dozen lifetimes.

"Mr. Matthews?"

But the voice. It was a bit timid and cautious sounding for Lydia, and the southern accent had a slight northern clip. But the sweet-as-honey intonation and the soft-as-silk inflection were definitely hers.

"Are you still there, Mr. Matthews?"

"Yes. Yes, I'm still here. I'm just . . . a little confused." *Make that a lot confused,* he added to himself.

"I'm sorry. I guess I do need to explain a little."

"Please."

He heard a slow, steady intake of breath. "Almost five years ago, sixteen days after Lydia Quinn's disappearance, I woke up in a Chicago hospital. I had been in a coma at least two weeks."

"Why? What happened?"

"I don't know . . . exactly. I couldn't remember." At least four seconds drifted by. "I still can't."

"*Still* can't?"

"That's right."

Daniel searched his mind and came up with only one possible answer. "Amnesia?"

"Yes."

His eyes slid shut. That explained everything. Why she hadn't come home. Why she hadn't called. She hadn't known *where* to come or *who* to call.

Opening his eyes, he pulled a pen from his shirt pocket and his plane ticket from the inside pouch of his blazer. "How do I get there?"

"Before I tell you, Mr. Matthews—"

"Daniel, please," he said with a grimace. If he didn't know better, he'd think he was talking to a stranger. He paused in the midst of balancing the plane ticket on his knee as reality sank in. They *were* strangers. At least he was to her. Right now, she didn't know him from anyone else she might pass on the street. How long before she regained her memory? *Would* she ever regain her memory?

"Okay. Daniel." Her wary voice interrupted his disturbing

thoughts. "I think you and I should meet first and make absolutely certain I am Lydia before we get anyone's hopes up."

Get anyone's hopes up? She had to be kidding. His were already flying way above reach. But she had the right idea. Why get her parents' and sister's hopes up until he was absolutely certain she was Lydia? And when he saw her, he would be.

"I agree," he said.

"And would you please not notify *Without a Trace* yet?"

Her request struck him as odd. She had never been one to shun attention. She would have wanted the whole world to know she'd been found. But now was not the time to ponder her reasons for wanting secrecy. He'd agree to anything to get her to tell him where she was. "Okay. If that's what you want."

"It is."

He trapped the ticket between his knee and the heel of his hand, ready to write down her address.

"I have my reasons," she added, as though she owed him some sort of explanation.

A chilly finger of foreboding slid up Daniel's spine. What had happened to her in the last five years? What had she done with herself? What kind of life had she led?

"This is where I live," came the mysterious yet oh-so-familiar voice.

Daniel snapped to attention and started writing down the information.

❧

Sara hung up the phone softly. She couldn't believe it. She had actually talked to someone from her past. Last night, after the show had ended, she had phoned directory assistance and gotten Daniel Matthews's telephone number, but she had waited until the morning to call. She'd needed time to think, time to figure out the terms on which she would meet him. After all, she had more to think about than herself. She had Chloe.

"Well," Mrs. Porter said from where she sat beside Sara on the family room sofa, "when do we get to meet Mr. Matthews?"

"Soon, I imagine. He's on his way to Kennedy Airport right now. He was in New York for the premier show last night and was on his way to catch his flight back to Quinn Island this morning. But now he's changing his plans. He's going to take the first flight he can get to Chicago. He could be here as early as this afternoon."

Rising, Sara crossed her arms and wandered to the tall window beside the stone fireplace. Sweeping aside the sheers that hung beneath tapered blue damask draperies, she looked out at the small oasis of flowers she had created. The miniature roses climbing a cast-iron fence were just beginning to burst open in brilliant shades of pink. The red azaleas lining the edge of the yard were in full bloom, and the blossoming impatiens in the small flower bed surrounding a cedar bird feeder nodded lazily in the crisp morning breeze.

In her other life had she loved the feel of the earth sifting through her hands? Had she found one of the most amazing things in the world planting a seed and watching it grow?

Had she believed in God?

Does Daniel?

So many questions to be answered. So much territory to be rediscovered. Sara had always thought if this moment ever came, she'd be ready. Now that it had, she wasn't so sure.

Mrs. Porter touched Sara's shoulder. Sara turned to face the closest thing to a family she and her daughter knew. With wise eyes full of understanding, the older woman clasped Sara's hands. "Sara, dear, I know you're scared. But, remember, God sees the big picture. This will all unfold according to His plan."

"I know," Sara said past the mixed emotions that clogged her throat. God had brought her through too much over the past five years for her not to realize He had a hand in her being found. She squeezed Mrs. Porter's soft hands. "It's going to be hard leaving you."

Mrs. Porter's eyes grew misty. "I know. But you'll soon meet a man who loves you so much he's never stopped searching for you. You have a family who's grieved for you for almost five years. Just think of the joy you'll bring them all when you return to them. And you know I'll always be here for you and Chloe, no matter what. I hope you'll remember that."

Sara's own eyes teared. "You can count on it."

The two women embraced in a hug that Sara knew marked the ending of one era of her life and the beginning of another. This heartfelt gesture was a symbol of time shared, joy experienced, and blessing, both great and small, they had brought to one another. The next would be to say good-bye.

3

ere we are," Daniel told the Chicago taxi driver.

The cabbie shot him an "I-think-I-know-where-I'm-going" look in the rearview mirror as he turned into the entrance of Twin Oaks Subdivision in Riverbend, Chicago.

Unperturbed by the driver's obvious irritation, Daniel grasped the back of the front passenger seat and slid forward, reading the house numbers. After his phone conversation with Lydia that morning, he had managed to secure a flight to Chicago almost immediately. Now, here he was, four hours later, on the brink of a long-awaited reunion with her.

The empty years of searching were almost over.

He craned his neck to read a number partially hidden by a tall flowering bush. Nothing about the affluent neighborhood surprised him. Class suited Lydia, and everything about the stately homes lining the well-kept street bespoke class. He was sure she had fit in well here.

"There it is," he said, pointing to the third house up the street. "Fourteen-oh-one."

The driver swerved up to the curb in front of the colonial-style brick home. Passing the cabbie a generous bill, Daniel said, "Keep the change," and vaulted from the car, hauling his overnight bag behind him.

He strode up the sidewalk and hurdled the two steps leading to the front stoop in one smooth motion. Without pause, he rang the doorbell. Impatiently, he straightened his blazer and finger-combed his hair. When the doorknob rattled, every muscle in his body tensed.

But the woman who opened the door wasn't Lydia. She was an

elderly lady with a short crop of silvery-white hair, immaculately applied makeup, and an out-of-style but elegant dark green polyester dress. Pearl-studded earrings as big around as quarters hung from her earlobes, and a generous row of pearls circled her aged neck.

He raised his brows. "Mrs. Porter?"

As she inclined her regal head, a welcoming smile brought a youthful sparkle to her light blue eyes. "So nice to meet you, Mr. Matthews." Her gaze swept down his body and back up again, making him feel like a ten-year-old under wash-up inspection before Sunday dinner.

When her eyes once again met his, one appraising brow inched up her forehead. "I must say, the television cameras didn't do you justice."

Daniel appreciated the woman's attempt at friendly banter, but at the moment he didn't want to waste precious minutes on idle small talk. "Thank you. Is Lydia here?"

"Yes. She's upstairs." Mrs. Porter stepped back, and Daniel entered the foyer. A crystal chandelier hung from a high ceiling, and the walls were dressed in burnished gold wallpaper. The mottled marble floor and the stairway's heavy wooden railing were polished to a glossy sheen. The faint scent of lemon oil and potpourri hung in the air. Obviously someone, perhaps the maid, had recently been cleaning.

Mrs. Porter closed the door and stepped around him. "I'll show you to the living room," she said, then led him toward double doors at the end of the foyer. Glancing back over her shoulder, she added, "Better known in my day as the courting parlor," and sent him a saucy wink.

Daniel couldn't help grinning. He had a feeling he was going to like this woman. The engaging way she combined flippant flirtation with elegant sophistication settled one or two of the butterflies swarming around in his stomach.

She swept open the mahogany doors and he followed her into a spacious, richly adorned room. In the center of the room, two Queen Anne sofas dressed in silken ivory faced each other over an ornately carved coffee table. On one side of the sofas, a mahogany baby grand stood in the slanted light of two tall-paned windows dressed in red velvet. On the other side, floor-to-ceiling shelves offered a versatile library of books.

"I'll go get Sa—" She paused an instant. "Excuse me, *Lydia*." With that, she turned and left the room.

Daniel drew in a deep breath and released it through pursed lips. The moment he'd hoped, longed, and prayed for over the past five years was finally within his grasp.

He paced the floor for a couple of minutes, glancing at the open doorway every ten seconds or so. Then he wandered to one of the tall windows next to the piano. To his far right, he noticed a well-tended flower garden. A hungry bird, pecking away at lunch, perched on the lip of a cedar bird feeder that served as a centerpiece for a circle of impatiens. Bits and pieces of seed husks drifted down like snowflakes to the colorful blossoms below.

One corner of Daniel's mouth tipped upward. Lydia liked flowers—the ones with long stems or in vases, the kind he used to send her in celebration of a special day.

All at once, gooseflesh raced across the back of his neck. Slowly, expectantly, he turned, and the vision before him stole his breath.

Her free-flowing brown curls fell in a soft cloud around her face and shoulders. Her delicate skin glowed with candescent purity. Her amber eyes captured his soul.

Was this really Lydia?

Her heart-shaped face and petite build matched that of his beloved, but that's where the likeness ended. All the classic professionalism that represented Lydia's ambitious character—highlighted hair blown and gelled straight and turned under at the shoulders, enough makeup to camouflage what she considered every minor flaw, a form-fitting business suit and matching pumps—were all gone.

This woman was dressed in a simple salmon-pink dress that molded her tiny waist, then blossomed into a full skirt of countless crinkling folds that flowed freely over her slim hips and swirled around her tiny ankles, exposing only her small, ivory-slippered feet. No long, polished fingernails. No jewelry, except a basic gold-tone watch with a white leather band. Her earrings, if she wore any, were hidden by her hair.

While Daniel thought this sprite of a woman charming, he knew, beyond a fraction of a doubt, Lydia would never dress in such a down-to-earth and casual way.

Had he been wrong? Had he come here with high hopes only to find the wrong woman?

He knew exactly how to find out. He took a guarded step forward.

❧

As he came nearer, Sara clasped her hands tighter to keep them from shaking. Since last night, she had imagined what this moment would be like at least a hundred times. But not even in her most vivid dreams had she captured the reality.

His mere presence was overpowering; it wrapped around her like a warm blanket after a long, cold walk in the rain. His hopeful expression drew her. His seeking brown eyes mesmerized her.

How did I survive these last five years without you?

The thought stole into her mind, scattering her rehearsed reserve. When he stopped with a meager foot between them, she had to remind herself to breathe. He said nothing, just stood staring at her. When the weight of his perusal became more than she could bear, she bit her lower lip and ducked her head.

She watched his right hand rise slowly, felt his forefinger curl beneath her chin. He lifted her head until she once again looked into those penetrating dark eyes.

"Smile for me," he said.

His voice tremored, and her heart contracted. But his request baffled her. She searched his face, then opened her mouth to ask *Why?*

"Please," he said, intercepting her intended question. "I just . . . need . . . to see you smile."

Her forehead creased. How could she smile on command?

Then she thought of the thing most precious to her, her daughter, and her lips curved of their own volition.

His gaze dropped to her chin, then slipped up to a spot an inch below the right corner of her mouth. She knew what had drawn his attention—a misplaced dimple, a unique oddity she never thought about until someone mentioned it. When he lifted his gaze back to hers, the tears in his eyes rocked her.

"Lydia," he whispered on a breath of wonderment. "It *is* you."

In less than a heartbeat, she found herself enveloped in his arms. His warm, male scent wrapped around her. She turned her head so that the side of her face rested on his chest. His racing heart kept pace with her own.

Her arms, with a sudden will of their own, rose and slipped beneath his blazer and around his waist. Her hands spread over the smooth material of the polo shirt that covered his muscular back. He buried his face in her hair and cupped the back of her head with one hand. A sob escaped his throat, shuddered through his body . . . and into hers.

Tears pushed against the back of her eyes as something strange, something wonderful flowed through her. Not a spark of recognition or even a trace of familiarity. Instead, she felt a long-awaited sense of belonging.

But her sanguine thoughts were shattered when he eased back, braced her head with his hands, and hungrily covered her mouth with his own.

꩜

She pushed so hard against his chest, he stumbled backward. The outward curve of the baby grand bit into his hip, saving him from falling, and the wide-eyed terror on her face and the trembling hand pressed against her chest brought him reeling back to his senses.

"I'm sorry," he said. "I shouldn't have done that."

She didn't move, didn't speak. Just stared at him in stunned silence. Reaching out a hand, he took one cautious step forward.

She took a defensive step back, halting his advance.

He let his hand fall limply to his side. "I truly am sorry. It's just that the shock of seeing you again overwhelmed me."

"It's okay," she said, although her shaky voice betrayed her wariness. "It's just that . . . I don't know you."

The meaning of her words slammed into him, clipping the wings of hope that had carried him since that morning, when he'd first heard her voice on his cell phone. She did not know him; therefore, she did not love him anymore. Some of his most treasured remembrances were of her—but her memories of him, of what they once had . . . were gone.

He'd shared her past, but what about her future?

⤙

With one shaky hand pressed against her stomach and the other against her chest, she willed her racing heart to slow down. She wasn't sure what shocked her most, being kissed by a man she'd met less than ten minutes ago, or her reaction to it. The second his lips had touched hers she'd been swept away by a heady sensation. She wasn't some wanton strumpet ready to fall into the arms of the nearest handsome man. At least, she didn't think she was.

When she felt she could speak again without stuttering, she swallowed and wet her tingling lips. "Why don't we sit down?"

He nodded, then waited while she perched on one end of the sofa like a nervous bird ready to take flight. He eased down next to her, settling back and crossing an ankle over the opposite knee.

How did he manage to look so composed after what had just happened between them? Had the kiss not shaken him as it had her? Apparently not, if appearances were anything to go by.

For a few tense seconds, she studied the hands she'd clasped in her lap; then she lifted her gaze to find his intense brown eyes on her. Releasing a shuddery breath, she raised her hand and tucked a curl behind her ear, then dropped her hand back to her lap. "I think we've just established that this is going to be a challenge for us."

A rakish grin pulled at one corner of his mouth. "Like starting over."

He said the very words circling in her mind. But she wasn't ready to broach the details of their relationship just yet. She wanted to start with something safe, something still detached from her addled emotions.

"Tell me about Quinn Island," she said. "And my family."

Lacing his hands over his stomach, he stared into space for a few seconds, apparently trying to decide where to begin. "Quinn Island consists of one small barrier island and about twenty-five thousand acres inland," he said at last. "It was named for its founder, Samuel Quinn. Actually, you're a direct descendent. He was your grandfather—ten greats back, I think—but I tend to lose count on about the fourth great."

She found herself smiling at his wit.

"He and his family sailed to the East Coast from Ireland early in the eighteenth century," he added.

"You mean my family has lived there almost three hundred years?"

"That's right. Although the only true Quinns living among the island residents now are your father's and his brother's families."

"Why's that?"

"The town lost many residents to malaria during the 1700s, when the rice crops were so prosperous. Then many more moved away when the Civil War and a series of hurricanes halted rice production in the late nineteenth century. But time passed, newcomers moved in, and now Quinn Island is a thriving little town by the sea."

As he continued telling her about her heritage, her home, and her family, his smooth southern drawl served as an antidote to the anxiety that had been growing inside her since the night before. She found herself relaxing, settling back at an angle to face him, one arm folded across the top of the sofa and one leg curled beneath her.

When he described the barrier island, she grew a little breathless. She could almost feel the cool damp sand beneath her feet, smell the salt in the air, feel the breeze tug at her hair. Almost picture herself there. Almost, but not quite.

"It sounds so beautiful," she said when he finally paused.

"It is." His grin sent a flutter through her stomach. "Actually, you own a beach house on the island."

"I do?"

He nodded. "Your late Grandfather Quinn left it to you seven years ago."

"And I lived there?"

His smile waned. "No. You preferred living inland. You rented a townhouse apartment in town, near your shop."

That bit of information surprised her. For the last five years, she'd lived with the dream of living on a beach. As he talked more, she worried her lower lip with her teeth and focused blankly on the space beyond his right shoulder. Apparently, a lot had changed, but the biggest truth staring her in the face was how much *she* had changed. Had she really been the sophisticated southern belle Daniel spoke of with such affection?

"Lydia?"

His soft voice penetrated her thoughts. "Yes," she responded hesitantly. Answering to "Lydia" made her feel uneasy, like she was infringing on someone else's identity.

Twin lines creased his forehead. "You don't have to talk about it now, if you don't want to, but I was wondering . . ." He swallowed, as if the rest of the sentence was lodged in the back of his throat.

She thought she knew what he wanted to ask. "You want to know what happened that night."

He answered with a somber nod.

"I really don't know. All I can tell you is what the doctors and police told me."

He reached over and wrapped his hand around one of hers, caressing her knuckles with his thumb. "Lydia, you don't have to—"

"No. It's okay. You need to know."

❧

Daniel's chest tightened with anticipation. He waited in silence for her to continue.

Finally, she pulled in a deep breath. "My first memory is of a faint beeping sound, which I later learned was a heart monitor. Then pain. Deep, heavy pain all over my body and inside my head."

He tightened his hold on her hand, but she didn't seem to notice.

"When the doctor managed to get some of the pain under control, I realized I was in a hospital. I asked him what I was doing there. He told me I had suffered severe trauma as the result of a physical assault. He asked if I remembered what happened to me. Of course, I didn't.

"Then he asked my name, and I couldn't tell him that either." She pursed her lips. "That was the most frightening thing of all, not knowing who I was, where I came from, how I had gotten there . . ." She sighed. "It still frightens me sometimes."

Her lips drew downward in a thoughtful frown. "When the doctor realized I couldn't remember anything, he explained I had been brought into the hospital two weeks earlier, unconscious and barely alive. I had been beaten and apparently left for dead."

"Who brought you into the hospital?"

"A truck driver, a man named Peter Maulding from Mobile, Alabama, found me at a rest stop just outside Chicago. He'd stopped to stretch his legs, and when he went to throw a coffee cup away, he noticed a bloody blanket rolled up around a large bundle inside the dumpster. When he looked closer, he saw a lock of my hair sticking out of one end. He called for help on his truck radio. The ambulance and police came and took me to the hospital."

Chewing on her lower lip, she glanced away. "The nurses said Mr. Maulding called every day to check on me. I finally got to talk to him a week after I regained consciousness. I thanked him for saving me. He simply said 'God be with you, ma'am,' and hung up. He never called back after that."

Daniel made a mental note to locate Peter Maulding and send the truck-driving angel of mercy his own personal "thanks."

"It took thirty-two stitches here," she continued, cupping the back of her head with her free hand. "And fifty-three here." Twisting around, she pushed back her thick curls, offering him a view of her left temple, where a jagged scar fanned out in several directions, like a web spun by a drunken spider. One rough side of the scar disappeared into her hairline.

She pulled her hair back over her temple, expertly concealing the blemish; a move, Daniel suspected, she'd practiced a million times over.

"There were other injuries. A lot of bruises, broken ribs, a broken shoulder, a collapsed lung . . ."

The more she told him about what some demented monster had done to her, the less he wanted to hear. When he felt he could bear no more, he searched his mind for a way to steer the conversation in another direction.

"How did you come to live with Mrs. Porter?" he asked when she paused to take a breath.

A smile touched her lips. "She was an auxiliary volunteer at the hospital. Still is. She visited me every day from the start. The nurses said she would talk to me, just like I was alert and could hear her, and she read passages to me from her Bible. They also said she prayed for me, for my healing.

"The visits continued after I woke, even though I was bitter and angry and not very pleasant company at first. I was so mad at God for allowing me to lose everything, even though I didn't know what it was I'd lost, I wanted no part of hearing that He loved me." A soft sigh drifted from her. "But Mrs. Porter was a stickler. She would say, 'Don't you worry, my dear. God and I are going to love that hate right out of you heart.'"

"And did they?"

Her delicate features softened even more. "Yes, they did. And when I was ready to leave the hospital and had no place to go, Mrs. Porter brought me here and nursed me back to health. When I got my strength back, she helped me find work."

"What kind of work?"

"Housework. I clean houses around the neighborhood four days a week. Fridays, I work here."

Daniel wouldn't have believed it if the words hadn't come from Lydia's own mouth. He couldn't think of an immediate response, so he simply stared at her.

She tipped her head to one side. "You look surprised."

"I am," he blurted, then shook his head to clear the fog that had gathered there. "I mean, someone called in during the program last night and said you looked like her cleaning lady, but I thought surely she was mistaken."

"Who was it?"

"A woman name Elizabeth Bradford."

"Yes." Lydia nodded. "I clean her house on Wednesdays. She lost her husband last year and she's having a hard time adjusting."

"Then you really do clean houses for a living?"

"Yes, I do."

He must have looked as dumbfounded as he felt, because after studying his face a couple of seconds, she said, "Why does that shock you so?"

"Because you hate housework. You used to hire someone to clean your shop and apartment once a week so you wouldn't have to do it yourself."

"Maybe I just didn't know how good I was at it."

"Are you saying you like it?"

She shrugged. "I can't complain. It keeps food on the table and a roof over our heads."

Another jolt of surprise pushed his eyebrows halfway up his forehead. "Our? You mean you keep up this entire house and feed yourself and Mrs. Porter on what you make cleaning houses?"

Her eyes widened and her mouth fell open.

Daniel's trained lawyer's eye read the expression. She'd let something slip unintentionally. He waited to see if she would explain.

She blinked, which seemed to snap her out of her stupefaction. "No. Mrs. Porter is financially secure. I merely rent two rooms from her for me and someone else."

A sharp, foreboding fear shot through Daniel. Was there another man? He'd never even considered the possibility.

Pulling her hand free from his, she leaned forward and opened a small coffee table drawer. Daniel held his breath. He felt like a loaded gun was pointed at his chest—and Lydia's finger was on the trigger.

She withdrew a picture in a gilded frame. Closing the drawer, she held the photo out to him. "This is Chloe."

With an unsteady hand, he reached for the frame. He found himself looking down at the image of a blond-haired, blue-eyed little girl with the face and smile of an angel. He felt his lips curve. "She's beautiful."

"She's my daughter."

His gaze snapped up to Lydia's. "Yours?"

She inclined her head. "She was born almost eight months after I was brought into the hospital. The doctors estimated she was one month premature."

Daniel tried to recover from the blow she had just delivered. She had a child. A daughter. How could that be?

She dropped her gaze to her lap and fidgeted with the creases in her skirt. "Daniel, ever since last night, I've wondered . . ." She pursed her lips, wet them, then swallowed. "I, ah, need to know . . ." Raising her lashes, she searched his face with beseeching brown eyes. "Could she be yours?"

Her question took him aback—and wounded his pride. "How could you even ask such a thing?"

She flinched like he'd raised a hand to strike her, and he would have given anything to take his sharp retort back.

"Lydia, I'm sorry." He reached for her hands. "For a second there, I forgot you couldn't remember."

"It's okay." She tugged one hand free from his and dabbed at a tear in the corner of her eye. "I just . . . needed to know for sure."

"No," he rasped, "she can't be mine. We were . . . are both Christians who had decided—well, we were going to wait until we married."

She bit her lower lip. A teardrop escaped, rolled down her cheek, and splattered his hand.

Cruel fingers of dread cut off the air in his lungs. *No, God, no! Please! Not Lydia!* A sick feeling churned in his stomach and burned his chest. He squeezed his eyelids shut. "You were . . ."

"Raped," she said in not much more than a whisper, supplying the word he couldn't speak. She followed up with an even softer "Yes."

Over the past five years, he had considered the possibility of a sexual assault. But since that morning, he had been so caught up in the joy of finding her . . .

The pain sweeping though him was more, much more than he'd ever imagined. If only he had been there . . . An almost unbearable weight bore down on his chest. He *should* have been there.

He felt her slim hand slide over his. "I'm sorry, Daniel. I just needed to know."

The coolness of her touch, like an early summer rain, and the sincerity in her voice, as though she owed him an apology, jerked him back from the dark hole into which he was slipping. He opened his eyes and looked into her solemn face. *Lord, if there is ever a time You're going to give me strength, please let it be now.*

He cradled her wet cheek in his palm. "No, Lydia. I'm the one who's sorry." He enfolded her in his arms. "This should not have happened to you."

If she wondered why, she didn't ask. She just slipped her arms up around his neck.

Cupping the back of her head with one hand, he buried his face in her sweet-smelling hair and began to rock her. "I am so, so sorry," he repeated.

But his words did nothing to ease the self-condemnation he felt. All the "I'm sorry's" in the world could never undo what he had let happen to her.

4

*L*ydia reined in her raw emotions. What was she doing, falling to pieces all over Daniel this way? Hadn't she known, deep down, that he wasn't Chloe's father? If the timing of her daughter's birth hadn't been enough to convince her, the sharp contrast between Chloe's fair complexion and Daniel's dark one should have been.

Still, since learning she had been engaged to him, a small part of her had hoped Chloe could be his, had yearned to know her child had been conceived in love and not violence. On the other hand, another part of her had feared if he were Chloe's biological father, the relationship could complicate things in the long run. She certainly didn't want Chloe trapped in the middle of a custody battle between an amnesiac mother and a father she didn't know.

Lydia released a shuddery sigh. At least she could find one consolation in confirming her daughter wasn't Daniel's child: She had been a woman of moral character, engaged to a man of honor. A deep sense of loss for what might have been, what would never be, washed over her.

Realizing she needed distance in order to regain her equilibrium, she forced her silent tears to ebb as she pushed away from him. She brushed at the shoulder of his sports coat as though the busy friction of her fingers would dry the dampness there. "I'm sorry. I didn't mean to cry all over you."

He captured a lingering tear with his thumb. A small gesture, but it almost unraveled her barely garnered emotions all over again.

"It's okay," he said. "It's turning out to be quite an eventful day for you. I think you're entitled."

Eventful didn't touch it. Spectacular. Out of the ordinary. All the things she thought she'd missed over the past five years rolled into one single day. How could she have ever thought she'd be ready for this moment? For facing her past? For a man like Daniel?

"Is she here?"

Daniel's question seemed misplaced, like he'd pulled it out of a trivia hat.

"Who?" Lydia asked, trying to think past the fog swimming around her brain.

"Chloe. I'd like to meet her."

"Oh."

Snapping back to reality, she stepped away, forcing Daniel to drop his hand from her face. She combed nervous fingers through her thick mane. "She's upstairs with Mrs. Porter. I'll go get her."

As soon as she was out of his sight, she once again pressed a hand to her quivering stomach. She couldn't believe the effect meeting him was having on her. The moment she had walked into the living room and he turned, looking at her with those dark eyes, she had felt a connection. Was it possible some dormant emotion from her past had been rekindled, even though she couldn't remember him? Or was she simply feeling the need to fill the unsatisfied longing that had grown over the last five years, the need to belong somewhere, to someone?

She hadn't known Daniel Matthews long enough for it to be anything more.

She found Chloe rocking in Evelyn Porter's lap, listening to a story.

"'The sky is falling! The sky is falling!'" Mrs. Porter's voice hip-hopped through the air.

Henny Penny doesn't have a thing on me, Lydia thought, stepping farther into the room. Her world couldn't be any more precarious right now if the sky really was falling.

"Chloe, are you ready to go meet Mr. Matthews?"

"Yes!" Chloe pushed aside the book and scrambled down from Mrs. Porter's lap, the ever-present George the Giraffe tucked under her arm. Ever since Lydia had talked to her daughter that morning about Daniel, the curious tyke couldn't wait to meet "a man Mommy knew before moving to Chicago."

Lydia straightened Chloe's hair bow while she delivered a lecture on the appropriate times to say "please" and "thank you." Then, after a quick inspection to see if the child's green empire-waist dress, white tights, and black patent leather slippers were still clean and intact, she grasped her daughter's hand and headed for the door.

As they descended the steps, the flutter in Lydia's stomach increased. What would Daniel think of Chloe? Could he learn to love this innocent child created out of an act of black rage? Or would he ultimately reject her?

Lydia paused outside the living room, looked down at her daughter, and gave the tiny hand inside hers a reassuring squeeze. Then, squaring her shoulders, she opened the door.

Daniel stood waiting for them beside the sofa, his hands tucked casually inside his pockets. His gaze met Lydia's briefly, then dropped to Chloe.

Lydia felt an insistent tug on her hand. At her daughter's silent prompting, she stopped just a few feet inside the door. The next move would have to be Daniel's.

He came forward slowly, his attention fixed on Chloe.

The child rarely met anyone outside her sheltered world within the neighborhood. What would she do? Hide behind her mother's skirt? Run? To Lydia's amazement, Chloe stood statue still, her huge blue eyes gauging Daniel's every move.

He got down on one knee and looked into her eyes. "You must be Chloe."

Still clutching George beneath her arm, Chloe gave an emphatic nod.

"Your mom's been telling me about you. I'm Daniel."

"My mama said your name was 'Mr. Matthews.'"

Lydia's lips twitched, and a chuckle escaped Daniel's throat.

Resting his forearm across his raised knee, he said, "Only to people who aren't my friends. But I can already tell you and I are going to be very good friends, which means you can call me 'Daniel.' What do you think?"

Like a rehearsed act, both faces tilted upward and two beseeching gazes locked on Lydia's.

She was a stickler for manners and respect, and she didn't want Chloe to get in the habit of calling her elders by their first name. But with the pair looking up at her like two kids campaigning for an ice cream cone, she felt her resistance slip away. "Sure." She knew when she was defeated.

Chloe gave Daniel her most charming smile. "She says I can call you 'Daniel.'" In the same breath, she added, "Will you come play in my sandbox with me?"

Before Lydia could protest, Daniel was standing and lifting Chloe to his hip. "Sure, I will." He passed George to Lydia.

She stood, mouth agape, the giraffe with a bad hairdo dangling from her hand. She wanted to remind Chloe that she had on her best Sunday dress, and Daniel that he had on a pair of professionally creased Docker pants and what looked to her like an expensive pair of penny loafers. But the words froze in her muddled brain.

She wasn't so surprised at Daniel being enamored with Chloe. Once the child warmed up to someone—and she had warmed up to Daniel in record time—she had a charming personality that drew people to her.

But what was it about Daniel that had allowed him to slip so easily past Chloe's usual reserve? He'd waltzed right up to the child and, in the space of a minute, maybe two, swept the little girl off her feet.

Like mother, like daughter. The old cliché popped into Lydia's head, poking fun at her usual levelheadedness.

But Lydia and Chloe weren't the only ones who had fallen prey to Daniel's magnetic charm. Mrs. Porter had raved about him, too. She had said, *"He's got to be one of the most engaging young men I've ever met,"* when she came upstairs to fetch Lydia after showing him in.

First Mrs. Porter, then Lydia, now Chloe. Did the man affect the entire female population this way?

He stopped before opening the door Chloe had pointed him to and turned. "Coming, Mom?"

Realizing her mouth still hung open, she snapped it shut. "Ah, yes. I'm coming." George in tow, she hurried to catch up with them.

Thirty minutes later, she sat on the steps of the patio, chin in hand, her long skirt draped over her feet and legs, watching Daniel and Chloe. At first, Lydia had contemplated joining them, then decided the four-by-four sandbox made of scrap lumber she'd salvaged during a neighbor's renovation was barely big enough for two playmates, especially when one was a guesstimated six-foot-two man.

Daniel and Chloe shoveled sand and built imaginary houses where imaginary stick people lived. They laughed and giggled. The well-dressed attorney who had stepped into hers and Chloe's lives less than two hours ago didn't seem to mind one bit that the seat of his pants and the soles of his polished cordovan shoes were nestled in gritty, clingy sand.

He had shucked off his blazer and tossed it over a nearby swing seat, revealing lean, muscled forearms beneath the sleeves of his white polo shirt. Whenever he tilted his head a certain way, the afternoon sun lit the chestnut highlights in his dark hair. Every once in a while, his laughter floated through the air, each time touching a place inside her she hadn't even known existed. He looked like a man in his element, a man carved by God's own hand for fatherhood.

Lydia realized where her thoughts were drifting, and she mentally rebuked her wandering mind. She could chase dreams of Chloe being Daniel's daughter until the sun set in the east. The truth remained that Daniel was not, and never would be, Chloe's biological father. Considering the circumstances of Chloe's conception, it would take a mighty big man to overcome that obstacle and accept the child as his own.

And this early in the game, Lydia didn't know if Daniel was quite big enough.

❧

An hour later, after tucking Chloe in for her afternoon nap, Lydia stepped outside her daughter's room ahead of Daniel. With little effort, Chloe had talked him into picking up where Mrs. Porter had left off reading *Henny Penny*. Then she had fallen asleep in his lap.

Lydia waited for the faint click of the closing door. "Chloe's quite taken with you," she said.

He grinned. "I'm quite taken with her."

Trapping her lower lip between her teeth, she looked down the hallway at nothing in particular. They had so many things to discuss. So many circumstances to consider. "You understand now why I didn't want any attention drawn to your finding me."

"To protect Chloe?" he guessed correctly.

Nodding, she turned her attention back to him. "I know the chances are slim, but if one of the men who attacked me—"

His eyebrows shot up. "Men? You mean there was more than one?"

Lydia closed her eyes ruefully and pressed a cool palm to her forehead. She kept letting things slip before she was ready to talk about them. Was she losing her mind now along with her identity?

Dropping her hand, she lowered her gaze to the base of his neck exposed by the V-opening of his collar. "Yes. The doctors said there were at least two." When she raised her lashes, he looked away, but not before she caught the pain in his eyes.

She knew, in many ways, his grief cut deeper than hers. He had lost someone very dear to him the night of her abduction. But she had no memory of the attack. When she talked about it, she felt as though she were talking about someone else, someone she'd read about in the newspaper or seen on the evening news but never met. She couldn't feel the fear, the horror, the pain she must have felt that night. Besides the physical scars her body carried, the only evidence left that such a violent act had been committed against her was something very dear to her—her daughter.

"Would you like some tea?" she suggested. She and Daniel could both use a break, take some time to calm their frazzled nerves before talking about the next step they should take.

Daniel nodded, then followed her downstairs and into the kitchen.

❧

Fury almost choked him. He wanted revenge on the demons who had violated Lydia. Even as his inner voice told him his thoughts were immoral, he envisioned himself torturing the life out of each faceless monster.

She refused his offer of help, so he pulled out a chair, sat down, and watched her flutter around the kitchen like an energetic butterfly. She filled a teakettle with water and placed it on the stove, then reached into the cupboard and pulled out two ceramic cups.

"We have chamomile and regular," she said. "Which would you like?"

Since he didn't know what chamomile was, he decided to play it safe. "Regular."

"Cold or hot?"

"Cold." Five years ago, she had known that.

"Sweetened? Unsweetened? Cream? Lemon?"

She threw the single-word questions at him like he was a dartboard, and he felt himself smile. She looked so captivating, standing there holding the cups against her chest like two cuddly kittens, her amber eyes wide in anticipation of his answer.

"Sweet," he said, referring to more than the tea. "No cream or lemon."

She had also known he didn't take cream or lemon in his tea five years ago, a little irritating voice inside reminded him, tempering the joy he felt at simply watching her putter around the kitchen. How was it that practically everything she did reminded him she couldn't remember him or what they had once shared, yet at the same time, charmed him so? In some ways, he felt like he was experiencing the rapture of falling in love all over again. In other ways, he felt as though he were groping in the dark, wondering which way to turn, what to reach for.

She set his iced tea in front of him, then returned to the counter where she added a teaspoon of honey and a tea bag to a cup of boiling water. Balancing the cup over a saucer, she padded to the table. "Would you like something to eat? I can fix you a sandwich."

He'd missed lunch, but the way he felt right now, his appetite might not ever return. "No, thank you. Tea's fine."

He waited until she sat down, then lifted his drink in a mock salute before taking a long, cool sip. When he set his dewy glass back down, he watched as she dipped her tea bag in and out of the steaming liquid in her cup. The water, he noticed, was turning a color that reminded him of stagnant pond water. Finally, she laid the bag on the edge of the saucer and took a careful sip of the pungent-smelling brew.

"What kind of tea did you say that was?" he asked as she settled the cup back in its saucer.

"Chamomile. It's supposed to have a calming effect." She shrugged one shoulder. "Most of the time it works."

Maybe that's what he should have had. He studied the fog rising from the cup, debating on changing his mind—until he caught another whiff of the acrid-smelling liquid. *Nope,* he decided without further contemplation. That chamomile stuff reminded him of the rabbit tobacco he and his cousins used to sneak to their grandpa's woodshed to chew during their rambunctious adolescent years. The aftermath was never worth the effort. Retching had never been fun.

Besides, the only thing he drank hot was coffee.

The contrary little beast inside him nudged him again, pointing out that Lydia had never cared for hot tea either. Water and diet soda had been the only liquid she'd ever let pass through her painted lips.

His gaze slid to her mouth. Those lips weren't painted at all right now, just barely moistened by a trace of the sheer gloss she'd been wearing when he first arrived. He had to admit, he liked them that way.

He took another long drink of tea, then studied the dew beading on his glass while he tried to collect his scattered senses. How could one experience so many conflicting emotions at once? Joy and sorrow. Pleasure and pain. Courage and fear.

So far, he'd found only a remnant of what he'd lost five years ago, and he didn't know if that was good . . . or bad.

❧

Lydia set her teacup in its saucer and studied Daniel. He looked so sad with his head bowed and his gaze fixed on his half-empty glass. What was he thinking? After learning all that had happened to her, was he sorry he'd found her? Was he tormented by what the attack had cost her? Cost him?

He'd said they were both Christians and had decided to wait until their wedding night to claim each other as one. He had been a man of honor about to marry a woman of purity. Lydia suspected he was still a man of honor, but she was no longer a woman of purity. And that was only one cold, harsh fact wedged between them. There would, she suspected, be many, many more.

Above all, there was Chloe. Right now, Daniel was caught up in the thrill of finding *Lydia*. But what about later, when the excitement of new beginnings died and the dust of celebration settled? Would he be reminded of how Chloe had been conceived every time he looked at her?

Was finding out worth the risk?

Lydia reached over and laid her palm on Daniel's forearm. When he looked up, the anguish in his eyes almost made her look away. Almost. But she somehow hung on to her resolve and pushed forward. "Daniel, I truly am sorry."

He frowned. "What for?"

"For all the terrible things you're finding out about me. That I'm not the same woman I was five years ago."

Abruptly, he stood. Caught off guard by the sudden action, she flinched. The heavy oak chair upset by the impact of the back of his knees teetered on its hind legs for a few precarious seconds, then settled with a dull thud on all fours.

Before Lydia could react, he captured her upper arms in his firm yet tender grip and lifted her. The space between their bodies vanished as she gaped up at him in surprise. He looked down at her with a turbulent expression in his eyes she couldn't define. Each of his breaths brushed her face like a swiftly passing storm.

"Lydia, what happened to you was not your fault!" he said through clenched teeth. "Do you hear me? It was *not . . . your . . . fault.*" He punctuated each of his last three words with a gentle shake.

Then, as swiftly as the storm came, it dissipated. His features softened and his eyes filled with . . . compassion, sorrow, remorse? She wasn't sure. She just knew the entire atmosphere changed from turbulent to tender in less than a second.

"It's not your fault," he repeated, each breath now touching her face as soft as a whisper. "And it doesn't change the person you are." He shook his head, gazing down at her in a way that made her feel like she had just stepped into a beautiful dream. "It doesn't change a thing, Lydia. Especially the way I feel about you."

He gathered her in his arms, cupped the back of her head with one hand, nestled her cheek against his chest. "I love you, Lydia. I always have. I always will."

She knew he meant it, just as sure as she knew the arms holding her were sincere, and the hands caressing her would never harm her. Regardless of what had happened, he still loved her and was willing to go the distance.

But was she?

She didn't know. She was afraid of getting hurt, of hurting Chloe . . . of hurting him.

She slipped her arms around his waist and allowed his strength to surround her. Each rise and fall of his chest, every heartbeat, seemed to mirror her own. Her resistance was gone, had vanished like a bad dream at dawn the moment he said, "I love you." What in the world was she going to do?

She released a shuddery sigh. "I can't pick up where we left off," she heard herself say. "You know that, don't you, Daniel?"

"I know." He drew back and braced her face with hands neither too big nor too small, neither too rough nor too smooth. "We'll start over, and take it slow." He caressed her cheek with his thumb. "You're my destiny, Lydia. We were meant to be together."

A look of deep longing rose in his eyes, igniting inside her a desire to fulfill his dreams. The atmosphere grew still, and for a moment they did nothing but stare at each other. Then his gaze dropped to her mouth. Her heartbeat accelerated in anticipation of his kiss—and the knowledge that when it came, she'd be powerless to resist.

But it never came. Instead, he simply slipped his arms around her again and held her. She marveled at the incredible feeling of being embraced by a man who loved her enough to remain loyal through five long years of separation.

But would that love survive the future? He'd said nothing had changed, but she knew it had. And he knew it, too, even if he wasn't yet ready to admit it. A chilly finger of foreboding brushed her spine, intruding on her moment of bliss, reminding her of the stark reality anchored to their reunion.

He remembered the woman she was.

She knew only the woman she'd become.

What they once had was gone.

Once Daniel figured that out, would he still think of her as his destiny?

5

*M*uch later that evening, Daniel all but collapsed when he sat down on the freshly made brass bed. When he'd earlier mentioned finding a motel room, Mrs. Porter had insisted he stay in one of the two empty bedrooms upstairs. He hadn't put up an argument—he wanted to stay as close to Lydia as possible.

He massaged the back of his neck where fibers of tension had gathered. He knew the night would bring little sleep, but he did need to get what rest he could. He hoped to get Lydia home by day after tomorrow, which meant tomorrow would be filled with hasty preparation.

But there was one task he couldn't postpone until morning. He fished his cellular phone out of his blazer pocket, flipped it open, and dialed. The phone on the other end rang once.

"Hello?" came the anxious voice of Margaret Quinn. "Daniel, is that you?"

"Yes, Margaret, it's me."

"Where on earth are you?" Lydia's mother wanted to know. "We called your office this afternoon and your secretary said there'd been a change in your plans. Did the television station receive any more calls after we spoke with you last night?"

Daniel decided to get right to the point. Lydia's parents had waited long enough for this call. "I'm in Riverbend, Illinois—"

"Illinois? Wha—"

"I've found Lydia."

Silence filled his ear, then a breathless, "Oh, dear heavenly Father," slipped from her lips. "Bill! Bill! Come quickly! Daniel's found Lydia! Where is she?" Margaret asked Daniel next in the same breath. "Can I speak to her?"

"I'd rather you wait until tomorrow to do that."

"Tomorrow!" Her voice was appalled. "You can't be serious. Tell me how to get there. We'll take the first flight out."

"Before you do anything, Margaret, I need to tell you a few things."

Daniel heard a faint click. "Daniel?" came the slightly out-of-breath voice of Bill Quinn. "Is it true? Have you really found her?"

"Yes, Bill, it's true."

"Oh, thank God." The older man released a sob.

Bill's reaction played havoc with Daniel's overwrought emotions, which he'd barely managed to temper before making the call. He squeezed his burning eyes shut. He had to get this out. He had to somehow tell them about Lydia without breaking down again himself. *Help me, Lord,* he silently prayed, and a fragile but definite sense of calm stole over him.

"There are some things you need to know before you talk to her," he finally managed to say, and without hesitation he plowed ahead, telling them about her waking up in a Chicago hospital sixteen days after her disappearance, her amnesia, and how she came to live with Mrs. Porter. He finished with "She has a daughter . . . as a result of the ra—" he closed his eyes, forcing down a sudden wave of nausea, "—as a result of the attack."

"Oh, my baby," Margaret said in a raspy, choking voice. "My poor, poor baby."

"The little girl," Daniel added, barely holding onto his brittle composure. "Her name is Chloe."

"Chloe," Margaret repeated.

"That's right."

For five full seconds, Margaret Quinn said nothing, as though she were giving the child's name a chance to take root somewhere. Daniel prayed it would be in her heart.

"What does she look like?" she finally asked, unable to disguise her concern and curiosity.

Daniel's anger at the torture Lydia had suffered returned, dropping on his chest like an exploding bomb that spread into each limb. "Not like Lydia." *And not me. She'll never look like me.* "But she's the most beautiful child I've ever seen," he added, and meant it.

Three seconds ticked away. "I'm sure she is, Daniel." The woman's timorous laugh brushed Daniel's ear. "What about that, Bill? We're grandparents."

Daniel breathed a sigh of relief. He couldn't help worrying about how Mrs. Quinn would take the news of Chloe. Margaret Quinn always had her family's best interest at heart, even when she was overbearing. But she sometimes focused too much on image and appearance, especially where her daughters were concerned.

"How is she, Daniel?" Bill cut in. "Is she there with you? When can we talk to her?"

"Physically, she's fine. Emotionally? I don't know. She seems to be okay, but quite honestly, it's too early for me to tell what kind of impact her memory loss has had on her. That's why I wanted to prepare you before you speak with her. She doesn't remember anything or anyone from her past before the abduction, so, please, don't expect more from her than she's able to give right now. I know you're both anxious to see her, but I think it'd be best to wait until we get home."

"When will that be?" Margaret asked.

"Hopefully, in a couple of days. Another thing, she wants to return quietly. No hoopla and fanfare." This he said more to Lydia's mother than her unassuming father.

"But so many of her friends will want to welcome her home," Margaret argued, as Daniel had expected her to. She probably had half the homecoming party planned by now.

"In time, they can," he responded, unbending. "But it will have to be when Lydia's ready. Remember, she's coming back to a place and people she doesn't remember. That's overwhelming enough in itself."

"I think Daniel's right, Margaret," Bill injected, and Daniel silently thanked the older man. "Let's keep the homecoming limited to family for now."

"Okay," Margaret relented, albeit reluctantly. "If you think that's best, Daniel."

"I do." He raked his hair away from his forehead. A rebellious lock flopped back down over his left brow. "Listen, I'd better go. I'll call back first thing in the morning. If she's up to it, you can talk to her then."

After hanging up, Daniel sat for a long time with his elbows on his knees and his hands clasped in front of him, staring at the darkness beyond the bedroom window. For some reason, the words of an old song he associated with funerals came to mind.

Precious memories, unseen angels,
  Sent from somewhere to my soul;
How they linger, ever near me,
  And the sacred past unfold.

As he sat there, with the lines of that old hymn floating through his head, the past did unfold, memory by precious memory, starting with the first time Daniel noticed Lydia as more than another kid in the neighborhood. He'd been home on Thanksgiving break his fourth year in college and had attended a high school football game with a friend. Lydia had been seventeen then, captain of the cheerleading squad, and to Daniel, the most beautiful thing he'd ever seen.

At least a hundred more memories played themselves out in his mind: her college graduation, the day she opened her dress shop, the evening he proposed. Right up until the day she'd left for the fateful New York trip, pouting in that pretty way of hers because he wouldn't postpone his first solo court case to go with her.

When the reflections came to a haunting end, he dropped his forehead to his hands. A harrowing question preyed on his mind: Would things between him and Lydia ever be as they once were? An even more frightening question followed, casting shadows of doubt over the first: Did he even want to return to the life they'd once shared?

He gave his head a disparaging shake. He didn't know. He truly didn't know. He never imagined finding her would bring so much confusion . . . and pain. "Oh, God, help me," he pleaded. "Please, please help me."

Daniel didn't know exactly what he was asking for. Only that he would need guidance in the days to come from One much stronger than he.

When he finished praying, he closed his eyes and wept.

❧

Lydia Quinn, she said to herself for about the hundredth time in half as many hours. She tossed a pair of socks in the open suitcase on her bed. *Lydia Anne Quinn. Ms. Lydia Quinn.*

No matter how she rehearsed the name in her mind, it still sounded as foreign to her as the first time she'd heard it. She paused in packing and stepped in front of her dresser mirror, trying to picture herself as a sophisticated southern belle. Like the dozen or so other times she'd stood there since the day before yesterday, all she saw was "Sara," mother of Chloe, close friend and companion to Evelyn Porter.

Shaking her head, she went back to packing. How was she ever going to step back into her old shoes? This wasn't some fairy tale where the peasant heroine slipped on the glass slipper and found a perfect fit. This was her own life, and she had a feeling her shoe size had changed dramatically over the past five years.

When she closed the case, the latch caught with an amplified click of finality. Her life here was coming to an end. In less than an hour, she, Chloe, Mrs. Porter, and Daniel would leave for the airport. In less than two, they'd be on a flight to Quinn Island—her home. She was so glad Daniel had invited Mrs. Porter to come along and stay for a few weeks. At least Lydia would have a confidant while she reacquainted herself with her family.

As she turned to her dresser and started tossing her meager toiletries into a makeup bag, her mind drifted back over the hours since Daniel had walked into her life. Yesterday had started out like a whirlwind. She had been moved by the conversations with her parents and sister over the telephone. Hearing the weepy joy in their voices was enough to toy with her own emotions. But that was it. She hadn't even been able to work up a tear at the prospect of returning home to these three people who obviously loved and missed her very much. A sigh escaped her lips. Surely, that would all change once she got to know them.

After the phone call, Lydia had made rounds in the neighborhood, saying good-bye and letting the families she worked for know Mrs. Porter's great-niece, a college student on summer break, would soon be taking over her cleaning jobs. By the time she returned, Daniel had booked a flight to Myrtle Beach International Airport, arranged to have a shuttle pick them up this morning and take them to O'Hare, and made plans to have Lydia's and Chloe's few material possessions—aside from their clothes—shipped to her parents' house.

Lydia wasn't quite sure how she felt about his assertive efforts. In some ways, she was grateful he was a take-action sort of guy. He had taken care of a dozen little details that would have been a bit overwhelming for her. After all, she was acquainted with very little of the world outside the subdivision she'd lived in for the past five years.

Even so, Daniel could have kept her better informed. Other than wanting to know how soon she could be ready to go home, he hadn't asked her opinion about anything. And that pricked an irritating little nerve in Lydia. She might have lost her memory, but she hadn't lost her mind. She still had the ability to think and make decisions for herself and her daughter.

She sensed another's presence and paused short of dropping her tube of lip gloss in the makeup bag. Even before looking toward the open doorway, she knew who she would find there. Deliberately, she set the lip gloss back on the dresser and closed her eyes, stealing a deep breath of fortitude. This was going to be the hardest good-bye of all.

Opening her eyes, she turned slowly to face the sad green eyes of her best friend. "Jeff," she whispered, and a lump lodged in her throat.

He stood with his hands shoved into the pockets of his khaki pants, his shoulders hunched forward. When their gazes met, he pursed his lips, and his chin quivered. Behind the lenses of his wire-rimmed glasses, his eyes grew misty. His desolate expression reflected the feeling rising in Lydia's chest. They had been through so much together, from the premature birth of her daughter, to the untimely death of his wife. And she would miss him—a lot.

But Lydia knew, as did he, things had changed. The love he had hoped would one day blossom between them would never come to pass.

"I'm going to miss you, kid," he said, his voice heavy with sorrow.

Three steps each and they were in each other's arms. "I'm going to miss you, too," she said.

"I love you. You know that, don't you?"

"I know. I love you, too."

But theirs was not the kind of love that made two people one—the kind he and his deceased wife had shared. And deep down, Lydia was sure he knew that, too.

❧

"I love you. You know that, don't you?"

"I know. I love you, too."

Daniel stopped short of stepping up to the open doorway of Lydia's room. What was this? Lydia proclaiming her love to another man?

He leaned against the wall for support. Why hadn't she told him this before now?

A brief silence followed, leaving Daniel to wonder what was happening between them. Were they holding each other? *Kissing* each other? The image of Lydia locked in another man's lent new strength to Daniel's limbs. He'd just found her, and he had no intentions of losing her—again. He pushed away from the wall and stepped up to the open doorway, bracing himself for the scene he expected to find.

Lydia apparently caught his movement out of the corner of her eye and stepped away from the strange man. When she turned to face Daniel, he expected a look of guilt or embarrassment, an expression that said "I wish the floor would open up and swallow me." Instead, she greeted him with an innocent smile.

She tucked her hand into the crook of the stranger's arm, and together they stepped forward. "Daniel, I'd like you to meet a very dear friend of mine."

The man stretched out his right hand. "Jeff Chandler. It's nice to meet you."

Yeah, right, thought Daniel, as he returned the handshake. Either the man really *was* just a friend or he was an idiot. If he felt for Lydia half of what Daniel did, he'd be bracing himself for a battle, not shaking the enemy's hand.

With a curt nod, Daniel pumped the man's hand, once. "Daniel Matthews. Likewise."

"Yes, I saw you on *Without a Trace* the other night." Jeff pushed his glasses up the bridge of his nose, then stuffed his fists into his pockets. "Sara's waited a long time for this day. I know you're happy she's going home."

Lydia. Her name is Lydia. He slipped a possessive arm around her, urging her to step away from Jeff. Daniel feared she'd stiffen, pull away, send some sort of silent signal that she didn't want him showing such an open gesture of affection in front of her "dear friend."

But she didn't. In fact, he thought he felt her lean into him a little.

"Words can't express how happy I am," Daniel said. "Her parents and sister, too."

Jeff's gaze held Daniel's for a moment, and Daniel got the peculiar sensation that the man was trying to convey some sort of silent message. Then a look of sad resignation rose in Jeff's eyes, and, in spite of himself, Daniel felt a thread of sympathy for Lydia's friend.

"You're a fortunate man," Jeff said. He turned his attention to Lydia, and his features softened even more. "I'm going to go say goodbye to Chloe now." He leaned over, kissed Lydia's cheek, and squeezed her hand. "Take care, kid. You know where I am if you ever need me."

Lydia nodded, and even though she smiled, Daniel noticed tears gathering in her eyes.

Jeff turned and walked away, and for a moment, Daniel looked after him. What did the man really mean to Lydia?

She stepped away from him, taking her comforting warmth with her. When he focused his attention back on her, she was standing with her arms crossed, glowering at him like a first-grade teacher ready to go head-to-head with a willful student.

"How much of that conversation did you hear?" she asked.

He decided to play innocent, see how much information she would volunteer about her relationship with Jeff. "What do you mean?"

"I mean, you came in here like a man on a mission. And I'd like to know how much of my conversation with Jeff you listened in on."

He took a few seconds to size her up. In the past, she'd never been so direct . . . or insightful. He rubbed his jaw. The determination and challenge in her demeanor told him there was no point in trying to continue with his charade. She'd already seen through it.

"I heard him tell you he loves you," he admitted. And with that admission came a feeling Daniel hadn't experienced in a very long time. A slip in control. It felt strange . . . like a shoe on the wrong foot.

"Then you heard me tell him I love him, too."

He inclined his head.

"I do," she said.

Hearing her confess her love for another man while she was staring him down had more impact on him than when he was standing outside her door. He thought he'd suffocate right there on the spot.

"But I'm not *in love* with him," she added.

He arched an inquisitive brow. "Meaning . . . ?"

She glanced away, a frown pinching her forehead. After a long, thoughtful moment, she looked back at him. "I met Jeff when I was in the hospital. His wife Caroline was one of my nurses."

Daniel perked up. Jeff had a wife. That was good.

"I don't know why they and Mrs. Porter chose to befriend me, but they did," Lydia continued. "They supported me emotionally while my body healed physically. They stood beside me during my pregnancy and Chloe's premature birth. They were, I suppose, a substitute family to me and Chloe."

An expression of deep pain clouded her delicate features. "Then the unthinkable happened and Caroline was diagnosed with Lou Gehrig's disease. I was with her and Jeff when she died eighteen months ago."

Now Daniel felt like a heel. The man had lost, big-time. A loss that, in many ways, Daniel could relate to.

Lydia drew in a deep breath, released it slowly. "After her death, I tried to help Jeff out with his kids when the burden of single fatherhood overwhelmed him. I tried to listen when he got so lonely for

Caroline he thought he was going to die. I tried to be there for him, like he had been there for me.

"The kind of love Jeff and I share is the kind between two friends who have been to hell and back with each other." Her light brown eyes sought for understanding. "Haven't you ever had a friend like that?"

A picture of Lydia's sister Jen floated across his mind. They had gone through the heartbreak of Lydia's disappearance together, had grown closer through it. He had to admit he understood exactly what Lydia was trying to say.

"Yes, I have," he said, pulling her into his arms. Resting his chin on the top of her head, he added, "I'm sorry I jumped to the wrong conclusion."

"You don't owe me an apology, Daniel. Considering you didn't know the circumstances, I'm sure what you heard sounded suspicious."

"Still, I shouldn't have barreled in here like 'a man on a mission.'"

She drew back, smiling up at him. "I don't know. I found it kind of flattering, myself."

A pleased grin lifted one corner of his mouth. "You did?"

"Yes. I did."

Like a warm cloak in a chilly wind, the air grew heavy with enthralling tension. Slowly, their smiles faded. She wet her lips. Her involuntary movement drew his gaze to her mouth, and a shudder of longing shook him. He became aware of her every breath.

He lifted his eyes back to hers. "I guess you know I want to kiss you."

Releasing a pent-up breath, she pushed away. "Please don't. Thinking about going to Quinn Island and meeting my family has me addlepated enough as it is."

Addlepated. Now there was a word he'd never heard her use before. But he thought he knew what she meant.

Patting her chest like she was trying to calm an unsteady palpitation, she turned to her dresser. She dropped a tube of lip gloss into a makeup bag, zipped it, and tossed the bag into a small open suitcase on the bed. After securing the luggage, she straightened and turned back around to face him. "There's one other thing I need to tell you—

"Outside, a vehicle horn blared.

A rueful smile tipped her lips. "I guess it can wait. There's our ride to the airport."

She slipped the thin strap of her purse over her shoulder and reached for the luggage lying on the bed, but Daniel was one step ahead of her.

"I can at least carry the small one," she said.

"I've got it."

She nodded, offering no further argument.

Standing in the middle of the room, she took one last lingering look at her surroundings. Then, drawing back her shoulders, she lifted her chin a determined inch, forcing more courage into her actions than her anxious eyes reflected.

"Well," she said, "I guess it's time to go home."

6

*H*ow many times have I done this before?" Lydia asked Daniel as she fastened her airplane seat belt with slightly shaky hands. A jittery knot bounced in her stomach.

"Five or six," Daniel answered, making sure Chloe was safely secured in her seat.

Daniel had been fortunate enough to reserve adjoining seats in the same row for him, Chloe, and Lydia. He—at Lydia's insistence—had taken the window seat, Chloe sat in the middle, and Lydia sat next to the aisle. She really wasn't interested in seeing how high the plane could fly.

Mrs. Porter sat in the aisle seat one row up.

Lydia rechecked Chloe's restraint. She knew Daniel had aptly secured the belt, but fidgeting gave her something to do with her hands besides wringing them in her lap. "Was I always this nervous?"

"A little the first time. But after that you always looked forward to the flight."

Mild turbulence during takeoff had Lydia clinging to her armrests; Chloe reached for Lydia. But once Daniel explained an airplane penetrating air pockets was like a pin popping balloons, Chloe found the occasional bump-bang rather amusing and began to giggle.

Lydia's uneasiness, however, didn't calm until the plane leveled off and the flight became smooth. Then, she realized, she didn't mind flying at all. She reminded herself of what Daniel had said about her enjoying flying in the past after she'd conquered her first-flight jitters. Maybe she had finally found something she had in common with her old self.

Her fit of anxiety returned full force when the pilot announced they were approaching Myrtle Beach International Airport. Meeting people who knew more about her past than she did weakened her fortitude, made her feel as though the thin shell of her self-composure might break under the mildest look of criticism.

"Are you okay?" Daniel asked as the plane rolled to a stop.

Lydia met his gaze of concern. "A little nervous," she admitted. "I never realized meeting my own family would be so . . ."

"Scary?"

She forced a smile. "Yeah." Looking down at her daughter, she pasted on a cheery expression. "Are you ready to meet Grandma and Grandpa Quinn and your aunt Jennifer?"

With a sparkle in her eyes, Chloe bobbed her head and raised her arms so Daniel could unfasten her seat belt. They fell in line and shuffled down the aisle. Daniel, with Chloe perched on his hip, led the way since he was the only one familiar with the airport and its unloading routine. Lydia followed Daniel, and Mrs. Porter fell in behind.

Lydia forced herself not to withdraw while people of all shapes, sizes, and ages craned their necks in search of their loved ones. She scanned the colossal wall of faces, hoping to locate those waiting for her. Seeing them first would at least give her a chance to brace for their reaction.

A man in a dark suit, carrying a briefcase in one hand and holding a cellular phone to his ear with the other, breezed by, bumping Lydia's shoulder and, for an instant, he drew her attention away from the crowd.

"Hey, do you know how to say 'Excuse me'?" she heard Daniel say.

The busy man just shot Daniel a flippant glance and kept on going.

Lydia's lips pinched together. Sure, the man had been rude, but that was no reason to solicit a brawl in the middle of an international airport. She was going to have to talk to Daniel about his impetuous overprotection.

"There they are!" A female voice rose above the crowd. "Lydia! Lydia!"

Before Lydia could lock onto the source of the voice, she found herself clenched in a fierce embrace. A blanket of blond hair brushed her face. Her nostrils filled with the sweet fragrance of expensive perfume. She tilted her head so her chin could rest atop the woman's shoulder and reminded herself to hug this still unknown member of her family.

Just as quickly as she'd grabbed Lydia, the woman set her back, keeping a hold on her upper arms. Lydia found herself looking into the misty blue eyes of a slim young woman at least six inches taller than herself.

Jennifer. Her sister. Lydia recognized the sibling from *Without a Trace*.

"Oh, Lydia." Tears streaming, Jennifer lifted her hands to frame Lydia's face. "Look at you. You look wonderful."

Jennifer's gaze zipped to the area beyond Lydia's left shoulder. "And this must be Chloe."

As Jennifer stepped aside and flitted toward her niece, Lydia saw the couple who had been standing a few feet behind her sister. The woman leaned on a cane; the man held a protective arm around her. They were looking at Lydia like a young mother and father admiring their newborn for the first time after a long, complicated pregnancy.

"Mom? Dad?" Her voice was as small as a frightened child's. Lydia stepped forward at the same time they did, and they all came together in a fervent embrace.

Almost immediately, a warm feeling of acceptance stole over Lydia. She might not know these two people yet. Their faces might not be familiar to her as they once were, and their names might still sound strange and foreign. But one thing she did know—they loved her, as parents love their children. She could hear it in the tremble of their voices when they spoke to her, feel it in the strength of the arms as they held her.

Maybe she'd arrived "home" after all.

❧

They claimed their luggage, then made their way out to the parking area where Daniel had left his sleek white sedan—a lawyer's car, for sure. They fastened Chloe's seat belt and then Daniel, Lydia, and Mrs. Porter got in his car with the child, while Bill, Margaret, and Jennifer left to retrieve Jennifer's car from another lot.

An hour later, Daniel turned onto a road marked Plantation Lane. He threw up his hand at the fourth deputy sitting in the fourth patrol car Lydia had noticed parked alongside the road since they'd entered the Quinn Island city limits ten minutes ago.

"Daniel," she queried, "are all these deputies for my benefit? Or is Quinn Island just well blessed with lawmen?"

"They're for your benefit and Chloe's. I called the sheriff yesterday and asked him to keep an eye out in case someone learned of your return. When the news starts spreading, it will draw a lot of attention. I didn't want you having to deal with that today."

"I appreciate that," she said. And she did appreciate his foresight—but not that he'd failed to inform her of his contact with the sheriff. She chewed her lower lip in frustration. What else had he failed to tell her?

"Also, Lydia," Daniel added, "I had to inform the sheriff you'd been found. Remember, you were the victim of a crime. There are going to be a lot of questions . . . interrogations in the days to come. I want you to be prepared for that." He glanced her way. "I'll be there with you through the whole thing. You'll not have to go through it alone."

Like ice cream in the summer sun, her irritation melted. She couldn't stay annoyed at him—he wouldn't let her. He was too gentle. Too kind. Too doggedly determined to look out for her and Chloe.

"Thank you," she told him. "That means a lot."

He turned his attention back to the road, and she turned hers to the roadside, where oleanders, palm trees, and other foliage that looked native to a tropical island lined the street. She made a mental note to ask Daniel the names of the plants she wasn't familiar with—and to buy a pair of dark sunglasses. The midafternoon sun seemed so much brighter here than in Chicago.

After they'd traveled about half a mile, Daniel turned the car onto a paved drive and stopped in front of a gate. When he pressed a button on a small box clipped to his sun visor, the black iron doors swung open. He maneuvered the vehicle through the gate, while Jennifer, Margaret, and Bill followed in Jennifer's car.

The narrow road was banked on each side by huge oaks. The branches of the mammoth trees, dripping with Spanish moss, offered a patchy overhead canopy that sprinkled the pavement with mottled shadows and sunshine.

They rounded a bend, and Lydia gasped in awe. The two-story brick house, a renovated and updated remnant of rice plantation days, with four heavy white columns and four second-story dormer windows, was like a regal queen on her throne. The house sat in the midst of acres of green lawn sparsely dotted with more oaks and native trees she couldn't yet name.

The house itself, with its tall bay windows and steep roof, was impressive enough. But the vast, wide-open space surrounding the building was breathtaking. A person could look out any given window and see nothing but nature, Lydia surmised. She had a feeling Chloe was going to love it here.

The rest of the afternoon Lydia spent getting acquainted with her family and her new surroundings. She toured the house, got familiar with the rooms she, Chloe, and Mrs. Porter would occupy, and looked at photo albums. She learned she had once taken ballet, voice, and violin lessons, and she wondered if she would still be able to dance, sing, or play the violin if she tried.

A stark reminder of what had been taken from her came when Jennifer pulled out Lydia's scrapbook of wedding plans. Everything had been organized with precision—bridesmaids' dresses, groomsmen's tuxedos, types of flowers—right down to how much each item would cost. The prices astounded Lydia.

How did I do it? she wondered. She could put a house in order faster than Mr. Clean, but thoughts of keeping books and organizing big events terrified her. From the looks of her wedding planner, her wedding was to have been a *big* event.

The final page included the wedding announcement that had been published in the local newspaper. She and Daniel had planned to marry in the First Community Church of Quinn Island, because, Jennifer said, it was the only local church big enough for the wedding party and anticipated crowd. Then, after a Paris honeymoon, they were going to live in Daniel's house while they built another.

Lydia closed the planner with a dismal sigh. What a charmed life she must have led. Too bad she couldn't remember any of it.

Daniel's parents arrived for supper. His father was also an attorney and shared his partnership with his son. Mrs. Matthews worked diligently in the Quinn Island Historical Society, the woman's club, and an organization that housed foster children until suitable homes could be found. They both greeted Lydia in a way that made her feel just as loved as her own parents had, then oohed and ahhed over Chloe like true doting grandparents.

Time passed. Mr. and Mrs. Matthews left. Chloe, who had missed her afternoon nap, and Mrs. Porter, who'd also missed hers, wore down and went to bed. Then a somnolent quietness fell over the five remaining adults, as though they were all tired and weary, with nothing noteworthy left to say. Eventually, Bill and Margaret retired, and Jennifer soon followed; she rented a town apartment, but she had decided to spend the night at her parents' home in celebration of Lydia's return.

Daniel remained until shortly before midnight, then stood from where he sat next to Lydia on the sofa and held out his hand. "Walk me out?"

When they stepped out onto the wide front porch, she turned around to face him. He captured both of her hands in his, and for a moment he simply looked down at her. She wished she could see his eyes, read what was in them. But the overhead light threw dark shadows over the deeper planes of his handsome face, concealing whatever silent message he held there.

"I'm going to miss you tomorrow," he finally said.

A thump of fear hit Lydia in the chest. Her eyes stretched wide. "Miss me? You mean, I won't see you tomorrow?"

A pleased grin pulled at the corner of his mouth. "Do you want to?"

Realizing how childish she'd sounded, she ducked her head.

He released one of her hands and curled his forefinger beneath her chin, lifting her head so that she was again looking at him. "I want to see you, too, but I thought your parents and Jennifer would want to spend some time with you and Chloe tomorrow."

Of course, he was right. But thoughts of being away from him for the first time since meeting him three days ago triggered a strange and inexplicable uneasiness inside her. But what could she do about it? Fall down on her knees and beg him not to leave her alone at the mercies of her new and unfamiliar world?

She thought not.

"You're right," she said, forcing so much bravery into her voice, she sounded like an amateur actor in an unrehearsed play. "I do need to spend tomorrow with my family."

What about the next day? she wanted to ask. After all, it was Saturday. Would he want to see her then? And why did she so desperately want him to want to?

"How about dinner tomorrow night?" He moved his hand from beneath her chin and brushed the backs of his fingers across her cheek. His gaze left hers and traveled over her face, like he was trying to carve her into his memory.

Her stomach fluttered. How was she supposed to focus on what he was saying when he touched her that way? "Dinner?" she finally managed to squeak.

He nodded. "We can call it the first official date of our new beginning."

"Okay," she agreed, her voice sounding small and faraway. Then her maternal instincts jabbed at her moonstruck conscience, reminding her she had one small priority. "What about Chloe?"

"I've already got that covered. She said she'd be ready at seven."

Lydia blinked. "You mean, you don't mind taking her along?" Jeff had often wanted to leave her behind.

He tugged on her hand, urging her to inch forward into his open arms. "Now, why would any man mind being the escort of the two most beautiful girls in the world?"

Lydia knew he was exaggerating, at least where she was concerned. But who was she to argue? He wanted to take Chloe along, and, whatever his reasons, that thrilled Lydia beyond description. She slipped her arms around his waist and rested her cheek against his chest. "Thank you, Daniel."

"For what?"

"For not leaving Chloe out."

"I like having her around."

Lydia closed her eyes. *So far, so good,* she thought with a contented sigh. *So far, so good.*

7

The next morning, Lydia stood on the sidewalk outside Lydia's Boutique, perusing the dress shop with her mother, her sister, her daughter, and Mrs. Porter. When Margaret had asked Lydia what she wanted to do that day, Lydia had told her mother she'd like to see the shop. She was curious to see the place that was once so much a part of her life, see if she could envision herself working there. So far, she couldn't.

"It's hard to believe I actually own this place," she mused out loud.

"Trust me, you do," her mother said. "Jennifer has done a wonderful job keeping it open and profitable while you've been away, but it was your dream."

Lydia squinted through the bright morning sun as she studied the calligraphic lettering on the windowpane and the decorative trim on the eve spanning the front of the white frame building. Then she scanned her mother's and sister's faces, noticing their proud expressions. *Whose dream is it now?* she had to wonder.

She couldn't picture it as hers. In fact, she didn't think she had much fashion sense at all. She wasn't even fond of shopping. Of course, her life in Chicago hadn't offered her the opportunity to shop often. When she did, her purchases were always based on affordability.

Mrs. Porter had surprised her sometimes with an outfit beyond her own means, usually on a birthday or Christmas. But, generally, once Lydia got back on her feet after her long trek to recovery, her friend and former landlady had respected her desire to provide for herself and daughter.

Lydia noticed Margaret leaning heavily on her cane, and she took the weary woman's arm. "Let's go inside so you can rest a little while."

Margaret gave her daughter a grateful smile, and the four women and Chloe went through the door.

Lydia had learned her mother's limp was a result of the surgery she'd had prior to Lydia's disappearance. Margaret had never fully recovered from the hip replacement, and Lydia couldn't help wondering what part grief over her abduction had played in her mother's incomplete recovery.

As she helped her mother negotiate the steps, a sad and discouraging thought filtered through her. She would never be able to replace all that was taken away that fateful night on a deserted highway. But she would do her best. She owed this woman, her sister, her father, and Daniel that much.

When Lydia stepped into the shop, she stepped out of her comfort zone. She glanced around in awe at rows and rows of stylish clothing, both women's and children's, hanging from wall racks and circular supports placed expertly across a polished hardwood floor. Lacy lingerie lined the shelves and supports at the back of the store. Two crystal chandeliers hung from a dazzlingly white ceiling, and soft classical music seemed to float through the walls. The two store clerks, one at the counter and one organizing a sales rack, both looked as though they had just stepped off the set of a classy New York fashion shoot.

Feeling a bit overwhelmed, Lydia drew in a deep breath, only to wish she hadn't. Even the air in the store smelled expensive.

"Mama, is this really your store?" Chloe asked, gaining her mother's attention.

Instinctively, Lydia lifted her daughter to her hip. She didn't want to be responsible for anything that might get broken by the curious four year old. "That's what they say, sweetheart."

"Can I have a new dress?"

"Of course you can, angel," a beaming Margaret answered. "In fact, you can have all the new dresses you want."

"Maybe one," Lydia injected, intentionally keeping her gaze

averted from her mother's. At some point, Lydia suspected she was going to have to talk to Margaret about who was mother to whom.

The salesclerk at the counter noticed the women and made her way to the front of the store, her gait reminding Lydia of a sleek, pampered house cat. "Hi, Jennifer," she said in a cultured voice that matched her cultured smile. "I thought you were taking the day off."

"I am. We just dropped by for a visit."

The two women engaged in what Lydia thought was an incomplete hug—they daintily grasped hands and merely touched cheeks together.

As they parted, the clerk, with her shiny black hair pulled back in a slick French chignon, fleetingly scanned each face as she turned to Margaret. Then her gaze snapped back to Lydia like a yo-yo on the rebound. After about two seconds of shocked paralysis, the elegant woman's painted mouth dropped open as though she'd just seen Lazarus raised from the dead.

Lydia forced herself not to withdraw. She figured she'd see many similar reactions in the next few days. She might as well start getting used to it.

Jennifer touched Lydia's arm. "Lydia, this is Jaime. She's the assistant manager of the store."

Lydia shifted Chloe to her left hip and extended her right hand. "Hi, Jaime. It's nice to meet you."

Jaime blinked like she'd been slapped. "Meet me? We went to school together. I was going to be in your wedding."

Lydia tried to muster up a smile but failed pitifully. "I'm sorry. I don't remember you. I have amnesia."

"Amnesia?" The clerk's voice rose and fell in a wave of shock.

"Yes." Lydia knew the woman deserved an explanation. But Lydia wouldn't go into the details of her abduction in front of Chloe.

As though sensing her sister's distress, Jennifer shuffled toward the door and hooked her manicured hand in the crook of Jaime's arm. "Come in back with me for a minute. There's something I need to show you." With that, she led Jaime away.

Lydia breathed an inward sigh of relief, making a mental note to thank her younger sister later.

"Now," said Margaret, hobbling to a dress rack and flipping through the dresses there, "let's see what we can do about getting you started on a new wardrobe."

New wardrobe? Lydia blinked. She already had a wardrobe. She looked down at her ribbed pink shell, full-length denim skirt, and navy sandals. Of course, her closet wasn't stocked with stylish designer classics, like her mother and Jennifer wore. One couldn't find many of those in discount stores and thrift shops. But her meager collection served its purpose.

"Chloe and I really need only one dress each, to wear on our dinner date tonight with Daniel."

Her mother didn't seem to hear her.

Lydia sent Mrs. Porter a *what-should-I-do?* look. The older woman lifted her shoulders in a *don't-ask-me* gesture, then turned and started flipping through some dresses on a sale rack.

"What about this?" Margaret turned to display a red dress designed to mold a curvy body.

Lydia didn't think she had many curves to mold. Even if she did, they weren't for anyone's eyes but her own and, maybe someday, a husband's. She shook her head. "It isn't me."

Puzzlement pinched Margaret's forehead. "You don't like it?"

"It's okay. It's just not something I would wear."

"Why don't you try it on and then decide?"

Lydia held up a hand. "Really, there's no need."

An injured look fell over Margaret's face as she turned and hung the dress back on the rack. She hobbled to a chair next to the dressing area and sat down.

Oh, great, Lydia thought. *Now I've hurt my mother's feelings.*

She set Chloe down and searched another rack, pulling out the first dress she came across in her size and style. Holding the garment up in front of her, she stepped up to her mother. "What do you think about this?"

Margaret critically eyed the dress, then lifted her gaze to her daughter's. "Do you want the truth, dear?"

The smile Lydia had pasted on for her mother's benefit wavered. "Of course."

"It doesn't suit you."

Well, touché, thought Lydia. She supposed one turn deserved another. Although she really hadn't meant to offend Margaret by rejecting the dress she'd chosen. Lydia was just stating a fact, her opinion, which, she'd noticed, didn't always set well with her mother.

"What are we looking for?" Jennifer asked, rejoining the group.

"Chloe and I need something to wear tonight. We have a dinner date with Daniel."

Jennifer's eyes lit up like a sunbeam. "Let me see what I can find." Like a kid on a treasure hunt, she scampered away and started digging through the racks.

Lydia's lips curved as she watched her sister retreat. Jennifer seemed so well suited for the affluent dress shop's environment. Much more so than Lydia herself did.

Margaret spurned Lydia's invitation to join her and Jennifer in their search, claiming she needed a while longer to rest her leg. So Lydia left the pouting woman and returned the dress she held to the rack. As she reached to hang up the garment, she caught a glimpse of the price tag and realized her mistake. The one hundred dollars she had removed from her savings pouch and tucked into her billfold before leaving the house was barely enough to buy Chloe an outfit, much less purchase one for herself.

She turned to Jennifer and Mrs. Porter, who both seemed intent on finding her the perfect garment for her evening out with Daniel. "You know what?" she said. "I think I may have something to wear back at the house, after all. Why don't we just concentrate on finding something for Chloe today?"

"Oh, come on, sis," Jennifer said, inspecting a short, black, sequined dress that sparkled like a blanket of black diamonds under the chandeliers. "What's one more outfit?"

About two hundred bucks, Lydia was tempted to say, but she decided to keep the quick retort to herself. Aloud she said, "One more than I really need."

Jennifer gave Lydia a baffled look. "That never stopped you before."

Lydia sent the baffled look right back. "It didn't?"

"Of course not." Jennifer held the dress up to Lydia. "Your philosophy was always that a woman couldn't have too many clothes. Your closet was the envy of every female in Quinn Island."

Perplexity creased Lydia's forehead. She knew Jennifer hadn't meant to be critical. She'd simply blurted out a statement of fact from one sister to another. Still, Lydia couldn't help feeling a little offended. She was also a bit unsettled by what this particular revelation about herself revealed. Had she really been so self-absorbed and frivolous with her money when so many people in the world were cold, hungry, and homeless?

Still trying to digest the information, she looked down at the dress Jennifer held up before her. Embarrassment crept up her neck just looking at the garment. She had T-shirts that were longer.

"Where are my old clothes?" she asked, figuring she might find something among her pre-amnesia wardrobe to wear for her date.

"We had everything put into storage when the lease on your apartment ran out. All that stuff is at least five years old. Why don't you try this on? I think it'll look great on you."

As gently as possible, Lydia pushed the dress away. "I don't think so. But, thanks, anyway."

Mrs. Porter, who'd been flipping through the sale rack all along, turned with a knowing grin and held up a dress that halted Lydia's ready protest. The younger woman stood dazed for a moment, admiring the sleeveless garment with its modest scooped cowl neck, trim waistline, and long skirt that graced yards and yards of silky beige material she knew would feel like luxury floating around her ankles.

She reached out and turned over the tag. Just as she feared. Even with the discount, she didn't have enough to buy a dress for both her and Chloe. And Chloe's needs came first.

She dropped the tag, brushing her fingers across the smooth material as she pulled her hand away. "It's a lovely dress, Mrs. Porter. But, really, I'd rather concentrate on getting Chloe one today."

Jennifer touched Lydia's arm. "Liddi, what is it?"

"Nothing," she answered, feeling the weight of her sister's perusal bearing down on her.

"Is it money you're worried about?"

"No," she lied. "I just didn't bring enough along today to pay for two dresses. I'll get Chloe one today, and come back and get mine later."

Understanding curved Jennifer's lips. "Lydia, that isn't necessary."

"Of course it is."

"Lydia," Mrs. Porter spoke up, "I think what your sister is trying to say is that you own the shop. The dresses won't cost you anything."

But Lydia had already thought about that. She gave the dress a palms-out gesture. "That dress cost this shop something. It's not right for me to just take it."

"Lydia—" Jennifer started, then stopped and rubbed her fingertips across her forehead, as though she were having second thoughts about what she'd intended to say.

"What?"

The younger sibling shook her head. "Nothing." She turned and motioned to Jaime, then reached for the dress in Mrs. Porter's hand. As the clerk stepped up to them, Jennifer said, "Jaime, go figure our cost on this dress and let me know what it is, please."

Jaime nodded and walked away. When the clerk was out of earshot, Jennifer turned back to Lydia. "Lydia, you have money. Since Daniel's the family attorney, we turned your finances over to him to take care of while you were away. I'm sure he'll go over everything with you when he has a chance." She squeezed Lydia's hand. "I just thought you'd want to know that."

Jennifer knelt in front of Chloe. "Now, let's go see what we can find you to wear, princess, while your mother tries on her dress."

Margaret decided she wanted to be a part of finding her granddaughter a frock. With the enthusiasm of two fairy godmothers contemplating a peasant maiden's costume for a ball, she and Mrs. Porter followed Jennifer and Chloe to the children's section of the shop, leaving Lydia to try on her dress alone. And to think.

So, I have money, she mused as she stepped into a fitting room. How much money? Enough to buy her and Chloe a small place of their own? Enough to help fund the new homeless shelter for which Jeff was trying to raise money? What about the missing persons' organization her mother had founded in her honor? Would a few extra funds help find another lost loved one?

She unzipped the dress and slid it from its hanger. What would it feel like having enough money to grocery shop without having to check the prices of every item on her list? Put more than a widow's mite in the offering plate on Sunday? Buy Chloe that one special dress?

Mentally, she pulled back the reins of her elaborate thoughts and slipped the dress over her head. She'd better wait and talk to Daniel about her net worth before making plans to build houses or fund homeless shelters.

As she twirled in front of the mirror, inspecting the most beautiful garment she ever remembered seeing, her thoughts turned to her and Chloe's dinner date with Daniel. With very little deliberation, she decided to buy the dress.

Chloe chose a purple frock with a high waistline and white lace trim, which didn't surprise Lydia. Purple was her daughter's favorite color.

With the outfits hanging from fancy silk-covered hangers and protected with long garment bags bearing the store emblem, Lydia left the shop with just over fifteen dollars in her purse. Hopefully, the White Seagull, her sister's restaurant of choice for lunch, would be easy on the pocket.

Fortunately, it was. Lydia breathed a sigh of relief as she glanced at the menu posted outside the café entrance. The quaint little establishment had outdoor seating with a view of the marsh channel that separated the island from the mainland. The table umbrellas flapped occasionally in a breeze brisk enough to offer comfort to the patrons but tame enough that it didn't send the eating utensils flying.

As soon as they all settled around the table, Margaret leaned on her forearms and looked at Lydia. "Sweetheart, why don't I call Judy Spivey, your old hairdresser, and see if she can work you and Chloe in this afternoon?"

The question—which sounded more like the follow-up statement to a decision that had already been made—caught Lydia off guard. She couldn't think of an immediate response.

"She always did such a good job with your hair before," her mother added. "And don't you think Chloe's hair would look better in a chin-length bob?"

Self-consciously, Lydia raised a hand to her thick, wind-tossed tresses. She was rather fond of her hair just the way it was, even if her corkscrew curls did usually have a stubborn will of their own. As for Chloe, well, she'd been a bald newborn and a fuzzy toddler. It had taken four years for her hair to reach shoulder length. No way was anyone going to lay scissors to those light blond locks just yet.

Silently praying she wouldn't offend her mother again, Lydia reached over and covered the woman's hand with her own. "Give us a few days to get settled in, then we'll see about making an appointment with the hairdresser."

"But what about your date tonight?"

Lydia squeezed her mother's hand. "We'll get by," she said with an appeasing smile, then gratefully reached for the menu the waitress had just laid on the table.

Thankfully, Margaret let the matter drop, but Lydia had a feeling it would be picked up again later.

Lydia had helped Chloe with the child's menu and was trying to decide between the homemade vegetable soup and the chef's salad for herself when she heard Chloe giggle. Curious, Lydia cut her daughter a sidelong glance to find the child cupping a hand over her mouth, trying to stifle laughter. Lydia shifted her gaze to the other women at the table. They were all looking at her with amusement in their expressions, like some sort of conspiracy was under way.

Then everything turned black.

8

*S*miling, Lydia raised her hands to the fingers covering her eyes. She'd known those hands only four days, but would recognize them anywhere—even if she went another five years without feeling their touch.

An unexpected yearning wove through her, and for the first time since seeing her face on *Without a Trace*, she felt grievously cheated. Half a decade ago, she had not only been robbed of her past life, but of her precious memories of Daniel.

She pulled his hands away from her eyes and twisted her head around, looking up into his handsome face. His muscular forearms were exposed by dress shirtsleeves rolled up to his elbows, and beneath the unbuttoned top button of his shirt, his tie hung loose like he'd pulled at the knot with his forefinger. The wind pushed his dark hair flat against his forehead. His smell, all man heightened by a faint scent of spicy cologne, wrapped around her senses like a silk thread.

He captured one of her hands before she could drop it back to the table. "Fancy meeting you here," he said. "I knew there was a reason I was craving one of the Gull's subs today. My guardian angel was sitting on my shoulder, pointing me in your direction."

He leaned down and kissed her forehead, and Lydia released an inward sigh of contentment. He seemed to know just what to say and do to make her feel cherished.

Before letting go of her hand, he gave her fingers a gentle squeeze. Then he turned to Chloe, lifting the eager four-year-old out of her chair and up over his head. "And what about you, angel face? Have you been keeping these ladies straight?"

Chloe's answer was an attack of giggles.

A stranger looking on would think he had made the move a thousand times. Was he this way with all kids? Or did he see something special in Chloe?

Or was Lydia engaging in wishful thinking?

"Me and Mama bought pretty dresses for our date with you tonight," Chloe said as Daniel lowered her to his hip.

Daniel flashed Lydia a pleased smile, then turned his attention back to Chloe. "You did?"

"Uh-huh." Chloe gave her head an emphatic nod. "Mine's purple."

"Purple? I like purple. You'll make all the other girls very jealous."

He tickled Chloe's stomach, sending her off in another fit of giggles, before setting her back in her seat.

"Why don't you join us, Daniel?" Margaret suggested.

"I believe I will. Let me go wash up and I'll be right back." With that, he headed for the indoor area of the restaurant.

Lydia returned to her menu and had just about decided on the soup when a hand holding a small tape recorder appeared in front of her face, blocking her view.

"Miss Quinn," an unfamiliar male voice said, "could you answer a few questions about your abduction and the five years you were away from Quinn Island?"

She tipped up her head and looked into the eager face of a young man in a crumpled gray suit with press credentials clipped to the jacket pocket. A thirty-five millimeter camera dangled around his neck, and the end of his tie lay across the top of his shoulder, like he'd been running.

Lydia blinked. "I . . . ah . . ." Words failed her. She stared up at the man, unable to react.

"I understand you have a young daughter. Is this her? Is she a result of the assault, or do you know who the father is?"

Seconds passed like long minutes. Lydia became aware that everyone in the busy eating area was staring at her. The invisible walls of the outdoor café started closing in on her, trapping her. Still, she couldn't react, couldn't speak.

Out of the corner of her eye, she saw her mother and Mrs. Porter start to rise; then, for some reason, both ladies sat back down.

That "some reason" appeared instantly at her side in the form of Daniel. He clamped his hand over the microphone end of the recorder. "No, Mark, Miss Quinn will not answer any questions."

The man swung toward Daniel. "As a member of the media, I've got rights—"

"So has Miss Quinn." Daniel's voice was calm.

"But—"

"I can go talk to the judge." Daniel's tone remained low and steady, but Lydia could see a vein throbbing beneath his ear, and she sensed the fury caged just beneath the surface of his dark eyes. "I'm sure he'll have no problem issuing a restraining order to anyone who comes within a hundred feet of Miss Quinn with the intention of invading her privacy."

Lydia thought surely the reporter would back down. Amazingly, the smaller man persisted. "Come on, Daniel. The people of Quinn Island have a right to hear her story."

Daniel pulled his hand away from the tape recorder. "Then there's always harassment. Did you get that on record, Mark?"

The reporter snapped off the recorder and crammed it in his jacket pocket. "I'll get my story," he sneered. "I have another source, you know." With that, the irate man turned and stalked away.

Lydia propped her elbows on the table, dropped her forehead to her hands, and started shaking.

Daniel slid a chair against hers and sat down, slipping his arm around her shoulders. "Lydia, are you okay?"

The words on the menu blurred. Her world tilted. Someone touched her arm.

"Lydia," came her mother's concerned voice, "can I get you something? A glass of water?"

She heard everyone calling to her, but the darkness closing in around her was stronger. She couldn't pull herself back from it. The menu started to fade.

"Mommy!"

That did it. The alarm in Chloe's voice jerked her up straight. She focused on her child, and the concern and confusion in her small face bruised Lydia's heart. "Mommy's fine, sweetheart." They reached for each other at the same time. Lydia shifted her daughter to her lap. With arms and legs, Chloe clamped onto her mother's neck and waist and laid her head on her mother's shoulder.

"Did that man hurt you?" the little girl wanted to know.

"No, sweetie. He didn't hurt me."

"Then why did Daniel make him go away?"

In her peripheral vision, Lydia saw Daniel open his mouth to answer. She held up a hand to stop him. When she felt assured of his silence, she took the same hand and rubbed her daughter's back. "Because the man was asking about things I didn't want to talk about."

"What kind of things?"

Lydia pursed her lips, thinking. "Private things."

"Like my private places, where no one's s'pose to touch me."

"Yes. Something like that." Lydia felt her face warm, but she was awed by how closely her daughter's comparison paralleled her own feelings. Chloe was a private part of Lydia she had always been able to protect from evil and harmful things. At least, she had until today.

Chloe planted her small hands on her mother's shoulders and pushed back. "We need to pray for him." She bobbed her head with each word for emphasis. "Like Moses prayed for his people."

Lydia tucked a wisp of stray hair behind her daughter's ear. "You're right. We should." But she wasn't quite ready to forgive the stranger who had so rudely intruded on her and her daughter's life.

The waitress appeared at the table and Lydia asked Chloe if she was ready to order.

Wrinkling her nose, the little girl shook her head. "I'm not hungry anymore."

"Me, either." Lydia glanced around the table. "I think Chloe and I will just wait in the car."

Daniel stood, reaching for the back of her chair. "Come on. I'll take you back to the house."

She looked up at him. "But don't you have to get back to the office? And what about lunch?"

"We'll fix us something there." He captured her upper arm and helped her stand.

"But I don't want to be an imposition."

He trapped her chin beneath his thumb and curled forefinger. "You, my dear, could never be an imposition."

Lydia had no more energy to argue. She turned to her longtime friend. "Mrs. Porter—"

Mrs. Porter waved a hand through the air, shooing Lydia, Chloe, and Daniel away. "You run along, dear. I'll come with Margaret and Jennifer."

With Chloe perched on her hip, Lydia left the restaurant under the security of Daniel's protective arm. But inside she felt like she was dangling from a faulty trapeze swing with no safety net beneath her. What had just happened back there with that reporter? When he had asked about Chloe, she couldn't move, couldn't speak, couldn't react. All she could do was sit there and stare at him.

Then there was Daniel, like her own guardian angel, putting the reporter in his place, taking care of her . . . and Chloe. What would she have done today if he hadn't been there?

Daniel took the initiative and fastened Chloe's seat belt, then opened the door for Lydia. She climbed in like a battery-operated doll with a weak battery. As she watched Daniel circle the front of the car on his way to the driver's side, the layers of numbness began to peel away from her brain, leaving her mind exposed to the stark reality of her situation.

She needed him.

She felt a crack in her wall of independence, a small piece chip away. She needed Daniel, but God knew she didn't want to.

Ever since the day she had recovered from the assault and started making her own way, she had been determined not to need anyone. Not Jeff. Not even Mrs. Porter.

Not anyone.

Because she knew too well that fate could deal a person a cruel blow—and he or she could find themselves alone, like she had five years ago. During her recovery—when someone else had held the soupspoon to her mouth, bore her weight every time she went to the bathroom, provided her with a roof over her head—she had discovered that dependence was not the kind of existence she wanted for herself. And when she rose above it, she vowed she'd never go back.

She might one day fall in love with Daniel, marry him, share his home and children. But she *did not* want to depend on him for survival. Because if she did, and then something happened one day to take him away from her, she feared she might curl up into a ball and die, like she'd tried to do before she had Chloe. She didn't want to risk going back to that terrible feeling of helplessness. She didn't want to care about anyone that much. But she had a sinking feeling it was too late—and an even deeper fear that her dependence on Daniel went beyond basic need. Far beyond.

He had stepped into her life, swept her off her feet, carried her over the rough places, and, so far, had refused to put her down. What would happen if he decided to? Would her heart survive it?

The leather seat of the car creaked a little under Daniel's weight, and he touched her face. She closed her eyes and tilted her head so that her cheek rested in his palm.

Heaven help her, she needed him.

❧

"What was the reporter talking about when he said he had another source of information on me?" Lydia asked while she and Daniel prepared two ham and cheese sandwiches. Chloe, who sat at the table engrossed in a coloring book and crayons, preferred plain cheese.

Since Friday was the maid's shopping day, Lydia, Daniel, and Chloe had the house to themselves during lunch, which suited Lydia just fine. Something about spreading her own mayonnaise and slicing her own tomatoes helped her corral her scattered nerves and made her feel more at home in the spotless plantation house kitchen.

"Mark dates Jaime," Daniel answered as he slapped two slices of ham on his sandwich. He started to follow suit with Lydia's, but she fanned away the second piece of meat with an inward shudder. Where did he put all the food he consumed? Certainly not on that lean, muscular frame of his.

She added the cheese. "You mean the clerk at the dress shop? The one who told me she was supposed to have had a part in our wedding?"

He added slices of tomato. "That's the one."

On went blankets of lettuce. "So, that's how he found out I was going to be at the White Seagull. We were talking about it at the shop when we checked out."

The top layer of bread fell into place. "I would say so."

The phone rang, and Lydia almost jumped out of her slippers. With one hand over her racing heart, she turned to pick up the wall receiver.

Daniel abandoned the glass he was filling with ice and grabbed her wrist. "Don't answer that."

She frowned up at him. "Why? It could be Jennifer or Mother. Or Mrs. Porter."

"Let me." He squeezed between her and the wall and picked up the receiver. "Hello."

Almost immediately, he scowled. "No, Miss Quinn will not be available to answer any questions this evening." A short pause, then, "No, she won't be available tomorrow, either." His scowl deepened. "Not then, either. She's not interested in talking to the press, period." His hand, which still circled her wrist, inched down to grasp her hand. "Not that it's any of your business, but I'm her attorney, and, no, I'm not interested in talking to the press, either. Thank you, and have a good day."

With that, he hung up and turned to her. He raked his free hand through his hair. A rebellious lock dipped toward his left brow. "Lydia, I don't think it would be a good idea for you to answer the phone for the next few weeks."

She didn't have to guess at the meaning of his words. "Daniel, exactly how many people do you think know I'm back by now?"

He pursed his lips, glancing into the distance over her left shoulder as though mentally stacking numbers, "Oh"—he cut his gaze back to hers—"I'd say about half the town."

Chewing her lower lip, she pulled her hands from his and turned, taking a few steps away from him. "Goodness, news travels fast here, doesn't it?"

"News like this does."

His hands cupped her shoulders. Drawn by his magnetic touch, she leaned back into him. His strong, comforting arms enveloped her shoulders. She raised her hands to his forearms and laid her head back against his chest. He rested his chin on top of her head and, ever-so-gently, began to sway from side to side. She closed her eyes and floated with him, feeling as though they moved as one, like ice dancers skating to a love song.

"I know your amnesia puts you at a disadvantage, love," he said. "Everyone here knows you. You don't remember anyone. But we'll get through this together, you and I."

She released a rueful sigh. "Seems like, Mr. Matthews, I've become somewhat a burden for you."

"On the contrary, Miss Quinn. You've given me back my reason for living."

A hand came up and brushed the hair away from her temple. His soft lips touched the jagged scar there. She felt the sting of tears behind her closed eyelids, and an overwhelming need to say "I love you." But the words tripped over the lump of emotion lodged in her throat.

He slid his palms up her arms, stopping when he reached her shoulders. Slowly, he turned her around. She knew he was going to kiss her and that she was going to kiss him back. A dizzy current raced through her as she floated toward him.

But ten small fingers crawling up her leg shattered her cloud of ecstasy in a million tiny pieces.

She pushed away from Daniel and looked down. What on earth had she been thinking? A trembling hand rose to her fluttering stomach. Obviously, she hadn't been thinking. Otherwise, she wouldn't have forgotten her daughter was sitting at the table less than six feet away.

She kneeled down in front of Chloe and grasped her daughter's hands. "What is it, sweetheart?"

Chloe tilted her head to one side, pushed out her lower lip in an artful pout, and looked at her mother with eyes that reminded Lydia of a wounded puppy. "I want you to hold me, Mommy."

Chloe only used "Mommy" when she really needed, or just plain wanted, her mother's attention. This was one of those "just plain wanted" times. But Lydia couldn't fault the timing. Had it not been for her daughter's interruption, she would have been engaged in the kind of scene she censored when Chloe watched TV. Lydia even blushed when she saw a man and woman locked in a passionate kiss on the television screen. That kind of intimacy, in her opinion, belonged to the privacy of the two consenting adults. Anything more belonged within the sanctity of marriage.

"Now, Chloe," Lydia said, "I think you're big enough to walk. Besides, if I hold you, who's going to carry our food to the table?"

Chloe turned huge accusing eyes on Daniel.

In answer to her daughter's silent message, Lydia said, "I was hoping we could eat out on the terrace"—she really needed the fresh air— "and I don't think it's fair to ask Daniel to carry all the food out there by himself. Do you?"

Chloe ducked her head and shook it.

When Lydia stood, she noticed a look of sincere remorse on Daniel's face.

"I'm so—"

She cut off his apology with an upheld hand. "It wasn't your fault." Scooping up hers and Chloe's plates, she headed for the terrace, knowing without looking that her daughter followed close behind.

"I'll be out in a minute," she heard Daniel say, but she never looked back, never broke her stride.

She didn't blame him for their momentary loss of self-control. He was a man. A passionate man who had, from day one, been honest and open about his feelings for her. She, on the other hand, was the mother of an impressionable four-year-old who had been sitting right there in the kitchen with her and Daniel when she had so willingly fell into his arms.

How could she have been so stupid?

❧

How could he have been so stupid?

Daniel berated himself while he stood, hands stuffed in his pockets, watching the two most important people in his life disappear through the kitchen door. In a moment of passion, he'd forgotten all about Chloe—and his vow to let Lydia make the first move.

She was so vulnerable right now, trying to find her place in a world she knew nothing about, live among people who unknowingly placed high demands on her. He didn't want to be one of those people. In fact, "those people," as well meaning as some might be, were exactly what he wanted to protect her from. Now, here he had gone and almost given in to his increasing desire to hold and kiss her. He would have if Chloe hadn't intervened.

He leaned back against the cabinet and scrubbed a shaky hand down his face. He needed to get out to the terrace and figure out how to worm his way back into Chloe's good graces. But he couldn't. Not right this minute. His insides were still quivering.

❧

Some two minutes later, when Daniel felt his emotions were under control, he carried his sandwich and the drinks—purple Kool-Aid per Chloe's request—outside on a tray. He cautiously sat down in the vacant seat next to Chloe, positioning himself on the side of the child that was opposite her mother.

The first five minutes, he got nowhere. He talked and asked questions he thought four-year-olds might be interested in answering. Chloe chewed on her plain cheese sandwich, sipped her purple drink, and pointedly ignored him. The heel of her tennis shoe tapped out a steady *thump, thump, thump* on the chair leg as she swung her short leg back and forth.

He looked to Lydia for help. She merely gazed back at him with a twinkle in her eyes, then glanced away and took a dainty sip of drink, trying, he could tell, not to laugh.

She was enjoying seeing him squirm. *Spiteful woman,* he thought with affection, then almost grinned himself. Guess it served him right for losing his head and crawling all over her in the kitchen in front of her daughter.

He heaved a sigh and went back to Chloe. He'd interrogated hardcore criminals who had been easier to crack than this kid. "You know what, Chloe? I know where there's an ice cream parlor that serves purple ice cream."

Her leg stopped swinging. She stopped chewing.

Daniel waited a few seconds, then added, "Do you like purple ice cream?"

One, two, three seconds passed before Chloe nodded, once, without looking at him, then went back to chewing. Her leg went back to swinging.

At last, they were getting somewhere. Daniel felt like raising his hands and physically praising the Lord.

After fifteen minutes and a promise of a purple ice cream cone the very next day, Daniel felt confident all was forgiven. Chloe was talking and smiling again at his corny jokes, and the untimely kitchen incident seemed to be fading quickly from her young mind.

At least he thought so until she twisted her head around, peered up at him, and said, "Are you going to marry my mama?"

Daniel blinked. Now, how was he supposed to answer that? He glanced at Lydia, who looked the other way. No help there.

He folded his arms on the table and looked down at Chloe. Wanting to stay on good terms with the child, he gave an answer he felt was both unassuming and honest. "Maybe. Someday."

"That's what she says about Jeff."

Lydia swung her head around, gaping at Chloe like the child had just revealed a well-guarded secret.

Daniel almost choked on the last bite he'd taken of his sandwich. "She . . . says . . . what . . . about Jeff?"

"Whenever I ask my mama if she's going to marry Jeff, she always says 'Maybe someday,'" The singsong innocence of Chloe's voice did nothing to calm the spasms inside Daniel's chest.

Seemingly oblivious to the earthquake about to explode in the man beside her, the child turned her attention back to the sandwich she held in one hand and took another bite.

Daniel lifted a sharp, questioning gaze to Lydia.

"I'll explain later," she said with a nonchalant shrug.

Had she lied to him in Chicago when she told him she and Jeff were just friends?

She started stacking plates on the tray, and he followed suit with the glasses. She could count on explaining about Jeff. *Soon.* Like, within the next hour. No way was he going to spend the rest of the day wondering how she felt about this other man. And if she had any intentions of "maybe someday" marrying him, Daniel would simply have to change her way of thinking.

Because he had no intentions of her marrying anybody . . . except him.

9

$\mathcal{I}$'m not sure going out tonight is such a good idea," Lydia told Daniel as she set the dishes in the sink.

Daniel understood her reservations, and he had already come up with a solution. Stepping up beside her, he slid his hands into his pockets so he wouldn't follow his instinct to touch her. "What if I were to take the afternoon off and take you and Chloe to a place where your privacy will be respected and no reporters will harass you?"

She shifted to face him. "I can't let you do that. You've already missed four days of work this week. You must have tons to do."

A sharp pang of regret jabbed at his chest. Once he had put his work before her, and his decision had cost them both—dearly. He would not make that mistake again.

"Only half a ton," he said, forcing a chipper note into his voice. "Which is nothing out of the ordinary. Besides, when I found you in Chicago on Tuesday, I went ahead and cancelled all my appointments for the week. The only thing waiting back at the office for me is a stack of paperwork, which isn't nearly as appealing as spending an afternoon on the island with you and Chloe."

Her eyes lit up with a childlike exuberance. "The island?"

He nodded.

Even as she shook her head, he could see her struggling to contain her enthusiasm. "Seriously, Daniel. I don't want you to feel you have to entertain us."

Chloe was back at the table engrossed in her coloring, but Daniel suspected she was keeping a keen eye on him and her mother. He resisted the urge to reach for Lydia's waist and risked capturing her hands instead. "The only reason I went into work this morning was because if I hadn't, I would have been on your parents' doorstep at dawn wanting to see you, and I really felt your family needed a little time with you."

A well of emotion still too raw to be contained rose in his chest, as did the conviction in his voice. "Lydia, I have waited for this day for so long that I live in fear I'll wake up and find it's all been just a dream." He squeezed her fingers. "There's nothing at work that can't wait until Monday. But there's something here I've wanted for five years. I'd like to spend every minute with you that I can. That is, if you have no objections."

"I don't," she responded, her voice sounding small and breathless. "We'd love to go to the island with you."

A small degree of satisfaction settled over Daniel. Maybe, just maybe, she was beginning to feel for him just a little of what he felt for her. "Great. Let me make a phone call, and in about thirty minutes, we'll be set to go."

"Do Chloe and I need to change?"

He considered Chloe's shorts and Lydia's casual skirt and top. "No. You're both perfect just the way you are."

He placed his call, making arrangements to borrow a car since his was too easily recognized. In addition to the vehicle, he requested hats and sunglasses for himself, Lydia, and Chloe so they could leave the grounds in disguise.

When he hung up the phone, he turned around and squared off to face Lydia, who stood about three feet away, her hands laced in front of her. For a fleeting moment, he lost sight of his purpose. Did she realize what a captivating picture she made, standing there mesmerizing him with those soft brown eyes of hers? Somehow, he didn't think so.

Mentally, he shook his head, reminding himself of his intention. "Now, I'm ready to hear about Jeff," he said.

She shrugged. "There really isn't much to tell."

"Then it shouldn't take you very long."

She glanced pointedly at Chloe, then looked back at him, clearly expecting him to relent and wait until later to hear what she had to say about Jeff.

Daniel merely leaned back against the counter, crossed his arms and ankles, and waited.

She studied him a moment, apparently contemplating what to do, then rolled her eyes and threw up her hands in defeat. "Come on, Chloe. Let's go see what's on PBS."

Chloe shot Daniel a wary look, and at first he feared she'd refuse to go.

Lydia held out her hand. "Come on, Chloe," she repeated with a mild note of firmness. "Daniel and I need to talk about something, then we're going to ride out to the island with him and see the ocean."

Chloe lit up like a sunbeam. "We are?"

Daniel sauntered to the table "That's right. We might even round up a bucket so we can play in the sand."

The child jumped down from her chair and, ignoring her mother's hand, dove for Daniel, wrapping her arms around his knees.

He peeled her arms from his legs and kneeled down in front of her. When she reached around his neck and planted a butterfly kiss on his cheek, his chest tightened. The sting of unexpected tears nipped at his eyes. He quickly blinked them away. The little girl's charms were as potent as her mother's, but in a totally different way.

Chloe followed her mother out of the kitchen with a jaunty bounce in her step and her ponytail swinging from side to side behind her. As soon as the door closed behind them, Daniel placed another quick call, adding a sand bucket, shovel, and a beach blanket to his earlier request.

When he hung up, he leaned back against the counter once again and tried to prepare himself for Lydia's return. What would he do if she told him she was in love with Jeff and was thinking about marrying him? He forced a deep breath into his lungs. He wasn't sure what he'd do. But, if he were a betting person, he'd wager he'd lay down and die, right there on the spot.

When she stepped back through the door, every muscle in his body tensed like a rope engaged in a tug-o-war game.

She stopped about three feet in front of him and crossed her arms. "You're buying her affection, you know."

One corner of his mouth tipped. "It's worth it."

Their eyes locked, igniting a bolt of electricity that crackled over several seconds of silence. Then she blinked, and he felt her pull herself back, as though she'd suddenly realized she was standing too close to a cliff ledge.

Shifting her weight to one foot, she said, "So, you want to know about Jeff."

He nodded, once. That was all the knot in his throat would allow.

"About two months ago he asked me to marry him."

He slowly arched an inquisitive brow. "And you were considering it?"

"I was . . . waiting."

"Waiting for what?"

"To see if something more than friendship would develop between us, or if a parental bond would develop between him and Chloe."

"And was anything developing?"

A soft smile curved her lips. "No. I realize now that Jeff and I are simply good friends. That's all we'll ever be. He knows that, too."

He heaved a deep sigh of relief. When he exhaled, his muscles turned to pulp as the tension drained from his body. He scrubbed a hand down his face. "I lost you once. I don't want to lose you again. To anything, or anybody."

They both grew still and very quiet, and Daniel saw a tenderness in her eyes he knew he'd never seen before. And in that single defining moment, he realized she cared about him. *Really* cared about him. About his thoughts, his feelings, and what he had suffered. Even after all she'd been through, she still found room in her heart to care about what her disappearance five years ago had done to him.

He was overcome with . . . something. He wasn't sure what. It was a feeling he'd never, until that moment, experienced. But whatever it was, it moved him. And humbled him.

"I was going to tell you about Jeff's proposal," she said, answering a question he'd asked himself at least a dozen times since Chloe had made her little earth-jarring statement a while ago. "Yesterday, before we left for the airport, I started to tell you, but the shuttle arrived and there wasn't enough time. Since then, I really haven't thought about it."

Daniel nodded, satisfied he knew all he needed to know. There was no one else, and she had planned to tell him about the proposal.

He eased away from the counter. "You know," he said, "I'd really like to hug you before we go, but I'm afraid to." Afraid Chloe would walk in. Afraid he couldn't let go.

Suddenly, she had the brown eyes of a minx and the mischievous grin of an imp. Strolling forward, she raised her hands to his waist. His throat went a little dry.

"Just don't forget my daughter's in the very next room," she said.

Daniel would have laughed out loud, but he didn't want to draw the protective four-year-old's attention just yet. Slipping his arms around Lydia, he said, "I think, *maybe,* I can manage that."

Her arms circled his waist and she laid her cheek against his chest. Feeling more contented than he had in a very long time, he rested his jaw on top of her head. My, but she was full of surprise. Why hadn't he ever noticed that about her before?

❧

"Mama, are we goin' in that?" Chloe said from where she stood on the top step next to her mother.

The old SUV sitting in the circular drive had an unpainted front fender and a creased back bumper. Under a multitude of dings, dents, and scratches, lay a dull coat of yellow paint. Daniel had borrowed the eccentric-looking vehicle from his eccentric-looking cousin named Steve.

Pasting on a bright smile, Lydia peered down at her child, who now wore a floppy straw hat and a child-size pair of oval-lens sunglasses. "We sure are, honey. Wasn't it nice of Steve to let us borrow it?"

Chloe scrutinized the vehicle, but she made no further comment.

She might not have been showered with many luxuries outside their basic needs, but she was accustomed to riding in Mrs. Porter's and now Daniel's comfortable, well-kept sedans.

Lydia donned her straw hat and sunglasses, and Daniel jammed a white baseball cap, bill turned backward, over his dark hair. He had also changed clothes and now wore an olive-green polo shirt, a pair of faded jeans, and a well-worn pair of running shoes.

He fastened Chloe in her seat and opened the door for Lydia. Amazingly, the inside of the car was as neat and clean as a king's castle and smelled as fresh as the morning sunshine. When Daniel fired the engine, it purred like a well-fed kitten.

Steve had left in Daniel's car about five minutes earlier, hoping to draw away any media or overzealous well-wishers who might be stationed at the front gate. Even so, as Daniel approached the entrance to the drive, unease stirred up a swarm of butterflies in Lydia's stomach. When the gate clanged shut behind them, she felt as though she'd been locked out of her house in the middle of a cold, dark night.

"Are you sure no one will bother us on the island?" she asked as Daniel eased out onto the highway.

He'd noticed how the knuckles of her clasped hands had turned white when he drove through the gate. Reaching over, he pried her hands apart and laced his fingers through hers. Her fingertips felt like icicles pressed against the back of his hand, but he wasn't surprised. Her hands had always gotten cold when she was nervous. Today, they had been cold a lot.

"If anyone sees you and recognizes you," he explained, "they may stop and say hello and tell you they're glad you made it home, but they won't bother you. Not like the people on the mainland who know you so well."

"Oh, Daniel, the people haven't bothered me so much, other than that nosy reporter." The last phrase she added as though she'd just tasted something sour. "It's just that everyone seems so thrilled to see me. Since I can't remember any of them, I can't empathize with their experience, because mine's a totally different one." She shook her head and turned her attention to the view outside the passenger window. "I don't mean to sound cold, but it's just going to take some time to recapture what I once felt for everyone."

Just like it'll take time to recapture what you once felt for me, Daniel thought. Something heavy settled on his chest. He shifted gears in the old five-speed. "You don't sound *cold*, sweetheart. I know it's going to take time."

And when she learned that five years ago a self-serving decision on his part had ultimately put her in the situation she was now in, would she even want to love him at all?

10

$\mathcal{F}$ifteen minutes later, Daniel drove over the bridge spanning the channel that separated the island from the mainland. About a quarter-mile after crossing the bridge, he veered to the right and drove down a street lined with sparse houses shrouded by verdant trees and lush landscaping.

Lydia eyed each home on the island with curiosity, noticing they were all modestly built, but well-kept and welcoming. When Daniel passed the first four without stopping, she said, "Which one belonged to my grandfather?" She simply couldn't see herself as the owner of one of these charming little cottages by the sea.

"You'll see," was Daniel's answer.

They passed a female jogger accompanied by a gorgeous collie on a leash. The runner gave the SUV a critical glower, but she showed no interest in the occupants.

A smile settled on Lydia's lips. So that was why Daniel had chosen such a deprived-looking vehicle for their outing. Onlookers paid more attention to the automobile than to who was inside.

"Mama, where's the ocean?"

Smiling, Lydia peeked around the bucket seat at her daughter, then looked to Daniel for the answer.

"It's on the other side of the houses, Chloe," he explained. "All those plants and trees around and between the houses were placed there on purpose, to make a shield between the road and the ocean."

"But when do *we* get to see it?" Chloe persisted.

He glanced at Chloe via the rearview mirror. "Soon, angel. We're just about there."

A kneeling elderly woman tending her flower bed raised her garden trowel in greeting. Returning the affable gesture, Lydia asked, "Are the people who live on the island friendly?"

"Very. They keep an eye out for one another, occasionally get together for things like barbeques and birthday parties. At the same time, they respect each other's privacy."

The small, wood-frame island church, supported by partially submerged stone pillars, appeared to be floating on top of the marsh. Daniel had told her the aged building had encountered at least a dozen major storms since it had been built over 120 years ago. Somehow, the old house of worship had withstood them all and was still standing.

As they drove past the church, Lydia decided Daniel was right when he had told her the island was like a world within itself. Strictly residential, no nightclubs, no bars, no social clubs that labeled one class or another. Just a safe haven for people who wanted to escape the madness of a harsh, demanding world and live in quiet tranquility.

A place for people like her . . . and Chloe.

The tension tugging at Lydia's nape began to ebb, heightening her awareness of Daniel's thumb caressing the back of her hand.

The road ended where someone's driveway began. Instead of stopping, Daniel pulled into the private road that was flanked on each side of the entrance by a replica of a ship's-helm wheel. He navigated a ninety-degree curve to the left and continued up a gently sloping hill, then stopped in front of a charming two-story cottage with a wraparound porch. The gray paint appeared fresh and unweathered, but the shrubs and flowers could have used the tender hand of a good gardener. The poor bushes either reached across the stone walkway like long, gnarly fingers or drooped in haggard disarray outside their intended boundaries. Lydia's hands itched to start pruning. The wide stone walkway that led up to matching front-porch steps added a pleasing touch of traditional grace and dignity to the quaint appeal of the structure.

Lydia studied the house and its surroundings with keen interest. It was the last building on the island, so there could be only one reason Daniel would stop here. "This . . . belongs to me?" Her disbelief spilled over into her voice.

"Yes. The cottage and the entire southern tip of the island is the property your grandfather left you seven years ago."

She shifted her gaze to his. She could tell from the expectancy in his expression he was waiting for her reaction.

So was she.

She studied the cottage once again. A lazy white cloud drifted behind the gabled wood-shingled roof. The sun, blazing high in the western sky, bathed the gray, trimmed-in-white house and its fertile surroundings in a soft blanket of white light, making it look almost ethereal. The fat leaves of two tall palm trees, one flanking each front corner of the house, swayed back and forth in a temperate breeze, as though beckoning her to step out of the car and come.

But something held her back. The excitement, thrill, and exhilaration she had expected to feel upon arriving at her island retreat had dwindled, leaving in their wake an odd sense of hesitation. How did she accept such a generous gift from someone long gone, someone she didn't even know?

A bump on her left elbow drew her attention. She swiveled her head around to find Chloe had unfastened her seat belt and scrambled to the space between the front bucket seats. Blue eyes wide, she gaped at the cottage "Is this our house, Mama?"

"Yes. I suppose it is." But it didn't seem real. In fact, nothing had seemed real since she left Chicago. Except Daniel. And, sometimes, she feared he was too good to be true.

"Are we gonna live here?" Chloe wanted to know.

"I don't know, honey. We'll just have to wait and see."

Lydia raised her eyes to Daniel's. The warmth in his smile eased some of her trepidation.

"Would you like to have a look inside?" he asked.

"Isn't it locked?"

A grin curved his lips. "Yes, but I have a key."

One corner of her mouth quirked in amusement. "Why doesn't that surprise me?"

When she stepped out of the SUV, she drew in a deep breath. The balmy air smelled faintly of the flowering shrubs huddled around the house and something else. The salt and sea, maybe?

Lydia was anxious to see the beach. She wanted to see if the earth merging with an endless plane of water was really as awe-inspiring as she thought it would be, and to discover why the ocean had been so alluring to her in her second life—the one she'd lived as Sara.

"I'm sorry the yards have been neglected," Daniel said as they approached the stone front-porch steps. "The landscaper I was using moved away from Quinn Island. What with getting ready for the *Without a Trace* show and all, I haven't had a chance to replace him. I'll get on it first thing Monday, though."

"You'll do no such thing," Lydia said.

He stopped short on the second step, prompting her to glance back over her shoulder at him as she stepped onto the porch. He was staring at her with a strange, somewhat stunned, expression. She shifted around to face him. "What is it?"

"Why don't you want me to hire another landscaper?"

"Because I want to do it myself."

"Really, Lydia, it's no trouble. In fact, I already have one in mind."

"I'm not talking about hiring a landscaper, silly. I'm talking about doing the landscaping myself. I love yard work."

He blinked. "Are you serious?"

"Of course I am."

He continued staring at her as though she'd just dropped in from outer space.

"I have a feeling I just said something out of character here," she said.

He took the final two steps, forcing her to tilt her head in order to maintain eye contact. He stared down at her. "You used to hate yard work."

"I did?" She found that a little hard to believe.

"Yes, you did." He grasped her fingers and lifted her hand. Dropping his gaze to their point of contact, he added, "You didn't like messing up your hands." His thumb traced the irregular plane across her knuckles. "You have the most beautiful hands." A wistful smile tugged at the corner of his mouth. "You loved having your nails done."

She pulled her hand free of his and curled her fist in the folds of her skirt. Obviously, Daniel had taken a left turn down memory lane, because she didn't have beautiful hands anymore. While living in Chicago, she'd barely had time to file her nails once a week. She certainly hadn't had the time—or money—for something so frivolous as a professional manicure. And four years of cleaning had left her skin rough and dry despite the hand creams she used daily.

Still, given the choice of an hour at a manicurist's table and one planting and pruning the neglected foliage around the beach cottage, she'd choose the latter.

How would Daniel feel about that? Sorely disappointed, Lydia suspected.

"Mama, when we gonna get to see the water?"

"In just another minute or two," Daniel answered, pulling a set of keys from his pocket.

Grateful for the timely interruption, Lydia kneeled in front of her daughter. "I'm proud of you for being so patient, Chloe. Sometimes, when grown-ups get to talking, we get sidetracked."

"What's sidetracked?"

"It means sometimes we forget what we're supposed to be doing." It seemed she'd been doing that a lot over the past four days.

Daniel pushed the door open and stepped back. "Well, ladies, here we are."

Reaching for Chloe's hand, Lydia rose and stepped cautiously across the threshold. Entering the house felt eerie, like entering a vacated office building long after business hours. Her sandals echoed with a dull, hollow-sounding thud against the hardwood floor. White sheets draped over furniture cast ghostly impressions around the large, dusky room beyond the foyer. Dust fairies, awakened by human presence, danced in the sunlight that sliced through the open door behind them.

Chloe pressed her small body against her mother's thigh. Laying her hand on her daughter's shoulder, Lydia stopped short of stepping beyond the foyer. "It's okay, honey. Those are just bedsheets, spread over the furniture to keep it from getting dirty."

Daniel stepped up beside them, flipped a wall switch, and the bright overhead lights chased the spooky shadows into cheery pale yellow walls. A painting of a sailboat in a heavy gilded frame hung over what Lydia guessed was the living room sofa.

She noticed immediately the absence of cobwebs and dust buildup. The house might not have been lived in for seven years, but it certainly hadn't been neglected.

She cut Daniel a sidelong glance. "Let me guess. You've looked after this place for the last five years."

He shrugged. "I've tried. I have someone come in and clean occasionally, and I try to get out here once every month or so to see that everything's okay."

Scanning the room, she heaved a deep breath. "I don't know how I'm ever going to repay you for all you've done while I've been away."

He caught her chin between his thumb and forefinger, tilting her face toward his. "Love is free."

The room swayed, and Lydia wondered if a wave had slipped beneath the house and carried them out to sea.

"Mama, look."

Lydia hadn't even noticed that Chloe had left her side. A wing of panic fluttered in her chest when she didn't immediately see her daughter. Then she noticed the backs of two tiny pink tennis shoes planted beneath a child-shaped lump under the curtain hanging over the back door.

Daniel led Lydia across the room and pulled back the curtain. There stood Chloe, her little nose pressed against the full-length pane of a French door, a ring of fog where her breath fanned the glass. Beyond the window was the site Lydia felt she'd waited an entire lifetime—at least, the only life she could remember—to see. White crested waves rolled into shore, spreading a soft sheet of foam over bright pale sand, then languidly drifted back out to sea. A sailboat bobbed up and down amid a rippled blanket of diamonds tossed by the sun across the blue-green water. Two silver seagulls rode on the wind.

Both Chloe and Lydia gasped and jumped back when three large pelicans dipped in front of the door window.

"It's even more beautiful than I imagined," Lydia said.

Daniel reached around her and unlocked the door. "I'm glad you like it."

Like it? She had a feeling she was going to love it.

Daniel opened the door and the wind rushed in, catching her and Chloe both off guard as it pushed them backward. The breeze grabbed their hats and tossed them across the room at the same time Daniel reached out to support mother and daughter. His body was a sustaining wall that kept them from falling.

When Lydia and Chloe were both steady, Lydia said, "Wow, I never realized the wind would be so strong." Fortunately, she had pulled her hair back in a loose ponytail at the nape of her neck. She could just imagine what her stubborn curls would look like after an hour's tryst with this breeze.

"We're supposed to have some rain showers coming in this afternoon, so it's a little more brisk today than usual. Even so, it should be a little calmer down on the beach. Up here on the knoll, you get the full brunt of the breeze coming in off the ocean."

"Good, because I know a little girl who's going to be very disappointed if she can't at least get her feet wet." She knew a big girl who would be, too.

"Do you want me to get the stuff out of the car now or later?"

"Later," she said. Grasping his hand, she pulled him out the door behind her.

Hand in hand, with Chloe in the middle, they descended the stairway leading down to the sand. When they were two steps from the bottom, Lydia stopped, halting Chloe and Daniel in the process. "Is it okay if we take off our shoes?"

"Sure, if you want to."

She glanced down at Chloe, who peered back up at her through the sunglasses that were a small replica of her own. "What do you say, Chloe? Do we want to take our shoes off?"

"Will the beach hurt my feet?"

Daniel kneeled down next to Chloe. "No, sweetheart. The beach won't hurt your feet as long as you don't step on the sharp shells."

"Then we want to."

Side by side, she and Chloe sat down on the steps and removed their shoes, Chloe tucking her white socks neatly inside her sneakers before setting them next to her mother's sandals.

"Aren't you going to take yours off?" Lydia asked Daniel.

He took off his hat, turned it around so the bill was in its proper position, and jammed it back down on his head. "Maybe later."

She guessed he had his reasons. At the moment, she felt too happy and carefree to stand around and contemplate what they were. "Okay." She shrugged, then looked down at Chloe. "Ready?"

Chloe gave an emphatic nod.

Instead of taking off in an eager run, like she was tempted to do, Lydia took the first step slowly, relishing the feel of the warm, dry sand beneath her feet. She didn't want to miss a thing.

She took a few more steps, then crouched down, encouraging Chloe to squat next to her. Lydia scooped up a handful of the soft ivory earth and let the granules sift through her fingers. Chloe mimicked her mother.

Lydia watched her daughter concentrate on the sand leaving her small hand to be carried by the wind to another resting place a short distance away. "Doesn't that feel nice, Chloe?"

With all the seriousness of a scientist on the brink of a discovery, Chloe bobbed her head.

They rose and traveled the short distance to a ribbon of shells that had been washed ashore and deserted by the previous high tide. Lydia and Chloe knelt to examine the abandoned treasures, testing the shape and texture of several in their hands. Chloe chose two that particularly struck her fancy and shoved them into her shorts pocket, along with a handful of sand.

When they were satisfied they had, for the time being, viewed enough of the sea jewels, Daniel lifted Chloe over the crusty string of shells, then insisted on doing the same for Lydia.

Here, the sand was harder, cooler, packed by the countless waves that washed over it in the course of a day. Daniel bent down, slipped off his shoes and socks, and set them aside. When he straightened, Lydia quirked a quizzical brow.

He simply shrugged. "'If you can't beat 'em . . .'"

Once again, they linked hands, this time with Lydia taking the middle position. It seemed appropriate, somehow, that she be linked to both her daughter and the man beside her—the man who had become such an integral part of her life in such a very short time—when she stepped out into the water for the very first time. Together, they walked to the line in the sand the last wave had made, then ambled a few steps further.

The next surge rolled in and surrounded their feet and ankles with a cold rush of water. Lydia and Chloe gasped. Chloe retreated a few inches, but made no effort to crawl up her mother's leg for protection, as Lydia had expected the child to do.

Then the wave rolled back out, and Lydia gasped again, instinctively tightening her hold on her daughter's hand. "Oh, my," she said. Something had slipped ashore and was pulling the sand out from under her feet.

In less than a heartbeat, Daniel's arm was around her. When the earth stopped shifting, she looked down to find a seemingly unperturbed Chloe watching the retreating water and grinning like she had just taken her first ride on a carousel and was awaiting her next. Had Lydia been the only one who had felt it?

She swiveled her head around and looked up at Daniel, whose face beamed with amusement. "I should have warned you," he said, without the slightest hint of remorse. "When the water goes out, it takes some of the sand with it. Makes you think the earth's opening up to swallow you."

She blinked. "Right. I suppose I should have figured that out." Somehow, the side of his shirt had gotten bunched up in her fist. She let go, cringing at the wrinkles she'd made.

Just as the next wave rolled in, Chloe pulled free. Lydia turned and started to reach for her daughter, but Daniel stopped Lydia with his hands on her waist.

"She's fine," he said.

Hesitantly, Lydia watched while Chloe started skipping in circles, giggling as the foamy water rolled in and swam around her feet, then eased back out to sea.

Lydia felt Daniel tug on her waist, urging her to lean back against him. A willing recipient of his support, she relented.

Once, Chloe glanced up at them and Lydia stiffened, remembering how her daughter had reacted the last time she was in Daniel's arms. But this time Chloe merely grinned at Lydia and Daniel, paying no mind to the cozy position they were in. "Look at me, Mama," she said. "I'm a mermaid." Then she went right on dancing with the sea, the sand, and the sun.

When Daniel chuckled, the muscles of his chest rippled across Lydia's back. After watching her daughter a long moment, a smile tipped Lydia's lips. She had never seen her usually reserved daughter so buoyant and deliriously happy. Lydia herself had never felt so buoyant and happy. So free.

Capturing the wind-tossed strand of hair that had escaped her ponytail, she looked out over the water. The sailboat was long gone, and now a fishing barge crawled across the horizon at a snail's pace. Overhead, in a sky-blue canopy blotted with clouds of cotton, a plane puttered by, towing a banner advertising where to get the cheapest beach towels and suntan lotion. Below, the cool water continued to tug around their ankles, shifting the sand beneath her feet.

Lydia rested her head back against Daniel's chest. He laid his jaw against her temple and started swaying from side to side in that steady, rhythmic way of his that made her feel they moved together as one. Closing her eyes, Lydia opened her heart and accepted the gift that her grandfather had so generously given. Contentment filtered in and filled a place inside her that for five long years had been empty. For the first time in her life that she could remember, she knew where she belonged.

11

*D*aniel laid Chloe on a freshly made bed in the cottage. Since the child was accustomed to an afternoon nap, she had worn down two hours into their beach excursion.

Instead of returning to the Quinns' so soon, Daniel had suggested they make one of the beds in the cottage for Chloe. He was thankful when Lydia agreed. Since their reunion, he hadn't had a chance to really talk to her, learn much about her life between Quinn Island and Chicago, simply be with her.

He pulled a thin cover up over Chloe's shoulders and kissed her soft, round cheek, lingering a few seconds. Beneath the sunscreen he'd insisted she and her mother apply while on the beach were several other refreshing scents: little girl, baby shampoo, and sunshine.

A longing so deep it hurt fisted inside Daniel's chest. In the short course of four days, he had come to realize he wanted to be this child's father. He wanted to be there to tuck her in every night, see her when she woke each morning, see her off on her first day of school, hear her excitement when she lost her first tooth. And he wanted to marry her mother. Wanted it so badly, his arms ached when he crawled into bed each night, alone.

What sometimes puzzled him, though, was that his feelings for Lydia seemed even stronger than they were before. How could that be?

He straightened the covers around Chloe's shoulders once more, even though they didn't need it. Maybe the old adage really did ring true. Maybe he simply hadn't known what he'd had until he'd lost it.

As he straightened, Lydia leaned over to kiss her daughter's cheek; then they crept from the bedroom and into the living room. He followed Lydia's lead as she wandered to one of the double windows overlooking the beach. Together, they opened the shutters. Dark, smoky-gray clouds were gathering on the horizon, and the waves breaking close to shore had grown more violent. The rain would be here soon.

Sliding his fists into his pockets, he shifted so that he faced her profile. In the silence that had fallen over the room, he watched as she stood, arms crossed, gazing out at the aggressive hands of Mother Nature.

He'd been doing that a lot today. Just watching her. At times, while they were on the beach, he'd wished he could see the world through her eyes. To her, every experience had been an adventure, every discovery a secret waiting to be revealed. Even though the light of eager excitement had shone in her lovely face as she canvassed the seashore, she had been a patient explorer, as though to hurry would be to miss something miraculous and spectacular. And her gentle endurance as she answered her daughter's one million and one questions had merely strengthened his growing need to become a father and a husband. Chloe's father. Lydia's husband.

His gaze slid to the view beyond the window. All ships and wildlife had run for cover in anticipation of the upcoming storm, leaving behind only the sand, the darkening sky, and the roiling waters. Daniel loved these waters. In fact, he jogged the island shores three times a week. Sometimes, more than that. Over the past five years, when the weight of the world, of losing Lydia, had become almost more than he could bear, he'd often found himself out there during the most desolate hours of the night. Something about feeling the damp, salt-laced wind whisper across his skin, watching the white-crested waves, like ghosts rising from the ocean, crash against the jetties, hearing the lone call of a night bird, left him with a sense of sanity he couldn't find anywhere else.

"Why me, Daniel?"

Lydia's soft voice penetrated his weighty thoughts. "Why you what?"

She angled her head and looked at him. "Why did my grandfather leave all this to me? Why not Jennifer, or my father?"

A smile of understanding tipped his lips. Her grandfather had once told him that when Lydia was a child, she would spend hours scavenging the beach with her grandmother, or digging up treasures in the sand, or simply watching the ocean. Even though that had changed as Lydia had gotten older, the late Otis Quinn had always felt she would one day return to the first place that had captured her heart—the island. That was why he'd left his beach cottage to her.

But Daniel knew that wasn't the answer she was looking for. "Your grandfather," he explained, "through inheritance and hard work of his own, obtained a substantial field of assets during his lifetime. Trust me, Lydia, everyone else got their fair share."

Shaking her head, she turned her attention back to the world beyond the window. "I wish he were here so I could thank him personally. This place feels like paradise to me."

"Me, too," he admitted.

A paradise that, five years ago, she had hated. The quiet seclusion, the boring neighbors, the remote solitude that Daniel found so calming. He studied her expression, fascinated at how she now looked at the capping waters through eyes of awe and wonderment. How long would it be before she remembered she wasn't interested in "living at the end of the earth"?

Daniel's last thought led to an even more perplexing question, one he was eager to have answered. "Lydia?"

"Hmm?" she muttered without looking at him, as though she were in a daydream and had no desire to leave.

"Will you ever regain your memory?"

She blinked, and that faraway expression of awe faded from her face. Slowly, she turned her head and looked at him with a mixture of trepidation and uncertainty, like a novice swimmer about to tread unknown waters. "We haven't had a chance to talk about that yet, have we?"

Cupping her shoulders, he urged her to face him, then grasped her hands. The forlorn look in her eyes tore at his insides. He didn't want to force her to talk about anything that might upset her. But her memory loss was an issue they couldn't evade. It was there, staring them both in the face, every minute of every day. They needed to deal with it . . . so they could move on.

"No," he said, "we haven't. But we need to. Don't you think?"

"Yes." Her shoulder dropped an inch in resignation. "We do." Her gaze skimmed the room, settling on the sofa. "Let's sit down."

He helped her remove and fold the sheet covering the sofa, then tossed it over the arm of a linen-covered chair.

They settled on the couch facing each other: she with her hands clasped in her lap, one leg tucked beneath her; he with one arm folded over the back of the sofa, a leg bent and resting on the cushion between them.

After only a slight hesitation, she began. "After a battery of tests and a failed attempt at hypnosis, the doctors determined my memory loss was permanent."

He took a moment to digest the information. She would never regain her memory. Her past—and her memory of theirs together—was gone. Forever. What did that mean? For her? For him? For them?

"Are they certain?" he asked, grabbing at a straw he saw slipping far beyond his reach.

She nodded. "The tests were actually just protocol. Their final diagnosis was based on the type of head injuries I sustained."

He'd half expected, half anticipated this. But the reality still hit him full force, like an unforeseen sucker punch to the chest.

She ducked her head and studied her hands. "Daniel, I know you had hoped my memory would return . . ." Pausing, she pursed her lips, then lifted a misty gaze back to his. He could see she was fighting tears. "I'm sorry," she added, as though that was the only thing left to say.

Seeing her struggle overrode his own confusion and pain, giving him the strength to offer her the comfort she needed. The comfort he owed her.

He cupped her cheek with his hand. "Lydia, you don't owe anyone an apology for what happened to you. Especially me." Forcing nonchalance into his voice, he added, "So, your memory will never return. We'll deal with it. The important thing is, it doesn't change the way I feel about you." He took a few heartbeats to scan her face, giving himself enough time to steel the courage to seek his next answer. "I guess the next thing we need to figure out is how you feel about me."

She raised a cool palm and covered the hand pressed against her face. "Oh, Daniel, I know I have feelings for you, and that those feelings run deeper than anything my limited memory has ever known." She gave her head a slow, regretful shake. "But right now, I have no idea who Lydia Quinn really is. Who *I* am." A long second drifted by. "I'm going to do my best to figure that out, but it's going to take time. How long? I don't know." Her eyes pleaded with his for understanding. "Are you willing to wait?"

"Of course, I'll wait," he said without hesitation. He'd waited five years to find her. He'd wait five more to win back her love if he had to. "I wasn't planning on going anywhere anyway," he added.

A garbled sound—half laughter, half sob—escaped her throat. Her arms reached out to circle his neck.

With a sigh of acceptance, Daniel enfolded her in his embrace. She had feelings for him. *Deep* feelings, she had said. He closed his eyes. He wanted more. So much more. But he knew what she was offering today was all she could give. For now, that would have to be enough.

Her sweet scent made him long to claim her lips, taste the sweetness in her kiss. But he quelled the urge to do more than simply hold her. He would wait. Because he knew, when he finally earned her love, that wait, no matter how long, would be well worth it.

12

$\mathcal{W}$hat do you think about this?" Lydia held up the dark pantsuit for her customer's approval.

With a disapproving frown, Mrs. Pratt shook her head. "I don't know about the navy, dear. Do you have something a little more colorful?"

Lydia managed to hold onto her smile. "I think so." She hung up the pantsuit and for the third time searched the garment rack in an attempt to find the mayor's wife a suitable outfit to wear to an upcoming Fourth of July celebration.

Lydia had been back in Quinn Island for a month, back working in the shop for three weeks. And for two weeks and six days, she had hated her job. Hated it . . . with a passion.

She hated trying to figure out which garments suited the tastes of Quinn Island's finest. And she hated it when, nine times out of ten, her patrons looked down their nose at her selection.

She hated wearing ridiculously expensive, and usually uncomfortable, clothes in order to blend in with the atmosphere of the store. And she hated that the mother in an average-to-low income household couldn't come into the shop and purchase a simple Sunday dress for her daughter without spending an entire week's wages.

But the thing she hated most about being the sole owner of an affluent dress shop was leaving Chloe behind in the mornings.

In Chicago, Lydia had been able to take her daughter with her on her housecleaning jobs. Determined to follow the same pattern here, she had set up a children's entertainment center in one corner of the store equipped with television, VCR, toys, and books. The play area helped in occupying young children brought into the store by their parents for short periods of time. But, halfway through Lydia's first day on the job, Chloe had gotten bored and restless. She didn't like being restricted to the four waist-high walls designed to look like a playhouse. And Lydia would often dash back to check on her daughter while waiting on a customer—which didn't set too well with her clientele.

She'd finally relented and taken her parents up on their offer to watch over her daughter during shop hours. To Lydia's dismay Chloe was thrilled. Lydia's parents—especially her mother—were constantly showering their granddaughter with gifts, taking her to fun places, doing things with her that had always been beyond Lydia's means.

Lydia paused, considering a flamingo-colored pantsuit. Deciding Mrs. Pratt wouldn't look good in pink, she moved on.

So far, Chloe's daily adventures with her grandparents didn't seem to be spoiling her. But Lydia feared it was just a matter of time. Oh, she had told her parents they were indulging their granddaughter too much, and her father seemed to take her concerns to heart most of the time. But her mother *never* listened to, or else she simply chose to ignore, Lydia's requests. And Lydia hadn't quite figured out what to do about it yet.

Turning, she held up a red outfit for Mrs. Pratt's approval. The woman, whose patience seemed to be wearing thin, shook her haughty head again.

Lydia gritted her teeth, biting back a sharp retort. She thought the pleasingly plump woman with the peaches-and-cream complexion would look good in the red.

Pivoting back to the rack, Lydia continued with her search. Why did the women who visited the shop feel she or Jennifer or one of the clerks had to help them make their selections anyway? Didn't anyone in this town have a mind of her own? On a whim, she whipped out the flamingo pantsuit she'd passed up a minute ago. Mrs. Pratt had already snubbed three of Lydia's choices. What was one more?

To Lydia's surprise, the woman's eyes lit up like headlights on high beam. "That's it." She grabbed the matching garments from Lydia's hand. "Wait right here and you can tell me how it looks after I try it on." With that, she did an about-face and shuffled to the dressing room.

Lydia gave serious thought to hiding beneath the garments hanging on the rack. She didn't want to give her opinion on the pink pantsuit, because she'd have to lie in order not to offend Quinn Island's first lady.

Like a perceptive angel of mercy, Jennifer appeared at Lydia's side. "You have a phone call, Sis."

Lydia looked heavenward and mouthed, "Thank You, God. Thank You." Then she faced her sister with an elated smile. "You don't mind finishing up with Mrs. Pratt, do you?"

The corners of Jennifer's lips turned down. "I knew I should have taken a message."

Lydia made her escape as Mrs. Pratt came out of the dressing room. "Oh, Jennifer, dear," Lydia heard the mayor's wife say. "If I had known you were here . . ."

With a subtle grin, Lydia circled the counter. Couldn't Jennifer see that *her* name belonged on the deed and ownership papers of the shop? Not Lydia's?

Sitting down on a stool behind the counter, she kicked off her two-inch heels. As she reached for the receiver, she crossed her legs and massaged one foot with her free hand. She had yet to figure out the reason for wearing pinching shoes for the sake of style.

"Hello. This is Sa . . . Lydia Quinn." How many more times was she going to do that? "May I help you?"

"Miss Quinn, this is Andy Kelley at Kelley's Used Cars. I'm just calling to let you know your car's been serviced and is ready for pick up."

Excitement kicked up a little dance beneath Lydia's ribs. Her car. *Her* car. The sweet little white number she'd closed the deal on last Friday was ready to pick up. Come tomorrow, she'd no longer have to depend on everyone else for transportation. She could chart her own course.

"Thank you, Mr. Kelley. I'll be there first thing in the morning to pick it up."

She hung up the phone, only vaguely still aware of her hurting feet. The timing was perfect. Tomorrow was her Wednesday off. And Daniel, who had just finished a time-consuming court case, was taking half the day off to spend with her and Chloe. Since they had made no definite plans, Lydia could pick him up and they could drive to the island for a picnic. Wouldn't he be surprised? She couldn't wait to see the look on his face when he saw what she had done.

The front door chimed, and Lydia glanced toward the entrance to see that another patron had arrived. She jumped off the stool and was halfway around the counter when she realized she could feel the coolness of the hardwood floors beneath her feet. She ran back behind the counter, slipped her shoes on, then headed for the front of the store, greeting her next customer with an enthusiastic smile.

~&

"Thanks, Dad. For everything," Lydia told her father the next morning as she stepped up to her new used car. Last week, he had helped her pick out, test-drive, and examine the midsize station wagon for operating efficiency. Today, he had driven her to the dealer to pick up the car.

She always had such fun with him. He was easygoing, sometimes funny, and would always share his knowledge when asked for advice. But he never insinuated he knew what she should like or what was best for her.

Like Mrs. Porter had always done, he simply let her be.

"Anytime, sweetheart. All you have to do is ask whenever you need me."

She kissed his cheek, then looked down at Chloe, who stood beside her granddad, holding onto his forefinger while nestling George the Giraffe under one arm. "Are you ready to go?"

Chloe cocked her head and peered at her mother through the sunglasses Daniel had given her the first day they had gone to the island. "Are you sure you know how to drive?"

Chloe had never seen her mother drive. In order to obtain a driver's license, one had to have proof of existence—a birth certificate, a social security card. Lydia had none of those things in Chicago.

But she had remedied that just last week. Plopping her fists on her hips, she leaned over so that she was practically nose-to-nose with her daughter. "I passed the driver's exam and got my license back, didn't I?"

Chloe pushed her glasses up on her nose and readjusted George. "Yes," she said, but her expression still looked a little wary around the edges.

After fastening Chloe in the car, Lydia kissed her father's cheek again and climbed in. Heat and humidity were already beginning to weigh down the late June morning. But when Lydia switched on the engine, instead of reaching for the air conditioner button, she pressed the control that zipped down the window. She wanted to feel and smell the fresh air as she drove *her* car for the first time.

At the beginning of her search for an automobile to suit hers and Chloe's needs, Lydia and her father had scavenged the new-car lots. But she had soon concluded it was senseless to pay five figures for a car that would depreciate several thousand dollars the minute she drove it off the lot. So she had settled for a two-year-old, average-sized, averaged-priced, four-door station wagon with a gray cloth interior and bright, white exterior. A car that had Sara Jennings's name written all over it.

No, she retracted her thoughts with a mental shake of her head. The car had *Lydia Quinn's* name written all over it.

She shifted into drive. No matter how hard she tried, she still sometimes had trouble thinking of herself as *Lydia,* Quinn Island's former prom queen, instead of *Sara,* Chicago's plain Jane Doe.

When she first pulled out onto the highway, her pulse quickened. But a couple miles into the trip, she was navigating the steering wheel like driving was second nature.

She stopped at the supermarket deli and picked up a lunch of fried chicken, fries, slaw, and banana pudding. On the way to the checkout, she grabbed a six-pack of soft drinks and some eating utensils. The reporters had finally stopped hounding her, and the towns-people had all gotten used to the news of her return, so she got in and out of the store with just a few polite greetings and inquiries as to how she and Chloe were doing. But, even if she had had to sidestep a member of the news media, the feeling of freedom would have been worth it.

At precisely twelve-thirty, Lydia pulled into the driveway of Daniel's one-level brick home. When she saw his car still sitting beneath the carport, she knew she had timed her arrival just right. She'd given him enough time to get home from his office and change clothes, but had caught him before he left to come and pick up her and Chloe.

As she and Chloe climbed out of the car, he ambled out of the front door, letting the screen door slap closed behind him. He approached with slow, curious steps. Lydia stopped beside Chloe's door, took off her sunglasses, and just watched him. The blazing midday sun lit chestnut highlights in his dark hair. His yellow polo shirt molded his sinewy shoulders, and his faded jeans could have been tailor-made to fit his slim waist and thighs.

Instead of stopping where she and Chloe stood, he continued on, strolling around the car with his hands in his pockets. A guarded look of bewilderment settled over his face.

When he had made a complete circle, he stopped in front of her. "What is this?"

Feeling about as proud of herself as a peacock, Lydia stuffed her fists in her overall pockets and rocked back on her heels. "It's my new car. Ya like it?"

Daniel scratched his forehead with his thumb. "Ah, when did you get it?"

She noticed he had evaded her question, which knocked her elation down a couple of notches. "Bought it last week. Picked it up this morning."

"All by yourself?"

She feigned offense. "What? You don't think I know cars? This baby has a V-6 engine, automatic transmission with automatic overdrive, antilock front and rear disk brakes, and gets twenty-nine miles to the gallon on the highway." She shuffled from one end of the car to the other like a seasoned salesperson while she shot off the list she had practiced with her father. And when she stopped, pivoted, and beamed at Daniel, she was pleased with the results.

His mouth dropped open like a trapdoor with a broken hinge. "Where did you learn all that?"

"From Grandpa."

Lydia's smugness fizzled like a drop of water hitting a hot skillet. She glowered down at her daughter. "Thank you, Chloe. I was really anxious to let Daniel know that."

Unperturbed, the informative four-year-old simply pushed her glasses back up on her nose.

Reluctantly, Lydia lifted her gaze to Daniel's face. Just as she expected, he was smirking.

"Your dad helped you pick out the car."

She lifted her nose an impertinent inch. "We picked it out together."

He scanned the vehicle again, front to back. "Why didn't you tell me you were buying a car?"

"I wanted to surprise you." And, even though she loved him—and she did love him, with every fiber of her being—she didn't want to be influenced by his sometimes aggressive decisiveness.

He scratched his forehead with his thumb again. "You surprised me all right."

Like a factory inspector, he ambled around to the driver's side, opened the door, checked the mileage and all the control gadgets—half of which Lydia still hadn't figured out. He requested the keys, then switched on the engine, and revved the motor. While the car was running, he checked the heat, the air conditioner, and the radio. Switching off the engine, he pulled a lever that popped open the hood, then got out and scrutinized the conglomeration of metal called a motor. Seemingly satisfied with what he saw, he closed the hood and got down on his hands and knees, looking underneath the car.

All the things her father had done when she'd expressed an interest in the vehicle.

Standing, he brushed off his knees and then his hands. "Nice car. Been well taken care of," he said, but it was what he didn't say that bugged her.

Crossing her arms, she shifted her weight to one leg. "What is it, Daniel?"

"Nothing," he said with all the innocence of a car thief.

She had learned enough about him to know when he was holding back on her. Tilting her head to one side, she leveled him with an unbending glare.

He opened his mouth to speak.

She pursed her lips.

His shoulders dropped in resignation. "I like the car, Lydia, I really do. It's just that—"

She held up a hand. "Wait a minute. Don't tell me it's not me. If I hear one more person say something's not me, I'll scream."

With a spark of amusement in his eyes, he grinned. "We wouldn't want you to do that, now, would we?"

She found herself smiling in return. "No. I don't think we would."

He crouched down to give Chloe his usual hug and nuzzle on the cheek. Sometimes, Lydia envied that little affectionate greeting from Daniel that belonged only to her daughter. All she ever got was his hand on hers or an arm slipped casually around her.

She appreciated Daniel's modest patience in courting her, but, good grief, didn't the twentieth date or so warrant at least a goodnight kiss?

"I smelled food in the car," he said as he stood. "Does that mean we're going on a picnic?"

"How does an afternoon on the island sound?"

"Sounds like my kind of date."

While he helped Chloe with her seat, Lydia skirted the front of the car and slid into the driver's seat.

Daniel opened the passenger door and poked his head inside. Arching his brows, he said, "You mean you're not going to let me drive?"

Caressing the steering wheel, she shook her head. "Not just yet. I feel like I've just gotten my first set of wings and I still want to fly."

She noticed a subtle change in his expression; the slightest hint of sadness rose in his eyes. "As long as you always let me fly with you." He folded himself into the passenger seat and closed the door.

Despite the elevated temperature, a chill raced down her spine. Something was wrong. She sensed it.

When he grasped her chin between his thumb and forefinger, leaned over, and pressed the softest of kisses to her forehead, she pushed her misgivings to a remote corner of her mind. *We're okay,* she told herself with forced conviction. *We're still okay.*

On the drive to the island, he started snooping, poking around in her dash pocket, thumbing through the owner's manual, studying the service record left by the last owner. But, Lydia noticed, he was quiet. Too quiet. And somber.

"Daniel, what is it about my getting this car that bothers you so?"

⚓

He kept his gaze focused on the owner's manual he held open in his hands. He knew it was petty, a grown man getting his feelings hurt because the woman he loved hadn't told him she was buying a car. But he couldn't seem to help it. She had once made him a part of her every decision. Lately, though, she was making more and more choices without consulting him. Sometimes, like right now, an ornery little monster would rear its ugly little head and set him to wondering if she'd eventually get to where she didn't need him at all.

"Daniel?" she gently prodded when he didn't answer.

He certainly wasn't going to tell her he was sitting there licking his wounds, so to speak. But he could ask her one thing. He returned the owner's manual to the dash pocket and closed it. All he'd really wanted to do anyway was make sure she hadn't forgotten proof of insurance. "I was just wondering why you bought this particular car?"

"It's practical for me and Chloe. It's in good running condition. It was reasonably priced."

It was practical for *her* and *Chloe.* Did he not fit into her picture anywhere? "But you could have bought any car you wanted."

"And I did."

He considered her answer. Before, she would never have settled for a used car, or one that she'd considered so "average." He raked his hair away from his forehead and heaved a sigh. That didn't seem to be the case anymore.

He studied her hauntingly familiar yet somehow-new profile. Since her return, she was always doing things that sometimes surprised him, sometimes shocked him, and many times delighted him.

Her former tastes for expensive toys had never really bothered him before, not much, anyway. After all, they both came from old money and had profitable jobs. They could afford it. But her more recent tastes for practical, more functional essentials with reasonable price tags charmed him—and paralleled his own way of thinking.

"What are you going to do with your other car?" he asked, referring to the sports coupe she'd been driving the night of her abduction. Right now, it was in her uncle's basement garage, where it had been towed after the initial police investigation.

"I'm going to sell it and give the proceeds to the missing persons' organization my mother founded." She shrugged a shoulder. "Who knows? Maybe the money will help locate another lost loved one."

His level of respect for her increased twofold. Reaching over, he laced his fingers through hers, leaving her with only one hand to drive. "Since when did you get to be so amazing?"

She didn't have an immediate comeback, and he couldn't help grinning. The way she now blushed at compliments was so appealing.

"Maybe . . . since I met you," she finally said, and started working her fingers free from his. "Now, give me back my hand before I run off the road."

13

"r. Matthews, you have magic hands."

Daniel smiled at the woman lying back against the settee arm, her eyes closed, looking thoroughly satisfied with the foot rub she was getting. "And you, Miss Quinn, have beautiful feet." Small and dainty. They fit perfectly in his hands.

"Mmm," was her only response.

Feeling quite relaxed himself, he settled further down on the sofa and propped his bare feet on an ottoman.

The afternoon had been glorious. They had eaten out on the back lawn, then taken a quick swim to combat the scorching temperatures. When Chloe had worn down, they had returned to the cottage, changed from swimsuits back to their street clothes, and tucked the little girl into the same bed she'd slept in the first time Daniel had brought her and Lydia to the island.

Laying his head back, Daniel scanned the living room of the cottage, which was beginning to look and feel more like a home than a house that had been forsaken for seven years. They had removed the linens from the furniture on their second visit and spruced up the yards on their third. Last week, Lydia had added a few personal touches—scented candles to the coffee table, a ginger jar to the mantle, and a silk flower arrangement to the dining room table. Today, she had brought a crocheted afghan and thrown it across the wicker rocking chair that sat next to the fireplace.

Little things that make a house a home, Daniel thought. And with just a little nudge to his imagination, he could picture this house as a home: his, Lydia's, and Chloe's.

With a circling thumb, he started working his way up from Lydia's heel. She shifted and gave a contented purr. He loved pleasing her, and since she'd returned to Quinn Island, that had been amazingly easy to do. The simplest things—a walk on the beach, a single red rose, an unexpected foot rub—brought her pleasure now.

His smile mellowed. She had been so flabbergasted, and so appealingly embarrassed, the first time he'd pulled her feet into his lap, slipped off her shoes, and started massaging. And so appreciative afterward. He couldn't have been more shocked than when she pulled his feet into her lap and returned the favor.

Mentally, he shook his head. That had been a first. But then, there had been a lot of firsts since her return. Some pleased him. But some he didn't quite know what to do with, like her showing up at his house today with a car she'd picked out and purchased without his knowledge.

He pushed the nagging thought to the back of his mind. Wasn't it enough to simply be with her like this? Something stirred inside him—a deeper longing, a stronger need. He struggled against the desire to move his hands to her slim ankles, to lean over her and satisfy his hunger with one sweet kiss.

She had given him no indication she was ready to move their relationship forward. What they presently had would have to be enough . . . for now.

She flinched when he hit a particularly sensitive spot in the middle of her foot. "Hey, no tickling," she chided, opening her eyes to level him with a halfhearted glare.

Just to see her eyes dance with laughter and feel her small toes curl beneath his fingers, he kept circling the end of his thumb in the center of her foot. Just before she reached the point of squirming, she jerked her feet away.

"You don't play fair."

He helped her sit up. "I couldn't resist," he said.

"No. You just wanted your own feet rubbed." Facing him, she scooted back, folded one leg in front of her, and patted her thigh.

Who was he to argue? Taking her cue, he propped one foot on her bent knee. She set to kneading, her smooth brow pinched in concentration.

He watched in fascination. He would have never thought that a woman rubbing a man's feet could be so enthralling. Of course, this wasn't just any woman. This was Lydia, and she was what made this simple act of altruism so attractive. He relaxed back against the sofa arm.

"Daniel," Lydia said as she started working on his other foot, "if this house were yours, would you move into it?"

"In a heartbeat," he answered without hesitation.

Her frown of concentration melted into a warm smile. "Good."

His brow dipped in befuddlement. "Why?"

She glanced up at him, her amber eyes all aglow. "Because I've decided to move out here."

Her answer brought him up short. He pulled his feet away from her hands and slid forward, his knee bumping lightly against hers as he draped his arm over the back of the couch. "Are you serious?"

Annoyance wilted her shoulders. "Daniel."

"I know. I know. If you hear 'Are you serious?' one more time, you're going to scream. But . . . are you serious?" His voice squeaked with surprise.

She shook her head like he was a hopeless cause. "Yes, I am. Why does that surprise you so?"

"I don't know." But really he did. She had been totally against living on the island in the past. She hated the feel of salt on her skin, the wind in her hair, and the quiet seclusion. "I guess because you liked living in town so much before. You were a people person."

She took a moment to consider his answer. "Well, I've changed my mind." From the tilt of her lips, she apparently found his stunned expression amusing. "That is a woman's prerogative, isn't it?"

"I suppose, but . . ."

"But?"

"You'll be so far away from everything."

"Just three miles from town."

"And it's so secluded out here. Suppose there's a break-in?"

"You said the island was the safest place on the coast."

"Well, yeah, but . . . what if Chloe gets sick?"

"I have a car. I know how to use the phone."

He opened his mouth, but, for the life of him, couldn't think of another justifiable argument.

She grinned in victory.

He scowled in defeat.

He knew he had a tendency to be overprotective, as she had so gently pointed out on several different occasions. But he couldn't help it. The thought of her being out here alone gripped his stomach with fear. What if something happened to her or Chloe? He couldn't go through losing Lydia again. And with Chloe in the picture, the stakes were now twice as high.

She bracketed his head with her hands and leaned forward until her face was only a breath away from his. "Daniel, I'm not a child. I'm a grown woman, with a child of my own."

He couldn't argue with that. Still, he had his reservations. "I know. It's just the thoughts of you and Chloe being out here all by yourself . . ." An old familiar weight bore down on his chest. "Sometimes, things can happen . . . *fast*. When you least expect them to. I'm entitled to be concerned."

Understanding softened her features. "I know. But you can't live in fear that something bad is going to happen every time I get out of your sight. And you can't put me and Chloe in a bubble and shield us from the world. Now, I can promise you I will do everything possible to ensure my and Chloe's safety." A knowing glint of laughter flickered across her lips. "And, I'm sure you will, too." Then the laughter was gone. She spread her fingers, as though trying to encompass his mind and conquer his fears. "The rest we have to leave up to God."

He closed his eyes, his insides quaking with the struggle between past demons and present rationality. Somehow, rationality won. "You're right," he begrudgingly admitted as he opened his eyes. "I can't lock you and Chloe away, and I can't be with you every minute of every day. But . . ." He scrubbed a defeated hand down his face, then desperately grabbed at one last straw. "How would you feel about me parking a camper in your backyard?"

She threw her head back and laughed. The infectious sound managed to calm, to a small degree, his inner turmoil.

He offered her a sheepish grin. He knew parking a camper in her backyard wasn't reasonable. But he'd do it, if she'd let him.

Following instinct, he pulled her close and wrapped his arms around her. She slipped hers around his neck. He could live to be a hundred and never get tired of the feel of her body in his arms. She raised a hand, combed her fingers through the back of his hair. Jolted by a strong need for more, he closed his eyes. Why didn't he just go ahead and kiss her? The worst thing that could happen would be for her to push him away, like she did that first day in Chicago.

He drew back, cupped the side of her face with his hand, and before he even had a chance to act upon his thoughts, she pushed him away.

"Oh, Daniel. Look!" She jumped up and breezed past him.

It took him a few seconds to adjust to the change in atmosphere. When he did, he twisted around to find she had opened the back door and was kneeling down to pick up something, her abundant curls fluttering in the breeze. She stood, and when she turned around, she was holding a kitten—if you could call it that. The neglected little thing looked more like two huge yellow eyes sewn into a scraggly coat of matted gray fur.

As though pleading for mercy, the haggard feline looked at him and released a weak "Meow."

"Poor baby." Lydia cradled the kitten against her chest as gently as a mother would a newborn. "She's scared to death and starving."

Standing, Daniel rubbed the back of his forefinger beneath the kitten's chin. The kitten turned her head and flattened her ear against his hand, touching a soft spot inside him. "I think Chloe had some milk left over from lunch. I'll go see if I can dig up a pan and warm it up."

While they waited in the kitchen for the milk to heat, Daniel watched Lydia lavish the kitten with attention. She set the scrawny thing down on the bar, then plopped her chin on folded hands so that she and the animal were eye level. The cat arched her bony body along Lydia's face, then it sniffed at Lydia's hair and was knocked backwards by a sneeze. Laughing out loud, Lydia picked up the stunned kitten and rubbed her cheek against the top of its fuzzy head.

Daniel stood awestruck. Lydia had apparently forgotten she hated cats. She didn't like animals, period. She detested getting fur on her clothes. Bemusement tugging at the corner of his mouth, he turned back to the stove and poured the milk into a bowl. He certainly wasn't going to be the one to remind her of that fact.

Five minutes later, they sat side by side on the floor, their legs crisscrossed, watching the kitten devour the warm milk.

"Where do you think she came from?" Lydia wondered out loud.

"My guess is some heartless jerk set her out thinking somebody here on the island would take her in . . . or that she'd starve to death."

The light in Lydia's eyes grew dim. "Poor thing." Reaching out with a forefinger, she ruffled the fur on the kitten's back. "Lost, alone, no place to call home." A brief silence filled with heavy thoughts passed. "I know exactly how you feel."

Daniel curled a finger beneath Lydia's chin and urged her to look at him. "You're not lost anymore."

Bitter tears stung her eyes. "Sometimes, I wonder . . ." The second the words were out, she drew back and swiped a hand across her face. She hadn't gotten through the last five years by crying on someone else's shoulder or playing off another's sympathy. And she certainly wasn't going to start now. "Sorry. I didn't mean to whine."

Apparently undeterred, Daniel grasped her chin and forced her to look at him again. "Lydia, why don't you let me in? Let me help you carry some of that burden while you're trying to figure everything out."

"I'm not a baby, Daniel." Pushing his hand away, she vaulted up off the floor and strolled to the window over the sink. Crossing her arms, she looked out at the waters battering the island's southern shore.

She was angry with herself. In a weak moment of self-pity, she had opened a door she had meant to keep closed. The past, the only one she could remember, was gone. She was no longer Sara Jennings. She was Lydia Quinn. She was *born* Lydia Quinn and, somehow, she had to accept that. She just never realized it would be so hard.

Daniel's hands, so understanding and tender, cupped her shoulders. Following his gentle bidding, she relaxed back against him. His strong arms enfolded her shoulders. She raised her hands to his forearms, laid her head back against his chest. Balmy scents of warm milk, saltwater, and the most intoxicating one of all that belonged only to him drifted through her head, filling her with a selfish yearning. Sometimes, she wished she could shut out the world and create one of her own that included only her, Daniel, and Chloe.

But even as the thought flitted through her mind, her pragmatic side reminded her that kind of thinking was unreasonable. She had responsibilities, people who depended on her, more demands than she could ever possibly meet. And she owed it to her loved ones to try to meet those demands.

Daniel's warm lips touched her temple. "I love you, Lydia. That's one thing you'll never have to try to figure out."

She turned in his arms, letting her palms rest against his chest. "How, Daniel? How can you love some crazy, confused woman who's nothing like the one you fell in love with years ago?"

He touched her nose. "First of all, you're not crazy. Secondly, who can explain love?" He shrugged. "I certainly can't. All I know is that it's still there, stronger than ever. I don't question it; I just accept it."

If he didn't question it, then why should she? Focusing on her hands, she fiddled with a button on his shirt. "Then why don't you ever kiss me?"

He tipped her chin. "Because you asked me to wait."

Her brow dipped in befuddlement. "I did?"

"Uh-huh." He nodded. "Remember the first day we came to the cottage? You asked me to wait until you figured everything out."

Closing her eyes, she pinched the bridge of her nose. "Daniel, I was talking about renewing our engagement. I figured, in the meantime, we would date and . . . you know . . . let our relationship follow the natural course of things."

He grasped the fingers she held to her face and kissed the back of her hand. "Why didn't you say something? Or at least give me a sign?"

She tried to focus more on what he was saying than the chill bumps racing up her arm. "Because I'm a woman," she answered, thinking surely that would explain it all.

Apparently, it didn't. "Yes," he said, his dark eyes roaming her face with a mixture of amusement and appreciation. "I'm well aware of that." He started rocking, carrying her with him in that gentle sway of his that kept time with a song only he and she could hear.

"The man is supposed to make the first move, not the woman."

The rocking stopped, and surprise lifted his brows. "You never felt that way before."

Her eyes opened wide. "What!?"

"Nothing," he quickly injected, then closed his eyes, giving his head a quick shake like he was trying to clear it of a distraction. When he met her gaze again, he added, "Forget I said that." He let go of her hand and captured her wrists, urging her to put her arms around his neck. She didn't resist.

"Now, about this kissing thing." He slipped his arms around her waist. "Seems like I was waiting on you. You were waiting on me."

Biting her lower lip, she nodded. She didn't have enough air to speak.

He pulled her closer. "What are we going to do about it?"

"I guess . . . this."

Following her heart, she rose on tiptoe and lifted her face up to his.

"Mama!"

Chloe's voice coming from the hallway shattered Lydia's moment of rapture. She squeezed her eyes shut against the impact as her emotions slammed back to earth. Then, lowering her heels to the floor, she opened her eyes and pressed a forefinger to Daniel's lips. "Hold that thought. Okay?"

He kissed her fingertip. "Got it."

They parted just before Chloe turned the corner coming into the kitchen, her small hands circling the ribs of the kitten Lydia had long forgotten. The neglected cat looked like she was frozen in a permanent state of shock, but she didn't seem to be in any pain.

Lydia rushed across the room to show her daughter how to hold the kitten properly. Chloe held up the furry, yellow-eyed skeleton and said, "Look what I found, Mama. A kitty cat."

Daniel was still holding onto Lydia's thought when she later drove him home so he could pick up his car and follow her back to her parents' house.

While swapping secretive little glances with Lydia, he suffered through a preplanned dinner at the Quinn's dining room table. Then he sat through an hour of some insipid game show Margaret insisted they watch, her idea of a family thing. Then came Chloe's story time and bedtime which he breezed through with utmost patience.

But after he and Lydia had tucked her daughter in, with kitten Mittens—named for her white front paws—in a basket beside the bed, and closed the bedroom door, he grabbed Lydia's hand, and together they rushed down the stairs like two kids on Christmas morning. They hit the foyer running, but Daniel stopped short when Margaret stepped from the living room into their path. Lydia, who was one step behind him, apparently didn't see the older woman and smacked into his back, almost catapulting him forward to the floor at her mother's feet.

He reached back with his free hand to steady her. "Mrs. Quinn!" *Uh-oh.* He'd called her "Mrs. Quinn" instead of "Margaret." He hadn't done that in years. He sounded just like a kid caught sneaking a cookie before lunch.

Out of the corner of his eye, he saw Lydia peek out from behind his shoulder. "Hi, Mom." Unfortunately, she sounded just as guilty as he.

With a quizzical frown puckering her forehead, Margaret Quinn looked from Daniel to Lydia, then back to Daniel. "Where on earth are you kids going in such a hurry?"

Daniel opened his mouth, but all that came out was a caught-in-the-act-sounding "Ahh." And Lydia was no help. She just stayed under cover behind him.

Then, like a perceptive guardian angel, Lydia's father appeared. "Come on, Margaret," he said, grasping her hand. "There's something on

TV I want you to see." Sending Daniel a conspiratorial wink, the older man pulled his thoroughly perplexed wife back into the living room.

The instant they were out of sight, Daniel and Lydia scrambled for the door.

They sprinted toward the side of the wraparound porch, startling the night creatures into silence. When they rounded the corner, where they knew they would be safe from windows and prying eyes, Daniel leaned back against the wall.

Slightly out-of-breath, he slid his back down the smooth plank wall far enough to compensate for their height differences. "Now, there's this matter of a—"

She grabbed his head and kissed him.

Daniel couldn't move. Couldn't breathe. Couldn't think. All he could do was stand there and receive what she was offering. Her love, without reservation. No, she hadn't actually said the words. But it was there. He could feel her pouring it into him, washing him clean, purest of mountain streams running down from the highest of mountains.

Fireworks exploded in his chest. The doors to his heart, soul, and mind—places that had been only half open before—swung wide open, the emotions flowing out of them. His throat ached.

And when she finally pulled back, looking up at him like he was her lifeline, he saw her in a completely new light. He couldn't explain it; he didn't even know if he wanted to. He just knew that things were different. A lot different than they were before. What he felt for her was deeper and more far-reaching than anything he had ever known.

And as new as the first rose in spring.

"Well," she said, her voice filtering into his awestruck thoughts, "aren't you going to say anything?"

"I'm . . . speechless."

She brushed her thumb across his lower lip. He felt the tingle all the way to his fingertips.

"There's something I need to tell you," she said. Dropping her hands to his chest, she raised her lashes and looked so deep into his eyes, he could feel her gaze touching his soul. "I may not have myself figured out yet, but I do know how I feel about you."

"I'm listening."

"I love you, Daniel. I love you with all my heart."

He cradled her face in his hands. He couldn't hold back the tears; he didn't even want to try. "Lydia. My precious, precious Lydia, you don't know how I've longed to hear you say that."

Her lips curved. "Well, get used to it, because I have a feeling you're going to be hearing it a lot in the future."

"Good, because I love you." He lowered his head to hers. "I love you," he repeated in a whisper against her mouth before he claimed her lips.

This time, it was he who gave. He willingly laid every fiber of his being in the palm of her hand, holding back nothing for himself.

And when she reached out with her heart to accept his gift, he knew, for the first time in his life, what it felt like to give freely and love without condition.

❧

Much later that evening, Lydia walked hand in hand with Daniel to his car. "I can't wait until Chloe and I get moved into the cottage," she mused out loud.

"Me, either. That way, we won't risk running into your parents when we're headed out to the front porch to neck."

"*Daniel!*" She smacked his shoulder with her free hand. "We did not neck."

Well, no, really, they hadn't. They'd just kissed, held hands, and each other. But he sure did love making her blush, even if he couldn't quite see the rosy color rising in her cheeks with nothing but stars and a half-moon for light. He knew it was there.

"Besides," she added, "we'll have an inquisitive four-year-old dogging our every step out at the cottage."

"She goes to bed early."

Lydia shook her head. "You're crazy."

"About you."

Her soft chuckle floated through the air. "I give up."

Her mention of moving to the island reminded him of something he had been curious about since early evening. Stopping next to his car, he urged her to face him and grasped both of her hands. "Tell me something, Lydia. When we were out at the island this afternoon, why did you ask me if I'd move into the cottage if it were mine?"

"Because, if you and I do make it to the wedding altar, I didn't want Chloe and me to move out there, fall more in love with the place than we already are, then have to pull up stakes and move again. Before I made my decision, I needed to know it was a place where you would want to live, too."

"You mean, you didn't make your final decision until you had my answer?"

"No."

Was it possible to love her more? He tugged her into his arms. "Thanks for thinking about me."

"That seems to be about all I do lately."

"Good."

He lingered over a kiss, then held her for a tranquil moment with her head resting against his chest, his cheek resting on the top of her head.

"We're going to make it, Daniel," she said with a sigh. "I have a feeling."

Daniel released a slow breath full of contentment. He had a feeling, too. And it was awesome.

14

$\mathcal{T}$hanks for allowing me to come in during my lunch break, Daniel. It's Lydia's Wednesday off, and that leaves us a little shorthanded."

"No problem," Daniel said, reaching for the sales contract on a piece of investment property Jennifer had recently acquired. "I should get this wrapped up with the sellers this afternoon. I'll give you a call as soon as everything's finalized."

Nodding, Jennifer stood.

Daniel slipped the contract into her file and reached for the phone, intending to call Lydia to see if she could meet him for lunch. She'd told him she was going to hang new curtains in the cottage today, but surely she could take a break.

But Jennifer lingered, so he stopped short of picking up the receiver and peered up at her. From the worry lines marring her pretty forehead, he could tell something weighed heavily on her mind.

He pulled his hand away from the phone, leaned back in his swivel chair, and laced his hands over his abdomen. "Wanna talk about it?"

"If you've got time."

He really didn't. Allowing her to come in and sign her contract on the spur-of-the-moment hadn't left him much time for lunch, and he really did want to see Lydia. But Jennifer had been there for him so many times over the past five years, he felt he owed her a sympathetic ear whenever she needed one.

He motioned to the chair she had just vacated, and she sat back down. Leaning on her forearms, she focused on her fidgeting red-tipped fingers while she apparently weighed out whatever it was she needed to say.

As patiently as possible, Daniel waited.

Finally, she looked up at him. "Daniel, I was just wondering what you think of Lydia?"

He approached her question with a lawyer's analytical caution. "I'm not sure I understand what you're asking."

"What I'm asking is, what do you think about the way she is now?"

"I still love her, Jen. That's not changed." And that, he thought, explained it all.

"I know, but . . ." She chewed her thumbnail for a long, thoughtful moment before adding, "Does Lydia sometimes do or say things that totally confuse you or catch you off guard?"

His lips curved in a slow grin. "All the time. I mean, sometimes when I'm with her I think I'm looking at Lydia, then she'll do or say something totally out of character, and I feel like I'm seeing someone else." He shook his head, slipping into a daydream filled with visions from the evening before. "When I hold her now, it even feels different."

❧

Lydia pulled into the parking lot of Matthews and Matthews, Attorneys-at-Law. Since Daniel was working on a property dispute set to go to trial tomorrow, she knew he might not take time for lunch. So, in an impetuous moment, she had decided to lay aside the curtains she was hanging, pick up some takeout, drop by his office, and have lunch with him. Granted, the local burger express didn't specialize in the healthiest food in the world, but at least she would know he'd eaten something to tide him over until their dinner date tonight.

As she parked her station wagon, she noticed Jennifer's car sitting a few spaces away. Her sister was probably there going over paperwork on some new investment. The shrewd businesswoman was always looking for a profitable deal.

Oh, well, Lydia thought as she grabbed the bags from the passenger seat, if Jennifer hadn't eaten, they could all have lunch together.

Even though she and Jennifer were as different as night and day, Lydia thoroughly enjoyed her sister's company.

Lydia stepped out of her car, inhaling the boggy, grassy scent of the saltwater marsh across the street. Would she ever come back down to feeling normal again? Not if the last two weeks were any indication of what the future had in store for her. Life had never been so near perfect. She and Chloe had gotten settled into their new home on the island, she was head over heels in love with the most wonderful man in the world, and, for the first time she could remember, she was looking forward to the rest of her life with childlike excitement.

Yes, she thought as she closed the car door, *things are about as perfect as perfect could be.*

As she reached for the entrance door with one hand, she reached for a small part of her that was missing with the other. She felt a little lost not having her daughter along, but the child's grandparents had confiscated her for an afternoon at the park. Since Lydia had planned a day of much work and little play, she had conceded to the outing.

The desk with a missing secretary gave the reception area a lulling out-to-lunch feel. Scanning the doors flanking each side of the workstation, Lydia noted the senior Matthews's door was closed. But Daniel's was standing wide open, which, she knew, meant "Come on in."

Catching her breath in anticipation, she tiptoed across the room.

"Does Lydia sometimes do or say things that totally confuse you or catch you off guard?"

Jennifer's voice, and the mention of her own name, stopped Lydia before she stepped into view of the doorway.

"All the time," came Daniel's answer. "I mean, sometimes when I'm with her I think I'm looking at Lydia, then she'll do or say something totally out of character, and I feel like I'm seeing someone else." A brief pause, then, "When I hold her now, it even feels different."

Nothing could have prepared Lydia for the forceful blow that knocked her cloud of joy out from under her or for the feeling of her newfound elation hitting the floor with such rock-solid impact. Before her weakening limbs could collapse beneath her, she turned. As quickly and quietly as possible, she left the office.

"But, you do think she's all right, don't you?" Jennifer said, continuing her conversation with Daniel. "I mean, you don't think there are any mental repercussions from the attack, do you?"

Daniel noticed that the lines of worry in Jennifer's forehead had deepened. She *really* needed assurance that her sister was going to be all right.

"No, Jen," he said. "With Lydia's permission, I spoke with her doctor and reviewed her medical file. There is no permanent damage other than the memory loss."

Jen's troubled eyes filled with tears. "But she's so different now."

Daniel retrieved a box of tissues from his credenza and offered it to Jennifer, then he leaned forward and folded his arms on his desk. "Jennifer, I don't think anyone can go through what Lydia went though and not be changed. I mean, think about it. She not only lost her memory that night, she lost me, you, your mother and father. Everything that made her what she was, including herself. When she woke up sixteen days later, her entire past, up until that moment, was gone.

"Then, out of sheer survival instinct, I think, she was forced to live as a woman named Sara Jennings for five years. Now, here she is, back on Quinn Island, trying to readjust to the life that really belongs to her. She's been jerked around a bit, to say the least, but she's trying hard to adapt, and every day she makes progress." He reached over and patted Jennifer's hand. "She's going to be fine, Jen. She just needs a little more time to figure everything out. That's all."

Jennifer sniffed, dabbing at her eyes with a tissue. "Do you think she'll ever go back to the way she used to be?"

As always, whenever he stopped to ask himself exactly the same question, a niggling fear wormed through him. "I honestly don't know." And he honestly didn't know if he wanted her to.

Pursing her lips, she lowered her gaze. "Can I make a small confession?"

"Attorney-client privilege. Your secret's safe with me."

"There are some things . . . many, really . . . about this new Lydia that I like better."

Me, too, Daniel said to himself. But out of loyalty to the Lydia of his past, he kept the admission to himself. "Lydia will be fine, Jen," he repeated. "You'll see. Just fine."

When Jennifer turned to leave, Daniel checked his watch, then combed a harried hand through his hair. No point in calling Lydia now. His lunch hour was almost over.

❧

After dropping her keys twice, she finally managed to unlock the door. Tears streaming, she flew through the house, out the back, stumbled down the steps, and fell to her knees on the beach.

When I hold her now, it even feels different.

The cold, cruel reality in those words almost choked her. She curled her fingers into the gritty sand. Daniel wasn't in love with her. He was in love with a memory.

She looked up to the heavens through bitter tears. The salty breeze stung her wet cheeks. An errant strand of wind-tossed hair plastered her cheek, clung to her mouth. This hurt. Hurt . . . worse than anything.

A sob tore through her body. "Oh, God, help me! *Please,* help me! I don't know who I am anymore."

Burying her face in her gritty hands, she bowed her head to the sand and continued to weep . . . and to pray.

❧

By the time she returned to the house an hour later, she'd cried so many tears, her entire body felt dehydrated. And the back of her neck, she could tell, was sunburned. She pushed her mangled curls away from her face. Maybe she should have just stayed down there and withered away in the sun. It wouldn't have been nearly as painful as facing the brutal reality in Daniel's words less than two hours ago.

She opened the door to a ringing phone. She had a feeling she knew who it was, and she wasn't ready to talk to him yet.

The phone stopped ringing; her recorded greeting played; the tone sounded. "Hi, hon. I just had a minute and thought I'd call. It's been a few hours since I talked to you."

She could hear the grin in his voice. She closed her eyes against the ache in her throat. He had called that morning before he left for work, and everything had been so wonderful then. If she could just roll back the hands of time for a few short hours.

No! She opened her eyes and brought herself up straight. Going back wouldn't do any good. She'd merely be looking at the world through the rose-colored glasses of blind love, and Daniel's heart would still belong to another.

"I guess you decided to go shopping for the cottage after all. If I don't hear from you in an hour or so, I'll ring you back. And, no, I'm not being overprotective and checking up on you. I simply called because I love you."

Anger shot through her like a hurling arrow, and she shivered. "Liar!" she sneered as the phone line went dead, then immediately wanted to recant the sharp retort. Why should she be mad at Daniel? He couldn't help how he felt. He didn't even realize yet he wasn't in love with her.

Like a back draft, another realization hit her. "Oh, God," she whispered through her fingers, "this is going to hurt him. Just as much as it's hurting me." Her pain heightened. Legs giving way, she crumbled to her knees. The flood of tears started all over again. "Oh, God, what am I going to do?" Wrapping her arms around herself, she began rocking back and forth. "*Please* show me what to do."

Miraculously, she found a small calm in the midst of her storm. And in that silence, a still, small voice spoke to her and told her what to do. Wearily, she picked herself up off the floor, scooping up Mittens as she did so.

A zombielike walk down the hall took Lydia to her bedroom, where an unhung curtain still lay draped over the ironing board. Setting Mittens on the sea-foam-green-and-rose spread that covered her iron bed, she opened her nightstand drawer and withdrew a cloth-bound book. Testing the feel of its satiny ivory-colored cover, she sat down on the bed. Mittens poked her curious nose over Lydia's arm to see what was so interesting.

Lydia had found the journal among her old belongings when she had taken them out of storage. At the time, she had been surrounded by her family and Daniel, so she'd tucked the book away to read at a more opportune time. She settled back into the mountain of pillows propped against the head rail. Guess this was that time.

Two-and-one-half hours, 177 handwritten pages, and one cup of chamomile tea later, she knew exactly who Lydia was—someone that she herself would never be.

She closed the journal and stared unseeingly at the waves crashing against the jetty beyond her window. "Sara," she whispered.

From beneath the pain of a broken heart, a tiny spark of peace winked at her. Then the window of her soul opened up and revealed the truth to her. *Sara*. That was it. That's who she was.

Not the owner of an elegant dress shop. Not a sophisticated southern belle. Not Quinn Island's golden girl. She was not the woman Daniel Matthews fell in love with all those years ago. She was Sara. Just plain Sara. And for her, that was enough.

She drew in a shuddery breath. She'd finally figured it out. The sigh that followed was painful. Now, all she had to do was tell Daniel.

Then, she would crawl to some private corner of the world, curl up, and die for a while.

~&

Daniel stood at Lydia's front door, waiting for her to answer the doorbell. He hadn't even gone home to change after work. When she had called thirty minutes ago and said she needed to postpone their dinner date because she wasn't feeling well, he had made a quick trip to the grocery store. He'd picked up soup, saltines, and soft drinks—all those things his mother used to push down his throat whenever he was sick—then driven straight to the cottage.

He shifted the grocery bag from one arm to the other. A full minute had passed. He pushed the doorbell again, shrugging off the uneasiness crawling up his back. Maybe she was in the shower, or maybe she was too sick to get out of bed and answer the door.

He was reaching in his pocket for his key when he heard the shuffle of her small feet.

"Daniel, you shouldn't have come," came her weary-sounding voice through the closed door. "I told you I wasn't feeling well."

"I just wanted to check on you, see if you needed anything."

"No. I don't! I just need to be left alone."

He flinched at her sharp tone. Something was wrong. *Very* wrong. And he wasn't going anywhere until he found out what.

"Daniel," she pleaded, her voice now sounding weak and defeated. "Please . . . just go home."

Didn't she know him better than that? "Lydia, I'm not leaving until you open the door and let me see for myself how you are."

Silence stretched tauter than a harp string.

"I have a key," he reminded her, and he was about to use it when he heard the latch give from the other side. Slowly, she opened the door, and what he saw almost bowled him over. Her hair was a mess, and she was dressed in a long, white, terry robe and fuzzy pink slippers. And she had been crying—hard. "Lydia. What's wrong?"

She stood, one hand still on the doorknob, the other fisted tightly at her side. Was that fury smoldering in her eyes? "I . . . told . . . you . . . I'm . . . not . . . feeling . . . well," she ground out through clenched teeth.

"I'd say that's an understatement." He pushed his way inside, almost tripping over Mittens. Closing the door, he set his loaded grocery bag on the floor and captured Lydia's forearms. His gut twisted at the sight of her tear-swollen eyes. "Talk to me."

She pulled away, as though his touch had burned her. Cupping her elbows, she took several backward steps. As she did so, Daniel sensed her erecting some sort of wall between them. But why?

Something dark and foreboding swept over him, leaving him chilled to the core. Cautiously, he took a step forward.

She took another back. Sorrowfully shaking her head, she said, "I don't want to do this tonight, Daniel. I'm not prepared."

He lifted his hands in a helpless gesture. "Do what, Lydia? For heaven's sake, tell me what's going on!"

A tremor shuddered through her body. Biting down hard on her lower lip, she closed her eyes.

He longed to reach for her, comfort her. But he sensed, somehow, if he did, she'd just slip farther away, farther behind whatever impenetrable wall she was building between them.

When her trembling ceased, she opened her eyes, turned, and wandered to a double window overlooking the sea. Slowly, he followed, stopping an arm's span behind her.

Seconds passed like hours. Daniel fought the choking hand of dread reaching for his throat. His hands sweat; his lungs burned; his head hurt. He didn't know what was coming, only that it was bad.

Finally, she said, "I've finally figured out who Lydia is."

In light of the uneasy currents ricocheting around them, he knew better than to say *That's good*. He somehow swallowed around the sticky dryness in his throat. "And?"

"It's not me."

He willed her to look at him, but he got no results. "What do you mean, it's not you?"

"Just exactly what I said. I'm not now, nor will I ever be, Lydia."

He trapped his temples between his thumb and second finger, trying to keep his reeling mind from crashing. "This doesn't make sense."

"It makes perfect sense if you stop to think about it. I don't act like Lydia; I don't think like Lydia; I don't like the same things Lydia liked." Her face was void of emotion and her body as rigid as a mannequin. It was clear she was trying not to feel. *Forcing* herself not to feel.

"I don't want to be a shop owner," she droned on like a robot. "I want to be an advocate for missing and abused children. I don't want someone telling me how I should dress or wear my hair; I want to decide those things for myself. I don't want to have to recoil every time I have something to say; I want to speak my mind without worrying that I'm going to offend someone every time I do so. I don't want to live in a town house; I want to live right here on the island for the rest of my life."

She finally stopped to take a breath.

"Do you think any of that matters to me?" he ground out.

"It should. It should matter a great deal to you." Her stoic features softened and her rigid shoulders dropped slightly. But she still refused to look at him. "Daniel," she said in a voice now laced with compassion, "five years ago, on that deserted Darlington highway, Lydia died. Sixteen days later, Sara was born. You didn't ask for it, and neither did I, but that's the way it is." Finally, she turned her head and looked at him, and the depth of pain in her eyes almost ripped him in two. "Lydia's gone, Daniel. I can't replace her. I've accepted that. Now you have to."

He shook his head in denial. "No way. This isn't right."

"Don't you see, Daniel? It's the only thing that is right. Everything else has been wrong up until now."

Fear as quick and sharp as a two-edged sword sliced through him. He pulled a face in disbelief. "What are you saying, Lydia? That you really don't love me?"

No, she wasn't saying that. She would never be able to say that. But she couldn't let him know it.

She turned back to the window. She was dying inside, and she needed to get him away from her. "I'm saying you need to go home and mourn Lydia, Daniel. Go home, and mourn the woman you really love."

He raised his hand.

She closed her eyes. "Please don't touch me," she said quickly, before he had a chance to. Because if he did, she'd shatter into a million pieces around his feet. Then she'd allow him to pick her up and put her back together again, regardless of the cost to her and to him.

When she mentally felt him withdraw his hand, she opened her eyes and continued staring out the window. But out of the corner of her eye, she could see his chest rising and falling with emotion. It took every ounce of willpower she possessed to hold back the tears filling her eyes.

"Okay," he said, then paused to take two more heavy breaths, like he needed them to replenish his strength. "You want me to go; I'll go. For now. But as soon as I figure out what happened between now and this morning, I'll be back. You can count on that, Lydia."

"Sara. My name is Sara."

He just stood there, chest heaving, hands clenching and un-clenching, staring at her like he didn't know what to do with himself.

She had to get him out. Now, before she broke. "You may hate me for this now, Daniel," she said softly. "But someday you'll thank me. Now, *please. Go.*"

He captured her chin and forced her to look at him. What she saw in his eyes was both frightening and promising. Anger, confusion, and pain were mixed together with love and determination.

"Hate you?" he said, his voice full of harsh incredulity. "Sweet-heart, I will *never* hate you. You can call yourself Sara, Jane, Polly, Sue. Pick one; I don't care." His grip on her chin tightened, stopping short of the point of pain. "I'm not in love with your name; I'm in love with you."

She almost reached out and grabbed the fragile thread of hope he was dangling in front of her. Almost. But just in time he dropped his hand, leaving her weak and incredibly weary.

"Now, I'm going to leave," he added, his hand now clenched back at his side. "Because I'm afraid if I don't, I'm either going to throttle you or knock a hole in your wall. But I'll be back. *Soon.* And that, my dear Sara Jane Polly Sue, is a promise." With that, he turned and stalked away.

She stood by the window and waited until she heard him drive away, then waited a few minutes more. When she was certain he wasn't coming back, certain he wouldn't come in and see her, she buried her face in her hands and crumpled to the floor.

❧

One-and-one-half hours later, Daniel walked out of the Quinns' home, climbed into his car, and headed home. Maybe he should feel guilty that he had just conspired with Lydia's entire family to find out what was going on with her, but he didn't.

He was a desperate man.

15

*H*i, Bill. Come on in." Daniel stepped back to allow the older man entry. "Have you talked to Lydia today?"

Bill shook his head. "Not today. I drove out to see her last night, but she's still not talking."

Daniel's stomach churned with disappointment. It had been three days since his and Lydia's perplexing parting. So far, no one had been able to get her to open up about what had happened that day to make her suddenly turn around and head in the other direction. She would open her door to her family, but not her heart. To Daniel, she would open neither, and it was driving him crazy. He was on the verge of claiming insanity and camping out on her doorstep.

"I did receive a call from Chicago this morning, though," Bill added.

Daniel arched his brows. "Mrs. Porter?" Lydia's friend had gone home several weeks ago; why hadn't he thought of her? If anyone could get through to Lydia, it was her former landlady. "Has Lydia talked to her?"

Bill nodded. "Mrs. Porter called her yesterday, just to see how she was doing."

"And?"

Bill grinned. "Why don't you ask me to sit down? Then I'll tell you what she said."

Chagrined at his lapse in manners, Daniel muttered, "Sorry," and led the way to the den. He'd been doing a lot of peculiar things over the past three days.

Bill settled on a forest-green leather sofa, and Daniel perched on the edge of a matching recliner seat, elbows on knees, hands clasped in front of him.

"Seems like . . . *Sara* overheard a conversation between you and Jennifer on Wednesday that made her feel you were disappointed in the woman she'd become since her abduction."

Daniel's brow creased in concentration. He had to jiggle his memory in order to recall his Wednesday meeting with Jennifer. "Jennifer came into the office that day to sign some papers. We did talk a bit about Lydia, but Lydia wasn't there."

"Yes, she was. Standing right outside your door."

"Eavesdropping?" Daniel couldn't believe it.

"No. At least not intentionally. She'd come to bring you lunch, but when she heard her sister ask you if she ever did things to confuse you, and you told Jen 'yes,' that even holding her was different now, she left."

"I also told Jen that my love for Lydia hasn't changed. Didn't she hear that, too?"

"Guess not."

Daniel flopped back in his chair. "So that's what this is all about. A simple misunderstanding."

Bill shook his head. "I'm not sure it's all that simple."

"Sure, it is. As soon as I explain to her that she didn't hear the whole conversation, she'll realize she jumped to the wrong conclusion, and we'll probably have a good laugh over it." After he kissed her until their breath was gone. But he didn't think her father would be interested in hearing about that.

Bill leveled Daniel with a somber look. "Did she jump to the wrong conclusion, Daniel?"

"Of, course, she did. What else could it be?"

"Perception. Insight. The sudden realization and acceptance of how things really are."

Daniel frowned. "What are you saying, Bill?"

"That maybe Lydia, as we knew her, really is gone, and we need to stop looking for her to come back to us."

Daniel shook his head in denial.

"Think about it, Daniel. She's known us only six weeks. *Six weeks.*

She's like a child who was stolen from her home in infancy and not returned until adulthood, or someone who's just moved here from out of town. We can't expect her to come back and step into the life that we all had planned for her." Tears brought a sad sparkle to the older man's eyes. "I know she's tried. She's given her best shot at giving us back what we lost, but for whose sake? Hers or ours?"

Propping his elbow on the chair arm, Daniel massaged his throbbing temple. He didn't want to accept what Bill was saying. Didn't want to accept that Lydia was really gone. Even though, deep down, he suspected he had known it for some time. "So what are you saying?" he repeated. "That we should just forget about the past? Pretend it never happened?"

Bill gave his head a solemn shake. "I don't think any of us could do that, or that anyone, including *Sara*, would expect us to. I'm just saying that maybe it's time we stopped trying to hold onto it, and accept the gift that we've been given in return." His gaze bore into Daniel's for a wise and perceptive moment. "A good place to start would be by letting go of all that guilt you've been toting around for the last five years."

Daniel shifted his gaze to the cold, empty fireplace. He still found it amazing that Bill Quinn had never blamed him for his daughter's disappearance, for not taking that trip with her.

"Fate dealt us all a bitter blow that night, Daniel," Bill continued. "There wasn't one of us who didn't stop and ask ourselves if there was something we could have done." Voice mellowing, he added, "No one blames you, Son. Don't you think it's time you stopped blaming yourself?"

Daniel continued to massage his temple, continued staring unseeingly at the fireplace. He didn't know how to respond to all that Bill had said. Daniel needed time to think, weigh everything out, and to pray.

As though sensing Daniel's need for solitude, Bill stood. Daniel started to follow suit, but the older man stopped him with an understanding hand on his shoulder. "Don't get up. I'll see myself out."

Daniel nodded and settled back in his chair. Would he ever muddle through all the confusion? With a sigh, he raised his hand and started kneading his temple again. Was anything in life ever certain? At the moment, he could think of only one thing.

"Bill?" Daniel called just before the man exited from the room.

In the open doorway, Bill turned back.

"This whole Lydia being Sara thing may still have me a bit addled," Daniel said. "But there is one thing I'm not confused about. I love your daughter. Of that, I'm certain."

A knowing gleam warmed the older man's eyes. "I know you do, Daniel. If I didn't, I wouldn't be here."

Bill started through the door again, then apparently struck by another thought, he stopped and turned around. "One more thing. You told Jen that your love for Lydia hasn't changed. Are you sure about that?"

"If anything, I love her more."

"More? Or different?"

Both came to mind so quickly that Daniel blinked in surprise. He did love her more, stronger, deeper than before. And that love was different, because *she* was different.

Daniel gave the man standing at the doorway a blank look of dawning enlightenment. Why, he'd gone and fallen in love all over again, with a woman named Sara.

Bill simply smiled. "That's what I thought. Now, all you have to do is convince my daughter."

❧

Dear Diary

Sara pulled her hand away from her new journal and studied the words she'd just written. For some reason, they didn't feel right. She drew in a deep breath and released it through pursed lips. Why did she feel a need to start a journal anyway? What benefit was there in telling your innermost secrets to a book?

"Mama, can me an' Mittens go climb on the rocks?"

Holding a strand of windblown hair away from her face, Sara looked up at the child standing beside her in a neon pink bathing suit.

A gray ball of fur swarmed around her ankles, sniffing at a bottle of sunscreen lying on the beach blanket where Sara sat. For some reason known only to a child's mind, Chloe was fascinated with the mountain of huge rocks that was an extension of the jetty at the end of the island.

"No, you may not," Sara answered, adjusting the strap that had slid off her daughter's shoulder. "You might fall and get hurt or slip and get your foot trapped between the rocks." She pushed Chloe's sunglasses up her nose. "Besides, the tide's coming in and you might get washed away. Then what would I do without my little girl?"

"You'd cry and cry, just like you do for Daniel."

Sara blinked back the stinging onslaught of tears. Why did the child have to be so perceptive?

Chloe tilted her head, the end of her ponytail brushing one shoulder. "Is he ever coming back to see us?"

Chloe had questioned Daniel's absence several times over the past four days, but Sara didn't have the strength yet to explain to her child that he would no longer be a constant part of their lives. She wanted to wait until she got past the stage of sporadic weeping that often hit her unawares at any given time of the day. "Honey, Daniel is your very good friend, and he loves you very much. I'm sure he'll find a way to see you soon."

"But don't he want to be your friend anymore?"

Probably not. But she couldn't tell Chloe that. "Daniel is everybody's friend," she said, hoping the answer would satisfy her daughter. Before the child could come up with a response, Sara added, "Now, you and Mittens go on and finish your sand castle. We only have a few more minutes before we have to go in."

Chloe and Mittens scampered a few feet away to a lumpy mound of sand that looked more like a range of bald mountains than a castle. The calming call of a seagull harmonized with the voice of the waves crashing against the jetty. While Sara listened to the beauty of the sea song, she watched her daughter and reminded herself that she was a woman truly blessed. She had a God who would never forsake her. A child who was healthy and happy. A family who loved her and—although they were still a bit taken aback—supported her desire to legally change her name to Sara Lydia Quinn. Oh, yes, and she had Mittens. The cat had promptly become a comforting, permanent member of hers and Chloe's family.

The only thing missing was Daniel.

She forced a breath past the catch in her throat. *Four out of five isn't bad,* she reminded herself. One couldn't have it all.

With a fingertip, she caught a tear trying to escape the corner of her eye. "'For I know the thoughts that I think toward you, saith the LORD,'" she whispered to herself, "'thoughts of peace, and not of evil, to give you an expected end.'"

The verse had given her a sense of peace in the midst of every storm she had ridden over the past five years, and it gave peace now. She had to be thankful she'd found out Daniel's true feelings for her before one day he woke up next to her and realize he'd married a stranger.

But peace did not take away the pain. At least, not yet anyway. She pressed a palm against the weight on her chest. Even when her heart was once again able to reach beyond pain to sweet remembrance, things would never be the same. There would never be another Daniel.

She turned her attention back to the book and poised her pen over the paper. *Dear Diary,* she read, then realized what was wrong. With one quick stoke, she marked through *Dear Diary* and wrote *Dear God.*

This would be her prayer journal. The place she went to daily to talk to God and thank Him for all the goodness and blessings He had brought to her life, a place to pray for others and ask for strength. Especially in the days of loneliness ahead.

She wrote nonstop for ten minutes, finishing her first entry with:

> *God, please help Daniel understand why I had to let him go.*
> *Help him get through the pain, for I know, right now, he is*
> *hurting. He's lost so much. Help him find the woman who is right*
> *for him. I know there's one out there somewhere. Someone who*

will make him happy. Someone as true and kind and as generous as he. He has too much love to offer not to share his life with someone like that. And I promise, when that time comes, I will be happy for him.

Love,
Sara

She blotted the teardrops from the page with the end of a beach towel and closed the journal. Then she wiped the moisture from her face with her hands. She'd get through this. Somehow, by the grace of God, she would survive.

She glanced up to check on Chloe. Her bucket lay overturned in the midst of the lumpy sand castle, and her blue shovel was stuck up in the sand. But Chloe and Mittens were gone.

"Chloe?" Her pulse quickened as she searched the shrinking beach, then surged with alarm when she located her daughter trying to climb up the jetty rocks. "Chloe!" She threw the book aside and vaulted up in a run. "Chloe! Wait!"

Thank God, Chloe complied.

Sara ran out into knee-deep water and scooped up her daughter off the rocks. She trudged back to dry land and set the child down on solid ground. Then, kneeling, she clasped Chloe's upper arms. "Chloe, what has gotten into you?" The child rarely disobeyed a request. "I told you not to climb on the rocks. You could get hurt!"

Sunglasses now gone, Chloe looked up at her mother through worried blue eyes. Her small chin quivered. "But I have to get Mittens. She's gone after the fish."

"What fish?"

Chloe pointed toward the water. Sara's line of vision followed her daughter's pointing finger, and sure enough, there was Mittens halfway out the jetty, slapping at small fish jumping out of the swirling waves. *"Mittens,"* Sara chided under her breath. Didn't the crazy cat realize her legs were three inches—not three feet—long?

"We have to get her, Mommy," came Chloe's small, panic-stricken voice. "Or she'll wash away."

Sara turned back to her daughter. "Okay, Chloe. I want you to go sit on the steps and don't move. No matter what."

"What are you going to do?"

"I'm going after Mittens."

"But what if you get washed away?"

"I won't," she said, hoping she was right. "I'll be very careful. But, if something does happen, and I can't get back, then you go to the house and call 9-1-1. Okay?"

"Okay."

"Now, go sit down, and stay there until I get back."

With bare feet, Sara gingerly negotiated the jagged rocks until the wind caught her off guard, making her lose her footing and scrape an ankle. She picked her way over the rest of the rubble on hands and knees, clenching her teeth a little harder every time Mittens ignored her summons.

"I'm going to wring your skinny little neck when I get you back to shore," she ground out as she crawled up onto the six-inch wide jetty platform. Her hand slipped and snagged a small splinter. Wiping the blood that seeped from her palm on the seat of her cutoffs, she added, "If you don't make me shark bait first."

❧

Cradling a small bouquet of mixed flowers in one arm, Daniel climbed the front steps of the cottage. He had no idea what he was going to say to her when she opened the door—and she would open it, even if he had to use his key first. He just knew that somehow he had to convince her he loved the woman she was now—not the woman she used to be. That was a love whose time was past. Like Bill had said, it was time to let it go. Accept what God had given him in return—and Daniel was wholeheartedly ready to do that. Now, if he could only persuade her to accept him.

He stepped up to the door, his stomach a knot of nerves and anticipation. He'd do whatever it took to plead his case. After all, it was a matter of life and death. *His.*

With a deep, bracing breath, he rang the doorbell. What should he say to get her to hear him out before slamming the door in his face? Maybe he could start with something like, *Hi. My name is Daniel. What's yours?*

Almost immediately, he shook his head. Too corny sounding. And she'd probably never fall for it, anyway. He glanced down at the flowers resting in the crook of his arm. He had chosen a mixture of painted daisies, sweet-smelling lavender, morning glories, and several other species he couldn't name, all nestled in a bed of pink baby's breath. They reminded him of a field of wildflowers, and he had known the minute he saw them in the florist's window that Sara would love them, a lot more than she would a box of long-stem roses.

He looked back at the door. Where was she? He'd expected to hear some activity from her or Chloe by now. He knew they were home; her car was in the garage area beneath the house.

He rang the doorbell again, waited about half-a-minute, then bounded down the steps and headed for the narrow path carved through the thick island flora that led to the back of the house. Maybe she and Chloe were on the beach, which would be even better. That way, she couldn't slam the door in his face.

When he broke through the thick cloud of plant life, he scanned the beach area. He found only an abandoned beach blanket and sand bucket. One corner of his mouth tipped. She and Chloe were probably exploring. His gaze drifted a little farther down the beach to the jetty, and his steps faltered. Sara was crawling out on the narrow platform, about to be swallowed up by the roiling waves of the incoming high tide.

Terror slammed into him at the same time adrenaline kicked in, and he didn't stop to think. Taking off in a dead run, he screamed, "Saaaaraaaa!"

❧

The waves slapped at Sara's hands and knees, but she was almost there. Only a couple more feet and she would have Mittens, who had realized the error of her ways and had climbed up onto the top of one of the poles anchoring the jetty.

Sara paused, listening. Had someone called her name? Her instant of distraction left her unprepared for the next wave that sloshed over the jetty, and her left knee slipped off the platform. A jolt of alarm quickened her pulse and she steadied herself. Best keep her mind on what she was doing.

She hooked her hand around the quivering cat; as she pulled the kitten to her chest, she hesitated again. Someone had called her name, and it sounded like Daniel.

Twisting her head around, she found him sprinting down the beach toward her, waving his arms over his head and yelling, "Sara! Wait! I'm coming!"

Something cold and powerful hit her on her blind side, and the next thing she knew, she was being swallowed by the churning dark waters of the Atlantic.

❧

"Sara? Sara? Can you hear me?"

There it was again. Daniel calling her name. Calling her up out of the darkness. She must be dreaming.

Something cold and wet covered her mouth and forced air into her lungs. Her body convulsed. She coughed as air rushed from her chest, then her body settled back down.

"That's it, baby," came that beautiful voice again. "Come on back to me."

Slowly, she opened her eyes, and there he was, kneeling over her, nursing the back of her head with one hand, his wet hair dripping on her face. Oh, but he was beautiful.

"Oh, thank God." He buried his face against her shoulder. "Thank God, you're alive. I thought I had lost you."

Instinctively, she raised her hand to the back of his head and held it there. As the fog evaporated from her mind, she struggled to sit up. "Chloe?"

He drew back, cradling her face with his palm. "She's fine. She's sitting on the steps with one of the neighbors."

"Mittens?"

"She's fine, too. You were still holding onto her when I got to you."

Assured her family was safe, she reached up and laid her hand against his cool, damp cheek. "Sara." It wasn't a question, but a statement of awe and wonder.

His eyes crinkled. "Yes, sweetheart. You're fine, too."

"No, you. You called me 'Sara.' When I was out on the jetty, and you were running toward me, without stopping or thinking or . . . anything, you called me Sara."

His brow furrowed in thought, then smoothed. "Yes, I guess I did."

The center of her being flooded with joy that extended to every fiber in her body. "Thank you, Daniel. You saved my life today, in more ways than one."

❧

"We're going to keep you overnight, just for observation."

Sara let her head flop back on the pillow. "Is that really necessary, Dr. Bayne?"

He shifted his gaze from the chart he was writing, peering at her over his reading glasses. "Probably not, but I'd rather be safe—"

"I know. I know. You'd rather be safe than sorry."

"That's right." He patted her knee. "Now, there are some very anxious people outside waiting to see you. I think I'd better let them in before they knock down the door."

Her father and Chloe came in first. After greeting them both with a hug and kiss, she settled Chloe on the bed next to her. "Where are the others?" she asked her father.

"They're outside. The doctor said we could come in only two at a time. Hospital rules." He eased himself down on the edge of the bed and picked up her hand. "Jen and Margaret will come in next, then your mother and I will take Chloe home with us for the night. Since Daniel's going to stay the night, he decided he'd take his turn last."

Her eyes widened. "Daniel's spending the night?"

Her father sent her a teasing wink. "I gave my permission, as long as he keeps himself in the guest cot."

A bit discomfited, she ducked her head. He lifted it back up with a finger beneath her chin. "I don't think we could run him out of this place tonight with a shotgun. That young man loves you, Sara. *You.* I hope you've figured that out by now."

"I have, Dad. And I love him, too."

"An' me, too," Chloe chimed in, and a round of laughter followed.

Her mother and Jennifer kept their visit short, then Mr. and Mrs. Matthews stuck their heads in to express their happiness that she'd survived her cat-rescuing venture unharmed.

The second Daniel's parent's left, Sara adjusted the pillows supporting her back and combed her fingers through her tangled hair. She'd give a week's wages for a mirror and brush right now. She had to be a mess. Wetting her lips, she straightened her covers and clasped her hands in her lap. She hadn't been this nervous the first time she had met Daniel, six weeks ago in Chicago.

He hesitated in the doorway, a dream in the shadows, then strolled into the glow of the overhead lights, her knight who had come to carry her away to happily ever after. A leather overnight bag dangled from one hand. Someone, his parents probably, had apparently brought him some fresh clothes, but he hadn't taken the time to change yet. His navy slacks and yellow pullover shirt were both pretty much a mess, and he hadn't even combed his hair. But he was the most beautiful sight she had ever seen.

He stopped a few feet inside the door and tossed the overnight bag to a nearby chair. "Hi," he said, dazzling her with a sheepish grin.

If she didn't know better, she'd say he sounded shy. "Hi, yourself."

"My name's Daniel. What's yours?"

A silent message passed between them. The promise of a new beginning was sealed. Anticipation and excitement danced across her skin. "Sara. My name is Sara."

"*Sara,*" he mused, as though testing the flavor of the word on his tongue. Slowly and deliberately, he ambled forward. "I like that name," he added as though he approved of the taste.

The fluttering butterflies in her stomach veered off course, darting around in a dozen different directions, bumping into each other. "Thanks. Daniel's nice, too."

"You think so?"

"Yeah. I think so."

He eased down on the edge of the bed, captured her hands in his. His tender gaze consumed her. "So, Sara. What are you doing tonight? And tomorrow night? And for the rest of your life?"

She shrugged a shoulder. "I dunno. Wanna get married?" It was bold, it was forward, and it was cheeky. But it was right. She *knew* it was right.

A spark of surprise and delight widened his eyes. Then, almost as quickly as his elation had come, it faded. He released one of her hands and pressed his forefinger to her lips. "Hold that thought."

She kissed his fingertip. "Got it."

Just before he dropped his gaze, she caught a glimpse of pain. A pain, she sensed, he had carried too long. She wanted to lift her arms and embrace him, comfort him. But something told her to wait. To let him explain.

He recaptured both of her hands, caressing the backs of her fingers with his thumbs. "There's something I need to tell you about the trip to New York."

"Okay."

Lifting his lids, he met her unwavering gaze. He could live an eternity drowning in those eyes, eyes that showered him with love and devotion. A quick wave of apprehension clenched his stomach. After he told her why she took that New York trip alone, would she still look at him like he hung the moon?

He wasn't sure he wanted to find out, but he knew she deserved to know the truth. "I was supposed to go with you on that trip, Sara. I had my room reservations made and my bags packed, but I backed out at the last minute because a court case got pushed up a week on the trial schedule."

She waited a moment, as though she expected him to say more. When he didn't right away, she gave a nonchalant shrug. "So? You're an attorney, Daniel. I was a dress shop owner. We were both doing our jobs."

"Yes, but I could have let my dad handle the case. I could have talked to the judge, told him I couldn't change my plans. I could have done a number of things, but I didn't." Shame pressed down upon him, almost choking him. "I chose my work over you, Sara, and because I did, you suffered a brutal attack and lost your memory. Can you ever forgive me for that?"

"There's nothing to forgive, Daniel," she said without hesitation.

Her lack of pause told him she meant it. She did not blame him for her abduction. But that didn't change the fact that it had happened, that because of his self-serving attitude, she had been alone that night.

"Daniel, do you ever ask yourself 'What if?'" she added after a prolonged moment of silence.

He studied her face, the wisdom in her expression, and found there a deep well of understanding. "Yes," he admitted. "All the time."

"I've done that a lot myself over the past six weeks. What if I hadn't taken that exit? What if I had stayed on the interstate? What if I had been a few minutes earlier and been involved in the accident that caused the traffic delay?" She pulled her hands free of his and framed her face with his palms. "What if you *had* been with me that night, and you too had fallen prey to the men who attacked me?" Her features softened. Her eyes grew misty. "If that had happened, I suppose I would have a pretty tough time forgiving myself, too."

He shook his head. "But it wouldn't have been your fault."

"Exactly."

She gave him a moment to consider her words. "Oh, Daniel, you're such a wonderful protector. You take such good care of me and Chloe, and I know you took good care of Lydia, too. That's one of the reasons you're finding it so hard to forgive yourself.

"But it wasn't your fault. God was in control of our lives, and *no one* is to blame. And no one is holding you accountable except yourself." He felt her fingers spread over his head, as though she were trying to encompass his mind with assurance. "Let it go, Daniel. I know for an honorable heart like yours, that's easier said than done. But you can do it. With God's help, you can do anything."

Daniel knew he was looking into the face of a woman who knew what she was talking about. A woman who had awakened one day wounded, pregnant, and alone. A woman who hadn't known who she was or where she came from. A woman who had crawled up from the pits of hell and learned to stand on her own.

A woman who had taught him how to give freely and love without condition.

Looking deep into her eyes at that moment, he knew nothing from the past would ever come between them. A shadow receded from his heart, and a burden he had carried for five long years grew lighter. She was right. With God's help and her love, he could do anything. Even, one day, forgive himself.

He felt a touch of God's grace flow through him, and a surge of love flooded his soul as the last chain of bondage fell from his heart. He shifted his head and kissed her palm. "You're something else. You know that?"

"I know," she said without a single shred of vanity. Then, with a minxish grin, she grasped the front of his shirt and pulled him forward. "Now, there's this matter of a thought . . ."

He stopped with his mouth less than a breath away from hers. "Oh, yeah, as I was saying. What are you doing tonight?" He brushed her lips with his. "And tomorrow night?" He brushed her lips again. "And for the rest of your life?"

"I dunno. Wanna get married?"

"Yes, Sara. Yes, I do."

The silence that followed was filled with faith, hope, and love. All three. But the greatest of these was love.

And in the midst of that love was forgiveness.

CROSSINGS®

THE BOOK CLUB FOR TODAY'S CHRISTIAN FAMILY

A Letter to Our Readers

Dear Reader:

In order that we might better contribute to your reading enjoyment, we would appreciate your taking a few minutes to respond to the following questions. When completed, please return to the following:

Andrea Doering, Editor-in-Chief
Crossings Book Club
401 Franklin Avenue, Garden City, NY 11530

You can post your review online! Go to www.crossings.com and rate this book.

Title _____ Author _____

1 Did you enjoy reading this book?

❑ Very much. I would like to see more books by this author!

❑ I really liked_____

❑ Moderately. I would have enjoyed it more if_____

2 What influenced your decision to purchase this book? Check all that apply.

❑ Cover
❑ Title
❑ Publicity
❑ Catalog description
❑ Friends
❑ Enjoyed other books by this author
❑ Other _____

3 Please check your age range:

❑ Under 18   ❑18-24
❑ 25-34   ❑ 35-45
❑ 46-55   ❑ Over 55

4 How many hours per week do you read? _____

5 How would you rate this book, on a scale from 1 (poor) to 5 (superior)?
_____

Name_____

Occupation_____

Address_____

City_____ State_____ Zip_____